1 1 MAR 2019

1 1 MAR 2019

2 8 MAR 2019

cecu HEA

NEW

SEA

East Sussex
County Council

Please return or renew this item
by the last date shown. You may
return items to any East Sussex
Library. You may renew books
by telephone or the internet.

0345 60 80 195 for renewals

0345 60 80 196 for enquiries

Library and Information Services
eastsussex.gov.uk/libraries

Also available from James Brogden and Titan Books

Hekla's Children

THE
HOLLOW TREE

JAMES BROGDEN

TITAN BOOKS

The Hollow Tree
Print edition ISBN: 9781785654404
E-book edition ISBN: 9781785654411

Published by Titan Books
A division of Titan Publishing Group Ltd
144 Southwark Street, London SE1 0UP

First edition: March 2018
1 2 3 4 5 6 7 8 9 10

A CIP catalogue record for this title is available from the British Library.

Printed and bound by CPI Group (UK) Ltd, Croydon, CR0 4YY

FOR 'BELLA'

MARY IN THE OAK TREE
COLD AS COLD CAN BE
WAITING FOR THE SKY TO FALL
WHO WILL DANCE WITH ME?

TRADITIONAL BIRMINGHAM SKIPPING SONG

PROLOGUE

5TH MAY 1945

NATURE ABHORS A VACUUM, OR SO IT IS SAID.

Sergeant Nicholas Raleigh and Corporal Rhys Hughes, both of the 9th Bomb Disposal Company, Royal Engineers, looked down at the smooth grey curve of steel, which broke the surface of the ground like a half-submerged sea monster. Surrounding them, the woods of the Lickey Hills were coming into leaf, bright with sunshine and the songs of birds. Meanwhile the bomb at their feet lay in the middle of it all, smug and insolent.

Sergeant Raleigh tilted his cap back and scratched his head, frowning. 'Thousand-pounder, you suppose?'

'Give or take an ounce,' answered Corporal Hughes. He was sitting on a log and eating a cheese sandwich. Coming from a long line of Welsh miners, he'd taken to the Royal Engineers as if born to it. The vast majority of the unexploded ordnance they encountered was in Birmingham

– spread out down at the foot of the hills in a grey haze – dealt with in a claustrophobic chaos of shattered buildings and the stench of burning, so he was enjoying the rare chance for a day out in the fresh air, and this place was as good as any for a picnic.

Raleigh didn't seem to be appreciating the occasion. He was tall and rangy, and some might have said humourless with it, but surviving three years in a post of which the life expectancy was normally measured in months would do that to a man.

'How long d'you reckon it's been lying there?' asked Hughes.

'Last raid was back in forty-three,' mused Raleigh. 'So two years at least. They'll have been trying to hit the Austin works. This one's fallen much too short for a simple miss. Probably found things a bit hotter than they expected and dumped the weight before scarpering.' He looked around. 'Good news is that there's nothing nearby.'

The Lickeys were a small range of hills to the south of Birmingham, a well-loved pleasure spot for city-dwellers looking to escape for day trips. A little over a mile from where they were standing, they could see the rooftops of the Austin works, pitted and painted green to look like ordinary farmland, where plane and machine parts for the war effort were made. The bomb had been found by a local gamekeeper who had alerted the Home Guard, and after checking to make sure there weren't any more in the vicinity, a wide safety cordon had quickly been established. There might have been a few folks up here strolling or picnicking, but nowhere near danger, and other than the tram terminus and the Bilberry Tea Rooms at the bottom, the nearest human habitation was a good half-mile distant.

Corporal Hughes stood, brushing crumbs off his knees and tugging his uniform jacket down over his comfortably proportioned belly. 'So are we going to blow it up then, Sarge, or not?'

Raleigh favoured him with a grim smile. 'Why yes, Corporal, I rather think we are.'

The explosion was quite literally earth-shaking. Birds burst from the trees as a massive geyser of dirt, leaves and bits of tree fountained into the air and rained debris over a wide area, just as echoes of the detonation rolled out from the hills and over the city below. The silence that followed it was almost as deafening, and in that frozen moment fearful and wondering eyes turned to the sky. When the last fragments had fallen, Sergeant Raleigh and Corporal Hughes approached to inspect the damage.

Hughes placed his hands on his hips and gave a low, awed whistle. 'Well that'll clear your tubes and no mistake,' he said.

It appeared as if God Himself had reached down and scooped out a sixty-foot wide handful of the hillside, leaving mounds of soil and rocks settling back into the crater in small avalanches, and splintered trees about the periphery. All that remained of the bomb was a twisted fragment of tail fin right at the very bottom and a litter of leaf debris that had been sucked into the crater by the blast's initial vacuum.

'You're not wrong,' Raleigh replied. 'Right, let's get the worst of it.'

They set to giving the immediate area a quick once-over for the largest and most obvious pieces of shrapnel, to be dumped in the crater and covered over. It would not be many more seasons before the woods reclaimed the spot as if nothing had ever happened; as if there had been no such things as war, or bombs. Already birdsong was slowly returning to the woods, filling the shocked silence.

Raleigh's explorations were interrupted by a sudden cry of alarm from Hughes. 'Sarge!' he called. 'Come quick!'

He found Corporal Hughes standing by the wide trunk of an old, dead oak tree. It had succumbed to either lightning or disease many years ago, and it had sheared off about seven feet from the ground, the remains of its limbs being little more than stark, fingerless stumps. The explosion had caused a great split to open up in it, a ragged fissure revealing that the trunk was hollow. At the bottom, in the shadow of a shallow well formed by the centre of the roots, he made out the deeper darkness of an eye socket staring back at him, and he recoiled.

'Sweet Mary mother of God,' he breathed.

The skull was lying on a pile of what he at first took to be old sticks, but then saw that they were ribs, leg bones, arm bones, the blocky lumps of vertebrae and a littering of fingers and toes. Stuffed into the hollow trunk, the corpse had been unable to fall and had simply rotted where it stood, the disarticulated remains collapsing through themselves and into a jumbled pile with the skull uppermost, staring up at the opening in the top of the broken trunk, which was forever beyond reach. There was fabric – too stained to tell the colour or whether it was shirt, trousers, or dress – and strands of dark hair still attached to the skull.

Hughes' normally ruddy face was pale, and he was making strange gulping noises as his cheese sandwich threatened to rebel.

Both men had seen their fair share of death: bodies mangled and torn apart by German bombs, burned in fires, lacerated by shrapnel, crushed by fallen buildings, or any one of a dozen other ways a person could be killed. Neither could claim to be unaffected, but you took a deep breath and you carried on and you did your job. It was horrific, but explainable, and hard to think of as murder. It was war. This, however, was something entirely different, and coming as it did in what should have been a place of natural beauty and tranquillity gave it a particular sense of violation.

Hughes had managed to get himself under control. 'Poor bugger. Who do you think he was?'

The police were called, but they could not discover the identity of the corpse beyond that it was the remains of a young woman. No witnesses came forward, and as the hills lay right on the boundary between the districts of Birmingham and Bromsgrove the investigation was passed back and forth between the two county constabularies until the threads of the investigation were hopelessly tangled and eventually lost altogether.

Still, nature abhors a vacuum, and no more so than the hole left by a soul taken friendless, anonymous and alone. Like air, or birdsong, myth floods in to fill the gap.

HAND OF GLORY

1

COLLISION

RACHEL COOPER STARES DOWN INTO THE BLACK GULF *where the two steel hulls meet. A second ago they were approaching each other with the ponderous inevitability of thunderstorms, and she was scrabbling with slippery feet to get out of the way. In a second's time they will rebound, and the two narrowboats will go on their ways, fifteen tons apiece. Her fascination lies in the fact that at this moment her lower left forearm is down there between the two of them, in the black canal water, and there is absolutely nowhere near enough space for something as thick as a human arm to be in such a place.*

At this moment there is no pain. Pain will come later – that and much, much worse. For now there is only a dull surprise, as if to say 'How on earth did my arm get down there?'

A stupid, meaningless accident, that is how.

* * *

Black Knight Boats operated a narrowboat hire company out of Stoke Pound on the Worcester and Birmingham canal, offering holidaymakers access to the heart of the country's inland waterway network at a sedate four miles an hour, and a slightly eye-watering price tag. It catered mostly to empty-nesters and young middle-class families with illusions of enjoying a carefree and nomadic lifestyle, and it had taken Rachel months to convince Tom that it was their sort of thing.

'I am not spending a week of my summer holiday farting around in the Black Country on a barge like some old man,' he'd protested. 'If you really want to see smashed-up warehouses and drowned shopping trolleys, get in the car, we'll be there in half an hour.' What was wrong with Greece? he'd wanted to know. It was hotter, it was cheaper, there was room service and a pool. Which meant it might as well have been anywhere, Rachel had countered; she wanted to see where she lived. Why didn't she just look out the bloody window, then? he'd hmphed.

Variations on a theme, all through autumn last year.

She'd clinched it on the traditional Cooper family Boxing Day canal walk, that feat of domestic organisation which saw Tom, his mother Charlotte and his dad Spence, Gramps, sister Rosie and her husband Clive and brood of four, not to mention assorted dogs, bikes, hangers-on, boyfriends, girlfriends, and newer additions like Rachel herself, all pile into a small fleet of SUVs to walk off some of the festive bloat with a slow stroll up the canal to the Tardebigge Reservoir and back. Coming as she did from a much smaller family of just herself, her mother, an elderly great-grandmother known to all as 'Gigi' and a variety of distant uncles and aunts whom she rarely saw, Rachel loved immersing herself in the fuggy, jumbling chaos of Tom's extended family, and even after three years was still surprised by how Charlotte welcomed her so unquestioningly and uncritically into the bosom of her tribe.

She and Tom had fallen back from the main mob and were walking with grandfather – fag on and fuck the doctors; Gramps had smoked since he was fourteen and what the bloody hell did they know about any of it – squelching along the muddy towpath, when they'd passed The Queens Head on the other side. It was busy with Boxing Day drinkers, many of them sitting muffled up in the beer garden under wide patio heaters.

Tom rubbed his hands against the chill. 'I could just about do with a pint,' he said.

Gramps snorted. 'You don't want to drink there. It's all beer with goblins on and pulled pork and quinn-ower. Get yourself over to The Weighbridge at Alvechurch Marina. They do a good drop of ale.'

'Could you get there by boat?' Rachel wondered.

'I should say so. It's only a couple of miles further up. You'd pass a few decent pubs on the way.'

'You don't say.' She nudged Tom. 'Quite a few decent pubs, the man says. Just think, darling,' she cooed, taking his arm and snuggling up against his shoulder. 'A week-long pub crawl through the Black Country, lazy summer days.

You, captain of your own vessel; me, lying on the roof, in the sun, in my bikini...'

Gramps sniffed. 'I'd take her up on that, son, before she changes her mind.'

So they'd walked up to the reservoir and back, and kept going down to where Black Knight had their office and dozens of boats moored in the pound being refitted for the tourist season, and booked it then and there.

Her wedding ring, she realises, is on that hand, down there, in the dark. In the frozen moment between when everything was perfect and when everything will be crushed and broken. Part of her hopes that it slips off and falls into the silt, because at least that way there's a chance that it might be rescued.

There was nothing lazy about the long, hot summer days that began that week. Tom was captain; that was non-negotiable. He even bought a hat. Rachel spent weeks putting together the most versatile wardrobe for a boating holiday – lots of Breton stripes and canvas.

A half-day's induction by the Black Knight people had shown them how to drive the boat, perform basic maintenance checks and operate the canal locks, and it was then Rachel realised how badly she'd misunderstood the role of first mate. She'd thought she'd be lounging on the roof in a wide-brimmed hat and sunglasses with a glass of wine and the latest Joanne Harris, while Tom took care of the mechanical side of things. Her only experience of boats had been as a child on Edgbaston Reservoir, where she'd been taught to sail by her dad in light, easily handled Picos. She hadn't factored in that a narrowboat would have to be manoeuvred while the locks were operated, and that this would be her job. Each lock had two pairs of massive swinging wooden gates that she had to open and shut, shoving at them like a donkey on a treadmill, and then she had to crank the sluice gates either open or closed with a metal device that looked like a tyre iron. Despite the fact that her desk job involved watching closed-circuit television monitors of a stretch of the M5 motorway for the Highways Agency and included the routine lifting of nothing heavier than a box-file, she kept herself reasonably fit by running – but lock gates involved a whole different set of muscles, and soon her back and arms were killing her.

What made it worse was that there were thirty of these locks on the Tardebigge Flight up into Birmingham. They had to stop halfway through for the night, during which she was good for nothing except demanding a back rub.

Stiffness and fatigue were mostly to blame for the accident. They'd made it into Gas Street Basin right in the centre of Birmingham, which was busy with the multi-coloured liveries of dozens of boat companies, polished brass glittering in the sun, cascading colour from hanging baskets and flower boxes, streamers and pennants. There were no locks to open or close, so she sat in the bow and drank in the life and colour, but it was more of a navigational challenge for Tom at the stern, avoiding so many other craft, and she could see that they were drifting dangerously close to one of them. It was a café narrowboat, with large windows where tourists sat eating their lunch, cruising even more slowly than themselves, and the captain at the back could see that Tom was having trouble keeping a safe distance.

'Oi!' he shouted. 'Watch yourself there!'

'It's okay, honey!' she called to Tom. 'I'll fend us off!'

There was a long wooden pole clipped to the roof which she should have used, but that would have involved climbing all the way up there and dragging it back down, whereas she was sitting at the front already, and the side of the restaurant boat was coming right towards her. It wasn't as if they were going to hit it outright – they were going to glance it at worst, and maybe not make contact at all. All she had to do was lean over and give it a good shove with both hands; mass and momentum being what they were, she wouldn't have to deflect it by much, and it only needed an inch or two.

The boats lumbered together. She leaned out, placed both palms against the cold steel of the other hull – close enough to make momentary eye contact with a woman in glasses who raised her eyebrows in surprise – braced her feet, and pushed.

And her feet slipped.

Instead of her rubber-soled deck shoes she was wearing sandals that offered no purchase at all. She fell forward, head and both arms over the rail of her boat, and saw her own shocked reflection in the black, oily water. She flailed with her right hand, grabbed the rail, and started to pull herself back up from the rapidly narrowing gap.

And then it was now.

This moment, the lightless pivot of worlds – between one in which there is sun on water and flowers and wedding rings, and one in which she is a broken, crippled thing – passes, and cannot be recalled.

The boats bumped and parted as if there was nothing dramatic to see here, people, move along. The sun was no dimmer, the laughter and music no quieter. The woman in glasses got on with her lunch. Rachel pulled herself up properly with her right arm, dragging something heavy that seemed to have clamped itself to her left. When she looked down at what remained of her left arm just below the elbow, she began to scream.

2

AMPUTATION

THE SURGEON WAS AS APOLOGETIC AS THE URGENCY of her injury would allow. His ID badge said MR ADENSON, VASCULAR SURGEON but he was just another in a long list of concerned faces and forgotten names. Names, tags, worried frowns, and the elephant in the room: the massive swathed lump lying in bed beside her. There was an oxygen mask on her face and an IV in her good arm, killing the pain from the bad one. There was even, she discovered with disgust, a tube coming from between her legs. There wasn't an inch of her that didn't feel bruised or invaded or like it had been pulled off, twisted, and stuck back on upside down.

A question had been asked, but she couldn't remember what it was.

'Mum?' Rachel moaned, and her mother was there, eyes puffy with weeping. 'It all hurts. Everything. I just, I can't…' She couldn't see her mother's face properly; it was blurry, and she couldn't work out why until Olivia wiped her face and she realised she was crying. 'I'm sorry...'

'Oh shh, my darling, whatever for?'

'Because of Dad... and you said... you said you never wanted to, to see the inside of a hospital again...'

'Shh, shh, it's not your fault, my love. You're hurt, not sick. It's not your fault.' Olivia turned to the doctor. 'And you're absolutely certain, then?' she sniffed. 'There's no way of saving it?'

Mr Adenson shook his head. 'The damage is simply too severe and too extensive, I'm afraid.'

Pulverised, they had said. *Massive vascular damage.* The two narrowboats hadn't just bounced together and apart with her arm between them, they'd skidded off each other, doing to her flesh what two bricks rubbed together might do to a worm. Her hand hadn't been squashed so much as smeared.

'Mum,' she said. 'Let them do it.'

So they did it.

While they operated, she dreamed, but as is the way with such things she could only remember fragments of images when she woke up.

She dreamed of a tree.

It was an ugly tree, ancient and broken. At some point in its history the upper portion of its trunk and boughs had been shorn away – possibly through lightning or storm winds – leaving a squat, wide stump just higher than a tall woman's head. But this had not killed the tree. A ragged crown of sapling limbs spread out from the blunt top, while thinner, sicklier shoots grew like the questing tendrils of a sea anemone further down the trunk, half-strangled by tumours of mistletoe and ivy, itself so old that its stalks were as thick and twisted and dry as the arms of old men. As she saw it, it came to her that the tree was hollow, and that someone was inside it, because from within that tangled mass she could hear a woman's weeping.

Then a bare arm pushed free and reached out to her.

The next time Rachel woke up, the mask was gone, along with the catheter and the worst of the pain, but the IV was still in, and even under all the dressings it was obvious that the limb on the other side was a lot shorter, ending halfway down from the elbow. *Thank God it isn't mine*, she thought.

There was another tube coming out of all the dressings, taking fluid away, as if the rest of her body were just some kind of processing plant for pain. The slightest shifting of position was enough to set her whole arm shrieking from shoulder to fingertips – never mind that her fingertips weren't there any more. Whoever was in charge of the pain centres in her brain didn't know that and was absolutely losing their shit, sounding the alarm that something was very, very wrong down there. Her throat was raw and her stomach rolled with nausea.

A hand stroked her brow: her mother murmuring, 'Oh my poor darling, there there, oh my poor darling,' over and over.

'Mum?' she croaked.

Her mother was instantly alert. 'Yes, darling? Can I get you anything?'

Rachel nodded towards the bandaged stump lying next to her. 'Whose arm is that?' she asked. 'What have they done with my hand?'

Olivia made a strange sort of choking noise and called for the nurse.

Gradually the nausea and disorientation passed, and Rachel was able to take clearer stock of her situation.

'Where's Tom?' she asked her mother, who was still there and seemed not to have left for – how long was it? Rachel had lost track of time. It must only have been hours, but it felt like days. Maybe she'd always been here.

'He's waiting outside, darling. We didn't want you to have to deal with too much too soon.'

'I already am. Tell him he can come in.'

Tom came in, and like everyone else the first thing his eyes travelled to was her bandages.

'Hey,' she said.

'Hey.' His face was haggard with shadows. He was still wearing the same clothes – cargo shorts, deck shoes and a checked shirt and gilet vest – he'd worn on the boat. She'd teased him about it at the time, asking him when the next Young Farmers' Association meeting was, back when any of that mattered, on the other side of before.

'Oi, I'm up here.' Rachel pointed to her face, and his eyes

finally met hers. 'At least you weren't staring at my boobs.'

He smiled weakly. 'This is all my fault,' he started. 'If I'd had the boat under better control…'

'And if I hadn't nagged you into it in the first place,' she interrupted. 'And if that other boat hadn't been there. And if I'd been wearing proper shoes. And and and. Nothing you or I can say will make this grow back.'

'I know, I just—'

'It is what it is,' she said, a little more harshly than she'd intended, but she didn't have the energy to put up any kind of façade, either brave or gentle. 'And apologies won't make it better. I don't need them. I will need your help, though.'

His eyes widened in surprise.

'I know,' she said. 'You can count the number of times I've asked for that on one hand, which is ironic, since that's all I've got now.'

She could almost hear her mother wince, but the smile Tom gave her was almost normal. *There you are*, she thought. *There's the man I need*.

'You're incredible,' he said.

'No, I'm shit-scared and on some amazing drugs, but I have no choice. What's happening with the boat?'

He blinked. 'Seriously? You're worried about *that*?'

'I need something to think about.' She glanced at her bandages. 'Something… else. See if you can get, I don't know, some kind of part refund for the days we didn't use. Is all our stuff safe?'

'It's okay,' Tom said, stroking her hair. 'Dad's got it under control. Oh, there's this, though.' He produced a small plastic grip-seal bag and showed her the contents. 'They had to cut it off you when they… you know.'

It was her watch – the Mondaine she'd been given for her twenty-first. The strap was sheared through, the glass face was smashed and both the hands were gone. *Ha*, she thought. *Beat you there. I only lost the one.* Compared to losing her hand, a broken watch was nothing, but it reminded her of something far more important. 'Oh shit!' She turned shocked eyes to him. 'My ring!'

He shrugged helplessly. 'It wasn't there.'

'What do you mean it wasn't there?' She struggled to sit up higher, but that sent a spike of agony into her elbow despite the painkillers, and she cried out.

Olivia leapt to support her. 'Darling, please, you mustn't—'

'What do you mean *it wasn't there*?' Rachel repeated between gasps of pain.

'What do you want me to say?' he asked. 'I mean that it wasn't there. If it had been, they'd have had to cut it off you too. It must have, I don't know, snapped under the impact and dropped off. It's probably at the bottom of the canal.'

'*No…*' she moaned. Her wedding ring. She'd never for one second begrudged the Cooper family's self-made wealth which had allowed them to bankroll the wedding, but all the same she'd been fiercely proud of having at least arranged the rings – designed by an old school friend who had made good as part of an arts and crafts collective in the Jewellery Quarter. Its twin was on Tom's hand – the one that was stroking her hair and trying to calm her – a simple band of white and yellow gold fused together.

'Hey, it's just a thing,' he said. 'Just a thing. It can be replaced. You can't. You're okay, and that's the important thing.'

She gave a hollow laugh and gestured with her bandaged stump. 'Yeah, what's left of me.'

Eventually even mothers and husbands had to leave, and night settled on the recovery ward. It was a false darkness, though, like trying to sleep on a long-haul flight with all the lights down and your eye mask on but still aware of the restless souls all around you, busy with whispered conversations and soft footsteps along unseen corridors. Her hand was the same, buzzing and jittering in the empty space below her elbow as if refusing to accept that it didn't exist any more. She was never going to be able to sleep, she thought, with her mind churning over the seismic effect this was going to have on her life, and the random shooting pains and starbursts of pins and needles.

But she did.

She surfaced from sleep just far enough to know that her mother was stroking her hand, telling her that everything was going to be all right without speaking; just loving, slow strokes across the back of her hand and down across her fingers.

But it must have been a dream, because when she opened her eyes the ward was still dark, and there was nobody sitting beside her bed.

And it was her missing left hand that had been so lovingly stroked.

31

3

RECOVERY

THE SURGEON MR ADENSON WAS TALL AND GANGLY, and his long fingers inspected her wound with as much delicacy and precision as any surgical instrument. Just behind him stood her physiotherapist, a small Nigerian woman who had been introduced to Rachel as Abayomi 'Call me Yomi; it's less embarrassing for all of us' Akinsanya. She had a northern accent as broad as her smile but stood very still and self-contained with her arms folded. Rachel watched her suspiciously; she'd heard horror stories about physios from one of her mother's golfing friends who'd had a knee replacement, and Rachel didn't want to think about what plans for her arm lurked behind Yomi's friendly smile. Rachel hissed as Adenson touched a tender spot.

'Sorry about that,' he frowned. 'Sensitive?'

'Just a bit.'

'It's bound to be at first. That'll pass. There doesn't appear to be too much swelling, though, which is a good thing. We'll aim to have that drain out tomorrow afternoon if all goes well, and then a compression dressing to help keep it down.'

'We'll sort that hypersensitivity, too,' nodded Yomi.

'I hope so. It's been going off like firecrackers all night.'

'Those phantom sensations will subside as your nerves get used to their new conditions, don't worry,' said Adenson. 'They can even be a good thing. Not the pain, obviously, but we have found that patients who have a good ability to imagine or mentally recreate the sensations from their lost limb often find it easier to adapt to the use of a prosthesis.'

'You mean like a hook?' Rachel shuddered. 'No thanks.'

'Don't worry, love,' said Yomi. 'You've got options.'

'The good news there,' continued the surgeon, 'is that you've got a nice amount of your lower arm to work with – we were able to save it down to just a couple of inches short of your wrist. The more muscle you've got to work with, the more control you have of whatever prosthesis you choose. Ms Akinsanya here will be working closely with you to maintain as much flexibility in your elbow as possible and develop those muscles.'

Yomi winked. 'You're going to have forearms like Popeye the Sailor Man by the time you're done.'

'But my elbow is fine,' Rachel said, and bent it to show them, despite the twinge this caused.

'I know, but the tension of the tissues in your arm will have gone skew-whiff, and a prosthetic's quite a bit heavier than a real hand, so you'll need a bit of building up.'

Rachel looked at her wound properly for the first time.

Her arm ended just where she would have worn her watch, the skin joined over the end in a line of black stitches. It was puffy and still stained yellow with surgical swab, but she could see that when it had healed properly she'd be left with a single straight scar. She waved her right hand in the space just in front of it. *My hand used to be in this space*, she thought. *My flesh. And now it's gone, but I'm still here. Maybe this is what it feels like to be a ghost.*

'Can I see it?' she asked Adenson. 'My old hand, I mean?'

He paused in his exploration of her arm, looking surprised. 'Ah, I'm afraid not.'

'Why not? Why can't I see my hand?'

'Because we don't have it any more.'

His bluntness took her by surprise. 'Well where is it, then? Have you *thrown away* my hand?'

She saw his eyes flick up and down the recovery ward; she was being loud. Too bloody right she was. That hand had learned to tie shoelaces and bake scones, played terrible recorder at school concerts and scored a decent number of netball goals, stabbed Sally Bonner in the leg with a biro for that thing with the rat in Year 10 Biology, slipped down the front of Ian Wilkinson's jeans in the back row of a cinema while watching *Inglourious Basterds*, and even had a wedding ring placed on it.

She was aware that people were talking to her.

'Mrs Cooper?' repeated Adenson. Her cheeks were wet. When had she started crying?

She shoved the tears away with the heel of her hand. 'Okay. Fine. It's gone. Just where? Tell me that.'

'Hospital regulations are that the ah, remains from an operation—'

'Clinical waste,' she interrupted.

He blinked. 'Beg pardon?'

'It's right there on the bin by the door: *please dispose of clinical waste carefully*. I'm sorry to ride you, Mr Adenson, I don't really mean to, but you've just cut my hand off and it's a bit late to be pussy-footing around trying to protect my feelings with euphemisms, don't you think?'

'Well then, clinical waste, like your hand, is collected and incinerated off-site by a third-party contractor. It really is gone, I'm afraid.'

'So it's ash.'

'Yes.'

'Well that's something, I suppose. Just as long as it's not sitting in a jar on someone's shelf for all the medical students to point at and have a laugh.'

'I assure you, nothing like that would ever happen.'

She looked at him sidelong. 'Really? I have a friend who used to work in a pub near the medical school; I've heard about you medics.'

'I'm sorry to disappoint you, but despite my job involving cutting parts of people's bodies off I am in reality a very boring man.'

She reached over with her good – her only – hand and wrapped her fingers in his. 'No, you're not,' she said. 'You're a miracle worker and I'm a mardy cow. Honestly, thank you for saving what you could.'

After he'd gone, Yomi showed her the stretching and

flexing exercises she wanted Rachel to do to keep the rest of her arm in the best possible condition for when she started physio, and when she left Rachel had a go at imagining the sensations of her non-existent hand. Somewhere in her bag was her phone and on the other side of it a whole world of friends, relatives and co-workers who would either need to be told or were already desperate for news, but she couldn't face that right now. Instead she concentrated on what it had felt like to wiggle her fingers and make a fist. It was strange seeing the tendons on the underside of her forearm twitching as they tried to move something that wasn't there any more, but she found that it actually did help to reduce the shooting spasms of pins and needles. Once or twice her imagination succeeded in convincing her that she could actually feel her fingers rubbing together and forming a fist. She imagined punching herself repeatedly in the head while muttering, 'Stupid! Stupid! Stupid!' until the nurse asked her if they could get her anything and she said no, she was fine thanks, just as shiny as could be expected given the circumstances. She smiled while giving them the imaginary finger, and then felt horrible about it afterwards.

She managed one hobbling trip to the loo, shepherding her collection of plastic tubes and bags like a mountaineer setting off to conquer Everest, and collapsing back into bed afterwards, just as exhausted.

She thought she was hungry and tried to eat a little hospital food, its blandness calculated to avoid upsetting delicate post-op stomachs, but couldn't manage it, so she asked for more pain meds to shut up the shouting in her arm, and even as she was marvelling at how much the operation had knocked out of her, slept.

When she woke up, Tom was there again.

'Hey,' she murmured.

'Hey.' He put away his phone and bent close, stroking the hair out of her eyes.

'How long have you been there?'

'I dunno. An hour?'

'You should have woken me.'

'No bloody way,' he said. 'The nurses in this place are terrifying. One of them said if I disturbed you she'd use me for spare parts.'

'Sounds about right. Could you—?'

He helped her sit up and got her some water. 'You know if I could have given *my* hand I would've,' he said.

'Don't be daft.'

'Honestly, though, I was just reading about it. They're getting really good at hand transplants. There's this pub landlord who had gout and—'

She reached up and stroked his cheek, shutting him up. It was bristly, which surprised her. One of the things that had attracted her to him in the first place had been how scrupulous he was about grooming. Her best friend Sandra had opined that it was vain, if not actually gay, for a man to moisturise and wouldn't she prefer a bit of stubble instead, to which she'd replied God no, who needed all that scratching about in your neck? 'Neck?' Sandra had retorted in horror. 'Girl, if he's going no further south than your neck you definitely don't want anything to do with him!' But here he was – unshaven, and it worried her.

'Are you looking after yourself?' she asked.

'Me? What about you? You're the one who's hurt.'

'Yes, but you're the one who's going to have to look after me – at least to begin with. Aren't you?'

'Of course I am.'

'Then please do me a favour: don't do the whole "I'd cut my arm off for you" thing. I know what you mean and I love you for it but it doesn't help. Or stories about arm transplants. It's hard enough trying to get my head around the fact that it's gone in the first place. I need you solid and down to earth, to help me cope.'

Tom nodded. 'Okay.'

'They say that if there's no swelling or infection and I'm strong enough they'll move me to an ordinary ward tomorrow or the day after.'

'That'll be good, won't it?'

Rachel fiddled with the dressing. 'I don't want visitors.'

'Okay.'

'I'm serious, Tom. I don't think I could handle your whole family, everyone, being all sorry and full of sympathy. I just want to deal with this. Does that make sense?'

'Absolutely. No visitors.'

'Or flowers. Or balloons. Or any of those horrible cuddly toys.'

'No hospital gift shop tat. Got it.'

'Chocolate's okay.'

'Well obviously.'

'Oh,' he said, 'I brought you a bag. I didn't know how long they'd keep you in, so it's just some spare clothes and stuff.' He placed a sports holdall beside her, being careful of all her various tubes and wires. She looked inside.

'Along with, it looks like, everything from the bathroom cabinet and off my bedside table.'

He shrugged. 'How am I supposed to know what's important?'

It might have been the drugs, but she didn't think she had ever loved him as much as she did right at that very moment.

The next day they removed the tubes from her arms and Rachel began to feel a bit more like herself and less of a battlefield between injury and surgery. They told her she was making excellent progress and arranged visits from a prosthetics specialist, an occupational therapist, someone from the West Midlands Rehabilitation Centre at Selly Oak and even a social worker. 'I'm an amputee, for God's sake, not an addict,' she complained to her mother. All of them had appointments they wanted to make with her and forms for her to fill in. 'My job has less paperwork than this. Sod's law it would be my writing hand that's perfectly fine.'

'You shouldn't make jokes about this,' Olivia tutted.

'I have to joke. It's just too tragic otherwise.'

* * *

They kept her on the surgical ward for three days and then moved her to a recovery ward, where any temptation she might have had to feel sorry for herself withered in the company of a middle-aged man occupying the cubicle across from her, who spent long periods of time just staring at the fat white stumps where his legs had been as if waiting for them to suddenly hatch like cocoons.

4

HOME

TOM PICKED HER UP IN THE VAN HE DROVE FOR HIS family's landscaping and gardening business. She'd made such good progress during her week on the recovery ward that they were letting her go straight home, albeit with a small pharmacy's worth of medication and a strict timetable of outpatient checkups to obey.

'There's somewhere I need to go first,' she told him, as she eased herself into the van. Her arm had been put in a hard cast to protect it while the stitches healed, and strapped up tightly to her body to prevent her from accidentally bashing it, but it was still the first time she'd had to manoeuvre with it outside the safety of the hospital and she felt like she needed a buffer zone of at least a metre around it at all times. The cab of the van felt horribly cramped, but it was still more spacious than Tom's car.

'Where?' he asked.

She showed him the address on her phone.

'Really?' He shrugged. 'Okay, if you say so.'

He drove them out of the city, through the suburbs and grim-faced estates, and into the industrial edge-lands where the skin of the city gave up even pretending to be green and became the concrete that it had always been.

ARJ Clinical Waste Management inhabited the same kind of small factory unit as any of the other dozens of interchangeable mechanical or engineering firms in the area: a square-framed prefabricated building with half a dozen forklifts and vans parked in the yard, all surrounded by a chain-link fence. The only notable difference here was the large number of bright yellow dumpsters, wheelie bins, containers and notices reading CLINICAL WASTE: FOR INCINERATION ONLY.

Tom parked up across the road and turned to her. 'I still don't understand why you need to come here,' he said.

Rachel carefully disengaged her left arm from the seat belt. 'You know you told me about that time when you were six and your great-granddad took you and Spence and Gramps to Normandy, to see where he fought?'

'Yes, but I don't remember anything about it.'

'And you know why people leave flowers at the sites of fatal car accidents?'

'Okay, I get it. Memorials.'

'Kind of. People need to see the places where their loved ones died.'

'But you're not dead,' Tom pointed out.

She held up her arm. 'This part of me is.'

He winced. 'Fair enough. But I'm coming with you.'

'I don't need you to—'

'Too late, already happening,' he said, opening the door and getting out.

There was a gate with a small booth, and a stubble-headed man with a hi-vis vest and a clipboard sitting in it. 'Help you?' he grunted.

Rachel turned on her best smile – granted, she was in a hoodie and sweatpants, didn't have a bit of make-up on and altogether probably looked like she'd been dragged through a hedge backwards, but it was the best she could do. 'Hello. Can you please tell me if your company handles waste from Heartlands Hospital?'

His small eyes narrowed with suspicion, if not actual thought. 'You got some ID?'

She could feel Tom bristling beside her and sighed. She hadn't wanted this to turn into a pissing contest.

'Why does she need ID?' Tom demanded. 'She's just asking a question.'

Rachel turned aside a little and murmured, 'She's right here, darling.' Then, stepping a little closer to the man in the booth, she showed him her truncated arm and smiled sweetly. 'I think you might have incinerated something of mine. Can I please see a supervisor or something?'

There was that wince again, this time from both of them. The booth guard muttered something that might have been 'I'll go get him', and scurried off without looking at her again. Whatever his job description was, it plainly didn't cover dealing with bolshie one-armed women. He returned with a version of himself who was younger, slimmer, and had slightly more hair.

'Good afternoon.' The newcomer smiled. His eyes flicked down to her arm but the smile didn't waver. 'Can I help? I'm told you have a complaint about something?'

'I'm sorry, there's been a misunderstanding,' Rachel said. 'There's no complaint, honestly. I simply wanted to know whether you handled the waste from the hospital that performed my operation. That's all, nothing else. No complaints.'

'Heartlands?' he asked. 'Yes, yes we do. Consignments are processed and disposed of within twenty-four hours.'

Waste, she thought. *He doesn't want to refer to my hand as waste to my face – and I wouldn't either if I were him.*

'I'm afraid I can't let you see,' he continued. 'Health and safety, you understand.'

'I understand. Thank you for your time. Come on, darling.' She led Tom back to the van.

'So,' he said, as they got in. 'That was fun. Are you done?'

She looked at the place, fixing it in her memory. There were no twinges from her absent hand. Everything below the wrist was quiet and dead. 'Yes. I'm done. It's gone now. Let's go home.'

Rachel explored her home for what felt like the first time, with eyes looking for the obstacles to a one-handed existence that they obviously hadn't anticipated when they'd bought the place. Tom's parents had paid the deposit on a detached family home in Shenley Fields, an area of town that had been smart and fashionable after the war, when building standards were more generous, and even though it had gone a bit to seed in later years it was still technically a part of Bournville Village Trust, which meant there was a decent amount of green space that was looked after and not so much of the cramped over-building that blighted a lot of the city. There was a large playing field surrounding a small lake raucous with Canada geese, care homes in quiet cul-de-sacs, the ruins of Weoley Castle just up the road in one direction and a large leisure centre in the other. The house itself had been rented out by the previous owners after the death of an elderly relative, and by the time it had come to Rachel and Tom it had needed a lot of renovation. He'd jumped at the chance to flex his DIY muscles, and she wasn't averse to living with a certain amount of chaos while walls were replastered and rotten woodwork replaced, but it wasn't anywhere close to being finished yet.

Rachel had claimed the garden as her own personal project, even though she'd had neither the time nor the inclination to do anything beyond move an outdoor table and some chairs onto the leaf-littered patio. Tom was more than happy with this, because the last thing he wanted to do was come home from working on somebody else's land and have to go straight out into digging his own.

The money from his parents hadn't been entirely without strings, even though they remained invisible and, for the most part, un-pulled. Charlotte hadn't exactly been subtle in her evaluation of how many children's bedrooms the property might allow. Tom had been suitably embarrassed by his mother's broodiness-by-proxy, but Rachel knew that he was watching his sister Rosie's growing family with interest and wasn't going to be content as just Uncle Tom for too many years. The room that had been worked on least was the rear upstairs bedroom; what Rachel called the 'spare room' but which she'd seen in his scribbled designs referred to as 'nursery'. Fortunately there was enough work needing to be done on the rest of the place before they began to have those arguments. She didn't know what kind of impact her injury was going to have. *Life-changing injuries* was what they called it on the news. *Let's just see if you can handle a tin opener first, shall we?* she told herself.

Inside the front porch she looked at the racks of shoes, with all their laces. Velcro was going to be her new friend, she decided, along with buckles, straps and pop-studs. 'Well the good news,' she said, 'is that I get to buy a whole load of new footwear.'

Tom was wrestling her bag out of the van. 'And the bad news?' he called.

She looked at him. 'There is no downside to this. Fancy a cup of tea?'

'Give me a chance, I'm not through the door yet.'

'It's all right, I'll do it.'

'Are you sure that's such a good idea?'

'It's a cup of tea, not juggling fire.' She scooped up the small drift of junk mail, pizza menus, and unpromising brown envelopes that had accumulated behind the front door, collecting them right-handed against her left instep. 'I have to start living with this,' she said.

It was good to be back in her own kitchen, surrounded by her own things, all exactly where she knew they should be – even the boiler, another of Tom's works-in-progress, which looked like someone was midway performing open-heart surgery on a robot. Looking through the cutlery drawer she chanced upon a potato peeler, and felt an odd pang at the idea that she might never use such a simple thing again. She found that the only difference having one hand made (at least in the case of tea-making) was that everything was just a bit slower and required a more methodical approach. The trickiest bit was spinning the lid off the milk bottle.

Tea made, she picked up Tom's mug to take it through to him, glanced at the surface of the brown liquid and stopped.

She couldn't breathe. At precisely the same time her heart began to race, and sweat broke out on her brow as if she had a fever, despite feeling freezing cold. Her left hand, the one that wasn't there, was frozen too – she could actually feel goosebumps rising on her dead wrist.

She wasn't looking into a cup of tea at all. She was staring at her own reflection in the dead black water of the canal between the two boats that held her trapped, still.

Then the face changed and a voice from the blackness whispered:

'Not dead.'

Rachel screamed and dropped the mug, which shattered into a hundred thick shards on the kitchen tiles, spraying a flood of stinking black canal water.

Then Tom was there, his hands either side of her face,

and it was just a spilt mug of tea, just a mess that needed cleaning up, and no whispering voice.

That night, as they undressed, she was aware of him looking at her sidelong – or rather, at her arm.

'What?' she said.

'Nothing,' he replied, and turned away, tossing his shirt in the laundry hamper.

'Bollocks nothing. Does this make you feel uncomfortable?'

'*Me* uncomfortable? No, I just thought... I don't want to... sharing a bed... what if I accidentally... I could make up the spare bed until you've gotten used to...'

'You're not going to squash my arm in the night,' she told him. 'And neither of us is sleeping in the spare room.'

And neither of them did. They just held each other for a long time, but afterwards she thought that he slept ever so slightly further away from her than was usual.

5

REHABILITATION

A WEEK LATER SHE HAD HER FIRST FOLLOW-UP examination in Adenson's office. He removed the dressings and examined her wound (she had quickly grown to hate the word 'stump'; it had an ugly, final sound to it), and pronounced her as having made excellent progress.

'The stitches will come out on their own, in time,' he said. 'You're keeping up with your physio?'

'Oh yes,' Rachel replied. 'I do not want to be in Yomi's bad books.' She'd even taken herself out for a few runs – just around the playing field next to the house and back, but it was a start.

'How are the phantom sensations?'

'I hear they're gigging the cruise ship circuit these days.'

He blinked. 'I'm sorry?'

'Sorry. Um, no. Nothing significant. No actual pain, anyway. Flashes of hot and cold, some terrible pins and needles.'

'They will subside over time. It's a—'

'Long process, I know.'

Nothing as bad as the incident with the tea had happened since, and she'd put that down to a simple anxiety attack – she certainly hadn't told anybody about the voice from the mug, convincing herself that it was just part of the post-traumatic stress that she'd been told to expect. Though there had been one odd moment a few nights afterwards. She must have fallen asleep on her arm, as everyone did once in a while, because the pins and needles had spread from her wound right up into her armpit, and she half-woke to find her arm lying across her chest like a large, warm, numb slug. Still half-asleep, she'd started to knead blood and life back into the other limb, and just for a moment she could have sworn that her living right hand had curled around the non-existent fingers of her dead hand, and that they'd squeezed each other like old friends hugging after a long absence. She could well understand the phenomenon of phantom sensations in her dead hand, but in her living one? In the sanity of daylight she'd convinced herself that it had been her half-dreaming mind playing tricks.

'Here,' said Adenson, handing her something which looked like a packet of department-store underpants. 'These are compression socks. Just a cotton-Lycra sleeve which fits over your stump – they'll help to prevent dirt getting into the stitches, as well as generally with the hypersensitivity and the swelling.'

Rachel fumbled the pack open and examined one. It looked like an ordinary sports support. It was heavily elasticated and she struggled to get it over the end of her stump, but when Adenson offered to help she swatted him away. When she finally managed to roll the material down over her wrist it made the buzzing from her nerve endings diminish immediately. 'Nice,' she said, relishing the relief. 'Hey, do you think they come in other colours?'

Tom drove her to her first outpatient appointment with Yomi at the West Midlands Rehabilitation Centre at Selly Oak, and she arrived with some nervousness, expecting everything that the word 'rehab' conjured up – grim-faced orderlies in white coats and flapping gurney wheels on scratched linoleum floors – but what she found were smiling faces, potted plants and a sense of hushed, unhurried concentration, like a private college or a conference centre.

'This is liable to take a good couple of hours,' said Yomi, glancing at Tom.

'You don't have to stay here for the whole thing,' Rachel said to him.

'It's okay,' he replied. 'I'm in no hurry. The more I know the better I can help you.'

Yomi raised her eyebrows, looking him up and down with approval. 'You hang on to this one, my lovely,' she said.

'Oh I absolutely intend to.'

They were shown to the Prosthetics Department, past treatment suites and a large exercise room where teams of blue-uniformed physiotherapists guided patients in the use of their mechanical legs – it looked to be painful and frustrating work – but when she reached their destination Rachel thought she'd been brought to the staff lounge by mistake.

'Welcome to your classroom,' smiled Yomi, ushering her into what looked suspiciously like an ordinary domestic kitchen.

'I thought this was occupational therapy,' Rachel said.

'It is. Did you think you were going to be weaving baskets and painting with a brush in your teeth?'

'Well, no, but…' Rachel stopped, took a deep breath and consciously unbunched her shoulders. 'Okay. What do we do?'

Yomi made a show of consulting a complicated schedule on her iPad. 'I don't know about you but I was thinking we start with a cup of tea and some biscuits and you tell me how you've been getting on with that arm of yours.'

'I think I can manage that.'

Over tea and chocolate Hobnobs she told Yomi about how she'd been looking after her arm and keeping the worst of the pain at bay with her medication but otherwise trying to tough it out. The longest she'd managed so far had been from breakfast until mid-afternoon before she'd been unable to bear it and was forced to pop a co-codamol. Yomi quizzed her on every aspect of her job at the Highways Agency, her home routine, what kinds of clothes she liked to wear, whether she cooked ('Does having the phone number of your local Papa John's on speed dial count as cooking?'); did she drive a car, ride a bike, have any hobbies, play any sports or musical instruments? Tom was banished briefly while she was taken to a small examination room and given a full physical check-up, as a result of which she was pronounced to be as physically fit as could be expected under the circumstances.

'Fine then,' said Yomi when she'd finished. 'Someone with a disease, unless it's a really nasty one, can go for a long time pretending nothing's wrong, telling themselves it's just a headache, a bit of tiredness, a patch of dry skin. Men are the worst.' She winked at Tom. 'But you don't have that luxury, I'm afraid. You can't ignore something that should be there but isn't, if you know what I mean. Our job here is to help you be able to do all of those things you need to do with the minimum of fuss and bother. Your arm's still got a lot of settling down to do, but now might be a good time to start thinking about whether or not you want any kind of prosthesis. Lots of people do. Lots don't. It all depends what you're comfortable with. That will help us decide what you need to learn and how – the fact that you're right-handed obviously makes things a lot easier from the start.'

'Well I don't want something that just looks like the real thing but doesn't do anything, I know that at least. What are my options?'

'Come and have a look.'

Yomi led Rachel and Tom back through the main physio studio and into a room full of arms. Some were simple hooks, some looked disturbingly realistic – hanging from pegs on the walls like serial killer trophies – and others were engineering confections of straps, cables and pulleys so elaborate Rachel couldn't imagine how they were even put on, let alone operated. They spilled out of boxes on shelves and lay disassembled in a workshop area, where a technician looked up briefly, said hi and then bent back to making the articulated steel fingers of a skeletal hand flex and un-flex.

'That's all very Terminator,' Tom observed.

'And yours for only about ten thousand pounds,' said Yomi.

Rachel whistled. 'Really?'

'You'll either need to go private or be in the army to afford something like that. Here, my common garden variety NHS patient, let me show you what's available to the great unwashed.'

'What did you make of those arms, then?' Tom asked, as they undressed that night. He was in the bathroom, brushing his teeth.

'Ugly,' Rachel said. 'Awkward. Honestly I think I'm going to be better off without.'

'Not even the myo-electric one?'

'Ha! At ten grand? Win the lottery while I was in hospital, did you?'

He spat, rinsed, spat again. 'No, but I have been talking with Mum and Dad.'

'You can't ask them for that. The house is one thing; that's for us.' *To raise a nice little addition to the Cooper dynasty*, she added silently to herself. 'My hand is mine. I'll pay for it, or not, thanks.'

'Asking for help isn't a crime, you know,' he replied.

She didn't want to have this conversation again, and especially not now. Her own mother – a woman whose life was a scrupulously accounted ledger of obligations owed and discharged – had been deeply reluctant but ultimately powerless over the extent to which Tom's family had supported them at the start of their marriage, and Rachel found herself fiercely protective of the empty space below her elbow.

She pulled her t-shirt off and went into the bathroom, turned her back towards him and fumbled with the clasp of her bra. 'Well in that case, mister, care to lend a lady a helping hand?' She was more than capable of doing it herself one-handed, but had no intention of letting him know that. 'Don't you go getting any ideas, though.'

He came to her, grinning, and undid the clasp. 'Nope, no ideas here.'

'None that you're thinking with your brain, anyway.' She could feel the reassuring solidity of his chest against her naked back, the hardness of him lower down in his briefs, his lips moving in the soft hair at the base of her neck, and the warmth of his hands as they reached around to cup her breasts. She sighed and relaxed back against him as his fingers teased. Her wound had enjoyed more than its fair share of attention over the last two weeks; time for the rest of her to have a go. She reached back over her head to run her fingers through his hair – reaching with both arms, of course, it being such an instinctive response, forgetting that she had only the one hand with which to do it, but reminded when the compression sock protecting her stump grazed his ear.

The unexpected contact caused a flash of pins and needles up to her elbow; not pain as such, more the zing of a sore tooth bitten carelessly. She hissed in discomfort.

Tom jerked his hands away. 'Sorry! Shit! I didn't mean to—'

'It's okay,' she said. 'Not your fault. Just a twinge.'

She turned to face him, putting her left arm around his waist and sliding her right hand down the back of his briefs to his bum and pulling him close. 'Let's try it this way round, what do you say?'

But the hardness had gone, which was ironic considering the rest of him was as stiff as a board.

'I'm sorry,' he whispered. 'It's just…'

'Still weird. I get it.' She pulled away, picked up her nightshirt and went into the bathroom, closing the door on him to finish undressing. Not to punish him – just so that he couldn't see how furiously embarrassed and stupid she felt. 'Tell me though,' she called through the door. 'Is it ever going to stop being weird, do you think?'

He didn't reply.

'Because this is never going to grow back, you know. This is me now.' She stared at her reflection in the mirrored doors of the bathroom cabinet, feeling all slanted and lopsided, her right arm hanging so much lower, like an orangutan's. Then she shook herself, squared her shoulders and put her head back. 'This is me now,' she repeated to her reflection defiantly. She half-opened the mirrored cabinet door, and placed its edge in the middle of her chest so that when she looked down at herself in it, the reflection of her right arm occupied the space of her left. She slowly opened and closed her right hand, imagining as she did so the feeling of her left hand doing the same thing. It was a simple technique that Yomi had told her about, which fooled the brain into thinking that the non-existent hand was still there, and supposedly reduced the stress on the nerves. She repeated this a dozen times, waiting for them to settle.

Gradually the buzzing ache subsided, but in its absence there was more than just a lack of pain. There was something that felt like cold – a chilly breeze playing with her dead fingertips. She almost fancied she could feel goosebumps rising.

'Oh just fuck off,' she whispered to her stump, then closed the cabinet and went to bed. Tom was already there, prodding at his phone.

'You know,' she said, 'if it helps, I bet we can get hold of some kind of sex toy attachment for one of those things.'

He snorted a laugh.

'There you go.'

Tom left for work early the following morning and Olivia came around with cards and flowers that she'd been stockpiling. 'Is there anything I can do?' she asked.

Rachel gestured at the hallway, with its ancient wallpaper half-stripped and its paint-spattered floorboards. 'That all depends on how good you are with a paper steamer.'

'Is there anything I can do for *you*?' her mother emphasised, indicating that since they had been the ones to pay for it, all matters pertaining to the house were a matter for the Coopers, specifically Tom.

'You can help me decide which clothes to keep and which to chuck?' Rachel suggested.

'That's more like it. I'll get these in some water while you make a start.'

Upstairs, Rachel opened her wardrobe as if expecting something to leap out at her. The smell of camphorated mothballs and dry-cleaning powder reminded her of the hospital. Everything reminded her of the hospital. Bits of it seemed to have followed her home. Her clothes hung tidily or were folded into neat piles. She had a little chart tacked to the inside of the door with hand-drawn cartoons of all the different permutations of which piece of clothing went with what. Newly added were the things that she'd bought for the canal holiday: French stripes, navy-blue three-quarter-length trousers, deck shoes, canvas and cotton. While Tom's holiday had begun when he'd started the narrowboat's diesel engine and his eyes had lit up at its throaty roar, hers had begun weeks earlier when she'd started shopping for outfits to satisfy a carefully curated mental image of sitting on the foredeck in the setting sun with a glass of wine, while Tom did something mechanical, or possibly involving long, heavy ropes, which required a v-neck tee and cargo shorts.

'Never going to happen now,' she told the wardrobe, and transferred them by the handful into a charity bag. They could have gone on eBay, but getting rid of them piecemeal like that would have been as painful as having her hand amputated finger by finger. A clean break was the only way to do this.

Then there were the suits. Technically she didn't need any as a regional control officer because Highways England had its own uniform, and watching three large monitor screens for an eight-hour shift didn't offer much opportunity for striding purposefully through a metropolitan cityscape, latte in hand, looking capable and sharp. But Olivia had instilled ambition in her daughter, and Rachel had had plans to enrol on a course in transport planning after the summer, to see how far up the civil service beanstalk she could climb. Now she'd been told that she couldn't return to work until the occupational health report on her was finished, and Yomi had said that might take a month, and she was already two weeks into her three months of sickness leave.

'Neither's that,' she said, and out came the suits too.

She'd never thought of herself as a superficial person before, but looking at all her outfits now she realised how many of them had been bought to satisfy one or other lifestyle fantasy, none of which involved her having only one functioning hand. She pulled out the rest of the clothes, first by the handful, then by upending entire drawers and flinging them across the bedroom in a sudden flood of rage and self-pity that seemed to come out of nowhere.

When Olivia came upstairs to investigate the commotion, she found Rachel sitting in the middle of it all. It looked like someone had taken off the roof of the bedroom and dumped the contents of a charity shop into it. Rachel was sobbing in great gulping breaths.

'I can't… do this!' she wept. 'It's not fair! I don't want to be like this!'

'I know, honey, I know.' Her mother gathered her in a hug and tried to shush her, and when that failed simply sat there and let Rachel shudder against her.

'I can't work, I can't even put a bloody necklace on! Tom won't come near me. It's like I'm a… a leper or something! What…' she gulped. 'What am I supposed to do?'

'Hmm,' Olivia replied, doing an elaborate show of thinking deeply. 'I think, given everything that's happened, what you really need to do is help me sort out what to do with all those flowers.'

Rachel eyed her sceptically.

The flowers weren't the half of it. There were also cuddly toys, chocolates, and even a bottle of Prosecco.

'What in God's name is that for?' Rachel said, horrified. 'Congratulations on your successful amputation?'

Her mother looked at the card. 'It's from Auntie Lydia. Bless, she means well.'

'And you think I'm actually going to write thank-you letters to all these people? It's not Christmas.'

'I think it's something to keep you busy and help take your mind off things.'

'My own self-pity, you mean.'

'If you want to put it that way. You can start with this.'

Her mother handed Rachel a small potted begonia with blousy pink flowers; *old-lady pants*, whispered a sly child's voice in her mind, and she had to stifle a smirk. 'You mean plant it?'

'Your Tom's a gardener, isn't he? I refuse to believe that there isn't a trowel hiding somewhere in all this chaos.'

'He's not a—'

'*Landscape* gardener, then,' corrected her mother, holding her hands up in surrender. 'Fine. Just put that poor thing in the ground where it belongs.'

Reluctantly, Rachel obeyed.

The garden was a mess, she would be the first to admit that. With all of their efforts going on the house she'd had no time to really address it, and as a result the long, narrow lawn was overgrown, the flowerbeds down the side were a wilderness of weeds, and the shaggy bushes at the far end were making a bid for freedom over the back fence. She found a relatively clear space in the flowerbed nearest the patio and dug a hole. The flowers got a bit crushed while she had the begonia upside down to shake the pot free, but soon it was in the ground. She had to get on hand and knees to pat down the earth around it, and obviously couldn't brace herself on a left hand that wasn't there any more, so settled for leaning on her forearm instead.

There was a spasm of pins and needles from her stump, and then, just like an old-fashioned radio dial tuning in from static to find a signal, the sensations changed. They settled down, smoothed out, and became intelligible.

Texture.

She could feel her non-existent fingers flexing and curling in a mulch of leaf and twig fragments, and soil below that, damp and loamy. She imagined clenching a handful of brittle leaf litter, crumbling it and digging again for more. It couldn't be real, obviously, but all the same she could see the tendons on the underside of her forearm working as if it was. She'd been told to expect all manner of peculiar sensations from her damaged nerves, and this had to be a tactile hallucination because even if her hand really were still there it would be lying on lawn grass, not this autumnal detritus. She dropped the trowel and with her right hand patted the grass in front of her stump just to be sure, and for a moment she even thought she could feel invisible dead leaves with that hand too, and pulled away sharply, sitting up.

Where her stump had been lying – where she was positive that there had been nothing but clipped green grass – lay a handful of brown and black leaves.

It was there all the time, she told herself. *You just didn't notice it when you knelt down, that's all.*

It was possible. Just.

What was absolutely not possible was the fact that the begonia – which a moment ago had been bright and blousy with old-lady-pants blooms – was now brown and shrivelled, and quite dead.

That night she dreamt of the tree again – the hollow oak with the hand reaching out from inside, and when the voice whispered, '*Not dead!*' and woke her sweating from the nightmare, she crept out into the garden in her nightshirt and stood in the shifting undersea shadows of streetlight through the overgrown bushes, looking down at the dead flowers for a long time.

6

THE DEVIL'S COACH-HORSE

RUNNING HELPED.

She'd started six months into her job at the Highways Agency when she'd realised how easy it would be for the sedentary nature of a desk job to turn her potato-shaped. At first it had been little micro-runs around the block – shorter even than the time it took her to get changed in and out of her running gear – but as her legs and lungs got over the shock of being forced into the kind of exercise she'd never done as a teenager, her runs became longer until her lunch hour couldn't contain them, and she was getting up before seven to put a few more miles beneath her feet before breakfast.

To her surprise, she quite enjoyed it. She wasn't training for anything; it was just the steady, unhurried plodding along a well-worn route, which allowed her brain to idle for a while. The plodding grind also quite nicely masked the jittering ache in her healing nerves. For the duration of a 5k run she could focus on the burning in her legs, and it was nice to know that there was still something that worked the way it should.

While running was her thing, working out at the local leisure centre was Tom's – not that he needed to. Gardening work – sorry, the *landscaping business* – kept him more active than most men his age, but even before that, when they'd both been working for Highways, her friends had been openly envious that she'd managed to snag not only a genuinely decent guy but gorgeous into the bargain. Part of her had felt that she'd been too lucky for too long, and that sooner or later the universe would slap her down to redress the balance. Now it had. Now she was a deformed joke of her former self whom her perfect husband couldn't bring himself to touch.

'We're quits, now, okay?' she growled at the world as she ran.

Her favourite route took her into Senneleys Park, a short distance from home; it was nothing spectacular, just a big open expanse of grass and bushes criss-crossed by paths, but it was easy to overlook despite its size and so usually wasn't too busy, and there was a number of fitness stations for runners where she could do her physio exercises. These were mostly to build up the strength in her left bicep and shoulder since the right was taking more than its fair share of the load these days. One exercise was a kind of plank where she rested on her knees and forearms and lifted one arm to point straight ahead and then the other, so each shoulder took an equal go at bearing her weight. She felt a bit daft because it wasn't a very picturesque position, but then none of the other runners or dog-walkers she saw were especially glowing endorsements of health.

She was balanced on her knees and right forearm, extending her left as far as it would go and giving the tendons a good stretch, when a lightning flash of pins and needles crashed through it and she collapsed back onto her elbows with a gasp. Fortunately the sensation passed just as suddenly, but in the black space that it left she felt leaves beneath her dead fingers again. She was tempted to pull away, pretend nothing was out of the ordinary, but the blunt stump of her wrist reminded her that nothing was ordinary any more.

This time she extended her imaginary fingers and explored.

Feeling around, she encountered something woody, a tree root, possibly, and followed it as it broadened and thickened to join a second root in a V of moss, rotting leaves and soil. To her eyes, there was nothing but the rubberised mat of the exercise area.

'Everything okay there?' someone asked.

Rachel looked around and saw a man – shaggy-haired, with a light beard that made him look oddly like Shakespeare, with a black Labrador panting happily beside him – looking at her in puzzlement and concern. She smiled politely, as if she wasn't still on all fours and presenting her arse to the world in black leggings. 'Dropped a contact,' she explained.

'Ah. Need any help?'

'No thanks, I got this.'

'Fair enough.' If he'd noticed that she was missing a hand,

he was too polite to draw attention to it. 'Good luck.'

'Thanks.'

He lobbed a tennis ball into the distance and the dog shot off after it, while he followed, hands in his pockets as if he hadn't a care in the world.

Rachel groaned. *Kill me now.*

Then something that felt like it had lots of legs skittered over her dead fingers and she jumped back with a yelp. She stared at the patch of empty ground where her arm had been. That had been no phantom pain.

'What the fuck is going on?' she whispered. The temptation to ignore it – to walk away as if nothing had happened – was strong, but ultimately overcome by the realisation that if she was going to take control of her situation she needed to deal with it. Even the bits that were impossible.

She placed her forearm back on the ground, kept her dead hand still and waited. Normally, creepycrawlies had never bothered her much – she was the household spider eviction specialist – though the general rule was anything bigger than a pound coin could expect the business end of a rolled-up newspaper. The skittering thing came back and she resisted the urge to pull away again. Part of her couldn't believe that she was actually doing this, but she reached across with her living hand anyway and, just like the leaves, plucked the creature out of empty air.

It was a small black beetle, about an inch long, with a pair of nasty-looking pincers on its head and a long segmented abdomen, which ended in two tiny white prongs which it raised and flourished at her as if it thought it was a scorpion.

'My, aren't you fierce,' she whispered to the tiny thing. 'Where did you come from, hey?'

Something squirted from the white prongs on its back – it had an acrid stench like rotting apples.

'Gross. Now that isn't very polite, is it?'

She took photographs of it with her phone and let it scurry off into the grass.

She was finishing up her stretches, her mind swimming with unanswerable questions, when she noticed that the beetle had come back. There were two of them.

'You've found a friend...'

It was joined by a third, then several more, and as she looked around she saw that dozens, hundreds, possibly thousands of them had appeared out of the grass, all flexing their scorpion-like tails and their head pincers.

All looking at her.

'Wait...' She backed away from them at a walk, determined not to give in to the unease she could feel building behind her breastbone.

But they didn't wait. They seethed towards her in a glistening black carpet.

Rachel turned and calmly jogged away.

She was easily able to outpace them, but more kept appearing out of the grass either side of the path, so she ran faster, but no matter how hard she pushed herself they were always a metre or so ahead as if they had been there all along, swarming, waiting to ambush her. At first she tried to avoid stepping on them, but that only slowed her, so she stamped them flat with a sudden savage glee that surprised her, except that some managed to get onto her trainers and crawl up onto her bare ankles, biting. She screamed and tried to slap them away even as she was running, terrified that she would fall and then they'd crawl into her ears and nose and mouth, and her hand came away sticky with their rotten-apple stink.

She fell through the park gate and landed in gravel, putting both hands out to break her fall and forgetting in her panic that she only had one. The compression sock did nothing to protect the tender flesh of her stump from taking the full brunt. Agony lanced straight up her arm and into her shoulder, and she screamed again. The pain was so bad she could barely see.

Concerned faces were around her, helping her up, asking if she was okay. She tore off the sock and examined her stump, half-expecting to see it split open, spraying blood everywhere, the ends of her bones gleaming pink and her nerve endings twitching like severed worms as her flesh sought blindly for the part that had been cut away. But there was just a bit of light grazing and a few pieces of grit stuck to the skin. Impossible that it could hurt so much.

Someone gave her a drink of water. When she was able to talk again and thank them, she looked around but there were no beetles anywhere – if they had even been there in the first place.

Hobbling home, she checked the photos on her phone. The beetle was there all right. The stinging abrasions on her stump and the bite marks on her ankles were still there too. Whatever this was, it was real.

* * *

Google told her that it was *Ocypus olens*, the Devil's coach-horse beetle. Superstition held that it was cursed on account on having eaten the core of Eve's apple, and using its tail to point the way for Judas when he was looking for Jesus to betray him in the garden of Gethsemane. Anyone who killed a Devil's coach-horse would be forgiven seven sins. *Well that's all right then,* she thought. *I must have cleared several lifetimes' worth.* There was, however, nothing on the subject of them swarming or attacking people.

'That's because those beetles weren't real,' she told herself in the bright silence of her kitchen. 'You do know that, don't you?' It was the kind of concerned yet patronising, passive-aggressive tone that her mother adopted from time to time, usually when Rachel had pushed her too far. *How can any of this possibly be real? You've lost a hand –* that's *real. That's about as real as it gets, my dear.* Maybe it was all part of the post-traumatic stress she'd been warned about. If she'd hallucinated the insect, she'd probably hallucinated its photo on her phone too. There was one way she could find out about that, at least.

She texted the photo to Tom, along with the message: *Made a friend in the garden today!* ☺

A few moments later he replied: *Ugly bugger. Seriously, you need to get out more.*

So Tom had seen it, which made it real. Unless she was hallucinating Tom's reaction too, but where did that line of reasoning end? That the whole world as she knew it was being fabricated by her traumatised brain while her body was strapped to a hospital bed in a psychiatric ward, drooling? If that was the case then she had nothing to lose.

If she assumed that it was all real, she reasoned, then it was replicable, and maybe even controllable. So, in the safety and sanity of her kitchen, where everything was in its place and Yomi's advice was written up on a chalkboard next to the fridge to remind her, she tried to stop worrying too much about whether or not she was going crazy and simply explored the scope of what her dead fingers could feel.

Where her eyes saw gleaming melamine cupboards and countertops, her fingers felt nothing, but when she moved closer to the walls she encountered flaking plaster and splintered wood. It was as if her dead fingers were ignoring the superficial skin of the world and probing deeper into the older, more essential fabric of the building itself. She picked a scab of plaster away and with her right hand brought it – across? through? – into reality. It crumbled to chalky powder between her thumb and forefinger, and as it did so a small crack opened in the wall before her eyes – the *real* wall.

Just like the begonia that had died when she'd brought the dead leaves through. Not random, then.

She bent to the floor, feeling around on rough floorboards where there should have been ceramic tiles, found a shard of broken glass, and watched the corner of an expensive piece of Italian floor slate spontaneously crack away in its place.

Plainly, the act of bringing something through from whatever world her hand inhabited caused a proportionate amount of damage to this one.

She was going to have to be very careful.

7

PROSTHESIS

FOR HER NEXT APPOINTMENT WITH YOMI, RACHEL took the bus. It was a much longer and more awkward trip, but it didn't have to rely on Tom's goodwill, which in any case was in scant supply. She'd waited for him to make the first move in bed, and when that hadn't happened she'd given it one last shot, ambushing him in the shower. It hadn't gone well, ending with a broken towel rail and harsh words on both sides. So she stopped trying. He'd been grumpy and withdrawn, throwing himself into the family landscaping business and using the long summer days as an excuse to return late at night – sweaty, exhausted, and good for only food and sleep. This was fine by Rachel, because she had more than enough to worry about with what was happening to her hand.

She had become used to the phantom pains, except they weren't really pains as such any more. She would regularly experience flashes of cold and warmth, and a sensation that could only be described as that of an icy breeze moving across her non-existent skin, but since the incident in the park nothing dramatic had happened.

Until, on the bus to Selly Oak, it began to rain on her dead hand.

What started as a familiar cold flush soon became a maddeningly specific pattering, and she knew that wherever her hand was (because she had by now come to the inescapable conclusion that it had to be *somewhere*, no matter that it was also ash), it was outside in the rain. But it didn't frighten her. At most, it was simply annoying because she couldn't wipe it. All she could do was shake the non-existent water off, and she knew how this must have looked to the other passengers: the crazy one-handed woman swatting the empty air with her stump. She reached across with her right hand, and even though neither could touch the other, the fingers of her living hand came away wet.

I bet my nails look atrocious, she thought, and laughed. Now she *was* a crazy one-handed-waving-at-nothing-laughing-to-herself woman on the bus, and she found that she didn't give a shit.

As she watched, rust bloomed on the metal rail of the seat in front of her. It started as a coin-sized patch but spread quickly, like frost forming in time-lapse, until a ruler's length of the bar was corroded and its powder-enamel coating was cracked and falling off in scabs.

She glanced around guiltily in case anybody else had seen – though what they could have accused her of was unclear – and then casually moved to another seat.

* * *

At the rehab centre, Yomi had a present for her. 'I thought we'd give this a bit of a go, my lovely,' she said, and held up the harness of a prosthetic claw.

Rachel shrugged. 'Why not? Things couldn't possibly get any weirder.'

Yomi helped her with the harness. It was less complicated than it looked, with a strap that went from a loop over her good shoulder, behind her neck and down to where the socket with its hook fitted on to her wrist. As Yomi was helping her fit the silicone cup she noticed the grazed skin on Rachel's stump. 'Looks painful,' she observed. 'How did you do that?'

'Cut myself shaving.'

The look that Yomi gave her suggested that facetiousness was not considered a constructive part of the therapeutic process.

'Okay,' Rachel admitted. 'I fell over running. Landed right on it.'

'I imagine that hurt.'

'Like an absolute bitch.'

Yomi inspected it. 'Any swelling or lingering pain?'

'Only to my pride.'

'Good then. Don't worry if this fitting is a bit uncomfortable. Whatever you decide to have will be custom fitted to you. I had to guess your size.'

Size. As if this was no more extraordinary than popping out to Marks and Spencer for a bit of clothes shopping. 'Do they come in different colours and patterns too?' she joked.

'Yes,' replied Yomi. 'Why wouldn't they?'

A cable ran from the hook, up and around to her other shoulder, so that when she reached forward the tension on the cable made the claw open, while relaxing her reach made it close.

'Hey, that's actually quite easy.' Arm went forward, claw opened. Arm went back, claw closed. Almost as easy as bringing bits of debris through from wherever.

'I'm glad you think so. How has everything else been?'

'Oh you know, the usual.'

Yomi sniffed, unimpressed. 'Really. Lost a lot of hands, have you?'

'No, I meant, you know, nothing out of the ordinary. The pain's almost gone entirely. Now it's mostly just pins and needles, flashes of hot and cold.' *And magic leaves and impossible rain and crazy dreams of hollow trees and my husband is too disgusted by my stump to sleep with me. Nothing major.* 'I've been doing my exercises and rubbing it for the sensitivity thing. Most days I don't even need the sock at all.'

'Hubby not with you today?' Yomi asked, adjusting one of the straps.

'No, he has a lot of work on.'

'Bet you'll be glad to get back to work yourself. There, that'll do it.' Yomi straightened up, smoothed down the front of her blue tunic and looked at Rachel closely. 'You're going absolutely doolally being stuck at home, aren't you?'

Rachel's shoulders slumped in surrender. 'Christ, yes.

My mother keeps "just popping round" with some new thing she's found on the Internet to help me cope better, like electric tin openers and weird little plastic clip things to hold books open, and in the meantime I'm sitting on my arse getting fatter and stupider every day. It's funny, all this happened on the holiday that was my idea because Tom and I were working so hard that we hardly saw each other, and now all I want is for you to sign off on my OT report so that work will let me back and I can sit in front of a computer screen all day essentially watching cars drive up and down. That sounds stupid, doesn't it?'

'Not in the slightest. Come here.'

Yomi led her to the suite of training rooms that included a small mocked-up office complete with filing cabinets, photocopier and computer. She pointed to a pot of pens sitting on the desk. 'Pass me one of those, would you please?'

Rachel reached out with her right hand.

Yomi gave her a look.

Rachel sighed and reached out with her claw.

By the end of that hour her shoulders were aching from the strain of pulling against the cable, she'd dropped that bloody pen God knew how many times and was more convinced than ever that she was going to avoid using a prosthetic as far as humanly possible. It wasn't that it was especially awkward, but it involved building up a whole new set of muscle memories – like having to pat one's head and rub one's stomach at the same time, but without being able to feel what one hand was doing. Worse, for the whole of the time she'd been wearing it, there had been no phantom sensations at all – there actually did seem to be nothing but dead, empty space from three-quarters of the way down her forearm, and even though the rational adult part of her mind said, *Good, that's how it's meant to be. It's gone and you better start getting used to that if you want your life back*, she hadn't realised until now just how frequent, and even welcome, those sensations had been. Wearing the claw felt like a bizarre kind of betrayal. When Yomi asked if she wanted to book a session to have a cast made of her stump for the Prosthetics Department, Rachel said she needed more time to think about it.

The day did resolve one thing, however: as she waited for her bus home again she decided that if nothing else she was going to bloody well start driving again. She didn't know how much difference the amputation would make – or even if the authorities would let her get behind the wheel at all – but she needed to regain as much control over her life as she possibly could.

> *'Mary in the oak tree,*
> *Cold as cold can be.*
> *Waiting for the sky to fall,*
> *Who will dance with me?'*

The children sing as they dance, holding hands, in a circle around the hollow oak. A woman's hand stretches out from a fissure in the trunk, beseeching, pleading for help, but the children laugh as they skip past just out of reach of her trembling fingers.

'Help her,' Rachel murmurs, lost deeply in her dream. 'She's not dead. Not dead.'

8

SMOKY

A DOZEN MILES SOUTH OF BIRMINGHAM, OVER THE Lickey Hills, past the affluent green-belt properties of entrepreneurs, football players and B-list celebrities, and on the outskirts of the dozing market town of Bromsgrove was a nineteen-acre pocket of Worcestershire countryside, which hid the Avoncroft Museum of Historic Buildings. The open-air space was landscaped to contain over two dozen buildings from all over the country and spanning seven hundred years, rescued from demolition, deconstructed, transported and rebuilt on the site. It made for odd juxtapositions, with a half-timbered Elizabethan merchant's house sharing its lawn with a group of Viking re-enactors, only a stone's throw from a working blacksmith's forge, a medieval barn, a windmill and a Second World War prefabricated house complete with vegetable patch and Anderson shelter.

It was here that Rachel's great-grandmother Caroline,

known to all and sundry as Gigi, celebrated her ninety-sixth birthday on a fine August morning, surrounded by the chattering chaos of her extended brood. While Rachel may have been an only child, the same was definitely not true for the other offshoots of her family. Aunts, uncles, cousins, nieces and nephews – many of whom she didn't recognise or even know the names – travelled from as far away as Sweden to pay court to the elderly matriarch at lunch in a large free-standing function hall beneath an ornately carved fourteenth-century wooden ceiling which had once been part of Worcester Cathedral.

Rachel found herself sitting next to twelve-year-old Alfie, the son of her second cousin Vicky. He was on her right-hand side, and making no attempt whatsoever to hide the way he kept trying to peer around her to catch a glimpse of her left arm. She'd chosen to wear a stump sock with a subtle flower print to match the colour of her blouse rather than her more obtrusive hook, even though her mother had asked if there was any chance she could get hold of a cosmetic fake hand so that it didn't 'distract' anyone. 'This is what I am, Mum,' she'd said. 'I'm not going in fancy dress.' The way Alfie was goggling, he'd have been distracted no matter what was on her wrist.

'I saw this really old film once,' he said to her out of the blue. 'Dad showed it to me. It was about this guy who gets shrunk in a spaceship and injected into some other guy's bum. And there was a bad guy with a robot hand that had all these attachments that he took off and stuck on. He had, like, one with a gun in the finger.' Alfie looked at her expectantly.

'I don't have attachments,' she told him. 'I have a hook, but not like a pirate's. Sorry.'

Alfie's face fell.

'I do have an unbelievably gross scar, though,' she added.

Alfie's eyes lit up.

'I can show it to you if you like, but you have to promise not to throw up.'

'Cool!'

'Rachel!' her mum admonished from the other side of the table. 'I don't really think that's appropriate, do you?'

'Sorry, Mum.' She smiled apologetically, and as polite conversation resumed across from her she leaned in closer to Alfie and murmured, 'Really, really gross. I'll show you afterwards.'

She showed him after lunch, outside on the garden lawn, but he wasn't impressed. 'That's it?' he said. 'That's just, like, a line.'

'Oh,' she said, looking at her stump in disappointment. 'So there's no danger of you throwing up, then?'

He made a *pfft!* noise.

'Right then.' She made a show of thinking hard, looking around at the buildings and tapping her chin with her forefinger. Gigi was being led along one of the gravel paths by Mum and Cousin Vicky, doing a slow tour of the site in the sun, pointing out the flowers. Meanwhile the smaller spawn had been taken by their parents and some of the older children to play on blankets in the middle of the wide central lawn. 'Tell you what,' Rachel said to Alfie. 'How would you like to see a mummified cat instead?'

Alfie looked sceptical; he'd been burned by her false promises once already.

'Seriously,' she said. 'An actual dead cat, dried out and mummified, in a wall of one of these buildings.'

At the end of the day, Alfie was a twelve-year-old boy, and the lure of a dead cat was simply too strong to resist.

She took him to the Merchant's House, a large Elizabethan town house two storeys high, with a sway-backed roof, half-timbered walls and slatted oak louvres for windows. It was open to the public, and often used on bank holidays by groups of historical re-enactors who would live in it over the weekend, cooking over the wide open fireplace and staging mock duels on the lawn outside. Rachel liked that it was still a working building; it smelled of smoke and was equipped with simple furniture which people actually used.

It was while the house was being disassembled for transportation to the site that workmen had discovered the mummified body of a cat inside the wall of one of the upstairs rooms, and when the house had been reconstructed the cat had been incorporated as a feature, in a glass case embedded in the wall with an interpretation board below.

Alfie stood with his nose literally pressed against the glass, staring. The unfortunate creature had been walled up alive and starved to death stretched out on its side, and having been propped up for better display gave the impression that it was lying sphinx-like, with its paws crossed serenely and its empty eye sockets staring at the ceiling.

'It's said that people used to do this for luck,' said Rachel. 'Nobody really knows why. Maybe the idea was that the ghost of the cat would keep away rats and mice. Maybe so it could keep away darker spirits like the Devil himself.'

'Is it cursed? Like in the film?'

'No. There are no such things as curses. There are only ignorant people and the cruel things they do. Come on, enough of this. Let's go get an ice cream.'

She let him go first down the steep, uneven staircase to the ground floor. It was when she was halfway down herself that she felt something furry slip past her fingers.

She stopped, and looked back. No animal had passed her. Even if it had, her dead hand had been the one to feel the contact; she'd left her stump sock off after showing Alfie her scar, to give it some fresh air, and hadn't bothered to put it back on again. It had felt just like a cat arching its back to rub against her in greeting.

Leaves. Broken glass and nails. Beetles. And if insects, why not larger creatures?

Rachel found herself alone; Alfie had run out of the house without stopping to see if she was following. The laughter outside was muted by the building's thick walls. The room above her was bright with sunlight spilling through the slatted windows while below her the main living space and kitchen were dim in smoky darkness. Halfway up the stairs, she knelt and offered her ghost hand to the shadows.

'Puss-puss-puss?' she murmured. 'Are you there, puss?'

For a long time there was nothing, and then the barest whisper of fur against her dead fingertips.

'Hey there, puss-puss. I'm not going to hurt you. Good puss.'

It came back more confidently, and she was able to follow the arch of its back, discovering a knobbled row of vertebrae and cage of ribs beneath the fur, then a whip-like tail.

'Oh my god, you poor thing, you're starving, aren't you?'

Its head butted her hand, the skull prominent. It was a friendly little thing, though that was likely because it was so obviously hungry. How many people must have passed it by every day, unseeing, while it tried to rub against their legs and coax titbits that never came? How could she leave it now?

'You're coming home with me,' she decided, and the next time its tail slithered through her left hand she reached across with her right and in the pivot moment between them she brought it through.

The cat looked as starved and pathetic as it had felt, its fur cloud-grey and matted. As a consequence its ears seemed as large as a bat's. When it meowed at her the sound was more of a thin, parched scratching, but as if in compensation its purr was that of a traction engine. She held her breath and waited for the world's reaction to her interference – for some part of the building to split or collapse, but nothing did. Meanwhile the cat twined its way back and forth between her ankles, producing its dry meow.

'Smoky, that's what I'm calling you. Okay, Smoky?'

Judging by the way Smoky butted against her legs like a small but determined head-banger, this seemed just fine. She checked between Smoky's back legs. Definitely a boy.

'So here's the upshot, dude,' she said, sitting on the stairs as he clambered all over her. 'You get life and food and fussing, but you're going to get stuck full of needles and those fluffy dice of yours have to go.' She tried to pick him up but he wasn't having any of it, squirming out of her arms like a fish and making for the front door. He paused at the threshold, sniffing the outside world.

'You sure?' she asked him. 'It's a jungle out there.'

He trotted out into the sun, then shot off across the grass in a grey streak to disappear into the bushes.

'That's gratitude for you.'

As Rachel was heading back to the party she saw Tom coming out of the ride-on miniature railway, which ran a wide loop of track through trees and bushes next to the site. He angled to meet her.

'I saw you hanging out with young Alfie just now,' he said.

'Don't worry, I'm not about to ditch you for a younger man,' she replied, taking his arm.

'I don't know why you always say you're no good with kids,' he said. 'He's been raving on about how cool you are.'

She sighed. 'Let's not have this discussion again, huh? Not today. It's too nice. Besides,' she said, 'why do I need a child when I have you to look after?'

At the end of the day, after Gigi had been chauffeured away like departing royalty, Tom was getting into the driver's side of the van when a thin grey shadow detached itself from the undergrowth and hurtled towards them. Before either of them could react, Smoky sprang onto Tom's lap, over his shoulder, and disappeared into the back of the van.

'What the hell was that?' yelped Tom.

'Hello, you,' said Rachel, turning around to look at the cat. He was crouched warily behind a pair of wellington boots. 'Decided which side of your bread is buttered, did you?'

Smoky narrowed his eyes at her.

'Oi!' Tom yelled. 'Out of my van! Bloody stray…' He opened his door again but Rachel put a hand on his arm.

'Tom, please. This is Smoky. Smoky, this is Tom. Play nicely together.'

'You mean it's following you?'

'I'm keeping him. Look at him, the poor love. He needs a home.'

'He needs *shaving*. He looks like a toilet brush! He'll be crawling with fleas and God knows what else!'

'I'll take him to the vet first thing. Tom,' she looked at him directly and made it clear that she was being serious. 'I need this.'

Tom sighed. 'All right – but your guest, your mess.'

'Of course!' she smiled. 'Buckle up, handsome,' she added, as Tom started the van.

'Don't worry, I am,' he replied, reaching for his seat belt.

'I wasn't talking to you.'

Smoky quickly put on weight and acquired a healthy sleekness. He was fitted with an ID microchip, given a full range of vaccinations and treated for fleas, a bad case of worms, and a bacterial infection in one ear; the bill for all of which was eye-watering. He was confined to the kitchen with a litter tray for the first week, while Tom fitted an electronic cat flap to the back door that opened only to his chip. On the first night he was allowed to have access to the outside, Rachel lay awake for a long time, worried that he would run away or fall foul of neighbourhood dogs, urban foxes, or any one of a dozen threats.

'Don't know what you're so worried about,' grumped Tom. 'Cat leads the bloody life of Riley. He's healthier than I am.'

The oak was hollow but not empty, she knew that well enough by now, but this time the dream was different. Something was raking in the leaf mould amongst the roots; something with a low-slung body and long digging claws. Something that raised its head...

Rachel was woken by an unholy row from the back garden. It sounded like a hyena attacking a coyote in a rubbish bin: high-pitched yipping and yowling followed by the crashing sound of garden furniture being knocked over and the violent flapping of the plastic cat flap as Smoky, presumably, threw himself inside without his feet touching the ground.

'Christ...' muttered Tom.

Rachel put on her robe and hurried downstairs. Opening the door to the kitchen, she found Smoky on top of the stove's smoke hood, growling with terror, and every hair on his body rigid. As soon as he saw the open doorway he leapt to the floor and fled past her into the living room.

'What the...'

There was movement on the other side of the cat flap. The plastic was transparent so that its user could check that the coast was clear, and through it she saw a pair of eyes. They glowed green in the light from the cat flap, slitted and wide enough apart for her to know that their owner was much larger than a domestic cat.

Whatever was out there suddenly threw itself at the door so hard that she actually saw it shudder, and she heard claws raking the wood.

Brooms and mops were clipped to the wall beside the door; she grabbed one, then the back door keys off their hook, unlocked the door, yanked it open and stepped outside, brandishing a broom like a baseball bat and yelling, 'Piss off!'

There was nothing outside – just a suggestion of movement further down the garden. Something long and low and incredibly fast disappearing into the bushes by the back fence.

Come the morning, Tom surveyed the damage to the back door with incredulity. 'What was out here last night?' he said, scratching his head. 'A fucking wolverine?'

The door surrounding the cat flap was scored with deep gashes, some severe enough to have torn away chunks of wood.

'I don't know,' said Rachel. 'A fox, maybe?' She didn't

really believe that – the thing that had vanished down their garden had been too much like the animal in her dream, grubbing around the roots of the oak as if looking for bones. Smoky was upstairs on their bed, having refused to leave all night.

'I've never heard of a fox doing this kind of damage before. They're scavengers.'

'Maybe it was rabid.'

'Great. That's all we need. Rabid bloody urban foxes.'

Over the next week there were two more attacks. In both cases there was a loud and violent struggle in the back garden between Smoky and his enemy, and in both cases his enemy tried to get into the house after him, causing more damage to the back door but escaping by the time Rachel got downstairs to confront it. Smoky became skittish and nervous about going outside, venturing only just as far as necessary to check his territory and have a crap before hurrying back to the safety of the house. On the second attack he suffered a long claw wound on his right hind leg, which required stitches at the vet.

'This is ridiculous!' Rachel protested to Tom. 'And it's not some random fox – this thing has got it in for him. It's deliberately hunting him.'

'In that case we're going to have to get rid of it, aren't we?' said Tom. 'The question is, how hard are we prepared to try?'

'What do you mean?'

'Well, we could call in an exterminator and have them set traps. It would take a long time and cost a lot of money – and it has to be said that this cat of yours has not been cheap so far – and it might not even work. It might even hurt Smoky by mistake.'

'We can't do nothing, Tom. The poor cat's a nervous wreck.'

'So back to the question: how hard are we prepared to try? How much do you want this thing gone? Enough to kill it?'

'I'd rather not,' she said. 'But if it came to it? Yes, probably, only as a last resort, though.'

'Well then, here's an idea I'm just going to throw out there for the sake of argument: one of the lads who my dad employs is a bit of a survivalist; likes his bushcraft and his Bear Grylls programmes, and he's always telling us stories about his adventures. We're pretty sure a lot of it is bullshit, but what is true is that he owns a crossbow. He brought it in one day to show us. Says he goes hunting up in Scotland. Massively illegal of course, but there it is.'

'Oh no, no, Tom, I couldn't. That's going too far. A crossbow? What is he preparing for, *The Walking Dead* to come true? No. I mean what if it's somebody's pet?'

Tom shrugged. 'There's the line then.'

Despite her misgivings, Rachel found herself seriously considering the idea, but the next attack took the decision out of her hand.

They snapped awake in the middle of the night to the familiar crashing and screeching, only this time it seemed louder, taking on a higher pitch and a more desperate cadence. Running downstairs with Tom close behind, Rachel flicked on the kitchen light and soon saw why. The thing that had been terrorising Smoky had finally succeeded in jamming its head right through the cat flap, where it was now stuck. It had torn the cat flap from its mounting and was wearing it like a collar as it snarled and thrashed and snapped at the empty air. Its head was long and narrow like a weasel, if a weasel had a wildcat's markings and had grown to the size of a badger. And no weasel, cat or badger had ever sported teeth like this.

'Jesus Christ!' whispered Tom, aghast. 'What the fuck is that thing?'

Rachel didn't know and didn't care. She grabbed the nearest heavy object to hand, which turned out to be the kettle – a wedding present of brushed steel with a hickory handle – and slammed it down on the creature's head. It shrieked and tried to pull away, but had got itself well and truly wedged in the hole. She could hear its claws on the other side scrabbling for purchase as it tried to escape.

'Oh no you fucking don't,' she told it, and brought the kettle down hard again. The animal snapped at her hand, whip-quick, and she nearly lost a finger to its jaws. Its breath stank of dead flesh.

'You fuck!' she screamed, and hit it harder, ignoring Tom who tried to intervene, and the creature kept shrieking and scrabbling and she kept hitting it until it stopped moving and all that was left was a badly misshapen and bloody mess with broken teeth and brain matter splattered up the door.

She was panting and crying by the time she stopped. The silence in the kitchen was heavy with shock and the stench of blood. Tom eased the gore-clotted kettle out of her hand and dumped it in the sink.

'Are you okay?' he asked.

Rachel's response was to run out of the kitchen and into the small downstairs bathroom under the stairs, where she was violently sick.

When it grew light enough they shovelled the thing into a gravel bag so that Tom could take it out into the countryside and dump it. Rachel didn't want to bury it in the garden; she didn't like the idea of its unclean flesh rotting in the soil underneath her feet. Even in broad daylight it was impossible to tell which species it belonged to. They didn't speak to each other as they worked; to have asked questions about what the thing was would have been to invite a reality into their lives which some instinct for survival, or at least sanity, told them to reject. All the same, Rachel knew what it was. It was the pushback for Smoky, the reaction that she had waited for on the stairs in the Merchant's House after she'd brought him through and foolishly told herself she'd avoided. But there was no avoiding it. The world would not tolerate her interference. This creature had come out of the same place as Smoky to claim him back because she'd broken a law by taking him in the first place.

But if everything else was real, including the weasel-badger, then the hollow tree that she'd dreamt it sniffing around must be real too, along with the woman trapped inside it.

9

THE MARY OAK

'I THINK I'D LIKE TO GO FOR A WALK,' RACHEL SAID.

Tom paused in his planing of a banister spindle. 'What, out to the playing field?' He shrugged. 'All right. I could do with a break.'

It was a Sunday morning, the weather was behaving itself for a change and being more or less sunny, and they were enjoying the chance to open up the house to a bit of fresh air. Since the walls had been stripped back, repaired and then repapered there'd been a smell of damp plaster and wallpaper paste which they were both glad to be rid of. Tom was putting in a banister of plain wooden spindles up the staircase, after which they'd be able to seal the upper and lower hallway floors and the landing and argue about carpet colours.

'No, not the playing field. I was thinking about the Lickeys.'

He put down his plane and looked at her as if she'd suggested taking up circus skills. 'The Lickey Hills? You? When did you join the beige anorak brigade?'

Rachel sniffed. 'Listen to yourself, Captain DIY. You know that toolsheds are gateway drugs for allotments, don't you?'

'All right,' he laughed. 'It's a nice day. But why there?'

'Used to go there with my dad before he got sick. It just seemed like a good idea. They have ice cream,' she added teasingly. *It's also that I've been dreaming about a certain tree pretty near constantly since the accident and I'm sure that's where it is, not that you need to know that.* He was never going to refuse her a trip down memory lane for her deceased father's sake.

'Fair enough.' He swept a pile of shavings onto the ground. 'I'll just get this little lot cleared away and put some decent clothes on.'

When he reappeared, rattling his car keys, she was already sitting behind the wheel of her Megane with the engine running.

She leaned out of the window and grinned. 'I thought I'd drive, darling!'

His face froze. 'You're kidding, right?' Although it didn't look like he thought she was joking.

'Not even remotely. I've been practising all week – just to the shops and back. It's really very simple.'

'You've been *what*?'

'Like I said. Driving. Shops. Back. Really simple. I've had quite a bit of time on my hand while you've been so busy at work.'

'But isn't that— Are you even allowed to— Why didn't you tell me?'

She frowned. 'Not sure that I needed to run it past you first, actually. I've told the insurance people and the DVLA and got a letter from Yomi to say that I'm basically competent; they've said that I need to have a test but until then I'm fine as long as I don't go on the motorway.'

'But what if you'd had an accident?'

She waved her stump at him cheerfully. 'Been there, done that, lost the limb. Are you coming? Because I'd quite like you to come with me – it'd make me feel a lot safer – but I'll go on my own if I have to.'

Reluctantly, he got in. 'So how does this work, then?'

'It's called an internal combustion engine. What happens is, a fine spray of petroleum gas enters a cylinder where a spark plug causes it to—'

'Just drive if you're going to drive.'

'I love you too.' She gave him a peck on the cheek. 'Anyway, I'm still a better driver than you even with one hand. You know it, I know it.'

He watched her every movement with the intensity of a sceptical audience member at a magic show determined to see the illusionist's sleight of hand, wincing with every gear change, which she accomplished by crossing her right hand over her body to reach the stick while holding the steering wheel steady with her knees and her stump between the gaps of the wheel. She'd bought a steering wheel spinner knob to help her right hand, like the kind she'd seen truck drivers use. She could tell that Tom was annoyed; she hadn't intentionally kept it a secret from him but what with the weasel-badger thing it had seemed like just one more thing that he hadn't needed to worry about.

She only made one mistake, going over a roundabout, when her hand slipped and she accidentally beeped the horn. A little old man wheeling his bicycle over the pedestrian crossing on the other side jumped and stared, nearly dropping his bike.

'Sorry!' she mouthed at him through the windscreen, holding her hands up in apology – and his eyes widened as he saw that she only had one. As they went past she caught the sound of him shouting something that probably wasn't very polite. She laughed and turned to Tom. 'Did you see the look on his face? I should have yelled, "Look, Grandpa, no hands!"'

'Just – please – keep your eyes on the road.'

On a Sunday morning the Lickey Hills Visitor Centre car park was packed, and the surrounding woodlands were raucous with families; small children and dogs chased each other amongst the trees while dads manoeuvred pushchairs along the paths after them and mums wandered behind, tapping away on their phones.

'So you used to come up here with your mum and dad?' Tom asked.

'Mm-hm.' She looked at him sidelong; there'd been something in his tone. 'Why do you ask?'

'Oh, I don't know,' he shrugged, doing a very bad job of trying to appear nonchalant. 'Just seems like a nice family tradition to keep up, that's all.'

Maybe it was the cumulative effect of several broken nights' sleep on top of the stress of everything to do with her injury, but the irritation boiled up inside Rachel seemingly out of nowhere, taking her by surprise and sweeping her words along with it so that before she even realised she was speaking she'd snapped, 'Well you know what, Tom, if you want to fill me with your little babies you're actually going to have to fuck me at some point, aren't you?'

He stared at her, open-mouthed. 'Where did that come from?'

Rachel didn't reply, instead starting off at a brisk walk. He followed her at a diplomatic distance as she strode along the trail out along Bilberry Hill until it dipped down to cross the road that wound its way between the reserve's three main hills. On the other side they climbed again, past the Old Rose and Crown Hotel and the golf club behind it. Then they were up into the thicker woods of Beacon Hill, where the paths became steeper, narrower, and labyrinthine. In places Rachel had to use her hand to steady herself on a tree trunk or branch.

'Are you sure this is a good idea?' Tom asked from behind her, concern in his voice.

'It's fine.' She stopped to let him catch up. 'Listen, Tom, what I said back there...'

He waved it away. 'Don't. You were right. You don't need that kind of pressure right now. I'm the one who should be apologising.'

She let him hold her for a moment and then disengaged. 'We used to come up here all the time. There's a little toy

103

castle up the top with a lookout. Let's talk properly up there.'

It would have required too much awkward explanation to tell him that she felt drawn to these woods by the dreams that were causing her so much trouble, because she was having a hard enough job trying to explain it to herself.

Tom nodded and walked on.

He was barely a dozen metres ahead of her when it happened. There was nowhere for another person to have come from unseen, but all the same a woman was suddenly standing on the path facing Rachel: young, slim, in a summer dress torn at one shoulder, her face deathly-pale beneath a layer of dirt and her dark hair tangled with leaves. The woman opened her mouth and a torrent of black beetles poured out around two words:

'Not. Dead.'

Rachel yelped and lost her balance. She slipped on a patch of leaf mulch, which skidded out from beneath her feet, and gravity carried her stumbling off the trail and down the slope, pin-wheeling her arms until her outstretched palm hit a trunk and she jolted to a stop. It was only once the first gasp of relief had subsided that she realised that it was the palm of her left hand that had arrested her fall, and that the trunk it was braced against wasn't there. Her eyes told her that there was nothing but empty space in the middle of a small clearing, yet the touch of her dead hand told her that the space was dominated by a large tree. She regained her balance and pulled back, breaking contact. There was no sign of the woman.

Rachel wanted to run after Tom, to tell herself that there

was not something fundamentally wrong with reality. Even if she was losing her mind, that was at least plausible. But the blunt fact of the stump at the end of her arm reminded her that she was no longer allowed the luxury of self-delusion.

She took stock of her surroundings, and realised that the trees all around the edge of the clearing had been decorated. Tied to one of the thin birch branches nearest her was a ribbon, either pink or red gone pale with time and exposure. There were other ribbons on other branches, of different colours and materials, along with bits of coloured string and strips of plastic, the foil from chocolate wrappers, feathers, scraps of lace, and pieces of paper; some were new and vivid, others so old they were faded to a ghostly white. There were dolls' clothes, crude mobiles made out of sticks and grass, and even small bones. She saw the skulls of rodents, and a large one that might have been that of a hare.

'Jesus,' she whispered. 'What is this place?'

She took a step forward and reached out, feeling with the imaginary fingers of her dead hand, concentrating on its phantom sensations. A breath of breeze where there was none. A coolness, as of being in the shade, even though she stood in an open woodland clearing under the sun.

There.

She felt leaves in front of her, in the empty air. She pinched one at its base and pulled, gently at first, then harder until it snapped and it felt so real that she almost heard the branch rustle as it sprang back. She brought her living hand up; she was holding a large bronze leaf – unmistakably that of an oak. She followed the branch she'd plucked the leaf from, her hands exploring the bole of the tree. It was large and ancient, she could sense that. The bark was not smooth but deeply corrugated, with patches of moss and dry pieces crumbling away at her touch. She explored tangles of ivy and something with thorns that pricked.

'Rache?' Tom scrambled down the slope from the path to join her. 'Are you okay? I heard you shout something and turned around and you were gone. Did you fall?' Then he saw the decorated trees. 'Whoa. What's this all about?'

'I was just wondering the same thing.'

'Looks like some kind of shrine, but to what?'

Not what, she thought. *Who. A young woman in a torn dress, trapped in a dead tree. I've been dreaming about her since the accident, darling, didn't I tell you?*

Tom started moving around the clearing, examining the rags and trinkets, and the sight of him passing back and forth over the space where the woman was trapped started to make Rachel twitchy. It felt like a desecration. 'Can we go?' she asked. 'This place is giving me the creeps.'

But something had caught his eye – a piece of standard printer paper in a plastic polythene wallet, smeared with rain and yellow with age. 'Look, a poem,' he said.

'Tom...'

'Her strong enchantments failing,' he read.

'Her towers of fear in wreck,

Her limbecks dried of poisons

And the knife at her neck.

The Queen of Air and Darkness

Begins to shrill and cry:

"Oh young man, oh my slayer,
Tomorrow you shall die."
Oh Queen of Air and Darkness,
I think the truth you say,
And I shall die tomorrow
But you will die today.'

He let the paper fall back to where it hung. 'Fuck me that's creepy,' he murmured.

'*Tom!*' Rachel all but screamed.

'What?' he said, blinking as if woken. 'Oh, sure.' He returned, and his eyes were clouded with a strange expression she'd never seen before. 'Let's go back to the visitor centre and ask someone. The rangers will know.'

The visitor centre was a large open-plan building with a café area overlooking a steep slope down to a playground, a classroom area, shop, and a large collection of glass cabinets and display boards offering information about the flora, fauna and geology of the Lickey Hills. They found the poster describing the walks around Beacon Hill, and the trail that they'd followed, but couldn't see any mention of the strange clearing. Nor was it mentioned in any of the leaflets on the history of the area, or in the many photographs framed on the walls. Eventually they found one of the park rangers, a wiry-looking young woman in hiking trousers, fleece top and a name badge that introduced her as Fiona, who was filling one of the leaflet dispensers, and asked her.

'Oh!' she said, as if they had confided a great secret.

'That's the Mary Oak. Not many people come asking after that. They either know where it is or they don't.'

'But there's no oak tree,' Tom pointed out.

Rachel bit her tongue.

'There used to be. It's a bit of a grim story, so we don't tend to publicise it. The oak in that clearing was cut down and burned over seventy years ago after the body of a woman was found in its hollow trunk.'

'I can see why that wouldn't be on the Family Fun Trail,' said Tom.

'Her murderer was never caught, and the police weren't even able to establish the woman's identity.'

'So why is it called the Mary Oak, then?' he asked.

'Well,' said Fiona, warming to her tale, 'on the other side of Beacon Hill is the Lickey Monument; basically it's a great big obelisk commemorating an important landowner or soldier or someone like that. Anyway, three days after the police printed an appeal for witnesses in the local newspaper, graffiti appeared on the base of the monument; someone had painted *Who danced with Oak Mary?* in big white letters all around it. The name stuck, even though it left the police none the wiser.'

I saw her, thought Rachel. *I heard her voice. She was alive. No, she* is *alive, still trapped in that tree. Oak Mary.*

Fiona's tale wasn't done. 'There are three main theories about who she was. Some say she was a victim of gypsy witchcraft, some that she was a German spy betrayed by her contacts, and some that she was a prostitute killed by a client.'

'What do you think?' asked Tom.

'Oh, I don't know enough about the case, although obviously I feel sorry for the poor woman. I don't think we'll ever know; she's passed into folklore now. Spooky, isn't it?'

Rachel was beginning to feel light-headed. There didn't seem to be enough air in the room, despite its size.

In contrast, Tom was clearly fascinated. 'So why all the ribbons and things?'

Fiona shrugged. 'Memorial, perhaps? The way people leave flowers by the side of the road for accident victims? And there is something of a wider tradition of decorating trees. There are rag trees all over Ireland and clootie wells in Scotland where they do the same thing; places where the old pre-Christian customs still survive. People leave rags for wishes, or to cure illnesses, or to beg favours of the dead...'

'I'm sorry,' said Rachel, swaying a little and putting her hand on Tom's shoulder. 'Do you mind if I sit down? I'm feeling a bit weird all of a sudden.'

A chair was found, and a cup of tea. By the time Rachel was feeling clearer-headed, Fiona had left to attend to other ranger business.

'I think I'll drive us home, if you don't mind?' said Tom.

Whether it was the day out, or seeing her drive, or the aphrodisiac effect of a good old-fashioned ghost story, or just something that had to click over in Tom's head in its own time, the drought broke when he and Rachel got home. She went to have a lie down and he came up later to see if she was okay, and she pulled him down beside her and said, 'No, not yet.'

She might have been missing one hand, but she still had two good arms for clutching him close, and two strong legs for clutching him even closer, and a mouth for kissing and sucking and biting and telling him how much she loved being taken by him and being filled with him.

Smoky peered in, sniffed disdainfully, and went to find something more interesting.

When they were finished and Tom was lying beside her, Rachel traced the planes of his back and buttocks, the slope of his neck, the groove of his spine, and saw that his shoulder blades were scored with the scratch marks of her fingernails. On both sides. Far from scaring her, she found this oddly comforting. At some point in the month since her accident she'd accepted that her hand, while physically absent, wasn't actually gone. She didn't know where it was, but she could move it, feel with it, touch the man she loved with it, and that had to be a good thing, didn't it?

She didn't appreciate how wrong she was in that sentiment until later that evening.

Tom was stacking the dishwasher when there was a tremendous crash. Rachel rushed into the kitchen and found him slumped in the doorway to the utility room, shaking his head woozily, surrounded by shards of glass and crockery.

'Tom! What happened? Are you all right?'

'I'm not...' he mumbled. 'Came over dizzy all of a sudden.'

She helped him to his feet, feeling his forehead. 'Jesus,

you're burning up.' This close, the heat from him was palpable. 'Let's get you sat down.'

'I'm fine.' He tried to wave her away, but weakly. 'Bit of man-flu is all.'

'Man-flu be buggered,' she snorted. 'On your feet, soldier.'

She got him as far as the sofa, where he collapsed, muttering incoherently. Then she called an ambulance.

10

INFECTION

RACHEL SAT IN THE BACK OF THE AMBULANCE, helpless and almost paralysed with a crippling sense of déjà vu, as the paramedic bustled about and the vehicle swayed. Tom was slipping in and out of consciousness, and muttering in his delirium.

'Rachel!' he called, with sudden and shocking clarity. 'Rache!'

She grasped his hand – it was sweat-slickened and hot. 'Hey, honey, I'm here, shh, I'm here.'

He turned and fixed her with urgent, red-rimmed eyes in a face the colour of candle wax. 'She's not dead!' he gasped.

Rachel didn't need to ask who 'she' was. Mary in the Oak Tree, who had appeared to her on the path above the clearing where she had been found seventy years ago, her corpse stuffed into a hollow tree – a tree that had been cut down and burnt and yet was somehow still there, in the place where Rachel's dead hand could still feel it, the place of dead leaves and rust and carrion beetles.

Rachel gripped Tom's hand tighter. 'Yes she is,' she told him. 'And if she's got any sense she'll stay that way.'

An unusually aggressive strain of Staphylococcus aureus, the doctors had said. Rachel looked at Tom, blurry through a haze of tears, as he lay in intensive care with tubes snaking in and out of him, and couldn't get her head around how he was the casualty and she was the one watching helplessly. This wasn't how it was supposed to be.

A nurse had sat down with her and explained how the bug often lived harmlessly on the skin and only caused problems when it got into the bloodstream; how the scratches on his back hadn't even broken the skin and so it was extremely unlikely that she was the cause; that by the nature of his job Tom probably suffered minor cuts and abrasions every day and could have infected himself days ago without any symptoms showing until now; that it was all probably just a horrible coincidence. He was a fit, strong man in his twenties and was responding well to the IV antibiotics, his temperature was already down and there was no obvious sign of any organ damage.

Rachel didn't believe a word of it. She knew that she was responsible – that the infection had come from her scratches, never mind whether or not they'd broken the skin. Her dead hand had brought the disease back from that other place.

She'd been twelve when her dad had died, but her

memories of the hospital were few and dim because her mother, wanting to protect Rachel when she couldn't protect herself, had left her with Auntie Bridget – one of many honorary 'aunties' who she only realised in her teens weren't relatives at all but a wide circle of old friends from school, the tennis club, and antenatal classes. All Rachel knew was that Daddy was sick and had gone away to get better, that from time to time Mummy went to visit him, and that when this happened she went to stay with Auntie Bridget, who didn't have children of her own and so treated Rachel to movies, shopping trips and let her have the run of the large manor house that she managed for the National Trust. It had priest holes and cellars and attics which were off-limits to the paying public, and Rachel was able to push the real world to one side for a few hours by exploring and pretending she was the heroine of a trashy teen horror novel. Given how depressed and angry her mother seemed to be most of the time, Rachel found herself looking forward to these visits more and more, which carried its own special kind of guilt.

She didn't know what made her mother relent at the very end and take her to see her father for that first and last time. Maybe because it was so near the end and the only thing big enough to override the imperative of protecting her daughter was the necessity to say goodbye.

It had not gone well.

There had been a book in the waiting room: a large picture book written to help small children cope with bereavement. It had illustrations of a tired-looking but happy old woman in a bed with a comfy patchwork quilt, surrounded by her loved ones, and at the end she smiled down on her family from out of the sun.

Rachel's father had been nothing like that. She couldn't recall the details of the room (though she was pretty sure there hadn't been a patchwork quilt), except for the smell: antiseptic and rubberised sheets and an underlying whiff of something sickly brown-yellow, which caught at the back of her throat. At first she thought there'd been a mistake – that they'd gone into the wrong room accidentally – because the bald, hollow-eyed old man in the bed wasn't her father. Her father was ten feet tall, with curly brown hair and hands that could fix anything. He sang terrible songs and listened to unfunny comedy shows on Radio 4. This old scarecrow of a thing looked like it would break in two if she blew on it hard. But then he smiled faintly and spoke, and even though it was a whisper it was still his voice: 'Hey there, Trub.'

A hand flopped out of the bedclothes in her direction; little more than a claw.

'Go on,' said her mother, urging her forward. 'It's your father.'

Rachel shook her head, mute with horror. She couldn't touch that claw.

'It's okay,' the man whispered to her mother. 'She's afraid. It's natural. It's okay.'

Her mother went over to the bedside, fussed with the sheets, stroked his brow and kissed it, murmuring to him. *How can she do that?* Rachel thought. Couldn't she smell that he was sick?

'Come and hold his hand,' said her mother. 'Nothing's going to hurt you. It isn't catching.'

Reluctantly she had approached and taken her daddy's right hand with her left. Except it wasn't her daddy's hand. How could it be? Daddy's hands had taken her sailing on Edgbaston Reservoir. They'd put up her framed poster of McFly. One time, when she'd had a bad reaction to penicillin, she'd hallucinated bugs crawling over her hands and Daddy had placed his strong hands over hers until the bugs had gone away. She knew that there were no such things as cancer germs, but at the same time it had felt like the hand she was holding was full of nothing but death.

'You said it was going to get better!' she insisted. 'It's not fair! You said!'

'I know,' he answered. 'And I'm sorry. But it isn't.' His responses were gasped and thready. The lung cancer had been stealthy and too far advanced by the time the doctors had spotted it, helped by the fact that – and here was the bitter, crushing irony of it all – her father didn't smoke and never had. Nobody had been able to explain it beyond something vague to do with passive smoking or environmental carcinogens. Years later, when she'd tried to explain to her best friend Sandra how unfair it all was during the course of a very drunken girls' night in, Sandra had flourished her wine glass and declaimed in an affected poetic voice, 'Death is the bitch brood-mother of us all, and we are her wayward litter. She takes us whenever she likes and owes nobody a reason why.'

At the age of twelve all Rachel could do to express her rage and helplessness was repeat, 'But it's not *fair*!' as if this was somehow all her parents' fault. She cringed at the memory now, at her own unthinking childish self-centredness, and wished more than anything that she could go back and tell the little girl not to be afraid, that her dad just needed a hug.

But she *had* caught the death in her father's hand; it had killed hers and left her with nothing but a stump. It had just taken a little while, that was all.

She looked at Tom, lying there waxy, pale and twitching in a troubled sleep as his body fought the illness that she knew she'd caused.

She takes us whenever she likes and owes nobody a reason why.

Rachel took his hand, disturbed by how hot his flesh was. 'Well you're not having this one too,' she said with quiet venom. 'You've got a fucking fight on your hands here.'

Then she went to call Charlotte and Spence to tell them that their son was in hospital.

Charlotte Cooper swept into the Intensive Care Unit's reception area where Rachel was sitting, trying to answer all of the texts and messages and well-wishes and questions from their wide circle of friends, even though she had next to no information herself. Tom's mother was small, with cropped iron-grey hair and a fierce no-nonsense attitude, which was the main reason why Cooper Landscaping was such a successful business. No invoice went unchased, no email unactioned, and she was equally uncompromising on the quality of the work that she expected from her husband and his men.

'Where is he?' Charlotte demanded. 'Where's my boy? You should have told us the moment it happened! The moment!' Having delivered this she left Rachel open-mouthed and strode over to where the duty nurse was angling in to intercept her. Spence followed a few paces behind, but stopped to give Rachel a hug.

'You all right, m'love?' he asked. 'Bearing up?'

Rachel just nodded, determined not to cry, but afraid that any reply would open the floodgates.

'She's worried,' he said, nodding at his wife, who was interrogating the nurse. 'Don't take it the wrong way.'

'I won't.' How could she, when she knew how cruel grief could make someone?

Rachel was allowed to see Tom again briefly that evening. Already he looked better; his skin had lost its waxy colour, but there were dark circles under his eyes, which made him look utterly exhausted.

'Hey,' she said, and squeezed his hand. The return squeeze was weak, but there.

'I've got this really weird feeling of déjà vu,' he replied. 'But like, in reverse.'

'You and me both.'

'I've got this really weird feeling of déjà vu,' he repeated, and gave her the ghost of a grin.

'Shut up or I'll unplug you.'

'Yes, ma'am.'

For a while she fussed ineffectually at his bedding and his dressings, keeping up a stream of cheery, inane chatter. 'They say I shouldn't kiss you because your immune system is pretty rocky and I might give you something.' She laughed. 'That'd be ironic, wouldn't it?'

'Why?'

Rachel swallowed nervously, and looked away. She hadn't been going to say anything for fear of his reaction. When their positions had been reversed she'd told him that she didn't need his apologies, just his help, but she hadn't considered how much he'd felt the need to apologise, even though the accident hadn't been his fault.

'I think I gave this to you,' she admitted. 'You know, on your back. When I scratched you. When we were, you know. I'm so, so sorry.'

'Bollocks,' Tom said. 'You didn't give this to me. The doctors said there are a dozen ways I could have got it. It was a freak, one-in-a-million thing.'

'But it couldn't just be coincidence.'

'Listen.' He struggled up onto one elbow. It cost him an effort and she tried to stop him but he brushed her protests aside. 'You did not do this to me. Just like I did not do *that* to you.' He nodded at her left arm. 'And even if you did, you didn't. Understand? We don't do this to each other. No blame, remember?'

She nodded, sniffed, and wiped away the tears that she'd sworn not to allow. 'No blame.'

'So just bloody come here and kiss me.'

So she did.

* * *

That night, sleeping alone in the house, the nightmares began. If she'd thought the dreams of the hollow tree had been bad, they were nothing compared to what she dreamt of its prisoner.

11

GYPSY WITCH

ANNABEL CLAYTON STOOD ON THE HEIGHT OF BEACON Hill and watched her city burn.

Even though the centre of Birmingham was miles away she fancied she could feel the heat of it rolling towards her on the great mumbling, snarling thunder of bomber engines, explosions, and the roar of the fires themselves. So great was the inferno that it lit up the underside of the lowering cloud cover as if it were the roof of a vast cavern of hell itself, stabbed with the scrabbling fingers of searchlights and the fitful sparks of anti-aircraft fire. It was nearly midnight, and the raid had already been going for six hours.

'All those people,' she said to the man next to her. His name was Brian, and he was a signaller for the troops manning the barrage balloon and gun emplacements on neighbouring hills. He was a good man in his own way, even though he had sneaked away from his unit for a crafty fumble. He tried to wrap a blanket around her shoulders but she shrugged him off.

'Come on, love,' he protested. 'It's freezing.'

'With all those fires?' she asked. Every now and then there would be a brighter bloom as one of the German bombs found its mark on a gas main or a fuel dump.

'That's miles away, silly. You can't possibly feel them from here.'

She liked him well enough for a *gadjo*, but didn't take well to his calling her silly, as if she was nothing but a *chavi* with wide eyes and legs for a handsome face in a uniform. He didn't believe in what she could See, but that was all right. He didn't have to.

'The year I was born,' she said, 'my family and all the other families were evicted off the Black Patch where we'd been living for half a century. The authorities didn't want it because it was all waste from the factories, and then they decided that they did want it, so we had to go. They said they were going to turn it into a park so the children in the slums thereabouts had somewhere outside in the fresh air to play, as if that wasn't how my ma and pa and all their brothers and sisters had grown up in the first place.'

Brian was stamping his feet and blowing on his hands but she paid him no mind.

'The families were offered council houses in the area, and some took them. Some, like my folks, didn't. They got back in their vardos and took to the roads like they'd always done. I was born on the road, and Ma reckons that's why I have the Sight – because I was born living the way my people ought to live. That's why we're safely out this way while my cousins and their kin are being blown to bits in their nice safe council houses. Of course, the children will have been evacuated to the countryside, probably moving from one place to another. So Romani becomes *gadjo*, and *gadjo* becomes Romani.' She laughed at the irony.

'I do wish you'd talk proper English,' he complained.

'I know you do.' She turned and entwined her arms about his neck, looking up into his face, smiling and dark-eyed against the fires. 'Except when you like me to whisper sweet gypsy nothings into your ear while you're taking me,' she murmured against his lips.

'Shameless,' he murmured back, and kissed her. For the life of her she couldn't work out why she'd taken up with someone like Brian – he was so completely the opposite of every man in her family. Maybe that was it. It made about as much sense as anything else these days. It certainly didn't take the Sight to see why he was besotted with her, or that the poor lamb thought he was going to be able to make a decent and respectable woman out of her when the war was over.

She pulled away and patted him on the chest. 'Right then,' she said. 'You have your soldiering to get back to. I have my thieving and poaching.'

'I never said...' he sputtered.

'Shh.' She laid a finger on his lips. 'I know. I'm only teasing. Off with you now, and keep an eye open for the laundry.'

Some of the women at her camp made a few pennies by taking in laundry for the soldiers billeted nearby; it was how she'd met Brian in the first place and provided a convenient method for sending messages back and forth, especially as how their fraternisation was likely to be frowned upon by both sides.

Annabel's husband would certainly not approve.

'I insist on seeing you back,' he said. 'It isn't safe.'

'That you shall not!' she replied. 'It would be better for me to meet robbers than be seen with you! Besides, I've been walking these woods since I was a child.'

'Well all right, then.'

Brian sauntered off through the trees back towards his unit, grinning like a man who'd had his oats – maybe a nibble rather than the whole nosebag on this occasion, but there was nothing wrong with keeping a man's appetite strong – and she set off in the other, down the steep slope towards the Old Rose and Crown where her people were camped.

She knew every path and hollow by heart and so didn't need a torch, which was just as well, given the blackout. The woods grew older and thicker down towards the road, and she made a detour to avoid one tree in particular – a certain old oak, broken and hollow, standing aloof in a clearing of its own as if avoided by the other trees. It was not that the oak was actually malicious, but such trees were long-lived, and a hollow heart was always a dangerous thing. Their roots reached hell itself, it was said, and allowed all manner of nastiness up into the world, like the demon huntsman Harry-Ca-Nab who roamed these parts. No, she didn't fear the hollow oak, but on a night like tonight, when so much death was in the air, it was wise not to tempt fate.

She moved silently through the wood and out onto the

road, the fires in the city themselves hidden but their glow still a poisonous orange twilight which allowed her to see the way home.

While she was glad that Brian hadn't made a fuss about seeing her home, she wondered all the same if he would have been more insistent if she'd been a nice, respectable village girl instead of Roma. No doubt he imagined that any unsavoury characters she might meet were of her people anyway, and while there was a grain of truth in that, there were more dangerous types than just her kin attracted to these woodlands – especially on a night when the chaos of an air raid was ideal cover for all manner of dark deeds.

She unfolded the blade of her clasp-knife and held it loosely in the folds of her shawl as she walked.

Of course, if she had been a young virgin there was no way on God's green earth that she would have been allowed out after dark, let alone unchaperoned. But she was married to a respectable husband and had three sons by him (though the Lord hadn't seen fit yet to grace her with a daughter), and she had the Sight. All of these brought her as much respect and trust as any woman could expect. And as she'd learned from her father, uncles, brothers and sons, what was that respect for if not to be exploited?

She'd Seen this raid, just as she'd been Seeing things for as long as she could remember: the weather; the hiding places of lost objects; the best horses to buy and sell. She gave the excuse that having predicted the raid, she had to watch it, and nobody had argued. Nobody had expressed any desire to come with her either, because although they profited from her Sight they also feared it. It was her business, just like horse trading was men's business, and the aggressive policing of a virgin's purity was women's business.

There had been a coaching inn at the bottom of the road for as long as anyone could remember – a place to change horses before the steep climb up and over the hills into Worcestershire. Her people had enjoyed its hospitality for generations, even when it was replaced by a large house-turned-pub called the Old Rose and Crown, whose stables were used for much the same purpose. In the blackout all that could be seen of it was the silhouetted peak of its gabled roof giving the impression that it was closed and deserted for the night, but she knew that the men would be having a lock-in, drinking grimly and listening to the raid, speculating pointlessly about what was being hit and whether the bombs were getting closer. Behind the pub were the stables, and in a field behind that were the tents and caravans of the camp.

For the same reason that the pub was dark, both the men's and women's fire-pits at the centre of the camp were dark and cold, but the darkness was busy with the chatter of women coming from the larger tents and vardos. Two boys screamed past her making *nnyeeoooww! dattadattadatta!* noises as they fought the air war with sticks and stones. She thought about all the terrified people huddling in air raid shelters waiting for their homes to be destroyed; those proud buildings of bricks and mortar were little more protection from a German bomb than a crude bender made from sticks and cloth.

She was tired – wearied to the soul with it all – but for

respect's sake made her way to the largest and most ornate of the caravans, climbed the steps and opened the door. Warm light and chatter, and the sweet tang of pipe tobacco washed over her as she stepped inside.

Mami Rudge was in her rocking chair smoking her pipe, with her feet up to the pot-belly stove, holding court over four other women who were embroidering the bodice of a wedding dress, which took up most of the vardo's floor space in a great confection of white lace. She didn't join in their chatter, content to observe with a shrewd eye and occasionally lean forward to point at something that needed attention with the stem of her pipe. As consort to the chief man, Bill 'Shiner' Rudge, together they'd shepherded the four families of the Rudges, Claytons, Smiths and Preddies to safety and prosperity through the thirty-odd years since the Black Patch, and Mami's power was on display all around her: the finest Worcester porcelain on the walls; the most delicate Nottingham lace on the table; rows of horse brasses and pewter tankards polished to mirror brightness. Now in her seventies, when she got about at all it was with a stick, but her presence roved the camp unimpeded. Mami might not have had the Sight, but she was *drabarni* all the same, and there was precious little in this world or the next that escaped her attention.

Annabel kissed the old matriarch on one leathery cheek and said, 'Hallo, Mami. You're well, I hope.'

Mami reached up to pat Annabel's hair briefly. 'Hello, duck. Did you see your bombs, then?' There was just a hint of disapproval in her voice.

'They're not my bombs, Mami. But I seen them, yes.'

'And did they do any-odd different from what you expected bombs to do?'

'No, Mami.'

'Well then.' Mami sucked on her pipe and nodded to herself. 'You'll take tea? Tilly!' she called, without waiting for an answer. 'Brew for Anna here, me duck.'

'Yes, Mami.'

Tilly was Mami's youngest married granddaughter and happy to oblige in this, as in most things. It was the last thing Annabel wanted, but refusing hospitality was unthinkable. While she was being poured a cup of sweet black tea, Mami's eldest daughter-in-law, Jess, passed her a needle and thread, and she set to work adding a cluster of forget-me-nots to the dress. She had to admit, it was a pretty piece of cloth. Maisie Smith was a lucky girl – lucky too to be marrying the youngest Clayton boy and Annabel's brother-in-law, Peter. Everybody knew it, and Mami most of all. A dress this expensive was impossible to refuse, and the obligation it created for Maisie's parents couldn't be avoided.

'Why on earth d'you want to go up Beacon Hill to watch folks gettin' bombed?' asked Jess with a shudder. 'It's morbid, that is.'

'Aye, and dangerous, too,' added Mami. 'Though not so dangerous as some other things folk could be doing, I dare say.' There was no tone to it at all, but just the same Annabel fancied she caught a glance from the old woman, nothing more than a sidelong flicker of an eyelid, and her heart suddenly beat hollow with fear. Did Mami know about

Brian? Was she fishing for a reaction? Or was Annabel's own guilty conscience making her see things? She forced herself to finish her tea calmly and join in with the gossip, and when she'd stayed long enough for politeness's sake she made her apologies and returned to her own vardo.

She looked in on her two youngest, who were sleeping soundly despite the excitement of the air raid, and took herself to bed. She lay there for a long time listening to the grumbling of the guns, and thinking about Brian's dear, infatuated fumbling.

When her husband Harry thumped into bed beside her, he reeked of beer and the smell of another woman. It wasn't the first time, and it amazed her that husbands thought that their wives couldn't notice such a thing; or maybe it was just that after so long Harry had finally ceased to pay her the respect of even pretending to disguise it.

'Where w'you earlier tonight?' he slurred, kicking his heavy boots off.

'I went up Beacon Hill to watch the air raid,' she whispered. 'Keep your voice down or you'll wake the babbies.'

'Should stay at home with the other wives,' he grumbled. 'Shaming to me it is, you tramping about like you do.'

She bit her lip and stayed silent.

'You 'ear me, woman?' he barked, and cuffed her. Even drunk and in the dark, his aim was damnably good.

'Yes, dear,' she whispered. 'I'll stay close to camp.'

* * *

The year turned and summer harvest work dried up. Rationing bit into householders' willingness to part with a penny for half a dozen wooden pegs, or a bit of laundry, or even a fortune told. Even though the horse trade boomed, food wasn't any easier to come by, and the women supplemented their larders by foraging in the woodland. By October there was plenty to find – late apples and hazelnuts, sweet chestnuts, sloe berries – but the wood was only so big, and as autumn deepened there was an increasing danger of running into locals who had the same idea, or worse still, soldiers.

When Harry eventually caught her with Brian, Annabel didn't feel fear or even anger. Both of those emotions were common enough in her marriage. What eclipsed her mind as he came storming through the bushes was the monumental unfairness of it all. He had no business being this deep in the woods when he should be off labouring for the army, or better yet drinking. If he'd come looking for her especially, he definitely hadn't expected to see what Brian was doing to his wife, because he stopped dead and his mouth dropped open.

She had her back against a tree, petticoat rucked up around her waist, one hand steadying herself on the trunk and the other clutching Brian's hair with his face buried between her parted thighs. It was almost funny, watching Harry's face as he tried to work out what Brian was actually doing; if it had been Brian's cock inside her instead of his tongue, that would at least have been understandable. Never mind that a woman's sexuality was corrupting to menfolk in the first place, that which lay below the waist was so unclean that to even wash shirts and skirts in the same basin was forbidden.

For a Roma, especially one with such a traditional cast of mind as Harry Clayton, it was hard to think of a worse act. What Brian was doing to her was literally unthinkable, but dear sweet *gadjo* that he was, he didn't care about any of that. He just wanted *her*.

She called out to warn Brian, but by the time he looked up Harry's shocked paralysis had broken and he was charging at them, bellowing.

He grabbed Brian by the back of his uniform and flung him at a nearby tree, then followed up with his fists as she pulled at his clothing and screamed at him to stop. Brian had some army training, but Harry was a veteran of dozens of bare-knuckle fights and poor Brian didn't stand a chance. All she could hear was Harry grunting, 'My *wife*! My *wife*!' to the rhythmic meat-packing slaps of his fists hammering into Brian's head and ribs. She couldn't honestly blame Brian when he reeled away in a crouching run, arms sheltering his head, and disappeared into the trees. She was half-tempted to do the same.

As Harry came towards her there was a hunger for blood in his eyes that no amount of begging or submission would feed, so even though her heart was beating hollow with terror, she stood her ground.

'You'll not touch me,' she dared him. 'I—'

'Shut your trap, whore!' he barked, and backhanded her, drawing blood. 'I'll not what? Eh? What will I not?'

'And why not?' she shot back. 'You make a *whore* out of Hettie Pritchard – don't think I don't smell it on you! What right have you to complain of another man making a *whore* of me?' He was so two-faced he even flinched at her use of the word.

She spat a mouthful of her own blood back in his face. 'I have the Sight, idiot!' she retorted. 'I am favoured! If you kill me you're cursed!'

That gave him pause. Like everyone else, he believed absolutely in curses and took such a threat seriously. Annabel might not be *drabarni* yet, but her gifts were unquestioned. It was only when he latched his hands about her throat and began to squeeze that she realised how badly she had underestimated the injury to his male pride.

'I'll bear it,' he growled, shoving her head against the tree. 'I'll bear your curse, witch, because there are some things that will *not* be borne!'

Choking, she pried at him with her fingers and beat at him with her fists, but she might as well have tried to uproot the tree itself for all the good it did. Her lungs heaved, burning. There was a fire in her chest, and its roaring was in her ears and its smoke was darkening her eyes.

'Be cursed then!' she mouthed, and her words formed out of the surrounding rustle of leaves and branches, the forest giving her a voice where she lacked breath of her own. He looked around in alarm, gave a little whimper and squeezed harder. 'I curse you and all that you do from this day forth,' she said in her forest-voice. 'Your horses. Your money. Your blood. I curse it all to dust.'

Then the darkness covered everything, and it became everything, and she died.

* * *

And she watched.

Harry Clayton dug a shallow grave in the soft earth, and covered the corpse of his wife. By the time he finished it was late afternoon and he hurried back to the Old Rose and Crown, but it was not yet open, so he shut himself in his vardo. He had a couple of stiff tots from a jar of homebrew while looking at Annabel's things: her skirts, her shoes, a half-darned stocking neatly folded on her sewing box. He had another tot, squared himself, and went out to start asking if anybody had seen his wife.

The men searched the woods while there was still light, and Harry made sure to be the one to check the spot where her body lay. He stood inches from her corpse, calling, 'Annabel! Anna, my love, where are you?' until the other searchers were safely past.

When no sign of her could be discovered and it was too dark to see, the men returned to the camp, intending to make further plans over ale, but the Crown remained closed and dark, and the landlord didn't reply to any shouts or thumps at his front door.

Then the soldiers appeared.

They weren't in uniform and some of them had masked their faces with hankies, and they carried sticks and clubs instead of guns, but it was obvious who they were. They outnumbered the Roma by at least half again. Their leader demanded that the gypsies hand over the man who had so badly beaten their fellow that he was pissing blood, and then the whole thieving pack of them could fuck off away from the homes of decent folk.

Shiner Rudge asked him was that what decent folks did, then – wore masks and threatened women and children with sticks?

The brawl that followed was short but ugly. The soldiers tore down the benders and tipped over the vardos, smashing crockery and furniture and trampling belongings into the mud. Mostly the women and children were left alone to scream uselessly, but those who tried to defend their battered husbands and fathers were given no quarter. When the soldiers left, the Romani camp at the Old Rose and Crown looked little different to any bombsite in the city.

Slowly and painfully, and with much bitter weeping, the Roma gathered their scattered belongings and prepared to move on. There were some sidelong glares and mutterings thrown Harry's way for the trouble that he'd brought on them, mostly from the women who plainly didn't believe his explanation that Anna must have run off to be with her soldier, but Shiner accepted that he'd been honour-bound to give the man a beating, and that was that.

They set out in the morning, shuffling through the early mist along the road like refugees, humpbacked with what they could carry and marshalling limping horses and vardos with twisted wheels. There was long debate about where to go next – some argued for further out into the countryside, others for back into the city, but with winter coming on and much repair needed before the children could have decent homes again, it was decided that they would split up: most of the men would find a new camp and set to fixing things, while the young, old, and injured would seek shelter with their town-dwelling kin.

So Harry Clayton took his sons and joined the city-bound exodus.

Romani traditions of hospitality meant that everyone had a place to sleep that night, though most found themselves on floors or in cramped and damp Anderson shelters.

Harry's sleep was plagued with the voices of trees whispering threats and obscenities at him in Anna's voice. During the day he wandered around in a foul mood looking for any work to be had, but despite the bomb damage and the need for strong arms to clear the debris and rebuild, there was nothing for the likes of him, he was told. Other Romani were getting work, he saw, but one site foreman after another turned him away. He took himself to a nearby pub with what few pennies were left in his pockets.

'I'll bear it,' he muttered into his pint of Ansells. 'I'll bear it all, you bitch.'

That was where his youngest, eight-year-old Dan, found him. 'Da!' he yelled, running into the pub. His eyes were wide and his face pale. 'It's Toby! A wall's fell on 'im!'

They had been hunting for shrapnel, Dan told him as they ran. Maybe someone had leaned against the wall or maybe it was set to fall on its own, but it had come down on him all the same, burying him under the rubble.

Harry dug his boy out from the bricks, pale with dust and unconscious. He gathered the child in his arms, snarling at the men who tried to help, and lurched through the streets to the house where Mami Rudge was staying with her sister-in-law. Toby was laid in the back bedroom and Harry hovered in a torment of waiting, chewing his nails while the old women in their black shawls busied about his son with cloths and poultices like solicitous crows. Eventually Toby came round, and if it hadn't been for the presence of womenfolk Harry would have wept with relief.

Mami took him into the kitchen and forced him to drink a cup of black tea.

'He'll pull through,' she said. 'They bounce, the little ones. Sometimes things bounce off them too.'

'It's my fault,' he muttered.

'Well now, there's taking responsibility and then there's just plain feeling sorry for yourself,' she replied.

'No. You don't see. It's my *fault*.' He took a deep, burning mouthful of the bitter brew and did the only really brave thing he'd ever done: he told Mami the truth about Annabel.

When he'd finished, he felt shrunken somehow, and Mami looked taller – a stern, towering figure of coldness with her arms crossed, glaring at him. 'Aye, and cursing is the least you deserve,' she spat. 'Hanging would fit you better.'

'I know.'

'You should have come to the *drabarni*. We would have dealt with it. This was women's business.'

'She was my wife—'

'She had the Sight!' Mami snapped. 'She was out of your hands to punish, either by right or power! Easiest way to deal with this'd be to let the law have you. Put a stop to her curse right and proper, maybe.' She sucked her teeth, thinking. 'Maybe not. If she was angry and strong enough, might not make any difference. It ain't just about you, in any event. Them boys don't deserve losing both parents so quick, and like that. Then your Peter and young Maisie Smith – she don't deserve to have to carry the burden of being married to the brother of a convicted murderer.' Not to mention the reputation of Mami herself, who had arranged the union.

She crossed to the kitchen window and looked out over the bricked yard with its string of grimy laundry and across to the back of the house opposite, whose roof was a burnt ruin. In more peaceful times the yards of back-to-backs like this would be noisy with children playing. 'No,' she decided. 'There's enough death in this world without thinking yours is going to help any of it. There are older ways of dealing with this.' She went to the back door, put on her coat, and turned back to him. 'Come on,' she said. 'You're taking me for a day out to the Lickeys.'

Annabel's body was in the same spot, though something had been at it – something that had dragged her left hand out from the covering leaves and gnawed off two of her fingers.

Mami looked at Annabel, narrowing her eyes and sucking in her breath. 'She's powerful angry, and powerful strong. No, I think she won't be satisfied with your blood any more.'

She shot Harry a dark look. 'Fetch me a rabbit, big man.'

It took him a few hours to catch one and return, by which time Mami had uncovered the corpse and done her best to clean it up, brushing out the hair and smoothing down the dress. She accepted the rabbit without a word and, taking a small knife from the front pocket of her apron, skinned, gutted and dismembered it. She arranged its parts around Annabel's body and used its blood to write – in letters of an alphabet that Harry had never seen – on the bare skin of Annabel's arms, legs, and face. All the while, she sang in a low voice – a murmuring, atonal hymn in a guttural language, which somehow melded with the whispering of the surrounding trees and stippled Harry's skin with gooseflesh to hear. It set his mind to wandering in the deep shadows between ancient trunks where there was only the old memory of ice, and if humankind was considered at all, it was as invaders fit only to have their blood spilled to feed hungry roots.

When Mami had finished, she sat back. 'Now we wait.'

'For what?'

'For the *lesh*. The eldest. The wood-born. Stronger than her.' She nodded at Annabel. 'Some say it followed us from the old country, but I think it's older than countries. I think it was already here too. The smell of that rabbit's blood will have carried my invitation to it, but it'll either come or it won't.' She shrugged. 'You better hope that it does.'

'Why's that?'

'Because the alternative for you is a long drop at the end of a short rope, me duck,' Mami laughed, but the echoes of it were swallowed by the trees as if they'd never been there, and she stopped quickly.

When the *lesh* arrived, it looked so ordinary – so much like just another tramp in a long, ragged coat with wild hair and a beard full of leaves and twigs – that Harry didn't understand what he was seeing and Mami had to lay a restraining hand on his arm to stop him leaping up and telling the old derelict to bugger off.

It circled them in the cover of the surrounding trees several times, perhaps suspicious of their intent, before approaching Annabel's corpse and staring down at it, then at them.

'This?' it said. Its voice was the creaking of tree trunks in a high wind, the soundless roaring of leaves.

Mami nodded. 'If you please.'

It regarded the corpse again. Bent low and sniffed it. 'She is angry.'

'She has reason to be.'

'And strong. Very strong.'

'You are stronger.'

The *lesh* raised eyes as black and hard as petrified oak to her. If her flattery had touched it in any way, it gave no sign. 'My price.'

'Is here.' Mami gestured at Harry, and stepped aside.

'Here!' Harry protested. 'What do you mean by that?'

'Harry,' she tutted. 'Surely you know that the oldest magic of all is that nothing ever comes for free?'

'But...' he faltered, stumbling backwards, face twisting between shock, rage at the betrayal, and terror of the ragged creature that was reaching for him. Its teeth were jagged shards of wood, and black beetles squirmed in its beard. The stench that came off it was the rot of soil and leaf-mould that had never seen the sun, the kind that brought forth only pale fungus in the ancient abysses between trees ten thousand years old. 'You old witch!' Harry snarled.

The *lesh* caught him by the wrist with fingers as unyielding as roots and then began to drag him away. Harry screamed and yelled, beating with his other fist at the grip that would not break.

'But you said!' he pleaded. 'My boys!'

'Oh they'll be looked after right enough,' Mami replied. 'And a damn sight better than by the man who killed their mother.'

Harry braced his feet, slipped and fell, but the *lesh* didn't break its stride. It simply dragged him bodily through the undergrowth like a doll, kicking and sobbing, and into the shadows between the trees. Mami listened to his screams escalate into shrieks and then stop abruptly.

When the *lesh* returned, its fingers were stained and the hair around its mouth was matted and red. Nearby stood the trunk of an ancient oak – leafless and limbless, its writhen wood looking almost fluid in the night. The *lesh* put its hands to the trunk as if to open a pair of curtains, and pulled the wood back, revealing the black hollow of the tree's rotten core. Then, without acknowledging Mami's existence, it stooped and gathered Annabel's body in its arms, placed her in the hollow and closed the wood over her pale face. Finally it favoured Mami with its recognition. 'Strong, yes,' it said. 'Not as strong as oak.'

With that, it walked away between the trees and disappeared from sight.

Mami let out a great, shuddering sigh that was part relief, part exhaustion, and part grief. She went over to the oak where the *lesh* had trapped Annabel's angry soul, and laid a hand on the trunk.

'Sorry, m'duck,' she whispered. 'If there'd been any other way.'

12

THE STAND-OFF

TWENTY-FOUR HOURS LATER TOM WAS SITTING UP
more comfortably and taking a little water, and he was
transferred to a recovery ward where the doctors continued
to monitor his progress, which, they openly admitted, was
astonishingly good.

'Your bloodwork is a lot better,' said the doctor, as
Charlotte, Spence and Rachel hovered by the bedside. 'We
should be able to send you home tomorrow, or the day after
at the very least.'

Tom grinned and danced a little bed dance. 'How soon
before I can get back to work?'

Charlotte shushed him. 'Don't you worry about that.
We've got it all covered.'

'Seriously,' added the doctor. 'It takes a lot longer to
recover from this sort of thing than you may think. Your
system has taken a battering and you'll still be on some

heavy-duty antibiotics for a while. I'd say at least a fortnight of solid home care before you can do anything remotely like heavy lifting.'

Charlotte leaned in and kissed him on the forehead. 'I've already got your old room made up.'

Rachel blinked in surprise. 'I'm sorry, what?' She'd zoned out. Her dream of Annabel Clayton had left her exhausted; she'd woken up feeling as if she'd lived through the fictional events that her over-stressed unconscious mind had conjured. 'Surely he's coming home with me.'

Charlotte turned a frown of concerned sympathy towards her. 'Really, dear? Do you think that's wise?' It was what the men who worked for Tom and his dad called her Mother Superior voice, though never to her face. Even though it was Spence's name on the sides of the vans and on the business stationery, Charlotte was the one who wielded the real power from the back office. Rachel had been on the receiving end of her ruthless pragmatism only once, during the arrangements for the wedding. It wasn't that Charlotte had overtly controlled things, or been as crude as to ride roughshod over any of the decisions that Rachel and her own mum had made, but everyone knew who was bankrolling the occasion and all it took was for Charlotte to produce that slightly puzzled frown, as if she hadn't already made up her stainless steel man-trap of a mind about whatever it was, and ask if you really thought that was *wise* to use *that* florist or *this* piece of music. And here it was again, at Tom's bedside. *Do you think that's wise?*

But this wasn't a dress or a bouquet; this was her husband.

'Well it's common sense, really, isn't it?' Rachel replied. 'You've got the business to look after, and I'm at home all day.'

'Hello,' Tom waved. 'I'm in the room.'

Charlotte continued to stroke Tom's hair. 'Yes, dear, and ordinarily of course you know there'd be no question of him going home with you, but – and sorry to have to mention the elephant in the room – you're only at home because you're recovering yourself. Are you sure you're up to the strain of looking after both of you, ah, on your own?'

That hesitation. *Single-handed*, Rachel thought. *You were going to say am I capable of looking after us single-handed.* Of course she was capable; Charlotte knew that as well as anyone. But Tom was opening his mouth to reply and she knew that he was going to have to choose between his wife and his mother. She couldn't force that on him.

'It's fine,' Rachel said, cutting him off. 'You're right. I wasn't thinking. He should go home with you. He shouldn't have to worry about how I'm coping too.' She produced an unruffled smile and held up her stump as if in apology, and took childish delight in giving Charlotte the phantom finger.

'Mum,' said Tom. 'This is ridiculous. Of course I'm going home with Rachel. What's she got to do that's so hard? Watch me sitting on my arse playing *Call of Duty* for a fortnight?'

'You might have a relapse, dear...'

'Then she can drive me to the hospital. She's still a better driver than me even with one hand.' He flashed her a quick wink, and she felt her heart swell with love for him.

'Well then,' sniffed Charlotte, 'if that's what you think is best, though I'm not sure what the doctor thinks about all of this.' She turned to him, the last resort when her own powers of persuasion weren't enough: the appeal to authority. But he simply shrugged.

'It's really nothing to do with me, I'm afraid,' he said.

Too true, thought Rachel. *Best keep yourself out of the middle of this one if you know what's good for you.*

'Just as long as he takes his antibiotics.'

Rachel saw then what few people must have seen, the shadow of defeat crossing Charlotte Cooper's face, though it was quickly smoothed over, and she felt a quick and guilty thrill of bitchiness. 'Well then,' said Tom's mother. 'That appears to be settled.' As if she'd been the one to settle it. 'But you will come around for dinner and let us feed you properly, won't you?'

Rachel was magnanimous in victory, and she let Charlotte have her dig at Rachel's home-making skills. She had intended to order pizza tonight anyway. 'Of course,' she said sweetly.

13

NAZI SPY

ELINE LAMBERT STOOD ON THE HEIGHT OF BEACON Hill and watched her city burn, and it filled her with a sick kind of satisfaction.

In contrast, beside her Nial Van Alst was becoming increasingly agitated, muttering angrily and swearing in Dutch, which he thought she couldn't understand. He was a tall man, and the long overcoat he wore only added to the impression of height. It was November, and cold, but she didn't think he was stamping and rubbing his hands just to keep warm. Steam puffed from his mouth like dragon's smoke.

'Fucking Luftwaffe!' he spat. 'Fucking Göring. He couldn't hit the ground with his fat behind if you cut his legs off. South, you fools!' he screamed at the bombers suddenly, shaking his fist at the sky where the Heinkels and Junkers were trying to evade the probing fingers of searchlights and the bursts of anti-aircraft fire. 'South! It's right there! *Right there!*' He stabbed with a finger at where the Austin factory works lay just below them in Longbridge at the foot of the hills. The works were carefully camouflaged by day and all but invisible at night.

Alarmed by the noise he was making, she tried to shush him. 'Do you want every soldier on this hill to hear you?' she hissed. It was possibly foolish to come up here in the first place, so close to the factory's defensive emplacements, but Van Alst had insisted. He had wanted to revel in the sight of the works being pounded into flaming wreckage.

Van Alst was an ass of the highest order. He'd been in the Midlands before the war started, as a perfectly legitimate salesman of printing presses, typewriters and sewing machines, which meant that for a very long time he avoided the attention of British intelligence and managed to facilitate quite a few of the Abwehr's agents and their nasty little games. The Abwehr were military intelligence, and although Van Alst would never have had the guts to put on a uniform himself, he had his uses.

Eline could tell that despite all the bluster and ranting he was a bit scared of her; and assuming that he had read her file, he was right to be, knowing what kind of violence she had both endured and was willing to inflict.

When the German tanks attacked Huy, Eline and her family were already on the road out of town with their belongings in an old pram: her father, her big brother Michael, and her little brother Carl. Her mother had refused to go, since her grandfather and grandmother were both so old and frail that they couldn't possibly have coped on the road, but she had made her husband swear to take the children safely to the Belgian coast. Eline, at fourteen, was hardly a child, but obeyed all the same.

Nobody knew how the Germans got ahead of the refugees so quickly. She learned later that a lot of troops had been parachuted on to secure key bridges and road junctions, and the line of refugees that her family was a part of walked straight into them. The soldiers told them to get off the road to make way for the tanks, and head off across the fields, which would have been straightforward enough except that they also demanded the refugees pay a toll of whatever money and jewellery they possessed. Most obeyed. Those that didn't were beaten with an almost professional detachment. One young man, seeing his wife in tears at having to give up her wedding ring while the soldiers laughed and made crude jokes, plainly reached the limit of how much humiliation he could tolerate, and pulled out a gun.

When the machine-gun fire and the screaming started Eline's family were at a point in the road where high, thorny hedges hemmed them in on both sides, too far away from the gaps where the soldiers had been telling the refugees to leave the road.

She remembered her father and brothers picking her up bodily and shoving her through the hedge while she cried that she didn't want to leave them, then screaming at the thorns that ripped at her face and hands, but there was so much screaming that her voice was lost. Screaming and machine-gun fire. It didn't last long.

She lay in a barley field on the other side and listened to the soldiers laughing as they first looted the bodies, and then dragged them away into the fields on either side to make way for the tanks. Too terrified to move, she lay there for hours tormented by thirst, even when armoured vehicles grumbled past in a seemingly endless line, like giant ants.

When it was dark she made her way back towards Huy, hiding every time she heard a voice or saw a vehicle. She knew it would be no safer at home, but at least what was left of her family would be together. Then she saw what the advancing tanks had done to her home, to the entire street.

Things became a little blurry after that.

When she came back to herself she was in Huy's Grand Place. It was the catcalls and leers of the soldiers lounging in the open square that brought her to her senses. She couldn't believe that what they saw was in any way appealing because she must have been in a pitiful state, but there was always that breed of man for whom the more pathetic you were the more they wanted you. She didn't like to think what they would have done if Madame Saunier hadn't chosen that moment to come out of La Taverne Meuse to empty the slops bucket down the drain. Madame scolded the soldiers and took Eline in, cleaned her up and gave her a place to stay at La Taverne.

Eline stayed there for the next two and a half years.

In that time she found that she quite settled to bar work. Before the war, like all daughters of good, respectable families, she had looked at girls who served in *tavernes* and cafés as a little too friendly with the male customers than was decent. True, a number of the girls from La Taverne Meuse went with German soldiers, either to get something or because it made them feel safer, or even maybe because they genuinely liked them. Eline found that she had a talent for singing and spent more of her time standing by the creaking old piano making the Germans tearful with love ballads than serving drinks, which suited her fine. She could lose herself in the music and not have to negotiate the wandering hands of men she despised.

It all unravelled when she overheard some unshaven lump of an Obergefreiter and his younger comrade-in-arms trying to impress each other by comparing scars. It didn't take that much 'overhearing' because they were loud enough to carry across La Taverne. The older one showed a semicircular scar in the muscle next to his neck and laughed about how it had been given to him by some 'filthy little Walloon bitch', and proceeded to regale the company with his hilarious account of what he'd done to the woman by way of punishment.

Eline walked up to their table and enquired politely if *die herren* had finished with their drinks, then she calmly smashed a wine glass against the edge of a table and drove the jagged point of the broken stem into the German's carotid artery, just where his throat met his chin.

She managed to stab him three more times before they pulled her off. Throughout the entire attack she didn't make a sound.

It would be a lie to say that she wasn't afraid when they dragged her outside. She knew that the best she could hope for was a quick bullet to the head, and that it could be much, much worse. But she neither cried nor begged, and maybe that was what convinced Abraham Scheller that she was worth saving.

Scheller was on the personal staff of Colonel Hans Piekenbrock, chief of Abwehr 1, the German army's intelligence-gathering division. His purpose in Huy was interrogating prisoners held at the town's ancient citadel, and he had been drinking at La Taverne Meuse for several nights. It wasn't exactly a lucky coincidence that he should be there in that back alley behind La Taverne to order the soldiers to let Eline go, but it certainly felt like it to her.

'You are good,' he said to her. She was lying in the garbage, curled foetally around several painful kicks to her ribs. 'You maintained an immaculate façade and when you attacked you did so effectively and mercilessly. You will be trained to be better.' He bent down closer, holding his finger and thumb an inch apart before her eyes. 'This is how close to death I am going to let them beat you, so that when you come to work for me you will know how close you are, and how little it will take to finish the job, should you betray me.' Then he said to the soldiers: 'Anything except her face,' and left her to them.

A year later, when the little fishing boat sneaked her ashore on the British coast just north of Scarborough, her orders being to liaise with Van Alst, her first action was to walk straight into the nearest police station and offer her services to the Allies.

* * *

So she stood on the hill and watched the city burn with a sick satisfaction because she knew it could have been worse; on their way in from the North Sea those bombers would have shed some of their ordnance on a non-existent coastal airfield that she'd convinced Van Alst of, and every bomb that fell on sand dunes was one less to fall on the people below.

She sidled up to Van Alst, wrapped her arms around his right one where it was jammed furiously into his coat pocket, and stroked his sleeve. He was rigid with tension. 'It's out of our hands now,' she murmured. 'There'll be other opportunities. We've done our best. *You've* done your best.'

The mollification of his bruised ego seemed to have done the trick, because she felt him slump suddenly, the rage draining out of him.

'Maybe you're right,' he said, and gave a rueful little laugh as he gestured at the flames, the explosions, the distant sound of sirens. 'It's not as if this isn't a glorious enough sight on its own, is it?'

Right then and there she wanted to kill him – to take the stiletto dagger that was nestling in the calf of her right boot and open another wider, smugger smile in the throat beneath his mouth – so she cuddled closer and said, 'It's beautiful.'

A few minutes later Eline shivered and complained about how cold it was, and he did the chivalrous thing by wrapping his greatcoat around her shoulders as they walked back to his car.

They went to the nearest public air raid shelter, under the picture house in Rubery, where they whiled away the rest of the raid just like all the other ordinary men, women and families crammed in like sardines: playing cards and singing songs. When the raid was over he drove her back to her digs and saw her to the door with an oddly chaste little peck on the cheek, as if they'd done nothing more dramatic than stepping out together to a dance.

Eline's boarding house had a telephone but she did not trust that old witch Mrs Higgins not to eavesdrop on her tenants' conversations, so she threw on a coat and went to the phone box around the corner. She had to queue for half an hour before it was her turn, by which time it had started to drizzle and she was cold and irritable, which was never the best frame of mind with which to approach one's superiors. The phone box was at least warm, if somewhat fuggy with the smell of other people.

She dialled the number that she'd been given, got through a number of secretaries with the correct pass codes, and was eventually put through to Colonel Robert 'Brass-Eye' Collins. She hoped she'd woken him in bed with his fat wife.

'It's done,' she said. 'You can bring Van Alst in now.'

'Hmm,' he said. 'Possibly. Possibly.' In the background she could hear a metallic clicking, which she knew to be the sound of him tapping his monocle against his teeth thoughtfully. He probably wore that stupid thing to bed, too. Just the sound of it gave her the shivers; it had been the accompaniment to long hours of interrogation at his hands as he worked to decide how much of her story he believed and how far he could trust her. The soles of her feet cringed at the memory.

'What do you mean, "possibly", sir?'

'I just wonder how much more our old friend Nial Van Alst is good for. One doesn't want to cook the golden goose before it's laid its last egg, after all.'

'But, sir, tonight's raid. The Germans will have bombed Starfish 12.'

'Yes, they will.'

'Which means that it's only a matter of time before their reconnaissance shows up that there aren't dozens of British planes wrecked on the tarmac, and that there isn't even any tarmac in the first place. He'll know that I've been turned.'

'Yes, I am aware of that. There's no need to harangue me, Lambert.'

'But, *sir*—'

'Twenty-four hours, Lambert. See what else crawls out of the woodwork and we'll bring him in. You have my word. In the meantime, business as usual, understand?'

'Yes, sir.'

Eline hung up and stood looking at the receiver for a moment. *Business as usual.* The man had no idea how paranoid and volatile Van Alst was. She wouldn't put it past Brass-Eye to have decided that she had outlived her usefulness and to let her swing in the wind. Her thoughts were interrupted by a tapping on the phone box window and she turned to see a man in a trilby huddled against the damp, waiting for his turn. She left and went back to her digs, filled with a profound unease.

* * *

157

To maintain the illusion of normality Eline went to her shift at Austin's 'shadow' factory at Marston Green the next morning, where the raid was all that anyone was talking about, at least during tea breaks. The factory floor was simply too noisy and the work required too much concentration for idle chit-chat. Eline was one of a gang of twelve women whose job was to weld fuselage sections of Lancaster bombers together. The sections were manufactured at the Longbridge's East Works and transported across the city to Marston Green because their runway was too short for Lancasters. Welding was hot, sweaty, exhausting work, but quick to teach and easy to pick up if you wanted a skilled trade and a good excuse to be hanging around planes. Colonel Collins could have wangled her an administrative post at RAF Cosford, with access to all sorts of classified information, but that would have looked just a bit too convenient for Van Alst. The Dutchman thought that the intel she passed to him about the Lancasters' ultimate destinations came from chatting with the female Air Transport Auxiliary pilots who ferried them from the factory to their operating bases, because he believed that women loved nothing more than gossiping to each other. The truth was that the workers on the factory floor rarely saw any of the 'atta-girls', and when they did it was like catching sight of royalty. In their flying jackets, the women pilots of the ATA knew that they were absolutely the most glamorous and inspirational creatures the welding girls had ever seen.

As the day went on, Eline's feelings of unease increased. She imagined high-altitude Nazi spotter planes photographing the ruins of the fake plywood airfield in Sussex where she had told them the Lancasters were being sent, the German analysts poring over those prints, radioing their findings to Van Alst, him coming to her digs that evening with several large friends...

It was time to disappear again and find another barley field in which to lie low. Sweden, possibly. During her lunch break she made another phone call.

Bill Heath was a thief, smuggler, and black marketeer. He had Brylcreemed hair and impeccably stylish tailoring, which was impossible given the rationing, but he wore it proudly as an advertisement for all the things he could get, no questions asked. The man was his own walking billboard. There was no way that the police didn't know about him, which only proved how effective his web of bribery and corruption was. He told Eline he could get forged papers and transport to somewhere northern, and she paid him with the cash that she'd been saving up from what both Colonel Collins and Van Alst had been paying her, which was nicely ironic.

At two o'clock on a freezing November morning she found herself, suitcase in hand, on a darkened street corner, jumping at every shadow and waiting for the sound of Bill Heath's car. She heard it a long time before she saw it; he was driving very carefully without headlights, only occasionally flashing a torch at the road signs to navigate.

If there had been any lights – anything, even the gleam from a window of some night-owl peering out – to let her see who was in the car with Heath, she would have taken to her heels.

As it was, when the torchlight swept briefly over her and Heath's voice said, 'Bloody finally. Get in the car, bab,' she did as she was told, opened the back door and got in.

Then she smelt it. Van Alst's cologne. It seemed like Heath's connections ran in all sorts of directions.

The unmistakable hardness of a gun barrel pressed into her side. Van Alst's profile was a black shadow against the car window.

'You know where,' he said to Heath, who set off carefully again.

'Sorry, bab,' Heath said from the front seat. 'But you know how it is.'

She ignored him. Her brain was a twittering aviary of panic and she could only afford to concentrate on one thing. 'Nial,' she started, hating the way her voice quavered. 'Listen…'

The gun jabbed harder, silencing her. 'I would rather not draw attention to myself by shooting you in the street,' he said. 'But I would not push it if I were you.'

Van Alst leant across and reached for her door, and in a single moment of gut-twisting certainty she knew that if he pushed down that lock button she was a dead woman. The sick sweetness of his cologne thickened as his face moved closer to hers; it was an awkward position for him and he had to twist slightly to keep the barrel of the pistol in his right hand pressed into her side, and she heard him inhale and knew that he was smelling her, enjoying it, probably excited by her fear, and the unspeakable vileness of him made her dart forward and sink her teeth into whatever flesh they could reach.

His right ear, as it turned out.

Van Alst howled and very helpfully pulled away, and with a snap something was left in her mouth. She spat it out and clawed at the door.

Something shoved her sideways, hard. At first she thought the most ridiculous thing, that he was actually trying to help her out of the car – then her fingers on the door handle were slippery and the stench of his cologne was replaced by something thicker and meatier. Blood.

Her blood. Her fingers left the door handle and went to her side, exploring. Her coat, jacket, and blouse – everything there was sodden.

Then the shock hit her, mercifully before the pain, and her head felt like it was being sucked inside out. Through the buzzing void that the world had become she was aware of Heath screaming at Van Alst, demanding to know what the fuck he thought he was doing, while Van Alst had one hand clamped to the side of his head and his pistol in Heath's face, ordering him to drive, or he'd do Heath too. Heath, quite rightly fearing that he was dealing with a madman, switched his headlights on and floored it as much as he could with hooded lights and without attracting attention. If anyone saw anything odd about the car, they stayed behind their curtains.

Heath drove them south, out to the Lickey Hills, and by the time they arrived the pain had started to cut through the grey fog of shock and it was like nothing Eline had ever experienced. The bullet must have passed straight through from one side to the other because it felt like she was being sawn in half with a length of red-hot barbed wire. She could barely pull together the strength to whisper, 'Please…' which they ignored anyway, as they dragged her out of the car and dumped her at the foot of a broken oak tree.

Almost worse than the pain was the knowledge that she was dying. Being hurt was awful, but soon she simply wouldn't *be*, and that seemed somehow offensive, aberrant, a mockery of everything that her family had endured.

'Hurry up!' hissed Van Alst to Heath, who was busy with a ladder of all things, reaching in through the top of the hollow trunk to pull out bags and boxes, which he piled up next to the car.

'I'm not bloody leaving this stuff in there with her, am I?' Heath shot back. 'There ain't room, for one thing.' This was obviously where he stashed his black-market goods, and just as suitable a place to hide a body. But Van Alst and Heath weren't going to wait for her to die, and the Dutchman didn't even have the decency to finish her off first. They picked her up, one under her arms and the other under her knees, and hoisted her towards the black, yawning hole, and despite the pain and weakness this was when she *really* began to struggle and scream, because to die was bad enough, but to die like this? They paused for a moment while Van Alst shoved something – a handkerchief, possibly – in her mouth as a gag. Then there was rough bark tearing the skin of her legs, something hitting against her head and then a sudden jarring drop, and…

Eline couldn't move. She could feel the roughness of the wood with her trembling fingertips, and the space was so tight that she couldn't lift her arms to her face to pull out the gag.

Then things started crawling over her feet.

She was screaming into the gag, into the blackness at the heart of the dead oak, which swallowed her pain, her rage, and even her death. She had thought that non-existence was the worst thing imaginable, but now she knew she was wrong, because this tree wasn't going to let her simply dissolve into nothingness. It would let her body die, but even after that it was nowhere near finished with her. It was greedy, this tree.

She was still screaming long after she died.

14

THE MIRROR BOX

TOM MADE A RAPID RECOVERY OVER THE FOLLOWING two weeks. Not wanting any more unwelcome distractions from her dead hand, Rachel took to wearing her prosthetic most of the time, and a compression sock for the rest, only baring the skin of her stump to wash it. And even though the prosthetic's harness and straps chafed her shoulders and the cup rubbed her stump, it worked – the phantom sensations stopped almost completely, except for a slight grumbling of pins and needles every now and then. With her husband to care for, it was easy for Rachel to dismiss the nightmares as the product of stress and anxiety.

Tom – in a fit of creativity brought about by the extreme boredom of an enforced convalescence – delighted her by cutting a slot for her iPhone into the prosthetic's plastic underside, exactly where she'd once worn her watch. Now she could use her phone without having to hold it in the same hand, even if she did feel like she was playing at being a secret agent by talking into her cuff. That was as far as she allowed him to go, however, despite the detailed schematics for a wrist-mounted crossbow that he drew up for her. 'If you want one of those you're going to have to cut your own hand off,' she told him, and menaced him with her claw.

'My very own Furiosa,' he laughed.

They took plenty of walks to build his stamina and she got back into her running, and for days at a stretch she could almost pretend that they were on holiday together. But before long he was fit enough to get back to work and she was left alone in the house again. Far from being peaceful, its emptiness seethed with the ticking of clocks, the buzzing of the fridge and a dozen other appliances, the whisper of traffic, the murmur of neighbours. There was no such thing as silence. She wondered, if she could silence all those things, what would emerge to fill the void? What fundamental whisper of the universe's heartbeat would she hear then? She thought it might sound like that place where her dead hand was.

She did her best to ignore it. She couldn't wear her hook in bed, of course, but covered that by getting some mild sleeping tablets and wearing her compression sock. While she waited for the wheels of bureaucracy to grind their slow way towards letting her have her life back again, she filled the silence of the days with the inane babble of daytime chat shows and soap operas. When Tom came home they watched movies or went out to the pub or played board games – something she normally detested, but if Tom noticed how out of character this was he didn't say anything. Maybe he liked the novelty of having chatty, sociable company in the evening instead of the pair of them staring like zombies at their phones in silence. She prayed that he wouldn't notice the desperation behind it – the fear of that buzzing silence and what lay on the other side of it, because the more she ignored it the louder and louder and louder it got.

In the brief moments when she wasn't wearing her hook or stump-sock, the phantom sensations in her ghost-flesh clamoured, becoming more insistent the more she tried to ignore them. It became so bad that Rachel dreaded showering and started having baths again, being careful to keep her left arm out of the water until she absolutely couldn't avoid it, washing her stump quickly while her ghost hand burned and throbbed.

During a physio session she told Yomi, who gave her two options: heavier medication, or a mirror box, which was basically a portable version of the bathroom mirror trick.

Rachel was about to reply but surprised both of them by unleashing a yawn so massive it felt like her head had hinged open behind the ears.

'Wow,' Yomi said, impressed.

Rachel grinned sheepishly. 'Sorry.'

'Tired?' Yomi peered closer. 'Lovely, are you getting enough sleep? You've got some dark circles under those eyes.'

Rachel waved it away. 'I'm okay. Been having some wacky dreams, that's all.'

'Nightmares?'

'No, nothing like that. Not about the accident. Stop worrying, I'm fine.'

Yomi opened a drawer in her desk and took out a leaflet, which she handed to Rachel. 'You're bound to be going through a pretty rough time, psychologically. There are some very good support groups you can talk to, you know.'

Rachel made a face. 'Um, thanks, but not really my thing.'

'Or maybe your church?'

Rachel laughed. 'Oh, now that is very definitely not my thing, I'm afraid. I don't have a faith.'

'Oh I'm sure the Lord doesn't mind about that.' How could it not have been until now, Rachel wondered, that she'd noticed the discreet gold cross that hung around Yomi's neck? The NHS probably had strict rules about the wearing of religious symbols on duty. 'Losing a limb can hit you just as hard as losing a loved one,' Yomi added. 'And produce the same grieving process. Learning how to cope with that can be just as important as learning to pick up a pen.'

'Well, I learned all I need to know about the grieving process when my dad died of cancer, thanks,' Rachel replied. It was more brutal than Yomi deserved, because she was only trying to help, but it was a raw nerve, and one that hadn't healed.

Yomi's hands flew to her mouth. 'Oh my dear, I am so sorry,' she whispered. 'I had no idea...'

'I know you didn't. I'm sorry to be a bitch. It's not your fault.'

'No, you had every right—'

'Can I borrow a tissue?' Rachel was crying again, but

these were tears that she'd shed hundreds of times before; they were almost old friends. Yomi passed her the box and Rachel blew her nose.

His funeral had been a humanist ceremony. Kieran Douglas Howson had chosen to be cremated and his ashes scattered at a woodland burial ground where the plots looked more like a well-tended municipal park than a cemetery. The 'chapel' had been bright and warm with polished wood, and a curved wall of tall windows, which framed the woodland as a backdrop. The religious trappings had been removed, leaving only flowers flanking a lectern. The celebrant had been a short Canadian woman in a neat suit, with eyebrow piercings and a broad stripe of purple in her hair, which twelve-year-old Rachel had thought was the coolest thing ever, despite her grief, and she'd listened to every word that the woman had said.

'If there is an afterlife, it exists in the stories told about us by those we leave behind, in the memories of those who loved us, who pass those stories on, laughing at the recollection of the times we made asses of ourselves, and crying at the recollection of the times we hurt them. Let's not do Kieran the injustice of pretending he was some kind of saint on earth. He wasn't. He was a human being and like all human beings he was capable of astonishing generosity and unthinking cruelty. The highest respect we can pay to those we love is to remember them honestly, with all their flaws and talents, and tell each other the stories of why we love them.'

'I prayed to God every night my dad lay dying, and nothing happened,' Rachel said to Yomi, 'except that he died in a lot of pain from a disease that wasn't his fault. So, you know,' she shrugged. 'You join the dots, don't you? If God heals the sick, why isn't there a single case of Him healing an amputee?' She gave a wry smile and held up her stump. 'If He can heal this, tell Him not to bother, I'd rather have my dad back.'

The mirror box, when it arrived courtesy of eBay, wasn't really a box. It was three folding panels, each the size of a large paperback book, one of which was mirrored, and they opened up into a right-angled triangle with the mirrored face standing vertical. Rachel put it on the breakfast bar with the vertical mirror facing her right hand and placed her stump on the other side of it, in the triangular hollow formed by the three panels. Smoky thought it was fascinating, and obviously provided for his entertainment, and she had to swat him away several times before he got the hint and retreated outside on garden patrol, but not before giving her a filthy look.

From her angle, the reflection of her right hand gave the illusion of an identical left hand where there was none. It operated on the same principle as her bathroom cabinet exercises, but Yomi had taught her a few extra tricks.

First there was what Rachel thought of as her musical scales: touching her thumb to the tip of each finger in turn and back again, slowly at first, then faster, concentrating on how her missing hand would feel doing the same thing, and seeing the reflection of her living one providing the illusion.

Then fist clenches, finger snaps, and writing letters in the air with her forefinger. F-U-C-K-Y-O-U, she wrote, and then, because that seemed just a bit too petulant, R-C- -T-C-4-E-V-A. She was just finishing up the last A and thinking that the aching in her stump really had subsided – score one more versus the craziness in her head – when she caught a flash of something metallic in the reflection. At first she thought it was something in the kitchen – one of the oven knobs, maybe, or the hanging cutlery above the hob. But it was neither of those. It wasn't anything in the room at all.

It was the ring on her finger.

Except that there was no ring on her finger. Her right hand was bare.

Yet there it was in the reflection, on the third finger where her long-gone wedding ring had been. She pulled her hand back as if burned.

Her eyes wandered up to the kitchen chalkboard on which she'd written, a thousand years ago it seemed, Yomi's advice: *You can't ignore something that should be there but isn't.*

She sat back in front of the mirror box, squaring her shoulders as if preparing to defuse a bomb. Slowly she put her arms back. The ring was still there in the reflection, and still stubbornly absent in reality. She prodded it with her thumb but couldn't feel anything. She turned her right hand to and fro, examining it. Stranger still, the ring wasn't hers. Her wedding ring had been very plain and two-toned: a strip of nine-carat yellow gold flanked by a strip of white gold. This was narrower and cheaper looking, the thin metal faceted to give it the illusion of weight and texture, and she found this oddly reassuring because if she'd been losing her mind and hallucinating it, surely she would have hallucinated her own wedding ring? Far from being afraid, she was fascinated.

As Rachel bent down to peer closer, the side of her face appeared in the reflection, and an eye that was not hers stared back: hollow and haunted, blue where hers was brown, and across it fell a lank curtain of hair. It had dead leaves in it.

She jerked away from the breakfast bar, knocking the stool over with a clatter, and retreated to the sink, arms crossed protectively in front of her chest, hand gripping stump.

'I'm getting very pissed off with this now,' she whispered to the empty room.

15

WHORE

DAPHNE MASSEY STOOD ON THE HEIGHT OF BEACON Hill, bent over the hood of a car and getting fucked from behind by a man she didn't know as she watched her city burn.

He wanted to fuck her while the bombs fell, that's what he'd said. She'd shrugged; it was his shilling, she'd told him. He could fuck her where he liked, just so long as he didn't get her arrested or blown up by a German doodlebug.

'The only doodlebug I've got for you is right here, darling,' he'd leered, and pressed her hand to the bulge of his crotch. She'd giggled, because that's what he'd wanted her to do, but heaved a huge inward sigh. It had been a long night – her feet ached, her cunt ached, everything ached. The raid had been going on for five hours when he picked her up in a Digbeth alleyway. Most of the other girls wouldn't come out during a raid, and the few that did had long since called it a night, telling her she was wampy in the head for turning tricks

173

while the streets were full of flames and sirens. Maybe she was. Maybe part of her liked walking around in the chaos. It made more sense than the way folks tried to carry on as if everything was normal when they weren't being bombed. She'd long since accommodated herself to the fact that a body could get used to anything; besides, work was work, and there were all sorts of tastes to be catered for, including men who got the hots for a big explosion. *The bulge in his crotch isn't all that big*, she had thought with a secret smirk.

He was utterly forgettable: middle-aged, balding and tubby with it, wearing spectacles and an overcoat that made him look like a low-rent Leslie Howard. His mouth was girlish and his hands were oddly delicate. At first she thought he was an accountant or a schoolteacher, but he had a car, and that was exciting.

It was entirely illegal to be driving during an air raid, and at one point they were flagged down by men in uniform demanding to know where the bloody hell the client thought he was going, but he showed them some papers, after which there was much saluting and they were allowed to pass.

That was the point when Daphne began to worry about who the client was.

The silly thing was that she hadn't even been looking for work this evening, not really. She'd been out with three of the other girls – Sally, Flo and June – for a drink and a giggle to take her mind off the fact that she'd been given the boot from yet another job. The Marston Green works, it had been, sweeping and tidying up after the women who were welding and riveting airplanes together. The woman at the Ministry of Labour – a sour-faced bint called Mrs Lewis – had given Daphne her work chit and ignored her protestations that it was all bound to go pear-shaped again. She had no technical skills to speak of, and had produced a receipt for her fine from the police to prove that she was a genuine working girl and not just some idler, but that hadn't made any difference.

'We must all do our part,' Mrs Lewis had said. 'Where would our boys be if they gave up after a few setbacks?'

'Back at home giving their wives a bloody good seeing to, I should think,' Daphne had replied, which had not impressed Mrs Lewis. Still, she'd taken the chit and gone to the factory the next morning.

By teatime she was out on her ear.

It had been the other women, of course, as it always was. As soon as they'd clocked where Daphne had come from they refused to have anything to do with her. Some of them refused to touch any of the tools she'd used, as if she had something contagious. It was one particularly snide remark from some posh wife of a well-to-do husband about how they were going to have to fumigate Daphne's overalls, 'Or better yet, burn them! Cheap tart!' and the accompanying duck-babble of laughter, which finally snapped the thin thread of her temper.

'I might only get a few quid instead of a nice big house,' she retorted, 'but we both earn them on our backs all the same, don't we, bab?'

In the cat-fight that followed it took three men to haul Daphne off the posh woman, who had a nice big house but for the next fortnight would have a black eye to remind her of those that didn't.

The police popped Daphne in a cell at the Steelhouse Lane lockup to cool down for a few hours, but evidently decided that it wasn't worth their while charging her as their night was already busy with more serious criminals such as thieves and looters. By the time they let her go she was sorely in need of a pint so she went straight down the road to the Eagle and Tun where she met up with Maisie, Flo and June.

There were no Yanks in the pub that night but there was a singer, which made them laugh. Hilariously, the closest category to 'prostitute' the Ministry of Labour had on its books was 'light entertainer'. They asked the singer if she knew 'The Deepest Shelter in Town', but she got sniffy at that so they sang it for her until the landlord booted them out, and they went laughing and singing into the streets:

So honey, don't get scared, it's there to be shared
And you'll feel like a king with a crown
So please don't be mean, better men than you have been
In the deepest shelter in town.

That was when the raid had begun and her three friends had scuttled off down the nearest shelter, ironically enough, whereas she had chosen to walk amongst the noise and flames.

* * *

The client took Daphne to the Lickeys, which made sense because from up there they had a magnificent view of the city as it burned. There was a barrage balloon station on Bilberry Hill opposite, probably manned by soldiers. That was likely part of what did it for him, the risk of getting caught. She remembered coming here as a little girl, on day trips with her brothers and sisters, watched over by Wendy, the eldest. There had been donkey rides and ice cream from a fat Italian man called Antonio who sang and wore a white apron and had a moustache that went out past his ears. Did families still come up here these days? Wendy had done all right for herself in the end, marrying an engineer and moving to Coventry, although that had borne the brunt of the German bombs and now there was no telling whether she was alive or dead.

And here was her little sister Daphne, skirt up around her waist, being fucked for two quid from behind over the bonnet of an Austin 10 by a small man with tiny hands as she watched her city being bombed in flowering explosions of orange flame and thinking it was funny how she wasn't sure whether she was alive or dead either.

Then an unexpected thought occurred to her: *I bet I could paint this.*

Art had been the only thing for which she had shown any talent at school, back in that impossibly distant other life when there had been such things as school and ice cream. She'd been indifferent at maths, uninterested in reading, and cack-handed when it came to housewifery lessons, but with a pencil or a paintbrush in her hand she could disappear for hours into a world of imaginary landscapes far from the back-to-back slums and endless rows of terraced houses that hemmed her in on all sides. She got into trouble several times for bunking off school to wander around the big museum and art gallery in the city centre. Her favourites were the landscapes of Rosa Brett; not just because they showed her hazy horizons and towering skies, but because she was a woman painter, largely ignored in favour of her more famous male Pre-Raphaelite colleagues. Daphne's mother, despite not really understanding, had been wise enough to know that the world was moving on and it might just be able to carry her strange, distant-eyed daughter into a future that wasn't limited to raising a family, and so had encouraged her, while her father humphed and snapped the pages of his newspaper.

Then the war had come, and soon there was no more ice cream, paper was rationed, and the world became more interested in blowing itself to bits.

All the same, Daphne thought she might be able to scrounge an old watercolour set from somewhere, and come back up here in the daylight to see what kind of horizon presented itself.

The small man's breathing was quickening and his pounding against her becoming more frenzied as he approached his end. The hands that held her hips crawled up her back and clamped her shoulders, forcing her down hard onto the metal. For a small man he was stronger than expected.

'Oi!' Daphne protested. 'Steady on there! I'm not a bloody rolling pin, you know!'

He ignored her, thrusting harder, grunting, and his hands moved to encircle her throat.

'Oi!' she repeated, louder. 'And you can stop that silly game and all!'

Maybe he didn't mean it, and this was just his way of getting off. He wouldn't be the first. But he was tightening his grip now, and she'd never put up with that nonsense before and she wasn't about to start tonight. She managed to squirm her right arm underneath herself, and reached back between her legs to where he was slapping into her, grabbed his bollocks and squeezed. Hard.

He screamed and fell out of her, stumbling backwards, clutching himself.

Daphne got to her feet, gasping, pulling at her knickers and her skirt. 'Tosser!' she spat. 'What part of "nothing funny" didn't you understand?'

He was groaning, cursing, tucking his wilting prick away.

'Take me back now,' she demanded. 'Or I'm going straight across to those soldiers, and I don't care what fancy bits of paper you flash around.'

'I'll show you what I find funny,' he growled. He wasn't just tucking himself in but also taking something out, and that was when she saw the knife in his hand.

'Wait,' she whispered, backing away. 'I'm sorry. You don't need that. I'll do whatever you want.'

'That's very obliging of you,' he said, and tilted the blade. 'But you misunderstand – this *is* what I want.'

Daphne ran, plunging down the slope through the trees whose branches whipped her face in the darkness, and screaming for help to the soldiers on the opposite hilltop. Even if they could hear her they were surely too far away to get to her in time. The small man was limping after her, calling, 'That's the spirit! Much more like it! Give me my money's worth!' Then her foot caught on something, and the world spun itself around her and smashed her in the back of the head.

He caught up with her as she lay dazed and unable to move, and took his money's worth of her with his hands and his knife.

And she watched.

The small man stood over her a while, panting with his exertions. The firelight in the sky gleamed on the blood that slicked him to the elbows, appearing quite black, as if he'd been dipped in tar. He dragged her body deeper into the woods, where there was a large hollow oak tree broken at the trunk and open at the top. He hoisted her over his shoulder and posted her feet-first into it like a parcel. Then he walked back towards his car, whistling.

Long after he had gone, her dead eyes remained staring upwards through the hole, the only horizon available to her now being the great shadow of the barrage balloon that hung in the sky and blotted out the stars, straining to fly, but tethered to the hard earth.

16

NIGHTMARES

'RACHEL! RACHEL, COME ON, WAKE UP!'

She was shoved out of sleep and into consciousness – panicked, thrashing, covered in sweat. The echo of an unremembered scream still stung her throat. She fumbled for the bedside lamp, knocking over a cup of water and rattling bottles of sleeping pills.

'Whuzz…?'

Tom was sitting up beside her, the hand that had awoken her still on her shoulder, now comforting and reassuring. Slivers of the nightmare scattered like frightened fish.

'You were having a nightmare,' Tom said.

'Really,' she muttered. 'And it felt so warm and fluffy.'

'Sounded like a nasty one, too.' He yawned, half-asleep himself.

Rachel checked the bedside clock. 1:47. *Christ*.

'You were yelling your head off,' he added.

She grimaced with embarrassment. 'Sorry. What was I yelling?'

'It sounded like someone was trying to kill you. Can you remember anything?'

'No!' she lied. 'And I don't bloody want to!'

She shook his hand off, got out of bed and went to the loo. When she came back to bed with a towel to mop up the spilled water, he was watching her with a wariness that made her feel guilty for having been snarky, but that just made it worse. Whatever was going on in her head was bad enough without having to deal with him giving her wounded puppy looks.

She'd been a gypsy... or a spy... or a prostitute... she couldn't remember. Someone had throttled her to death... then something even worse had come for her...

Wordlessly, she cleaned up the mess, refilled her glass and popped another Nytol.

Tom frowned. 'Are you sure you're supposed to be taking another one?'

'Relax,' she said. 'It's not like you can overdose on this stuff.' She switched her light off, but in the darkness she could *hear* him staring at her. Eventually the tension was too much to bear. 'What?' she demanded.

'Well, it's just that I thought those things were supposed to help you sleep, not give you nightmares.'

'It's just a one-off. Nothing to do with the tablets.'

He laughed shortly.

'What?'

'A one-off? Hon, the last few nights it's been like sharing

a bed with an epileptic octopus, and it's getting worse.'

'Well why didn't you say something then?'

'Because you've been on edge, that's why, and I didn't want to make things worse. I've been hoping that whatever's going on would sort itself out, but it obviously hasn't.'

There was a protracted silence. Rachel could feel from the tension in the long muscles of his legs that there was more Tom wanted to say. 'Oh for God's sake just say it,' she sighed.

'Say what?'

'You think I should see a shrink. You think I'm going mental.'

'I think,' he replied carefully, 'that you losing your hand and then my infection coming on top of that has all been a lot more stressful than either of us has realised. I don't for one second think that you're mental. I think you might benefit from talking to someone about it, that's all.'

It was funny, she thought, how in the darkness a lie like that could burn so brightly. She got up, clutching her pillow. 'I think I'm going to sleep in the spare room, you know, to save you from another broken night.'

'Oh no, Rache—' he began, but she shut the bedroom door on her way out, cutting him off. At least he had the sense not to come after her.

The pre-dawn chill had yet to lift from the clearing where Mary's Oak had once stood when Rachel arrived, at nearly seven in the morning. The density of the surrounding trees and the northward-facing slope of the hillside conspired to keep light and warmth at bay for as long as possible, as if they were unwelcome. The votive ribbons and scraps of paper hung motionless, and even the birdsong seemed muted. The clearing mocked her with its false emptiness.

'What do you want from me?' she demanded, not knowing whom or what she was addressing. 'What the fuck is all of this about?'

She pulled off her stump-sock and a tumult of undammed sensation flooded into her ghost hand – it was like plunging her fist into a blender full of razor blades and a candy-floss tumbler and the backwash of a jet-ski and a bucket of worms and a hundred other tactile hallucinations and it only stopped when she stepped forward and placed her palm against the invisible Mary's Oak, and then it was just bark. Rough. Unyielding. Real.

She braced her weight against her palm, head down, breath heaving. *I can't do this. Whatever it wants, I can't do this.*

It was definitely the tree from her dream. Exploring, she encountered the curving shoots of branchlets emerging straight from the trunk and, stretching up to the limit of her reach, confirmed that this was because it was broken about seven feet from the ground – whether by fire or storm she couldn't tell. Here the ivy and regrowth was thickest. She traced it, walking a wide empty circle as she explored fissures in its bark and the bulbous swellings of cankers. Her fingers brushed something smoother, warmer, and slightly yielding which branched into several drooping...

...fingers.

Hand.

It was a living human hand.

She recoiled, stumbling backwards until she collided with something else, which dropped long arms over her shoulders, and she screamed and whirled around, but it was only a normal birch tree on the fringes of the clearing.

It couldn't have been a hand. It must have been a leaf, or a particularly smooth patch of trunk that had just happened to feel like a human hand.

Except her nightmares had taught her otherwise. Stepping forward again as gingerly as if the clearing were seeded with landmines, she reached out into the empty air.

The hand was still there. Warm and alive, not a corpse's hand. It protruded through a fissure in the trunk, as if its owner was reaching out for help.

You know who this is. Oak Mary. The Queen of Air and Darkness, just like in the poem.

The hand closed on her wrist.

'Shit!' Rachel pulled back instinctively, but Mary's grip held with the strength of desperation. The more Rachel pulled, the tighter Mary gripped, and Rachel was seized with the sudden certainty that Mary would drag Rachel into the hollow oak with her, into the claustrophobic darkness where there was only mould and swarms of black beetles, and the two of them would be trapped cheek to cheek for eternity like dead twins in the womb of a corpse.

'No!' Rachel moaned. 'Please God no...' She brought up her right hand, thinking to pry the dead woman's fingers from her wrist, and forgetting in her panic what had happened every other time she'd brought her living and dead hands together with something held between them. The tension snapped like being on the winning end of a tug of war, and she fell backwards with the weight of another human being across her legs. She kicked out, shoving the body off her, and scrambled away with her heels and elbows to the edge of the clearing, panting, waiting for the figure to move, to attack her.

It lay still. One arm flopped to the side, and a voice whispered, 'Not... dead...'

Mary. She's a person, remember? Her name is Mary. Or Annabel. Or Eline. Or Daphne.

'Oh Christ,' said Rachel, appalled. 'What have I done?'

At the sound of her voice, Mary's head turned. Hers was the same face that Rachel had seen in her dreams, in the mirror box, and on the trail above the clearing. A slightly square face with dark hair and blue eyes.

'You were trying to bring me down here, weren't you?' Rachel asked her. 'You wanted me to rescue you.'

'Please...' whispered Mary.

Rachel shook her head, not just denying Mary's plea, but her very existence. 'I can't help you. I don't know what's happening. I don't know what you are.' She picked herself up and backed away from the clearing, past the encircling cordon of offerings, and her eye caught sight of a Barbie doll hanging from a branch; whoever had put it here had made the doll a dress which was an exact miniature of that worn by the woman who lay with hand outstretched, begging for help.

Which one of them are you going to abandon? Rachel

asked herself. *The brutalised wife, the traumatised refugee or the slaughtered prostitute? Which are you going to leave at the mercy of whoever else happens by?*

None of them, was the answer. Reluctantly, as if approaching a wounded animal that could turn and bite her at any moment, she went back into the clearing and took Mary's hand. It was warm with life, but pale and weak. Perhaps the last shreds of her strength had been spent clinging on to Rachel. 'Can you walk?' Rachel asked.

A faint nod, and a whisper: 'I think so.'

'Then let's get you up and find you a doctor.'

HER STRONG
ENCHANTMENTS

17

THE HOSPITAL

Extract from Preliminary Medical Report re. 'Mary' by Dr Philip Jackson, Heartlands Hospital:

The patient is a white Caucasian female in her early twenties. She is of slight build, 157cm tall and weighing 46kg, giving a borderline underweight BMI of 18.6. Multiple minor abrasions to her face, neck, shoulders and arms, with more severe injuries to her right hand: swelling and bruising of the knuckles and the loosening of fingernails on the index and middle finger. Several splinters of wood were removed from the nail beds.

No evidence of physical or sexual assault; however perineal scarring suggests at least one vaginal delivery.

Blood work shows borderline anaemia (12.6gdl) and vitamin-C deficiency; these indications of malnutrition tally with the low BMI. Lack of viral antibodies suggests that childhood inoculations against TB, polio,

MMR, or meningococcal B or C were not carried out, possibly due to parental preference or social isolation. Given the patient's presentation in old-fashioned clothing, the concern is that she may have delivered into the same environment one or more children who are in need of medical attention.

'She's asking after you,' Nurse Moran said.

Rachel looked up from her phone. There were three missed calls and a clutch of increasingly terse texts from Tom wanting to know where she was; her single response of *Am fine, went for walk to clear my head* obviously wasn't cutting it. After three hours sitting in Heartlands' Accident and Emergency waiting room under fluorescent lights that flickered at a frequency just short of migraine-inducing, her eyeballs felt like two sandblasted marbles. Nurse Moran looked like she felt, but to be fair Nurse Moran had already been six hours into her shift when the ambulance had brought in Rachel and her mysterious companion.

'Not that she knows who she's asking for, mind you,' she added. 'But she's asked for you all the same.'

Rachel got up, not realising until that point how painfully numb her arse had become, and followed the nurse towards the examination rooms.

'All she can tell us is that her name is Mary,' said Moran as they walked. 'Beyond that she apparently has no memory of who she is or how she got here. We're going to schedule a CAT scan to check for a head injury, but her condition could be psychological, caused by whatever trauma she was running from when you found her.' Rachel had told the paramedics that she'd found Mary unconscious in the woods, which nobody had cause to question. 'She's going to be up on a ward while we try to work it out, so best to see her now before she's moved.'

The clinical surroundings of the hospital bed and gown in which they'd put Mary accentuated how slight she was and made it impossible for Rachel to tell her age. She could have been anything from a teenager to an early thirty-something. There were cuts and bruises all over her arms and face, cross-hatched with surgical tape. Her right hand was more heavily swathed; she'd lost three fingernails trying to claw her way out of the tree, though there was no way Rachel could explain that without sounding insane. There were so many questions she wanted to ask Mary but couldn't with Nurse Moran standing right beside her. *Will you all please just fuck off!* she screamed silently. She just wanted five minutes alone with the woman she'd pulled out of the dead oak.

The woman in the bed gave her a tired smile. 'Are you Rachel?'

'Yes. Hi, Mary.'

'Yes. Thank you for saving me.'

Rachel shrugged, embarrassed. The clarity of Mary's eyes was a little unsettling when they were fully focused on her. 'I'm glad you're okay.'

'"Okay". That's peculiar. You sound like an American.'

Rachel didn't know what to make of that. For her part,

Mary had an accent she couldn't place. It sounded vaguely European.

'May I please hold your hand?' Mary asked.

Rachel and Nurse Moran traded a brief, bemused glance. 'Sure.' She held out her hand.

'No, not that one,' Mary pointed. 'The other one.'

Rachel flushed. 'Sorry to disappoint you, but I don't have another one.' She showed Mary where her left arm ended, but Mary didn't seem to understand.

'I mean the bright one,' she said. 'The one you used to pull me free. You know.'

Nurse Moran drew Rachel gently aside. 'I'm sorry. Obviously she's more confused than we thought. I think it's probably best if we leave her to get some rest.'

'Of course.'

'The police have her clothes and they'll be doing everything they can to work out who she is and get hold of any relatives who might be looking for her.'

'And what if they can't?' Given where she'd come from, Rachel had her doubts that the authorities would find anyone.

'Well then she'll either go into sheltered accommodation or, depending on her needs, somewhere she can be treated by specialists.'

'An asylum, you mean.'

'Perhaps a psychiatric unit.'

'Same thing.'

Nurse Moran's long-suffering smile thinned ever so slightly. 'Not remotely.'

'I'm sorry, I didn't mean to be snarky. It's just that, well, you've seen her. She's so...' Rachel fished for the right word.

'Vulnerable?'

'That's it. I hate to think of her being caught up in all that. What if I were to give her a place to stay? You know, a friendly face, a bit of stability to help her remember?'

'I'm sorry, but I'm afraid it just doesn't work like that. Mary needs the care of trained professionals. The best I can do is to make sure they have your contact details so that if she asks for you again they can get hold of you.' Nurse Moran patted her arm reassuringly. 'She's going to get the best possible care. Trust me.'

And Rachel did trust her. It was just the rest of the world that couldn't be relied on.

Rachel was in a twitchy state all the way home, preoccupied by the morning's events, and more than once her right hand slipped while crossing over to change gear or use the indicators, earning her some beeps and headlight flashes of irritation from other drivers. *Fuck you*, she thought. She was just about in the mood to face off against some road-rage dickhead so she could see his expression when she showed him her hook. *My very own Furiosa.* Tom could fuck off with that and all. As if her disability existed so he could live out some film dominatrix fantasy. She knew she was being uncharitable but right now she didn't care. She'd come so close to getting answers about what was going on with her hand, and they'd been snatched from under her nose.

'And there we have it, ladies and gentlemen,' she said aloud. 'The holy trinity: Pettiness, Bitchiness and Self-Pity.' She was on a roll today.

Underlying all of this, of course, was fear. Leaves and cats were one thing, but her stomach churned at the thought of what the fallout might be for bringing an entire person through. The weasel-badger had been bad enough.

When she pulled into her drive she sat in the car for a long time, listening to the engine tick as it cooled and scrutinising the house as if there might be snipers behind the curtains. It all seemed perfectly safe. Tom's van was gone. Impossible as it seemed, it was still only eleven in the morning; he would have been at work for hours by now.

She unlocked the front door and tiptoed around the house, listening at the door to each room before she entered and checking all the locks and bolts. The silence felt like the indrawn breath before a scream.

She dug out her phone with trembling fingers and dialled Tom.

'Where the bloody hell have you been?' he demanded. 'I've been worried sick!' She'd never been so relieved to hear him annoyed. His voice was raised above the racket of something like a chainsaw or a wood chipper.

'I'm sorry,' she replied, hoping that she sounded like she was. 'I just had to get out for a bit of a walk. The same four walls were doing my head in. Are you okay?'

'*I'm* fine. And what do you mean a bit of a walk? You've been gone for hours. I was really worried.' His voice softened, and the background buzz grew fainter, as if he'd cupped his hand over the phone or moved away. *What is that thing?* she wondered. *Jesus, Tom, be careful.* Unlike her mother she'd never been the fretting sort, but now all she could see was Tom stumbling while talking to her, losing his balance and pitching into some piece of machinery, all grinding wheels and clashing teeth, his flesh pulped, his blood bright crimson, his screams...

'I'm fine now,' she lied. 'Much better. The walk really cleared my head.' *I pulled a dead woman out of a hollow oak tree and took her to hospital where she's recovering nicely.* 'I'm going to take a couple of happy pills and have a lie down, try to catch up on some sleep. I'll make an appointment with Yomi first thing.'

'Good for you,' he said. 'We'll talk about it when I get home. I'd better get on. Love you.'

'Love you too.'

The tree trunk in which Oak Mary's remains were found had been hacked open and burnt long since, but the woodland had never grown back properly, as if shunning the spot. Still, within a few months day-trippers had been wandering through that part of the Lickey Hills again as if a dead woman hadn't rotted to bones there, but a few remembered and left gifts and offerings.

Now, where the oak had once been, there was a new crater. It was several metres across and waist deep, raw-edged and funnelling dirt and leaf litter back down into itself as if it had only just been made – as if a great hand had reached down from the sky and scooped a massive handful out of the ground, or a long-dead tree had been pulled up in its entirety, roots and all. Or as if something had crawled out of the bowels of the earth.

Three human figures stood equidistant around the hole, blinking in confusion at their surroundings and each other. One was a small man, perfectly ordinary in appearance: balding, tubby, bespectacled, dressed in a jacket, gloves, a checked scarf and shiny black shoes. The second was taller, leaner, and darker, despite his shock of white-blond hair and the ice-blue eyes that swept the clearing suspiciously. His long black coat made it seem as if he were perpetually wreathed in shadow, and he was missing half an ear. The third man was a ragged, hulking thing dressed in foresters' green plaid, caked with filth and glaring belligerently with hazel-coloured eyes that glinted through a wild tangle of hair. While the others stood, he squatted, running his fingers through the soil, raking it with fingernails that weren't flesh but wood.

The Small Man mopped his brow, uttering a *phew!*, and started to unwind his scarf. At this, the Dark Man pulled a handgun from the pocket of his greatcoat and levelled it at him.

'Easy there!' exclaimed the Small Man in alarm, palms out. 'No need for that, chum. I'm just a bit warm, that's all.' He continued to remove his scarf, then his jacket, and placed them carefully on the ground. He had braces holding up his trousers and sweat patches under his armpits. 'Neither of you feel a tad warm?' he asked.

'Why would we feel this?' replied the Dark Man. His English was accented, though not strongly. The Green Man simply grunted, which could have meant anything.

The Small Man gestured around. 'Feels like summer to me. Look how green it is. Doesn't it feel like summer to you?' he asked the Green Man and gave a little laugh. 'You look like you'd know, if anyone.'

The Green Man unfolded himself and rose to his full height, which was impressive, easily a head taller than the Dark Man. He wore heavy woodsman's boots. A beard spread over his barrel chest like undergrowth, bristling with twigs and crawling with black beetles. 'What do you think you know about me?' he growled.

The Small Man's eyes narrowed. '*Lesh*,' he said, and his tone was cold. 'The gypsy witch's death. And you,' his glance darted back to the Dark Man, whose gun so far had not wavered an inch. 'The spy's death.'

'You cannot know this,' sneered the Dark Man.

'Oh, one always knows one's brothers.'

The Green Man spat. 'No kin of yours.'

'And which of her deaths are you?' asked the Dark Man, looking the Small Man up and down with disdain. 'Something sordid and pathetic, by the look.'

The Small Man yawned. 'Sticks and stones, *mein herr*, sticks and stones.' He took his spectacles off, gave them a quick polish on his shirt, and when he replaced them his façade of bonhomie had returned. 'So here we all are!' he smiled. 'All come to look for our wayward damsel. The Three Stooges of Death. You're Moe, obviously,' he added, winking at the Dark Man. 'The really interesting question, though, is how she managed to escape in the first place.'

The Green Man shrugged. 'Doesn't matter. It happens. Rarely, but it happens.'

The Dark Man pointed at the three of them in turn with his gun. 'Nothing like *this* has ever happened: for one soul, three deaths? Never.'

'Can either of you two feel her?' asked the Small Man.

Silence settled over the clearing for a moment. The Dark Man frowned, as if listening. The Green Man sniffed the air.

'No, thought not.'

'Impossible,' growled the Green Man.

'How can this be?' demanded the Dark Man. 'How can none of us feel her soul? She must belong to one of us!'

'You know,' mused the Small Man, 'I actually don't think she does.' He was investigating the trees at the edge of the clearing, with their clutter of ribbons and trinkets. 'Observe,' he said. 'These appear to be offerings. This isn't a normal grave. Doesn't it look rather more like a shrine?'

The Green Man spat his contempt.

'A shrine!' scoffed the Dark Man. 'She is no saint.'

The Small Man picked up a grimy teddy from the leaf mulch and sniffed at it. 'Yes, you can smell the belief. It's faint, but it's there.' He produced a knife from his trouser pocket, opened the blade, and then opened the teddy. With a little chuckle of satisfaction, he dropped the shredded remains to the ground, put the knife away and dusted off his hands. 'It complicates things.'

The Dark Man ripped a handful of ribbons from the

branch nearest him and flung them away in disgust. 'But how are we to find her if we cannot feel her?'

'Oh, she'll come back,' said the Small Man. 'Sooner or later they always come back. They can't resist the pull of the place where they died. All we have to do is remain calm and patient.' He dug in his pockets for a packet of cigarettes, lit one, and stood smoking and admiring the dappled light through the leaves as if he were out for nothing more than a leisurely morning stroll. 'Summer,' he repeated and laughed softly to himself.

The Dark Man tilted his head at him. 'Your laziness and complacency sickens me,' he sneered, and put away his revolver.

'As well it might,' the Small Man responded, and blew a serene cloud of smoke at him. 'I am you, after all. And vice versa.'

'I will not sit around idly and just hope that she takes it into her head to wander in my direction.'

The Small Man waved his fingertips as the Dark Man stalked off between the trees like a funereal heron. 'Toodle-oo then, old bean.'

Voices and the barking of a dog came faintly through the trees. The Green Man scowled, and without seeming to move, the shadows, hues and contours of his body blended more and more closely with the background until he had disappeared altogether.

18

THE MONUMENT

KINGFISHER HOUSE ACUTE PSYCHIATRIC CARE UNIT was part of the sprawling Queen Elizabeth Hospital complex in leafy Edgbaston, and felt to Rachel what she imagined a first-class airport departure lounge would be like, rather than a facility for the mentally ill. Mostly, she decided, it was the light. It streamed in through skylights and glowed through glass block walls, gleaming from polished veneer floors as they followed the sweep of white, curved walls. It softened the air and muted the noise just as effectively as the carpets, the sofas and armchairs, all of which were in plain, uncomplicated colours. This was not a place for shadows to linger in sharp corners. Pot plants softened the edges, and the artworks on the walls were gauzy abstracts.

Patients either sat in the open common area and chatted, played games and did crafts, or were else in smaller rooms off the main corridor, reading, blogging, meeting their case-workers or relatives. The unit was generous with its visiting hours, and Rachel was able to spend a lot of time with Mary, helping her get to grips with the era in which she found herself, and trying to jog her memory.

But their discoveries were few and made for grim reading.

Some things are so alien and beyond the capacity of the human mind to process and fit into a sane picture of the world that the brain simply throws its hands in the air in surrender and accepts that what is in front of it is true. It seemed that for Mary, Rachel's tablet was one of those things. For Rachel, it was Mary herself, standing just behind her, leaning forward slightly to read the screen, the living weight and breath of her warm next to Rachel's shoulder. She'd expected Mary to be full of questions about what a computer was and how it worked, and dreaded having to display her own ignorance, but she was spared that because Mary seemed to take it in her stride. She was much more interested in what was scrolling up the screen. If 'interested' was the right word. 'Appalled' might have been closer, and Rachel couldn't blame her.

The website they were on was called 'The Hollow Isle', a forum dedicated to the paranormal, hauntings, esoteric locations, UFOs, crop circles, disappearances and unsolved murders. The section on Oak Mary ran to hundreds of separate conversational threads and dozens of pages. There were the inevitable slanging matches, but also scores of official documents, witness accounts from the soldiers who had found the body, and seemingly endless amounts of conjecture, hypothesising, claims and counter claims. Here was laid out the details of the urban legends that Fiona the park ranger had mentioned, and Rachel and Mary read them together with deepening unease.

'I've dreamt this,' Rachel said, and told Mary about the nightmares. Mary listened with her eyes wide and spilling tears of horror.

'I don't remember any of that,' she whispered.

'But how can that be?' Rachel protested. 'How can I have dreamt these stories so exactly?' She pointed at the screen. 'They're the same! How can I know that and you *not*? How can you be her?'

'I just remember the tree,' Mary replied. 'I'm inside it, that's all. Except...' she swallowed. 'Except that it's aware of me, the tree. It wants me and it will never let me go.'

'But you're here,' Rachel insisted, and pulled up an artist's sketch of how Oak Mary might have looked in life. 'Those are your *clothes*!' She'd been drawn wearing the dress and cardigan found on the body; the same items that were now folded in the chest of drawers in Mary's small room. 'How can you not remember, seriously?'

'I don't know! What does it matter, anyway? I'm here! I'm alive! Who cares how I got here?'

'Because it's in my head!' Rachel tapped her forefinger against her temple, like she was trying to drive in a nail. '*You're* in my head! All of it! All of that... that horrible...' She couldn't bring herself to finish, and instead held up her stump. 'And because of this! If you really were...' but she faltered again.

'Go on, say it,' prompted Mary. 'Dead. If I really was dead. Yes?'

'If you really were dead, then what have I been touching all this time? The place where dead people go?' Rachel laughed, because fuck it, why not go all the way? '*Hell?* Have I been bringing back bits of Hell? Because every time I have, something has retaliated. Tom nearly *died*, for heaven's sake. And now I've brought you through from – wherever – and you're a bloody sight bigger than an insect or a cat. What if something bigger comes after me? What if it comes after Tom again, or my mum, or his family? I can't not know. And how can you not want to know who you are?'

'Well which would you want to be?' Mary demanded. 'A prostitute, a gypsy witch or a Nazi spy? Which death would *you* like? And maybe none of them are the truth, just stories. I know I died – isn't that enough? I died and someone put me in a tree! What version of that story do you think I could possibly want to be true?'

A nurse, hearing raised voices, stopped by the room with a smile of concern. Rachel discreetly hid the web pages with their images of ghosts, corpses and spectral trees. Kingfisher House was not likely to approve of that as reading material for its patients.

'Hi, Mary,' the nurse said. 'How's everything going in here?'

'Everything's fine here, thank you.'

The nurse glanced at Rachel, but kept addressing Mary. 'I think five more minutes, don't you?'

'I'm sorry,' said Rachel. 'I've taken up too much time. I'd better go.'

'No rush,' smiled the nurse, 'just, I think maybe a change

of scenery in a bit would be a good idea, yes?'

'Of course.'

As the nurse moved away, Mary said, 'She thinks you're upsetting me.'

'Am I?'

Mary sighed. 'Yes, but you have a right to, I suppose. I wouldn't be here at all if it wasn't for you. Fair's fair. I'll try to help you however I can, but I don't know how much good I'll be.'

Impulsively Rachel folded her into a hug, and only then realised how thin Mary was, and how brittle her bones felt. 'Everything will be fine,' she said. 'You're away from that place now. You're safe.'

The doctors at Kingfisher House, satisfied that Mary didn't pose a threat to herself or others, were happy to let Rachel take her out the following day. When Rachel came to collect her after breakfast, Mary didn't look too thrilled at the prospect. 'Are we going to try and jog my memory today, then?' she asked, in tones of glum resignation. 'Is that the plan?'

'Eventually,' said Rachel. 'I thought we might get you some new clothes first, though. Fancy a spot of shopping?'

Mary's eyes lit up.

It hadn't been Rachel's intention to deepen Mary's feelings of culture shock – at the back of her mind had been a vague idea of seeing how much of the modern city centre Mary

recognised and using that as a way into her lost memory –
but just parking the car was adventure enough, never mind
actual shopping.

For Mary, absolutely everything was astonishing. The
concrete ring-road and flyovers, the glass-fronted high-
rises which reflected the clouds like a second sky, the
outlandish way everyone was dressed, and all walking
around apparently talking to themselves or into their hands.
They ate sushi and took selfies on Rachel's phone and Mary
marvelled at the image of herself.

The novelty was short-lived, however. For each new wonder
there were a dozen things to increase Mary's anxiety: strange
sounds that made her jump, and flashing advertisements
that made her wince. The multimedia LED billboards in the
shape of huge eyes over the entrances to New Street Station
absolutely terrified her, and she wouldn't go near them. By
lunchtime Rachel decided to abandon their shopping mission
and head out of town for the relative calm and hopefully
more familiar surroundings of the Lickey Hills.

Rachel drove herself and Mary to the picnic area on Beacon
Hill, the westernmost of the Lickeys, as it seemed like the
most obvious place to start. 'There used to be trams running
along here,' Mary said as they drove along the A38, pointing
at the dual carriageway's central reservation, which was
green with grass and tall horse-chestnut trees, none of
which had been planted when she had been alive, but which
to Rachel's memory had been there forever.

'There've been no trams down here since the sixties,' said Rachel. 'Although the council has just started putting them in the city centre, actually.'

Mary laughed. 'Oh well, looks like I'm just in time,' she said, but as an attempt at humour it felt strained. She twisted the strap of her seat belt with white-knuckled fingers. Neither of them was able to forget that Rachel was driving her back to the place where she'd been murdered.

Beacon Hill was a wide sward of open grass rising in a gentle slope to a lookout point built out of stone in the form of a small castle. Like pretty much everywhere else on the hills it was bustling with families, while older couples sat on park benches overlooking the panorama of the southern reaches of the West Midlands urban sprawl. Suburbs spread out into an umber haze of air pollution. The weather had turned overcast, and a chill wind tugged at them.

'I remember generalities,' said Mary, as they approached the lookout. 'Like this thing – this wasn't here. It was just one of those big brass plates that pointed out where everything was, on a big lump of concrete. But I don't know how I know that. I can't recall a specific time when I was up here. I just know I was, once.'

'So no memories being jogged free, then?'

Mary shrugged. 'Sorry.'

'That's okay. We're just scratching the surface.'

Rachel took out her tablet, called up a page from the Hollow Isle website and read:

'"On Friday 11 May 1945, the *Birmingham Post* ran a feature article on the Oak Mary mystery, prompted by the police who had by that point drawn a blank with their initial investigations into the woman's identity. It included an appeal for witnesses and an artist's sketch of what the body was found wearing, which consisted of—" blah blah blah we know all this, "—which prompted the journalist to venture the entirely unfounded opinion that the girl had been murdered while out for the evening at a nearby dancehall. There was absolutely no reason to suppose this, except perhaps that it allowed him to conclude with the portentous question: 'So, who did Mary enjoy her last dance with?' Several days later a piece of graffiti appeared on the base of a nearby monument; in large, stark white letters was written *Who danced with Oak Mary?* Soon copycat messages began appearing on walls all over Rednal, Rubery and Northfield, and it quickly passed into local legend. Even a schoolyard skipping rhyme developed:

> *Mary in the oak tree*
> *Cold as cold can be*
> *Waiting for the sky to fall*
> *Who will dance with me?*"'

'Please stop,' said Mary, and hunched her shoulders tighter against the wind. 'Please. Let's go and see this monument, and get it over and done with. I need to walk.' She strode off ahead, a small, hunched figure.

A few hundred metres down the road from the Beacon Hill car park there was a gap in the hedgerow just about wide enough for a vehicle, and then a track that soon opened out into a wide space hemmed in on all sides by tall groves of oak and yew. In the centre of it a huge column of stone thrust itself into the sky like an accusatory finger. The obelisk must have been twenty metres high; it was made of grey, unadorned granite so dour-looking that despite the bright sunlight it seemed to radiate its own chill. In two places birch saplings had taken root in cracks between the blocks. It was supported by a wider plinth and surrounded by a spiked metal railing from which the black paint was flaking away. The plinth itself carried a plaque dedicated to some long-forgotten eighteenth-century nobleman, but the lettering was obscured by the faded ghost of crudely painted words:

WHO DANCED WITH OAK MARY?

Evidently some attempt had been made to scrub them away in the distant past, but without much success, and the effect was that the message seemed translucent, hovering just above the surface, or below it, as if instead of stone it were the ice of a frozen lake.

Abruptly, Mary began to giggle, and it made Rachel's blood run cold. It was too high-pitched, like the sound of a rusty sign flapping in a gale.

'I remember now, he did his knee in,' Mary said, and something was wrong with her voice, too. Her accent had broadened, with a lilt that might have been Black Country or Irish. 'We crawled under that gap there so he could do me standing up against the stone, but it were slippery and with his kecks around his ankles he bashed all the skin off his knee.' She laughed, and turned to Rachel. 'That Brian, he really were a proper twonk.'

Her eyes, which had been a clear greyish-blue, were now a deep chocolate brown.

'Mary—' Rachel started.

'I'm not Mary!' the other woman laughed. 'I'm Annabel. Annabel Clayton.'

The *lesh* was deep in the rootweb, its awareness threaded through the trees and copses of the surrounding woodland, dormant and drifting in a world of rustling green, when it felt the gypsy witch awaken in Oak Mary.

'Annabel,' it grinned. 'My girl.'

The Green Man emerged from the tangle of root and branch and set off at a wide-legged lope through the woods to claim its prize.

'This isn't funny,' said Rachel.

'I know,' Mary replied, just as suddenly sober as she'd been giggly the moment before. 'Harry beat him terrible bad. Not as bad as what he done to me, of course. Ah, Lord,' she grimaced, as if in physical pain. 'I genuinely don't know which is worse: the forgetting or the remembering.'

'No,' said Rachel. 'I mean, this isn't a joke. Mary—'

'I'm telling you!' Mary flashed at her. 'I ain't your sodding Mary! I'm—'

That was when the *lesh* attacked.

It came at them out of the dense shadows between the yew trees, quite silently, but unbelievably fast. Rachel caught an impression of wild hair and a beard, ragged clothing, and long reaching arms, before it grabbed her by the scruff of her jacket and flung her away.

'Rachel!' Mary screamed.

Rachel pinwheeled and fell, wrenching her hip, but glanced back to see the man (*that's no man Jesus Christ look at his skin what's it made of, wood?*) had Mary (*Annabel?*) by the throat and was lifting her up, her feet kicking and dangling centimetres off the ground while her fists beat uselessly at the arm (*it's a branch it's a fucking branch!*) that held her aloft.

The *lesh* wore Harry Clayton's face, and it snarled into Annabel's, its breath stinking of rotting wood, fungus, and stale beer. 'You come back with me now, woman,' it growled. 'Back to the camp, where you belong.'

Annabel spat in its face. Unmoved, it turned and headed back for the yews, moving more slowly as it dragged her along by the throat. She was making awful choking sounds.

This is it, Rachel thought. *This is the pushback, the punishment for interfering.*

She looked around for help, but this was a dead end of the country park seldom visited by day-trippers, and she hadn't seen another human being since they'd arrived at the monument. Meanwhile the *lesh* had almost reached the treeline.

'No!' Rachel picked herself up and leapt at the creature, not at all sure what she was going to do, certain only that she couldn't let whatever it was escape unchallenged. 'Put her down, you bastard!'

The *lesh* turned to meet her challenge, one long arm sweeping around to backhand her, and she instinctively tried to shield her face. Blindly, her non-existent left hand caught the creature's arm at the wrist and stopped it in mid-swing.

She stared at it, gaping idiotically.

So did the *lesh*.

To anybody watching, it would have looked like her attacker's arm had paused, hovering six inches in the empty air above Rachel's stump, but there was nothing empty about that air. The *lesh* turned fully to face her, and she felt its muscles straining in her dead grip but knew that she was stronger – finally stronger than whatever had been terrorising her for months. She held fast.

It snarled at her in baffled fury. 'Let. Me. Go.'

'Put her down,' she repeated, first in a whisper, but then with more confidence. 'Put her *down*!'

'I will kill her.' It squeezed Annabel's throat with its other hand.

'*NO!*' Rachel twisted inward and down savagely, feeling first her enemy's wrist dislocate, then its elbow, and finally its shoulder in a series of splintering crunches. The *lesh* howled in agony and dropped Annabel to tear at Rachel's grip with both hands. She let it go and it reeled backwards, arm flopping. Crouching protectively over Annabel, who was coughing and retching into the grass, Rachel glared up at the *lesh*. 'Touch her again,' she warned, 'and I'll rip both your fucking arms off.'

For a moment it looked like the *lesh* might attack her all the same. But distantly there came the sound of barking, and that seemed to clinch it. Throwing Rachel a last look of absolute hatred, it loped off into the trees, and seemed to dissolve into the foliage.

As Rachel crouched, chest heaving for breath and trying to believe what had just happened, two large dogs tore past her and into the woods after the creature, barking and snarling. A few moments later a man ran up, out of breath.

'Are you two all right?' he panted. 'What the hell was that?'

Rachel helped Annabel to her feet. She was sobbing and clutching her neck, where bruises had already started to appear. 'That was...' Rachel started, but had no idea how to finish. 'We were attacked,' was the best she could manage.

The dog owner was young and dressed in jogging gear, and his eyes were out on stalks. 'But you...!' he stammered. 'His arm...!'

Rachel ignored him and turned to Mary. 'Are you okay?'

Mary nodded. 'Think so,' she croaked.

The dogs returned, two beautiful huskies capering with excitement, and the young jogger clipped leads on them. 'I'm going to call the police,' he said, taking out his phone.

'No!' said Rachel, a little too fiercely, then added, 'No, please,' more calmly. 'I'll do it, but I want to get my friend back to the car first. Please, it's tricky.' Then a sudden inspiration hit her. 'It was her husband. He's been stalking her since they split up. The police already know about him, but I'll definitely call them from the car. There's no need for you to get involved in it all. You've been more than enough help already. Thank you.'

Plainly the notion of becoming involved in someone's domestic troubles was too awkward for their Good Samaritan, because he put his phone away quickly, made some embarrassed-sounding apologies, and left with his dogs.

'My hero,' Rachel muttered after him, then turned back to the woman she wanted to call Mary, but who insisted that she was Annabel. 'Let's get you out of here.'

19

ANNABEL

RACHEL MANAGED TO DRIVE THEM DOWN TO THE
bottom of the hill and onto Rednal High Street before the
adrenaline wash-out hit and the hand holding the steering
wheel started to tremble. It was tricky enough driving one-
handed without this. She also began to feel woozy, but didn't
realise that she'd actually greyed out until the car jerked,
snapping her back to awareness of the fact that Annabel
had reached over to grab the wheel.

'Pull over,' Annabel demanded. Her voice was raw and
rasping. 'Before you kill the pair of us.'

Rachel did as she was told, then she sat back and just let
everything go away for a while. When the world drifted back
into focus, the woman in the passenger seat had polished
off most of the bottle of water that Rachel kept by the
handbrake, swearing at the pain in her throat in a language
that most definitely was not English. She was Mary, but at

the same time Annabel. Her face had the same shape and her hair was still brown, but somehow both seemed fuller, more really there. Rachel also saw that they had parked quite neatly outside a pub called the Old Hare and Hounds.

'Well will you look at that?' she said. 'Come on. If anyone ever deserved a drink it's us.' She got out of the car but Annabel hung back, hesitant. 'What's the problem?'

'We can't go in there!' Annabel croaked, then coughed, and took another mouthful of water.

Rachel frowned. 'I rather think we can.'

'What?' Annabel scoffed. 'Just waltz on in and buy two pints of bitter like a couple of men?'

Rachel realised what her concern was. 'Oh no, look, seriously, it's okay. It's the twenty-first century. Women do this all the time. The times, they have-a-changed.' She opened Annabel's door and held out her hand, which was still trembling.

'Well all right, if you say so.'

As they went in, Annabel stared around at the polished woodwork, the recessed halogen lights and faux-retro furnishings, and Rachel became aware that it wasn't just the fact that they were two unaccompanied women which she was finding hard to cope with.

'Even the menfolk wouldn't come in here,' Annabel said. 'They'd have been out on their arses before anybody could shout thieving gyppo scum.'

Rachel collapsed into a chair, plucked the lunch menu off the table and tossed it at Annabel, who sat down opposite her. 'Here,' she said. 'Anything you like.'

'Oh, you choose,' said Annabel, in a manner that was just a little too offhandedly casual.

'No, seriously. Anything. The cakier the better.'

'Um.' Annabel bit her lip. Her face had gone bright crimson, and with a sudden flush of embarrassment Rachel realised what the problem was.

'Oh, honey, you can't read, can you?'

The other woman cursed low and hard, in a language that Rachel didn't understand but had a funny feeling was probably Romani.

'But I thought – back at the psych unit – we read that stuff about Oak Mary together…'

'You and *Mary* read it,' Annabel replied, with surprising venom. 'I'm. Not. Her.'

'Okay, okay, I'm sorry.' Rachel ordered a pot of tea for two, and they sat in strained silence while it arrived. The normality of tea seemed to thaw the ice between them, but Rachel didn't like the way her own hand trembled as she poured.

'You all right?' asked Annabel.

'I don't know. I feel like my skeleton's turned to jelly. You seem to be taking this in your stride, though.'

Annabel smiled. 'I've had a scrap or two in my time.'

'Really? How many times have you had a scrap with anything like… that thing?'

Annabel's face grew dark again. 'It had Harry's face,' she said. 'I wasn't expecting that.'

Recollections of the fight at the monument fought their way through Rachel's wooziness, and she shuddered. 'What was it?'

'A *lesh*. A forest guardian from the old world. Mami Rudge called it up to deal with me.' Annabel produced a ghastly grin. 'On account of the fact that I wasn't going to die easy. Not for that sod Harry. Still.' She subsided. 'I weren't expecting it to come for me wearing his face, and that's a fact.'

'Jesus,' Rachel whispered. 'I think I nearly took its arm off.'

Annabel barked a laugh. 'That you did, my dear! I'll bet that put the wind right up him!'

'And you know all this because you're...' Rachel looked around and lowered her voice. 'A witch?'

Annabel grimaced. '*Drabarni*, please. It ain't witchcraft, it's knowledge. It gives you power over the way of things. Also I have the Sight, but that's different. That's something I was born with. Being *drabarni* is about learning the old ways, and passing that on.' She reached out a hand to Rachel's stump. 'May I?'

Rachel hesitated. After the surgery, nobody but Yomi and Tom had ever touched it. Still, she nodded, and Annabel laid her cupped palm over the end. It felt like an odd kind of intimacy.

'You've got some power there too,' Annabel said. 'To do what you did. To pull me through, and to beat the *lesh*.'

'Maybe the Touch instead of the Sight, though,' Rachel joked, but Annabel remained deadly serious, nodding.

'Yes, maybe so.'

'So you're really not Mary?'

'I was, when there was nobody else to be, but you helped

me remember. I'm Annabel Clayton. Pleased to meet you.'
She stood up from her chair and ducked her head, dipping
one knee slightly.

Rachel stared. 'Did you just... curtsey to me?'

'Would you rather I shook your hand like a man?' Annabel
replied, and began to laugh as if this was the most hilarious
idea she'd ever heard. Rachel found the sound infectious
and began to laugh with her, realising that it didn't matter
what the woman sitting opposite called herself. It might just
have been the reaction to the fight, but both of them were
still laughing like drains by the time their food arrived.

'So what do we do now?' asked Annabel. She'd polished
off most of the tea, drinking it scalding, unsweetened and
black, several scones and a piece of carrot cake with her
fingers, and was busy licking cream cheese topping off them.

'We get you back to the hospital and tell them that you've
recovered your memory,' said Rachel. 'And your appetite,
apparently. We probably leave out the bits about witches
and forest demons – somehow I don't think that's going to
help your case.'

Annabel looked alarmed. 'I can't go back there!'

'They're only trying to help—'

'No!' She shook her head vehemently. 'They put chemicals
into you that make your blood slow and cold so that you
can't fight them, and to make you forget who you are and
what you come from. They'd take away my Sight. They'd
call it madness and they'd put electricity through my brain
to burn it out of me, and I'd end up no better than some
gadji housewife never seeing the outside of her own four

walls. And anyway, the *lesh* is still out there. It's going to keep coming for me and I don't want to put innocent people in its way.'

'But you can't just run away.'

'Oh yes I suvvin' well can! You should be waving me on my way; you didn't ask for any of this.'

'Neither did you. And you're being stupid. Where are you planning to go? What are you going to do? It's great that you've started to remember who you are, but you've got no identity that you can use in the modern world, no money or credit cards; for God's sake, you probably don't know what a credit card even is. We can help you. Tom's family business can give you a job, we can fix you up with somewhere to live, and you can be Annabel – but not if I'm in jail for harbouring an escaped psychiatric patient. What do you think the doctors and the police are going to do when you fail to turn up at dinnertime? Who do you think they're going to blame?' She pointed at herself. 'Muggins here. I'm the one supposed to be responsible for you. Plus, in case you hadn't noticed, I already beat seven bells out of that *lesh* thing once, even though I still don't have the faintest idea how. If you really want to help me you can start with that.'

'Start with what?'

'So far you're the closest I've got to anybody who might have a clue about how this whole coming-back-from-the-dead thing works. I don't mind admitting I'm in over my head here. I could really do with some advice, or at least a second opinion. Please?'

'Fine then,' Annabel sighed. 'I'll go back, and tell them I

had a lovely day shopping. But you better be waiting in your car for me somewhere tonight because I'll be letting myself out of there by morning.'

Rachel paid the bill and they went out to the car, but before they reached it Annabel's shoulders slumped and her hands came up to her face, and Rachel realised she was crying.

'Hey, what? I'm sorry, what did I say?'

Annabel's voice escaped from between the cage of her fingers, muffled. 'My boys. What you said about where was I going to go. I just realised that they'll be old men, if they're even alive at all.' She pulled her hands away. 'Mami called the *lesh* on me because I cursed them. I cursed my own family. My own *children*. What kind of a person does that? And you think I can help you?'

Rachel put her arms around her, felt her stiffen and then give in. 'Someone who is very angry and scared and in a lot of pain,' she said. Tom's expression of confused hurt when she'd gone to sleep in the spare room floated clear in her memory. 'It's not just you, trust me. I'm the last person to ask anything about kids. Come on. We can't stand about in the car park hugging all day.'

The three deaths reconvened at the clearing of Mary's Oak. The Green Man looked considerably the worse for wear; his left arm dangled and was bent in several directions that it shouldn't.

The Small Man was picking his fingernails with his knife.

'Well that answers one question, at least,' he observed. 'We should have guessed that she had help. Nobody escapes without help. She was too weak to remember even her own name, never mind regain flesh. No.' He picked and picked. 'A wayward soul is one thing. To aid and abet that, to wilfully tamper with the boundary between life and the umbra – that's nothing short of criminal. It requires punishing.'

'That is beyond our remit,' warned the Dark Man. 'We are only here for Mary.'

The Small Man paused in his picking, having drawn blood, and examined a crimson bead, which trickled from underneath his fingernail and over the soft pad of his thumb. 'I don't know about you,' he said, 'but I like the flesh. I like the freedom it gives, for example, to redefine one's remits.'

The Dark Man snorted with contempt. 'I like how you stood back and waited to see what would happen.'

'Who would have thought our colleague would find her so quickly? That was almost an utter disaster.'

'So close,' the Green Man growled. 'She changed. She was mine.'

'So close?' sneered the Small Man. 'Look at you. That woman nearly ripped your arm off! And do you know why? Because you're weak.'

'You too, and him,' the Green Man replied. 'Weak because we are three. Split. Diluted.'

'Pah. You thunder about like a god of tree stumps but you're just an implausible bit of folklore. Oak Mary the gypsy witch is a pretty enough fairy story but don't seriously expect anyone to believe it. And as for being a Nazi spy,' he looked the Dark Man up and down disparagingly. 'Only a cretin would believe such tripe...'

'You talk altogether too much,' snarled the Dark Man, and drew out his revolver and shot him.

The Small Man yelped and clapped his hands to his ears, dropping his knife. At such close range there was no chance that the Dark Man could have missed, yet his target remained standing as the echoes crashed through the trees and dissipated.

The Small Man turned and looked at the tree directly behind him, which sported a fresh, splintered bullet hole. 'That,' he said through gritted teeth, 'was wholly unnecessary, not to mention futile. We cancel each other out, you fool. We are mutually exclusive. Each one of us precludes the true existence of the other two. Therefore we cannot take direct action against each other, you must know that.'

'Indeed we do,' agreed the Dark Man.

'Then why on earth did you try to shoot me?' The Small Man sounded decidedly peeved.

'Because you annoy me,' the Dark Man replied. 'And I find that I enjoy watching you flinch.' He shot him again. The echoes rolled back and forth between the hills like bowling balls.

'Will you stop that!'

'As much as it sickens me to admit it,' said the Dark Man, 'it is evident that we have misjudged our situation. Our triumvirate nature would suggest that Mary's soul comprises three distinct and divergent identities, and is moreover protected by someone who possesses an unaccountable talent to reach beyond the physical state. I propose that we pool our resources and find Mary first, deal with the woman who guards her most severely, and then settle the matter of ownership afterwards.'

The Small Man raised an eyebrow at the Green Man, who thought about it for a moment and then gave a cautious nod and a grunt. 'Very well,' sighed the Small Man. 'So, when shall we three meet again? In thunder, lightning or in rain?'

'*Ach, hou je smoel*,' the Dark Man muttered, exasperated.

The Green Man suddenly raised his head, sniffing. 'Someone…' he murmured.

'You see?' The Small Man waved an accusatory finger at the Dark Man. 'You draw attention to us with your childishness. And where are *you* going?'

The *lesh* was dissolving back into the background foliage. His voice was a dim rustle of leaves and branches. 'Following.' Then he was gone.

'Well you just be careful!' the Small Man yelled after him. 'Or she'll rip your arse off and feed it to you!' After a moment of silence while the woodland settled around them he turned to the Dark Man. 'He is correct, though. We are diluted.'

'I know. See to it. I'll find us a vehicle.' And he too left, heading for the car park.

The Small Man lit a cigarette and puffed an irritated little cloud of smoke. 'See to it,' he muttered. 'See to it, the man says.'

Rachel, that was what Mary had called her. It seemed that this Rachel had a talent that was prodigious to say the least, and he wasn't about to chance *his* arm against that – especially not with only a third of the strength he should have had. He took himself for a stroll back through the woods, nodding and smiling politely to the couples and families he passed, and returned to the monument. He read the graffiti on its base: *Who danced with Oak Mary?* and stroked the handle of the knife in his pocket. 'Why I did, of course,' he told the monument, and grinned. 'And I shall dance with her again before long.'

For eyes that could see past the living world this message was imbued with power. He stepped through the railing and close to the stone, trailing his fingers across the ghosts of the letters. They tingled. It was belief, that power – no, it was myth, something far stronger than simple, dumb belief. It was the same power that invested the offerings in the clearing, and was similarly weak with age and faded with forgetting. To be of any use it would need to be refreshed, and the Small Man was intimately familiar with the ingredients necessary to accomplish this.

He headed towards the large play-castle on Beacon Hill, busy with families and strolling couples, toying with the knife in his coat pocket and looking for someone who could supply both:

Fear and blood.

20

THE SIGHT

ON THEIR WAY BACK TO KINGFISHER HOUSE, RACHEL found an obscure spot in a side street near the hospital where she would pick up Annabel later that evening, then walked her to the front door and into the care of the nurses, with waves and smiles all round. The prospect of acting as getaway driver for an escaped psychiatric patient didn't daunt Rachel half so much as the conversation she needed to have with her husband first.

She tackled it over dinner, which they ate at the table instead of in front of the television, so he knew from the start that something was up.

'Tom,' she said. 'You remember that time when Tracey from work got her phone stolen and she tracked it to that pub, and you and some of your dad's lads went round and got it back, and there was that big fight?'

Tom grunted, scowling. 'Arseholes. Remember it? I'm

not likely to forget.' He'd needed four stitches and spent an hour in a police cell. 'Why?'

'Well, I have this... friend, and she needs my help.'

'From work?'

'An old friend.'

'School?'

'Kind of. Her name's Annabel. She's having trouble with a fella, and she needs somewhere to stay, and I wondered if she could stay in our spare room for a bit.'

'The nursery, you mean?'

'Tom, please—'

He put his hands up, grimacing in apology. 'Sorry, that was unnecessary. Look, I'm not saying no, but this place is not exactly fit for guests, is it? Plus it's been a busy month what with one thing and another; I was kind of hoping for a bit of a break for us to catch our breath before the next life-or-death emergency.'

She bit her tongue at his unintended irony. 'I know, I'm the same. It's just that the man in question is, ah, a bit nastier than those kids in the pub.'

'Surely if he's that nasty a piece of work she'd be better off going to the police?'

'Come on, Tom, you know how useless the police are. The news is full of stories about women who report stalkers and the police don't do anything and then they get attacked, or even killed. One poor girl in Sussex had her throat cut – and the only help she got before she was killed was a fine for wasting police time. It would only be a temporary thing. Just until Annabel gets herself sorted out.'

'Well,' he said, his wariness plain. 'If it's that serious, I suppose so. Of course she can stay.'

'Thank you.' Rachel leaned forward across the table to kiss him. 'You're my white knight.'

He ignored that. 'But she goes to the police first thing tomorrow, and I'm going to want the full story when she gets here. I don't want any nasty surprises coming through my back door wearing balaclavas.'

'Full story,' she agreed, and took a big gulp of water without quite meeting his eyes. 'No nasty surprises.'

Despite telling Tom that she was only going to be gone a little while, Rachel had to wait in the car for two hours before Annabel appeared, becoming increasingly paranoid that something had gone wrong. The suburban street where she was parked was narrow and curved, with large plane trees planted at intervals in front of steeply gabled older houses and their well-established gardens; she'd chosen it for the cover it provided, but it was a breezy evening and as nightfall deepened the streetlamps threw furtive, rustling shadows through the foliage. She kept catching glimpses of movement in her rear-view mirror, convinced every time that it was the *lesh* that had somehow found her again, and becoming even more frustrated when it turned out to be a branch or a cat instead of Annabel.

Another shadowy waving movement caught her eye and her breath. But it was just a branch behind a row of three wheelie-bins, which themselves were little more than squat shadows against a hedge.

'Come on, where the fuck *are* you?' she muttered.

Wait – hadn't there only been two bins before? She checked the mirror again. Yes, there were only two bins. So why had she thought there were three?

She twisted her head around to see through the car's rear window directly instead of using the mirror – because even mirrors weren't necessarily to be trusted – and could only see two bins. But now that tree next to them; had it been that thick before? Had that branch, which right now looked so much like an arm, bent in that direction? She was peering at it so closely that her neck muscles twanged like guitar strings, and when someone rapped on the passenger window she screamed and twisted back so violently that a sharp pain flared in her shoulder.

Annabel was at the window with a bundle slung over one shoulder, bouncing up and down and casting nervous glances all around. She rapped on the window again. 'Open up!'

Rachel unlocked the doors. 'Jesus!' she said as Annabel tossed her bundle into the back and jumped into the passenger seat. 'You scared the shit out of me!'

'Get us out of here!' Annabel demanded. 'Seggo! Quickly!' She smelled of smoke.

Rachel started the car. 'How did you get out?'

'Chucked a couple of matches into the kitchen bin. When the fire alarm went off they herded us outside. I had to climb over a wall. I don't know if they've noticed I'm missing yet.' She was craning her neck around, trying to look in every direction through the windows as Rachel pulled away. 'Have you seen it?'

'The *lesh*?'

'No, Father Christmas! Yes, the *lesh*! I'm sure I smelled it out there.'

'I don't know. Maybe. Look, let's just get home, okay?'

As they pulled out onto the dual carriageway a fire engine swept past with its lights strobing, but Rachel calmly steered them in the opposite direction, doing her best to control her nerves and stick to the speed limit, and hopefully doing nothing that would draw unwelcome attention to them. She had an uncomfortable feeling that she'd already drawn enough.

Tom was on his hands and knees in the hallway, draught-proofing the skirting board with a tube of silicone sealant when Rachel walked through the front door. 'Hello,' he said, looking up. 'You took your time, didn't you? Oh, sorry!' he added, seeing Annabel behind her. He straightened up, brushing the dust off his knees. 'I'm Tom.' He held out his hand. 'You must be Annabel.'

Annabel gave him a small, cautious smile and a duck of the head.

'Tom was just going out, weren't you?' said Rachel.

'I was?'

'Yes,' she replied, giving him a big, tight hug. 'You were going out to the Black Cross for a couple of drinks with your mates and leaving me to settle Annabel in so that we can have a nice girlie talk without feeling awkward having a horrible great clomping man around, weren't you?' Her hug turned into a gentle shove towards the front porch and his coat.

Tom sighed. 'When you put it like that, of course I was.'

'Where's your man's tool kit?' Annabel asked.

'In his van,' said Rachel. 'Why?'

'Chalk. String. Torch. Has he got those things?'

'More than likely. And again I ask: why?' Annabel hadn't relaxed a bit since arriving, and her terseness and distraction put Rachel's nerves on edge.

'The *lesh* is still out there, and it's coming for me. We need to defend your home.'

Fortunately Tom had walked to the pub, leaving his work keys behind, and Annabel found what she needed in the back of his van. The first thing she did was chalk a large, many-spoked circle on the front door, filling the spaces between the spokes with strange marks that looked like astrological symbols.

'I thought you couldn't read or write,' Rachel said. She would never have described herself as a suburban curtain-twitcher, but caught herself casting anxious glances up and down the street and wondering what the neighbours would be thinking if they were watching this.

'This isn't writing,' Annabel replied. 'At least, not in the way that you would understand it. These are *patrin*.' In her accent it sounded like *patreen*. 'Romani signs. Here,' she added, pointing to one of the marks. 'Warning threats, protections, prayers to saints and so on. We put one on the back door too, and then we make *patrin* out of sticks to hang in the windows.'

They foraged in the bushes of the nearby playing field by torchlight for the twigs and feathers she claimed to need; Rachel found herself shoving through clumps of brambles and undergrowth littered with plastic bottles and crisp packets. 'No way does this look dodgy,' she muttered to herself. 'This is what they call hedgerow magic, is it? Dog shit and needles. It wasn't like this in *Charmed*.'

Back inside, Annabel began assembling a series of crude mobiles out of the scraps, while all Rachel could do was watch and make supportive cups of tea, since she lacked the manual dexterity to make anything else.

'Holly,' Annabel explained. 'The autumn is only young so the *lesh* will still be oak until the year turns, but holly is a winter wood so it will sap his strength. Ha. Sap. That's a witch joke, you know.' She winked, and carefully bound two holly sticks together in a cross with a feather at their junction. 'Birds are air and fire, trees are earth and water. It's not foolproof but anything that weakens him makes it easier for us.'

'Also it's a cross,' Rachel pointed out. 'Like against vampires.'

Annabel grunted. 'I used to have faith, back in the day. Not for any particular reason, just because you did; the Romani are a very religious people. Being trapped in the oak put paid to that.'

'Why?' asked Rachel. 'You know that there's something after death. Surely that would prove that God exists or something?'

'Because it isn't really death. It wasn't really life, either. It was…' She stopped, trying to put into words something that must have felt, at best, like a nightmare. 'There's a word: limbo. You know it?'

Rachel nodded.

'Like that, then. I didn't see heaven or hell. I certainly didn't see God. There was only the tree, and nothing outside it. Just cold, and dark, and not being able to move, forever. Then all of a sudden a hand appears in front of me, so I grab it and hang on like – well, like grim death, so.' And she laughed.

'So what I was touching,' said Rachel, 'it wasn't, you know, oh God it sounds stupid just saying it.'

'Then just say it,' Annabel said lightly, working at another twig cross.

'The land of the dead?'

Annabel mulled this over. 'When you put it that way, yes, it does sound stupid.' Then she nudged Rachel with her elbow and grinned.

'Piss off!' Rachel laughed. 'Just answer the question. Did I touch the place where dead people go?'

Annabel's grin sobered to a frown, and Rachel found herself struggling to keep up with her rapid shifts of mood. 'Truthfully I don't know. I'm not dead now, so I don't see how I could have been dead before; not properly dead, at any rate. As far as I know, dead means dead.'

'Maybe you were improperly dead.'

Annabel chuckled – a throaty, dirty sound. 'Well I was bloody improper when I was alive, I tell you that.'

'Really? Do tell.'

'No chance!' She laughed. 'You'll think I'm an absolute slut.'

'Honey, I dreamed how you died. I'm already there. Brian was a very obliging young man, wasn't he?'

'Now you piss off!' Annabel blushed, and changed the subject. 'You've got an unfair advantage. I don't know anything about you. What about you and Tom?' she asked. 'How did you meet?'

'At the Highways Agency. He used to do maintenance and clean-up. If a lorry shed its load or a barrier needed mending, he was one of a team that dealt with the mess or made repairs. I worked, still do, in the control centre at Quinton. My job is to watch a stretch of the motorway and if anything like that needs sorting, I call out a team. So one day, a really hot summer's day three years ago, a scrap metal merchant's truck loses its load all over the northbound carriageway – there's bits of tricycle and washing machine all over the place – and I call out a team and it's Tom's. And it takes them a while, because there's a lot of mess, and like I say it was a very hot day, and he's wearing the standard hi-vis jacket, and it must have been sweltering. Oh God...' She broke off, and it was her turn to blush.

'What?' Annabel leaned forward, intrigued.

'This is awful. It's like one of those bloody Diet Coke ads.'

'I have no idea what that means. Keep going.'

'So they take a five-minute break, and they go up on the grass verge for a drink of water and he takes his jacket off and lies back in the grass, sort of propped up on his elbows, you know? And he's just got this t-shirt on and he's absolutely wet through with sweat, and he's just so fucking *hot*, you know?'

'I'll bet he was, in that weather.'

'No, I mean... never mind.'

'And you're watching all of this on your cameras?'

'Yes.'

'You're spying on him, being all hot and sweaty.'

'I'm a terrible person, I know.'

'And you looked at him and you thought, he'll do me nicely.'

'Oh yes.'

Annabel arched her eyebrows and leaned even closer. 'And does he? Does he do you nicely?'

'You were right – you *are* a slut.'

They laughed. Rachel found it hard to believe that they were gossiping about men at the same time as talking quite calmly about life after death and making wards against a supernatural entity as if these things went together naturally.

'What is it like?' asked Annabel. 'You know, the limbo place, when you touch it?'

'It's different depending on where I am. Around here there are lots of old brick walls and bits of crap – nails, wood, broken glass, things like that. I wondered if it was because this whole estate is built on an old factory works, and that it was some sort of echo of that place.'

'Have you ever tried to see it?'

'Now how would I go about doing that? It's my hand

that's over there, not my eyes, and I'm not about to poke one of them out, am I?'

'No, but there's sight and there's Sight, if you know what I mean.'

Rachel stopped what she was doing and stared at Annabel. 'Are you saying that you can teach me how to actually see what I've been touching?'

'I'm saying that you lose nothing by giving it a try.' Annabel put down the sticks and string she'd been holding and moved to kneel in front of Rachel, taking Rachel's right hand and wrist stump in her own hands. 'Do you know how to make an "okay" sign with your fingers?'

Rachel formed a circle with her right thumb and forefinger and showed it to Annabel. 'This? So?'

Annabel averted her gaze and gently moved Rachel's hand away as if it were a torch shining directly in her face. 'It's also, in the right kind of circumstances, a sign of the evil eye, so let's be careful with that. It has a name in Romani: *barjok*. Now, can you imagine making it with your dead hand instead? And then holding it up to look through, like an imaginary telescope?'

Rachel closed her eyes, feeling oddly like she was somehow betraying Yomi by actively trying to summon up the phantom sensations that she'd spent the last several weeks trying to eliminate. In the end it was as if she'd never bothered in the first place; she could clearly feel her left thumb and forefinger touching each other. She traced the smooth hardness of her index fingernail with her thumb. 'Ha,' she said. 'I've just thought: I bet my nails are in an absolute state. Do you think there are any decent nail bars in limbo?'

'Any decent what?'

'Never mind.' She raised her empty wrist to her face and peered through where the loop in her fingers should have been, not expecting to see anything except her own living room.

'Oh. My. God.'

A hole had opened in the air in front of her left eye and through it she saw the place that she'd only ever touched blindly and fearfully – the limbo realm that hid behind the world. It was like looking through the lens of a telescope while keeping your other eye open, and feeling your brain perform acrobatics with focus and perspective as it tried to reconcile two conflicting images – first superimposing one on the other, then vice versa, then both at the same time. At first it was difficult to make out much detail because it was a lot darker there, but it seemed to be a vast indoor space, like a derelict warehouse. Its walls were indistinct in the gloom, but fissures in the roof allowed an unsteady violet light to spill through, which hinted at things visible only in stranger spectrums still, and picked out the silhouettes of vast, dead machines rearing up like statues in a cathedral to alien gods.

Her new sight caught movement: human figures shambling in the shadows of these looming colossi. She couldn't pick out details of clothing or expression but she knew from the listless way they trudged amongst the ruins that they were alone and utterly lost. Once she'd recovered from her initial shock, she tried to describe to Annabel what she was seeing.

'You said that this estate is built on an old factory site?' Annabel asked.

'Yes – you think that's what I'm seeing?'

'I don't know. I think that maybe a fair few people die in factories. I wouldn't be surprised to find more than one trapped somewhere like that.'

'But that's...' Rachel shuddered. One shuffling figure had paused, and now changed direction, heading back towards her. If this factory was analogous to the living world, that would put it somewhere in the street outside. 'You mean all those times I was reaching into this place I could have touched one of those... I don't know what to call them. Ghosts? Spectres? I could have touched one at any time?'

'You did, remember?' Annabel replied, indicating herself. 'I'd be careful about drawing attention to yourself. If their experience is anything like mine they'll be desperate for any way to escape, and they won't be gentle about it.'

Rachel dropped her dead hand and blinked as the bright warmth of the living room re-established itself around her. Annabel was watching her with concern. 'Are you all right?'

'No,' Rachel answered. 'How could I be all right? Is that what it's like for you, having the Sight? Can you see that too?'

'It's not the same thing. It's more of a knowing thing.'

'But it's all just there! Around us, right here! Behind it all, I mean.'

Annabel seemed to be taking it all quite calmly, picking up the sticks she'd discarded and tying them together with string. Rachel found her nonchalance infuriating. 'How am I supposed to be all right, knowing that?'

'You already knew it was there, though,' the Romani woman pointed out. 'You've known about it for weeks, by your own admission. You've touched it. You've messed about with it. You saved me from it. Does it make that much of a difference actually seeing it?'

'Yes! Yes it does!'

Annabel's gaze was stern. 'Well it shouldn't. Stop your blartin and grow up, woman. You're stronger than this. Something came out of that place after me and you almost tore its bloody arm off, remember that? It'll come for me again and so we need to be ready when it does – more importantly your man needs to be ready too and he doesn't know a thing about any of this. You're going to have to explain it to him and make him follow your lead, and you can't do that if you're flapping all over the place like a pigeon trying to catch a taxi, can you?'

Despite herself, Rachel smiled. 'A pigeon catching a taxi?'

21

TELLING TOM

'WHAT'S THAT MESS ALL OVER THE FRONT DOOR?' demanded Tom when he came back from the pub. He found Rachel sitting at the breakfast bar in the kitchen with a large glass of red wine and an almost empty bottle. Lined up in front of her on the counter was a pile of dead leaves, a piece of broken glass, and a small black beetle. 'And what's this all about?' he asked, half-smiling, half-frowning. 'Where's your friend?'

'She's gone to bed. Bit of a busy day, what with one thing and another.' Rachel took a large gulp of Shiraz. 'Honey, sit down. There's something I need to show you.'

She decided that he took it quite well, all told. He didn't freak out, accuse her of attempting to trick him, or try to have her sectioned. If anything he seemed hurt that she hadn't told him before, but accepted her misgivings about what his reaction would have been. He got her to produce things with her dead hand several times, watching her like a hawk, and inspecting the damage that was caused whenever something came through: a cracked tile, a sudden stench from the fridge as a perfectly ripe cauliflower spontaneously rotted in seconds, a glass shattering in the dishwasher, and other incidents until he'd seen enough to satisfy himself that it was real. He prodded at the detritus from the other place.

'So how does it work then – touching the other side, I mean?'

Rachel snorted. 'You think I know?'

'No, I mean how do you bring things through? And how does it feel?'

Rachel considered, finding it hard to put into words something that half her mind continued to insist was impossible, despite the truth of it right in front of her. 'It's funny,' she said. 'You'd think there would be, I don't know, ectoplasm or a flash of light or something, but it's just, I hold something with the hand that isn't there any more, then bring my other hand up—' she mimed the action '—I transfer it from one to the other and...' She shrugged. 'Alakazam. It appears.'

'Have you ever tried sending something the other way?'

The question was so simple that it stunned her to realise that she'd never even considered it. 'Wow. No. I never, I mean, why would I?'

'Why does anybody do anything?' Tom asked. 'To see if you can?'

Rachel picked up an apple from the fruit bowl on the breakfast bar. It was glossy and green, and had a pleasingly solid heft to it; it felt real, like it couldn't possibly just vanish out of the world.

'I'm not sure about this,' she said. 'Whenever I move things from one place to the other something causes damage in response. That's how we got into this whole mess, remember?'

'Maybe that's because you're stealing something from limbo that's already there. You're not doing that in this case – you're putting something in instead.'

Rachel looked at him. 'And all of a sudden you're the expert.'

'You lose nothing by trying.'

'Really. Well if I do this and your chair collapses and dumps you on your arse, don't blame me.'

She concentrated on the phantom sensations from her left hand, imagining her unseen fingers reaching to grasp the apple and what its weight and smoothness would feel like, and she brought her right hand across – and it was gone. In the end it was no more difficult to pass it from one hand to the other than if she'd been a whole-bodied person. She brought it back again, and tensed, waiting for the backlash.

Nothing happened.

'Well what do you know?' she said in soft surprise. Then she laughed.

'What's so funny?' asked Tom.

'Oh I was just thinking of the glorious life of crime I could lead doing this. Imagine what I could smuggle through airport metal detectors.' She passed the apple back and forth a few more times before another idea struck her. 'What if...' She tried to hold the apple in both hands, living and dead, at the same time. It felt slippery, like a magnet trying to skid past another with the same polarity, and a shimmering violet haze began to form in the air between her hand and her stump. She cried out in disgust as the apple rotted in her grip and abruptly exploded, showering the pair of them with decaying fruit.

Tom and Rachel stared at each other for a moment with bits of apple on their faces and in their hair, and abruptly burst out laughing.

'Entropy,' he murmured, picking bits off himself and examining them. 'Something like that, anyway.'

'What's that?' said Rachel, surprised. Bless him, but it seemed altogether too scientific a word for her husband to have come out with.

'There's this bloke works for us, Jules, big fella, beard, reads loads of science fiction – all that stuff about parallel universes, quantum this, that and the other. He tried telling us once about this type of energy called entropy, the tendency of things to fall apart, and said it was the handyman's best friend because no matter how much you fixed anything it was always going to collapse. We said that was just a piss-poor excuse for why he couldn't mix concrete properly. But what if there really *is* a parallel universe that you're somehow touching, and it's got too much entropy, and every time you bring something through from there a bit of entropy leaks through with it?'

Rachel didn't like to contradict him, because Tom was

a fundamentally practical man and the ability to put a scientific label, however inaccurate, to the phenomenon was a crutch that he needed to support his suddenly skewed notions of reality, but she felt instinctively that the other place wasn't just a parallel universe. Somehow that seemed even less believable than the idea that she was reaching into the world of the dead.

'Can I just point out,' she said, 'that you're taking this an awful lot better than I was expecting.'

'What *were* you expecting?'

She shrugged. 'You screaming something like, "Holy fucking shit what is that thing burn the witch"?'

Tom was silent for a moment. 'Rache,' he said eventually, 'something happened to me once, that I've never told a soul before, not even you. Back before we met, when I was working for Highways, I was on a cone crew with two other guys – chap called Neil driving the truck, while me and this older bloke everyone called Boffey walked along behind, picking up the cones and stacking them on the back, as you do.

'Anyway, it was eleven at night, and the motorway was virtually empty. We're not going very fast, literally walking pace, and this traffic officer in his big black and yellow four-by-four zooms past and pulls in diagonally right in front of us with his hazard lights on, blocking the way. He doesn't get out but just sits there, and I don't realise it at the time, it's only later I think there are supposed to be two to a patrol, but this guy is on his own.

'This gets up Neil's nose, of course, so he gets out of the truck to ask the idiot what does he think he's doing. But the guy doesn't even turn his head to look while Neil is tapping on his window. He just sits, staring straight ahead like a shop window dummy.

'And as we're standing there scratching our heads and discussing whether we should call it in – because we figure maybe he's stoned or drunk or he's broken up with his wife and we don't want to get him on a discipline but at the same time this isn't normal at all – an articulated lorry coming down the opposite carriageway loses control, goes straight through the central reservation, across all three lanes of our carriageway, smashes through the guard rail and goes down the embankment literally twenty feet from where we're standing.

'If that traffic officer hadn't pulled in and stopped us, we'd have been right in front of that lorry and wiped out completely. Turned out the lorry driver had been on the road from Montenegro for twenty hours straight.

'So obviously we're staring down at the wreck and Neil runs for the radio in our truck to call it in and me and Boffey turn back and see that the traffic officer's gone. We didn't hear any engine, and we didn't see him drive off. He was just gone. We hadn't thought to check the registration number so there was no way of telling who it was, and there was no CCTV as evidence that it happened at all, except that there were three of us there and we know what we saw.

'Now I'm not saying that it was the ghost of a dead traffic officer patrolling the motorway who saved our lives that night, but in the absence of another explanation I'm open to the possibility. Likewise, I have to believe that you pulled those leaves and stuff out of somewhere, because as crazy as this sounds it's actually easier to believe that than the alternative.'

'What's the alternative?' she asked.

'That you've been secretly training as a street magician and you're deliberately messing with my head to gain access to my family fortune.'

She stared at him for a moment, trying to work out whether or not he was being serious. He winked at her and she burst out laughing. 'You dick,' she said, and swatted him.

'Seriously though,' he added. 'Don't you think you should tell the doctors?'

'Tell them what, exactly? What do I tell Yomi? That her physiotherapy has had some unexpected side effects?'

'I don't know. But you don't know what this might be doing to your nervous system or your cells or something. You need to get advice from someone, I don't know who.'

'What if it was a ghost?' she said. 'Your traffic officer. What if it really was someone back from the dead. Do you think that's possible?'

'Fifteen minutes ago I wouldn't have said it was possible for a person to materialise stuff from a parallel universe, so what I think is or isn't possible is a bit up for grabs at the moment. But people are different, though, aren't they? They have to be.'

'Why? If there are leaves and wood why can't there be flesh and blood?'

'Because people have minds, and souls…'

'What if, when you die, something of you stays in that

other place, just like something of this leaf? Some kind of echo, or like when you make a photocopy of a photocopy. According to Google, throughout the whole of human history, about 107 billion people have ever lived, which if you divide that by the world's current population means that fifteen people will have died for every person alive on the planet. Maybe not everybody goes to the other place and becomes a ghost; maybe it's only one in a thousand, but even that would mean 107 million ghosts in the world. If ghosts exist, we must be absolutely surrounded by them. And if they are in that other place, is it really surprising if from time to time they come back through?'

Tom heaved a huge sigh and rubbed his eyes with the heels of both hands. 'This is a lot to take in,' he said. 'We've both been drinking. I think I need to sleep on this for a bit...'

Rachel shook her head and placed her hand over his. 'Sorry, can't let you do that, I'm afraid. There's more, and I'm not doing it with a hangover. It's hard enough sloshed.'

'More?' he laughed. 'What more could there be?'

'What if,' she said slowly, watching him from under her lashes, 'one of them were to have come back through and was asleep in our back bedroom right now?'

She watched him process this: the little snort of disbelief, the sideways glance to see if she was making fun of him, the slight widening of the eyes as he saw that she wasn't, the deepening of his breathing as the adrenaline kicked in, and the sudden rock-hard tension in the sinews of his hand as he pulled it away. He lurched towards the hallway and the staircase.

'Tom! Wait!' She hurried after him, putting her hand on his shoulder, but he shook her off.

'No. Just no. I have to see her.'

'But, Tom—'

He stopped halfway up the stairs and turned on her. 'You're telling me that you've brought the spirit of a dead woman back from limbo and that she's in our spare room? I'm seeing her for myself.'

She caught him again at the door to the spare room. 'You can't just barge in there!' she hissed. 'She's a guest!'

'*Guest?*' He stared at her, incredulous. 'This isn't a fucking hotel for ghosts!'

'Well at least keep your bloody voice down!'

He opened the door.

Annabel was far from asleep. She was standing at the window, wrapped in a quilt, gazing out into the blackness of the garden and the rustling shadows of the bushes at the far end. Smoky had draped himself across her shoulders. She turned as the door opened, half-lit by the night, her dark hair framing her face and her steady eyes regarding them with a calmness that seemed to take the wind out of Tom's sails.

'Um,' he said.

'Hello, Tom,' Annabel replied. Her voice was pitched low, and it even made Rachel's heart skip a little. Lord knew what effect it was having on him. 'I heard you and Rachel talking downstairs.'

'Look—'

'Everything she told you is true. I know it all sounds very complicated but it's actually quite simple. With her help I have escaped from a terrible place, where I thought I'd be forever, and someone has come after me to take me back – someone who means to do me harm, and against whom I can appeal to no earthly authority. Helping me will put you in the path of that, but all the same, Thomas Cooper, will you help me or will you not?'

For a ridiculous moment Rachel had an image of her husband dropping to one knee and offering a sword in Annabel's service, but all he did was give a resigned, helpless shrug and say, 'Okay.'

Annabel smiled, and in the dark it was radiant. 'Thank you. This place is as secure as I can make it,' she added, shifting her attention to Rachel. 'If neither of you mind, I'm very tired.'

'Of course,' said Rachel. 'Come on, dear.' She had to pull him out of the room. He was murmuring something that she couldn't quite catch. 'What was that?'

'Nothing,' he said hastily.

But it had sounded like, 'Oh queen of air and darkness…'

Later, in their own bed, Tom turned to Rachel in the darkness and said, 'What she said about someone coming to take her back – that's where Smoky came from too, isn't it?'

Rachel nodded.

'And the thing that came for him—'

'We killed,' she finished. 'I smashed its brains out of its skull, and I'll do the same to anyone or anything that comes after her too.'

'She's certainly not what I expected.'

'Hmm, yeah, I noticed that.'

'What's that supposed to mean?'

'Oh nothing.' She snuggled up to him. 'Really, it's nothing. We're both knackered. Like you said, we need to sleep on this.'

She felt him drift off quickly, but lay awake in his loose embrace for some time afterwards, listening to the small noises of the house as they settled around the unaccustomed presence of another woman in her home.

22

NOZ

CONNOR LEANED BACK AGAINST THE OBELISK, PUT the balloon to his lips and inhaled, tasting the noz, all cool and sweet and chemically. Jake said it was a colourless, odourless gas and he was imagining it, but Jake also said that you could get high if you licked enough pencils, which pretty much proved that Jake knew shit all.

Around them the fir trees of Beacon Hill rose in long straight columns of shadow into the night sky. It was mild with only a slight breeze, making them sway and whisper to each other. Connor breathed in and out into the balloon, mixing the nitrous oxide with his own carbon dioxide so it started getting all warm and wet and funky and rubbery. They were pink birthday balloons with unicorns and princesses, which he'd nicked from his little sister Lucy's stash of party treasures. Two more were inflated and ready to use, but kept safely away from a small fire of twigs and leaves that they'd lit, because you always had to have a fire.

Jake turned to him. 'Is it good?'

The buzz was starting to fizzle out his nerve endings like slo-mo sparklers, spreading a tingling warmth through him. 'Yeah,' Connor grinned. 'Safe as,' and put his lips back to the balloon while Jake reached for the cracker tube and inserted a fresh noz cylinder. There was a crack and a hiss, and Jake inflated his own magic unicorn.

As Connor lay on a blanket of fir needles and the noz buzz kicked in, perspective flipped and he wasn't lying down looking up any more but looking out at the rays of some hyperspace tunnel speeding past him to infinity, like he was Han Solo in the Thingy Whatsit Falcon, which made Jake Chewie and that was pretty fucking funny, and he started to giggle.

Jake paused from dragging on his balloon. 'What's funny?'

But the giggles had taken over and Connor couldn't catch his breath to reply, which Jake took to be a sign that all was well and carried on inhaling, and soon the pair of them were hysterical with laughter, catching it from each other and giving it back as it subsided. Somewhere in the glowing nebula that used to be his brain, Connor thought that it was always better to do this with your mates. Sure, Jake was a dick, but he was all right.

And then a man was there, standing over them, looking down. He looked like a hipster version of Wolverine, and this was just fucking *hilarious*, and Connor was off harder than before.

But the more he looked, the less it resembled a man. It was

hard to tell because whether it was the jumping shadows of the fire or the noz fucking with his brain, or both, the guy's face seemed to keep changing shape, and the same with his clothes. Sometimes flickering, sometimes melting. Somewhere deep in Connor's brain a voice was yelling to him that it was the feds – someone had shitted on them and the feds had found them and his mum was going to fucking kill him – and suddenly it wasn't as funny any more. The nitrous oxide was wearing off, but there was still enough in his system that he couldn't do much more than lie there shaking with the aftershocks of his giggling fit as it leaned close.

'Who danced with Oak Mary?' it growled, and its voice was just as bad as its face, sounding like too many throats were trying to control one mouth.

'I... what? Oak... uh... wh-wh-who...?' Connor stammered.

'I did,' it answered, grinning. 'And I'm going to dance with you, too.'

Then it stopped even trying to look human. It swooped down on Jake with its... hands? Dear Jesus God were those its *hands*?... and literally tore him apart before Connor's eyes. At Christmas his mum had made a pulled pork roast, which was basically a packet of processed meat and juices, and when it was cooked she cut it open and shredded it with a pair of forks, and that was basically what the thing was doing to Jake, who shrieked and begged as he came apart in a spreading lake of his own juices.

That was when Connor got his ass up and ran, but the gas made him clumsy and he got maybe a dozen yards before his foot caught on a root and he fell face first. Wet agony exploded in his head as his nose broke. He couldn't breathe, couldn't move. This wasn't remotely amusing any more. He rolled over onto his back and saw it coming for him, carrying a pink princess-and-unicorn balloon like an eager child who had just seen a big piece of cake that it wanted to eat.

'Run, boy,' it told him. 'Run and tell them who you danced with.'

Connor took to his heels and pegged it into the trees, only paying slightly more attention to where he was going this time, still careening off trunks, getting lashed by leaves and stabbed by branches, falling and picking himself up and stumbling onward, sobbing all the while, until he lost it again and cartwheeled down a steep slope to fetch up hard on tarmac, fracturing his skull in a white starburst and dislocating his shoulder.

The shocked driver who found him lying in the middle of the Rose Hill road couldn't make out what Connor was saying at first, but it sounded like he was babbling, 'Pulled pork! Pulled pork! Pulled pork!'

23

STATIC

'...MUTILATED BODY OF A FIFTEEN-YEAR-OLD BOY, found at the Lickey obelisk...'

'Both of you shut up!' Tom flapped at Rachel and Annabel, while turning up the volume of the kitchen radio. They stared at him, Rachel with a spoonful of muesli halfway to her mouth, Annabel in the process of buttering a piece of toast.

'...by police following up reports from a local boy that he and his friend had been attacked. The investigating officer, Detective Inspector George Sanders, stated that this is by far one of the worst crimes of its kind that the West Midlands Police have seen in a long while.'

'What's going on?' Annabel mouthed to Rachel, who could only shrug, as perplexed as she was.

The newsreader resumed: 'A source within the police has revealed that the unnamed victim's blood was used to write graffiti down the length of the twenty-metre obelisk, spelling out the message "I danced with Oak Mary", though police are at a loss to explain how anyone could have scaled the obelisk to do so. The graffiti refers to the local urban myth of Oak Mary, the skeleton of a…'

Tom switched the radio off. 'I think we know the rest,' he said bleakly.

Rachel returned her spoon to the half-empty bowl. Her appetite seemed to have disappeared. A few miles away a young man lay murdered, his blood used as paint.

Annabel munched her toast. 'It's a warning,' she said.

'Well I'm considering myself fucking warned!' said Tom. 'What do we do about it? I'm assuming we can't call the police and leave an anonymous tip that a vengeful demon from limbo did it?'

'Tom,' said Rachel. 'You need to calm down. This isn't helping.' She was already on her phone, checking out the Hollow Isle's Twitter feed. 'Jesus,' she whispered, and turned the screen so that they could see.

Someone had been to the scene early, before the police had cordoned off the area, and taken a photo. The angle was from right up against the guard railings, and the foreshortening effect made the obelisk loom even taller still. The very top of it was slightly hazy with the dawn mist that wreathed the Lickey Hills in late summer, but nothing could hide the starkness of what had been written down it in broad sweeping strokes as if painted on with a hand, the letters a foot high each, the blood dried to a rusty brown:

I DANCED WITH OAK MARY

The 'I' had been underlined three times, as if whoever had written it was keen to take the credit.

The image had only been uploaded half an hour ago but already had over eighty re-tweets, and seventeen likes.

'Sick fuckers,' said Tom.

'Who?' asked Rachel. 'The killer or the likers?'

'Both.'

'It wants me to run,' said Annabel. 'It's trying to scare me, letting me know that it's coming for me, that it has a claim on me.' She rinsed her plate under the kitchen tap. 'I'm not going to.'

'So what are you going to do instead?' asked Tom. 'Sit here and wait for that *lesh* thing to come and get you? That doesn't strike me as much of an alternative.'

Rachel was flicking through other photographs of the hills and the surrounding park area, thinking of the poor murdered kid and how there'd be no day-trippers there today. 'We can't stay here,' she said.

'Why?' asked Annabel. 'I've made this place as safe as I can.'

'I don't mean for our sake.' Rachel turned to her husband. 'Tom, it's the playing field next to us. All the kids and families from the estate use it. We can't draw that thing right into the middle of a bunch of innocent people. Who knows what it'll do?'

'Well where can we go then?' he asked.

'Doesn't the business have anything we can use?'

Tom thought. 'Well, we do have the caravan and prefab on the works site.' As the family business had grown, Spence and Charlotte had bought five acres of farmland a few miles away in Hagley to store materials and the larger pieces of machinery. They'd also bought a static caravan and an old post-war prefabricated house to accommodate itinerant Polish workers employed as cheap seasonal labour. 'I don't know if they're empty,' he said. 'I don't even know if they're liveable. They're nice and remote, though.'

'Could you go and check them out?'

'I think I probably could.'

'It wants us to run,' said Annabel.

'So then we give it what it wants,' said Rachel. 'But we run somewhere of our choosing. And there's got to be something more we can do. Something we can find out about it. Some way of hurting it.'

'You've already hurt it once yourself,' Annabel pointed out.

Rachel looked at her stump, flexed her imaginary fingers and made a fist. 'That was luck.'

'Okay, well I'll leave the *Stranger Things* side of all this to you two,' said Tom, heading for the front door. 'I'm going to sort a place to stay and some muscle for backup. If anything happens – anything – call me.'

During the foot and mouth outbreak of 2001, Colin Elmdon watched his dairy herd of 110 Friesian cows be tested, slaughtered and burned in the space of six hours. Undaunted, he borrowed from the bank and started again, because he had a wife and two sons to support. Over the following fifteen years he built a prize herd of pedigree Guernseys, in the face of tightening legislation from the European Union and supermarkets cutting their prices a little at a time, until he was losing money on every pint of milk and the only way he could keep his herd alive was on government hand-outs. Neither of his boys stayed on at the farm, having seen what it did to their father, but he carried on after they went to their city jobs because he was a dairy farmer and there was nothing else he could do. Then a new government blood test – a cheaper one, of course – said that his Guernseys all had bovine tuberculosis, and would have to be killed. He pleaded with the ministry to test his animals again with the standard skin test, but they refused because it was too expensive and the new test was just as reliable, or so they said. So he watched his prize herd being slaughtered, including the dry milkers who were in calf, and the sight of the unborn animals struggling inside their dead mothers broke his heart. The compensation money was barely a tenth of the hundreds of thousands of pounds that his slaughtered herd was worth, and subsequent skin tests on the dead animals revealed that the cheaper blood test had been wildly inaccurate – all but eleven of the dead Guernseys had been healthy. So, on a blustery April morning Colin Elmdon took a shotgun and sat under a large spreading yew tree with a view over his empty fields and blew his brains out, because there was nothing left for him to do.

His sons auctioned off the farmland to pay their father's massive debts. Most was absorbed by neighbouring farms and housing developers. The farmhouse was bought by an eighties pop star who turned the outbuildings into a recording studio, and a five-acre slice was bought by Cooper & Sons Landscaping.

Rachel had never involved herself with Tom's family business and so had never visited the yard before. There were rows of wooden pallets piled with trade-sized bags of compost, bark chippings, and decorative aggregate; bricks, cement, and stacks of paving slabs for patios; fence posts and panels lined up like huge racks of toast.

As Tom's van pulled into the yard two men looked around from where they stood by a tower of unused wooden pallets. They were pinning a large paper target to it.

'That's Callum and Jeev,' said Tom. 'Come on, I'll introduce you.'

Jeev was short for Jeevan, but it was the only thing short about him. He was Bangladeshi, well over six feet tall, and he ducked his head respectfully as Tom introduced Rachel and Annabel. Callum was short, wiry and Scottish, with a close-cropped head of red hair and a wild bush of beard as if to balance it out, and dressed in a camouflage jacket and hiking trousers. He also had a crossbow slung over his back.

'Callum is the one I was telling you about before,' Tom said. 'You know, with the thing with Smoky.'

Rachel eyed the crossbow warily. 'I really hope you're not planning to use that,' she said to Callum.

'Course not!' he grinned. 'I'm just here, on private land with permission of the owner, doing a bit of perfectly legal target shooting with perfectly legal target points fired from a perfectly legal weapon. Wouldn't hurt a fly, me. Unless that fly was feckin' stupid enough to break into my boss's yard and attack his wife and her pretty friend.' He winked, and Rachel couldn't tell whether he was being conspiratorial or cheeky. Bit of both, she decided.

'The courts can be surprisingly lenient,' added Jeev. Callum nodded sagely.

'These two are going to help keep an eye on things,' Tom explained. 'I know you said that you didn't want to put anybody else in harm's way but trust me, Callum and Jeev can look after themselves.'

'I hope so, Tom. I really do.'

She wasn't at all sure that Tom bringing his friends into this business was a good idea, and had told him as much. Callum and Jeev were clueless about the *lesh* but if she'd tried to tell them they wouldn't have believed it. She wasn't even sure that Tom believed it; he accepted that she and Annabel had been attacked, but he hadn't seen the thing that had done it and obviously didn't appreciate how dangerous it was. He probably thought it was just some maniac in a monster suit, though he'd never say that to her face. Regardless, he point blank refused to go ahead with the plan without some extra muscle. All Rachel could do was hope that she got to the *lesh* before it could hurt any of them.

An old shipping container was both yard office and garage to a forklift and a pair of quad bikes – the latter having nothing to do with the business, Tom told her, but great for just bombing around the unused remainder of the property, which was overgrown with nettles and dock.

On the edge of the property up against a patch of woodland were the static caravan and the single-storey prefab house he'd mentioned. Both were ancient; the caravan was a dirty green, the prefab made of corrugated asbestos sheeting bolted together under a tin roof.

'God knows where Dad got this from,' said Tom. The prefab was the cleanest, he told them, and when he showed Rachel inside it made her wonder what the caravan was like. He'd cleared up the worst of the mess, but it still bore obvious signs of having accommodated itinerant young seasonal workers with no responsibilities, high spirits and dubious hygiene practices. The interior walls were made of plywood, and some of the light fittings were so ancient they were actually made of Bakelite.

The first thing she did was open a window.

'There's mains water and power on an extension from the office,' Tom explained, showing them past the small kitchen. 'And a full canister of camping gas for cooking and hot water. Lounge is through there. There's even a bath.' He opened a door onto an avocado-coloured bathroom with a short bath, a rubber shower attachment which fitted over the taps, and a sink, all of which looked like they gave worse than they got. 'Chemical loo, main bedroom here, spare at the back.'

'Let's hope we don't need to be here long enough to have to actually use any of this,' Rachel said.

'Me and the lads will stay in the caravan next door. But you know I'm not happy about it.' Annabel had been extremely reluctant to accept Tom's original suggestion that he stay in the prefab with them, but he'd grudgingly acquiesced to the peculiar aura of almost regal authority which she bore about her.

'I know,' said Rachel. 'But you're literally only a few metres away and I don't think either of us is going to be falling asleep, somehow.'

When he'd gone, Annabel busied herself redrawing her *patrin* on the front door and hanging the others in the windows, and then started cleaning the prefab while Rachel checked her newsfeeds. The obelisk murder was everywhere, the absence of any new information filled in with endless vox pops of dog-walkers and residents saying How Terrible It All Was and How You Just Didn't Expect This Sort of Thing Around Here, along with lurid click-bait sensationalism and conspiracy theories in which the original Oak Mary mystery featured prominently. The famous photos of her skull were shared and re-shared and gained thousands of likes as the competing theories about her identity were trotted out, none of which seemed to bear any relation to the young woman humming to herself as she swept floors and scrubbed surfaces.

The case for 'Mary' being a victim of witchcraft, or even a witch herself, Rachel read, *is too wonderfully lurid and sensational to bother with anything so inconvenient as a total lack of evidence, either of witchcraft having been practised in the area, or of gypsy communities living locally. Why would a coven of witches pick such a heavily frequented part of the hills, popular with day-trippers, for any kind of ritual, never mind human sacrifice, when there are many more obscure patches of woodland within easy reach? As to the presence of gypsy communities – either Romani or Irish Traveller – wartime census data gives us no reason to believe that these people settled anywhere other than the Black Country districts traditional to them.*

There was a lot more like this on the Hollow Isle website, and Rachel lost herself in the maze of links and references. The Oak Mary mystery went a lot wider than a simple historical curiosity; there were poems, stories, and even fan art. A play had been taken on a short-lived but critically well-received national tour, and a long-running BBC detective series, set post-war, had used the 'spy' theory of Mary's identity as its narrative hook. Spy Mary had been played by a little-known actor at the time who had subsequently gone on to star in a string of successful Hollywood blockbusters, and Rachel was looking up her profile on IMDb when the realisation hit: Mary was a celebrity, of sorts. Not film-star famous, obviously, or as well known as the victims of Jack the Ripper, but still a celebrity in the sense that she had a public, online identity quite separate from her true one, which in any case was non-existent. *Look at stars like Bowie and Prince,* she thought, *changing their names, appearances, even their sexualities like a painter choosing a palette, assembling identities out of art and pop-culture references.* Who had they been in their private moments? Had they ever lost their sense of themselves and had to turn to other people's stories about them to anchor their identities? *If there is an afterlife,* the celebrant at her dad's funeral had said, *it exists in the stories told about us by those we leave behind.*

Even if she could provide incontrovertible DNA evidence

that Annabel was the body in the tree, people still wouldn't believe it. She decided not to trouble the body in question with what was happening in the digital world. The real one was proving to be dangerous enough.

There was a blackened patch of ground between the caravan and the prefab where fires had been lit, and as the afternoon drifted into early evening the men brought over some wooden pallets and began breaking them up for firewood. Callum set up a tripod of metal poles over it with a length of chain and a hook hanging from the apex, and from this he hung a large cast-iron pot. Rachel, who had some experience of pulling things out of thin air, marvelled as he also produced onions, carrots, celery, potatoes, half a dozen different kinds of herbs and spices, and a large Tupperware box of raw lamb. There he paused. 'I take it neither of you is a veggie?' he asked, eyeing Rachel and Annabel with suspicion. They both said no. 'Thank Christ for that.'

Annabel took the chopping board and knife and started cutting up the vegetables.

'Here, what d'you think you're doing?' Callum protested.

'Making supper, what else?' she replied.

'Oh no you're not, not with my knife.' He reached over and took it out of her surprised fingers. 'There's only one chef around here and that's me.'

Annabel burst out laughing.

'Oh and what's so funny, exactly?'

'You're cooking! Over a fire!'

'And?'

'Well – you're a man!'

'I should feckin' well hope so!'

'She has somewhat traditional values,' explained Rachel.

'She sounds feckin' Amish if you ask me. Well, she's more than welcome to do the washing up if that'll make her happy. In the meantime, keep your hands off my meat and two veg, thank you very much. Go and do some knitting or something.'

The stew that Callum produced could have given a decent restaurant a run for its money, and the five of them sat back with full bellies and firelight on their faces, finding it hard to believe that there could be anything beyond the range of the flames that meant them harm. As conversation drifted, Annabel began to sing; it was soft and low, and in a language none of the others understood, and carried such a weight of melancholy that they found themselves haunted by it long after it was finished, each staring into the glowing embers, lost in their private thoughts.

'What was that?' asked Jeev.

'Just a song my pop used to sing while we were travelling. It's called the Romani Rai. It's about the road and the sky and being your own man.'

'It's one of the most beautiful things I've ever heard.' Jeev's eyes were shining.

Annabel blushed.

Callum shoved Jeev sideways. 'Give over, you big girl! Come on, you miserable feckers, let's get this camp sorted out.'

They decided to split the night into thirds, with each of

the men taking a couple of hours to stand watch by the fire. When Rachel objected that she and Annabel were as capable of sentry duty as any of them, Tom took them out of earshot of the other men and pointed out that Annabel was the one they were supposed to be protecting, that as far as they knew Rachel was the only one that could hurt the *lesh*, and that having either woman alone was therefore not a good idea. Rachel couldn't fault his logic.

As she and Annabel were sorting out their sleeping bags in the prefab's main bedroom, Rachel said, 'I still think we should have let Tom sleep in here with us.'

'Why? Do you want him to get hurt?'

'God no!'

'The *lesh* just wants me. It has no reason to go for anyone else unless they get in its way.'

'You mean like that kid who it tore apart at the monument? It didn't seem too picky then. What's to stop it carving its way through everyone else before it gets to you?'

'I don't want to sound callous, Rachel, but if that's what it's going to do then we can't stop it. If Tom were here he would want to defend us and then it most definitely *would* carve its way through him. Believe it or not this is the closest thing to keeping him out of harm's way that I can think of, short of telling him to go home, and do you honestly think he'd do that?'

'Never.'

'Well then.'

They busied themselves with their bedding in silence until Rachel said, 'Annabel?'

'Hmm?'

'This is going to sound stupid.'

'Probably. Say it anyway. I could do with a giggle.'

'Cow. No, I mean back there, when you were singing – and last night, when you met Tom…'

'Yes?' Annabel stopped unrolling her sleeping bag and looked at her.

'Did you… did you cast a spell on those men?'

Annabel laughed. 'What, because I am ze mysterious Gypsy Vitch?'

'You're right. It was stupid. Forget it.'

'There are no such things as spells, Rachel.'

'But there is magic.'

Annabel considered this. 'There are talents. If there are things you can do that nobody else can, like making something appear out of the air or making a man like you, is that any more magical than singing a song or cooking a nice meal?'

'In that case, ladies and gentlemen,' Rachel said, climbing into her sleeping bag, 'prepare to be astounded as I demonstrate my uncanny talent for lying awake all night fretting about things I can't control.'

24

ATTACK

OAK MARY'S THREE DEATHS HAD WATCHED THE CAMP from the treeline since before nightfall. Twenty-four hours of fear and rumour about the murder at the obelisk had energised all three of them; the Green Man's arm had healed and he was restless, shuffling from one foot to the other.

'You're afraid,' the Small Man said, smiling.

'I got you here,' growled the Green Man. 'Get me inside and we'll see who fears who.'

'So we're agreed, then,' said the Dark Man. 'You draw the woman out, I neutralise her. You keep the others out of the way,' he added to the Small Man.

'Neutralise,' snickered the Small Man. 'Are you actually trying to sound like a cheap gangster? I still don't see why we can't just kill them all and have done with it.'

'The more shades we make the more complicated it gets. We are already three when we should be one. How many deaths do you want to be?'

'All of them, of course!' grinned the Small Man. 'I want to be the death of the whole world! Your problem is that you lack ambition.'

'Very well, on your own head it is, then. You will have to answer for it.'

'Not to you, though, brother.'

The Green Man growled with impatience and sloped off into the trees.

Once he was safely out of earshot the Dark Man turned to the Small Man. 'Do you think he suspects?'

'No!' scoffed the Small Man. 'I doubt that he's thinking of anything much at all. Mary is the gypsy witch, he is her death, and he's got the scent of her blood in his nose. He's like a dog after a bitch in heat.'

'Good then.' The Dark Man drew his gun and moved towards the buildings.

All Callum knew was that Tom's wife's friend was being menaced by some dickhead of an ex-boyfriend and that the police were too useless to do anything about it; an assessment of the police that he wholeheartedly shared. He couldn't see how the dickhead in question would have been able to find them all the way out here in the middle of nowhere, but crazy-jealous dickhead ex-boyfriends had a tendency to discover these kinds of things. The good news about them being out in the middle of nowhere was that any headlights coming down the road wouldn't be there accidentally. That was why his attention – such as it was at three in the morning – was focused on the front gate to the yard, and not on the trees behind him, which was the direction his attacker came from.

He was sitting cross-legged in front of the fire with his crossbow in his lap, and the first he knew about it was a heavy metallic click and something like the end of an iron bar pressing into the back of his head.

'Yes, it's a gun,' said the accented voice of a man. 'I doubt you were expecting that.'

Callum froze.

'Spit into the fire,' said the voice.

Callum didn't know what the fuck was going on but he did as he was told, and spat into the embers.

'You hear that sizzling sound?' asked the voice. 'That's the sound your brains are going to make if I have to blow them out through your face. Nod if you understand.'

Callum nodded. He could feel his bladder threatening to let go. 'Listen, man—'

The end of the barrel pressed harder, forcing his head down and forward, closer to the heat of the red-hot coals.

'We are not here for you,' said the man. 'If I were you I wouldn't do anything to change that. We only want the girl.'

We?

The Small Man watched his companion drag the whimpering prisoner away with amusement. 'Here,' he offered. 'Let me.' He took hold of the human by the scruff of the neck.

The Dark Man observed the knife in his other hand, and his lip curled. 'You call it ambition – it's bloodlust, plain and simple.'

'You know what they say, to thine own self be true,' the Small Man grinned.

'Dress it up any way you like, it's still unnecessary butchery.' All the same, the Dark Man relinquished his captive. 'But be quick about it, at least.'

'*Ja, mein herr.*'

The Small Man dragged the human into the bushes. His cheeriness had evaporated. 'Plain and simple,' he muttered. 'I am neither of those things, brother.' Safely out of sight, he flung the human down and waved at him with his knife. 'Go on, bugger off. Get.'

The human hesitated, obviously suspicious of a trap.

'Go! Find a way to help your friends before I change my mind!' He advanced a step with the blade and the man took to his heels.

The Green Man wedged a large length of fence post against the door of the caravan where the other two men were sleeping. Meanwhile the Dark Man inspected the symbols chalked on the door of the prefab with interest. They carried something of the same kind of charge that the monument graffiti did; no doubt they were intended to protect those inside from occult threats, and judging from the way the Green Man was hanging back and squinting sidelong at the door as if at something which blinded or burned, they were working quite well. But not against him, because he was not the gypsy witch's death, nor was his small brother. They had no power over her, and so she had none over them.

'Get me in,' growled the Green Man.

The Dark Man smiled and swiped the palm of his hand through the protective sigils, smearing the chalk, then turned to the Green Man with a wave of his pistol barrel. 'After you.'

Despite being so tired that her eyeballs felt like marbles swivelling in sand, Rachel had thought she would be too stressed to sleep. Instead she was surprised to find herself dreaming that Tom was talking close to her ear, low and urgent: 'Wake up, girl! Wake up!'

She snapped awake, squirming into a sitting position. Other than the sleeping form of Annabel, she was alone. Her phone told her it was just after three. She parted the curtains a finger's width and saw the low red glow of the fire between the caravan and their prefab. There was no sign of anyone sitting at it. She couldn't remember who it should have been; maybe they were patrolling the yard, or having a whiz in the bushes. Maybe not.

She shoved Annabel awake none too gently. 'Wake up.'

Annabel knuckled sleep from her eyes. 'What?' When she realised what time it was she began cursing in Romani.

'Never mind that,' hissed Rachel. 'Shut up and listen. Or use your Sight or whatever. Is it here?'

Annabel scowled. 'The Sight doesn't have an on-switch,

you know. Where are the men?'

'I don't know. What do we do?'

'Trust to the *patrin*. And if they fail, we trust to your Touch. The *lesh* knows who it's up against now, and it will be afraid.'

'Fuck that,' said Rachel, and reached for her phone.

Tom was dragged out of sleep by the buzzing of his phone. He blinked at the screen, first registering the time and then the caller.

3:07.

Rachel.

Panic was an adrenaline spike to the heart, yanking him fully awake and he clutched the phone to his ear. 'Rache! Are you okay?'

Her breathing rasped down the receiver as if she had her phone cupped in her hand, trying to shield it. 'I don't know,' she whispered. 'I think…'

Then there was a tremendous crash of splintering wood and a scream, both in stereo: from the phone at his ear and from outside, barely metres away.

'Rache!' he screamed, then ripped open his sleeping bag and leapt for the door, slapping Jeev to wake him up as he passed. He tore at the door handle. It moved, but the door didn't. Something was jamming it closed from the outside.

Then the screaming began in earnest.

* * *

'Annabel!' called the Green Man. 'Anna! I know you're in there!'

Annabel squeezed her eyes shut and wrapped her arms tightly about herself. 'Sweet Mary Mother,' she groaned. 'It's got his voice too.'

Rachel knelt close and laid her hand on Annabel's cheek, forcing her to look up. 'It's going to be okay,' she said, with considerably more confidence than she felt. 'He can't get in. And if he does I'll rip something off him a bit more precious than his bloody arm.'

'Anna!' called the *lesh* in the voice of her dead husband. 'Enough of this! It's time for you to come home!'

'Leave us alone!' Rachel screamed. 'Just fuck off!'

The Green Man roared and threw himself at the door.

Rachel had just enough time to think *He doesn't look very fucking afraid to me* before the door gave way and he was lunging at her. She brought her left hand up to defend herself and his headlong charge threw him right into her grasp. She felt her dead fingers close around his throat, deep into the rancid mess of his beard. Though she was looking at flesh she felt bark, despite seeing his skin stretch and distort in her grip.

He can't be stupid enough to do this again, can he?

He wasn't. He gave ground and she followed instinctively, pushing him back to the threshold, down the single step into the open space between the caravan and the prefab, and that was when she saw two others, one of them raising a gun to point at her, and realised how easily she'd been played.

* * *

'*Rachel!*' screamed Tom, throwing himself at the door. '*Rachel!*'

Jeev joined him, and the plywood-and-fibreglass structure began to splinter.

The Dark Man aimed carefully, right between the woman's shocked, cow-like eyes, and thumbed back the revolver's hammer.

And waited.

'Shoot her!' bellowed the Green Man over his shoulder. 'What are you waiting for?!'

For whatever reason, the *lesh*'s companions weren't moving to help him, but Rachel cared no further than the opportunity this gave her. She gathered her strength and braced her feet, bringing her living right hand up to join the dead one. She felt for that pivot point, the crushing gap between worlds into which she had lost her hand, that blank space where she could touch the other side of the air and move things between death and life.

The *lesh*, realising too late that he had been betrayed by his companions, roared and fought back, tearing at the flesh of her arms with wooden-clawed fingernails and trying to break her grip.

'I said *fuck off*!' Rachel yelled, and pulled him apart.

She felt something elastic in the air – or behind it – stretch like a rubber sheet and then give suddenly, causing her to stumble forward, and for a terrifying moment she saw her left arm disappear up to the elbow as the *lesh* collapsed in an abattoir mess of rotting wood and putrescent flesh. She imagined herself overbalancing completely and following it into the nothing place behind the world, and a small crazy part of her wanted to give in to that temptation, but then Annabel grabbed her by her shirt and hauled her back, and the rest of her arm reappeared.

When Rachel gathered enough of her scattered wits to look around, the man in the dark coat was still pointing his gun at her.

'That was most helpful of you,' he said.

Before he could pull the trigger, the other, smaller man stepped in front of him. 'Now let's not be hasty about this,' he said, and placed the palm of his hand close to the pistol's muzzle, though it appeared to Rachel that he was unable to actually touch it.

'Are you out of your mind?' snarled the Dark Man. 'Step aside!' He did so himself, but the Small Man followed, blocking his shot again.

'Think!' said the Small Man. 'How does this benefit us?'

'She's dealt with him! We kill Mary's protector and we take her back! What is complicated about this for you?' He sidestepped again and was blocked again.

'She can reach into the umbra!' protested the Small Man. 'Do you know how rare that talent is? We can use it! If you kill her now only one of us can claim Mary but if we can use the woman's talent maybe *both* of us get to exist!'

The Dark Man hesitated. 'How?'

'I don't know yet! But you can't just blow the brains out of the possibility!'

But the Dark Man shook his head. 'I don't know what game you're playing. You may be under the impression that I'm as easily manipulated as our brother. I am not, and you cannot stop me. Remember the clearing?'

'What about the—'

The Dark Man pointed the gun at his face and fired.

There are some things from which one simply must flinch, whatever one's nature, and being shot point blank in the face is definitely one of them. The Small Man screamed even though the bullet ignored him and ploughed into the wall of the prefab behind him, where Rachel had been standing.

But by that time Rachel had ducked back into the kitchen, where Annabel was hiding.

'Who the fuck was that?' Rachel gasped. 'And why is he shooting at us?'

'Don't know. Don't care.' Annabel was fumbling in a cutlery drawer, and brought out a knife as a second gunshot tore through the wall above their heads.

Then Rachel heard Tom yelling, 'Rachel! Get out of there! Run!'

The door finally splintered apart under Tom and Jeev's combined blows and the fencepost propped against it fell away. He stumbled down the step barefoot onto the grass, and saw a pistol buck and flash in a tall man's hand.

'Rachel! Get out of there! Run!'

Tom threw himself at the Dark Man. They fell heavily to the ground together and the gun went flying. Jeev punched the Small Man in the face, and the Small Man staggered, blood squirting from his nose. Snake-quick, he lashed at Jeev with steel glittering in his hand, and Jeev screamed, falling back and clutching his arm.

Although Tom was well built, he still hadn't recovered fully from the septicaemia, and after the initial surprise of his attack the Dark Man was able to throw him off, and wheeled on him with his greatcoat swirling like the cloak of a vampire.

'*Kutkop!*' he snarled, and drove the point of his shoe into Tom's ribs. 'Interfere with death's business, would you?' He reached down, grabbed Tom's shirt and hauled him close to his face. 'You will beg for your own death to save you before I'm done!'

Tom recoiled from the graveyard stink of his breath. 'Whatever,' he coughed. 'I've already called the police, and they come quickly when there's gunfire. You're fucked, mate.' It was a lie, but it had the desired effect nonetheless.

'He's right!' yelled the Small Man, retreating to the treeline. 'We're done here! We should go!'

'We're. Not. Done.' The Dark Man reached into his coat pocket with one hand, coming out with a fist that gleamed with brass at each knuckle. 'I think I may have just enough time to pound this fool's brains out of his skull first.'

'Try it,' said Rachel, and backhanded him in the head with Callum's cooking pot.

The Dark Man collapsed like a coat off a hook, and as he crawled for the treeline, groaning, Rachel helped Tom to his feet and they retreated towards the prefab. Tom was clutching his ribs and gasping with every indrawn breath. Jeev was clutching his arm, which was dripping red. Annabel, who had followed close behind Rachel, stooped to pick something up from the ground.

The Dark Man's pistol.

'Well now this is interesting,' observed the Small Man, right at the edge of things. He had a bloodied handkerchief pressed to his nose. 'What might happen if she shot you with your own gun, do you think?'

'Shut up,' hissed the Dark Man.

The Small Man ignored him, continuing to talk as he backed slowly into the shadows. 'Would it even work? Can we even die, especially since neither of us is her death? See, this is what I mean about keeping the possibilities alive. It's tempting to let her try.'

'Don't push your luck,' warned Annabel, pointing the gun at him. But there was an unsteadiness to her voice and the gun shook in her hand. She looked like she was about to throw up.

'It is you who should be careful, I think,' said the Dark Man, crawling painfully to his feet. 'You know what that weapon has done – what it means to you. The real you. My you. You are no more a gypsy witch than that is a fairy wand.'

Annabel blinked, tottered, and held out a hand to balance herself. 'Rachel?' she murmured. 'I don't... I can't...'

'I'm here, right here.' Rachel slung the outstretched arm

over her shoulders, holding Annabel up. The gun tumbled from her grip.

'What's the matter?' asked the Dark Man, mockery dripping from every syllable. For someone who had just taken a lump of cast iron to the head he was recovering very quickly. Of the Small Man there was no sign. 'Are you experiencing perhaps a change of heart?'

Then a high-revved quad bike engine roared and headlights speared the darkness as Callum returned to the scene. At the sound of reinforcements, the Dark Man's face twisted with frustration. Sizing up the strength of the opposition, he snatched up his pistol, turned and ran into the darkness.

The figure in Rachel's arms collapsed to the ground and began to convulse.

25

AFTERMATH

'GET HER IN THE CARAVAN! QUICK!'

Rachel was cradling Annabel's head as she jerked and fitted. Tom moved to help but Callum jumped off the quad bike and strode over, his face twisted with fury, and shoved Tom with both hands.

'You told us it would just be the one guy!' yelled Callum, shoving him again. 'And you never mentioned any feckin' *guns*!'

Tom recovered his balance and shoved back. 'Do you think I fucking knew?'

'Boys!' snapped Rachel. 'Shut it, the pair of you, and do something useful!'

Jeev plopped down heavily on the ground, groaning and clutching his arm.

'Sort him out,' Tom said to Callum. 'I think he's going into shock.'

'He's not the only feckin' one,' muttered Callum, and went over to his friend.

Tom took hold of Annabel's knees and Rachel her shoulders, and between them they managed to carry her into the caravan and lay her as gently as they could on one of the sofas in the living area. From outside they heard Callum exclaim, 'Aw fuck, man, that's going to need some stitches.'

'Can you keep an eye on her?' Tom asked Rachel. 'I need to check on Jeev.'

Annabel's convulsions were lessening, but Rachel wasn't terribly reassured. 'I have no idea what's wrong with her,' she said. 'She's having some kind of seizure.'

'If she stops breathing, yell.'

'Oh you can count on that. Tom,' she added, as he was heading out of the door.

'What?'

'We can't take her to hospital. We can't let the authorities find her. She doesn't have any identification. They'll separate us and then she'll be vulnerable again. The police can't protect her from those men.'

'I'm thinking that might not be such a bad idea. Look at the mess she's caused.'

'Tom!'

'Jesus Christ, Rachel, one thing at a fucking time, okay?'

Tom slammed outside, where Callum was kneeling beside Jeev, who had collapsed onto his back. Callum had taken his hoodie off and wrapped it around Jeev's wounded arm, which he clutched in both hands. 'Cal! You got pressure on that?'

'Sorted. You calling an ambulance or the SAS?'

'Neither. We'll get him to A&E ourselves – quicker than a bloody ambulance, anyway. There's a big first aid kit in the office. Wait here.'

Cal uttered a hollow laugh. 'Going nowhere, boss.'

Tom ran across the darkened field towards the shipping-container office, which had a first aid kit. Halfway across he stopped as dizziness washed around inside his head like water down a plughole, and braced his hands on his knees as it flooded into his stomach. He fought the urge to throw up, swallowing bile. 'No,' he mumbled to himself. 'No you fucking don't. Keep your shit together.'

He kept it together and ran on.

By the time he and Callum had finished getting a dressing on Jeev's arm, Annabel had started to come around, and as far as Rachel could tell she'd suffered nothing more serious than a bad case of shock – certainly nothing worth taking her to Accident and Emergency for. But Tom wasn't having any of it.

'No. No fucking way. I am not leaving you here, not with her, and not with those bastards still lurking around. This was a stupid idea from start to finish.'

'But—'

'Yes! I get it! She might get locked up in a loony bin! Good! But you come with me now and I'll keep my mouth shut, or I will go without you and tell the cops everything, because we are *not equipped to deal with this*!'

He was red-faced and yelling by the time he'd finished.

Even during their most heated arguments she'd never seen him so furious. She knew it came from a combination of shock at the attack and fear for her safety, but she also had no doubt that he'd make good on his threat.

'Okay,' she said quietly. 'Whatever you say. Hospital it is.'

They delivered Jeev and Cal to the A&E department at the Queen Elizabeth Hospital. A simple lie about an accident at a party was enough to satisfy the paramedics and there was no need for Tom, Rachel and Annabel to wait for the hours that it would take for Jeev to be treated and discharged. There was no question about either of the men telling the truth about the attack; when Tom mentioned it to Cal he received a filthy look and a mouthful of abuse in return.

They drove home in silence along the empty early morning roads with Annabel passive and listless in the back. Rachel watched her out of the corner of her eye, and the more she looked the more she was convinced that it didn't look very much like Annabel any more.

'Anna?' she asked. There was no response. 'Anna, are you okay?'

Still nothing.

'Mary?'

The woman's glazed eyes swung toward Rachel. 'Yes?' she replied, in Mary's mouse-like voice.

'Nothing,' said Rachel, and turned to face forwards again. 'Just sit tight. We're going home.'

* * *

After Mary had let herself be put to bed like a child, Rachel and Tom sat at the breakfast bar in the kitchen with cups of tea going cold in front of them. Dawn was still a good couple of hours away, but both knew that any more sleep was impossible.

'There's no way we could have known there'd be three of them,' said Rachel.

'No,' agreed Tom.

'You were right. It was a stupid idea from start to finish.'

He shrugged. 'We had to try something.'

'All right, stop.' She turned to face him squarely. 'Just stop it.'

'Stop what?'

'Being so bloody agreeable about all of this! You should still be furious!'

'And what good would that do?' he asked, taking a sip of lukewarm tea. He looked absolutely done in. Rachel wondered why she wasn't freaking out herself, but then remembered how severely she'd reacted after the attack at the monument, almost crashing the car. Had that really only been yesterday? It seemed impossible that she could have changed so much in so short a time. But her stump was a constant reminder of how the impossible insisted on happening. You either coped or – well, you coped. There was no alternative, it was simply a question of how well or badly. *I took my enemy by the throat and tore him apart.* What were a couple of gunshots compared to that? She didn't know who those other two figures had been, but if they were all working together then they'd just had a taste of what she could do if they came after her or the people she loved. It should be the tall man with the gun and his tubby sidekick who were running scared.

'I will tell you this, though,' Tom said, breaking the silence, 'I haven't changed my mind about Mary, or Annabel, or whoever she is. I don't trust her. I think she's dangerous.'

'*She's* dangerous? What about those men who came after her?'

'Or if not actually dangerous herself,' Tom continued, 'dangerous like a lightning rod. Not something you want to hang on to for too long. I was tempted to go to the police at the hospital anyway and say that I thought she was part of something gang related just so they'd arrest her. But if you are determined to hang on to her then I'm going to stick as close to you as I can and try to minimise the damage, because I love you.' He grimaced at the tea and put it to one side. 'So what next, boss?'

'I don't know,' she confessed. 'To be honest, I thought that was going to be the end of it. I wasn't expecting the *lesh* to have friends. But maybe death always comes in threes, like three wise men or three blind mice. Except there was something the one with the gun said – about her not really being a gypsy witch. "The real you", he said. "My you".'

'What do you think it means?'

'I'm not sure.' Outside came the first twitterings of the dawn chorus as the world began to wake up.

'Right,' he said, slapping the worktop decisively. 'This is

no good. My head keeps going around in circles; I have to be doing something. I'm going to start getting the stuff in from the van. Are you going to bed?'

'I think I'll look in on Mary first, but yes.'

'Okay then.'

He shifted his stool back and made to leave, but Rachel caught his arm. 'I'm sorry,' she said.

For a moment it looked like he was going to say something, but instead he leaned down and kissed her, which was all the reply he needed to give.

Tom went out to the van, so wearied by everything that had happened that he didn't notice the figure in the shadows of the bushes bordering the drive until it *ahemmed* at him.

It was the Small Man.

Tom opened his mouth to yell.

'Shut your hole,' the Small Man ordered, and for a flicker of a moment allowed Tom to see the real face that hid beneath the glamour of his human disguise. Tom gasped and fell back a step, stunned.

'Sorry to have to do that,' the Small Man added, his plump and complacent smile restored. 'But I really don't have either the time or the inclination to have to persuade you, especially when all I want to do is help.'

He stepped forward and Tom flinched, then darted a glance in the direction of the house; Rachel might still be awake. It wouldn't take much to attract her attention. Then again, it didn't look like it would take much more for this man – this *thing* – to do him serious harm.

'Take it.' The Small Man was holding out a piece of paper. '*Take it.*'

'What... what is it?'

'Something to help you get rid of Oak Mary. She's dangerous; I know you know it.'

That got Tom's attention, and he looked more closely at the piece of paper being offered. Just something torn from an ordinary notebook, its leading edge perforated. But trust was not so easily won. 'I'm supposed to just believe that you've actually got our interests at heart, after you attacked us? After you shot at her?'

'I think you'll find it wasn't I who pulled the trigger. I actually stopped him from putting a bullet in the brain of your pretty little wife. I even let your ginger friend go; ask him if you like. But look, I understand your indecision, so I'm going to do something I almost never do: I'm going to explain.

'Your wife Rachel, for reasons I will confess to not having the foggiest clue about, has somehow acquired a talent for reaching through the barrier that separates the world of the living from that of, for want of a better word, the dead. This is problematic. Each time it causes an imbalance and a reaction to the interference, and this reaction is proportional, obviously. With little things like fiddling around with inanimate objects...' He waved his hand with a dismissive *pfft!* 'However, should one become ambitious or stupid enough to liberate an entire human soul from the umbra, well, the reaction takes a somewhat more dynamic form.' He gestured to himself and sketched a little bow.

'So, what— you're Death?'

The Small Man sighed. 'No, I am not Death. I am one of Oak Mary's potential deaths. I am a narrative, if you like. An urban myth looking for someone to believe in him.'

'So you're three possible deaths trying to claim her soul?'

'You catch on quick. Except there's only two of us now, thanks to your wife helpfully removing some of the competition.'

'But why?'

'Because Rachel subscribes to the philosophy that what makes us immortal is the stories that people tell about us when we're gone, and because she pulled Mary through from the umbra, it's her rules that apply. Damn atheists,' he spat. 'If she was Christian we could have settled this much more simply in a demonic cloud of fire and brimstone.'

'I don't understand.'

'Look,' said the Small Man. 'Who I am and what I am isn't really the point. But understand that my brother and I will never stop until we claim Mary and take her back where she belongs, because it is our function to do so. Your wife cannot protect her forever. Can you imagine living like this for the rest of your life? Because I assure you, that life will not be very long.'

'For someone who claims to want to help, you seem to like threats a lot,' said Tom.

'Suit yourself,' shrugged the Small Man, and moved to tuck the paper away.

'Wait a minute. What are you offering?'

The Small Man grinned as Tom took the paper and unfolded it, revealing a series of numbers and letters.

'These are packet references for the archives in Worcester library: the original police case files for the Oak Mary investigation,' the Small Man explained. 'She needs to know who she really was so that she can drop this absurd persona and I can take her off your hands and back where she belongs. You say I threaten. I say I offer the truth, the restoration of the natural order, and a return to normality for you and your wife. The decision is up to you.'

Tom didn't notice where or how the Small Man departed. He stood thinking about the chaos of last night. If the bullet that had hit the doorframe of the caravan had been ten centimetres to the right, he'd be mourning Rachel. In the end it wasn't any kind of a choice.

26

ELINE

RACHEL CATNAPPED FOR A FEW HOURS AND WOKE UP to find Tom crashed out on the bed beside her, fully clothed. The bedside clock told her it was mid-morning. Feeling groggy and light-headed, she pulled on some clothes and went in search of tea. As she padded downstairs she caught a waft of coffee and heard the sound of the kitchen radio burbling and the telltale chink of a china mug. Good, Mary was up, and she'd put the kettle on, bless her.

'Morning, Madame Mysteriosa,' she yawned. 'What's for—' Rachel froze in the doorway.

There was a strange woman in her kitchen.

She was sitting on one of the breakfast stools with her back to Rachel, the newspaper spread out in front of her, and Smoky parading himself back and forth across the paper, purring like a small furry motorcycle. She was dressed in one of Rachel's old blouses and a pair of dark trousers.

Her dark hair was wet and hung long and straight down her back.

'Hullo, Rachel!' the woman replied, and turned around with a smile. 'Did that little zizz clear your head? There's tea in the pot.'

It was Annabel, and yet at the same time it wasn't. Her voice no longer had the broad, round vowels of a Black Country Romani accent. It was clearer, crisper, and with a slight but unmistakably French lilt. Her face was the same shape, but the expression it wore was completely different – where Annabel had been quick and open, this young woman regarded her with cool appraisal and a slight arch of amusement to one eyebrow. Rachel was tempted to believe that Annabel was playing a practical joke on her, were it not for the very obvious lines of old scars on her forehead and cheeks which hadn't been there last night, and the fact that her eyes were bright blue again.

'You've changed,' Rachel said, trying not to appear too rattled.

The other woman looked at what she was wearing. 'I hope you don't mind,' she replied, then looked up with an odd, small smile. 'I don't think that is what you mean though, no?'

'Not really.' Rachel moved carefully around the end of the breakfast bar and switched the kettle on. The woman had found her old cafetière and a packet of ground coffee and was drinking from a breakfast bowl with both hands. 'Oi, scumbag,' Rachel said to Smoky. 'Off there.' She shooed him to the floor, where he moved to sit directly underneath the woman's stool and gave Rachel a filthy look.

'So,' Rachel said. 'Which one are you?'

The woman's smile broadened. 'Oh you catch on quick, I like this. I am Eline Lambert. Very pleased to make your acquaintance.' She gave a little dip of her head.

'So what happened to Mary, then?'

'Mary is nobody. Mary is...' Eline paused. 'Do you enjoy the cinema?'

'Sometimes, except when it's all remakes and superheroes. Why?'

'I love it. I read all the magazines. Do you know what a stand-in is?'

'Vaguely. I'm still not sure what that has got to do with anything.'

'If it takes a long time to set up a particular shot, the actors do not wish to be standing around with hot lights pointed at them, so the director will use a stand-in – this is just any nearby person to stand or walk around or read through the lines. Then when it is all set up, he calls the stars back in and shoots the scene. Well, Mary is my stand-in.'

'And you're the star.'

Eline grinned and spread her arms. 'Ta-daa!'

'So how can you just not be Annabel any more? What about all the things you remembered and knew? Was that all just lies? Or make-believe?'

'Being Annabel was like one of those dreams which seems so real that you cannot tell whether or not you have woken up. I have woken up. I know who I am now.'

'But *I* dreamed about being Annabel too! I dreamed

about being you. Why should one be any more believable than the other?'

Eline laughed lightly, but there was a note of mockery in it, which Rachel didn't like. 'A gypsy witch trapped in a hollow tree by a wood demon to contain her undying curse? That is no better than a fairy tale.'

'So is coming back from the dead,' Rachel pointed out. 'Anyway, that's a bit rich coming from someone who claims to be a Nazi double-agent female super-spy.'

Eline's face darkened instantly, and her eyes narrowed. 'I was never a Nazi,' she growled. 'The Abwehr were military, not that it makes any difference. They are all murdering bastards.' She gripped the bowl so tightly that coffee slopped over the rim and onto the newspaper.

'I'm sorry, I didn't mean…'

'There are things you do not joke about. Ever.'

Into the frosty silence stumbled Tom, yawning.

'Morning, Anna,' he said, going straight to the fridge and opening it without looking at her. He frowned into the fridge. 'Now what am I getting here – breakfast or lunch? I feel like I've got jet lag.'

'Tom,' said Rachel. 'This isn't Annabel. This is Eline.'

He turned around and Rachel saw her own surprise mirrored on his face as he noticed Eline's scars and eyes. A different personality looking out from the same face. Eline blew him a kiss. His shoulders slumped in defeat. 'Eline. Of course it is.'

'You don't seem surprised,' said Eline.

'Nothing surprises me about this freak show any more.'

'Brunch,' she said. 'The meal you're looking for is brunch.'

'The meal I'm looking for is beer,' he grunted, and started opening cupboards.

The business of putting a meal together was conducted in silence; a decompression airlock in the conversation. Knives, forks, spoons; bread, jam, tea – the unspoken rituals of these things were a common language which diffused the tension, and by the time the dishwasher was being filled they were almost comfortable in each other's presence.

After Tom and Rachel had showered and dressed, the three of them reconvened on the back patio where Eline sat on the low wall bordering the lawn and picked restlessly at the grass.

'So,' said Tom, 'we need to know more about what we're facing. There's too much conflicting information out there. I did a bit of digging, and I found out that the original police records for the Oak Mary murder are archived at the main library in Worcester. I think we should check them out. Maybe we can find something we can use.'

Rachel looked at him in surprise. 'You did a bit of digging?'

'Yes. Why? You're not the guardian of all things Mary-ish, you know.'

'Okay, no need to bite. I was just surprised, that's all.'

'It's a good idea,' said Eline. 'But I doubt whether we'll find anything that can help us against Van Alst – not that it actually is Van Alst, I mean. It's just something using his shape to come after me, just like the other one used the *lesh*'s shape to go after Annabel.'

'Something came after Smoky too,' said Rachel, 'but it didn't take the shape of a person – it was more like a badger-weasel-fox thing. Do you have any idea what they really are underneath?'

'Agents of death?' Eline shrugged. 'I don't know.'

'So let me get this straight,' said Tom. 'The badger-weasel was Smoky's death. The *lesh* thing was Annabel's death and then Rachel killed it, and now you're Eline because you picked up that tall bastard's gun and it – what – shook you loose? Woke you up? And he's your death.'

'Van Alst, yes.'

'So who was the other guy – the smaller one who looked like a geography teacher?'

'I don't know.' She waved her cigarette airily. 'An accomplice, I should imagine.'

Rachel shook her head. 'No, not from the things he said. He knew too much about what was going on. He was more interested in me than Annabel, because of what I can do.' Her skin crawled at the thought.

Tom pursued the point. 'So if he's another one of them, whose death is he? Which version of Oak Mary is he after?'

'Forget about him, he doesn't matter,' said Eline casually, but there was a higher, waspish tone to her voice that told Rachel she was becoming uneasy at where Tom's questions were going. 'Anyway, I'm not sure that it matters much. Compared to what you can do with your magic hand, there's nothing in the library that can help us. Still, I'd like to go. The police might have gained access to declassified MI6 information over the years; I might be able to find out what happened to the real Van Alst and Bill Heath.' She produced a mirthless smile. 'If by any chance either of them is still alive, I aim to fix that.'

'Chances are both of them are long dead by now,' said Rachel. 'I think your vengeance window is pretty much closed.'

'Then it's a good job I know someone who can open it again, isn't it?' Eline replied. 'You can bring them back for me.'

'I'm not bringing anybody or anything else back, period!' Rachel was becoming more than a little alarmed at how cold-blooded this new version of Mary was. 'I'm especially not bringing someone back just so that you can kill them all over again!'

Eline's eyes glittered, and she tore out little bunches of grass. 'It's not revenge. It's justice. When you've been murdered and denied the peace of a decent Christian burial and forced to scream away the decades, then you and I can have a conversation about vengeance.'

'Okay, let's bring this back down,' said Tom, intervening. 'We're agreed that, whatever our motivations, we need more information, and the archives seem to be a good place to start, yes?'

'Yes,' agreed Eline.

Rachel nodded.

'Fine then. Let's just try not to get caught up in any fire-fights this time.'

* * *

As they set off for Worcester, Eline asked Tom to take a small detour into the Jewellery Quarter. It wasn't on their way – in fact it was in exactly the opposite direction to the way they needed to go and into one of the busiest parts of the city – but it was, she said, important. There was something she had to pick up.

'Pick up?' Tom asked. 'Where are you going to be able to pick anything up after seventy years?'

'A graveyard,' she said, as if it were no more surprising than a trip to the supermarket.

'You're taking the piss now, right?' he said.

'I wouldn't dream of it.'

Warstone Lane Cemetery had been called Brookfields when she'd known it, and it was right in the heart of the city's famous jewellery-making district, surrounded by goldsmiths, diamond sellers, watchmakers, family businesses generations old and cooperative start-ups that would fold in a month. Rachel and Tom's wedding rings had been made in the next street. Heritage-themed pubs and cafés catered to shoppers and tourists who gazed through windows at trays of glittering treasures. 'This place has improved,' Eline said, as they crossed Vyse Street. 'There were munitions factories the last time I was here.'

They turned into the cemetery, which was overcrowded with headstones and in a sorry state, as it hadn't taken any new burials for thirty years and only a handful of the dead had living relatives left to mourn them or tend their graves. The headstones were blackened with pollution and eroded with time, the gravel sprouted with weeds, and the blunt stumps where statues had broken away looked disturbingly to Rachel like amputated limbs. There were large tombs and looming family monuments with many spires and crosses, but oddly no angels. Nor were there any people, despite how busy the surrounding streets were.

At the heart of the cemetery were three tiers of catacombs in a wide three-quarter circle like an amphitheatre; their doorways had been bricked up long ago to deter junkies and prostitutes, and untended curtains of ivy hung over the balustrades of each tier.

'These were air raid shelters,' Eline commented as they passed. 'People who had been bombed out of their homes used to live here. Can you imagine having your children sleeping in a place like this?' She shook her head in disbelief. 'Right next door to the dead, wondering how soon you'll join them?'

She strode off, leaving Tom and Rachel to hurry behind.

'So,' said Tom, catching Rachel's arm. 'Do you buy it?'

'Buy what?'

He gestured at the woman slipping between the headstones. 'Eline. Do you think that's who she really is? After all, there's no reason to suppose that she is any more likely than Annabel. She wasn't too keen on talking about the other chap, the small guy. Maybe she *should* be someone else.'

'The third possibility for Oak Mary's identity is that she was a prostitute,' said Rachel. 'I'm not surprised she doesn't want to be that. I suppose we're going to have to hope that we can find something in the archives to clear it up.'

Further downhill, towards the far edge of the cemetery, Eline found what she was looking for, and heaved a huge sigh of relief. 'I thought it wasn't going to be here!' she called back to them. 'Come and see!'

It looked no different to many of the other graves: not especially ostentatious, with lopsided kerbing around a patch of overgrown gravel and a large memorial stone in the shape of an open bible. There had been a cross at the head end, but at some point it had fallen, or been vandalised, and so as with many others the sextons had laid the broken decoration on top of the grave, which was the simplest and cheapest solution.

'Can you give me a hand, please?' Eline asked Tom. 'I need to move this out of the way.'

'Why?'

'Because I need what is underneath.'

'Oh no!' said Rachel. 'We are not desecrating any graves.'

'This was never a grave,' said Eline. 'SOE were inhuman, but not monsters.'

The cross was solid granite and difficult to shift, but between the three of them they managed to tip it over and onto the grass. Eline turned her attention to the bible-shaped memorial stone, then stopped and laughed. 'Look!' she said, pointing at the words engraved on the open pages.

In Loving Memory of
Mary Olivia Deveraux
Devoted Wife and Mother
1837–1902

'Of course it would be Mary, wouldn't it?' Still chuckling, Eline bent to the stone bible, hooked her fingers around the top edge and pulled at it.

It refused to budge.

'Excuse me? I believe you were helping, yes?'

Tom stooped beside her and heaved. Slowly, and with a horrible metallic grating noise as seventy years of rust gave way, the memorial stone tilted up on hinges hidden under its bottom edge to reveal a square, stone-lined hole in the ground. Rachel watched apprehensively as Eline reached in, still half-prepared for her to pull out a skull, but what she produced was a large rectangular object wrapped in cloth. Eline unwrapped it to reveal a leather suitcase. It was battered and dusty, but in remarkably good condition. She popped the locks and lifted the lid with a little crow of delight.

Inside were a number of cloth-wrapped bundles, which gave off a strong smell of oil. Eline picked one up and unwrapped it to reveal a bundle of documents including an old passport – the old-fashioned blue version – and a wad of money. 'Hmm,' she said, 'probably all obsolete by now,' and tossed them back. The next was heavier. 'Ah, here we are.'

Wrapped in the protective oilcloth was a handgun. In the next parcel was a cardboard box of bullets.

'Um...' said Tom.

Eline ignored him, inspecting the pistol closely. It was a semi-automatic with a square grip and short barrel; small, sleek and rounded. The magazine ejected smoothly, and the slide action was clean. 'Incredible,' she breathed.

'I'll say,' replied Rachel. 'As in what the fuck do you think you're doing?'

Eline opened the box of bullets and started reloading

the gun's clip. 'I would say that was fairly obvious. I'm protecting myself. I could have done with it that night, but I could not be sure that old Brass-Eye's men weren't watching this place.' She chuckled. 'I think it is fair to say they are probably not any more.'

Tom was doing a passable imitation of a meerkat, trying to look in every direction at once in case they were being watched. 'You can't wander around with a fucking gun!' he protested.

'Why not? Our enemy does. Or did you enjoy being shot at yesterday?' Neither Tom nor Rachel could find an adequate reply to that, and Eline went on. 'This,' she said, 'is a Browning FN 1910 – Belgian-made as all the best things are, obviously – nice and small, no external sight to snag on your underwear when you whip it out, very reliable. It was one of these that started the Great War. I think that you didn't know that.' She slotted the magazine, chambered a round, and fired a shot into the earth just to make sure. It made a surprisingly quiet, dry-twig cracking sound but Rachel and Tom jumped nonetheless. 'And still in fine working order,' Eline added.

'Great, the weapon of choice for assassins,' said Tom. 'You're going to get us arrested.'

'Nonsense. Nobody heard that. And if they did they thought it was a branch breaking.' She pocketed the pistol, threw everything else back into the suitcase and snapped it shut. 'Okay, now we go.'

27

THE HIVE

THE HIVE, HOUSING WORCESTER'S CENTRAL LIBRARY and historical archives, looked like a space fortress from a low-budget seventies science fiction show. It was clad in plates of a gold-coloured metal overlapping like fish scales, and rose to seven chunky square towers that didn't have a single right angle between them – a deliberate architectural conceit designed to create the impression of something orderly but created naturally, possibly by bees as its name suggested. Giant, super-intelligent space bees. It looked like it had not been built so much as landed, in an open area bordered by a grimy Victorian railway viaduct on one side and a shopping centre on the other.

Rachel, Tom and Eline found the main entrance via a series of wide ramps and walkways over a sunken grassed area like a drained moat. Inside, the historical archives reading room was just as disconcerting. Maybe it was because she'd been spending so much time in the company of Mary/ Annabel/Eline visiting places where the skin between the worlds of the living and the dead seemed so tissue-thin as to be invisible, but she was expecting dusty shelves and heavy furniture, cobwebby corners and crackling, ancient tomes. Maybe it was simply too much television.

She wasn't expecting a large open-plan space with modern glass museum cabinets displaying artefacts from the city's history and tables of gleaming white melamine and grey steel, overhung by large light panels, which provided a clean and directionless illumination.

Rachel had to produce her driver's licence and register for a research card before they were allowed access to the Oak Mary case files. The archivist – a slender Asian woman with bright henna tattoos decorating her hands – brought out six large brown cardboard boxes, weighing each of them first on sensitive electronic scales and recording the results, a precaution to make sure that nothing went missing. Rachel opened the first box; the battered, seventy-year-old manila folders inside looked incongruous in such a twenty-first-century setting, like a pensioner in an Apple store.

'Right then,' Rachel said. 'Six boxes. That's three each.'

'Three?' asked Eline. 'What about me?'

'Do you really think you're up to this?' Rachel asked, and laid her hand on the nearest box. 'The details? The photos?'

'My dear,' said Eline with heavy scorn. 'I've seen and done far worse things than were done to me. I know who I am. Nothing in any of these boxes is going to change that.' She pulled two boxes towards her. 'Come on.'

'And have we got any more of a clue about exactly what we're looking for?' asked Tom.

'Anything that mentions Bill Heath,' said Eline.

'Anything we might be able to use against what's after Eline,' Rachel added. 'I don't know what it would be. Something small, something that hasn't made it into the stories online. Maybe someone named here is still alive – a witness, a reporter, a policeman. I don't know.'

They were able to disregard three of the boxes straight away; they contained large ring-binders of photocopies of original documents from the other boxes, as well as a load more stuck to large pieces of backing board as part of some kind of old display. The other three had original material, but in bewildering array. There were dossiers on each of the many possible victims, sheaves of yellowing press cuttings, maps and charts of the Lickey Hills, manila folders for suspects and witnesses, receipts, references, telephone memoranda, typewritten versions of illegible handwritten notes, and multiple carbon copies of everything. It appeared that every single scrap of paper pertaining to the Oak Mary investigation had been collected from every police station that had ever been involved with it – no matter how tangentially – and bundled into these boxes without any regard for how many of them were duplicates or irrelevant to the case.

'God,' said Rachel, surveying the expanse of it spread out over their worktable. 'This is going to take days.'

Tom soon found the photographs. They were in a wide brown cardboard envelope sandwiched between the script for a local opera production of an Oak Mary musical and a lurid fifties true crime article featuring two soldiers goggling with horror at a skull, which leered at them from out of a hollow tree.

Rachel looked at Eline, concerned. 'Are you okay with this?'

'Do not treat me like a child,' Eline snapped. 'I have seen many dead bodies.'

'Yes,' replied Tom, 'but your own?'

He began laying out the photographs. They were old-fashioned and heavy, glossy and curled at the edges. There was only a handful of distinctly separate images: three of the tree, a pair of shoes, some heavily soiled clothes, a dental x-ray, a disarticulated skeleton laid out with the toe bones in a neat line along the bottom, and three close-up angles of a skull. It lay on a policeman's gloved hand as if being offered as a gift, and was devoid of flesh except for a knotted clump of hair still attached to the right temple. Rachel watched Eline looking at it, and saw her hand creep unconsciously up to stroke her own hair on that side of her head. Like all the other documents there were multiple copies collected from different police forces – prints and reprints – and Tom laid them out side by side, forming a collage on the table of Oak Mary's remains repeated over and over again.

'Christ that's grim,' Rachel murmured.

The smell of all those old photographs – the sweet-dry chemical tang of their emulsion and the dusty funkiness of the thick paper – reminded her of a time in her great-grandmother Gigi's house in Kings Norton. Rachel had been eleven, a year before her father's death and another five before the family was able to convince Gigi that only a nursing home could cope with her worsening dementia. Rachel had found a spare bedroom that she hadn't been in before, and in there a tall mahogany wardrobe, and in that a battered old suitcase covered in stickers, and inside *that* a shoebox labelled STEPHEN.

Granddad Stephen, he'd have been called, to go with Grannie Alice, if he'd lived long enough to be called anything by his granddaughter Rachel. Her daddy's daddy. Gigi's son. For an eleven-year-old the gulf of time between generations was almost impossible to conceptualise; you were either a child, a mummy, a daddy, or Old. The fact that there might be different degrees of Old was problematic because it forced you to think of someone who was Old as having once been a child, and it was impossible to see either Gigi or Grannie Alice in such a way. She knew they were mother and daughter, but not like Rachel and her own mummy, surely? Not *really*. She couldn't imagine Gigi brushing Grannie Alice's teeth and putting her to bed with a story.

So even though the box said STEPHEN, it was hard to imagine the name belonging to a child. Nevertheless, inside the box that was exactly what she found: piles of photographs of, mostly, a young boy. Her granddad. At school they were doing a project on My Family Tree and she'd been pestering her mum for old photographs. Gigi was always giving her little gifts of old coins, stamps, and buttons; there couldn't possibly be any harm in her borrowing one of Granddad Stephen's baby photos, could there? She'd only be borrowing it, anyway. She'd bring it right back when she was finished with her project.

She chose a photo of Stephen as a newborn, wrapped in a tartan blanket, his eyes tight shut. On the back of the photograph was a stencil of the photographer's address:

Harold K Jones
Commercial Photographer
873 Oldham Road, Manchester

Scribbled underneath it in pencil – smudged but just legible – were the words:

Born Wythenshawe General Hospital 9/12/42

It was only a little detail and in the ordinary course of events one which she would have forgotten, but it was branded on her memory because when she finished her project and showed it to her mum she got one of the most frightening tellings-off in her life. It wasn't that her mum was angry – quite the opposite. She seemed cold and absolutely matter-of-fact when she told Rachel she was wrong, that Granddad Stephen hadn't been born in Manchester. But it was there, Rachel had said, on the back of the photo. She didn't understand why her mother was making such a fuss. No, her mother said, and her face closed like a door. That was the thing that frightened Rachel the most: that terrible blankness.

Your father's family is from Birmingham, Rachel was told. They have been for generations. There are no relatives in Manchester and never have been. Nobody has ever been born anywhere else. It was the sheer blatant ugliness of the lie that had made its impression on her, the utter incomprehensibility of it. Why would her mother lie about such a trivial matter?

And why should that incident step into the footlights of her memory just now?

After staring at the photographs for a while, Eline shook herself as if coming out of a trance and took a deep breath. 'Let's get on, shall we?' she said, and resumed examining packets with brisk determination.

Rachel looked at Tom and raised an eyebrow in a silent question. He shrugged.

Half an hour later Rachel found something in a dog-eared police witness dossier that made her sit bolt upright as if stung. 'You mentioned Bill Heath?' she said to Eline.

Eline looked up. 'Yes?' she replied avidly.

'Found a file for a Lorna Heath,' Rachel said and tossed it over. 'It seems that Bill was never questioned during the original investigation, but his wife went to the police after he died with a very interesting story.'

Eline opened the folder and read the faded transcript of a letter written in 1957 – over a decade after the investigation had stalled.

Dear sirs,

You will wonder why I have chosen to wait this long to tell what I know, and to that I say that for all his faults Bill was still my husband despite everything. I cannot say that he was even an especially good man, he had fingers like a sieve when it came to money and couldn't hold a decent job down for more than two weeks straight. He had his moods, but then don't we all. Somehow he always managed to look sharp and was very generous with his gifts when he was flush. It was when he fell in with that Dutchman Van Alst that things turned bad. Van Alst would turn up at all hours of the night (and it was always night), in his shiny Rover, and off Bill would go with him, sometimes for days on end. Sometimes there would be a woman with them, and I asked Bill straight about that but he said that she was the Dutchman's piece and nothing to do with him, that he had always been faithful only to me, and I believed him.

Eline broke off. '"Piece",' she laughed, her lip curling in scorn. '*Il est bien culoté!*'

Bill stopped pretending to be doing honest work but he had more money than ever before. But then one night he came back on his own, with his flash suit all covered in mud and leaves and he was shaking like a leaf too – pale and staring, wouldn't say what it was that had scared him so badly. All he would say was that he wanted 'no more to do with the Dutchman or his piece of skirt'. Neither of them came calling again.

There was only one time I ever got anything more out of Bill about what happened that night. He was having nightmares – he'd never been that settled a sleeper at the best of times but these were full screaming night terrors – and after one particular bad one I found him sitting at our kitchen table and he stared at me with a face that looked like he was coming down with a fever. I don't think he was properly seeing me, though. I don't think he was even awake.

He said, 'I keep seeing her! In the tree! I keep seeing her eyes! Her eyes were open!' I was too shaken up to ask him what he meant by that, and he took himself back off to bed after that and slept like the dead for the rest of the night.

The next morning he denied he'd said anything of the sort, and I think maybe he really didn't remember saying anything because he definitely hadn't been all there. Three weeks later he was shouting and raving so much that they took him away to Scoles Farm Asylum in Rubery. Two days ago the asylum wrote to tell me that he'd died of apoplexy and I thought well finally I can tell someone what I know. I saw all the news reports and the appeals for information at the time and no doubt you'll say I've been obstructing the course of justice for not having said anything before now, and yes I pity the poor girl for what she went through, but I pity Bill too. For good or ill he was

319

my husband. So you can stop your searching for
that poor girl's killer, because the only ones who
know what happened are all in the ground, where I
hope you will let them rest.

Yours respectfully,
Lorna Heath

Eline tossed the letter back on the pile. 'I was never anybody's piece. Not Van Alst's, not Scheller's, and especially not old Brass-Eye Collins, who thought he owned my soul. I would dearly love to know if any of those old men are still alive. Imagine the look on their faces seeing me walking up to them.' Her sudden laugh rang clear across the open-plan space, and heads turned to show disapproving frowns.

'Shh!' said Rachel. 'People are staring.'

Eline flapped a dismissive hand. 'Let them stare.'

That was when all the fire alarms went off.

28

FIRE

TO A LIBRARY, FIRE IS THE WORST OF ALL THREATS and so the Hive wasn't taking any chances. The alarm was a great, raw, braying sound, which filled the space like tear gas, and left no room for people to so much as ask each other what was happening, let alone carry on anything resembling a conversation. All that Rachel, Eline and Tom could do was collect their belongings and join the crowd of people who were being marshalled down the main staircase by library staff and out through the main doors into the wide paved space outside. They moved as far back as they could and scanned the roofline of the building anxiously, looking for smoke.

'Is it a drill, do you think?' asked Tom.

'I'm not sure,' said Rachel. 'Did you see the way the staff were all rushing around? I don't think they knew it was going to happen.'

Eline was lighting a cigarette, unconcerned with the irony

of her action. 'Probably some little horror of a child,' she puffed. 'Did it on a dare.'

Inside, the Small Man sauntered up the main staircase, hands in his pockets. The noise didn't bother him, nor did the librarians and security guards who scurried past him, up and down, oblivious to his existence. He was still high on the buzz generated by the obelisk sacrifice. The newspapers had picked up on the Oak Mary story, obviously, but he hadn't anticipated how much power there was in this new Internet and its social media for spreading a simple narrative and strengthening it into something approaching myth. A person could make anything true: invent massacres, deny moon-landings, present the most obvious of lies as 'alternative facts'. Why, with judicious manipulation of people's basic fears, and a smidgen of luck, a small man could set himself up as King of the World.

It was all so very short-lived, though. He knew that in a few days, at most, the butterfly attention of the world would move on. It was like a sugar rush, this boost, but it was enough that he could make himself unseen for a while and take advantage of the distraction he had caused.

He made his way to the first floor and the reading table at which Mary and her protectors had been working, and surveyed the documents spread out there.

'Now then, Mr Thomas Cooper,' he said, sitting down and cracking his knuckles. 'Let's see if you've found the right breadcrumbs.' It was impossible to predict exactly what they might have found, but then a certain level of improvisation was always necessary in great works. When he got to Lorna Heath's letter, a slow smile spread across his face. 'Oh well done. Jolly good show. Shall we play a game of follow-my-leader, Mr Cooper?'

He folded the letter and tucked it into his pocket. 'Oh no! Not the asylum!' he chuckled to himself, sauntering out of the library as anonymously as he'd arrived. 'Whatever you do, don't go to the old asylum!'

It was the best part of an hour before anybody was allowed back in the library; the local fire brigade was nothing if not thorough. By that time Eline was bored and Rachel's arm was aching. All Tom had managed to discover from Google was that the Scoles Farm Asylum had been closed and condemned for decades, so there was no chance of following up any records there. Between the three of them they decided to call it a day.

They were in the process of packing everything carefully into their respective box files when Rachel saw Tom frowning and turning the same documents over and over again. It was the way he looked for his keys or his wallet or pretty much anything in the fridge – looking but not finding, despite it probably being right in front of him.

'What are you man-looking for?' she asked.

'That letter...' he muttered, looking under a folder he'd looked under three times already. 'You know, the one from Bill Heath's wife. Can't find it.'

'Here, let me.'

She looked, convinced it would be on top of the nearest pile, but it wasn't. The three of them scoured the table and the neighbouring ones, underneath, and even the surrounding shelves, but it simply wasn't there.

'It can't have just disappeared,' Tom protested. Then he saw the way Rachel was looking at him, and reddened. 'Oh, I really did just say that, didn't I?'

'Out of the mouths of babes,' said Eline.

'Maybe that's exactly what it did,' Rachel said. She made the sign of *barjok* and put it to her eye. The other side of this place was dim and almost completely formless; possibly the building was simply too new to have left bits of itself in limbo, and there were no lost spirits nearby to give it memory. The old documents were another thing entirely. Having been the focus of so much attention for so long, they had clarity, like projections of themselves thrown onto the backdrop of limbo by the light of the living world. But the letter wasn't there either.

'Somebody must have taken it,' she decided. 'No way is it just lost.'

'The creature pretending to be Van Alst?' asked Eline.

'Or his small colleague. I can't think of anyone else who might be interested in this information.'

'Or interested in keeping it secret,' Eline suggested.

'That was a very convenient false fire alarm, now that you mention it,' said Tom.

Rachel slapped the table. 'Shit! So what was in it that he could want to stop us knowing?'

'It was all about Heath,' said Eline. 'Van Alst's accomplice. Maybe he knew something that his boss did not want revealed.'

'But that doesn't make sense,' objected Tom. 'Everything that the police could find out is in these files, and they tell us nothing. How can stealing one piece of paper possibly make the slightest bit of difference?'

'If there's something they don't want us to know, I want to know what that is,' said Rachel.

'But we've read the letter – we already know whatever he's trying to hide. There's no point in him taking it.'

'He cannot be sure that we have read it,' put in Eline. 'Likely he is just being thorough.'

'So?' Tom protested. 'What good can the information do us anyway? Heath's long dead. They're *all* dead.'

Rachel smiled. 'Just because all the witnesses are dead doesn't mean we can't still ask them a few questions, does it?'

'Really?' asked Eline. 'You said you would not bring anybody else back.'

'I'm not talking about bringing anybody back. Just asking a few questions. That's if he's even there at all.'

'Where?' said Tom. 'Where exactly are you going to go looking for the soul of a dead World War Two black marketeer?'

'I imagine I'll start where he died.'

Tom laughed in disbelief. 'A lunatic asylum?' He shook his head. 'I don't like the sound of where this is going.'

'Neither do I,' Rachel conceded. 'But you have to admit there's a certain mad logic to it.'

'You can't just... just...' Tom dragged his hands down his face, looking utterly out of his depth. 'I can't believe I'm even saying this. You can't just go around talking to the spirits of the dead!'

Eline *ahemmed*, picking at a fingernail.

'That's not the same thing!'

Rachel looked at him closely. 'Why are you so sceptical all of a sudden? After everything you've seen in the last few days?'

'Because,' he answered, enunciating as if speaking to an idiot, 'you are basically talking about conducting a séance in a derelict lunatic asylum! You know that bit in a horror movie where they go down to the cellar and everybody says, "How fucking stupid, you never go down to the cellar"? This is that bit! Does it not strike either of you as being just the slightest bit out of order?'

'Oh I'm well aware of that!' Rachel shot back, stung by his attitude. She knew that he was struggling to process something that she'd had a lot more time to get a grip on, but she couldn't help herself. 'My whole life has been out of fucking order since my hand was cut off, you know? Bit of a sliding scale of abnormality from day one. Sort of like...' She bent and held her palm an inch from the floor. 'Here: learn to tie your shoelaces one-handed.' She straightened up and raised her palm over his head as if measuring his height. 'Here: learn to communicate with the dead. Somewhere around here...' She lowered her hand to chest level and waved it around. 'Try to maintain a functioning marriage without your husband thinking you're losing your fucking mind. I know exactly how ridiculous this sounds, Tom, because I am living it, but I am going to do it anyway because the alternative is to let those bastards call the shots. They killed a kid and used his blood as *paint*, Tom. They're still out there, and they don't give a toss about what you think is "out of order". So man up and help me like you promised you would or piss off!'

He stood gaping at her for a moment, then surprised her by grinning. 'Did you really just say "man up"?'

'Yes.' She glared at him. 'Problem?'

His grin widened. 'No, sir.'

The Dark Man watched Eline and her two protectors leave the library, and followed them. As with his small brother, the energising effect of the sacrifice at the obelisk enabled him to move unseen amongst the people milling around in the busy plaza, and there was nothing to hinder his approach.

He drew the revolver from his pocket and aimed it at the back of the human woman's head, pacing steadily behind. It would cause a stir, of course, but that didn't matter any more – the important thing was to get to Eline before his treacherous bastard of a brother.

Then the woman's hand telephone rang, and she answered it, still walking. 'Hello... yes...' She froze in mid-stride. 'How did you get this number?' she demanded. 'Leave us the fuck alone!' Whatever she heard in reply must have scared the wits out of her, because she looked around wildly.

'He's found us!' she yelled, then grabbed Eline's hand and began to run.

'What?' called her husband, evidently as confused as the Dark Man was himself, running after them.

'That was him!' she shouted back. 'The small guy. He said Van Alst was pointing a gun right at us!' The three of them were tearing through the crowd, trying to look in every direction at once. Any hope of stealth was gone.

The Dark Man swore, dropped his invisibility, and gave chase.

Some pedestrians saw him coming and managed to get out of his way in time. Others didn't, and were sent flying. He saw a man in a uniform – policeman, security guard, it didn't matter – turn and brace himself to meet the Dark Man's charge, balling his fists. The Dark Man grinned as he feinted right, dodged left and clotheslined him with an outstretched arm as he passed. There was an *oof!* as the human collapsed, and the Dark Man continued.

Then his brother was standing in his way.

He knew that the Small Man couldn't touch him, but his condition carried enough human instinct to have to flinch at the sudden appearance, and he skidded out of the way, losing his balance and sprawling in an ungainly heap.

'I know what you're thinking,' said the Small Man. 'And you're wrong. You're making a rather large assumption here.'

The Dark Man picked himself up and looked past his brother. Eline, Rachel and Tom had disappeared in the direction of the car park. There was no chance of catching them now.

'What?!' he barked. 'What assumption am I making, *paardenlul*?'

'I—'

'You betray me at the caravan, you get in my way now, and you say I am *wrong*? How have I misconstrued your intentions?' He spat the words with venomous sarcasm.

'You assume that I'm still interested in Mary.'

That brought the Dark Man up short. 'What?'

'I tried to tell you at the caravan, but you wouldn't listen. It's your own stubbornness that forces me to intervene. You can keep Mary – it's the woman Rachel I want.'

'For what conceivable reason? Her ability to reach into the umbra?'

The Small Man delivered another one of his infuriatingly enigmatic smiles. 'Possibly.'

'If you are thinking that you can somehow use her to build yourself a following in the umbra, I assure you, They will not stand for it.'

'You just let me worry about Them. If you could just refrain from trying to kill her for five minutes, then maybe both of us can come out of this with something. Tell me, brother,' he smiled smugly again. 'Would you like to know where they're going?'

29

ASYLUM

WHEN BIRMINGHAM BOROUGH COUNCIL BOUGHT A hundred and ten acres of land at Scoles Farm to build a lunatic asylum in 1852, the city's populace was insulated from the inmates by several miles of open countryside. They therefore remained largely untroubled by the plight of the nearly two hundred pauper lunatics who were locked away in conditions little better than one of the great city penitentiaries upon which its design was based. By the time Bill Heath was incarcerated there in 1947, the institution had increased to a population of nearly a thousand, with the addition of outbuildings, accommodation blocks, workshops, rambling wings and annexes, a high-vaulted chapel and even a patients' farm, making it a small village in its own right. It was invisible to the wider world, unreached by any roads that a stray traveller might chance upon, a hidden fiefdom of the confused and desperate.

The great economic rationalisations of the late twentieth century saw its slow starvation and ultimate demise as care was returned to 'the community', and the newer buildings were sold off and demolished to make way for a new housing estate. Behind neat wooden fences, new families erected swing sets and paddling pools on tidy lawns of turf laid over the substrate of crushed brick and plaster that was all that remained of cells where inmates had screamed and laughed and wept mere decades earlier; the gardens of suburbia fertilised by the rubble of madness.

Meanwhile the original Victorian building was slapped with a preservation order as being historically significant while simultaneously anybody who wanted to develop it into flats or sheltered accommodation were refused planning permission and so, trapped between layers of bureaucracy, the asylum was left to rot into itself. It squatted in the middle of the estate behind high wire fences and a screen of overgrown trees and bushes, ignored except by stray cats and teenagers, existing in a collective blind spot like the hollow and rotten heart of an old tree.

Four storeys high, its long frontage was opened by dozens of tall, rectangular sash windows with scrolled corbels like a Georgian mansion; every pane was broken. When the place was first abandoned an attempt had been made to board the doors and windows in the ground and first floors with sheets of bright blue plywood, but many had been torn away or burned. Numerous arson attacks had left the roof a charred ribcage and straggling greenery was reclaiming the eaves and gutters. There was no point in security guards or warning signs, or even in repairing the many holes made in the perimeter fence. The ruin was its own warning: *Come in*, those gaping windows said. *Have a look around, make yourself at home – we've got loads of broken glass, rusty nails and rotten floorboards for you to play with.*

It was not hard for Rachel, Eline and Tom to find a way in. The problem lay in where to start.

There had been a brief debate about whether to explore the old asylum during the day or under the cover of darkness, but Tom had flat out refused to go into the place at night, not just because it was creepy, but also he didn't fancy ending up in Accident and Emergency. Again. Sense had prevailed and they approached the ruin of Scoles Farm in bright midmorning sun the following day.

They climbed in through an arched ground-floor window, which was half-obscured by a buddleia bush growing out of the wall. The heavy scent of its flowers mixed with that of damp plaster and scorched wood as they found themselves in a wide hallway running the length of the building. Their feet crunched in a litter of broken glass, splintered wood, dead leaves and plaster.

'Still fucking creepy if you ask me,' Tom said, keeping his voice low, as if fearing the building was so dilapidated that the ceiling would collapse on them at any loud noise. 'Has it occurred to you that if they didn't want us to know about this place they might be waiting here to stop us finding whatever it is?'

'Of course it has,' said Rachel. 'I'd be worried if they weren't – it would mean we're on the wrong track. Look,' she added. 'That thing with the fire alarm? He's keeping his distance. He's scared, and he should be. I can do something that I don't think they've ever come across before. That gives us an advantage.'

'So does this,' said Eline, and from a deep pocket in her coat produced the Browning.

'Just be bloody careful where you point that thing,' Tom grumbled.

'*Mon chéri*,' she replied, 'I was doing this before your grandmother was born.' She began picking her way along the corridor. 'Come, let us find these ghosts.'

Taking a deep breath, Rachel made the sign of *barjok* and looked into limbo. With the exception of a strange violet light coming from outside, and the fact that she couldn't see Eline or Tom, the corridor looked exactly the same. There was no shadow of an older place underlying the physical ruins, no suggestion of the asylum as it had been, or remembered by any souls who still lingered here, no sign of any souls at all. It was actually something of a relief; the soul of a person dying in such a place as this couldn't be a pretty sight. Still, her frustration mounted as they explored the ruins and she saw absolutely nothing.

'You'd think there'd be *someone* lost here,' she said.

'Nothing?' asked Eline.

'Pardon the pun, but this place is dead.'

'We should try upstairs,' suggested Tom. 'That's where their dormitories will have been. Down here will be all meeting rooms and offices.'

Rachel shrugged. 'It's worth a try.'

They backtracked down the long corridor towards the building's centre, where twin flights of metal stairs curved upwards. Rust and paint flaked off them in equal measure, and they creaked alarmingly underfoot. The open centre of the stairwell was screened with heavy wire mesh, presumably to stop suicidal inmates hurling themselves straight down the middle, and the screens had caught burned and sodden wreckage from the upper floors. On one landing was a rusted wheelchair tipped forward onto the stumps of its axles where its smaller front wheels had been, like an animal with its forepaws amputated, and Rachel's stump gave a sudden furious burst of phantom pins and needles in sympathy. Looking up, she could see daylight through rents where the ceiling had first bowed inwards and then ruptured.

At the top of the stairs was another long corridor at right angles, leading deeper into the building with numerous dark doorways all down the right-hand wall, but the left had completely collapsed into a vaulted space which must have been a grand hall behind the hospital's main doors. What had once been a corridor was now a wide ledge between the rooms on their right and an echoing gulf, which the doors looked over. The void was bristling and cross-hatched with old scaffolding, put there in years past to shore up the fire-damaged roof.

'Fuck this,' said Tom. 'This is *not* safe.'

'I have to say—' began Eline in agreement, but Rachel shushed them both. She was looking through *barjok*, and she'd seen someone.

It was the shade of a woman in a ragged smock, so

emaciated that it was impossible to tell her age; she was all angles and shadows, like a marionette made of dead sticks. She'd been standing in one of the doorways, but as if aware that she'd been spotted, turned to look at Rachel, who gasped despite herself.

After a moment – in which Rachel realised that she had no idea what to say, if in fact she could communicate at all – the shade turned and walked away along the open-sided corridor.

'Wait!' she called, and followed.

'You've seen something?' asked Eline, hurrying after.

'Rache, be careful!' warned Tom. 'The floor is fucked!' He hung back, indecisive. 'Jesus, Rache, you're going to get yourself killed!' Eventually he too followed, wincing at every creaking floorboard.

The thin woman disappeared around a corner. Rachel followed but stopped short, blinking, as her sight tried to reconcile something impossible: there was a pair of swinging double doors which her right eye, looking at the living world, saw lying on the floor covered in debris, and another large room beyond. Her left eye, however, looking through the hole that her fingers made into limbo, insisted that the doors were still standing – one was still swinging slightly from the phantom woman's passage into the room beyond.

'Still,' she said to herself. 'At least something's different. That's promising.'

'What was that?' asked Eline, catching up.

'She went in there.' Rachel pointed, and explained what she'd seen. The room looked like it had once been some kind of day room before time's decay had ravaged it. Carpet tiles, stinking with damp and rot, were peeling from the floor like scabs, while sofas and armchairs sat amongst the shredded debris of their own insides. Someone had collected scores of old plastic seats and jumbled them into a mountain of jutting, rusted legs in the centre of the room, as if in offering to something. Of any inhabitants, living or dead, there was no sign.

Rachel frowned. 'I don't get it.'

Eline and Tom could only watch, perplexed, as she peered around the room in confusion. There was no evidence for her to think so, but the scribbled ziggurat of chairs gave the impression that it had been built and taken down and rebuilt over and over again in an act of obsessive and mindless construction only momentarily interrupted by their presence. The air crawled with unseen activity waiting to resume after their departure, like cockroaches inside the walls.

'She came in here, I'm certain of it. So why can't I see her?'

Tom went over to investigate a warped noticeboard hanging diagonally from one wall, and the tatters of yellowing paper still attached to it.

FRIDAY NIGHT IS BINGO NIGHT!
Please replace all board games in the cupboard after use.
Would you know the signs of a stroke if you saw them?
Think F.A.S.T.!

'Wait,' Rachel said. 'Maybe if I...' She went back to the doorway, but instead of using her left hand to see the room she reached out and her dead fingers touched the shadow door that still stood in the frame that her living eyes insisted was empty. She pushed, and felt it move, vibrating slightly as its hinges gave a creak she couldn't hear. She pushed it open fully and stepped over the empty threshold, hoping that when she looked through *barjok* this time she would see the ghost woman who had so unaccountably managed to hide. There was still so much about this talent that she didn't understand. She felt like a chimpanzee with a smartphone, prodding until something happened and trying to make sense of the funny lights and sounds.

Then an ice-dead hand closed over her left wrist, and she yelped with surprise.

Christ, not again. I'm not dragging anybody else through.

Tom, at the other side of the room, was turning with surprise and Eline was just opening her mouth to ask what the matter was when two more hands latched themselves onto Rachel's dead wrist, and sudden terror swamped her.

Oh fuck, how many of them are there? They can't all want...

As one they *pulled*, and she screamed as she recognised the trap for what it was, too late.

And her arm disappeared up to the elbow.

It was just like when she'd pulled the *lesh* apart, except this time her flesh didn't come back. More hands grasped at her, scratching, clamping on her like frozen manacles, and before she could brace her feet she was yanked again and her arm disappeared to the shoulder.

'No!' she sobbed. 'NO!'

The more of her arm they took, the more purchase the dead had on her, and the harder they pulled.

'*Jesusfuckingchristgetthemoffme*GETTHEMOFFME!' she howled.

Eline grabbed her right arm and yelled 'Hang on!' as Tom lunged from the other side of the room. Her left arm, now completely in limbo, was busy with dead hands from knuckle to armpit, fighting amongst themselves, tearing each other away and taking their places, and it was simply too much to oppose, even for the pair of them. With one final despairing shriek Rachel was pulled bodily into limbo, and Eline tumbled after.

Tom stumbled into the empty space where his wife had been a second before, and stopped, gaping.

'Rachel?' he whispered.

There was no response. Maybe it was his imagination that made him think the shadows were busier here than they had been – but maybe not.

'Rachel!' he bellowed, and the reverberations brought a sifting of plaster debris from the ceiling but nothing more.

'*RACHEL!*'

30

THE SMALL MAN'S PRIZE

THE ROOM WAS IN THE SAME STATE OF DECAY ON THIS side, Rachel saw, but it wasn't empty. It was thronged with the shades of the dead.

They let go of her as soon as she was through, and retreated slightly, forming a shuffling mob in a tight circle around her and Eline. They were gaunt and grey, all hollow eyes, gaping mouths and shuffling limbs. Most wore the tattered rags of their institutional smocks, some were in straitjackets and muzzles, and quite a few were naked, their rake-thin bodies like concentration camp victims. Some carried the marks of their deaths: gaping wrists, burns, blackened tongues and throats livid with the marks of homemade nooses.

But for all that, their individual personalities had been winnowed away over the years down to a single dumb imperative to simply exist. They were pathetic things, Rachel saw, and now that they'd accomplished their purpose they didn't seem actively malicious. Eline, on the other hand, was shrinking from them in terror, moaning deep in her throat like a trapped animal, which was probably the more normal reaction to being surrounded by a horde of the dead. So why didn't they freak Rachel out as much as they did Eline? Was she that far gone? Anger quickly rose to replace her fear.

'What do you want with me?' she demanded. 'I'm not taking any of you back.'

'No, you most decidedly are not,' responded a familiar voice.

The crowd parted to reveal, enthroned on one of the crumbling plastic chairs, the death that wore Van Alst's face. He'd swapped his long dark coat for doctor's whites, though they weren't especially white, blotched as they were with old bloodstains and filth.

'You will never interfere with this place again,' he added, with venomous intensity. 'They don't know that, of course. As far as they're concerned I've brought you here so that they can claw their way back to the living world through your screaming soul. Not that it will work.' The dead milled uncertainly at his words but he shrugged, unconcerned. 'But they'll try it anyway because they literally have nothing to lose and you'll be insane long before they realise that, and I'll finally have what is mine.' He pointed at Eline, who cowered. This made Rachel angrier still: that Eline, who had been so strong, could be made to fall apart so abjectly.

'You'll have to get through me first,' she said.

The Dark Man laughed. 'You will find that here, in the

umbra, *my* world, you are not quite as strong as you think.'
He raised his left hand. 'Hm?'

Rachel looked at her stump, and her sudden shock
eclipsed everything that she'd seen so far, because it wasn't
a stump any more. Here, her left hand was real again. 'Oh
my God,' she whispered. She held it up before her eyes and
flexed her fingers. It looked no different than it had in the
last moments before it had been crushed. The only thing
missing was her wedding ring.

The Dark Man waved at the restless crowd of impatient
shades filling the room.

'She's all yours,' he said.

They shuffled forward avidly. Rachel easily shoved them
away but there were so many that when one staggered back
three more took its place. Cold fingers pawed at her – at her
hair, her skin, her clothes – too weak to harm, only to clutch
desperately, and their voices as they begged were whisper-
thin, a susurrating chorus of pleading. Their breath, what
little they had, was in her mouth, dry and dusty and sickly-
sweet with rot.

'I can't help you!' she pleaded. 'I don't know what to do!'

They might be pathetic and deserving of pity, but they
were so many, so close, fighting with each other to touch
her, to be inside her, and through her to be alive again that
their collective insistence would kill her just as surely.

Eline was screaming and thrashing out at them, even
though they weren't interested in her at all, but they pressed
in on all sides and prevented any escape.

Then Rachel must have blacked out for a moment, because

it felt like a great shadow had thrown itself over both her and Eline and then turned itself inside out like an umbrella, because when she blinked again the dead were gone, along with Van Alst, and she was in an entirely different part of the asylum.

Standing before her was the Small Man, doing his best to look anxious and concerned.

'We don't have much time,' he said. 'My brother will find out where I've brought you soon enough. Come on.'

He set off along a corridor but when Rachel and Eline didn't immediately follow he looked back, frowning. 'Or did I get it wrong and you were actually enjoying yourselves back there?'

A sudden attack of vertigo seized Rachel as her brain tried to cope with the situation. She tottered and Eline caught her.

'Why did you save us?' Eline demanded. '*How* did you save us?'

The Small Man pinched the bridge of his nose, reining in his obvious impatience. 'As my brother said, you are in my world now, and I make the rules. Do you want to see Bill Heath or not?'

'How do you know about that?'

'For God's sake, woman!' he snapped. 'Yes or no?'

Yes was the only answer they could give, though it lessened Rachel's distrust of him not one bit, and as they followed him she couldn't shake the feeling that far from this being a rescue they were only being led deeper into the trap.

They were in a corridor somewhere on the asylum's top floor, she guessed, from the fact that just overhead through the space where the ceiling had been and the blackened ribs of the roof joists beyond, she could see the violet light of whatever passed for sky in this place. The doorways down each side of the corridor were open and dark, except for one where the door remained closed – it was heavy wood, hinged and banded with iron, more suitable to a dungeon than a hospital. Here the Small Man took out a ring of heavy cast-iron keys and fitted one into the lock.

'It wasn't easy keeping Heath out of the way,' he said over his shoulder. 'Van Alst's myth is very strong in this place. But then that was inevitable, of course. Heart of the labyrinth.'

'I have no idea what you're talking about,' said Rachel.

He looked at her, one hand on the door. 'Of course you do. You knew there was something you could use against him here and so I've brought you to it.'

'But why?'

'Because the enemy of my enemy is my friend,' said Eline scathingly. 'He's using us, just like he used you to kill his other brother, the *lesh*.'

The Small Man winked at her. 'Catches on quick, don't she?' He pushed the door open.

The cell was as ruined as Rachel had come to expect: big chunks of plaster had fallen from the walls, leaving red bricks exposed like raw muscle, and black mould covered what was left. A rat-eaten mattress sagged on a rusted iron-framed bed, on the edge of which sat the shade of a man with his head in his hands. He looked up as they entered, and Eline gasped.

'Bill? Bill Heath?'

His eyes widened as he saw her, and began to spill with tears. 'It's you!' he wept. 'I'm sorry! I'm so sorry! I should have told somebody. But I was scared. I shouldn't have left you there. I should have done something the moment we found you.'

'What do you mean, "found me"?' demanded Eline. 'You put me there, you and that bastard Van Alst! Shot me and dumped me like so much rubbish!' The Browning was in her hand and pointed at his face. He gazed at the muzzle vacantly. 'You killed me, you bastard. You watched him shoot me and then you drove me up to that place and you put me in that tree and you left me to *die*!' She was shrieking now, her cheeks wet with tears.

'No...' Heath murmured, in tones of great puzzlement. 'No, that's not what happened...'

The Small Man, who had his ear pressed against the door, cursed. 'He's here. Shit. Heath, just *tell* her. You!' He pointed at Rachel. 'Help me hold this door shut!'

Rachel leaned against the cell door next to the Small Man. Despite being a good six inches shorter than her, this close he was even more unpleasant. There was a sweet smell about him, like a teenager's antiperspirant, but it also reminded her of the rot on the dead patients' breath.

'A simple ambush,' he tutted. 'That's all it was supposed to be. And then you had to bring her along and now I've got to protect the pair of you.' He shook his head. 'Sickening.'

'So sorry to have inconvenienced you,' she retorted.

Heath was shaking his head slowly. 'But… no… we didn't shoot anybody. We found you there. You were already in the tree when we got there. You were dying. I left you to die. I'm so sorry…'

Rachel felt a sudden sick realisation unfolding within her. 'Eline…' she warned.

Heath's eyes wandered to her. 'Eline? Who's Eline?'

'Me!' screamed Eline. 'I am! Eline Lambert! Van Alst's "piece", you lying bastard! He was spying for the Germans and I double-crossed him and he killed me for it!'

Heath shook his head again. 'But… I don't understand… You're not Van Alst's girl. She was drunk so we took her back to her digs after the pub. Then we went up to Beacon Hill, to the tree. It was hollow. Good for hiding things we stole. Cigarettes and stockings and such. He wasn't a spy. Nor was she. She worked in a grocer's. And her name wasn't Eline – it was Sally. *You* were in the tree. I'm so sorry…'

'You're lying!'

Something threw itself heavily at the other side of the door, and it shuddered.

'What are you doing with my girl, little brother?' called Van Alst from the other side. 'I thought you just wanted the woman.'

The Small Man made a face. 'Little. Always going on about the height. You see,' he said to Rachel, 'he and I are what you might call mutually exclusive. For one of us to exist, the other logically cannot. Therefore we cannot confront each other directly, and so we must act through proxies. Which is why you currently are the only thing holding this door shut.'

'What?!' The door was struck again, opened an inch and then slammed shut as Rachel planted her feet and shoved back hard. 'Lock this fucking door!' she demanded.

The Small Man stepped towards Eline and Heath, twirling the key on his forefinger. 'Now if I did that, you'd be free to interfere again, wouldn't you?' he said. 'No, I think it's better if you stay right there.'

Heath was imploring Eline to listen to him. Her gun was pointed straight at his face. 'You were already in the tree when we got there! I don't know who you are but I swear, we didn't shoot you! We didn't even have a gun! You were already there! And your head... there was so much blood... you *must* have been dead. I didn't do it!'

The door was rammed again, harder, and this time the gap was wide enough for an arm to come darting through just as Rachel pushed back again, trapping it, and the Dark Man howled in rage and pain. 'Eline!' she screamed. 'Whatever he's saying, it's all lies! Don't believe him! It's a trick!'

'Oh no,' said the Small Man, taking the knife out of his pocket. 'It's the truth, from the very lips of the dead, and they never lie.'

'And then you opened your eyes,' said Heath. 'I was looking down into the tree and you... opened your eyes and looked right up at me! You knew I was there! You knew I could see you and that I wasn't going to do anything to help.' He buried his face in his hands again, sobbing.

'For God's sake, why didn't you?' Rachel demanded.

'Yes, why didn't you?' echoed the Small Man. 'Go on, Heath, tell her.'

'Van Alst,' Heath whispered. 'He said we'd get blamed. That we'd hang. I'm sorry. I'm so sorry. I was scared!'

The Dark Man threw himself at the door again. 'You lying mongrel!' he snarled at the Small Man. 'You never said anything about Heath being here! You said you wanted the woman!'

'And you just keep on believing me, don't you, *mein bruder*?' the Small Man sighed, shaking his head.

'Heath!' the Dark Man screamed. 'Keep your trap shut, you gutless little turd!'

'Eline!' cried Rachel. 'Please, help me! I can't hold this much longer.'

But Eline's attention was fixed on the shade of Bill Heath, who was rocking back and forth on the edge of his bed, weeping. She was pale and shuddering, and the gun wavered in her hand. The Small Man was right behind her, close enough to be nuzzling the hair above her ear, but she didn't seem to notice that either.

'Thank you very much, Bill,' said the Small Man. 'You've been most forthcoming. Now if you'll just be so kind as to—'

'Then Van Alst picked up a big pile of dead leaves,' Heath continued, ignoring the Small Man, his eyes fixed on the woman in front of him. 'And he... dumped them straight on your face and he said, "That's that then," and walked off. But I saw you spit the leaves out, so I know you were alive for at least a while. Don't you remember?'

'No!' Eline whispered, backing away now, her pistol drooping. 'This didn't happen! This *can't* have happened...'

'You only said one thing—'

'We don't need to know any more!' said the Small Man sharply. For some reason he seemed surprised, and even afraid of what more Heath might say. But Heath's confession, once begun, wouldn't rest until it had run its course.

'Just one word... just a name.'

'Heath! For once I agree with my brother: keep your trap shut!'

'What name?' moaned Eline.

'Stephen.'

The shock made Rachel lose her balance; at the next shove the door crashed open and sent her sprawling to the floor as the Dark Man stood at the threshold.

'*She's mine!*' he bellowed.

'So you see,' murmured the Small Man into Eline's ear. 'It wasn't you, was it? You're not her. How could you be? Nobody shot you, you weren't a spy, and your name isn't Eline Lambert, is it?'

The gun hung from her trembling fingers for a moment more, then tumbled from her grasp. 'No,' she whispered, and she wasn't Eline any more. Rachel saw it leave her as clearly as a candle being blown out. Without a hair on her head changing, she seemed to become smaller, and her features less clearly defined. She was Oak Mary again, the stand-in, pale and indeterminate. The Small Man's face split into a victorious grin as the taller version of himself in the doorway unravelled in the air like ink dissolving in water.

Even the gun that Eline had dropped disappeared as if it had never existed.

'My God,' whispered Rachel, appalled. 'What have you done?'

'Dispelled another myth,' the Small Man said, smiling. 'Don't tell me you actually believed that she was a Nazi spy, did you? Or a gypsy witch?' He tutted. 'Honestly, the things you people read. No.' He stroked Oak Mary's hair, and she shuddered a little. 'Spy, witch or whore – there really is only one option left for you now, isn't there, my dear?'

'Mary, don't listen to him!' Rachel pleaded.

But it was already too late. 'I'm not Mary,' said the woman, her eyes dull and defeated. 'I'm Daphne.'

'That's my girl,' said the Small Man, stroking her hair. She shuddered again, but still didn't move. Why didn't she fight him? Why didn't she just run? Rachel's head was pounding with sick rage.

'Fuck you!' spat Rachel.

'Oh no,' he replied with a leer, and his hand crept down to cup Daphne's left breast. Her face clenched as if she was about to vomit. 'But she will. Fuck me, that is. Fuck me and let me kill her, over and over again, forever.'

Rachel got to her feet and clenched her fists – both of them. She was damned if she was going to let him do this unchallenged. 'Leave her alone!'

'*Or you'll what?*' he barked, his sudden vehemence catching her by surprise. Daphne flinched. 'You should be grateful! I've taken her off your hands and she'll be at peace now she knows the truth; don't be so selfish as to deny her that.'

Rachel appealed directly to Daphne. 'But it's a lie, can't you see that? Just like the others!' Daphne was standing with that same terrible listlessness she'd had when Rachel had first pulled her from the tree, similar to the way Bill Heath's ghost was still sitting on the edge of his cot, clenched and unmoving. 'This can't be all that's left! This can't be true! Why did he say that the last thing she said was Stephen? That's my grandfather's name!' She grabbed Heath by the shoulders and shook him. 'What did you mean?' His head just lolled.

The Small Man shrugged. 'Lies, truth, at best they're just... what's that phrase? Ah yes, *alternative facts*. Only the living have the luxury of time and energy to bother about the differences. When you're dead you'll be thankful for whatever pitiful remembrance there is, before even that fades and you're left like these pathetic shades, trapped in the crumbling remains of a nightmare that you can't let go of because at least it's *something*. There is nothing after this. No heaven or hell or pleasure or punishment. Just a whimpering echo of existence maintained by the fading memories of whoever's left to remember you. You brought her back into a living world that had made a legend out of her, only it couldn't decide what that legend should be. *You* did this!' He laughed. 'You're even responsible for me! I didn't exist, nor did my brothers, until you broke her out of the umbra and forced death itself to intervene. Action and reaction, crime and consequence. She was nothing in that tree, and if she's nothing more than the ghost of a dead whore now, that is your fault.'

'No.' Rachel shook her head. It was unthinkable that she was responsible. 'I didn't ask for this. I did everything I could to stop it. But *she* forced herself on *me*. Mary... Daphne... whoever you are – why did you choose me?'

'Visiting hours are over, I'm afraid,' said the Small Man. He let Daphne go, shifted the knife into his other hand and lunged at Rachel, but by then she was already running.

She had no idea where she was going; she took corners at random and dodged around piles of debris and threw herself down a flight of stairs three steps at a time and jumped over holes in the floor and ducked under sagging doorways, her lungs bursting with panic. When the Small Man caught up with her, she was halfway along a creaking wooden balcony, which ran around the upper level of the great central hall. There was that strange sense of the darkness folding itself inside out and then he was standing in front of her. She skidded to a halt.

Beneath her feet, something cracked, splintered and fell away to the ground floor with an echoing crash, and the whole balcony lurched.

The Small Man didn't seem concerned, however. He'd taken his jacket off and rolled up his shirtsleeves. With his belly and knitted sleeveless jumper, his slacks and shiny shoes, he looked like he should have been on a seaside pavilion. 'I told you,' he said. 'This is my place. My rules.'

'Fuck your rules.' Desperate, Rachel lunged to the wall, and pushed with her left hand as hard as she could, enjoying the fleeting look of surprise and panic on his face. Something ripped free from the wall and the balcony lurched. He tottered, then came at her with a snarl and his knife upraised and she pushed again, harder, and the rotting wooden balcony came away from its anchoring points in the brickwork with a horrific groaning, splintering noise, and the entire framework collapsed down into itself and sideways in a tumbling chaos of timber and masonry, taking both of them with it. Plummeting, she had just time enough to think, *Well that was —*

Tom heard the collapse and knew instantly that his worst fears had been realised.

'Rachel!' he yelled, and sprinted in the direction of the noise.

When he reached the main hall and saw the wreckage of the balcony, his guts twisted with the certainty that she was dead. Beams and planks jutted at crazy angles from a cloud of dust, and fragments of plaster continued to rain down. He waded into the wreckage, tossing it aside and calling her name.

An arm...

He heaved away several bricks and a table-sized section of floorboards which had fallen across her, and found Rachel lying on her back, covered in dust. Blood trailed from one nostril, showing starkly against the white.

'No,' he moaned. 'No-no-no-no-no...'

He checked for breathing or a pulse, and nearly burst into tears when he found both – weak, but there.

'Hang on, honey,' he begged, as he dug out his phone and dialled 999. 'Hang in there, just for a bit, please.'

Presently, there came the sound of sirens.

THE UMBRA

31

NEAR DEATH

RACHEL WAS IN THE BOW OF A SMALL SAILING BOAT, in bright white fog. Almost motionless, with just the faintest suggestion of a breeze for the sail to catch.

Her father was at the tiller.

She stared, dumbfounded. He wasn't looking at her, but peering past her, into the fog.

'*Daddy?*'

His gaze shifted to her and he smiled.

'Hallo, Trub,' he said. 'Want to take a turn steering this thing?'

She couldn't reply. She couldn't do anything except stare at him. He didn't look sick, or pale, or tired, as he'd done in those last months. He sat easily, his face unlined, his curly brown hair full where chemotherapy had once made him bald. He saw her staring and raised an eyebrow.

'Try not to drill a hole right through me, okay?' he said.

One of the clearest memories she had of her father was sailing on Edgbaston Reservoir. There was a youth sailing club that met every Sunday morning and Thursday afternoons after school, and he would potter around in a canoe while the instructors taught her how to steer one of the little Picos. Her mother never came to watch, saying that she was worried sick that there'd be an accident and couldn't bear to be on edge while her daughter was out on the water. Rachel knew it was because she was an only child, but at the age of eleven didn't yet have an inkling of the frustrating and expensive IVF treatment which had made this so. She heard her mum and dad arguing about it sometimes – Mum found it incomprehensible that he was prepared to risk Rachel's life, while he wasn't prepared to let his daughter grow up wrapped in cotton wool. Being the astute politician that all eleven-year-olds are, Rachel said nothing for as long as the status quo held in her favour and enjoyed her sailing for as long as she could. It was the control she loved. The sense that she could take the apparently random movements of the air and instead of having to put up with whatever it threw in her face, trap it, control it and make it work for her.

All of that stopped the day he died – not just the sailing, but the notion that if the world really chose to get in your face there was anything you could do about it. The narrowboat holiday with Tom had been the first time she'd set foot on any kind of boat for years, and look how that had turned out.

She looked down at herself – she was still an adult, not a child, so this wasn't a memory, and her left hand had returned. She recalled the sensation of falling, her body being hammered by huge, heavy objects.

'Am I dead?' she asked him.

'Good heavens no!' he laughed, then cocked his head to one side and frowned slightly, as if listening. 'Maybe halfway.'

Halfway dead. She knew she should be freaking out – panicking, crying, *something* – and yet the news passed into and through her without causing a ripple. She felt a strange, drowsy numbness, as if the blankness of the white fog had entered her and laced itself through her blood like a dull opiate.

He patted the tiller. 'Seriously, come and take this thing. It's your turn. We'll get back to the boathouse and be home in time for eggy bread.'

Eggy bread. Dad's guilty pleasure breakfast choice of old. White bread soaked in beaten egg and fried until crispy golden-brown and dripping with oil, eaten with brown sauce and a mug of builder's tea. Everything her mother detested about food in one meal.

'I don't want this,' she said, a little surprised at how small her voice sounded. 'Daddy, please. I'm not ready.'

'Nobody ever is, Trub, that's the truth of it, not even if they live to be a hundred. But don't worry, I know what's best. Everything will be fine. All you've got to do is come over here and take your turn at the tiller.'

'You're not my father,' she said, and the horror of it unfolded inside her like dark wings.

'No,' conceded the being that looked like him. 'I'd rather

thought that went without saying. In my defence,' he added hastily, seeing her tense, 'what I am is partly based on your own memories and feelings for your father so I'm not like those others you met. I'm nice.' He smiled hopefully, and despite every nerve screaming at her that this was *Death*, she was in a boat with *Death*, she felt the corners of her own mouth curving up in response because it was her daddy's smile.

She forced them back down again.

'What are you then? Death?'

He laughed. 'No, I'm not Death. That's like asking a farmer if he's Agriculture.' He sighed. 'Okay then. I suppose it can't hurt. I'm a psychopomp.'

'A *what*?'

'I know,' he grimaced. 'It sounds like a bad seventies prog rock band. Blame the ancient Greeks. I'm here to make sure that you get to the next place safely.'

'What is the next place?'

'That depends.'

'On what?'

'Oh, all sorts of things. You won't know until you get there.'

'That's not very helpful, for a guide.'

He shrugged. 'I just guarantee safe passage. The destination is up to you.'

'But I'm not done! Mary is out there in the umbra, and she still needs my help!'

'Does she? She has a death that all parties are satisfied with.'

'How can you say that? She thinks she died a prostitute, at the hands of a client! And it's bullshit – just another story like being a witch or a spy. Are those all the options she has?

Which one would you pick for me, *Dad*?' She threw every ounce of sarcasm she could muster into that word. 'Which bullshit misogynist fantasy would you like to see your little girl spending the rest of eternity living out, over and over again?'

'Trub, listen to me very carefully. Your actions on her behalf, laudable though they may have been, have got you noticed – and not by simple bully boys like the three that came after her, but by... other things. If this boat we're on now were an ordinary human soul, they would be like aircraft carriers in comparison. You do not want to piss them off any more than you have already done, trust me. Cut your losses, accept your death and take this tiller.'

'If you knew anything about my father you'd know that he would never say such a thing.'

'Ha!' He shook his head, more exasperated than angry. 'Oh my dearest baby girl, how certain you are. Your mother obviously never told you, did she?'

'Tell me what?'

'That she was in the middle of divorcing him when the cancer was diagnosed. That once they knew it was terminal there didn't seem any point in carrying through with it, and they decided to let you have what little happiness there was left. That your cosy image of Mummy and Daddy is just another bullshit fantasy, as you put it. Your happy little family tree is hollow right to the core, Rachel, and has been for generations.'

The fog seemed to have got into Rachel's throat, because she couldn't speak. She could barely even breathe.

'You're lying,' she whispered.

'Sorry, Trub, but only the living lie. The dead have no need of it; death is the final, absolute truth.'

'*Shut up!*' she screamed, and jumped to her feet, making the boat rock violently. 'You're not my father!'

'Watch out!' he warned, holding out a hand to steady her. 'You're—'

'Get the fuck away from me!' She recoiled, overbalancing as the deck rocked like the floor of a fairground haunted house, and toppled over the side.

Freezing black water closed over her head, crushing the breath from her lungs. She flailed, panicking, unable to tell which way was up or down, and big flowers of colour grew and burst in her oxygen-starved brain, swelling faster and brighter while her lungs screamed for air until everything was a burning brightness behind her eyelids and

Bed.

She was in a bed.

In hospital.

Tubes: going in, coming out.

The nerve endings in her shredded left hand buzzed and jumped like a dying light bulb.

She'd dreamed about going home and discovering how to touch the limbo world on the other side of reality and rescuing a dead woman and fighting with death itself which had come to claim her threefold but that was ridiculous, wasn't it? The crazy dreams of a brain shocked by the trauma of having her hand first crushed and then amputated. It could never have happened.

She moved her mouth, trying to make sounds, trying to ask somebody where she was.

Am I dead?

A nurse's face swam into view: young, pretty, dark-haired. 'Now then, lovely, of course you're not dead,' she said, smiling and tucking the blankets around Rachel's body, her hands sure and capable. 'You're getting the best care possible. Soon have you fighting fit.' Her face went away, but before it did Rachel caught the impression that she was wearing more make-up than was normal for a nurse, and the starched cap on her head was like something out of an old film.

The light bulb buzzed, flickered, and went out, taking her with it.

32

GHOSTS

'WE HAVE TO STOP MEETING LIKE THIS,' SAID TOM, putting a bag with some fresh clothes for her at the foot of the bed. 'People are starting to talk.'

Rachel struggled into a sitting position. '*Déjà vu* sucks,' she groaned.

'You can say that again.'

'I just did.'

He laughed. 'We're here all week, folks. Try the peppered steak.'

She'd broken both bones in her lower right leg, her collarbone, cracked four ribs, and the doctors wanted to keep an eye on a nasty concussion. Lucky, in other words. The painkillers they had her on were old friends – they pushed the pain to the other side of that wall of dense white fog which allowed just enough recognition of how badly she'd messed herself up again. To paraphrase Oscar Wilde, to hospitalise yourself through one dumbass accident may be regarded as unfortunate; to do it twice looked like carelessness. Something like that, anyway. At least they hadn't cut anything off this time.

He passed her a bottle of water and she swallowed down two small orange pills. His forearms were covered in plasters and a large dressing swathed the last three fingers of his right hand where he'd suffered some cuts and scrapes trying to dig her out.

'Are you okay?' she asked.

'Don't worry about me. If I was any fitter I'd be dangerous.'

She looked around to make sure that they weren't being overheard, and said, 'Tom, when they brought me out, was there any sign of Mary?'

'You need to rest,' he said, patting her hand. 'Your priority now is to get better. Just focus on that.'

'But what about Mary, Tom? Did you see her?'

'I'll be back in a bit with something for you to read – you know, to keep you occupied, stop you worrying about things. *The Guardian*, yes?'

'*Tom—!*'

He stroked her hair away from her brow and kissed her on the forehead. 'Back in a bit,' he repeated, and was gone.

She stared after him. He'd never kissed her like that. Even when she'd been in hospital the first time for her hand, he'd never kissed her like she was a child or an invalid. Nor had he met her eyes when she'd asked after Mary.

That set the tone for his visits from then on. He was by her side as always, loving and patient, but he absolutely refused to discuss anything to do with Mary or the umbra. It was as if he'd simply decided that it hadn't happened, and his brain had reconfigured itself so that whenever she did try to raise the subject, she became inaudible. He would change the conversation, and if she persisted he simply left the ward on some absurdly trivial errand. It was like a curtain coming down between the acts of a play; he brought down a barrier in his mind as strong as anything between the lands of the living and the dead.

And it was maddening.

He was literally the only living human being she could talk to about any of it, and he was pretending like it had never happened. Of two things only was she certain: that Oak Mary was no more a prostitute than a witch or a spy, and that she was determined to get to the truth no matter how much Tom buried his head in the sand. Unable to get answers to her questions, they chased around in her head like cats during the long periods of time when she had no visitors to distract her.

That was why, when she started to see dead people on the ward, she dismissed it at first as the product of her frustrated imagination and the painkillers.

No amount of renovation or twenty-first-century medical equipment could disguise the fact that Birmingham's Royal Orthopaedic Hospital had old bones. In the bed opposite her was a young man who had the look of a surfer or skateboarder – shaggy ginger hair, improbably good-looking – with both legs in plaster to the hip and sprouting pins and braces from them at all angles. For a moment it seemed that his high-tech bed with its servo-controls and monitoring equipment had been replaced by something like a single narrow cot with tubular metal rails and a woollen blanket. Rachel blinked, and the modern bed was back, but she could see the echo of the older model hovering behind. She shook her head harder, closed her eyes and counted to ten, and when she opened them again even the echo had gone. But the ghost bed came back several times over the rest of that day, flickering in and out of her vision.

The phantom sensations had moved – now they were in her head. Maybe the accident had knocked them loose somehow. Maybe part of her was still in the umbra. The buzzing, flickering, twitching, tickling pins and needles that she'd been able to translate into physical sensations had taken root behind her eyes and between her ears, causing shadows to dance at the edges of her vision and echoes to whisper behind the sounds of the world.

Not that this made any difference to the young man; he lay in his bed just as easily either way. Nor did he seem to notice the ragged old woman who appeared once, sitting on the edge and staring vacantly into space, even though her appearance made Rachel recoil so sharply that she smacked the back of her head.

Once spotted, the dead were impossible to ignore. Mostly they were patients in tattered hospital gowns, wandering past with empty expressions as if looking for something they'd lost or couldn't remember. Some were so emaciated that when Rachel first saw one her heart seized in terror at the thought that the inmates of Scoles Farm had found her, and that she'd be besieged in her bed by clinging, desperate shades, unable even to run. They weren't, of course – just souls looking for doctors who couldn't help them or relatives who were themselves long dead. All the same, Rachel sank a little lower in her bed whenever she saw any of them, just to be on the safe side.

She smiled at the nurses who looked after her, responded to their cheerful small talk, and cooperated with the doctors when they did their tests. Sometimes she could tell that they were dead from their old-fashioned uniforms or the fact that they spoke with nobody except her. Other times it was more difficult to tell.

The dark-haired nurse in the starched cap stopped by her bed once in a while to ask how she was doing but never checked her drips, tubes, or dressings, seemingly happy just to hear that her patient was feeling much better. She wore an old-fashioned tunic with a prominent red cross, which might have been from the early twentieth century. She clearly didn't know she was dead, and Rachel didn't have the heart to tell her. It would have seemed rude, if nothing else.

More than anything she wished she could tell Annabel that she now had the Sight too.

Rachel's mother Olivia delivered the news that the Council wasn't going to press trespass and criminal damage charges with regard to Scoles Farm, but she didn't look happy about it. Quite the reverse: she had the pursed, long-suffering look that Rachel had seen many times as a teenager – usually when she'd been determined to do something of which her mother disapproved but couldn't prevent. The look that said *All right then, if you think it's a good idea. I can't stop you of course but I will be right here to pick up the pieces as usual.*

It was possible that Rachel was feeling sorry for herself just the tiniest bit.

'If you ask me,' continued her mother, 'I think they were afraid of the bad publicity they'd get for prosecuting a "disabled person".' She put little air quotes around the words as if they couldn't possibly apply to someone like her daughter. 'You're lucky.'

That word again.

Rachel snorted. A severed hand: the gift that keeps on giving.

'Yes! Lucky! Not to have been killed, for one thing!'

'If I didn't know better,' said Rachel, 'I'd think that you actually wanted us to get arrested.'

'Of course I didn't want you to get arrested,' she replied, and began polishing her glasses. 'What were you doing there?' she asked eventually. 'That's what I don't understand. If you could just give me a reason.'

'I told you why. I was doing a favour for a friend.'

'Yes, so you say. But what friend? The same friend who was with you in the prefab at the Coopers' yard? Oh yes,' she added, seeing Rachel's mouth drop open in surprise. 'I know all about that. Tom and I had a long chat about a lot of things while we were waiting for you to wake up.'

Rachel uttered a hollow laugh. 'That's rich. He'll talk to

you but I can barely get the time of day out of him.'

Her mother sniffed. 'We're not ganging up on you – I don't have an awful lot of time for Tom at the moment. I'm still not convinced that it wasn't all his idea to rope you into going scavenging who knows what from that horrible old building.' She ploughed on as Rachel opened her mouth to protest. 'Oh, I know exactly what these builders get up to. Stealing the lead from church roofs and old copper cables and things like that.'

'Now you're being ridiculous. You *know* Tom! He'd never do anything like that!'

'Do I? Wouldn't he? He was the one who was driving the boat that crushed your poor hand, and I refuse to believe that he couldn't have stopped you going into that place if he'd really tried; he must have known how dangerous it was.'

'Right, let's clear one thing up at least.' Rachel pulled herself higher in the bed, ignoring the pain in her ribs. 'Tom didn't cause the boat accident. I was the one who put myself in harm's way; I was wearing stupid shoes and was too lazy to use the boat pole instead of my hands. If the accident was anybody's fault, it was mine. Still, at least this all explains why you never come to visit me at the same time.' She shook her head. 'I can't believe the pair of you.'

'Can you believe that I am this close to telling the police about this "friend" of yours who you allegedly "found in the woods" and who escaped from the psychiatric institution?'

'Mum, look, it's not that simple—'

'Yes! Yes it is that simple! It's exactly that simple! You

didn't seriously think you could keep me from finding out that you'd almost been shot, did you? Good lord, Rachel, what's been going on with you?'

Rachel could see the wet mirror shine of tears in her mother's eyes, and felt her skin crawl with guilt. Her mother didn't deserve this. None of them did.

'You were making such progress,' Olivia sniffed. 'I don't understand. Your rehab was going well, you were close to going back to work. And now I find out from Tom about the nightmares and the hallucinations, that you're getting mixed up with strange people and, and *violence*? If you could just explain it to me, if I could make some kind of sense of it all…'

But all Rachel could think, as this spilled out of her mother, was what the creature in the boat had said – *They decided to let you have what little happiness there was left* – and she felt the cramping guilt harden into something cruel.

'Were you going to divorce Dad?' she interrupted. 'Before the cancer, I mean?'

Her mother blinked as if she'd been physically slapped, and her face went pale. 'What? Who told you that?'

'Never mind who told me. Is it true?'

'I really don't see what it's got to do with—'

'Because you seem to think I owe you an explanation for everything that's going on in my head and outside of it, and I just think, if it's true, it's a shame you couldn't have extended the same courtesy to me. You must have thought you were doing me a favour – and you probably were, when I was *twelve* – but that was a long time ago.'

Her mother began fussing with her handbag, unable to meet Rachel's eye. 'I don't know where this has come from. It doesn't have anything to do with your situation.'

'It has everything to do with it!' Because if it was true then what the psychopomp had said about their family being hollow might also be true, and Rachel was starting to have some very uncomfortable ideas as to where Oak Mary fit into it all. Why had her last words been the name of Rachel's grandfather? Why had she fixated on Rachel at all? 'Just tell me. Were you going to divorce him?'

Her mother sighed and took a Kleenex from the box beside the bed and dabbed her eyes. When she spoke, it was to the tissue in her hands, not Rachel. 'Your father was a charming man. He could talk the birds out of the trees and then the feathers off the birds, my mum said. Except what she really meant was that he could talk the knickers off the birds, which is what he did. Frequently. Charming men need to be seen to be charming – they need to be appreciated – but it stops being fun when the little birdies stop being dazzled by the shiny surface and start to notice what's underneath, because they're afraid that what's underneath isn't very nice. The tragic thing about your father was that he *was* nice underneath – his penchant for young office assistants aside, of course – but he just couldn't see it. And eventually I stopped trying to help him see it because it became just too bloody humiliating.'

Rachel reached for her mother's hand, and felt her fingers stiffen for a moment as if about to flinch away, but then relax and allow themselves to be held.

'Yes,' her mother continued. 'I should have told you a long time ago. But ask yourself, when do you think is a good time to tell your daughter that the dead father she adored was a philanderer?'

Rachel couldn't answer that.

'I'm sorry,' Olivia said. 'I shouldn't have pushed you just now. I can't imagine the kind of stress you must be under.' She gathered her things together and got to her feet. 'I'm going to leave now. But you need to know what else Tom told me.' She fidgeted, plainly uncomfortable with what she had to say next. 'He said that you think you've been talking to dead people.'

The extent of Tom's betrayal stunned Rachel into a silence that her mother obviously mistook for guilt. 'I don't think you're... *well*, darling,' Olivia went on. 'I've called in a personal favour and asked someone from the hospital's psychiatric liaison service to stop by, unofficially. I can't force you to talk to her, but I hope you're going to co-operate because, frankly, I'm at my wits' end.' She shrugged. 'I don't know. Maybe you'll just be as prickly with her as you are with me.' She turned to go, and then half-turned back. 'There's nothing...' she started, then seemed to choke on something and tried again. 'It isn't... you mustn't feel... afraid. Of asking for help.'

She placed a dry kiss on Rachel's forehead and left.

Ashamed, Rachel thought. *You were going to say I shouldn't feel ashamed.*

33

LIAISON

THE NEXT TIME OLIVIA VISITED, SHE BROUGHT WITH her a serious young woman who spoke with the soft, rounded tones of an East European accent as she introduced herself as Ms Dasha Korovina, a member of the hospital's liaison psychiatry team. She was eating a sandwich.

'I'm not a doctor,' she said. 'This isn't even an appointment. I'm on my lunch break, actually. Do you feel up to having a chat?'

Rachel darted a swift look at her mother and smiled. 'Of course.'

Korovina sat on the chair beside the bed. 'It's important that you understand I'm not trying to trap you into saying something that you don't want to say; I'd just like to find out how you feel about some things.'

For some reason Rachel found the way Korovina sat so casually, eating her lunch and flicking stray crumbs from her blouse, a bit disconcerting. 'Aren't you going to take notes or something?'

'Would you like me to?'

'No, it's fine. I trust you.'

'You know, I don't often hear that phrase.'

'That's because you spend all your time talking to crazy people.'

Korovina smiled politely while her mother winced. She started by asking about how Rachel had lost her hand, how she was coping physically, did she find it frustrating, did she blame anybody for the accident? Then, how was she eating? Sleeping? Did she have any pets? (Yes, Smoky, though Rachel didn't think it wise to explain where she'd found him.) Did she take any exercise? How did she feel about the prospect of being in a cast for the next couple of months? Did she enjoy her job? Did she have friends there? Old school friends? Had she made any new friends either through rehab or since losing her hand? How had she felt when her father had died? Had there been arguments at home? Had she self-harmed, either then or ever?

Rachel carefully avoided mentioning Oak Mary or any of her incarnations, and for her part Korovina asked nothing specific about the events either at the prefab or the asylum. The whole process lasted for the better part of an hour.

'I'm afraid this last one is going to sound a little extreme,' Korovina admitted. 'And again you don't have to answer, but I have to ask: have you ever had suicidal thoughts?'

'No,' replied Rachel instantly. 'Never. The absolute last thing I want is to die.'

Korovina gave Rachel her card and said that she was free to call if she ever changed her mind about seeing a doctor, or just wanted to talk, and recommended the names of some mild anti-anxiety medications if she thought they would help in the meantime. She thanked Rachel for her time, and her mother saw her out of the ward. Rachel watched them go, talking quietly between themselves.

When Olivia returned, Rachel gave her a thin, cold smile. 'Well,' she said, 'we're having conversations about drugs, then. Good job. I should be much easier to control now, shouldn't I?'

'Darling—'

'Drugs won't make any difference.' She didn't bother trying to explain why. There was no way to tell her that throughout the duration of her conversation with Korovina an old dead man had been sitting on the end of the bed, dressed only in grubby striped pyjama trousers, the skin of his rake-thin chest blooming with tumours as he wept silently and inconsolably.

The dark-haired nurse in the starched apron and cap was back, and Rachel discovered with surprise that she'd been missing her and looking forward to her next visit.

'Thank you,' she said, as the dead woman fussed around her. 'What's your name?'

'My name?' asked the nurse. 'Why, it's Patsy. Patsy Humphries. And may I say, thank you for taking the trouble to thank me.'

'Is that unusual?'

'Most of my patients aren't what you'd call the talkative type.'

Probably because they're not even aware that you're there, Rachel thought. She was going to have to phrase her questions carefully. She wondered how she appeared, and what the hospital looked like from Nurse Humphries' point of view. 'I imagine they're probably not feeling very well. How long have you been working here?'

Nurse Humphries laughed. 'How long is a piece of string?'

'I mean you must see an awful lot of sick people through here.'

'Some times more than others, but don't you worry yourself with what you read in the papers. This little Spanish flu thing will burn itself out before you can say *olé!* She laughed again and snapped her fingers in the air like a flamenco dancer. Turning serious again, she regarded Rachel sadly. 'I hope you don't mind me saying so, but I couldn't help overhearing you and your mother arguing.'

'Oh that,' Rachel snorted. 'Don't pay any attention to us. She means well but there's nothing she can do to help and I can't tell her without having her think I'm a mental case. I'm afraid it's making me a bit of a pain. At the end of the day she and I are all we've got. You should have been a fly on the wall when I was fourteen.'

'Well, if you say so. Now you get some rest and I'll be back soon.' And with that, Nurse Humphries strode off smartly to visit another patient. Whether they were living or dead, Rachel didn't think it mattered all that much.

* * *

'Mum,' Rachel said, on Olivia's next visit, 'what did Gigi do during the war?'

Her mother looked up from the bedside flowers she'd been arranging. 'What an odd question. Why do you ask?'

'I don't know, I sort of got the impression she was a nurse or something like that. Humour me. It helps to take my mind off my leg.'

Put like that, her mother could hardly refuse. 'She was in the Women's Volunteer Service. I believe she was a driver for a while, delivering all sorts of things all over the country. At least until she and your great-grandfather got married, then she stayed home to look after her family.'

That was a surprise. 'Gigi, a truckie?' Rachel thought of the articulated lorries she saw from the screens of her operator's station, endlessly plying the routes of the motorway network, and tried to imagine her urbane great-grandmother with a beer belly and tattoos and a filthy teddy bear tied to the front of her rig – then immediately regretted it because, despite the pain meds, laughing felt like being stabbed with knives.

'Apparently so,' her mother murmured.

'So she got to travel all over the country but when she had a baby she hung up her air horn and settled right back in Birmingham to be a housewife with Great-Granddad Albert?'

'That's the way it happened, my love, for most people. When the men came back from the war everybody settled back into their old roles.'

Except that their son Stephen, Rachel's grandfather, may have been born in Manchester. It was nothing, a tiny thread out of place in the grand tapestry of her family history, barely worth worrying over, especially from a time so long ago when so many records had been destroyed and so much was confusing. But Rachel couldn't stop herself from plucking at it, even though she was afraid of what knotted secret might come loose. Heath had said that Oak Mary had been dying when they'd found her, and with only one word on her lips. *Stephen.* It was tempting to think that a connection was impossible – that it was just a coincidence of a mocking universe. But why was there such a strong connection between her and Mary? Rachel had dreamed Mary's life – or versions of lives – in vivid detail. And anyway, 'impossible' was a fine word to use when you'd fought hand-to-hand with death itself.

'Will you please take me to see her?'

This seemed to genuinely surprise Olivia. 'Gigi? You want to visit her now? I don't think you're in any kind of state to go anywhere. And it's not as if you've been particularly interested in spending time with her before.'

'There's an awful lot of old people in this hospital, Mum. I've been watching them.' *And not all of them are alive, either.* 'And I just... after what happened to me... oh God this is going to sound so stupid. It's all so brief, you know? Life? So easily taken away.'

This had started out simply as an attempt to persuade her mother to give her a lift, but Rachel soon felt the truth of it welling up inside her, filling her throat, and brimming from her eyes. 'I thought I was going to die, Mum, you know?' Her voice was thick with tears. 'I really thought I was going to die.'

Then her mum was crying too and holding her, and for a moment there were no hidden agendas, no point scoring or hinted accusations – just her mum, holding her, and everything was okay.

34

GIGI

OLIVIA WAS AS GOOD AS HER WORD, AND, ON A drizzling afternoon in September after Rachel had been discharged, took her to see Gigi.

Her great-grandmother was sitting in her customary wingback chair by the front bay window of the nursing home, looking out over the green sweep of lawn and the driveway that curved up to it, bordered by neat flowerbeds and a line of whitewashed stones. It was a still, dripping Thursday afternoon. The ache in Rachel's leg wasn't too bad, and her mum had phoned ahead to be told by the duty nurse that Gigi was having one of her good days.

She tutted when she turned from the window and saw Rachel limping across the residents' lounge, crutching one-handed. 'Oh my dear,' she said. 'Look at you! You have been in the wars!'

Rachel gave a wry smile. 'You could say that. Hello, Gigi.'

She bent to kiss Gigi's cheek. Her skin was so feather-light with age that Rachel could barely feel it at all. She was wearing slippers, a simple peach-coloured dress and a pale yellow cardigan embroidered with flowers. Her hair was so fine that it was more of a silver nimbus around her head, but an attempt had been made to style it and there was a suggestion of colour on her cheeks and lips. The nurses had obviously helped her to make an effort because she was having visitors, and it made Rachel feel guilty because if there hadn't been something she wanted from the old lady she wouldn't have come.

Rachel's mother followed and also planted a dutiful kiss.

'Thank you for bringing her, Olivia,' said Gigi.

'You're welcome, Gigi. Are you well?'

'I'm ninety-six years old – of course I'm not well,' she chuckled. 'I'm a bloody miracle.'

The nurse – a permanently smiling young man with an alarming monobrow – brought tea and biscuits. Gigi drank something from a cup and saucer which looked like diluted dishwater, and clucked and tutted as she watched Rachel handle everything one-handed.

'Such a shame about your poor hand,' she said. 'It must be awful for you.'

'Oh I don't know,' Rachel replied. 'You can get used to anything after a while.'

There was talk, then, of hospitals and doctors, medicines and maladies, and the fluctuating fortunes of distant family members whose names meant nothing to Rachel, and may not even have still been alive. The Canadian branch of the clan was considered, and plans put forward for Christmas, and Gigi asked after Tom and how work was progressing on their house.

'Oh no!' Rachel slapped her forehead in what she hoped was a convincing show of surprise, and turned to her mother. 'I printed out some photos of the house and I've left them in your car. Sorry – could you please get them for me?'

Her mother rolled her eyes in mock despair, and left to get them.

Rachel pulled her chair a little closer to Gigi and lowered her voice.

'Gigi,' she said. 'I've really come to ask about Grandpa Stephen. Your son.'

Her great-grandmother heaved a deep sigh and was silent for so long, gazing out at the grey-gleaming afternoon, that Rachel thought she hadn't heard her. How much time did they have until her mother returned?

'He was so like your father,' Gigi said eventually. 'So handsome. So clever. And he was such a good man. Albert and I couldn't have wished for a finer boy of our own.'

'Of your own? What do you mean?'

Gigi's voice was faint and murmurous, as if she were talking to herself. 'He made so much noise, that was the thing. Albert and I could hear him clear through the walls from next door, every night, night after night. The bombs scared him, poor little mite. Lord knows how that poor girl coped. "Good lungs on that lad," Albert would say. "He'll make a proper opera singer."'

There was another long pause while Gigi stared out of the

window, though it was obvious that whatever she was seeing, it wasn't the lawn and the drizzle-glazed driveway. Rachel began to worry that she'd unwittingly triggered an episode of her great-grandmother's dementia. Was it anything like what Rachel herself saw when she looked into the umbra? The thought of what shades might inhabit a nursing home daunted her, but despite her misgivings she let her Sight slip into the umbra to see what Gigi was looking at.

The bay window was replaced by a gas fireplace in a small, dark sitting room, made to feel even more enclosed by floral wallpaper and heavy furniture. Rachel found herself sitting on a dining chair at a small table. In an armchair was a young man she didn't recognise, with Brylcreemed hair and a pencil moustache, frowning at a massive old radiogram set, which lay in pieces on the coffee table before him. Across from him...

Rachel gasped when she saw how young Gigi looked. She was darning a sock, but still managed to look like a movie star: her hair was dark and lustrous, unlike the wispy cloud of old age that showed the shape of her skull, and even though she had no make-up on the unexpected smoothness of her skin gave her an almost visible glow. She wore no glasses and wasn't even squinting as she worked. Her eyesight, like everything else, was perfect in youth. She couldn't have been much older than in her early twenties; the man opposite must be her husband, Rachel's great-grandfather Albert, who she'd only ever seen in fading black-and-white photographs. Neither of them seemed to have noticed her, intent on their make-do-and-mending.

Rachel's confusion deepened as she realised that this wasn't a decaying echo of the nursing home; these weren't the hollow shades of the dead. This place felt real and alive. Then it hit her: this was a memory. Gigi's mind was wandering in the past and somehow shaping the umbra around her as she relived her youth. Whatever the umbra was, it was more than simply a parallel existence for everything dead – maybe it was somehow reactive to the memories and yearnings of the souls that inhabited it.

Then Rachel heard it – through the walls, faint but insistent: the crying of a baby. The infant's squalling was inescapable, a hoarse, pitiless sound, as if the baby had been screaming for many hours already. It desperately needed feeding, or changing, or both.

Then Caroline turned to look straight at her and said: 'Honestly, Bea, I think it's about time you came back and saw to the little mite, don't you?'

Rachel recoiled and her Sight returned to the living world where Caroline was Gigi again, gazing out at the watery daylight through thick spectacles. A moment later Rachel's mother returned, holding the photographs that Rachel had strategically left in her car. 'Here you go,' she said, handing them to her daughter and looking around. 'Now then, who does one talk to about scaring up another cup of tea?'

* * *

NAME: **Beatrice Rebecca Eaton**

Rachel stared at the name on her tablet.

BORN: **22 October 1919**
MARITAL STATUS: **S**
OCCUPATION: **labouring; factory worker**
ADDRESS: **34 Queens Rd, Birmingham, Warwickshire**
OTHERS AT THIS ADDRESS: **Stephen Arthur Eaton (b. 1942)**

Even though many census records had been destroyed and electoral rolls suspended during the war, the information had been surprisingly easy to find. There were any number of ancestry-tracing websites available, and all of them at some point linked to the archived database of the wartime Identity Card Register. Knowing Caroline's and Albert's full names returned their address in 1943, and with that Rachel had checked the records of the houses on either side. She even looked at it using a street view app: a steeply gabled little terraced two-up two-down with a neat front garden and a Neighbourhood Watch sign on the lamppost out front.

Beatrice's son was Stephen Arthur Eaton. He'd been born in Manchester. Her grandfather's name had been Stephen Arthur Howson. She found a record of his death, but no evidence that he'd ever been born.

'What did you do, Gigi?' Rachel whispered to the screen. 'What did you and Albert do?'

35

THE TALE OF BLACK MEG

FOR ALMOST A MONTH AFTER THE HOSPITAL SENT Rachel home, she did everything she could to make Tom believe that she'd put the business of Oak Mary behind her. She did her physio exercises, watched television, drank tea, completed what chores she could, and even started hobbling around her old running routes. On the last Sunday in September they ordered an Indian takeaway, and on the Monday morning he left for work with a peck on the cheek which turned into a longer kiss that told her he evidently thought they were on the long, slow road back to normality. She waved him off with her single hand, the very existence of which should have told him that normality was beyond her reach forever, and went inside to call a taxi.

* * *

The cab ride to the Cooper's yard was expensive, but there was no way she was going to beg a lift off anyone; the chance that they might have told Tom was too great. She asked to be dropped off on the empty roadside and then made her halting, stumbling way on her single crutch to the old prefab house through the woodland just as Mary's deaths had done, but once she got there she realised that her efforts at remaining hidden had been unnecessary – for the moment, at least, the place was deserted.

Except that it wasn't entirely deserted, just by the living.

Rachel remembered the voice that had awoken her before the attack. *Wake up, girl! Wake up!* She'd thought it had been the remnant of a dream, but now she knew better.

She let her Sight slip into the umbra and saw that where, in the living world, the prefab was surrounded by nothing more than overgrown grass and weeds, in the umbra it had a neat picket fence, tubs of flowers and a wicker chair out the front. A sandy-haired man in a string vest and baggy trousers was digging in a small vegetable garden behind the house. He was forking over clumps of earth and had a sheen of perspiration on his face, and looked so alive that if she hadn't already known he was dead it would not have occurred to her for a moment. It was nearly October, harvest time was all but done, and he was putting his vegetable patch to bed for the first frost. Were there even seasons in the umbra? Maybe there were if you wanted them strongly enough.

'Excuse me,' she said, in a tiny voice of which she was instantly ashamed, so she went around the side of the prefab to where he was working and said it louder, adding: 'I can see you, you know.'

He stuck his fork in the soil and turned to look her up and down. 'Oh you can, can you? And hear me too, I'll bet.'

His manner was more curious than aggressive. He had a narrow face with a big nose and wonky teeth, which might easily have seemed threatening, but his smile was warm and wide and made deep dimples appear in his cheeks.

'I'm Rachel,' she said, putting out her left hand – she could see it, even though it wasn't there. 'I think you might have saved my life. I wanted to say thank you.'

He eyed the offered hand with amused scepticism. 'I think you might have the wrong idea about me, miss.'

'Humour me,' she replied.

Slowly, he reached for her, and his eyes widened in surprise as their fingers made contact and she shook his hand firmly. His grip was warm, the skin roughened by labour; nothing like the shades at Scoles Farm Asylum and not in the least like that of a ghost.

'Well go to the foot of our stairs!' he laughed. 'How'd you pull that trick?'

'Make us a cup of tea and I'll tell you,' she said.

The interior of the prefab was utterly different to what she remembered: the random clutter and mess left by the Coopers' itinerant workers had been replaced by an immaculately tidy, if spartan, home. There was a newspaper folded on the coffee table and a pipe in an ashtray next to a radiogram like the one she'd seen in Gigi's memories. He walked through to the kitchen and put a kettle on the hob, which he lit from a pack of Pilot matches.

'Have a seat,' he said, shaking out the match. She could smell it, the pungency of sulphur. 'You look like you need it.' He nodded at her crutch and cast. 'You've been in the wars, eh? Oliver,' he added. 'Sewell. Sorry, I should have said before. I'm not used to this. Chatting. I don't get much opportunity to. Not with, you know…' He stopped, embarrassed.

'The living?' she finished for him.

'Hmm.' He took down a battered tin and spooned loose-leaf tea into an old brown teapot. 'No. Women.'

She laughed.

'I shouldn't have been surprised, though,' he went on. 'That you could, you know, with the hand. I saw what you did to those others, the ones that came for you and your friend. Handy, that was. 'Scuse the pun.'

'You saw what happened?'

'Yep. Saw it all. I should've helped more, sorry.'

'Oh no, no. You helped just enough. Besides, those others? I don't think you'd have come off well against them somehow.'

'Hmm.' He reached down a biscuit tin covered in pictures of daisies, removed the lid and offered it to her. 'Custard cream?'

She hesitated, wondering what the damage might be, and decided that a single biscuit couldn't do much harm. 'Why not? Thanks.' She took one with her dead hand and transferred it to her living one, thinking, *Ghost biscuits!*, and had to stifle the urge to laugh. She didn't want to have to explain it to him; maybe the word 'ghost' wasn't politically correct. *Corporeally challenged*, she thought, and this time had to disguise her laugh as a coughing fit.

'Are you all right?' he asked.

'I'm fine,' she waved it away, pointing at her throat. 'Just a crumb. Went down the wrong way.'

'Well don't choke to death, will you?' he replied. 'You're pretty and all, but I'm not that desperate for company.' And he actually winked at her.

'Are you… are you flirting with me?'

'I may be dead,' he said, 'but I'm not that dead.' The kettle started to boil, so he filled the pot and put a knitted tea cosy over it, blew the dust out of a decent cup and saucer for her, and found a chipped old mug for himself. Beneath her hand a patch of mould had bloomed on the table's linoleum surface in reaction to her taking the biscuit, but he didn't seem to have noticed.

'So you know you're… I mean you don't mind…'

Oliver let her flounder for a moment. 'Well I'm not sure what else you'd call it. How is your friend? Is she all right?'

It was like cold water to the face. 'No. No she's not at all right, I'm afraid.'

'Ah,' he nodded sadly. 'Redcaps got her after all, did they?'

'Uh, Redcaps?'

'I'm sorry. Army slang for military police. Closest thing I can think of to what they are – you know, keeping the troops in line, sticking to curfew. Dragging them back if necessary.'

'You know them?' She leaned forward eagerly.

He made a face. 'I wouldn't say *know* them. I don't think they've ever been men, or even alive, really. But I've seen them. Seen one, anyway. My one.'

'*Your* one?'

'We all get one, on the day we pass. You'll get one too,' he added, and the matter-of-fact way in which he referred to her death raised gooseflesh on the back of her neck. It briefly crossed her mind to tell him about the being that had worn the face of her father, but it was still too raw. He checked the pot, poured tea for them both, added milk for her and sugar for himself, then sat back and sipped. 'They're guides, or maybe guards. For me, it was the eleventh of March 1982. I was sixty-four years old, just like in the song. I know I don't look it but this is what I always looked like on the inside, so.' He shrugged. 'It was in the room next door.'

'Wait,' she said. 'You died in this building?'

'Of course – why do you think I'm still here? It was quick; there was a growth,' he shrugged again. 'You don't want to hear the details. My Ruthie was there, and my boys. They wanted me in a hospital but I'm a stubborn old bird and I wasn't having any of that. I was given this place on Wake Green Road when I was demobbed and me and Ruthie lived in it for over thirty years, and if you'd grown up in the slums I grew up in you wouldn't want to leave neither.

'So I'm lying there and it doesn't even really hurt that much any more and that's how I know I'm close, and there's Ruthie and Nick and Peter and a doctor whose name I forget, and behind them...' He laughed shortly, shaking his head at the memory. 'Sister Margaret,' he said. 'Black Meg, we used to call her in school, dressed in her nun's clobber like a big black crow, and with that look on her face, the one she had when she was beating you for whatever little thing you'd done wrong. Like she was hungry and about to puke both at the same time. She looked at me with that look and said, "Are you about ready now, Oliver?" as if I'd been keeping her waiting for something more important and I said, "Yes, Sister," so she sort of reached past my family without moving and took me by the hand and I got up and left myself behind and that was that.'

'So Sister Margaret was your Redcap?'

'Yes she was. That was the first and last time she ever touched me. She wiped her hand on the front of her habit like she'd touched something filthy and said, "Well come on then if you're coming." So I went with her and she took me to the front door – same front door you came in by just now – and there was something outside, something that she'd brought with her, that I just wasn't ready for. I was in the Normandy landings, did you know that?'

Rachel shook her head.

'Sword Beach, Third Infantry. Coming off those landing boats into German machine-gun fire was the single most terrifying experience of my life, next to my wedding day, but I'd have done it a hundred times rather than face what was on the other side of that door. I looked back at my family and my home and I turned to Black Meg – or the Redcap that looked like her, anyway – and I said, "Begging your pardon, Sister, but if it's all the same to you I think I'll stop here for a bit."'

'And what did she say?'

'Well you could tell that she wasn't happy. She said, "Are you sure that's what you want, Oliver?" with a kind of sneer like I was eleven years old again and too thick to decide which nostril to pick first. I squared myself and said, "Yes, Sister." She gave a sniff like it was nothing to her one way or the other. "Suit yourself," she said. "But just you mind my words, boy. Not everyone gets offered this, and rarely more than once. You'd better be damned sure."

'The thing is, I knew I should have left, but Ruthie was still crying over my body and the lads were having to hold her up. "I'm sure," I said.

'Then Black Meg was gone, and whatever she'd brought with her was gone too, and outside it was just the road. When my estate came to be settled nobody wanted to keep this place so it got sold and moved and I came with it. Ruthie passed a while later, and I really thought she'd come here with me, but she didn't. That broke my heart, and I came this close to calling for Black Meg and asking if whatever had been on offer was still there.

'But then Amy – that's my eldest boy Nick's daughter – turned up one day with *her* children. I don't know how she found it, out here in the middle of nowhere. She was telling them stories of how their granddad had fought in the war and how their own dad had played in this house, and I watched them playing in this kitchen where their dad used to watch Ruthie baking cakes, and I knew why I was still here. Am I making any sense?'

'More than you know,' said Rachel.

'I saw them all joined together, sort of in a line, like. I'd heard the word bloodline, but never really thought about what it meant. Or more like a ribbon. Everyone joined to

398

everyone else, and I knew that as long as they kept coming and remembering me, then I'd be here. Because there's nothing stronger than that line. It doesn't matter how far it stretches or how thin it gets, it doesn't break.'

Oliver gave a little shudder, as if coming back to himself, then saw the rapt way Rachel was staring at him and ducked his head, reddening. 'I'm sorry,' he said. 'Wittering on like that. Like I said, it's been a while since I've actually talked to anyone – least, anyone that could hear me.'

'Please,' she said. 'Don't apologise. This is exactly the sort of thing I've been desperate to find out for ages now.'

He shrugged. 'I can't claim to be an expert. You might want to be talking to a priest. What do you want to know?'

'Well, about your vegetable garden, for a start.'

He laughed in surprise. 'You want to know about my broad beans?'

'In a manner of speaking. How can they be there? I mean, the place where you are – the Redcaps call it the umbra – as far as I can tell it's a shadow of the world; the world that's dead and gone. I'm pretty sure there wasn't ever a vegetable patch where this building is now, so how can there be one on your side of things? How can something be growing?'

'I put a lot of work into that garden,' Oliver said proudly. 'You don't think I was going to give it up that easy, do you?'

'So it exists because you want it to strongly enough.'

'Maybe. So did the Redcaps get your friend, then?'

'Yes.'

'Ah now, that's a shame.'

They sat there for a while in silence, the living and the

dead. Finally Oliver cleared his throat. 'I saw everything that happened, that night,' he said. 'Heard everything you and your friend said. I want to help if I can. Those Redcaps are bastards. Always have been.'

'That's very kind, but I don't think you want to get mixed up in this business. You've been more than helpful as it is.'

'No, but see, I can help you look for her. On this side. It can be… unpredictable. You could do with a guide.' There was an edge to his voice that was more than just the desire to help; he was tapping the side of his mug with one fingernail, and it made a nervous little *tik-tik-tik* noise. 'I just…' he faltered, swallowed, and tried again. 'I know you brought her back. And I just thought, if I helped you find her you might, in return…'

'Oh no,' said Rachel, suddenly realising what he was getting at and shaking her head firmly. 'No way. You don't know what you're asking.'

'Not permanently!' His desperation was naked now. 'I'll go back, you have my word! Just for a day, maybe not even that. Just so I can talk to my boys properly, one last time. Please!'

'No.' Rachel's heart twisted for him, but there was nothing she could do, and it made her refusal brutal. 'Black Meg will come for you, and she'll carve her way through anyone and anything to take you back. I've seen it happen. I won't do it. Please don't ask me.' She drained the last of her tea in a hasty gulp and stood. 'I'm sorry. I shouldn't have come. It's not fair on you.'

'What's not fair is that you've got this wonderful gift and you refuse to share it!' he retorted.

'It's not a gift,' Rachel said. Memories of the emaciated shades at the asylum hovered around her like shadows. Oliver seemed nice enough, but she didn't want to see how far his desperation might push him. 'It was an accident.'

'Please! You don't know what it's like! You don't know what—'

Rachel withdrew her Sight from the umbra and tugged her stump-sock back on to deaden her Touch, cutting off the sight and sound of him instantly. She was standing in the prefab's dingy kitchen with nothing but sunlight and birdsong for company. All the same, she knew that he was just on the other side of the bright air, probably still pleading. It wasn't fair. He had no right to ask that of her.

'I'm sorry,' she repeated to the not-empty room, knowing that he could hear her but not respond, and feeling an utter shit about it. 'For what it's worth, I am grateful though.'

Rachel stepped out of the prefab and flicked up her hood, wondering how long she'd have to wait for a taxi to take her home again. She was so distracted that she didn't spot the Peugeot that must have pulled into the yard while she was talking to Oliver. Then she heard an 'Ahem!' and a man walked out from around the side of the prefab.

Tom's dad Spence did not look happy.

36

SHUFFLING OFF

SPENCE'S PEUGEOT WAS FULL OF TOOLS AND REEKED of dog, and the air in the car was thickened by the tension as Rachel's father-in-law drove in silence. Finally, however, it became too much.

'For God's sake!' he burst out. 'What was I supposed to do? Leave you in there talking to yourself?'

'I suppose that's what it must have looked like,' Rachel agreed.

'Must have looked like? Your mother and Tom both think you're having some kind of breakdown, do you know that?'

'No, but it doesn't surprise me.'

Spence peered at her so intently that Rachel began to be afraid that he'd forgotten he was driving. 'Well they might think you're going wampy,' he said. 'But you're not fooling me.'

'I'm not trying to fool anyone. I just want people to stop interfering in my business.'

Spence hmphed. 'Business, she calls it. Men with guns on my property and she calls it "business". Guns! In my yard! And that's the best explanation you can come up with?'

'I'm sorry,' she whispered.

'Sorry,' muttered Spence, scowling at the road. 'She's sorry.' He drove one-handed as he took out his phone and called his son.

Rachel shouldn't have been surprised to see Tom's van and her mother's Audi in the drive, but there was a third strange car – something small and powder-blue. When Rachel let herself into the house she found out why: Ms Korovina from psychiatric liaison was sitting on the sofa in the living room next to her mother, while Tom was doing something with a screwdriver to one of the kitchen cupboards, which was a sure sign that he was agitated.

'I've got her,' said Spence, as they entered. Her mother rose from the sofa and Rachel saw with wry amusement the restraining hand that Korovina put on her arm. Tom stopped fiddling and came over.

'Is she okay?' he asked.

'I'm fine, thanks,' Rachel retorted. 'Busy day at work, darling? Oh wait, it's only lunchtime. Must be the *drugs*.'

Her mother winced at the word. *Good*.

'She was at the yard,' continued Spence. 'She was in the prefab, talking to herself.'

'Is this true?' asked her mother.

'Actually, no,' said Rachel. She pulled off her stump-sock,

balled it up and tossed it to Tom, who caught it in surprise. 'I was talking to a very nice, sad man called Oliver Sewell. He's been dead for some time so his social skills aren't quite what they were, but then whose are, eh?'

'And have you spoken to him before?' asked Korovina, in the calm and non-judgemental professional voice of a mental health worker talking to a paranoid schizophrenic.

'No,' Rachel replied. 'But it's not the first time we've met. The first time, he woke me when I'd fallen asleep so he probably saved my life – mine and Annabel's. That was the night her deaths tried to claim her back and shot up the prefab. But Tom knows all about that, don't you, dear? You were there, after all.'

All eyes in the room turned to Tom. 'Rachel, I—'

'What? You what, Tom? You agree with me? You admit I'm telling the truth? You've finally decided to man up and talk to me about all of this?'

'I thought,' he replied carefully, 'that if I went along with it and said I believed you, I could find a way of making you see that it was all in your head.'

'Oh no!' Rachel laughed, wagging her stump at him like an admonishing finger. It also had the effect of getting the pins and needles going. Waking up the phantoms. 'No, you don't get away with it that easily. It was your idea to go to the library, remember? You weren't just humouring me, you were actively encouraging me. You know that everything I've said is true and that everything that's happened is real. It put you in hospital, remember? It came through the cat flap after Smoky. You told me about the ghost that saved your life, that night on the motorway. So why are you lying?'

Maybe it was her scornful laughter, or the accusation of lying, or the weeks of bottling up what he knew to be true, but something snapped in her husband.

'Because I have to protect you!' Tom yelled. 'That's what I do! I'm the one who's supposed to stop all this shit from happening to you, not cause it!'

'You still blame yourself for the narrowboat, don't you?'

'Of course I do! I was driving the bloody thing, wasn't I?' She saw the way his eyes darted to her mother, and a second sharper realisation stabbed her.

'And you do too, don't you?' Rachel asked Olivia. 'You blame him. Did you threaten him with going to the police after the asylum?' She turned back to Tom. 'Is that why you stopped talking to me about all of this? Did she get to you?'

'Get to him?' said her mother. 'Listen to yourself, darling.'

'I know exactly what I sound like, thanks. You've all done a very good job of making me out to be some kind of mental case. And I know,' she closed her eyes and breathed deeply, trying to calm herself. 'I know that's how it comes across. But *he* knows differently,' she added, opening her eyes again and pointing at Tom. 'And that's what really hurts.'

'You want to know what really hurts?' he shot back. 'Seeing you sitting around here like a junkie – you don't wash, you don't get dressed, you don't do anything around the house except stare at that fucking tablet of yours googling death and ghosts and your own bloody family tree, and what's *that* about anyway?'

Olivia turned to Tom. 'I thought you said she was getting better.'

She glared at him through slitted eyes. 'You've been spying on my browsing history? You dick!'

'Rachel,' interrupted Korovina. 'I don't blame you for feeling stressed and angry, and I want to help. Do you accept that?'

'Yes,' Rachel sighed, suddenly bone-weary. There was no point fighting any more. They'd left her with only one option.

'Perhaps it would be best if you could have a timeout for a couple of days, somewhere away from the people and the places that are upsetting you. We can go in my car right now. Would you like that?'

'Yes,' Rachel repeated. 'I would like that very much.'

Her mother clasped her hands together and gave a little tearful cry. 'Oh my darling, that is so good to hear!'

'Do you mind if I pop upstairs and get some things first?'

'Of course not, darling, of course not. Let me help.'

'Thanks, Mum.'

Taking her handbag, Rachel let her mother follow her upstairs. 'I'll go and get a suitcase from the back bedroom,' she suggested. 'Can you just pick me out whatever you think would be useful? Nothing with too many laces or buttons, though.' She held up her stump with a rueful smile. 'Bit tricky these days.'

There was actually nothing tricky about them at all, but it had the desired effect of making her mother's eyes tear up. Now she would focus on finding exactly the right clothes, and not for one moment would it enter her head that Rachel might be more capable than she'd been before the accident. Her mother folded her into a hug, stroking her hair, and for a moment Rachel almost let herself enjoy it.

'It's going to be okay,' Olivia said, her breath hot against Rachel's ear. 'It's all going to be okay.'

'I know, Mum. I know.' She pulled away.

While her mother went into the main bedroom at the front of the house and started opening drawers, Rachel went into the back bedroom, closing the door very quietly. She crossed to the old sash window which overlooked the kitchen extension and opened it, wincing at the squeak of unoiled pulleys, and eased herself over the sill and onto the flat tarpaper roof, pulling her crutch after her. Her leg cast clattered against the wood, and she expected someone to come running to stop her at any moment. She limped to the far end of the roof and peered over the edge at the patio, the garden tubs, the jungle of untended lawn and shrubbery that had become overgrown in the last month, and finally the back fence. If Tom was looking through the kitchen windows he would see her drop down and she would be screwed. She had to hope that he, his dad and Ms Korovina were in the living room talking about her.

This was going to be awkward, and quite likely very painful.

She turned her back on the drop, knelt on her good left leg with her cast sticking out, and eased herself over, bracing her left elbow on the edge and gripping with her right hand. It made her hang diagonally and when she dropped to the patio with a grunt, the impact shot a jarring pain up her injured leg and into her groin.

Move! she yelled at herself. *Stop being such a baby! They're going to see you!*

She dragged her crutch off the roof with a clatter and set off at a lurching stride up the garden path and through the back gate, sparing one quick glance behind her, but the reflection of the sky and trees on the kitchen window meant that she couldn't see whether or not she'd been spotted, and so she pegged it along the alley to the road, where she dug out her phone and called for a taxi.

When Rachel arrived at Providence Nursing Home, Gigi was snoozing in her chair by the window, spectacles hanging at her chest, a book in her lap, hands folded over the top. Rachel could see how the old skin had sunk into every hollow, showing the sinews, veins and knuckles, like something vacuum-packed for storage. She wore a plain gold ring on her right hand; something about it was familiar but Rachel couldn't spare the time to puzzle it out now when there was much more important business to take care of. Gently, Rachel laid her own hand over Gigi's and squeezed.

'Wake up, Gigi,' she whispered. 'It's Rachel. I've come to see you.'

Gigi stirred, licked her lips and slowly opened her faded, sticky eyes. 'Rachel?' she murmured. 'Is it teatime?'

'No, Gigi,' she smiled. 'It's not. I'm sorry to disturb you, but I need to ask you a question and I don't think I've got very much time.' How long would it take them to work out where she'd gone?

'Question…?'

'Yes, Gigi.' Rachel took out her phone, opened the photo gallery and scrolled through the images to the one she needed. 'Do you recognise who this is? I know it must have been a very long time ago, but I hope you will.'

Gigi fumbled her spectacles on, and peered at the image. She moaned softly and closed her eyes.

'You know her, don't you?'

'That poor girl…' Gigi whispered. 'That poor, poor girl.'

'She was your neighbour, wasn't she?'

'Beatrice. Her name was Beatrice. Bea.'

Gigi was looking at a picture of Mary that Rachel had taken on the day of their disastrous shopping trip.

Oak Mary.

Annabel Clayton.

Eline Lambert.

Daphne Massey.

Beatrice Eaton.

'I'm so sorry,' Gigi whispered. 'Please.'

'She was your neighbour and Stephen was her son, wasn't he? My grandfather wasn't your child.'

Gigi's eyes were pleading. 'She didn't come home!'

'When didn't she come home?'

'I'd babysit for her, when she worked nightshifts at the Longbridge works, and when she was out with her fella.'

Rachel leaned closer. 'What fella?'

'Soldier, he was, or so she told me, finally. That wasn't her story at first. She moved down from somewhere up north with a wedding ring on her finger and a story about how her husband was away at the war. And why wouldn't he be? So many young women exactly the same. But then one night she came clean, swore me to secrecy and said that there was no husband but she'd just met a new fella who she really liked and would I look after little Stephen if she went out dancing? I was so happy for her – she always seemed sort of sad. I thought if anyone deserved a shred of happiness it was Bea. So she left her pretend wedding ring at home and went out with her fella.

'One night, she simply didn't come home. Well the night went by and then another and Albert and I looked at each other and said she isn't coming back, is she? I said give her another day, she's in love. It can make a girl do all manner of peculiar things. So we waited another day and she still didn't come home. Call the police, said Albert, but I said no, they'll take him away from us, won't they, meaning little Stephen, and I couldn't bear that, because we had no babies ourselves, though not for lack of trying. I said if she turns up I'll give him straight back of course, but why have him go to an orphanage when he's got people here who love him? So I talked Albert round.

'I went next door to her house and found Stephen's ration book and the rest of his bits and bobs, and on Bea's dresser I found the wedding ring that she'd taken off to see her fella. I want you to know that I took it for Stephen. I always meant to tell him, whether she came back or not, but somehow I never did.

'And then a year and a half later they found her in that tree. I knew it was her straight away from the police sketches in the newspaper, but I'd have known it was her even without. And I know we should have gone to the police, but little Stephen was walking! He'd learnt to walk in *our* home, and he was starting to talk, and we were his parents. They'd have taken him away from us and given him to some auntie or uncle who didn't know him or love him, and I wasn't having that.

'But that poor girl. In that tree.' Gigi reached up to cup Rachel's cheek.

'I'm going to find her, Gigi,' Rachel promised. 'I'm going to tell her her own story, so that she can be at peace.'

Her great-grandmother fumbled at the ring on her right hand; it hung loosely on her shrunken finger and came off easily. She pressed it into Rachel's palm and closed her fingers over it tightly, with surprising strength. 'When you see her, give her this, and tell her that Carrie said she's sorry.'

'I will, Gigi. I promise.'

The nursing home had been converted from a large Edwardian town house, and its gardens survived as the grounds where patients strolled and took the air. It was easy to find a secluded corner from which to call Tom, hidden by heavy rhododendron bushes and the towering forms of thick-trunked beeches and sycamores. Ignoring the clustered blinking icons telling her how many missed calls and message notifications she had, she made the only call that was really necessary.

'Rache?!' Tom's voice was raw with disbelief. 'Christ, Rache, where the fuck are you? Your mother's beside herself!' His voice had a tinny, echoing quality, which told her he had her on hands-free.

'Are you driving?' she asked.

'What? Yes! I'm bloody looking for you!'

'Pull over, right now. I'm not having you crash. And don't hang up and call anyone else. If you hang up, I hang up, and that's it.'

'Just tell me—'

'*Now!*' she yelled.

She heard him muttering obscenities as he pulled over, and the swoosh of other vehicles going past in the background. When he spoke again, his voice was clearer.

'Right,' he said. 'Happy? Now tell me where you are.'

'Is Mum with you?'

'No, she's with the police, and like I said, absolutely beside herself. Let me come and get you – they're talking about having you *sectioned*, for God's sake.'

'I remember you threatened as much not so very long ago.'

He made no reply to that.

'But then you saw that it was all true,' she went on. 'I know that you've been lying about all of this because you think that's going to make it go away and that it's the only way to protect me. You're wrong on both counts.'

'Rache, I—'

'Just shut up and listen. I love you and I wish there was some other way but there just isn't. There's nobody listening to you now, you have nobody to be brave and sane for, it's just you and me, so tell me: you saw it all. You believe me. It's true.'

The cars continued to swoosh past in the background, and she realised that she was holding her breath.

He said 'yes' on a great expulsion of air as if they'd been holding their breath together. 'But you don't know it all,' he added. 'How much of a shit I've been.'

'What do you mean?'

'The library.'

'What about it?'

'The whole reason we went there in the first place...' He gulped, and she could hear the tears in his voice. 'I said I'd done some digging and found out where the Oak Mary case files were, but I lied. I hadn't. I was told.'

'By who, Tom? Who told you?'

'The Small Man. He set us up right from the start and I went along with it because I thought it was the best way to protect you and now everything's fucked up...'

Rachel was surprised to find tears of relief streaking down her cheeks. 'I want you to know that I don't blame you for anything,' she said. 'And I'm sorry. I wanted to make a home with you and yes, have babies with you and watch them grow up, and grow old and die with you, and now none of that is going to happen because I have to go away, and I won't be able to come back again.'

'No you don't,' Tom said, and his desperation nearly broke her. 'Or I can come with you. We can go together. Please, Rache—'

'No. Not where I'm going.'

It took a moment for him to register what she meant. 'Not that place. You can't. It nearly killed you!'

'I have to!' Rachel said. 'Beatrice – that's Mary's real name – is still trapped there. She thinks she's a prostitute called Daphne Massey; she's forgotten that she's Beatrice because there's nobody left to remember her. That's why she reached out to me, because I'm all the family she has left. Oak Mary is my great-grandmother, Tom. She just needs to know the truth so she can be at peace.' Suddenly Rachel was weeping. 'If I hadn't pulled her out of that tree she'd still be Oak Mary, which would be better, because the Small Man is killing her! He's raping and killing her over and over again, and she thinks that's who she is, and I can't bear it! I have to stop it, and you have to let me go and do it.'

'There's got to be an alternative,' Tom insisted.

'There is.' Rachel sniffed and wiped away the tears with her stump. 'It involves me being tranked up to the eyeballs on antipsychotics for the rest of my life. Do you remember we talked about what each of us would want if we were brain-dead and on a machine? You said you'd want to be alive as long as possible because it was the only life you were going to get.'

'And you said you'd want to be switched off.' She could hear the tears in his voice now.

'That's the alternative, Tom – the machine. You promised you'd switch me off.'

'Yeah,' he said thickly. 'Yeah I did, didn't I? Fuck that, though.'

'Tom, I—'

'No, you listen now. Go, save Mary, or whoever she is, and come back to me. You've got that hand of glory – you can punch a hole into limbo, right? Well when you get there and take care of business you punch one the other way and get your arse back home.'

'I don't think that's—'

But he'd hung up.

She stared at the phone. Part of her wanted to call him back and demand to know what he thought he was doing hanging up on her. It might be the last time they'd ever speak. He hadn't even said he loved her. But then of course that was the point: it would have been the same as saying goodbye. She put the phone away, shivering; it had grown cold in the garden. The trees and bushes seemed to be leaning over her, eavesdropping on her conversation; they made her feel small and powerless.

She took out the fake wedding ring that Gigi had given her and passed it into the umbra to her left hand. For a moment she thought it lucky that Beatrice hadn't had tiny fingers, but then realised that if that had been the case then Rachel herself would probably have inherited them, so it wasn't such a coincidence that the ring comfortably filled the gap where her own wedding ring had been. It felt like it belonged there.

She went back inside and could tell straight away from Gigi's listless, glazed stare that she was having another episode. Which memory from her long, long life was she reliving in the umbra? Rachel wondered. She extended her Sight. There was blazing sun, but even here it had the peculiar violet tinge of limbo, and sand, and the glitter of an ocean. Gigi was reclining on a deck chair in a navy-blue one-piece swimsuit and a sunhat with a brim so wide that it must have been a metre from one side to the other. Gigi was older than she'd been the last time Rachel had spied on her (because that was what it felt like: spying), in her forties or maybe a well-preserved fifty-something. That would make this the seventies – was she enjoying the new fashion for package holidays to sunny Europe? Given how grim the post-war decades had been, Rachel couldn't blame her. She looked happy and relaxed, in the prime of life.

The problem was that this didn't help Rachel get any closer to Beatrice. She needed Gigi's wartime memories – they were her way into the umbra where Beatrice was trapped. Feeling sick with shame, Rachel whispered, 'I'm sorry about this, Gigi, but there really is no other way,' then cleared her throat and said in a much louder voice: 'Hello, Carrie, it's me. Bea.'

Gigi turned to her in surprise, and as she saw Rachel her eyes widened and changed. Shadows rose from the sand like ground mist, wreathing themselves into the shapes of walls, furniture, floor and ceiling. Decades melted from Gigi's face, and she was Carrie again; Gigi was sixty years in this young woman's future. The sun hat had been replaced by a headscarf and the one-piece by a flower-print dress and apron, and she was standing in the open front doorway of her house on Queens Road, blinking at Rachel.

'Bea? Is that really you?'

'Of course it's me!' said Rachel, plastering a big smile on her face. She held out both hands – living and dead. 'Aren't you going to invite me in?'

Carrie shook herself, smiled, and held her hands out to grasp Rachel's. 'Of course!'

Rachel took a deep breath and, bracing herself against Carrie's grip, pulled herself into the umbra.

37

UNREAL CITY

THE TRANSITION WAS MUCH QUICKER AND SMOOTHER than it had been in the asylum, because here she was willing rather than resisting. Instead of spasmodic pins and needles, all she felt as she stepped over the threshold and into Carrie's home was a cold shiver run through her.

Someone just walked over my grave, she thought.

Carrie's memory clothed her in the mustard-brown overalls of a factory worker and gave her longer hair, curled and pinned back in victory rolls. Her left hand was solid and whole again, and the ring on it caught the dim light, shining with a preternatural lustre. Her right leg was healed, while her breath moved in and out of her lungs without pain from her cracked ribs. In the land of the dead, she felt more alive than she had for a long time.

Rachel stepped into Carrie's front hallway. 'Come in,' said Carrie, heading into the lounge. 'Stephen's asleep – minor miracle, that is – let me get you a cuppa.'

'No, thanks though,' Rachel replied. 'You're all right. If he's down I'll just pop my head in, then go next door and get changed. I'm a right sweaty Betty.'

Carrie waved at the staircase. 'You know the way.'

'You're an angel, Caroline Howson. You know that, don't you? Seriously,' she stopped Carrie in the kitchen doorway with a hand on her elbow. 'Thank you so much for looking after him all this time.'

Something clouded Carrie's face, some dim recognition of her older self that 'Beatrice' was thanking her for far more than just a spot of babysitting, but then it disappeared and she grinned and swatted Rachel with a tea towel. 'Don't be daft,' she said. 'It's no more than anyone would. You can return the favour when me and Bert finally catch.'

Rachel had intended to sneak out the front door and start looking for Beatrice as soon as possible, but found herself climbing a narrow staircase to a crooked upstairs hallway, and a back bedroom made even gloomier by the closed blackout curtains. As her eyes adjusted, she saw the cot and the small, pale form curled up beneath a patchwork quilt. Closer, she could hear the baby's soft breathing and see his fine, wispy hair.

'You're not my grandfather,' she whispered to him. 'You're just Gigi's memory of him. All the same.' She laid a hand gently on the soft rise and fall of his sleeping form. 'Sweet dreams.'

As she made her way back downstairs, Carrie called out to her, asking if she was sure she didn't want that brew, but she ignored it and tiptoed out through the front door, and Carrie's voice cut off as if at the flicking of a switch.

Looking back, Rachel saw that the house was dark and silent, barely even distinct; it was hard to make out specific features any more. Above it, and the saw-toothed ridge of the terraced rooftops, the sky looked like a ceiling of violet granite shot through with veins of saffron orange, which pulsed slowly as if it were a living organism, or a vast conflagration glowing through cracks in the stone. She'd only ever seen glimpses of it before, through windows or holes in roofs, and seeing it now in its crushing vastness she understood that whatever this umbra really was, it was not a place where human souls belonged. Still, they *were* here, recreating their last living moments and most treasured memories either in terror of what might come afterwards or simple ignorance of the fact that they had died. They weren't being punished for anything or given a chance to purge their sins in preparation for some final Glory. There was no purpose here. This was just the desperate, mute denial of a man clinging to a cliff edge by his fingertips afraid to let go. They deserved better. Beatrice deserved better.

The house next door was hers, and it was just as dark and featureless as Carrie's. Rachel knew that she'd find nothing useful there – Beatrice thought she was Daphne Massey, and the Small Man had her hidden away somewhere in her limbo of blitz-era Birmingham, but Rachel knew where she would inevitably end up. Every night he would take her up to the viewpoint on Beacon Hill, rape her, murder her, and put her corpse in the hollow oak tree, whereupon the nightmare would begin all over again. That was where Rachel had to go.

It was hard to tell how long she had been walking, as the houses remained anonymous cyphers of themselves and the sky was unchanged, but in time she heard the sound of children singing. It was a simple, lilting up-and-down refrain, like a nursery rhyme. Soon she saw the source.

A group of six children – three girls and three boys – were holding hands and dancing in a circle in the middle of the empty road. The boys wore long shorts and knitted sleeveless jumpers over shirts, while the girls wore dresses and long socks. War-era clothing.

> *Mary in the oak tree,*
> *Cold as cold can be*
> *Waiting for the sky to fall*
> *Who will dance with me?*

She remembered the images of the Lickey obelisk graffiti, *Who danced with Oak Mary?*, and the gloating, triumphant response daubed in a murdered youth's blood: *I danced with Oak Mary!* She knew who was responsible for that now.

'Excuse me?' she said, approaching carefully, afraid to scare the children away. 'Do you know where Mary is? Have you seen her?'

The kids saw her and took to their heels, shrieking.

'Hey! Wait!'

They scrambled up a slope of pulverised brick, which was all that remained of a bombed house, and disappeared over the top. Rachel followed, picking her way over the rubble: bricks, plaster, burnt timbers, and mangled items of furniture. She was so intent on finding safe footholds in the sliding debris that she didn't notice the man in the uniform standing at the very top until he shouted at her.

'Oi! You can't come through here, miss! It ain't safe!'

He was an air raid warden in dark overalls and wellington boots, wearing a broad-brimmed tin helmet with a letter W on the front and a large satchel around his neck. He made violent shooing motions with his arms as he shouted.

'You have to go back!'

Rachel had absolutely no intention of going back. She carried on climbing, ignoring his increasingly strenuous protests.

'You want to have a building fall on you, do you? Silly cow!'

'Tried that,' she grunted, coming level with him. 'Didn't work.'

The ARP warden was red-faced and blustering by this time, jabbing a finger in her face and spraying her with spittle as he sputtered, 'I'll have to call the authorities, you know! You leave me no choice!'

'Good,' she said, and grabbed his finger with her left hand and twisted, forcing him to his knees in the rubble as he yelped. 'You do that. Go and tell the authorities that Beatrice Eaton's great-granddaughter is here to rescue her soul – then maybe we can end this quickly without too much dicking around.'

She let him go and he slithered and scrambled down the other side of the debris hill, kicking up dust and sending small avalanches ahead of him. She saw that the back of his uniform had been burnt away, along with most of the flesh and muscle from his back; his ribcage and spine were charred black and shed crumbling fragments as he moved.

There was no sign of the children, but there was an awful lot of bustle and chaos in the road on this side for them to have disappeared into. Several buildings were on fire, and fire crews were sending streams of water into the flames with little obvious effect. The air was full of smoke, steam, the roar of water and fire, the chuntering of the diesel pump and the shouted commands of men. A crowd of onlookers had turned out to watch, every single one of whom was dead.

Some, like the ARP warden, wore their deaths openly: burns, eviscerations, crush injuries and distorted limbs. Others were less demonstrative or else had died of more subtle causes, but still had the same hollow-eyed pallor. Rachel didn't know whether they would be able to see that she was different, but didn't want to draw the attention of so large a crowd for fear that they would mob her as the shades in the asylum had, so she picked a careful way around them, using piles of smoking debris for cover.

Above them, the city skyline had changed – it was now a jagged silhouette against the lurid orange of burning, shot through with the questing fingers of searchlights and the fat bumblebee shapes of barrage balloons. Formations of bombers passed in an unending swarm far above even these, the droning snarl of their engines filling the air like the stink of burning. This part of the umbra belonged to the victims of the Birmingham blitz: their memories of three years of air raids shaped and condensed into a single unending night of devastation and horror.

She saw a tree festooned with the contents of someone's wardrobe, along with red, dripping ropes of intestines. She passed a woman in a gas mask pushing a pram, her muffled voice singing, 'Mary in the oak tree, cold as cold can be,' to something swaddled in blankets which was burned black but still twitching. A housewife sat amongst the ruins of her home and drank tea from a cup and saucer, weeping silently.

Eventually Rachel found herself in a wider thoroughfare that was almost entirely empty of traffic, which made sense during an air raid. But if the umbra mapped onto the living world as it seemed to do, and she needed to get to the Lickey Hills in time to stop the Small Man from killing Daphne again, then she was going to have trouble flagging down a lift.

An ambulance screamed by, its bell clanging frantically, followed by an army truck; as it passed her, rows of grim-faced soldiers stared out from the back.

With a heavy sigh, she picked a direction that felt like south and started walking again.

It had been raining all day, and the M5 was a wide mirror-sheened ribbon as it curved away from where Tom had parked on the hard shoulder. He put his hazard lights on;

there was no need to risk anybody else's life.

He got out of the van, shrugging on his waterproof against the downpour, and wandered a little way along the breakdown lane, peering at the tarmac and kicking bits of debris out of the way. It would have been somewhere around here, he reckoned – four years ago but just as fresh in his memory as if it had happened yesterday. Lorries hissed past, buffeting him with their slipstreams. He knew he was being watched on motorway CCTV, but he had a little while before anybody called a patrol four-by-four to check on him; they'd assume he was waiting for his own breakdown service.

'Come on then!' he called into the shifting veils of rain. 'You want me, here I am! Let's talk terms!'

For a long time, during which he strode up and down the hard shoulder, yelling into the rain, nothing happened. When he finally saw the checkered yellow-and-black livery of a Highways Agency Range Rover approaching slowly with its hazards on, he wasn't sure if it was a real living rescue driver or the one he'd been calling for. By this time he was drenched and shivering despite his waterproofs.

'I know you can hear me!' he called. 'I want to make a trade!'

The four-by-four rolled to a halt a few metres from him, its windscreen wipers flicking. Through them, he saw the face of the driver who'd saved his life all those years ago, gazing impassively back. Tom reckoned that if anybody *were* watching this on a screen, all they would see was a crazy man standing in the rain staring at an empty breakdown lane. And they might well have been right; this was crazy.

'Finally,' he said. 'What, were you on a tea break?' Nerves made him flippant, even though his heart was hammering with terror. 'Get out and talk to me. There's something I want.'

The face remained impassive for a moment longer, and then the driver's door opened.

38

APPETITES

RACHEL WALKED UNTIL HER FEET WERE NUMB, BUT her surroundings hardly changed. One burning, devastated neighbourhood gave way to another, populated by shambling figures. She found tram rails, but nothing passed by in either direction. She was beginning to wonder whether somehow her journey was being deliberately elongated; some power of the Small Man, alerted to her presence, that was stretching out the distance to obstruct her. But if that were the case why not come at her directly? It was tempting to think he was still scared of her.

It wasn't long before she saw the first 'wanted' poster. Beneath the words 'Do You Know This Woman? She May Be a Spy! Please Alert the Authorities if You Have Seen Her!' was a photograph of Rachel. Half a mile further on she ran into a Home Guard patrol. If they hadn't been making so much noise she'd have walked right into their arms, but as it was the sound of ribald male laughter made her duck behind a section of half-collapsed wall just as a quartet of Home Guard soldiers came around the corner. Only one wore a uniform and a peaked cap; the three following him were in civvies with armbands, tin helmets rattling on their heads and rifles loose in their hands. The rearmost was struggling to hop along while scraping something off the side of his boot against the pavement, and the other two were winding him up.

'Trust Paddy to step in the only dog turd in a hundred yards...'

'Chaps, wait up...'

'Aye, Paddy's a regular shit magnet. Have you seen that girl of his?'

'Oh, come on now, chaps...'

Only their uniformed leader seemed to be paying attention to anything around him. Rachel watched him carefully from a crack between two bricks: his quick, dark eyes glancing left and right. She held her breath as they passed, and only when the sound of their banter had disappeared into the background rumble of war did she peep out, then scurry off in the opposite direction.

That was when she heard the car. It pulled past her – a Morris Ten with high curved wheel arches and owlish headlights – slowed, and the driver wound down his window. She picked up her pace, glancing sidelong at him and angling away from the pavement because there was no world, living or dead, in which a strange car slowing down for a woman walking alone was a good thing.

'Rachel Cooper!' he called. 'I've come from Tom. He seemed to think you might need some help.'

She stopped and backed away warily. 'Sure,' she said. 'Because there's Uber in hell. Leave me alone.'

'Suit yourself,' he said. 'But a quarter of a mile in the direction you're going is a roadblock, and they're checking identity papers. I don't think you want to try to talk your way through that. The man they answer to now is no friend of yours.'

'Cheers for the heads-up,' she answered. 'I'll find a way around, thanks.'

'That one, yes, you might. But not the others, or the Home Guard patrols. And the place you're heading to in the hills is even more tightly guarded.'

She looked more closely at the driver. He had fair hair and a wide face with a neat ginger goatee, and even though he was driving a thirties automobile he was dressed in a modern hi-vis jacket with orange shoulders and a uniform she knew very well: the Highways Agency. 'Who are you? Why would Tom send you? *How* could he?'

'Look, it's all the same to me whether you get in or not. I've kept my side of the bargain. If you're too stubborn or too stupid...' He shifted the car into gear and started to move off.

'Wait!' Rachel yelled, and ran after him. 'What bargain? What deal has Tom done with you?'

The car stopped again. The Highwayman leaned over and opened the passenger side door, saying nothing. After a moment's agonised indecision she got in, and he set off.

The inside of the Morris smelt of vinyl, Bakelite and cigarettes, but at least it was warm. The driver was larger than he had first seemed, filling his side of the car, and she saw that his seat was shifted back as far as it would go but his knees were still bent. 'I know what you are,' she said.

The psychopomp glanced at her. 'Good,' he said. 'Then you'll know exactly what kind of deal your husband made.'

'Is he…?' She couldn't bring herself to say the word.

'No. Not yet. How long exactly?' He shrugged. 'Nobody ever knows. Not even us. But he's been living on borrowed time, and all borrowing has its cost.'

'What would it take…' She swallowed, fearing the consequences of her question. 'What would it take for you to leave him alone?'

'You misunderstand. Death is simply a biological process that cannot be bargained with. We are not death, we simply guarantee safe passage to what comes next. This hell you see around you is made by the dead for themselves. Would you rather he be left to something like this?'

'So why did you save him that day on the motorway? You just said that death can't be cheated.'

'I said it couldn't be bargained with. Cheating it is an entirely different thing.'

'But why do it anyway? Why not just take him?'

The Highwayman simply smiled cryptically. 'Your Small Man is not the only one who likes to play games.'

Rachel closed her eyes and let the tears come. 'He was just trying to protect me,' she whispered. 'That's all he's ever tried to do.'

The psychopomp grunted. 'Then make it count.'

A few minutes later he added, 'Start now – get in the back. We're coming up to the checkpoint.'

She could see brighter lights in the road up ahead so did as she was told, climbing over and into the back. There she found a tarpaulin bundled up on the seat and lay on the floor, pulling it over her.

The car slowed, stopped, and footsteps approached.

'Got some ID, pal?' asked a voice.

'No,' said the Highwayman. 'You know what I am. You'll let me pass.'

This was met with mutterings of consternation from further off. The first voice returned, nervous and bullish. 'We know all right. Whether we let you pass is another matter, pal. There's new orders. You've got to answer to the new authorities just the same.'

Rachel heard the springs in the driver's seat creak as he shifted his considerable weight.

'What I answer to,' said the Highwayman, 'will do much the same to your new authority as *this*.' There was a sudden scream from his interrogator, which turned into a series of choked squawks as the car rocked, and then something that sounded like a very large chicken drumstick being pulled apart. There were screams of 'Let him pass! For God's sake let him pass!' The Highwayman grunted with satisfaction, started the car and set off again.

When he signalled that it was safe to do so, Rachel climbed out of hiding and rejoined him in the front. Through the windscreen she saw that the burning cityscape had been replaced by a line of dark hills, above which floated a single fat barrage balloon.

'Your Small Man has done a good job of consolidating his power in this part of the umbra,' said the Highwayman. 'His brief existence in the world of the flesh has given him a taste for power. Power!' he laughed shortly and shook his head. 'There is no god, or gods, or devils after this. No. But there are... appetites. Hungers. Aspirations. There is nothing which aspires which was not first human.'

'I have no idea what you're talking about.'

'I and your Small Man and others of our kind were human once. It is possible that the reason I saved your Tom was out of... nostalgia, perhaps? We exist to service those appetites, which were themselves once human, and thus we may be seen as guides and guardians or reapers and demons, depending.'

'Depending on what?'

He shrugged. 'How you die, whether you are ready to die, where you choose to go after you die—'

'Wait – we get to *choose*?'

He blinked at her as if the question was so stupid it surprised him that she would even utter it. 'Of course. What else would be the point?'

'And which of these appetites do you serve? Where are you going to deliver Tom's soul?'

'Have you not been listening? That depends on him, not me. But your Small Man, now, he wants to be Big. He has acquired an appetite. He aspires. He has kept Oak Mary for himself when he should have delivered her, because her belief – and the belief of others in her – makes him strong. She is the saint around which he will build his church. In so doing he has overstepped the bounds of his condition, and that is a very dangerous thing. You have set yourself against him and have the means to destroy him because his power, like the power of any death, is founded on the belief of its victim and for the moment Oak Mary believes that he is her killer. Convince her otherwise – convince her of her true death – and he will no longer exist, just as the two others who appeared with him ceased to exist when they were disproved.'

'I was going to do that anyway,' Rachel pointed out.

'Yes, but now you know there is a bigger picture. Do this, and you draw the attention of those appetites. That may be something you wish to avoid.'

'Are you offering me a chance to back out?'

The Highwayman merely stared ahead at the road and grunted, which could have meant anything.

'One of your lot dressed as my dad tried to tell me the same thing, a little while back,' Rachel said. 'My answer's the same as it was then: fuck that. And just so you know,' she added, 'I don't care about your bigger picture. I don't care what kind of a deal Tom made with you. You come near him again, you and I are going to have words.'

He looked at her, and there was a new wariness in his expression. 'That will be an interesting conversation,' was all he said.

* * *

They drove past the broken chimneys and shattered windows of the Longbridge works where Eline had claimed to have worked, though Rachel knew now that it had just been an echo of Beatrice's life. In the same way, Annabel's accidental cursing of her son had simply mirrored Beatrice's grief at abandoning Stephen; her false lives had all carried within them some element of the truth that they unconsciously acknowledged.

The Highwayman seemed not to need headlights, steering confidently in the almost pitch dark as the road rose, taking them right into the shadow of the hills, and the houses began to give way to woods. The black silhouette of the barrage balloon, moored in the hills to protect the factory, seemed to hang directly over the car, like a massive, impossible weight ready to crush it.

He pulled over at a bend in the road. 'Here's where you get out. Take the trees for cover and make your way up the slope to the oak; that's where he has her.'

'What will you do?'

The Highwayman grinned, and she saw his teeth gleam in the dark. It was the first time she'd seen him smile, and it wasn't an altogether reassuring sight. 'I am going to keep his men up there very busy on your behalf.'

She got out of the car and stood at the roadside. 'Thank you,' she said.

'Don't thank me. Thank your Tom, for as long as you can.' Then he flicked the headlights on high beam, gunned the engine loudly and set off up the hill at a roar, leaning on the horn.

Rachel wasted no time, and began clambering uphill through the bushes. She knew these hills so well that she could have found the Mary Oak easily, even in the dark, but it seemed that even the vegetation was under the Small Man's control; she was snagged and tripped by brambles, stabbed by gorse thorns, whipped across the face by thin branches and stung by nettles. In a strange way, though, it was exhilarating to be able to grab at branches and roots with both hands to haul herself along. If she'd remained an amputee her progress would have been much slower.

A distant commotion erupted: shouts and gunfire and flashes of light through the trees. The Highwayman was making good on his distraction. She gritted her teeth, braced her feet and pushed onwards.

39

QUEEN OF AIR AND DARKNESS

AND SHE WAS THERE.

The Mary Oak, which had been cut apart and burned after the discovery of Beatrice's remains, was here in the umbra a towering memory of its former self. Shattered by an ancient bolt of lightning, its wide trunk ended eight feet above the ground in a blunt stump like an amputated arm raised defiantly at the heavens, except that the sky was blotted out by the vast bulk of the barrage balloon directly overhead. The broken prongs of dead limbs jutted from its trunk, bleached and pale with age, like bone.

'Daphne!' Rachel hissed. 'Daphne! Are you there! Can you hear me?'

A woman's voice, muffled, cried out in response.

Rachel ran to the tree, scanning it for any cracks or holes through which she could speak. Short of using the broken stubs of branches to climb to the hole in the top, she couldn't think of any way to free its prisoner. 'I'll get you out,' she promised. 'Hang in there, honey. I'll get you out.' This close, Rachel could quite clearly hear Daphne crying inside the tree.

She explored the trunk with her fingers, hunting for fissures or crevices. To her surprise, a large chunk peeled away in her left hand like papier mâché, but when she put her right hand to the hole it was solid and refused to budge so much as a splinter, so she simply braced herself with her right while tearing at the widening hole with her left. She flung aside chunks of dead oak until the breach was big enough to see Daphne's pale, tear-streaked face and wide eyes, and Rachel reached in to take her hand. Cold fingers gripped hers tightly.

'I've got you. It's okay. You're safe now.'

Someone started applauding from the shadows, slow and sarcastic. 'And the winner of this year's award for most obvious distraction goes to,' announced the Small Man, stepping forward. He had swapped his cardigan and braces for a general's uniform, resplendent with gold braiding and medals. 'Rachel Cooper, and her overdeveloped sense of importance.'

Rachel ignored him and turned back to Daphne. Her eyes were fixed on the Small Man's approach and she'd shrunk back as far into the claustrophobic space of the hollow trunk as she could, but she kept her grip on Rachel's hand.

'Listen to me,' said Rachel. 'You are not Daphne Massey. You're not Oak Mary either. Your name is Beatrice Rebecca Eaton. You came from Manchester to Birmingham with your son Stephen...' The other woman's eyes darted back to her and she frowned slightly. 'Yes! That's it! You remember! You wore this ring – take it…' The thin gold band was loose enough for Rachel to be able to push it off with her thumb and she felt it drop into the tree just as a hand grabbed her by the shoulder and spun her around. The Small Man's face was inches from her own and twisted with fury.

'Don't turn your back on me, bitch!' he snarled, and backhanded her. Rachel felt her lip split and tasted blood, and its redness rose up to fill her mind. She'd never hit another person before, so the punch she threw at his face was badly timed, off balance and with little force behind it. All the same, it was with her left fist, and it sent him sprawling as if he'd taken a sledgehammer between the eyes.

'Keep your hands to yourself, little man,' she spat.

He reeled. Blood was pouring from his nose. He put a hand to it and stared in amazement when it came away red.

'You like the flesh so much,' she added. 'You better get used to that. But you don't touch me or her ever again, understand?' Adrenaline and rage were buzzing in her veins at the same time as a tiny voice at the back of her head was whining, *Don't make him angry, just give him what he wants and maybe he won't hurt you*, but she ignored that too, because it sounded uncomfortably like her mother's voice. Besides, the stinging in her lips suggested that bridge was already burned.

The knife appeared in his hand, and he leered at her with bloodstained teeth. 'She dies for me every night, and she does it so well,' the Small Man said. 'You'll only get to do it the once, but if it's any consolation I promise to make you feel like it's lasting forever.'

He started towards her, but she saw him pause mid-step and his eyes widen.

There was a sound of cracking wood from the tree at her back.

'I remember now,' said a voice from inside.

40

BEATRICE

THE DAY SHE FINDS OUT SHE IS PREGNANT IS simultaneously the best and worst day of her life. There is no way that Stanley is ever going to acknowledge the child as his, and not just for the sake of his marriage – he has an important position in the Civil Defence Report and Control Centre in Salford to think about, much more important than that of a ten-a-penny secretary like Beatrice, no matter how pretty she is.

It is the best day of her life because she has a baby growing inside her. She is a mother, right now, regardless of what happens in the next nine months, and she's seen so many people die because of the war that even though having a baby terrifies her it feels right and necessary. She already knows that if it's a boy he will be Stephen and if it's a girl she will be Joanne.

She manages to hide her bump for almost six months

before anyone notices, and when they do the news is like a bomb dropped into the middle of her family. As good middle-class Catholics with an unimpeachable reputation in the community, the shame cannot be borne. She is accordingly shut away for the last months of what her parents, without a trace of irony, call her 'confinement' in a private women's hospital in Wythenshawe, where she gives birth to Stephen, and this is where things get really awkward because everybody is under the assumption that she is going to have him adopted.

She has absolutely no intention of giving up her baby. She is prepared to name the father and drag her family's name into the gutter if necessary, because if they're going to steal Stephen away from her that's where they might as well be.

Bridges are burned. Ties are cut. And when she departs Manchester Piccadilly station with only a suitcase and her child, she has all she could possibly want in the world.

Birmingham is an alien city. It has no easily definable centre, no names that she recognises, and the people talk strangely. She tells the local Food Office that her husband Larry is away at the war, stationed in Singapore, that all of her paperwork was destroyed when her home up north was bombed, and she's come to stay with cousins, and nobody questions the wedding ring that she bought at a market stall on Church Street before leaving home. She is issued with the appropriate ration books – one for her, and one for Stephen. The Ministry of Labour gets her a job making airplane parts at the Austin works in Longbridge and a place is found for Stephen at a nearby day nursery. On the first day she drops him off she is surprised to see so many mothers as young as herself doing exactly the same thing; it seems that nobody is keeping house any more, and she imagines whole streets of empty, echoing homes. It's hard work and long shifts but she is surprised to find herself enjoying it; there is a camaraderie of a kind that she has never known, and the girls come from all walks of life and muck in together without judgement. Nobody wants to know where she's from or who her family is – or if they do, it's because they're interested in *her* rather than the judging of her.

When Stephen is three months old, workers clearing the rubble from a bombsite near the nursery accidentally hit a gas main, and the fire which follows forces the nursery to close temporarily. Taking time off from the factory would mean losing wages, which Bea can't afford, so with heavy reluctance she knocks on her neighbours' door for help. She is already on pleasant enough terms with Carrie and Bert – a childless couple, he an engineer on the railways and therefore protected from the call-up, she a housewife – but even though they've traded rationing coupons and gossip Bea has never asked for anything really important until now.

'I hate to ask,' she says, over tea in Carrie's sitting room. 'It would only be temporary, just until the nursery opens again, and of course I'll pay you.'

'You jolly well will *not* pay me!' Carrie laughs. 'I won't take a penny!' On her lap she is dandling Stephen, who is trying to pluck at her ear with his pudgy fingers. 'No I won't, will I?' she repeats to him in a baby voice. 'No I won't!'

Stephen gurgles, and that seals the deal.

It becomes more than a temporary arrangement, of course. Carrie babysits whenever Bea can afford to pay her, despite her protestations, and often when she can't. It is a relief to Bea that her baby is being cared for more closely than in a large, busy nursery, and having Stephen around helps distract Carrie from her sadness at the fact that she and Bert are having such trouble getting pregnant with their own. Sometimes she watches the glee with which Carrie receives Stephen into her arms, and something cold turns over inside her, for just a moment, and then mercifully is gone. Carrie will have her own baby soon enough, she knows, and then their sons can grow up together as neighbours and friends. It's all just a matter of time.

Longbridge is close enough to the Lickey Hills that every so often Bea can hop on a tram and take a lunch break at the Bilberry Hill pleasure grounds and tea rooms there, watching families picnic and children ride donkeys, or just sitting on the broad sweep of Beacon Hill overlooking the city while she eats her cheese sandwiches.

It is here that she meets Billy Marriner.

He is a private in the 1st Battalion Worcestershire Regiment she learns later, on convalescent leave with malaria from fighting the Japanese in Burma. He is tanned and floppy-haired, and her first sight of him is chasing a donkey, which has taken it into its stupid head to make a bid for freedom.

He catches hold of its harness and brings it to a skidding halt only yards from her, sees that she's watching and tips her a cheeky wink before returning the errant animal to its owner. A few minutes later he plonks himself down on the grass next to her, introduces himself and asks if she'd like to join him for a ginger beer at the pavilion.

Beatrice, being very careful to remove her fake wedding ring and hide it in the pocket of her factory overalls, says yes.

And that is that.

They have lunch twice more on the hill and go to a dance at the West End in Suffolk Street. She tells Carrie that some of the girls from the works have arranged to go out on the town, which isn't a total lie because they have – she just chooses to omit the fact that she's meeting a young man there. Afterwards he offers to see her safely home, which alarms her, because the last thing she needs is for her neighbours to see her stepping out with a soldier.

'I'm more than capable of finding my way home safely, Billy Marriner,' she tells him.

'I don't doubt that,' he replies. 'But there's all manner of nasty types out on the streets at night. Thieves, looters, ruffians.'

She arches an eyebrow at him. 'Ruffians?'

'Or worse, maybe even Americans.'

She gives a gasp of mock horror and clutches at her throat.

'And so what kind of gentleman would I be if I let you take your chances alone? I fear you'd have no respect for me.'

'Well then,' she replies, 'I expect you to see me home like a gentleman.' She places a kiss on his cheek and takes his arm as they go in search of a tram. All the same, she insists that he leaves her at the corner of Queens Road, about which he is not happy.

'Look how dark it is!' he insists. 'I couldn't live with myself if something happened to you in the last few yards.'

'It's light enough,' she says. 'You can stand here and watch me wave to you from my front door and that will have to do.'

'But why?' he protests.

'Shh! Keep your bloody voice down!' she hisses. 'Because I don't want my nosey parker of a neighbour getting the wrong idea about you, that's why!' It's unfair on Carrie but seems to convince him. Reluctantly he agrees, and when she waves to him from her front step he waves back – and then, in a voice that rings down the street, he calls out with a laugh: 'Farewell and goodnight, sweet Beatrice!'

Bea winces. 'You ass,' she mutters, and glances fearfully at the neighbours' windows on either side. With their blackout curtains it is impossible to tell whether anyone is in and awake or not, but there is no movement so she tells herself that nobody has heard him.

All the same, as she closes her door she thinks there might be a flicker in her peripheral vision, as of a chink in a curtain in Carrie's upstairs bedroom quickly closed, but she tells herself that it's probably just a gleam of light on the glass pane.

* * *

On the third of these 'girls' nights out' there is a strange, small smile playing about the corners of Carrie's mouth as she takes Stephen, and a tone in the way she says, 'Well you be sure to have a good time, all right?' which sets Bea's heart fluttering with the panicked certainty that somehow she knows about Billy. Bea thinks she might be able to brazen it out but it seems worse than the original lie, almost insulting to her friend, so she sighs, crosses her arms, and sets her jaw defiantly. 'You know, don't you?'

And bless her, Carrie actually blushes as if *she* is the one caught in a deception. 'Yes, I do. Sorry, bab.'

'No need for you to be sorry. But how?'

Carrie shrugs. 'I've got eyes and ears. You seem far too happy for someone who's just going out with her girl friends.' Stephen is pulling at her lip.

Bea scuffs Carrie's hall rug with one toe. 'I thought I was being so clever, too.'

Carrie points to Bea's left hand. 'That and the fact that you've forgotten to put your "wedding ring" on again.'

Bea curses, in the kind of language nice girls from respectable families never use unless they've been working for months on a factory floor. 'You mustn't tell anyone!' she insists. 'Carrie, please, promise me you won't tell a soul.'

'Of course not. You wouldn't be the first, you know.' She shifts Stephen into the crook of her other arm where he starts grabbing her headscarf. 'Gerroff, you little tike!' she laughs, pulling his hands away, and Bea feels a sudden stab of jealousy. 'Is he nice?' Carrie continues. 'This fella of yours?'

Bea's smile is reluctantly drawn. 'Yes, he's nice.'

'Nice enough to be happy that your ration book comes with a bit more than he might be expecting, so to speak?'

'Truthfully? I don't know. He's very young.'

'They all are, bab,' Carrie sighed. 'They all are. Of course I won't tell a soul, no catches, no conditions. Just...' She hesitates, plainly wondering how much of Bea's business she wants to be part of, despite the other woman's baby wriggling in her arms. 'Just find out, that's all. Find out. And if he's not the kind that'd be happy, best break it off sooner rather than later.'

Bea nodded.

'Because no man likes to be strung along, no matter how much fun he's having along the way.'

'I know, I know.'

The problem is that despite Carrie's wise advice, it is Bea who is having altogether too much fun. Billy is a local boy and knows a hundred secret places around the city to show her. She leaves her ring at home and doesn't tell him about Stephen because she's enjoying herself for the first time in a long while with a fella. And he is very young, it turns out; nineteen compared to her twenty-four. It shouldn't make a difference but it does, and the more often they see each other and she reinforces the illusion that she is free and single the harder it becomes to tell him the truth.

The thing is, she's not sure that she even wants to tell him the truth. He's sweet and attentive and makes her laugh, and she might even be falling for him, but if she were to introduce him to her child he would become a potential father, and she absolutely does not know him well enough for that. Maybe, in time.

So when he proposes to her, it makes things somewhat awkward.

They are walking in the woods of the Lickeys in the saddle between Beacon and Bilberry Hills, and it is a perfect afternoon of light and birdsong. Without warning, he stops and seizes both of her hands.

'Will you be my girl?' he asks earnestly.

'I thought I already was!' she laughs.

'No, I mean really. The doctors say I'm nearly well enough to be sent back to the regiment, and I wanted to know... wanted to ask...' He stammers to a halt, blushing. 'Will you be waiting for me when I get back? I'm not asking you to marry me now, because I think that would be cruel – I mean I might not make it back – but if I do, what do you say? You and me, a little house, we can bring our children up here—'

She puts a hand on his chest to stop him right there. 'Billy,' she says, 'there is nothing I would like more—'

He whoops and crushes her in his arms and swings her around and when she is deposited back on the ground, a little breathless, she continues: 'But there's something you need to know first.'

His beaming face clouds.

She swallows. 'I already have a son.'

He backs away a step, frowning. 'What do you mean?'

She offers him a shy, embarrassed smile.

'But I thought...' He turns away, baffled, then turns

back. 'You mean you're not...'

Now his manner is starting to irritate her a little. 'Not what, Billy?'

'Not, well... pure.'

She laughs. She knows she shouldn't, that this is precisely the wrong thing to do, that he will think she's laughing at him, and she genuinely isn't, but there's something so deliciously old-fashioned about the word 'pure' which surprises the laugh out of her all the same.

'What's so funny?' he demands.

'Nothing, I—'

'How dare you laugh at me! You lead me on—'

'Oh that's unfair, I never led you on—'

'Letting me think you were a decent—'

'As opposed to what, Billy Marriner? What am I now? No, don't answer that. I don't want to hear those words from you. Bad enough I had to hear them from my own father. Talk about leading somebody on; I thought *you* were better than that.'

She turns to leave but he grabs her by the sleeve of her dress. 'Don't you dare turn your back on me!' he shouts, and the material tears, along with what remains of her temper. Rationing is tight enough as it is, and she's spent twelve of her clothing coupons on the dress to look pretty for him.

'You ass!' she shouts, and slaps him in the face.

Afterwards, trapped in the tree, she is never quite sure whether he deliberately intends to punch her in retaliation, or whether some combination of anger and a fighting man's reflexes take over and make his fist crash into the side of her head. Certainly the look of shock on his face seems genuine enough as she falls backwards down the hill. Her feet tangle in each other and her hands grab for something – a branch, a leaf, finding nothing – and the world pinwheels before her eyes, sky replacing trees, and the back of her skull hits a large rock with a sick, wet crunch and everything stops.

She is being lifted.

There is sobbing.

She cannot move.

She is swung over, upside down, carried, hair dangling, arms dangling, legs dangling, unable to move or cry out that she is not dead not dead not dead.

Maybe it would make no difference even if she could.

He is sobbing.

Fuck his sobbing.

She is upended and falling, knees collapsing under her own weight but they jam against something hard and she is left in a half-squatting position in a narrow chimney-like space with her cheek resting against spongy, rotten wood. Something crawls across her neck, up her chin and over her lips. She cannot even flinch.

What will happen to her baby?

What will happen to Stephen?

She wants to scream *not dead not dead not dead!* but instead everything stops again.

* * *

A face. Staring down, shocked.

Not his – someone else. Someone who can get help.

She summons every last scrap of life and strength left in her dying body and forms it into a word for the single most important thing to her in the entire world.

'Stephen?'

The face screams and disappears.

No help comes – just things that crawl and bite.

For the third and final time, everything stops.

Not dead! Not dead! Not dead!

41

THE HOLLOW TREE

THE CREAKING OF WOOD AT RACHEL'S BACK EXTENDED into a deep crunching, splintering noise. A long black fissure opened up in the oak's trunk, rising from the root to the very tip, and two pale hands appeared, one of which was wearing a cheap gold wedding ring, to grasp the edges on either side and pull, as if opening a pair of curtains.

'No!' shrieked the Small Man. 'No! Don't you dare, Daphne! *Daphne! Get back in that fucking tree!*'

But the woman inside was beyond his control now. She tore the tree open with her bare hands and stepped out into the open air.

'My name is not Daphne,' she said. 'It's Beatrice. And you are not my death.'

The Small Man let loose a howl of denial and ran at her with his knife upraised, but stopped halfway and collapsed to his knees as if stricken by some terrible agony. Then he began to unravel, coming apart in ribbons, which writhed in torment as they dissolved into the air, and for a fleeting instant Rachel saw the psychopomp naked: a smudged watercolour of a human figure, its limbs blurred strokes suggesting movement, its face nothing more than a group of screaming holes too crude even for a skull. This moment of having its identity stripped was like a physical flaying, and she watched without pity as it howled. But it also seemed to be drawing something through the air from Beatrice, coils and streamers of brightness to replace what was lost, and when the spasms subsided the figure got shakily to his feet like something newborn, and he'd changed.

Beatrice approached him with a smile of welcome. 'Hello, Billy,' she said.

The psychopomp looked at his new hands, then ran them over his new face and through his new hair. His bloody nose had healed, and he was wearing a soldier's uniform.

'I'm sorry!' he whispered.

'I know,' she replied. 'So make it right, now.'

'You know I'm not him, don't you? Your Billy had his own death, years after yours.'

'I know,' said Beatrice. 'But humour me for a little while, will you? Just until we get where we're going. Please, take me to my boy.'

'Are you sure you're ready?'

'Oh yes,' she sighed, and it was seventy years old, that sigh. 'I've been ready for a long, long time. There's just one last thing.' She turned and approached Rachel. 'Thank you doesn't really cut it, I'm afraid. I'm sorry for the hell you've been through.'

Rachel found herself tongue-tied. All three of them were there in the figure of her great-grandmother: Annabel's majesty, Eline's fierce beauty, and Daphne's sorrow.

Beatrice reached up and gently laid a hand on Rachel's cheek. 'I see him in you,' she said. 'I never saw him grow up or knew what kind of man he became, but if he fathered your father he must have been a good man.'

'You can stay!' Rachel blurted, finding her voice at last. 'Come back with me, get to know us. You could live a full life this time!'

Beatrice shook her head. 'And fall in love and build a family and then at the end of everything die and have to say goodbye to it all, again? Thank you, but no. Once was enough, as brief as it was. Will you and Tom be all right?'

'Honestly? I don't know.'

'Be patient with him. He's only a man, after all.'

'Come on then, bab,' said Billy. He crooked his elbow out for her and she linked her arm with his, and they strolled together like lovers in a sunlit park until they reached the split-open trunk of the hollow tree, and disappeared into its shadow.

There was a grunt of approval from beside Rachel. She turned and saw the Highwayman had also been watching Beatrice's departure. He nodded. 'That's a good job, there,' he said. He looked the worse for wear, scuffed and bloodied, his hi-vis jacket with the orange shoulders in tatters.

'I think I could say the same about you,' she replied.

'I am to say—' he started, then cleared his throat as if embarrassed. 'I am to offer you this. This,' he repeated, indicating the tree, himself, and everything around them.

It took a while for her to realise what he meant. 'You mean to be like you?' She stared in disbelief. 'A *Redcap*?'

'You have strength, and determination. Your heart is right. You are not swayed by pleading or flattery. You have seen how pitiable and confused the dead are. You would be... effective at guiding them onwards.'

'You make it sound like a job promotion.'

He considered this. 'An elevation. There is much more to this than what you have seen.'

She laughed, long and clear. It was a strange sound in this gloomy place, and the Highwayman looked around as if expecting it to have disturbed something. 'After everything I've seen,' she said, 'you seriously think I want to be one of you?'

'There are many who aspire to this kind of power,' he replied, a little stiffly.

'I'm sorry, did I hurt your feelings? No, my only aspirations are to be happy, to be loved, and to do right by the people who depend on me. That's not too much to ask, is it?'

The Highwayman made no reply to that, but simply turned to leave.

'Where are you going?' she asked.

He turned back. 'You've made your choice to go back. I can't help you in that, only to go on. But I wish you well, all the same.'

'But what am I supposed to do now?'

His eyes narrowed at her in irritation. 'You spurn something that only a handful of people have ever, *ever*, been offered, and then you demand help? Tell me, why should I? Why shouldn't I simply let you wander here until you go insane and fade away into a desperate shade?'

'Because of this.' She flexed her left hand and made a defiant fist, raising it at him. 'You've seen what I can do with this. If I'm trapped here with no alternative, God only knows what kind of damage I might do. Who knows what I might aspire to become? You're going to show me the way out of here because it's a lot less trouble for all of us.'

For a long moment he scrutinised her, as if assessing her capability to make good on such a threat. What he saw must have worried him, because he nodded towards the tree.

'There are places in the umbra where the dead scratch at the skin of the world to get back in,' he said. 'These places become... thin. You found one before, in the asylum. This is another. If you really are as strong as you think, you might be able to scratch all the way through.'

She looked at the lightless fissure torn into the trunk of the hollow oak. Beatrice and her guide had gone that way, presumably to whatever came after for her – but before that she'd been trapped there for over seventy years. What made Rachel think she could do any better? *Because I'm alive*, she thought. Beatrice hadn't had anybody's remembrance to give her strength except for the haphazard and contradictory offerings at the Mary Oak – toys, scraps of ribbon and poems. Rachel had... who did Rachel have?

'Mum, Tom,' she said, and then with a little laugh: 'Smoky.

That's who.' She turned back to the Highwayman, but he'd disappeared. 'Huh. Typical.'

She faced the darkness of the hollow tree, flexed the fingers of her left hand, squared her shoulders, and stepped inside.

She knew instantly that this was a mistake. For a start, ground level was a lot lower inside the trunk, and concave, as she should have remembered from looking at the photographs of Beatrice's remains. Like finding an extra, unexpected step on a staircase in the dark, she stumbled, disorientated, pitching forward, arms outstretched to arrest her fall, palms hitting wood, and she fell to one knee in damp soil and leaf mould. Regaining her balance, she looked back, but couldn't see the crack she'd just fallen through. She stood up and felt back in the direction from which she thought she'd come, but encountered only more dead wood in the absolute blackness.

No, not absolute. Above her – far, far above where the oak opened out – there was a bruise of violet light. It was so far on the edge of the visible spectrum that it hardly seemed to come from the outside world at all, more like the afterimage of a bright light on her retinas. So far away; but maybe not so far away that it was impossible to climb.

Trying to gauge the circumference of the space, she stretched out her arms, but found that there was barely room for her to unbend her elbows before her hands encountered cold, dead wood in both directions.

'Wait, this isn't right,' she murmured. It had been a lot wider than this a moment ago. Now, she could just about turn in a circle on the spot, but even then her shoulders brushed the sides. 'No...'

That bastard Highwayman had lied to her: there was no way out of here. This was no thin place.

Or maybe you're just not as strong as you think you are.

She felt panic begin to clutch at her like dead hands, and forced herself to take long, even breaths. 'You've beaten worse than this,' she told herself. 'Don't lose it now, you stupid cow. You're the Queen of Air and Darkness.'

Yeah, but she died, remember? Beatrice's body rotted where it stood and the bones collapsed into themselves right where you're standing...

Rachel punched the wood and the flare of pain in her knuckles silenced that voice.

'Shut the fuck up and *think*.'

She looked up again. Maybe she could use the fact that the hollow tree had narrowed to her advantage. She'd never done any rock-climbing but she knew about the principle of chimneying: she could brace her back and hands against one wall and her feet against the other, and inch herself upwards. From the outside the trunk had looked to be only a few metres high.

It looks a lot further than that from in here, don't you think? What if it got taller the same way it got narrower? What if it's...

She punched the panic silent again, and before it could start up its whining she braced her back and feet, and pushed.

It was a lot easier imagined than accomplished. She actually managed to shove herself upwards about half a metre, which by her reckoning brought her to ground level outside, but by then her leg muscles were quivering with the strain and the palms of her hands were sweaty and slipping on the dead wood beneath them, which was smooth and offered almost no grip. Then her right hand skidded away and she tumbled diagonally, cracking the side of her head so hard that she saw stars. She would have fallen if there'd been room, but now she couldn't even kneel – her knees would only bend halfway before her bum got stuck on the opposite side.

The hollow tree was getting narrower.

She let the panic come, then.

When Rachel came back to herself, her throat was sore from screaming. She'd screamed for Tom, her mother, her father, Beatrice, the Highwayman – anybody or anything which might have been listening – and after that she'd just screamed. Her fingers stung, too, from where she'd scratched at the dead wood, and several of them were sticky with blood.

This was how Beatrice had died. Except Beatrice had suffered a blow to the skull, which had at least given her the comfort of unconsciousness. Rachel was going to be fully aware as she expired.

Then the skin of her left ankle was tickled by something tiny with lots of legs. She knew what it was without having to look. It was a Devil's coach-horse beetle, and soon it would be joined by lots of its friends.

Panic and screaming took her again – utterly and completely.

42

CATS FOR YOU

WHEN THE HOUSE PHONE RANG, TOM LEAPT TO ANSWER it before it stopped its first shrill. In his mind two equal certainties fought for space: it was Rachel, calling to tell him she was okay; at the same time it was the police, calling to tell him that they'd found her body. Caught between the two, all he could manage was a thick-sounding grunt of 'Hello?'

He hadn't slept, eaten or changed his clothes in the two days that she had been gone. Despite his last conversation with her and his bargain with the ghostly Highways Agency man, he'd driven to everywhere and anywhere he could imagine she might conceivably have gone, knowing that she wouldn't be there, but knowing equally that he had to do something or else go insane. That had ended in a near miss with a cyclist and a mouthful of abuse which told him that he was doing more harm than good, and he had come home to spend the hours channelling his stress and fretfulness into fiddling pointlessly with half a dozen DIY jobs that didn't really need doing.

'Is this Mr Cooper?' asked a female voice on the other end. Not Rachel.

'Yes. What? Have you found her?'

'Her?' the woman asked. 'Don't you mean him?'

'What? Him? Him who? What are you talking about?'

'Your cat, Mr Cooper,' she continued, a little frosty. 'Smoky. I'm phoning from Rednal Veterinary Surgery. He was brought to us this morning by one of the rangers at the Lickey Hills. We scanned his chip and found your details.'

'Smoky.'

'That's right. He's perfectly fine – would you like to come and pick him up?'

Tom rubbed his palm over his face, rubbing his itchy eyes and feeling several days' worth of stubble. He didn't know whether to laugh or cry. The cat. They'd found the fucking cat. He hadn't even noticed that Smoky had disappeared too. Part of him wanted to say, 'No of course I don't want to come and pick him up, it's my *wife* that's missing; put the bastard thing to sleep for all I care,' but Smoky was Rachel's, and there was a good chance that the scrawny animal might be all he had to remember her by, so he said, 'Of course. Thank you.' Then he hung up and went to find a clean shirt.

Rednal Veterinary Surgery was a clean, bland facility staffed by people who were probably lovely and friendly if you weren't half out of your mind with worry for your missing wife, and Tom took Smoky away in a heavy-gauge wire mesh cat carrier after signing some paperwork that he didn't bother to read. He was tightening the passenger seat belt around the carrier when something that had been said to him earlier broke through the fog in his brain and flashed at him. He went back inside to the receptionist.

'I'm sorry – where did you say they'd found him, again?'

'The Lickeys. A ranger found him. We're the nearest practice.'

'Did they say exactly where in the hills?'

'Something about trees covered in ribbons? Apparently he was found playing with them. But then that's cats for you, isn't it?' She smiled helpfully.

'Yes. Yes it is. Thanks.'

He went back out to the van, got into his seat and looked across at Smoky, who was sitting in his cage, legs neatly tucked away, perfectly content.

'What were you doing all the way out there, hmm?' asked Tom. 'You can barely get your lazy arse downstairs for feeding time. You got something to tell me?'

Smoky just narrowed his green eyes at Tom and kept his own counsel.

It was a long shot, Tom thought, quite ridiculous, but then in the grand scheme of things no more ridiculous than bargaining with death on the hard shoulder of the M5, so what did he have to lose?

He stopped at the Beacon Hill car park, leaving Smoky in the van, and set off across the grass. It was a blustery September afternoon and children were back at school, so the only other people up there were older couples and dog-walkers. Normally he would have stopped to enjoy the view over the green suburbs of southern Birmingham and the bristling towers of the city centre, but there didn't seem much point without Rachel to enjoy it beside him – and he knew that somewhere down there, hidden within the neatly plotted estates, were the ruins of an asylum that had nearly claimed her life. So he struck off through the woods to the clearing of the Mary Oak.

It seemed no different from the only other time he'd been there – with Rachel – fascinated by the fluttering collection of tattered remembrances that clustered the branches and roots of the trees surrounding the clearing. It had been quaint, he'd thought, a bit of harmless folk tradition. If Rachel were to be believed, the hollow oak was still there, in the umbra; if this were not all madness, it was where she had pulled Oak Mary back into the living world.

And if he never saw his wife again, he supposed it would be as fit a memorial as any.

'Rachel,' he said to the empty air. 'I don't know if you're anywhere that you can hear this, but I just want to let you know that I'm sorry. I should have trusted that you knew what you were doing. I shouldn't have tried to pretend that none of it was happening. I made a deal with my death that I would go with him willingly at a time of his choosing if he helped you, but it must not have worked because you're not here, and I don't know what to do about that.' Suddenly his pent-up fury at the unfairness of it all boiled out of him. '*You fucker!*' he screamed. '*I'm not the one who's supposed to still be here!*' He sank to his knees in the middle of the clearing and wept. 'I don't know what to do,' he moaned. 'Somebody please just tell me what to do.'

But nothing happened. The woodland swallowed his apologies and his pleas alike into the mindless white noise of rustling leaves, leaving him with nothing. No answers. Nobody was listening. Nobody ever had. The prayers and offerings in the trees around him were no longer a quaint folk tradition; they were a cruel hoax perpetrated on the desperate by themselves, and suddenly their blind, complacent hope enraged him. Tom lurched to his feet like a drunkard and roamed around the clearing, grabbing the ribbons off the trees, tearing up the poems, stamping the toys underfoot and snapping the mobiles into kindling, sobbing as he did it. Finally, exhausted, he looked around at the wreckage he'd made and nodded, wiping his face. Good. Fuck it. Fuck it all.

He turned to leave.

Tell me what to do.

Voices.

That one had sounded almost like Tom.

But there had been so many voices: whispering, hectoring, shouting, begging, cursing. Most of them came from inside her own skull, but she suspected not all of them. She dipped in and out of consciousness like an oar rowing a boat over a black river, welcoming those moments of oblivion because living was torment. Her throat was swollen and raw with thirst; her head burning with a fever which had spread upwards from the roots of her infected fingers, hollowing her out, turning her into a husk. Sometimes she was as tall as an oak; sometimes, as small as the beetles that busied about her – in her ears, in her nose, at her mouth. She'd soiled herself at some point, and already stank like something dead. She *was* dead. It was just that her body hadn't caught up yet.

Please, Rachel, tell me what to do.

An outside voice, that one.

Tom's voice.

Her paper-dry lips mouthed the shape of his name: 'Tom?'

Tom stopped at the edge of the clearing and looked back. He thought he'd heard Rachel's voice, but there was nothing except the wind in the trees.

'Face it, mate,' he said. 'You're losing it. Time to go home.'

This time he heard it distinctly, the rustling of leaves and branches in the wind assembling themselves into intelligible syllables which repeated, 'Tom!'

'Rachel!' he yelled, and ran to the other side of the clearing, but there was nothing except more scattered ribbons and trampled toys. He ran back and found exactly the same thing, and then realised his mistake: her voice wasn't coming from somewhere hidden amongst the trees, it was coming from the middle of the clearing, hidden behind the air itself.

From where, out of the empty space about a foot above the ground, emerged his wife's left hand – the one that shouldn't exist.

Tom threw himself full length on the earth, clutching at her hand before it could disappear. Her fingers clasped his weakly, and he saw that they were filthy and bloodied, the nails splintered and ragged. He pulled, not too hard, not wanting to hurt her, but either her own weight or some other force was resisting. He scooched backwards on his knees and elbows, and more of her left arm appeared, then her shoulder, then her lovely, haggard face blinking in the bright sun, and as if that were the point at which the ghost of the Mary Oak conceded defeat, the rest of Rachel fell out of the air and onto the grass. Her hand was nothing more than a stump again, but she clutched him tightly all the same, and he thought she'd never looked so beautiful.

AFTER

GIGI'S FUNERAL WAS HUGE. IT WASN'T JUST FAMILY members – although they were many, and quite a few came from unexpected corners of the world – but also retired co-workers from her time in the council housing department, members of the congregation of St Hilda's which she had attended for as long as she was physically able, a group from a homeless charity where she'd volunteered, and even a minor government minister there to pay tribute to her work in the Women's Volunteer Service during the war. But there were few mourners from Gigi's own generation, as so few remained.

Rachel sat with Tom and her mum, listened to the eulogies, sang the hymns, and mingled with the murmuring groups eating church sandwiches afterwards. She didn't need the Sight to see the ribbon that Oliver Sewell had described threading all of them together. In some places its loops were so wide and loose that it might not have been there at all; in others, so tight that they could barely speak to each other for the pain of Gigi's passing, but simply stood close and quiet together, taking what peace they could from each other's presence. For the first time she thought that adding her own small loop to this beautiful, intricate pattern might not be such a bad thing.

She and Tom slipped out of the wake in the church hall and found a quiet place in the cemetery away from the kids who were, inevitably, running around the gravestones.

'She lived so long,' said Rachel. 'I never knew she was so many people.'

He nodded. 'I hope you're not expecting me to say something profound here.'

'Hmph. Chance'd be a fine thing.'

They walked on amongst the graves. *All the dead*, she thought, *and the only thing keeping them alive is us, the living*. Somewhere in a quiet and shady corner nearby there was a new headstone which Rachel had paid for very quietly out of her own money – a plot without a grave because there was no body to bury, and a headstone which read simply:

In Memory of Beatrice Rebecca Eaton
1919–1943

'I bet you can't wait to be away from here,' Tom said, startling her out of her reverie.

'How do you mean?'

'It can't be a fun place to be able to see into the hereafter with all these dead people around.'

'It's actually okay,' Rachel replied. 'Very quiet. The dead linger in the places that meant something to them when they were alive – the last place you're going to see a ghost is in a graveyard.'

'Now that's what you call ironic.'

They walked for a while more, through the dappled light underneath the trees.

'I thought I wouldn't have this long,' Tom said suddenly.

She waited for him to continue, knowing that if she pressed him he'd clam up out of embarrassment.

'When I made that deal with the Highwayman,' he added. 'I expected him to take me right then, or soon afterwards. I was ready to go.'

'Yes, well I wasn't. I told him I didn't care what kind of deal you made with him, if he ever showed his face around you again he and I would have words.'

'My hero,' Tom replied, with only the tiniest trace of irony.

'Anyway,' she added. 'His kind don't make the decisions. We do.' She took a deep breath and his hand. 'So,' she said. 'Want to make a baby?'

A surprised grin lit up his face. Then he looked around in mock confusion. 'What, here? Bit public, isn't it?'

She shook her head. 'You are such a dick.'

'You say that like it's a bad thing.'

* * *

The day Rachel brought baby Oliver home from the hospital, the umbra behind her home changed. Where once it had been the desolate echoes of factory units, there were now the dim but unmistakable shapes of the walls and doorways of her own house. To her Touch they were as insubstantial as memory itself, but she thought that over time they would become more solid, acquiring existence from the slow accretion of her new family's past, like a pearl building itself layer by layer. She didn't know what had happened to the shades of the dead that she had seen shambling there. It seemed unlikely that each had finally chosen to go with their own particular Redcap; more likely they had finally succumbed to the emptiness of their own existence and simply guttered out like candles.

It was as she watched her son grow and learn – first how to smile, then crawl, walk, and utter his first babbling words – that more and more the words of the Highwayman came back to her: *You have seen how pitiable and confused the dead are. You would be effective at guiding them onwards.*

She kept an eye out for the Highwayman, ready to confront him if he chose to make good on his threat to come for Tom, but it wasn't the psychopomp who found her in the end.

On a bright morning in early November, while Tom was at work and Ollie was down for his mid-morning nap, Rachel was enjoying a rare moment of peace with a book in the living room when she heard a loud and persistent scratching at the front door. Her heart did a quick two-step at the memory of a weasel-faced monstrosity snarling and tearing its way through the back door, and then she realised what it was.

'Smoky!' she called. 'You have a cat flap, you know!'

The scratching continued.

'Awkward sod,' she muttered, getting up. 'Don't make me manicure you again.'

In the hallway she found Smoky with both forepaws up against the inside of the front door. He turned to look at her, dropped to all fours, gave a hoarse meow which said 'Finally!' as clearly as if he'd uttered it in English, and then sauntered past her with his tail aloft.

She stared after him. 'So what was all that about?'

It was then that she noticed the blurred shape of a human figure through the frosted glass of the door's central panel. There was no reason to think that it was anyone other than someone selling double-glazing or religion, except that they were just standing there and hadn't even knocked.

You come near him again, she'd told the Highwayman, *you and I are going to have words*.

She flexed the fingers of her dead hand and with her living one opened the door a crack.

The man standing outside wasn't a psychopomp – but the reason why he hadn't been able to knock on the door was because he wasn't alive either. At first she wasn't entirely sure that he even was a he. Despite stubble crusting the lower half of a tanned and creased face in which dirt lined every furrow, the figure was dressed entirely in women's clothes: Ugg boots, yoga pants, a denim jacket with a heavy fur collar, and rainbow fingerless gloves. The left side of his head was thickly matted with gore, testifying to the manner of his death.

'Are you Rachel Cooper?' His voice was the sound of broken reed husks.

'Who wants to know?'

The harlequin figure broke down sobbing, tears cutting through dirt and heavily smudged eyeliner. 'Oh thank God!' he wept. 'They told me you were real but I didn't want to believe it. They said you can help me. Can you help me? Please?'

They?

'Help you? Help you how?'

'I'm so confused. I don't know what's going on. I don't know where I am. I think... I think something terrible has happened to me. And—' he glanced around fearfully. 'I'm pretty sure someone's after me. Please!'

Rachel looked past him into the street – both in the living world and the umbra – but saw nothing. No Redcaps, not yet, but they wouldn't be far behind. She thought of her son, vulnerable in his cot upstairs. And she looked at the shade again, at his terror and desperation. She remembered the pathetic spectres at Scoles Farm, and the pleading of Oliver Sewell – the man for whom she had named her baby. She didn't know how rumours and gossip spread amongst the dead of the umbra, but she knew that this weeping soul wouldn't be the last to come to her door begging for help.

So she opened it wider.

'Come on in,' she said. 'Let's get the kettle on and you can tell me all about it.'

AFTERWORD & ACKNOWLEDGEMENTS

OBVIOUSLY *THE HOLLOW TREE* IS A WORK OF FICTION, but I suspect like most writers I am a jackdaw for shiny pieces of other stories to steal, and so much of this novel is heavily inspired by an urban myth local to me – that of Bella in the Wych Elm.

On 18 April 1943, four lads poaching in Hagley Wood south of Birmingham found the skeletal remains of a woman hidden in the hollow trunk of an ancient elm tree. The resulting police investigation created more questions than it answered, especially when graffiti appeared in Birmingham which read 'Who put Bella down the Wych Elm?' and she changed from being an anonymous corpse into a woman with a name, and hence a family and identity. That identity has never been established – let alone that of her killer or killers – a situation not helped by the loss of her remains during the war.

Cue all manner of conspiracy theories.

In some she is a British double agent – a cabaret-singer-turned-spy betrayed by her wartime contacts and murdered to stop her revealing their secrets, her remains having been destroyed by MI5. In others she is a prostitute, killed by a 'client'. The discovery of bones from one of her hands in nearby leaf-litter was clear evidence of gypsy witchcraft, proof that she had been sacrificed and her hand severed in an attempt to create a 'hand of glory'. All of this is despite the fact that there is no evidence of gypsies or witches ever being active in the area, and the one cabaret singer who might have fitted her description was still recording songs several years after Bella's body was found. Given the chaos of wartime, the police did their best to find any 'Bellas', or variations on that name, who had been reported missing, but came up with nothing. To this day Bella's death remains unexplained. The case is closed, officially unsolved.

The danger in writing her story was, as I saw it, of falling into the trap of trying to uncover the 'truth' of her death and ending up with a historical murder-mystery. If that's what you're interested in there are any number of excellent books on the subject, picking apart the evidence for and against the various theories. Steve Punt made a particularly thorough documentary for Radio 4, and a recent independently produced short film by Thomas Lee Rutter is well worth a watch. My reason for playing fast and loose with the historical details was in an attempt to get at something deeper than a simple 'solution' to the mystery – something about the different people that each of us is in life and what that might mean for us in the afterlife, if there is one.

So Bella became Mary, the elm became an oak, and Hagley Wood became the Lickey Hills, near my home.

The real Bella graffiti also appeared on the base of a large obelisk in a field near the woods where her remains were found. The monument was erected by Sir Richard Lyttelton, owner of nearby Hagley Hall, as part of the then-fashionable vogue for manufacturing picturesque landscapes. The lettering is refreshed from time to time, always anonymously, and is something of a macabre navigation point if you're rambling the fields around Hagley. There is also a much larger obelisk in the Lickeys – this one raised in the 1800s to the memory of the 6th Earl of Plymouth who went by the improbable-sounding name of Other Archer Windsor, which suited as a replacement for the purposes of the story. We do love our tall, phallic monuments.

There are no rag trees in the Lickeys – at least not to my knowledge – but there is a clootie well a few miles away in St Kenelm's Pass, which runs between the Clent Hills. Folklore has it that Kenelm, a Mercian prince, was murdered by an ambitious relative and his body hidden there, and that when it was discovered and disinterred a freshwater spring burst out of his grave. That spring is now in the grounds of St Kenelm's Church, and the trees around it are decorated with ribbons, shoelaces and scraps of paper.

The Old Hare and Hounds where Rachel and Annabel have their drink after battling the *lesh* is real, as is the fact that next to the pub was once a cottage where a certain Mr

Tolkien lived for part of his childhood. This has nothing to do with *The Hollow Tree* except that I enjoy these kinds of coincidences. They happen much more frequently in real life than a writer can ever get away with in fiction.

In shamelessly plundering this hoard of local folklore I am indebted to Dan Williams, who knows far more about the area than I suspect he is letting on, and who marked my first draft for spelling, punctuation and grammar. Any geographical or historical inaccuracies are entirely my own. I'm also indebted to the staff at the archives of the Hive in Worcester where, if you choose, you can find the original police records of the Bella case, pretty much as I've described them.

I owe huge thanks to my agent, Ian Drury, for finding this tale a home, and my editors Miranda Jewess and Cat Camacho at Titan for making sure that it was properly housetrained when it was finally allowed in; to Odile Thomas for help with French cursing, and the Balti Boys (Pete, Mike, Stan, John and Adrian) for restorative curries. As ever, and eternally, to TC, and my daughters Hopey and Eden.

ABOUT THE AUTHOR

JAMES BROGDEN IS A PART-TIME AUSTRALIAN WHO grew up in Tasmania and now lives with his wife and two daughters in Bromsgrove, Worcestershire, where he teaches English. He spends as much time in the mountains as he is able, and more time playing with Lego than he should. He is the author of *Hekla's Children*, *The Narrows*, *Tourmaline*, *The Realt* and *Evocations*, and his horror and fantasy stories have appeared in various periodicals and anthologies ranging from *The Big Issue* to the British Fantasy Society Award-winning Alchemy Press. Blogging occurs infrequently at jamesbrogden.blogspot.co.uk, and tweeting at @skippybe.

HEKLA'S CHILDREN

JAMES BROGDEN

A decade ago, teacher Nathan Brookes saw four of his students walk up a hill and vanish. Only one returned – Olivia – starved, terrified, and with no memory of where she'd been. After a body is found in the same woodland where they disappeared it is first believed to be one of the missing children, but is soon identified as a Bronze Age warrior, nothing more than an archaeological curiosity. Yet Nathan starts to have terrifying visions of the students. Then Olivia reappears, half-mad and willing to go to any lengths to return the corpse to the earth. For he is the only thing keeping a terrible evil at bay...

"A VISCERAL, SEAT-OF-THE-PANTS THRILLER"
The Guardian

"AMBITIOUS, SKILFULLY PLOTTED
AND EVOCATIVELY REALISED"
SFX

"A SMART BLEND OF SCIENCE
FICTION AND HORROR"
Barnes & Noble

THE SILENCE
TIM LEBBON

In the darkness of an underground cave system, blind creatures hunt by sound. Then there is light, there are voices, and they feed... Swarming from their prison, the creatures thrive and destroy. To scream, even to whisper, is to summon death. As the hordes lay waste to Europe, a girl watches to see if they will cross the sea. Deaf for many years, she knows how to live in silence; now, it is her family's only chance of survival. To leave their home, to shun others, to find a remote haven where they can sit out the plague. But will it ever end? And what kind of world will be left?

"A TRULY GREAT NOVEL WITH A FRESH
AND ORIGINAL STORY"
Starburst

"A CHILLING AND HEART-
WRENCHING STORY"
Publishers Weekly

"*THE SILENCE* IS A CHILLING STORY
THAT GRIPS YOU FIRMLY BY THE THROAT"
SciFi Now

AN ENGLISH GHOST STORY

KIM NEWMAN

The Naremores, a dysfunctional British nuclear family, seek a new life away from the big city in the sleepy Somerset countryside. At first their new home, The Hollow, seems to embrace them, creating a rare peace and harmony within the family. But when the house turns on them, it seems to know just how to hurt them the most – threatening to destroy them from the inside out.

"IMMERSIVE, CLAUSTROPHOBIC
AND UTTERLY WONDERFUL"
M.R. Carey, *New York Times* bestselling
author of *The Girl With All the Gifts*

"THOROUGHLY ENJOYABLE,
MASTER STORYTELLING"
Lauren Beukes

"DESERVES TO STAND BESIDE
THE GREAT NOVELS OF THE GHOSTLY"
Ramsey Campbell

For more fantastic fiction, author events, competitions,
limited editions and more

VISIT OUR WEBSITE
titanbooks.com

LIKE US ON FACEBOOK
facebook.com/titanbooks

FOLLOW US ON TWITTER
@TitanBooks

EMAIL US
readerfeedback@titanemail.com

Eighth Grave
After
Dark

Darynda Jones

piatkus

PIATKUS

First published in the US in 2015 by St Martin's Press
First published in Great Britain in 2015 by Piatkus

1 3 5 7 9 10 8 6 4 2

A CIP catalogue record for this book
is available from the British Library.

ISBN 978-0-349-40348-9

Printed and bound in Great Britain by
Clays Ltd, St Ives plc

Papers used by Piatkus are from well-managed forests
and other responsible sources.

MIX
Paper from
responsible sources
FSC
www.fsc.org   FSC® C104740

Piatkus
An imprint of
Little, Brown Book Group
Carmelite House
50 Victoria Embankment
London EC4Y 0DZ

An Hachette UK Company
www.hachette.co.uk

www.piatkus.co.uk

For the Grimlets.

I am honored beyond measure that you

take the time to read my books,

post photos of coffee and half-naked men,

answer the many calls to arms,

and pimp the ever-lovin' heck outta
Charley and the gang.

Thank you, thank you, thank you!

Acknowledgments

Every book creates new challenges and opportunities, and each is a joy to write, but none of them would be what they are without the help of a few friends and colleagues along the way. I am forever grateful to the following radiant beings:

- Alexandra Machinist: for putting up with me!
- Jennifer Enderlin: also, for putting up with me! (No, really.)
- Josie Freedman: for the kind words and enthusiasm
- Eliani Torres: for not putting out a hit on me
- Everyone at St. Martin's Press: for being awesome
- Everyone at Macmillan Audio: for being amazing
- Lorelei King: for bringing my characters to life
- Dana Crawford: for what little sanity I have left
- Lacy Fair: for precious time saved
- Jowanna Kestner: for the giggles and the tears
- Theresa Rogers: for the incredible insight

- Robyn Peterman: for YOU! (and for my boyfriend Kurt)
- DD: for the underwear story :)
- Ashlee and Rhia: for allowing me to pillage your childhoods
- The Grimlets: for help with the you-know-what, especially,
  - Patricia Dechant
  - Jennifer Coffman Love
  - Trayce Layne
  - Wendy McCall Beck
  - Laura Harrison Burleson
- Patricia Whitney: for the sign
- Netter and Kinter: for the light in my heart
- The Mighty, Mighty Jones Boys: for my reason to breathe
- The Readers: for the fact that you love to read as much as I do

THANK YOU SO VERY, VERY MUCH!!!

Eighth Grave
After
Dark

1

Sometimes I crave pickles.
Other times I crave the blood of my enemy.
Weird.
—CHARLEY DAVIDSON

There was a dead tax attorney in my closet, sobbing uncontrollably into the hem of her blouse. She'd been there a few days now. It made getting dressed in the morning awkward.

I would've avoided her altogether if I could, but it was my only closet. And it was microscopic. Tough to ignore chance encounters.

But I had to get ready for a wedding, and sobbing tax attorney or not, I had to get into that closet. I couldn't let my bestie down. Or my uncle, the man with whom my bestie was gracing her presence for as long as they both shall live.

Today was the big day. Their big day. The day they'd been waiting for since they first laid eyes on each other. It took some finagling, but I finally got them to admit their feelings for each other and commit, and I wasn't about to let a tax attorney ruin it. Unless, of course, she was there to audit me. I didn't think so, though. Usually the person crying at an audit was the client, not the tax attorney.

No more stalling. I braced myself and opened the door. She sat curled in a ball in the corner, crying like there was no tomorrow. Which, for her, there wasn't. A name tag she was wearing when she'd died read SHEILA with TAX ATTORNEY stamped underneath that. She must have been at some kind of convention when she died, but her cause of death was not immediately apparent. She looked disheveled, her chocolate-colored hair mussed, her tight bun askew on her head, but that could have happened when she was attacked. If she was attacked. Or it could have been the result of a few too many mojitos during the after party.

There was just no way of knowing her cause of death without talking to her, and God knew I'd tried to do that on several occasions. She wouldn't stop sobbing long enough for me to get a word in edgewise. I could've told her I could see her because I'd been born the grim reaper. I could've told her I'd help her find whoever did this. I could've told her she could cross through me whenever she was ready to see her family, those who had passed before her.

Most people who died went either north or south immediately following their deaths. But some stayed behind. Many had unfinished business of some kind, just like the ghosts and spirits in folktales, but some stayed behind because they'd died traumatically. Their energy grabbed hold of the earthly realm and didn't let go. They were anchored here, and until they healed, they would never cross to the other side.

That was where I came in. I helped the departed any way I could. I found their killers, righted their wrongs, sent messages to their loved ones, all so they could heal and cross to the other side, which they then did through me. Through my light. A light that was supposedly so brilliant, it could be seen by the departed from anywhere on earth.

But Sheila wasn't talking, so there was little I could do at the moment.

As carefully as I could, I pulled a cinnamon bridesmaid's dress through her quivering shoulders. "Sorry," I said as I patted her dark hair. She released another loud wail of sorrow before I closed the door. Thankfully, it was a thick door.

"What?" I asked as I turned back to Artemis, a departed Rottweiler who'd been dubbed my guardian by the powers that be. And ever since a dozen testy hellhounds had tried to rip out my jugular, Artemis refused to leave my side.

She sat there, ears perked, head tilted in curiosity as she pawed at the closet door.

"I've tried talking to her." I walked to a full-length mirror and held up the dress. "She only cries louder."

I rubbed to soften the worry line between my brows. As far as bridesmaid's dresses went, this one wasn't the worst. It would've looked even better if I weren't the size of the Chrysler Building. I was currently incubating the girl who would save the world, according to prophecies, but that wasn't what had been worrying me that morning.

Being a matron of honor was just that, an honor, and part of my job was to make sure the bride showed up for her wedding. Cookie had yet to arrive. It was probably that third margarita she'd had last night. Or the ninth. That girl could knock 'em back. In her defense, she was drinking for two. Since I was pregtastic, I'd been restricted to sparkling grape juice. Didn't have quite the same effect, but it was fun watching my sister and BFF belt out show tunes while channeling Christopher Walken.

I dialed Cookie's number to make sure she was headed my way when a voice, deep and sultry, wafted toward me from the door of my bedroom. If that was Cook, she'd had way more to drink than I thought.

"Closing the door on a traumatized dead chick isn't your style," the man said.

Artemis yelped and leapt toward the door, her stubby tail wagging with unmitigated joy.

I swirled to face my husband, the devastatingly handsome supernatural being who'd been forged in the fires of sin, created in hell by the very creature we were in hiding from. As far as we knew, Lucifer, Reyes's father, had sent the Twelve, the hounds of hell, the most vicious and bloodthirsty creatures ever to exist. And he sent them here to destroy us. Our only salvation was literally the land we stood on. The sacred ground that the Twelve couldn't traverse, as we were now living in a convent. An abandoned convent, but a convent—with the requisite sacred ground—nonetheless.

And we'd been here for months in an attempt to avoid being ripped to shreds by the hellhounds that patrolled the border. With help, our job had been to scour ancient texts and prophecies as we searched for a way to kill them. Only Reyes and I were at risk. We seemed to be the only ones the hellhounds wanted for breakfast. Everyone else could come and go as they pleased, which would go a long way toward explaining the lateness of the bride to prepare for her own wedding. We had hours yet, but I figured Cookie would've been at the convent at the butt crack of dawn, waking me up to do her hair. God only knew what would come of that.

Still, my immediate company was nothing to scoff at. His disheveled appearance every time he entered a room of late caused the blood in my veins to surge, the pulse at my throat to quicken.

He bent to pet Artemis. I watched as he gave her a final pat then indicate the Barbie closet with a nod and a gently arched brow. I followed his gaze. The closet had been made for a person with few worldly possessions, aka a nun. And though I was now living in the aforementioned convent, I was not a nun. Not by a long shot. Proof resided in the ever-expanding girth of my midsection.

His signature heat drifted toward me, blisteringly hot, a by-product of his being forged in the fires of hell, and I turned back to him. His hair, thick and unruly and in dire need of a trim, curled over his collar and around his ears. He still wore the button-down from last night. It hung open, revealing the wide expanse of chest he'd crossed his arms over. The cuffs of the shirt had been rolled up to his elbows, showing his sinuous forearms. Beneath them, a rock-hard waist tapered down to lean hips that rested comfortably against the doorjamb. He let me absorb every inch of him, knowing it gave me a thrill. Knowing he'd reap the benefits later.

After taking in his form, my attentions unhurried, languid, I slowly returned to his face. He'd let a small grin soften his mouth. His deep brown eyes sparkled beneath dark lashes that were spiked with the remnants of sleep. As though he'd just woken up. As though he had no idea how sexy that was.

Normally, I would've chalked up his appearance to the bachelor party they'd had for my uncle, but he'd looked like that for weeks now. Exhausted. Disheveled. Sexy as fuck. I could hardly complain, but I was beginning to worry about him. I noticed that he grew hotter when he was trying to heal from an injury, and his heat had been growing hotter by leaps and bounds lately, but he hadn't been injured in months. We'd both been stuck in the convent, on sacred ground, since I was about a month pregnant. That was almost eight months ago, and we hadn't been stabbed, shot, or run down with a runaway vehicle since. I'd have to keep a close eye on him. I did that anyway, so I'd have to keep a closer eye on him.

"Hey! Wait!" I threw the cinnamon dress at him. "You're not supposed to see me before the wedding."

He flashed a set of startlingly white teeth. "I think that only applies to the bride."

"Oh, right." When he indicated the closet again with a questioning gaze, I decided to question him back. "Do you know how many times I've tried talking to her? She won't stop crying long enough to catch her breath, let alone tell me what's wrong. Why did I get this closet?"

His grin spread. "Because it's the only one in the room."

He had a good point. He'd been forced to use a closet in the next room, but still.

"Want me to take care of her?" he asked.

"No, I do not want you to take care of her. Wait, you can do that?"

"Just say the word."

Sadly, I considered it. Her sobbing was taxing, probably because she was a tax attorney, and yet I heard her only when the door was open.

"Check this out," I said, walking to the door. I opened it, and we were met with loud wailing. After a moment, I closed the door again. Crickets. Metaphorically. "This door is incredible," I said, opening it again and closing it several times in a row to demonstrate.

"You need to get out more," he said.

"Right? I'd kill for the delightful décor of Macho Taco."

His face held his expression steady, not wavering in the slightest, but I felt an involuntary pang of regret ripple through him.

I let go of the door and straightened. "No," I said, walking to him.

He pushed off the doorjamb and waited to wrap me in his arms. His heat whispered across my skin and bathed me in warmth as one arm slid around my back while he let his free hand caress Beep, the fugitive I'd been harboring for almost nine months. I felt it was about time to evict her, but the midwife Reyes had hired told me she'd come in her own time. Apparently, Beep lived in a different time zone than I did.

"No," I repeated, blasting him with my best stern face. "We've done okay. We now have a semi-solid plan in place to blow this Popsicle stand once Beep is born that could actually work, if the planets align just so. I've had lots of time to practice my mad skills in grim reaperism slash supernatural being. And I've learned a lot about why I never became a nun: no closet space. This is not your fault."

"At least your father isn't trying to kill us." He stilled, shocked at his own statement, then said, "I'm sorry. I didn't mean—"

"Don't be ridiculous." I dismissed his statement with a wave of my hand. My father had died a few days before we sought refuge at the convent, and I was still searching for his killer. Well, my uncle, a detective for Albuquerque PD was, but I was helping every chance I got. "Reyes, it's not your fault your father is evil. Or that he's the most hated being this side of Mars."

"That's not entirely true," he said. When I silently questioned him, he added, "Not everyone believes in the devil."

"Good point." I was not about to argue with him about his father. He felt guilty that his father would do anything in his power to kill us. To kill Beep, actually. She was the one prophesied to destroy him. I'd tried repeatedly to convince Reyes that this wasn't his fault—to no avail, so I changed the subject instead. "What's with all the dead people on the lawn?"

Departed had been showing up for about a week, standing in what would be considered our front lawn. If we had a lawn. If this were a house and not a converted convent.

A worried expression flashed across Reyes's face so fast, I almost missed it. Almost. "I wish I knew."

He'd been worried a lot lately. I could tell the situation was draining him, and I couldn't help but wonder if he didn't feel like he was in prison again. He'd spent ten years there for a crime he didn't commit. And now once again, for all intents and purposes, he was incarcerated. We both were. We were prisoners of a sort, stuck in this place, and while I was certainly going a bit stir-crazy, my restlessness couldn't compare to his. Still, one foot across that invisible line, the one that marked the sacred, blessed ground from the rest of the area, and that foot would be gone. Along with part of a leg.

We'd fought the Twelve before, and while we didn't exactly lose, we sure didn't win. They came back angrier than ever. Their snarls every time I stepped too close to the border were proof of that. They wanted a piece of me, but it was hard to blame them. I did have a killer ass. Or, well, I used to.

I walked back to the mirror and held up the dress, the one that had to be let out due to the fact that my ass had grown in sync with my belly. Reyes stayed close behind, his hand warm at the small of my back, his heat seeping in and easing the ache there. He was very therapeutic, especially now that the nights were getting cooler.

"They won't talk to me," I said, trying to decide if cinnamon had been my color all along and I just didn't know it. It did match my eyes quite nicely, which were the color of the amber in which the mosquito was preserved in *Jurassic Park,* but it also made me look a little deader than I liked. "The departed on the lawn. I keep thinking they need help to cross, but they just stare straight ahead, their expressions completely blank. Maybe they're zombies." I turned this way and that. "Either way, it's unsettling."

Reyes pressed into my backside and rubbed my shoulders with what I'd come to realize were magic hands. He was clearly the Magic Man Heart had sung about. I'd had no idea anything could feel that good. On bad days—the days there was just no settling Beep—it rivaled an orgasm.

Wait, no, it didn't. Nothing rivaled an orgasm. But it came damned close.

"You're bright," he said, bending until his breath fanned across my cheek.

"I know, but—"

"You're *really* bright."

I laughed and turned into him. "I know, but—"

"No," he said, his eyes sparkling with humor, "you're even brighter than normal. Your light is so bright, it fills every corner of the house."

Of course, only he would know that. I couldn't see my light, which was probably a good thing because how would I put on makeup if all I saw was a bright light? No, wait, he wasn't the only one who would know that. There were others who could see it. The departed, obviously, but also Osh, our resident Daeva, a slave demon who'd escaped from hell centuries ago. And Quentin, a Deaf kid we'd adopted as part of our gang, who mostly hung out with Cookie's daughter, Amber. And Pari, one of my best friends. And Angel, my departed thirteen-year-old sidekick and lead investigator.

I blinked, realizing all the people who would have known that my brightness levels needed adjusting. "Why didn't anyone tell me?"

He lifted a shoulder. "There's not anything you can do about it, right?"

"Right."

"Then why bring it up?"

"It's important, that's why. Maybe there's a reason. Maybe I'm sick." I felt my forehead. My cheeks. My chest. Then I lifted Reyes's hand and pressed it to my chest, glancing up from beneath my lashes as impishly as I possibly could. "Do I feel feverish?"

He darkened instantly. His gaze dropped to Danger and Will Robinson, aka my breasts. His gaze did that often, unruly thing that it was. Danger and Will loved the attention.

"You shouldn't tempt me," he said, his voice growing ragged.

A tingle of desire sparked to life, causing a warmth to pool in my abdomen. "You're the only one I should tempt, seeing as how we're hitched."

He wrapped a hand around my throat ever so softly and led me back against the mirror. It wasn't his actions that jump-started my heart, but the raw lust that consumed him. The dark need in his eyes. The severity of his drawn brows. The sensuality of his parted mouth. My girl parts tightened when he dipped his hand into my shirt. His thumb grazed over a hardened nipple, and a jolt of pleasure shot straight to my core.

"I'm here!" Cookie called from down the hall, her voice breathy, winded from the stairs.

I almost groaned aloud at the interruption. Reyes's grip on my throat tightened. He tilted my face up to his and whispered, "We'll continue this later."

"Promise?" I asked, unwilling to relinquish the impish bit.

He covered my mouth with his, his tongue hot as it dived inside me, as he melted my knees and stole my breath. Then, a microsecond before Cookie walked in, he pushed off me with a wink and strolled to look out the window. Still weak from his kiss, I almost stumbled forward.

"I'm here," said Cookie Kowalski, my assistant who moonlighted as my best friend, as she rushed into the room.

It took me a sec, but I finally tore my gaze off my husband. Cookie's short black hair had been flattened on one side, making her look lopsided. Her mismatched clothes were rumpled and a purple scarf dangled off one shoulder, perilously close to falling to the floor. Though Cook was considered large by society's standards, she wore her size well. She had the beauty and confidence of an eccentric, wardrobe-challenged countess. Normally. Today she looked more like a frazzled scullery maid.

I fought a grin and chastised her for her tardiness. "It's about time, missy," I said, tapping my naked wrist to make my point clear.

She gasped audibly, then looked at her watch. Her shoulders sagged in relief. "Charley, damn it. The wedding isn't for hours."

"I know," I said, stepping closer as she sat some bags on a bench at the end of the bed. "I just like to keep you on your toes."

"Oh, you do that. No worries there. I'm like a ballerina when you're around."

"Sweet." I leaned over to peek inside a bag. "I also want to thank you again for having the wedding here." She did so to accommodate Reyes and me, since we couldn't leave the grounds.

"Are you kidding?" she asked. "This place is perfect. Who gets to have a wedding in a historic convent surrounded by a lush forest adorned with the colors of autumn? Me. That's who." She gave my shoulders a quick one-armed squeeze. "I am beyond thrilled, hon."

"I'm glad."

"And, by having it here," she continued, pulling out a fluff of pink material from one of the bags, "neither you nor Reyes will be ripped apart by hellhounds during the ceremony. I'd love to get through this without getting blood on my wedding gown."

"It's so always about you," I said, and she laughed. Mission complete.

She took a ribbon off the material, then noticed Reyes's tousled state. "I'm not interrupting anything, am I?"

He turned, but only slightly, not wanting to expose the evidence of exactly what she'd interrupted. "Not at all," he said, pointing outside. "We were just talking about all the departed—"

"—who have passed on over the years," I said, stopping him from making a grave mistake. "And, boy, are there lots." I snorted. "Like millions. Maybe even billions."

Cookie stopped what she was doing—namely rummaging through another shopping bag—and turned toward me, her movements slow. Methodical. Calculated. "There—" Her voice cracked. She cleared her throat and started over. "There are dead people on the lawn, aren't there?"

"What?" I dismissed her suspicions with a wave of my hand. Because that always worked. "Pfft, no way. Why would there—? I mean, what would they be doing on—?"

"Charley," she said in warning, her hangover voice low and alarmingly sexy.

I bit down, cursing myself for my utter lack of finesse. This was her wedding day, and her nerves had been stretched thin enough without a last-minute addition of the recently departed to the guest list.

"Only a couple," I said, strolling nonchalantly to Reyes's side and looking out the two-story window. I was such a liar. There were at least a hundred departed standing in front of the convent. Silent. Unmoving. Unblinking. This was going to be the creepiest wedding ever. At least they weren't coming inside, but the wedding was actually outside in a little clearing behind the convent. Thankfully, they hadn't invaded that area. Much.

Reyes leaned down to me and whispered into my ear. "Your nearness isn't helping my condition."

I glanced at his crotch. The fullness caused a flush to rise in my cheeks. But he was right. Now was not the time. "Sorry," I whispered back before turning to Cookie again. "What's that?"

She was busy staring out another window, and I thanked God she couldn't see the departed. "The curtains for the nursery came in," she said absently.

"Oh!" I rushed forward, snatched them out of her hands, and shook out a panel of pink taffeta. "I sure hope it's a girl," I said, trying to change the subject.

"Of course it's a girl," she said, scanning the grounds. "All the prophecies say so. Where are they?"

"The prophecies?"

"The dead people."

"Right." I looked out over the weathered grounds. The grass had yellowed over the last month, the trees burning with the bright oranges, golds, and reds of autumn.

"They're gone now," I said, adding to the long list of sins I was committing in a house of God. "Those people love playing hide-and-seek. Seriously, it's like a thing with them."

I looked up at her, worried she wouldn't believe me, but her gaze had drifted somewhere else, namely to Reyes's reflection in the window. His shirt still hung open, the white material a stark contrast to the dark skin beneath, the muscles leaving shadows along the upside-down T of his chest and the rungs of his abs. "Good Lord," she said to me, her tone silky soft.

I agreed completely. "Good Lord indeed."

We both gawked a solid minute before he realized what we were doing. He dipped his head, unable to suppress a brilliant smile, and cleared his throat before announcing he got the first shower.

"I don't know how you do it, hon," Cook said when he left.

The communal shower was down the hall, a rustic imitation of my shower at home. And the thought of him in it, with steaming hot water cascading over his shoulders, down the curve of his back, sent a tiny shiver through my body. "Do what? Keep my hands off him?"

"No. Well, yes, but also keep your composure around him." She sat against the windowsill. "I'm not supernatural or anything, but even I can feel his power. His . . . allure. Does that make sense?"

"Damn straight it does."

"There's just something so primal about him. So ethereal."

"And?" I ventured. Cookie didn't usually say much without an ulterior motive.

"I worry about him. About him being a dad."

Surprised, I stopped and straightened my shoulders. "What do you mean?" Then, as a possible explanation sank in, I felt my eyes widen. "Do you think he'll be a bad father?" I turned and looked toward the door to make sure he'd left.

"No," she said with a soft chuckle. "I'm afraid he will sever the spine of any boy who breaks our girl's heart."

"Oh," I said, relief flooding me. But she had an incredibly well thought-out point. "Oh. You're right. I didn't think of that."

"You might want to discuss dating guidelines with him now. You know, before she turns five."

"Five?" I screeched. "Why five?"

The smile that spread across her face was one of practiced stoicism, as though she were talking to a mental patient. "And just when did you become interested in boys?"

"Oh, shit."

"Exactly."

2

IRONY: THE OPPOSITE OF WRINKLY.

—T-SHIRT

Two hours later, a wonderful woman named Hildie was doing Cookie's hair—thankfully, because I had no idea what to do with it—Amber was reading nursery rhymes to Beep, and I was eating strawberries atop my lofty position on a very swank divan named David Beckham. David sat by the window so I could look out at all the colors of autumn. He was thoughtful that way. He knew how much I loved fall, and fall in the Jemez Mountains was nothing short of spectacular.

"Humpty Dumpty sat on a wall," Amber said, reading from a picture book she'd bought Beep. She glanced at my belly as though to check if Beep were paying attention.

"Humpty didn't have much of a life, did he?" I commented.

"Humpty Dumpty had a great fall," she continued, ignoring me. It was weird.

"Lack of exercise. No hand–eye coordination."

"All the king's horses and all the king's men couldn't put Humpty to-gether again."

"Okay, stop right there," I said, a strawberry hovering near my mouth. "How are the king's horses going to help put an egg back together? Seriously. They're horses."

Amber was Cookie's thirteen-going-on-thirty-year-old daughter. She had what I'd begun to suspect was a touch of clairvoyance. She'd surprised me on several occasions with her knowledge or her visions of things to come, and she seemed to have a special connection with Beep. If I didn't know better, I'd say Beep was calmer when Amber was around. It was uncanny.

She sat in a chair beside me, her dark hair hanging in long ringlets down her back, her huge blue eyes concentrating on the pages before her. We were all in slips and robes—except Cookie, who was only in a slip underneath a massive hairdresser's cape—even though the wedding wasn't for another couple of hours. But both Amber's and my hair had been done already, our nails appliquéd to perfection, our makeup soft and sparkly. It had a hint of glitter in it. I argued that my face was shiny enough without adding glitter, but Cookie insisted. She wanted princesses in her wedding, and by damn, we were going to be princesses. I refrained from telling her princesses didn't wear glitter. Pole dancers wore glitter.

"It's a fairy tale," Amber said with a giggle, looking toward the door again. Uncle Bob was bringing Quentin up for the wedding. Quentin was her best friend and the current love of her life. I had to admit, the kid had stolen my heart at first glance. I couldn't imagine what he'd do to an impressionable girl. Thankfully, Cookie was too old for him.

"Do you think anyone will show up?" Cookie asked me. Again. While Amber was keeping a constant vigil on the door, Cookie was keeping watch over the drive to the convent.

"Yes," I said, trying not to laugh at her impatience. "Now, stop fidgeting." Poor Hildie. "Do you guys want anything?" I stuffed the last of the strawberries into my mouth and picked up my phone.

"Again?" Cookie asked. "That poor man."

"Are you kidding? Have you seen my ass? This is all his fault."

"Okay, then I'll take a water."

"And I'll take an orange soda," Amber chimed in.

"You got it. Hildie?"

"I'm good," she said, her brows furrowing in concentration.

I texted Reyes. I'd been doing that a lot. Texting demands to my minions. Being fertilized had its upside. Two minutes later, Reyes, wearing a T-shirt and jeans, had raided the kitchen that was down the stairs, past the foyer, and through a great hall—in other words, way too far for me to walk at the moment—and delivered our order.

He handed me a water with a wink. He'd showered, but had yet to shave. Or comb his hair. Or groom himself in any way. Gawd, he was sexy.

"Is that what you're wearing to the wedding?" I asked, teasing him.

In an act that stunned me to my toes, my uncle had asked Reyes to be his best man. They'd grown very close over the past few months—a good thing, since it was basically my uncle Bob who'd put Reyes in prison. But even Reyes had to admit to the insurmountable evidence against him. Earl Walker, the monster who'd raised him, made sure Reyes would be convicted of his murder, and convicted he was. At least until the cops found Earl very much alive.

"This doesn't work?" he asked.

"It works for me, but—"

"Me, too," Amber said, her crush on Reyes adorable. He flashed that brilliant smile of his. It was very unfair of him.

"Me, three," Cookie added.

Reyes walked over to Cookie as Hildie teased her hair. Or tried to tease her hair. She slipped several times, her hands suddenly useless in the presence of the son of what was once the most beautiful angel in heaven.

"I promise I'll look more presentable than this when the time comes, but until then." He took out a small box and handed it to her. "I wanted you to have this before everyone else demands your attention."

"Reyes," she said, her eyes wide. She opened it, absorbed the meaning of what it was he was giving her, then threw her arms around his neck.

A gold chain dangled from her fingers, and she flashed me the pendant, a diamond-studded infinity symbol.

"It's perfect," she said softly, her eyes wet with emotion.

He dipped his head in a bashful smile as she kissed his cheek. Then he turned back to me before I could hide the loving astonishment on my face.

He enchanted.

He simply enchanted.

Stopping in his tracks when he saw my expression, he studied me a long moment before walking over to me and placing a kiss on my cheek. The act was an excuse to whisper in my ear. "You have to stop looking at me like that if we're going to make it through the day without losing our clothes."

I turned to kiss him back. "I have no intention of making it through the day with you fully clothed."

He grinned again. "Do you need anything else?"

"Pitocin?"

One corner of his mouth rose. "What's that?"

"It induces labor. It's about time for Beep to move out. Cut her hair. Get a job. I need a flat belly."

"Have you tried crunches?"

"I just don't get it. I'm supernatural. You're supernatural. Why can't we have one of those quick pregnancies like Bella and Edward? Gwen from *Torchwood*. Scully. Deanna Troi. Or even Cordelia when that demon impregnated her. Twenty-four hours later, bam! Demon child."

"Aren't they all?" Cookie said, garnering herself a glare from her daughter. Ah, to be thirteen again.

"Seriously, what's with this nine-months crap? This is torture." I grabbed my belly and scrunched up my face. "Agony. It's worse than scurvy." I didn't actually know what scurvy was, but it sounded bad.

Reyes chuckled softly, kissed the top of my head, and walked out. Walked out!

"I'm not kidding!" I called after him. "I'm not putting up with this crap much longer."

"He's gone," Cookie said.

"Oh, okay." I cut the act short. "I have to admit, I feel wonderful. Nobody told me it would be like this. I have all this energy. I'm revved up, like, all the time."

"You're nesting."

My brows slid together in doubt.

"You know, getting ready for the baby to arrive."

"So, no actual nests?"

Hildie chuckled as Cookie said, "No actual nests."

"Is this what it was like for you?"

"I enjoyed my pregnancy quite a bit."

"Really?" Amber asked, grinning proudly from ear to ear as though it were because of her instead of in spite of her.

"That's good to know," I said. "What about your labor? How was that?"

"That was fun, too," she said without missing a beat, her smile suddenly as fake as the lashes Hildie had glued onto her eyelids.

"Cookie, I know when someone is lying to me."

"Okay, okay. Fun might be a bit of an exaggeration, but it was, you know, interesting. It was a learning experience. You just have to remember it's not forever. The good part is when you have to push. That's when it feels better. But you can't push too early."

I scanned the area for a pen and paper. "Do I need to take notes? Wait, what happens if I push too early? Katherine the Midwife didn't say anything about pushing too early."

Katherine was the midwife Reyes had hired. I was surprised she hadn't checked in yet. She'd been coming every day, since I was so close to my due date. That woman loved to poke and prod. I only liked being poked and prodded by one person, and his name was not Katherine.

"What'll happen?" Cookie asked, incredulous. "Are you crazy? If you push too early, you'll— You'll—" She stopped and stared into space.

"Did you just have a seizure?"

She blinked back to me. "No, it's just I have no idea what'll happen if you push too early."

She glanced at Hildie. The woman shrugged and kept teasing and tugging Cookie's hair this way and that.

Amber shrugged as well when I glanced at her askance.

"You guys are no help. Now I'm going to be scared to death to push."

"Oh, you'll push," Cookie said.

Hildie snorted and nodded in agreement.

So did Amber, as though she were very aware of what happened during childbirth.

"Someone's here," Amber said, jumping up and running to the window. Artemis, who had been snoring into the pillows on my bed, followed suit, barking at the car pulling into the drive.

"Are guests showing up already?" Cookie asked, panicking. "The food hasn't arrived yet. The decorators aren't finished. The flowers are still in the basement."

I considered getting up for a look, but that's as far as it went.

"Oh," Amber said. "It's just your stepmother."

Just when my day was going so beautifully. At least my sister, Gemma, would be with her, the silver lining to that dark cloud. My stepmother had also been coming to check on me every day. The woman who'd never lifted a finger to help me in her life, who had so little interest in me, she never glanced in my direction unless I was bleeding profusely, was suddenly vying for Mother of the Year. Gemma begged me to be patient with her. Said she was lonely after my dad's death. Said she wanted to make amends.

Maybe she did, but a lifetime of disdain was enough to drive anyone away. I had no interest in anything she had to offer, including an excuse for her behavior. She'd been trying to get me alone to talk to me, but I'd managed to dodge that bullet every time thus far. I just didn't want to listen to anything she had to say.

"And someone else is here. A black SUV."

I finally rolled off David Beckham to take a gander. "Special Agent Carson," I said, a little surprised. I hadn't seen her in months. We'd talked on the phone a few times and emailed quite a bit, but that was it.

"Oh, the FBI woman. She's so cool," Amber said, her voice forlorn. "I want to be in the FBI."

"I thought you wanted to be a hairdresser," Cookie said. "Or a brain surgeon."

"I changed my mind. I want a job where I get to carry a gun."

That was a scary thought. "Why?" I asked.

"Guys dig chicks with guns."

"Excellent reason," I said, giving her a high five.

Cookie shook her head.

"I'll go see what's up. Be back in a jiff."

"Wait!" Cookie said, ducking out of Hildie's grip. "I'll go, too." She unsnapped the cape and handed it to Hildie.

"Cook, no. It's your wedding day, for goodness' sake. And Hildie isn't finished."

"Kit might have a case for us. I need to be there to get the lowdown. Hildie can work on Amber." She raised her brows at Hildie, waiting for confirmation.

Amber had decided she wanted her hair up, and Cookie was game, provided there was enough time to change the style. Apparently, there was time.

"Okay, but as much as I love your undergarments, you're going to need pants."

———————

Cookie and I went downstairs in our robes and pajama bottoms, leaving Amber to be pampered and primped by Hildie. Artemis bounded down the stairs right behind us as we padded across the wood floor to the front door.

I opened it and welcomed Kit with open arms. Literally. She eyed me a long moment, then let me give her a hug, patting my back as though she didn't know what else to do with her hands.

"You're very . . . sparkly," she said, her voice sounding a bit like she'd sucked helium from a balloon. Probably because I was crushing her larynx.

I didn't hug halfway. If someone's larynx wasn't being crushed, I was doing it wrong.

"Am I interrupting something?"

I set her at arm's length and took a moment to gaze at her. It made her even more uncomfortable. Score!

But, truth be told, she looked really nice. Her hair had been curled, her suit fit a little tighter than usual, and she was wearing makeup. Stranger things had happened, but not many.

"Not yet. We're having a wedding, but not for a couple of hours."

She gasped. "I'm so sorry. I should have called."

"Don't be ridiculous," I said, ushering her into the foyer along with another agent I'd never seen before.

Every move I made, every step I took, was fashioned with a singular focus in mind. I had to be careful not to look at Cookie. Her hair had been only partially teased, which meant it looked like a hairball with spikes on her head. I'd studied something similar in advanced biology in high school. Knowing a virus like that existed in the world had scared me, had given me nightmares. Or it might have if I'd cared. But I was in high school. All I cared about was boys.

Still, seeing it in person sent a tiny quiver of terror lacing down my spine. Terror that I'd burst out laughing and embarrass her. I had to force myself not to snort every time I looked her way. I had to focus. Concentrate. Channel my inner ninja. They had lots of focus.

"What's up?" I asked Kit as I showed them to our makeshift living room.

I had a feeling the room had formerly been an area for silent reflection for the sisters. I could only hope God wouldn't mind that we'd turned it into a place to entertain guests. On the plus side, we'd partied in it only once. Last night, actually. But I didn't drink, so I was safe from any ramifications we might incur as a result of partying in a house of God. Cookie, on the other hand, was screwed six ways to Sunday. Poor kid.

"I have something I want you to look into," Kit said. "But just so you know, Special Agent Waters was very against my coming here."

I turned to the man trailing behind us. "You must be Special Agent Waters."

"I am," he said, his tone brusque. The energy radiating off him fairly vibrated. He was seething underneath his starched collar. So this would be fun.

All in all, he was very nice looking. Medium height. Slim build. Exotic coloring. His accent would suggest a local upbringing. I got the feeling that in his spare time he liked wearing feather boas and singing karaoke. But that could just be me projecting.

"I'm sorry to hear you won't be happy with my involvement."

"I just don't think there's anything you can do. I don't understand why we're here." He shot Kit a hard gaze.

My protective instincts bucked inside me, but I smiled as graciously as I could. "Well, I hope to disappoint you."

I'd startled him. After a moment, he said, "If you can do what Agent Carson says you can, the last thing I'll be is disappointed."

"Wonderful." I showed them to our limited seating choices, which consisted of a couch, a chair, and a wood bench under a large, bright window. "Then we're in agreement."

The moment we crossed the threshold, I stopped mid-stride, almost causing a three-person pileup behind me. But something had registered in my periphery, and I had to turn to see if my eyes were playing tricks on me.

They weren't.

He was here.

Mr. Wong was hovering in a corner of my living room, just like back at my apartment in Albuquerque. He had never moved from the corner back home in the three years I lived there. Not once. And he was already there when I'd rented the apartment. I just figured he came with it as an amenity, like granite countertops or radiant heating. But now he was here. Hovering. Nose in the corner as always. Toes inches off the floor. Nothing at all had changed except his location.

Artemis noticed him, too. Her stubby tail wagged so fast, it blurred like the wings of a bumblebee. She tugged at his pant leg. Crouched down. Barked. Rolled onto her back with a whine as I stood there, stunned. Cookie covered for me, leading our guests all the way into the makeshift living room. I wanted to cry out Mr. Wong's name, run to him, and throw my arms around him. I'd missed him so. But doing so would probably freak out my unwitting guests.

Agent Waters took the chair and left us womenfolk the couch. Giving up on Mr. Wong, Artemis trotted to the bench and splayed across it to get some sun. I finally forced one foot in front of the other and strolled over to join the gang. As we sat down, we once again did our best to avoid looking at Cookie. It was rather like trying to avoid the hovering ghost in the room. At least for me.

"So, what's up?" I asked Kit after pulling myself together. My mind had instantly jumped to a thousand different reasons Mr. Wong might be there. Departed were showing up by the truckloads, kind of like distant relatives during the holidays. And now Mr. Wong? Why? How did he get here? How had he even found me? Like sands through the hourglass, those were the questions of my life.

Some of them. I actually had quite a few more.

Kit handed me a file. I shook out of my stupor, opened the file, and looked at the picture of a beautiful young girl. She had large, expressive eyes and a sweet smile.

"Missing persons case," Kit said. "Fourteen-year-old female. Last seen with friends at a park in Bernalillo. Her parents noticed she was missing when she didn't come home—"

"—from school one day," I finished for her, scanning the file. "I saw this on the news. Faris Waters." I looked up at Special Agent Waters and saw the resemblance immediately.

"She's been gone for two weeks," he said.

"Is she your daughter?" The anger and helplessness radiating out of him would certainly indicate that.

"My niece."

I bowed my head. "I'm sorry."

"I'm sorry we're wasting your time when you clearly have better things to do."

"Not at all," I said, ignoring his double meaning—as in, I was wasting their time—as I thumbed through the pages, looking for the vital clues. A dark green pickup with tinted windows was seen driving through the area for hours at a time several days before Faris's abduction. It hadn't been seen since. "According to this, she was supposed to meet some friends to go to a party after school, but she never showed up."

"Her parents didn't know anything about the party, but her texts would suggest that was her plan. A classmate was having a birthday party that Friday afternoon."

"I'll need those texts and all her emails," I said without looking up. "I'll also need a list of her closest friends and their contact information."

Kit took out a memo pad and started taking notes. "You got it. I'll get you everything we have by the end of the day."

Agent Waters stood and turned to look out the window. His frustration level showed in the rigid set of his shoulders.

"Agent Waters," Kit said, a hard edge to her voice.

He turned back. "Why are we here? We're wasting time. What can she do that we haven't already done?"

Kit stood. "Jonny, I told you. She solves cases. It's what she does. She's very good at it. These two ladies," she said, pointing to both Cookie and me, "have solved cases that were considered unsolvable. They have closed three cold cases for me over the past year. They found evidence where no one else thought to look. Remember that scumbag in Alaska? That was them."

I was thrilled that she'd included Cookie in her praises. I couldn't do anything without my sidekick.

Agent Waters, or Jonny, raked the fingers of one hand through his hair. I was surprised he had any left when he was finished.

"Now, sit down and pay attention," Kit continued. Her tone was alarming and very curious. These two clearly had a history, especially if the glare he gave her was any evidence.

He rounded the chair and sat back down.

"Have you interviewed all her friends?"

This time the glare was directed toward me. Agent Waters was taking my questions as an indication that he was incompetent. I didn't mean that at all, but he was clearly sensitive about the case.

"Why the guilt?" I asked him. I felt it there, weaker than the other emotions shooting out of him, but it was there nonetheless.

"What?" He acted as though I'd slapped him.

"You feel guilty. Why?"

When he spoke next, he did so through gritted teeth. "Fuck you."

I braced for an attack. If that upset him, what I was about to say was likely to send him over the edge. "Until you explain why you feel guilty, I'm going to have to consider you a suspect."

Both Cookie and Kit gasped aloud. Cookie did that a lot, but Kit was normally so unflappable.

"Charley," Kit said as Cookie placed a hand on my arm. It was an involuntary reflex when Agent Waters stood to tower over me. Not that he was that tall, but I was sitting down. Our positions gave him a distinct advantage. I'd definitely have to go for the crotch if he swung at me. "Jonny—" She caught herself and started again. "Agent Waters was working in the field office in Dallas when this happened. He's been there for two years."

"I'm sorry," I said to her, still doing my best to egg the man on. I hadn't been kidding. Until I knew why *Jonny* felt so guilty about his niece's disappearance, I was going to have to assume he had something to do with it. "But you two have clearly had a relationship in the past. Your assessment can't be trusted at this point in time."

That did it. He came unglued and I prepared for war. Then again, would he really hit a pregnant woman? He lunged forward and I felt certain he would. Reyes exploded into the room incorporeally, his heat like a nuclear blast over my skin. I held up a hand, and though it was meant for Reyes—he had a tendency to sever spines first and ask questions later—Agent Waters stopped instantly. By then, his face was mere inches from mine.

"You are treading in unsafe waters."

Kit rushed between us, pushing the agent back. It was too bad, really. I wanted to see what he was capable of.

"What are you doing?" she asked him.

The agent turned his back on her, and Reyes dissipated only to walk up to the doorway physically and lean against the jamb. He watched Agent Waters, but I nodded my head toward Mr. Wong, trying to clue Reyes in to his presence as nonchalantly as I could. Reyes didn't bite. He wasn't

about to let his gaze stray one iota off his target. He had the best attention span.

Agent Waters scraped another hand through his hair, sat back down,
then began to rub the palm of one hand with the thumb of the other. "This
may be my fault."

Kit had started to sit down again, but she rose to her feet with his confession. "What do you mean?"

He pressed his mouth together before saying, "I think she was trying to figure out who was following her."

"You never said anyone was following her." She snapped up the file
and thumbed through it.

"No, I— I didn't want my brother and his wife to know she'd
come to me."

Kit sank back onto the couch.

"About a month ago, she emailed me. Asked me how to tail someone.
Said that there was a strange man hanging out in their neighborhood, and
could I run his plates?"

"Why isn't that in the report?"

"It wouldn't have helped," he said, his ire—and guilt level—spiking
again. "She never gave me any more information than that. Just that
some creepy guy was hanging out near the park she and her friends
hung out at. She's always wanted to join the FBI, and I think she was
going to try to investigate this guy on her own."

"What did you tell her?" Cookie asked.

"I told her—" He bowed his head. "I told her that it was illegal for me
to run the plates for her. I told her to let her parents know about the man."

"That's not anything to feel guilty about," I said.

He shook his head. "No, but she emailed me again a few days later.
She said she figured out who the guy was and asked if I could come to
New Mexico and arrest him."

"And?" Kit asked.

"And I told her to give all the information she had to her parents and have them call the police. I told her I didn't have time."

While it sounded pretty legit to me, Kit bolted out of her chair. "You selfish asshole," she said, her jaw locked in anger. "You know how much you mean to her."

Like a dog being scolded, he ducked his head even lower.

"You know how much she admires you," Kit continued. They definitely had a past. "And you know she would do anything to get you to move back here."

"Exactly," he said, raising his head at last.

Kit let that sink in, then scoffed at him. "That's it, isn't it? You thought she was just doing all that to get you to come home."

When he lowered his gaze again, Kit turned away from him in disgust.

"Were you close with your niece?" I asked him.

"Before I moved away, yes. Very."

The interesting part about that statement was not his emotions, but Kit's. The rigid line of her back softened and a sorrow swept over her. Kit straightened her shoulders again, then said, "Now tell her the rest."

For a moment, he didn't understand her meaning; then his gaze narrowed. "Are you kidding me?" When she didn't answer, he asked, "What does that have to do with anything?"

She turned back. "Either you tell her, or I will."

"It doesn't mean anything, Kit. Why even bring it up?"

She stepped closer. "A year ago, I would've said the same thing. Then I met Charley."

His gaze bounced from Kit to me, then back again.

"Tell her."

"Jesus Christ." He stood again as though unable to face me when he gave the next bit of information. "She's been telling everyone for years, since she was about four, she's going to die before she turns fifteen."

I blinked, confused. "And when does she turn fifteen?" I asked.

The next word was spoken so softly, I almost didn't hear it. "Tomorrow."

Cookie placed a hand on her chest in shock.

Kit turned to me. "Like I said, a year ago, I wouldn't have given her premonition a second thought."

"Then you met me."

"Something like that. Do you think it has any merit?"

"Let's just say, I don't believe in coincidences."

"I need to get some air," Agent Waters said. He stood and started for the door, stopping short when he came face-to-face with my husband. My angry husband. As far as he was concerned, Agent Waters had almost attacked me. The agent stopped long enough to let the full effect of Reyes's glare make its point, then stepped past him and strode out the front door, his movements brusque and sharp.

After he closed the door, I turned to Kit. "All right, what gives?"

"What?" she asked.

"I'm sensing a lot of hostility between you two. What's going on?"

She glanced toward the door, then said, "Jonny's my ex."

"You were married?"

"Don't act so surprised."

"No, I'm not. It's just—"

"You think I can't land a man?"

"Kit, that has nothing to do with that. You're just so all-business. I'm a little surprised you took the time."

"Well, I've been married."

"And to a Fed, no less. Aren't there rules against fraternizing with the help?"

She lifted a shoulder. "Kind of. Not really. It depends, but yes, he's a Fed."

I sat taken aback.

"I like to call him my FedEx." A tiny smile broke through her severe expression. "He hates that shit."

"Too bad he didn't take your name."

She groaned. "I know, I know. His name would have been Jonny Carson. I can't imagine why he wouldn't go for that."

"Did you ever go by Waters?"

That rankled her feathers. "No, I'd already been established in the bureau, so I kept my name."

"Maybe that was the problem." I raised my brows, chastising her with them. They were quite unsettling at the right angle. "Maybe you weren't totally committed to the marriage."

Her jaw dropped. "You're going to give me marital advice? You've been married, what? Eight minutes?"

I gasped. "More like eight months."

"And have you taken his name?"

I cringed, glanced over my shoulder at my totally understanding husband, then said, "We were pressed for time."

"Ah, yes." She nodded, taking in the surroundings. "You had to drop everything and get to the 'safe house.'" She added air quotes.

"Exactly."

"Are you going to tell me why you're out here?"

I pulled my lower lip in through my teeth. "You don't want to know."

She leaned closer. "What if I did want to know? Would you tell me?"

An uneasy smile spread across my face. "Probably not. Some things are better left unknown. I'm just so floored you were married," I said, expertly changing the subject. "There's so much about your life I don't know."

"Look who's talking. The woman who solves crimes using almost supernatural methods and yet won't tell me anything about how she does it."

I checked my watchless wrist. "Well, would you look at the time."

"Charley."

"We have a wedding to get ready for, right, Cook?"

Cookie nodded her frazzled head as I shoved Kit past Reyes and toward the front door. I opened it and saw two vans parked in the driveway. One from the caterers. One from the florist. And Jonny was standing on the porch, one hand holding a bottle of water, the other stuffed into a pocket. He straightened when we walked out.

I still couldn't believe it. Kit had been married. I also couldn't miss the spike of emotion that leapt inside her when she saw him again. She was still in love with him. I wondered if I should tell her that he was still in love with her, too.

He turned to us as Kit addressed Cookie. "I'm so sorry. I didn't mean to interrupt your wedding preparations."

Cook waved a dismissive hand. "Oh, please. We've been cooped up here for months, going a little crazier with each passing day."

Before she could run in the opposite direction, I lunged forward and gave Kit another quick hug, but it was an excuse to whisper in her ear. "I'll call you tonight and let you know if she's alive."

Kit nodded, deciding not to question in front of Jonny how I could possibly know that.

When I released her, I added, "I'll do everything I can. I promise."

"I know you will."

Jonny didn't seem quite so confident, but he did have the decency to apologize for his behavior. "I'm sorry I lost my temper."

"Don't give it a second thought. You're upset. I understand upset."

He nodded, probably relieved I wasn't threatening to file a complaint against him.

After waving them off, we hurried back in and closed the door before God and all his creation saw us in our robes.

Reyes walked up to us, and Cookie, suddenly self-conscious, tried to smooth down her hair. It was a bit like trying to tame a hurricane. He wrapped an arm around my waist and I leaned into him, reveled in his heat.

"Did you see him?"

When he finally tore his gaze off the door, he raised a brow in question.

"Mr. Wong. He's here."

The slight lifting of one corner of his mouth would suggest that he already knew.

"How long has he been here?"

"Since this morning. You didn't feel it?"

"Feel what?"

"The shifting of energy." He turned toward Mr. Wong, though we couldn't see him from where we stood, as there was an adobe wall between us. "I just wonder what he's doing here."

"Me, too."

"Me, three," Cookie said, wringing her hands.

I took another look at her, and I couldn't hold back any longer. I burst out giggling.

"What?" she asked, patting her hair. "I'm getting ready. What's the big deal?"

I strode forward and gave her one of my larynx-crushing hugs. "You," I said into her robe. "You are the big deal."

"I think two of the three people standing here would argue with you on that," she said, crushing my larynx back.

The door reopened. A frazzled Gemma tiptoed in and closed it behind her. My blond-haired sister was already sporting her wedding attire, a powder blue cocktail dress with matching ankle boots, only she'd added huge, dark sunglasses that didn't make her look like an insect at all, and she'd gathered her bangs into a pointy ponytail. She'd always loved unicorns growing up, but this was taking it a bit far.

She stopped when she noticed us. "What are you doing?" she said in a hisslike whisper, and I could've sworn she slurred her words. "Cookie, you're getting married in an hour and a half. What are you doing down here? In your robe? With your hair?" Horrified, she pointed at Cookie's head. Then her demeanor changed. "Unless that's how you're wearing it, in which case, it's so pretty. I love it. It looks really good on you."

I laughed out loud and she slammed an index finger over her lips. "Shhhh," she said, hushing me way longer than was necessary.

"Are you hungover?" I asked her softly, appalled. "How many drinks did you have?"

"I don't know. I lost count at three. Or twelve. I'm just not certain."

"What were you doing?" My astonishment knew no bounds. "Why would you drink that much when you knew we had a wedding the next day?"

"I was trying to keep up with Cookie."

"Are you insane?"

She swayed back against the door and shushed me again.

"Cookie's like a competitive connoisseur. The last guy who tried to outdrink her ended up in traction for a month."

Cookie came to her own defense. "Only because a man named Jose Cuervo convinced him he could fly. Not my fault."

But Gemma wasn't listening. "What is up with your hair?"

"Gemma, she's not wearing her hair like that."

"Oh, thank God." She placed a hand over her chest to still her racing heart. "I was worried. Okay, in, in, in." She shooed us forward. "We have a lot of work ahead of us."

I turned toward Reyes and raised a brow. "Some more than others," I teased. He could go naked for all I cared, though I doubted Uncle Bob would appreciate that as much as us girls.

Reyes gave me a quick squeeze, then left us to it.

"Where's Denise?" I asked. Not that I cared where my stepmother was, but I wanted to be prepared for her grand entrance. It always caused an unsettling sensation in my stomach.

"She's out back, ordering the decorators around," Gemma said.

"Sweet. Keeps her out of my hair."

With a chastising sigh, Gemma placed her manicured hands on her hips. "Charley, you have to promise me, for Cookie and Uncle Bob's sake, you will be nice to Mom today."

"What?" I asked, incredulous that she would even say such a thing. That she would trust me so little.

Her expression didn't change. I caved. She was going to be one of those stern mothers all the kids on the playground talked about as though she were something to be feared.

"Okay, whatever. I'll be nice. At least until the wedding's over. But once the rings are on the fingers, it's every evil stepmother for herself."

Gemma rolled her eyes. "You guys need group therapy so bad."

"Oh, hell no," I assured her. "I've had more than enough of that woman over the last eight months."

Denise had been coming out to the convent several times a week. Each time, she had another excuse. She noticed we were out of dish soap or she wanted to make sure I was okay. She was apparently a pediatrics nurse when she'd first met my dad, and that gave her another reason to invade my much-loved privacy. To bombard me with questions about how I felt, my blood pressure, was I taking the vitamins she brought, did I have any swelling? She had never, in my entire existence, paid so much attention to me. I'd learned long ago to be wary of any attention she tossed my way. Everything she did had an ulterior motive. Perhaps without my dad around to give her a sounding board for all things horrid and bizarre about Charley Davidson, she had no one else to turn to. But I was hardly a good alternative.

"She's lonely, Charley." Gemma's expression turned sympathetic.

"Well, let her go be lonely at your house."

"I work. I can't very well have her hanging out at my office all day, scaring my clients away."

"So she has to come here and scare all the dead people away instead? I have clients, too."

"She's hurting right now."

"I know, I can feel it. The sadness. Every time she comes over, all I can think about is Dad, and it breaks my heart all over again. As long as she keeps coming over, I can't heal."

"Charley, maybe she needs to heal, too."

"I'm sure she does. I just don't care."

"You can't mean that."

"You can't be serious. After everything she's put me through, you would still defend her?"

"Maybe she needs your forgiveness. She knows what she did was wrong."

"What she did?" I asked, growing more annoyed by the second. "You say that as though there was only a single transgression. She did everything wrong, Gem."

While Denise took to Gemma like a duck takes to *à l'orange*, she'd never quite bonded with me, if the menacing scowls and the constant digs were any indication. Any mother—step or otherwise—who tries to get her daughter committed to a psych ward because she's a little different from the other kids at the park doesn't deserve that daughter's love. But I'd tried. For years, I'd tried to be more like Gemma so our stepmother would like me. I once studied for two days for a spelling test just so I could get an A on a paper that would sit next to Gemma's on the refrigerator. I was so proud when I'd succeeded that I ran all the way from the bus stop to show it to her, and I fell on the way, but I made it home relatively unscathed. Denise took the paper with the bright red A on it out of my hands, gave it a quick glance, then sent me to my room without dinner for ripping my backpack when I fell.

That night, when I snuck out of my room to get a spoonful of peanut butter, I found the test wadded up in the trash. About three seconds later, I had an epiphany: There would be no winning her over. Denise despised me. Period. It's hard when the only mother a girl has ever known despises her. To learn that at age seven was quite the blow to the ego. I took the test back to my room, smoothed it out the best I could, and pinned it to a corkboard where I kept pictures my dad had taken of my real mom while she was pregnant with me. Before she died giving birth to me. They served as a reminder. Anytime I tried to gain Denise's approval, I looked at that crinkled A and rethought my objectives. The way I saw it, my acceptance of Denise's indifference saved a lot of heartache for me and a lot of disappointment for her.

"And she knows that," Gemma pleaded. "She knows she did everything wrong. What she doesn't know is how to talk to you about it. How to apologize. You make it so difficult."

"I make it difficult?" I asked, astonished.

"Charley," Gemma said, using her clinical voice, soft and nonjudgmental, "until we talk about it, until we sit down and really delve deep into our pasts, none of this is going to be resolved."

What Gemma so often forgot was that no matter how soft and nonjudgmental her voice was, I could feel the emotions raging beneath her calm exterior. We'd been having this same conversation for weeks. No, months. And I could feel her frustration. Now that Denise was open to the idea, Gemma wanted us to bond. To be besties and go shopping together.

I'd rather walk into a den of hellhounds.

"You mean if we don't have a long heart-to-heart, issues that have gone unresolved for decades will continue to be unresolved?" I asked, feigning horror at the thought before lifting one shoulder in an apathetic shrug. "Works for me." I turned and climbed the stairs, effectively ending the conversation.

I heard Gemma release a sad sigh.

3

I decided to finish getting dressed in the bathroom while Cookie and Amber put on their final touches in the bedroom. Walking down the narrow hall, I felt the history of the place leach out of the walls. The wood slats creaked beneath my weight, and I could just imagine what it would have been like being a nun here two hundred years ago. Well, not a nun, but a person, interacting with the Native Americans, watching their children play, growing food in the gardens below. What a rewarding life they must have led. And they were brave, the women of the frontier, whether a nun, a native, or a homesteader.

Yet their lives must have been so hard, especially without cell reception. I balked at the challenge of having only one bathroom on the entire floor. Every room had a sink and mirror, but when you had to go, you had to go. Thankfully, Reyes had added central heat and cooling, but I feared him changing the tone of the place, its historical feel, so we hadn't upgraded too much. We kept the rooms upstairs small and sparse, with stoves in each one. Even though they were no longer used, they still worked and could heat the tiny rooms quite nicely. We also kept the downstairs almost all original, patching the walls here and there and fixing the flooring. The former convent would make a great restaurant and B and B for the right owner, but it needed to be registered with the Historical Society to preserve its richness.

Another small renovation we did was add a working bathtub and separate shower in each of the two bathrooms, one upstairs and one down. Though not so fancy as George—that is, the stone shower in Reyes's apartment—the bathrooms had really come along, compared to the originals. While they'd been updated back in the 1940s, plumbing had improved by leaps and bounds since then.

I knocked softly on the bathroom door and, receiving no answer, opened it. A burst of steam hit me in the face, and I could only pray the glitter wouldn't melt off my face. Or melt my face off. Either way. I swiped at the steam and walked in on a half-naked slave demon as he was wrapping a towel at his waist.

"Osh," I said, covering my eyes. "I knocked. What the hell?"

A wicked grin spread across his handsome face. I knew this only because my fingers were accidentally open. It wasn't my fault I could see him in the almost-buff. While he looked nineteen, he was centuries old. Older than Reyes, actually. But somehow that knowledge didn't make me feel less perverted every time I took in his slim, muscular form. Created a slave in hell—or a Daeva, as they were called—he had lived a hard life. I couldn't imagine what he'd gone through. To be a slave was one thing. To be in hell was one thing. But to be a slave in hell? The concept boggled my mind.

Why did they need slaves in hell anyway? What exactly did they do? The only inkling of their duties I had was that some of them were, for lack of a better phrase, pressed into service, forced to fight in the demon army. I first met Osh while he was trying to win souls in a card game. He'd won one from a client, which I wanted him to return. But that's what he did. He supped on human souls. Fortunately, I'd convinced him to sup only on the souls of humans who did not deserve them, like murderers, drug dealers, child molesters, and lobbyists.

But that's where I'd first learned that Osh, or Osh'ekiel as he was called down under, escaped from hell centuries before Reyes did. In fact, he was the only Daeva to escape from hell, and though Reyes didn't trust him at first as much as I did, he'd grown to depend on him for Beep's sake. The demon did seem to have Beep's best interest at heart.

Reyes had once told me that the major difference between Osh in hell and Osh on earth was that his scars were not visible in his human form.

It made my heart ache for him. Normally. Not today, though.

Osh looked me up and down, a wolfish grin softening his youthful face. "I heard you. I was just getting kind of lonely. Figured I could use some company in here."

After giving up the pretense of purity, I lowered my hand and rolled my eyes. "Please. Like you could handle this." I hitched a thumb over my shoulder. "Scoot. I need to finish getting ready."

"I need to shave," he volleyed.

"You can shave in your room."

"My room is the size of a broom closet."

"So is mine. You didn't have to move out here, you know. You could've stayed in your posh house in the city." We'd secretly put him in a broom closet, but what he didn't know wouldn't hurt him.

"And leave you guys to fend off the hounds of hell without me? No way. But, yeah," he said, giving his head a shake, "this place is weird." Water droplets flew off his shoulder-length black hair and onto my face.

I pursed my lips as though that would faze him. "I agree. It's a good thing I was never a nun in the 1800s."

His grin reappeared in full force. "Somehow I don't think, even if you'd been born in the 1800s, you would've become a nun."

He had a point. I shooed him out and turned to the mirror to freshen my makeup, but as the steam cleared out of the room, I saw something unexpected. Names carved into the walls behind me.

Horrified, I looked up as though I could see into the attic. "Rocket!" I shouted, stomping my bare foot.

He appeared instantly. Rocket had died sometime in the 1950s. He was big, over six feet, and cuddly. He always reminded me of a giant bear I'd had as a child.

"What are you doing? I told you, you can't write the names on the walls anywhere but in the attic." Reyes and I had added extra Sheetrock up there so Rocket didn't damage the original structure.

"But, Miss Charlotte, I'm running out of room up there."

"Well, you're just going to have to go over the names that you already have. Think layers. Like you did at the asylum."

"Fine, Miss Charlotte, but I'm going to scratch through the paper. Nurse Hobbs doesn't like it when I do that."

Nurse Hobbs must have been a nurse at the asylum where Rocket had grown up. From what I could gather over the years, which wasn't much, Rocket had been committed to an asylum when he was very young. He'd probably had his gift even when he was alive. He knew the names of every human ever to exist who'd passed away, and he made it his personal goal to document them all. I couldn't imagine what his parents must have thought when he was a kid as he wrote name after name of those who'd passed on anything he could find. Back then, having him institutional-ized would have been the norm.

I grinned at his analogy. Anyone who thought of walls as paper needed to get out more. "We'll get new paper. It's okay."

Rocket had moved in shortly after we did. He'd had something to tell me one day that was apparently of vital importance. It involved a kitten that had wandered onto the property and got stuck in the asylum. It had likely been abandoned by its mother and Blue, his five-year-old sister whom I rarely saw, was very worried about it. So part of Cookie's job for a couple of days was to go search for the kitten at the asylum and bring it to the convent, because by then Rocket had moved in. He said Blue had moved in, too, but I had yet to see her here. Of course, in all the years I'd been going to visit Rocket in the asylum, I'd seen her only three times. She was painfully shy. But I also knew that where Rocket went, Blue was sure to follow.

Unfortunately, so was a sassy little girl named Strawberry. I called her that because she'd drowned when she was nine in Strawberry Shortcake pajamas. She had long blond hair and bright blue eyes and a bluish tint to her pouty mouth, evidence of her cause of death.

She appeared in front of me, hands on hips, glare firmly in place. "Why are you yelling at Rocket? You're scaring Blue."

"Rocket is writing names where he shouldn't. It's against the rules. No breaking rules—right, Rocket?"

He hung his head in utter shame. "No breaking rules. Right, Miss Charlotte."

"Okay, no more names except in the attic. Is that a deal?"

"Deal."

Rocket disappeared, but Strawberry unfortunately did not. I'd gotten to know Strawberry through a mutual acquaintance. She was the departed sister of a cop I knew: Officer Taft. I'd told him that Strawberry moved in with us some time back, so he'd come to the convent a few times to visit her. Not that he could see her, but I was a decent interpreter.

After Strawberry got the glare out of her system, she looked at my face and did a 180. Her huge eyes rounded in awe. "You're sparkling," she said, reaching up.

I kneeled down to let her touch my face, her hand icy against my skin as she patted my cheek.

"You're like a fairy princess."

Utterly flattered, I said, "Thank you."

"You're not as pretty as one or anything. And you're really fat. But you sparkle like one."

I forced my smile to remain steady in the heat of battle. Never retreat. Never surrender. "Thank you again," I said through clenched teeth.

"You're welcome."

"Hey, is Jessica back?" Jessica was my former BFF from high school who'd decided to make my life a living hell by moving in with me when Rocket, Blue, and Strawberry did. But I hadn't seen much of her lately.

"No, she's been staying with her sister a lot."

"Oh. I hope everything is okay."

"It is. I think she's scared of the dogs outside."

"Right. Can't blame her there."

"Okay, well, Blue and I are going to play with Sheets."

"Awesome. Are you going to drape them over you and play ghost? It's really appropriate."

"No, *Sheets,*" she said, her indignation over my ignorance exasperating her. "The kitten."

"Oh, of course. Sounds like a plan." Then, before she could disappear on me, I asked, "Why 'Sheets'? He's black."

"Because he's shiny and black, like David's sheets."

Ah, her brother, David—aka Officer Taft—had shiny black sheets. That was so much more information than I needed today. "Gotcha. Well, have fun."

"Okay." She popped back out, leaving me to my own devices. Probably not a good idea. After all, I had glitter on my face.

Guests started arriving soon after Amber and I finished getting dressed. Amber looked adorable, her hair piled high on her head and sprinkled with tiny bronze butterflies. She was also over the moon that Uncle Bob had showed up. Not because he showed up to marry her mother, but because he'd brought Quentin—*the* Quentin—with him.

Quentin Rutherford was a kid we essentially adopted when he'd been possessed by a demon. He'd been possessed because he could see into the supernatural realm, and at the time, the demon was after me. It had used Quentin as a guide, following my light, the light he could see. Once we'd rid him of said demon, we found out he'd been born deaf. Because he had no family to speak of, we, along with the Sisters of the Immaculate Cross, had adopted Quentin. And it didn't take long for Amber to appreciate that fact. According to the extremely detailed report she gave us, he was dressed to the nines. I was excited to see him myself.

We changed into our dresses while Hildie finished Cookie's hair. I ran to get our bouquets and check on everything while strategically managing to avoid my stepmother. The guests were in the back, where we'd set up several rows of white chairs. But knowing my sister, the whole affair would be absolutely lovely. At least she got to plan one wedding, since mine didn't turn out quite as expected. It became an impromptu thing in a hospital room, and all Gemma's hard work had been for naught. Now she got to start from scratch with a brand-new venue and a fresh set of victims.

When I got back to the room, Amber and I watched as guests got out of their cars. Gemma's former client and current boyfriend, Wyatt, pulled up, as well as Ubie's boss, Captain Eckert, a few detectives I'd seen around and Strawberry's brother, Officer Taft. Garrett Swopes, a colleague, showed next, looking rather delicious in a charcoal coat and tie. Amador, Bianca, and the kids showed up. They'd been coming out on a regular basis to see Reyes, and we'd had several amazing cookouts as a result. In the process, Cookie had grown quite fond of them, inviting them to the wedding. Their seven-year-old daughter, Ashley, would be the flower girl and five-year-old Stephen the ring bearer. I watched as a few other people I didn't recognize got out and walked around back to the makeshift chapel. Several were young girls between the ages of nineteen and twenty-three. Cookie said she had several second cousins. With the stunning array of men who were to attend the wedding, the cousins were sure to have fun.

I relayed to Cookie all the information I could about the guests showing up to set her at ease. She was nervous enough as it was. I'd assumed her knowing that people were showing up would calm her nerves. Instead it made her even more nervous. Go figure.

"Well," she said at last, standing behind me.

I turned and was stunned speechless. Cookie looked incredible. Her short, dark locks had been swept back and made to look like she had an intricate French braid. Just like Amber and me, she, too, wore tiny bronze butterflies in her hair to match our cinnamon dresses. But her dress was a creamy ivory wrap sprinkled with pearls. Her makeup was simple yet dramatic. She was breathtaking.

"Cookie," I said, unable to tear my gaze away from her. "You look magnificent. You look like a movie star from the '40s. You are utterly elegant."

She laughed softly, the act easing some of the tension from her shoulders. "Do you think Robert will like it?"

"Please," I said, astounded she had to ask. "Uncle Bob is going to trip over his own tongue when he gets a load of you."

She crinkled her nose and giggled like a schoolgirl.

"Mom," Amber said as she stared in awe. "You're so beautiful."

"Thank you, sweetheart. You're gorgeous."

Amber dropped her gaze and kicked an invisible layer of dirt bashfully.

"Are we really doing this?" Cookie asked me.

"Hon, if we don't do this, I think that man of yours is going to kidnap you and take you to Mexico. Or Vegas. Or Romania. You two are getting married one way or another."

She dropped her gaze. "I'm sorry we're getting married now of all times."

"What?" I asked, my voice an octave too high. "What are you talking about?"

"I just, I don't want to take away from the birth of your first child. This is such a special time for you."

"Cookie Marie Kowalski, how dare you even think such a thing."

"Are you sure?"

"As sure as I am that my uncle will disown me if I don't make certain you walk up that aisle in the next few minutes."

She laughed and hugged me. Amber joined us in a three-way just as Gemma walked into the room. My sister stood taken aback, a hand placed gently over her mouth for a solid thirty seconds before she shook out of her stupor and waved us forward. Thick droplets glistened between her lashes as she rushed us out of the room and down the stairs. We met Bianca and the kids at the bottom. Ashley's dress was a smaller version of Amber's. Her curls were also piled high on her head with tiny bronze butterflies inhabiting the thick mass. Stephen looked dapper in a black tux and bow tie to match the men's. After Bianca explained their roles again, she went to sit with her husband, Amador, as Gemma escorted us to the back door, where we would step onto the strip of green turf that led to the altar.

Ashley kept twirling in her dress, leaving petals in her wake, while Stephen fidgeted with his tie.

"We'd better do this before we lose them," I said.

Gemma gave us all quick hugs, then went to join Wyatt.

We all took deep breaths as the wedding music started. We sent Stephen down the aisle first, carrying the pillow with the quintessential promise rings. Ashley was next, dropping amber rose petals as she waved and posed for pictures.

I turned to Cookie, forcing myself not to cry. Not yet. There was a time and a place for tears at a wedding, and this was neither. But I couldn't help it. I leaned in and gave her one more colossal hug as a tear escaped despite my best efforts. I gave Amber a quick peck on the cheek, turned, and walked down the aisle.

I had it all planned. I was going to stare straight ahead. I was going to concentrate on my breathing. I was going to focus on not tripping. And it was all going according to plan. I looked at my uncle as he stood waiting for his bride. He looked amazing. Hair and mustache neatly trimmed. Black tux. White shirt. Crisp bow tie. The fact that he looked uncomfortable made me crack a minuscule smile, but I managed to keep my composure as I kept walking, kept breathing, and kept the tears at bay.

Then it happened. My eyes landed on Reyes Alexander Farrow. My uncle's best man, standing in the same black tux, starched white shirt, and black bow tie that my uncle wore. But they seemed worlds apart. Reyes looked like he was born for the finer things in life. His hair had been trimmed since that morning. How any man could look just as sexy in a dirty T-shirt and ragged jeans as he did in a formal tux and bow tie was beyond my immediate comprehension. But the pièce de résistance was simply Reyes himself. His wide shoulders, powerful even beneath the layers of tailored clothing. His face startlingly handsome. His jaw strong, his mouth sculpted to perfection. His thick dark lashes casting minute shadows across his cheeks. And his hair. It was shorter now, but thick dark curls still hung over his forehead. Curled around his ears. He looked like a supermodel. Something exotic and rare. Something not of this world.

One corner of his full mouth tipped up as he watched me watch him. Then the slightest arching of his left brow, and my knees almost gave beneath me. I had never seen anything so beautiful in all my life.

Then I heard a whisper beside me. I looked to my left. Denise sat glaring at me while Gemma's eyes were wide with panic. My heart sped up. My eyes widened to match hers. I was suddenly panicking, too, only

I had no idea why. She nodded toward the front, and I realized I had stopped. The moment my gaze landed on Reyes, I had stopped.

I quickly stared straight ahead, squared my shoulders, and continued down the aisle, wondering if anyone noticed the five-minute pause in the procession. Hopefully not. And if they did, I had a kid fermenting in my belly. I could chalk it up to Beep. But my cheeks burned either way.

I thought Reyes might laugh at me. Or at the very least, find my faux pas amusing, but when I looked over at him again, he was not laughing. He was not even smiling. He had darkened again, his expression almost dangerous as he took me in. He could feel my reaction to him and I, in turn, could feel his reaction to me. How he could have such a reaction with me looking like the Pillsbury Doughboy astonished me. He was kinky. I'd take it.

Once I got to the front, I stepped aside and turned, waiting for the gorgeous bride. The "Wedding March" began to play through the speakers and everyone stood as Cookie and Amber stepped out into the light of the warm fall afternoon. They strolled to the front slowly, taking their time, letting people snap pictures and whisper words of praise.

But my attention had turned to Uncle Bob, and I wished I'd thought to have someone record him, because his reaction to Cookie was worth all the coffee in Albuquerque. No, New Mexico. No! The world!

He sucked in a sharp breath of air at the sight of her, his mouth slightly open, his expression reflecting all the amazement and doubt that was so Uncle Bob. I could tell right then and there he wondered what she saw in him. And I wanted to tell him: *That*. That humbleness. That appreciation of her. That love for both her and Amber. No, not just love. Respect. He respected her. He respected Amber. He was truly grateful for them both. There was no greater gift.

When they reached the front, the minister raised his hands and gestured for everyone to sit. After the guests settled, he asked, "Who gives this woman to be married to this man?"

Amber spoke, her voice quivering only a little. "I, her daughter, Amber Kowalski."

She turned to Cookie, her blue eyes shimmering. She gave her a quick hug, then took Cookie's hand and placed it gently into Uncle Bob's, giving him permission to marry her mother. There was no higher honor. The happiness ricocheting inside me for my cantankerous uncle knew no bounds.

The minister smiled his approval, and I nodded to Quentin, who was sitting in the front row. He stood, took Amber's arm into his, and led her to her seat. The whole exchange was formal and sweet and reverent, and once again I fought with every ounce of strength I had to hold back the floodtide threatening to erupt within me.

The minister went through the vows quickly, garnering an "I will" from both the bride and the groom. And while it wasn't easy for me to take my eyes off the beautiful couple in front of me, I simply could not keep from staring at my husband. I had never seen anything so stunning. His dark skin in stark contrast to the white stiff collar beneath his jaw. His fresh haircut. His cleanly shaven jaw. Although I loved the scruffy Reyes more than pumpkin pie with whipped cream, this one was breathtaking. He was like Tarzan, Clark Kent, and James Bond all rolled into one. I half expected an Aston Martin to be sitting in our drive.

After being given the go-ahead, Uncle Bob wrapped one arm around Cookie's waist and lifted her chin. Only then did I realize she'd been crying. He gave her the gentlest of kisses, the kind that attested to the immense love and respect he had for the woman he'd just married, and the crowd erupted in celebration. It was over. After all the preparation, all the work, all the anxiety, it was over. Fast. Much too fast. We still had the reception, of course, and then I would get to work on the case while Cookie enjoyed her pre-honeymoon honeymoon. It would consist of only one night at Buffalo Thunder, a stunning resort and spa in the Pojoaque valley north of Santa Fe.

Cookie had insisted they hold off on their real honeymoon until after Beep arrived. Odd how Beep had changed all our lives so implicitly. She even added her own little kink in the wedding when the guests started giggling because my dress was moving. I couldn't tell if she was just trying to get comfortable or hosting a kegger. Either way, she was already stealing the show, trying to upstage.

I looked down at her with an *attagirl* grin.

The moment the crowd erupted, Uncle Bob whisked Cookie back down the aisle, which worked for me, as that was where the food sat.

"I have to admit," I said to Gemma as we loaded our plates, "you did good." I chose a kale salad with grilled salmon and an elegant cup filled with macaroni and cheese. I'd definitely be hitting that again, though I needed to leave room for pumpkin mousse, tiramisu, and chocolate truffles. And wedding cake! Couldn't forget the wedding cake!

Gemma had decided on much of the wedding's fanfare. The decorations. The type of food. All the extra stuff that made Cookie's day so special. I owed her. There'd be no living with her now.

"Thanks, sis." She shouldered me playfully.

Wyatt, her beau, asked, "How are you feeling?"

Reyes was close, as in right next to me, so I had to make it good. "Oh, it's awful. I have to pee every thirty seconds. My ankles are swollen. I drool when I least expect it. And I keep getting this weird craving for sardines and green chile on melba toast."

Wyatt had the decency to look aghast, but Reyes just grinned, focusing on the food instead of my suffering. The scoundrel.

"You hate sardines," Gemma said to me.

"Exactly. It's like I'm not me anymore and someone—or something— has taken over my body." I gasped. "It's *Invasion of the Body Snatchers*!"

Gemma giggled. "I think it's called being pregnant."

"Nobody cares about my suffering," I said as Reyes took both our plates to a table.

Gemma and Wyatt followed us. "We care," Gemma said. "Just not a lot."

She was so sweet.

As the afternoon wore on, Reyes and I got to sit back and watch Cookie in action. For once in her life, my very best friend was the absolute center of attention. And she glowed.

"She's really something," Reyes said to me.

I turned to him, his eyes sparkling with appreciation as he watched her and Ubie. "You know, every time you say something like that, I fall a little more in love with you."

His shimmering gaze landed on me in surprise. But he recovered quickly, his expression intensifying as he took me in. It made my insides tighten.

"I wanted to thank you for being Uncle Bob's best man."

He didn't respond. His gaze dropped to my mouth and lingered there as his heat feathered over my skin. He let one finger slide under the hem of my dress and up over a knee. His touch sent a shiver of delight racing up my thigh to settle in my nether regions. He was so darkly sensual, the moment didn't last long. There were too many other women clamoring for his attention, and I sat floored at their brazenness. No idea why. It was like that everywhere we went. Well, when we went places. One actually asked him if he could go out front to check her tires.

Man, Cookie had a fertile set of relatives.

Most people stayed outside to mingle. Fortunately, there weren't many departed in the back. They were mostly on the front lawn. As Reyes helped pull tables together, I chatted with Swopes and Osh, much to the chagrin of Cookie's second cousins, who were vying for their attention at the time, then with my good friend Pari and her beau, Tre. Then I sought out Quentin and Amber after Cookie and Uncle Bob cut the cake. We'd asked Quentin beforehand if he'd wanted an interpreter and he said no, informing us that nobody listened to the words anyway. He just wanted to enjoy the ceremony. What he'd really wanted was to whisper—aka, sign small where no one else could see—back and forth with Amber through the whole thing. They were absolutely adorable together.

The next obstacle I faced that afternoon was of the four-legged variety. Thrilled that Reyes and I were outside, and taking that as her cue to get her freak on, Artemis ran around like a gerbil on meth, turning occasionally to make sure we were still watching. And God help us if we weren't. Every time we turned away, she charged. That was fine for most involved, but she was solid to Reyes, Osh, and me. So while she flew through the guests with the greatest of ease, she'd almost taken me out. Twice. Fearing for my and Beep's safety, Reyes escorted me inside, where more food awaited and guests stood around chatting and eating and generally enjoying the afternoon. But we weren't in there long before he was needed elsewhere.

Turned out, Cookie had a whole plethora of family that I didn't know about. They were all aunts, uncles, and cousins. No siblings and her parents had passed away years ago, but she still had family showing up to represent like true homies. She even had that gaggle of second cousins. Five young women who had decided that Reyes, Osh, and Garrett were the most delicious beings they'd ever seen. Even Quentin and Pari's tall drink of water, Tre, weren't exempt from the Flirtatious Five. I was right there with them, but I did fear for one's life when she made googly eyes at Quentin. Amber's hackles rose to needlelike points, and I was afraid the other girl would not make it home with all her hair. Or all her limbs. Or both eyes. Or a full set of teeth. So many body parts could go missing in such a scenario.

Thankfully, Reyes headed that confrontation off at the pass, and Amber led Quentin to a quiet little table away from most of the guests. But that put Reyes back in the fray. I watched as the five practically assaulted him, each trying to get closer than the next. He took it all in stride, not that I was surprised. He'd been getting that kind of attention his entire life.

And he knew I was watching from inside. I sat at a window as he endured their attention, but the more I watched, the more flirtatious glances he shot my way. The more winks he offered. The more lopsided grins he wore. It was all quite enchanting, but the one that got me, the killer movement that almost sent me into orgasmic bliss, was when he glanced at me from across the sea of guests, gave me a long, languid once-over, then pulled his lower lip in through his teeth. To say the move was sexy would have been like calling a tsunami a ripple in the ocean.

I stood and walked to the door that led outside, about five seconds away from ordering him in, when I heard a female voice.

"Hi, pumpkin head."

I turned to see my aunt Lillian standing behind me, trying to see over my shoulder. Aunt Lil had died some time in the '60s. She was part world traveler and part hippie. Since there were so many people around us, I had no choice but to put my phone to my ear so I could talk to her without looking like a mental patient.

"Aunt Lil," I said, giving her a quick hug before anyone saw us. "When did you get back?"

"Just now, sweet cheeks. What's all the hubbub about?"

"Cookie got married today."

"Cookie?"

I nodded. "She married Uncle Bob."

Aunt Lil cackled with delight at the thought. "'Bout time that boy got hitched. I been worried about him ever since that yogurt incident when he was seven."

I didn't dare ask. "So, how long are you staying?"

"Until you pop, I suppose. I got to see this girl everyone is raving about. Whole place is jumping. Nobody will stop talking about her. Even had to call in the riot police, just in case."

No idea.

"That's so great, Aunt Lil. I'm thrilled you'll be here when Beep arrives."

"Wouldn't miss it, even though I did have to pass up the chance to go skinny dipping with the seventh Tsar of Russia." She wriggled her brows at me. "Now, where is the sexy beau of yours? I need something tall, dark, and scrumptious to look at, if you know what I mean. Men on this side aren't always easy on the eyes."

I laughed softly. "He's right over there, being accosted by Cookie's second cousins."

"Perfect. I'll join them."

I almost doubled over when Aunt Lil disappeared, then reappeared behind Reyes to give his ass a squeeze. He glanced at me, his face accusing as though I had something to do with it. Not to worry. Aunt Lil soon spotted Osh, who was fending off an elderly woman who'd had one too many Chardonnays. The best part, though? Reyes had blushed, and I fell a little further.

4

The day had turned out beautiful in every way possible, but one person was missing through all of it: Angel, my departed thirteen-year-old sidekick. He never missed a party. I considered summoning him, but he already knew about the wedding. Surely he would have come if he'd wanted to. He did a lot of stuff with his own adopted family. Maybe they had something going on today as well.

Still, I doubted it. Angel had been acting strange lately. More so than usual. He popped in at the most inopportune times, acted like he had somewhere else to be when he did stop by, and hadn't hit on me in months. Maybe he was accepting my marriage with Reyes, respecting our union, better than I thought he would. Or maybe the pregnancy freaked him out. Every time he did pop in unexpectedly, he seemed to avoid looking in Beep's direction. I needed to talk to him about it. Get him counseling. Though that could be difficult, considering the situation. If only Gemma could interact with the departed.

After two more hours of mingling, guests started to slowly dissipate.

Not literally, as they were corporeal, but they began giving their final congratulations and saying their good-byes. I wondered why they were leaving before Cookie and Uncle Bob did. The happy couple was supposed to head off to its pre-honeymoon honeymoon bliss while being pelted mercilessly with rice. It was tradition, and it wasn't often I got to throw things at my BFF or my uncle. I had every intention of making every throw count, but they wouldn't leave. Cookie was still in her wedding dress and Ubie in his tux and they were mingling and dancing and eating and drinking as though they had no intention of leaving.

Didn't they just want to be away from it all? I wanted to be alone with my sexy-as-hell husband so bad, I ached. But I didn't want him changing out of that tux before I had my way with him. How many opportunities would I have to rip a tux off him? I could reenact all those James Bond fantasies I'd had since I was, like, two. But I had another appointment to attend soon, so the clothes ripping would have to wait. It was probably a good thing Reyes was being kept so busy. He had checked in off and on, but his attention was always needed here or there. He did give an incredible toast that only once mentioned the fact that Uncle Bob had wrongfully convicted him of murder. So that was nice.

When yet another woman old enough to be his grandmother headed Reyes off and demanded his attention before he could get to me, I giggled at the forced smile on his face. She flirted, batted her lashes, and patted his biceps about twelve times too many for his comfort. He took out his phone and typed as the woman spoke to him, her movements exaggerated. I couldn't be certain, but I had a feeling she was talking to him about how she used to be a pole dancer until her hip gave out.

My phone chimed. I took it out of the delicate clutch that matched my dress and read Reyes's text.

Aren't you going to save me?

I don't know. I'm having a lot of fun right now. Wanna sext?

He crossed an arm over his chest while holding his phone. One corner of his mouth twitched as he leaned back against a tree and typed.

Absolutely.
Sweet. What are you wearing?

His eyes sparkled with mirth.

Animal print boxers and striped socks.

I burst out laughing, gaining the attention of everyone around me. I texted back, only this time I wasn't teasing.

You are so beautiful. How are you even real?

He sobered, staring at the phone a solid minute as the woman described her hip replacement surgery. At least, that's what it looked like from my vantage. He lifted an index finger to put the woman on pause right when she was getting to her recovery and strode toward me. His gaze didn't waver from mine as he walked, his gait like that of a panther on the prowl, the tux adding to the allure, and my body flooded with a molten heat that pooled deep in my abdomen. He took the three steps to the kitchen with one long stride and stopped in front of me.

I looked up and let my gaze trace the outline of his full mouth, the angles of his strong jaw.

After a moment, he wrapped a hand around my neck as though to pull me to him, but Ashley called out.

"Aunt Charley! Uncle Reyes! Mom says we have to go."

After several seconds, he managed to catch her just as she jumped into his arms.

"Can I stay the night? Pleeeeeeease."

Bianca walked up behind her and shook her head at us, adding a threatening glare should we even think about defying her.

I patted Ashley's back, in awe of the death grip she had on Reyes's neck.
She put her head on his shoulder and offered me her prettiest pout.

Amador stepped up to take her. "Uncle Reyes has enough women in
his life today," he said, peeling Ashley off him with a chuckle. "He doesn't
need a fluffy orange tornado following him around." He had been calling our dresses orange all day, mostly because Ashley was not a fan of
anything orange.

"Cimmanom," Ashley said, disappointed we weren't having a slum-
ber party.

"Aunt Charley needs to rest," Bianca said, taking her hand when
Amador set her down.

"We can rest together," she argued.

I'd spoiled her with our movie nights, not that I regretted a second
of it.

"We watch movies while Uncle Reyes makes cockporn."

Everyone in the immediate area stilled while Reyes and I pressed
our mouths together, trying not to crack up. This was a serious situation,
and cracking up now would just be wrong.

"Popcorn, honey," Amador said. Then he looked at Bianca. "Hon, she
really needs to learn how to say that word."

My laughter came out as more of a snort. I coughed to cover it up.
Reyes just turned his head, unable to lose the grin.

"I've tried," Bianca said, flustered. "Tell you what, we'll go to Mc-
Donald's when we get home. How does that sound?"

That was a pretty big deal. Bianca did not believe in feeding her
children fast food.

"Yay!" Stephen said as he ran up, zigzagged, feigned a left turn, took
a right before circling the parental units and shooting off in the opposite
direction. Reyes caught him just as he sped past. He giggled as he was

lifted high into the air, then brought back down into Reyes's arms. "I'm going to be fast like you," he told Reyes.

"I bet your dad's faster," he said.

Amador scoffed playfully. "Don't even start with that crap. I learned my lesson long ago."

Bianca tickled Stephen's bare foot. "If we're going to McDonald's, you'll have to put your shoes on."

Stephen had never been a big fan of shoes. Or socks. Or clothes in general. He'd once escaped from his house in his skivvies. They found him running down the street, telling anyone who would listen that his mother had been abducted by aliens.

"I don't like those shoes," he said, wiggling into the crook of Reyes's neck to get away from his mother while she tried to slip his socks onto him.

"Do you remember what the sign at McDonald's says when you go in? 'No bare feet.'"

He stopped wiggling and looked at her as though she'd lost her mind. "I'm not a bear."

I fought yet another giggle.

"He has a point," Reyes said.

"Yeah, laugh it up, *pendejo*," Amador volleyed. "Your time is coming."

"I can hardly wait," Reyes said to me.

We hugged good-bye, my heart full of hopes and dreams for Beep. Watching Reyes with Ashley and Stephen was one of the highlights of my life. I couldn't wait to see how he'd behave with Beep. If she was half as charming as Amador and Bianca's kids—

Then the truth hit me. I looked down at Beep, then over at Reyes. She would have him wrapped around her little finger in no time. "We could be in trouble."

He laughed and pulled me into his arms. "I have no doubt," he said, walking me to a dark corner of the kitchen.

I giggled when he pressed himself into me. Gasped when he bent to nibble an earlobe. "I'm the size of Nevada. How can you even want me?"

"I happen to love Nevada," he countered, his voice as deep and soft as his kisses.

If it weren't for the lady standing right beside us, the moment would have been perfect.

"You are the oldest soul I've ever come across," she said, astonished as she gazed at me, her eyes unblinking.

"Um, thank you?" I said as Reyes lifted his head at last.

I looked over at the woman. She wore an outdated floral dress and had clearly forgone a bra. She really needed the support a bra could offer her. I'd seen her piddling about, looking in our drawers when she thought no one was paying attention. I was certain she'd gone through the medicine cabinet in the bathroom.

"You're ancient."

That wasn't offensive at all. I straightened. "I'm only—"

"You are older than the stardust in the sky," she said, interrupting. Her eyes were glassed over, and I decided right then and there, no more open bars at weddings. Brought out the crazies.

Reyes stepped out of my arms then, as though something outside had caught his attention, and said, "I have to go check on Artemis."

"Artemis?" I asked, baffled. Since when did he have to check on a departed dog? Seriously, what kind of trouble could she get into?

"You are as old as time itself."

"Look," I said, growing frustrated, "that's just not something a girl wants to hear."

"You are older than—"

"Wow, you know what?" I said as I led her back into the kitchen where Denise was cleaning up. "There's even more champagne in here. Don't let anyone try to convince you we're out. You call 'em on it, okay?"

Cookie walked in then, a horrified expression on her face.

"Lucille, why don't you go find Uncle Tommy? He's been looking for you."

"Oh, my," said the woman, rushing back outside.

"I am so sorry," Cookie said. "Lucille won't bother you again. Uncle Tommy has been gone for decades. She'll never find him."

"Oh, no. How did he die?"

"Oh, he didn't die. He just packed up one night and left to live in the wilds of Alaska. We still get a postcard every few years."

"You have a very eclectic collection of relatives." I looked at Denise as she tried to scrub a stain out of the tablecloth. "But don't we all?"

"No, you're right. Mine is a little more eclectic than others, which is why you're only just meeting most of them."

"They're great. Really, Cook, but you never told me your cousin Lucille was clairvoyant."

"Oh, yeah, she's . . . different. Remember? I told you that one night we were playing Screw Your Neighbor with that couple from the first floor."

"Yes, you told me she's different. You didn't tell me she's clairvoyant."

Cookie cast a doubtful gaze. "Like *clairvoyant* clairvoyant?"

"Yep. Maybe that's where Amber gets it."

Cookie's expression did a 180, shifting from doubt to horror. "Bite your tongue. Amber is nothing like Lucille." I felt a spike of fear shudder through her. "That woman has sample packs of Preparation H from the 1970s."

"That may be, but it must run in your family. There is something very special about your daughter."

"Yes. Special. Just not *that* special."

I cracked up. "You're right. Odds are, Lucille was labeled insane at a very young age. But she's really just—"

"Eccentric," Cookie finished. "I get it. I just didn't know she was gifted."

"I doubt anyone does. But at least you know to nurture Amber's gifts. Not suppress them before they have a chance to bloom and then she becomes the lady that collects samples of hemorrhoid medication."

"I will do anything to avoid that." She indicated Lucille with a nod. The poor woman was asking everyone who was left if they'd seen Tommy.

"Hey," I said, frowning at her, "aren't you supposed to be on your way to your one-night stand? I mean, your pre-honeymoon honeymoon?"

She laughed. "Well, we were, but there is a missing girl out there. She takes precedence."

"What?" A jolt of alarm swept through me, not unlike a body shot might have. "Cook, no. This is your wedding day. You are not, under any circumstances, working. Oh my God, I can't even—"

My phone chimed and I looked down. It was the text I'd been waiting for.

"I have to go—"

"Go?"

"—but you are going on your pre-honeymoon honeymoon, and that is an order."

"Where are you going?"

"I mean it, Cook," I said as I hurried—aka waddled faster than usual—past her. "I don't want to see you when I get back."

"You can't leave the grounds."

I grabbed a sweater, then rushed out the front door, saying just before it closed, "Go!"

I walked quickly past some guests loitering by the cars out front, hoping they wouldn't wave me down for a chat. I also avoided eye contact with the departed who stood between me and my destination, winding through them, hoping I didn't look drunk to the loiterers. Seriously, didn't they have homes? I kept my head down and my stride quick. I had places to be, and I couldn't risk Reyes coming back to find me gone. He would definitely come looking for me.

Fortunately, he wouldn't see me go into the woods from the backyard unless he was specifically watching. I made sure to go straight for the cover of trees and stuck to them until I came around to a path that led to an access road about a hundred yards from the convent. I hurried as fast as my legs could carry the two of us, wobbling through the brush and dry yellow grass, dodging tree branches and departed alike. Even though I knew the Twelve couldn't come onto the sacred ground, I still kept a constant vigil. I'd been attacked more than once. Their teeth were like razors set on thick, powerful jaws. It was not something I wanted to experience again.

I could hear them growling in the distance, the sound a low rumble over the land, reminding me that in all the months we'd been here, they'd never stopped patrolling the borders. The access road came into view at last. The deeper I ventured into the woods, the more nervous I became. A blue sedan sat parked there. I stopped, my ankles aching from traversing the uneven ground. The growls had grown louder, echoing off the trees around me and reverberating in my chest. I fought to control my fear lest I accidentally summon the one man I didn't want to know I was meeting another of his gender. Alone. But it wasn't easy. The hellhounds knew I was taking a direct path to their jaws. I could go only a few more feet before they would latch on to me and pull me off the blessed dirt. I glanced back one more time to make sure Reyes hadn't followed me; then I called out to him.

"I'm here," I said.

A man, tall, in his early sixties, wearing a suit and a military cut, stepped from behind a tree and walked toward me.

"Mr. Alaniz," I said as he greeted me with a once-over.

"Ms. Davidson. I didn't realize this was a formal affair."

"This old thing?" I asked, teasing. "I just threw this on at the last minute." When he winked at me, I added, "Actually, my best friend got married today. I didn't have time to change."

"I understand, but I would advise against walking out here in those shoes again, especially in your condition."

"I know, but I had to sneak away. Thanks again, by the way, for meeting me like this."

"My pleasure," he said, his curiosity about me and our clandestine meetings clawing at him. I could feel it, but it wasn't his place to ask.

Mr. Alaniz was the private investigator I'd hired a couple of weeks after we'd absconded to the convent. Since I couldn't be out there trying to figure out firsthand who murdered my father, I'd hired someone who could. True, Uncle Bob and the entire Albuquerque Police Department were on the case, but I'd never felt so helpless, so useless. Freedom meant a lot more to me than it used to, and I had to conduct my own investigation one way or another. I had to do what I could, and if that meant doing it against Reyes's and Uncle Bob's wishes, so be it.

He looked past me, then said, "I'm not going to ask why we meet in secret like this, but I have to know if you are in danger."

I listened to the heavy breathing of the hounds. If he only knew.

"No," I said, dismissing the thought with a wave. "Absolutely not." And I wasn't. Not in the way that he meant. He wanted to know if I was in any danger from Reyes or anyone else who could stumble upon us.

"And if you get caught? What then?"

What then, indeed. "Let's just say my husband would be upset with me, but, no, I would never be in any danger from him. Never."

He seemed satisfied with my answer but looked past me again for good measure.

"What did you find out?" I asked, trying to hurry this along. Reyes would notice my absence soon. I was a little surprised he hadn't figured out my secret meetings with Mr. Alaniz before now. I was bright, according to everyone around me. So bright, I could be seen from anywhere on the planet. Why, then, didn't he see when I snuck out of the convent? How did he not know where I was every minute of every day?

A growl rumbled not ten feet away from me. I stilled and watched as a glistening of silver appeared, then disappeared in the trees. Fear tightened around my chest as Mr. Alaniz scratched his chin where a smattering of blond stubble grew. He pulled out a notepad.

I'd been to this spot a dozen times. They had never gotten this close. Right after we'd escaped to the convent, Osh had marked the sacred grounds with stakes, then threaded string around the entire area to indicate the border. Either I was closer to the border than I thought, or Osh's calculations were wrong.

I saw another flash of silver as a hellhound's muscles rolled in the shadows of the trees. I could hear its breathing, causing me to retreat involuntarily, but it kept its distance. As long as we had an accord, I didn't feel the need to run screaming back to the convent, but an uneasiness settled in my shoulders and neck, my senses on high alert.

"Your uncle is on the right track," Mr. Alaniz said.

I blinked back to him. "In what way?"

"You were right. After the last time we met, I staked out the place." He gestured toward another small access road above us. "I waited there, and sure enough, a man showed up and parked right about where I am parked now." He indicated his car with a nod, and an excited thrill ran up my spine.

"Were you able to follow him?" I asked. The entire police department had been looking for this guy, but he seemed to be a ghost. Until now.

"I was."

I clapped. It was the first good news we'd had in months. Apparently, some guy had been following me my entire life. My father figured it out and had been tailing the man when he died. We found pictures that my dad had taken of him, but we could never get an ID. So while my father was able to track him, we couldn't get within a mile of the guy. That we knew of, anyway. I began to wonder if he'd vanished until I was out walking Beep and Artemis one day and saw a car parked on the access road. The moment I looked up, the driver started the car and sped off, but I recognized him from the pictures my father had shot of him.

When my dad went missing, we found those pictures along with a whole slew of other photographs in the hotel room where he'd been staying. Photographs of me growing up. Some were as recent as mere days before my father died, and it couldn't have been a coincidence that he died soon after finding this guy. Whoever he was, he could have had something to do with my dad's death. And even if he didn't, I really wanted to know why he had been following me, literally, since the day I was born.

"But there's more to it. While you were right, he does have pictures of you from when you were very young, when I tailed him back to his apartment, I managed to snap some shots through his windows. Just like you said, he had pictures of you, articles, yearbook photos, pretty much your entire life pasted on his walls, but some of them were from just after you were born."

"And?"

"And, he isn't old enough to have been following you that long. He's barely in his thirties. Unless he took up stalking at age five, someone else is involved. Has been involved for a very long time."

He was right, and I had a feeling I knew who—or more precisely, what—was behind this.

Mr. Alaniz handed me a photograph.

I nodded. "That's him. That's the guy from my dad's surveillance photos."

"Then you were right. He does work for the Vatican."

I knew it. A former client, Father Glenn, had clued me into the fact that the Vatican had been keeping a file on me since I was born—but why? And if my dad discovered the truth, would the Church have had him killed? Over a few photos? Either way, I needed proof of this man's existence. And his address.

But first, "How do you know he was working for the Vatican for sure? Do you have any proof?"

"They're paying his bills, for one thing," he replied with a shrug. "He also gets a call from a number in Italy about once a week, a number registered to an office in Vatican City. I don't know much about the Vatican, I have to admit, but I'm sure they have several dozen departments. I couldn't determine which one this number was registered to, however."

"And how did you find out he got a call from them at all?" I asked, liking his results.

"It was weird. The guy just left his phone on a table at a restaurant," he said, lying through his teeth. "By the time I ran it out to him, I'd accidentally scrolled through all his incoming calls. And read his texts."

"One of those freak occurrences?"

"Exactly." He handed me a manila envelope. "And all that information may or may not be in this envelope."

"I'll have to think positive," I said, taking it from him, already coming up with ways to sneak it into the convent. "Did you find a connection between him and my father? Something that might implicate him in my dad's death?"

"No, and I don't think you will."

"Why?"

"He just doesn't seem the type to kill someone and leave his body in a storage shed."

The reminder of how my father was found shuddered through me. "Why do you say that?"

"He's a vegan, for starters. Most vegans are nonviolent. And he never misses Mass."

"Makes sense. He does work for the Vatican."

"I think his only job is to observe and report. For some reason, the Vatican wants to keep a very close eye on you. I just don't get a killer kind of vibe from this guy."

I nodded, trusting his instincts. "I don't suppose you got a name?"

"Howard, if that's his real name."

"Howard?" I asked, a little disappointed. I expected something exotic and Italian like Alberto or Ceasario. But Howard?

"Howard Berkowitz."

"Now you're just teasing me."

He grinned. "Nope. That's what he goes by."

"Okay, I'll look this over. In the meantime, I need you to grab Howard and bring him here."

He chuckled softly. "I'm sorry, Ms. Davidson, but I don't kidnap people."

"I don't mean kidnap. 'Kidnap' is such a strong word. I mean coax. Encourage. Maybe roofie him."

"Well, again, I can't do that. I have a better idea."

"There can't possibly be a better idea," I said, deflating. And here I was, thinking his ethics were on the same level as mine: practically nonexistent.

"How about we tell your uncle, *the APD detective,* so he can at least bring the guy in and question him."

I toed a rock at my feet. "That might work, but I won't be able to be there."

"You don't trust your uncle to get to the truth?"

Not when I could tell if he were lying instantly, but I wasn't about to tell Alaniz that. "No, I do. I guess I'll have to. But we have to get this information to my uncle without him knowing I was involved."

"I think I can handle that."

"Perfect." At least it was a step in the right direction. I scanned the area to make sure they hadn't sent out a search party for me. So far, so good. "Okay, what about that other thing we talked about?"

"Which one?" he asked, his voice full of amusement.

I had him working on several cases for me at once. "The brother thing."

"Ah." He flipped through his notepad.

This was the tricky part. The part Reyes didn't want me looking into. The part where Mr. Alaniz's fears for my safety could actually come to fruition. Reyes would never hurt me, but I couldn't say the same for any unfortunate passerby should my husband find out I'd been delving into his past.

5

SOME DAYS I LOOK BACK ON MY LIFE
AND I'M EXTREMELY IMPRESSED I'M STILL ALIVE.
——T-SHIRT

When Reyes, aka Rey'aziel, had decided to be born on earth to be with me, he chose a wonderful couple to raise him. Or that's the story I got. But he was kidnapped as an infant. I thought he'd been kidnapped by Earl Walker, the monster who raised him. I didn't find out until just before being banished to the convent that Earl didn't abduct him. A couple in Albuquerque, the Fosters, did. They'd abducted him from a rest stop in North Carolina.

How Earl Walker got ahold of him was a little less clear. Perhaps the Fosters feared they were about to get caught and sold him to Earl, and now they had another son. I'd asked Mr. Alaniz to find out two things: One, was the man the Fosters claimed as their son really their son, or had they abducted him as well? And, two, who was the couple that Reyes had been abducted from, the one he'd originally chosen to be his family?

The latter boiled down to one thing: That couple still lost a child thirty years ago. Their hearts were still broken, their dreams shattered, and I wanted them to know that their son had grown into a wonderful and honorable man.

Because I knew the time frame and the area where Reyes had been abducted—a rest stop in North Carolina about thirty years ago—it wasn't difficult for Alaniz to find his birth parents. But if he knew I'd sought them out, Reyes would be livid. He told me so, made me promise not to look for them, but after becoming pregnant with Beep, after knowing that bond that exists between a parent and a child, I couldn't let them go to their graves wondering whether their son was alive or dead. If he was happy. If he'd suffered.

They didn't need to know that he had indeed suffered. Beyond belief. But I felt they did need to know that he was alive and healthy and happy . . . for now, anyway. Hopefully he wouldn't find out what I'd done, and he would remain happy for a very long time to come. My meddling was a grave violation of his wishes, but I couldn't imagine losing Beep. I couldn't imagine her vanishing without a trace and me not knowing what ever became of her. No parent should ever have to go through that, and if it meant risking my husband's wrath, so be it. At least I would sleep better at night with them knowing what a wonderful man their son had become.

So, I devised a plan once Mr. Alaniz found out who Reyes's birth parents were. I wrote a letter as though it were coming from a neutral private investigator, and he would send it anonymously. I didn't tell them Reyes's name or where he lived or what he'd gone through. I'd told them only the essentials, just enough to bring them closure and allow them to move on with their lives.

Or that was the hope.

"I'm fairly certain, judging from the Fosters' son's coloring and age, he is one of three children that went missing around the time the Fosters adopted him."

"So, he'd supposedly been adopted by the Fosters. Are you sure he wasn't?"

"The adoption agency is out of business, but from what I could find out, they were in business only a few months and facilitated three adoptions."

"Three?"

"Exactly. But I have to admit, he seems . . . okay. Are you sure you want to open that can of worms?"

"Are you kidding? I love worms. And if they abducted him, his birth parents have the right to know. He has the right to know. Wait, do you think he knows?"

"I doubt it. According to his records, he was only a few weeks old."

"Okay, well, we have to decide how to handle this. What about the other thing?"

Writing that letter, the one where I told Reyes's birth parents their son was alive and well, that they could rest easy, knowing he'd grown up an honorable man, was a lot harder than I'd expected. I couldn't find anything about how to tell the grieving parents of a missing child that their son was A-OK in any of Emily Post's books.

Then there was the tiny hiccup in which Reyes had forbidden me from contacting them, so I didn't. I had nothing to do with sending that letter. Mr. Alaniz did. Of course, I failed to mention to Mr. Alaniz Reyes's habit of severing spines before he did it. My love muffin would never in a million years find out anyway. A good thing, because if he did, the power of his anger could destroy this side of the world. Thankfully, I covered my tracks beautifully.

"Well, funny you should mention them."

"Them?" I asked.

He cleared his throat. Studied another envelope in his hands. Glanced over his shoulder.

"Mr. Alaniz?"

"Um, your husband's birth parents."

"Did you send the letter?"

"Yes. Yes, I did." His sudden discomfort had me a little worried.

"And?"

"They're here."

"Who's here?"

"Your husband's birth parents."

It took a long moment for his words to sink in. When they did, a shock similar to being taken from a sauna and thrown into a frozen lake slapped across my body, my nerve endings firing all engines as I gaped at him.

He scratched his head in a nervous gesture. "They . . . my assistant—"

"Please tell me you're kidding."

"—put a return address on the letter you wrote."

"No."

"Yes. And—"

"No."

"Well, yes, she did."

"No." The ground tilted beneath my feet. "Please no."

"Ms. Davidson, they threatened to call the FBI—"

Everything around me blurred, and for the first time in months, I almost passed out. Only no one had hit me or drugged me or run over me with their car. This was au naturel. This was a boiling combination of dread and alarm and stark raving terror.

"—if I didn't explain what was happening. How I knew about their son. I knew you wouldn't want that, so I thought you could explain and—"

The edges of my vision darkened. He was going to kill me.

"—work out some kind of schedule."

Wait! I was pregnant. With his child, even! He couldn't kill me. It was illegal most everywhere.

"You know, maybe you could break it to your husband gently and then introduce them later. Over a bottle of wine."

The last thing I remembered before the ground slipped out from under me was how fluffy the world had become. Then everything went dark.

"Let's get her to my car."

I groaned as an arm went around my shoulders. Then another scooped under my legs followed by a labored groan as I became weightless. My lids fluttered open. Mr. Alaniz was hefting me into his arms and, with the help of two other people, began to carry me off.

I was being abducted!

No, wait, this was worse. I was being taken over the border. Deep, rich growls thundered around me as he carried me closer to my untimely death.

"Wait," I said, trying to blink past the fog. "Wait, Mr. Alaniz, put me down. I'm okay."

He lowered himself to one knee. "Are you sure?"

"Yes, I'm okay."

The minute he lowered me to the ground, I scrambled back. The hellhounds were inches away from me. They could have lunged at me or grabbed a foot and dragged me across, but they didn't. They did, however, growl. Their jaws snapped, their teeth clinking together with each gruesome promise.

I clambered to my feet, then came face-to-face with the woman I assumed was Reyes's birth mother. She was beautiful. With soft blond hair and gentle gray eyes, she'd aged gracefully despite the stress of living with what had happened. They had never had any other children, their sorrow so great. Or that was my guess.

"Mrs. Loehr," I said, trying to calm my racing heart.

"You know what happened to my son?" she asked, her features

suddenly hard, and I could tell she wasn't sure if she could believe that. If she could allow herself to hope after so many years. "You know what happened to Ryan?"

That had been his name at birth: Ryan Alexander Loehr. The fact that he had the exact same middle name and that all three of his first names—his birth name, current name, and celestial name, Rey'aziel—started with an R had boggled my mind since I first learned of it.

I looked over my shoulder toward the convent, the roof barely visible from my vantage. While no one had noticed my absence yet, it wouldn't be much longer before they did. I turned back. Mr. Loehr. He had dark hair and brown eyes, which could explain away Reyes's coloring, because he got none of his features from his birth parents. I could only assume he actually did look like Lucifer. He was certainly handsome enough. But I had to stave them off. Even for just a little while.

"Let me start by saying I am married to the man I believe to be your son."

Mrs. Loehr covered her mouth with a small hand, her eyes glistening already.

"If you will go back to Albuquerque, I promise I will get in touch with you. This is something I'm going to have to break to Reyes slowly."

"Reyes?" she said, her voice soft. "His name is Reyes?"

I didn't give his last name. I didn't want them Googling their son and discovering anything before I had a chance to explain.

"Will you please trust me and not call the FBI until I can tell my husband what I've done?"

"You wrote the letter," Mr. Loehr said.

"I did." I placed my hands on my belly. "I wanted you to know that your son was alive and well. That he was beautiful and wonderful and the most amazing person I've ever met."

"I don't understand," Mrs. Loehr said. "Why didn't he contact us? Why haven't you told him you found us?"

I closed my eyes and lowered my head. "He was violently against my contacting you."

My statement hurt her. I could feel a sharp pang pulse through her.

"Not for the reasons you might think."

"Then why?" she asked.

"Because he feels he no longer deserves you."

"What?" Her face showed her astonishment.

I took her hand in mine. "I'm not going to lie to you. He's had a hard life. A very hard life."

She pressed her mouth together to keep from sobbing.

"He doesn't want you to know what he's gone through. He doesn't want you to feel any more guilt than you already must."

She covered her mouth again as Mr. Loehr wrapped an arm over her shoulders.

"Please believe me, he is not going to be happy when he finds out I contacted you."

"Will you be okay?"

"Yes. He won't do anything drastic. He might, I don't know, storm out or something else guys like to do, but that's about it. He dotes on me."

"Can we just—?" Mr. Loehr began, but his voice cracked with the weight of emotion roaring through him. It took my breath away.

"Can we just see a picture of him?" Mrs. Loehr said.

"Of course." I brought up my photos on my cell, scrolled through until I found a shot that wasn't of him half naked, and handed it to them.

They gasped. Both of them.

In the picture I'd chosen, he was wearing a nice button-down. It was casual but nice. Really, really, really nice. Hell, they all were.

Mrs. Loehr touched the screen in disbelief. "He looks like your uncle Sal."

"He looks more like my great-grandfather."

Maybe there really was a family resemblance. Once we got to the point where I could talk to them in public without risking my marriage, I'd insist on full access to the family albums.

"He's beautiful," she said, her voice forlorn.

"That's what I keep telling him," I said, completely serious.

Mrs. Loehr smiled sadly. "When? When can we meet him?"

I bit my bottom lip in thought, then said, "If you will just give me two days, I promise he'll come around."

"Is that our grandchild?" she asked, and the question stunned me to my toes.

I ran my hands over my baby bump again in awe. "Yes," I said, suddenly thrilled Beep would have real grandparents. Denise didn't count. "Yes, she is."

"May I?" She stepped forward, hesitant.

"Of course."

She rubbed a hand over my belly as though I were Buddha. Which made sense. I felt like Buddha.

"What's her name?"

"Um, well, Beep. For now."

They both laughed softly. Even Mr. Alaniz laughed.

"Okay, well, I'd stay longer, but I have to pee."

"Oh, of course," Mrs. Loehr said. She leaned in and gave me a quick hug. Mr. Loehr did the same, and I was overwhelmed by the emotions coursing through the three of us. How was I going to hide this from Reyes until I could talk to him about it? Really talk to him.

Mr. Loehr gave me his business card. "My phone number is on there. We're staying at the Marriott on Louisiana."

"Got it. I will call you the minute I've talked to him."

"Could you tell him—?" Mrs. Loehr started. "Could you tell him we love him? We only want the best for him."

"Absolutely."

I watched as they hiked up the trail that led to the access road above us. They got in Mr. Alaniz's car and drove off as I fought another wave of hysteria.

How on earth was I going to tell Reyes?

I looked toward the Twelve as they paced just beyond the border, their hides glistening like silver fish in a pond. I could only see bits that appeared occasionally, like a mirage of crystal reflections that disappeared as quickly as they'd appeared, their muscles bunching and rolling with sheer power. They growled as I got closer, their snarls vicious and their teeth snapping like starving piranhas, begging for a piece of me. How close could I get? How long was their reach? Could they reach across the border and drag me to them?

I didn't dare get any closer. I couldn't risk Beep, but I was looking for their mark. According to Osh, all creatures from hell had a mark, a symbol of what they were and where their power lay. I thought that perhaps if I could see their marks, if I could draw the shape of them, that would somehow lead us to an answer. It would help us in our investigation. It would help us figure out how to kill them.

But even as close as I got, I couldn't see a mark. I really didn't know what to look for. I saw the silver of their hides, but they were black, so black that they absorbed light rather than refracted it. The silver was literally a reflection off such eternal blackness. But I didn't see a mark. I had yet to see what other supernatural beings saw, though. Maybe if I were more in tune with who I was, with what I was, I would see right through the beasts.

One growled and I saw another flash of silver, this time off a set of razorlike teeth. It lunged at me and I stumbled back, tripping on the low heels of my ankle boots. I caught myself before tumbling onto my backside. Thank goodness, because Beep would not have been impressed with my coordination.

Just as I regained my footing, I heard a male voice from behind me. "One p-push, and you'd be their next m-meal."

Startled, I turned to see Duff standing behind me. He was a departed man in his late twenties who wore a baseball cap, glasses, and a stutter. I'd always found him adorable. The stutter got me every time. But lately he was kind of creeping me out. No idea why, considering almost everything he'd said to me lately seemed to hold a veiled threat.

He smiled when he saw me, but he hadn't been wearing a smile when I first turned around. He'd been transfixed, mesmerized by the beasts snapping and snarling a few feet away, pacing beyond the border, waiting for me to stumble into their grasp. It seemed as though he admired them, but he recovered quickly and forced a warm expression.

"What are you doing, Duff?"

"J-just checking on you."

"Why?" I asked suspiciously. "Did Reyes send you?"

"N-no. No, I just came on my own. I s-saw you leave. I thought m-maybe you were in trouble."

"Why would you think that?"

Duff had been creeping around a lot lately, appearing at times and places where he had no right. He was turning into quite the stalker, and after Vatican Boy, I'd had about enough of stalkers. I kept meaning to talk to Reyes about him, but I also didn't want to ban him from our lives without cause. I feared, however, it was coming to that. He said some strange-ass things. Then again, maybe he just had really bad social skills. I'd met people like him. Cookie's cousin Lucille, for example. Or her second cousins. Or her uncle on her mother's side. Her whole family, in fact, was a Harvard study waiting to happen.

But Duff was getting a bit weird for my taste. I liked weird, don't get me wrong, but he was creepy weird, as though every move he made had an ulterior motive. As though he were testing his boundaries, pushing his limits to see how far he could go with me. He was about to find out.

But nothing could have prepared me for what he said next. "I wonder what would happen if someone just pushed you over the line."

I followed his gaze to the string that marked the boundary; then I turned back to him. "Are you threatening me?"

His eyes widened. "N-no. I would never. I just, I mean, I j-just wonder what they'd do. The hounds."

"Rip me to shreds." Well, that was enough crazy for me for one day. "Excuse me, Duff. I need to get back to the wedding party."

"S-sure," he said before disappearing. I couldn't help but notice the short but intense glance he'd placed on my midsection. Beep, seeming to notice as well, did a somersault. At least it felt like it. I turned to leave and slammed into a departed thirteen-year-old gangbanger.

"Angel," I said, enthusiasm raising my voice an octave. I threw my arms around his neck and kissed his cheek. I hadn't seen him in a while, and his presence had been sorely missed.

He hugged me back carefully, as though he might squish the baby between us.

"Where have you been?" I asked after setting him at arm's length. He wore the same red bandanna over his brow and a dirty T-shirt. The peach fuzz on his face still tickled when I kissed him. And he brandished the same wicked grin as always, the one that made me wonder what he'd been up to.

"Here and there. You're still hot, you know. I'd still do you."

"Wow," I said, forcing my smile wider. "You are too kind, but I'm good."

He lifted a shoulder. "If you ever change your mind, you have my number."

I snorted. "I've missed you. How's your family?"

He lowered his head, still not able to fully accept that his best friend's family had become his. "They're good. My mom and her nieces made tamales all day."

My mouth flooded with saliva. Pavlov totally could have studied me.

"I just wanted to tell you something."

"That sounds serious," I teased.

"You need to stay away from him."

Was this about Reyes? Again? "Sweetheart, I'm married to him, remember? I'm having his child."

He ducked his head to hide his face. "Not him. That guy that was just here. That cracker *pendejo* who pretends to be your friend."

My brows slid together in thought. "Duff?" I asked, surprised. He was the only cracker I'd spoken to in the last few minutes besides . . . My heart skipped a beat. Did he hear me talking with Mr. Alaniz and the Loehrs?

"Whatever his name is. Four-eyed bitch. He looks like a serial killer."

"Angel, it's not nice to judge based on looks. Not all people who wear glasses are serial killers."

"That's not what I mean."

"I know, sweetheart." I put my fingers under his chin and lifted his face to mine. "Are you okay?"

"I just don't trust him with you."

"You don't trust Reyes with me either, if I recall."

He shrugged and ducked his head again. "He's okay."

"I'm sorry. What did you just say?"

"Rey'aziel. He's okay, I guess."

Angel couldn't have shocked me more if he'd slapped me. "Are we talking about the same Rey'aziel? The one you warned me about? The one you've hated since . . . forever?"

He kicked at a rock, missing it since he was incorporeal and all. "He keeps you safe. That's all that matters."

"That's so sweet." I pulled him into an awkward hug since he wasn't really joining in. "You are the sweetest gangbanger I know."

"Okay," he said, wanting the nightmare to end.

"I wish you were alive." I set him away from me again. "I'd totally get you a Charley's Angel T-shirt."

One side of his mouth lifted into an adorable lopsided grin. "Like I would wear it."

"Oh, I'd blackmail you into wearing it." We started for the convent arm in arm. I really did have to pee. "You'd wear it every day and thank me."

"I don't think so, freak."

We trounced through the brush back to the party, and though I had a lot on my mind, Angel helped keep my mind off my impending doom. Reyes's birth parents showing up out of the blue was going to be a tad difficult to explain. Maybe the hellhounds weren't such a bad alternative to life without Reyes Farrow, because that was exactly what I risked by defying his wishes.

Angel gave me a kiss good-bye, saying he had to check on the tamales before trying to slip his tongue into my mouth, at which point I had to swat his ass. Sadly, I think he enjoyed it. I walked around to the front door, noticing most of the cars were gone now, but that the departed had multiplied. There were more now than when I'd left. All staring straight ahead. Waiting for something, which did nothing to put my mind at ease.

I would have to tell Reyes what I'd done. I would have to face the music, a term I never understood because it made whatever confrontation one had to endure seem bearable. I mean, it was music. How bad could it be to face it? The saying should have implied something direr, like, I would have to face the executioner. Much better.

I grabbed the door handle, but before I could open the front door, Denise opened it for me.

"Where were you?" she asked, almost frantic. "We've been worried about you."

Gemma walked up behind her and did the crazy sign, which since she was a psychiatrist seemed very unprofessional.

"You can't just go traipsing through the woods like that and not tell anyone where you've gone."

"But, Mo-o-o-o-om," I said with a schoolgirl whine, "all the cool kids are doing it. And I'm clearly not a virgin, so I'll survive a traipse through the woods should I come across a slasher."

She tsked while dragging me in the front door. "I don't understand half of what you say."

This was like a nightmare. My father gone and my stepmother deciding to pay attention to me after twenty-seven years. Then it hit me. I stilled. It all made sense now. We weren't on sacred ground. Reyes had lied to me. We were in hell!

"You need to go upstairs and rest while we clean up."

I flashed a boastful smile at Gemma and raised my arms in a long, languid stretch. "You're right. I'm awfully tired. And Beep has been especially active today. She's just worn me ragged."

Gemma narrowed her gaze before I giggled and hurried upstairs, hoping the loo was *desocupado*. It was. Thank goodness for small favors. As I washed my hands, I noticed a movement behind me. I turned quickly to find my dad, my wonderful, beautiful father, standing there. I'd caught glimpses of him off and on since we moved to the convent, but he never stayed. He never talked. In fact, every time he showed up, he glanced around nervously, as though he were being watched.

"Dad," I said, walking up to him. Even these few seconds were the longest I'd been able to see him since he passed, and my mind reeled with questions. "Dad, are you okay? What's going on?" I put my hand on his cold face for the first time, and a sob escaped my throat. "Why can't you talk to me?"

"Charlotte," he said, his voice soft. He stared in amazement, as though seeing me for the first time. "My Charlotte. I had no idea what you are. How important you are."

"What? Dad—"

"I'm so proud of you."

As long as I kept contact, he couldn't disappear on me. "Stay and talk to me. Please. I have so many questions."

"*You* have questions?" he asked with a light chuckle. But something caught his attention. He looked toward the bathroom door, breaking my contact, then was gone. I held my hand in the air a few seconds more, savoring the coolness he'd left in his wake, wondering why he disappeared so abruptly.

A knock sounded at the door, followed by a deep, smooth voice. "Charley?"

Even through the door, I could feel my husband's heat. His inferno. Then I looked back to where my dad had just stood. Was it Reyes? Was he afraid of Reyes?

I opened the door, a new worry creeping into my mind to add to the other one already running rampant. Why would my dad be afraid of him?

"Hey," he said, narrowing his lashes on me. "You okay?"

"Me? What? Of course."

He pressed his mouth together, the act causing the most sensual dimples to appear. "Spill."

At least I had an excuse for my nervousness now. I could use that to keep the truth at bay a little while longer. Once Reyes learned what I'd done, he may never talk to me again. The thought made my throat constrict.

"Dutch," he said, almost in warning.

"It's just, I saw my dad."

He glanced inside the bathroom. "Just now?"

"Yeah, but he disappeared again when you walked up."

He frowned at me, his gaze darting to his left, but he didn't say anything. I looked over his shoulder, and he took the opportunity to nuzzle my neck.

"Where did you go?" he asked.

"For a walk."

"An odd time for a walk."

"An odd time to go check on Artemis," I countered.

He stepped back in alarm. "What did you see?"

It took me a moment, but I realized he thought I was checking up on him. If he thought that, then he was hiding something. Crazy how guilt worked. "Trees. Grass. Bushes. The silvery black hides of hellhounds."

A muscle in his jaw flexed with tension "How close to the border did you get?"

"Not very. I was just at the gazebo. But I could see them in the distance."

"If they're that close, maybe you need to stay away from the gazebo."

"Maybe you need to tell me why you were checking on a departed dog who couldn't possibly get into any trouble."

He grinned. "Have you met your dog?"

He was right. I relaxed my shoulders. "Okay, she can get into trouble, but—"

"She's been trying to fight the hounds."

I gasped in surprise. "Artemis? Are you kidding me?"

"I've been trying to keep her away from the border."

I let out an astonished breath. "Thank you. Why would she even do that?"

"She's your guardian and she sees them as a threat to you. She's very perceptive."

I nodded absently.

"So, we're grilling. You hungry?"

"Aren't I always?" He had been a fantastic cook before, but put that man behind a grill, and the heavens opened up to watch him work.

"I'll bring you a plate."

"Perfect." He was still wearing the tux, the sight of him breathtaking. "You can't change, though."

"No?" he asked, the dimples back in full force.

"No. I have this whole James Bond fantasy going on."

"You know, I don't have to return this until Monday."

I curled my fingers into the lapel and pulled him close. "I have a feeling this is going to be a very *Moonraker* kind of evening."

Reyes left me at the door to our bedroom, where Cookie and Amber were changing. I joined them, changing out of my dress into a pair of stretchy pants—they had to be stretchy to accommodate my girth—a sweater, and a soft pair of boots.

"Okay," Cookie said as Amber helped her out of her dress, giggling when her mother's hair got stuck in the zipper, "what's on the agenda?"

I put my hand on my hip. "Your pre-honeymoon honeymoon." When she started to argue, I added, "Amber, Quentin, and I are going to make popcorn and watch *The Rocky Horror Picture Show*."

Amber nodded exuberantly.

"You're just saying that to get me to leave," she said, freeing her hair at last. "I know you. Quentin and Amber are going to watch *The Rocky Horror Picture Show* while you work the case."

She had me dead to rights. "True, but I can do this while you're banging my uncle."

A loud bark of laughter burst from Amber before she contained it.

"I promise to fill you in the minute you get back. This is your wedding day, Cook."

"Yeah, Mom," Amber said. She winked at me. "I have your six, Aunt Charley."

We high-fived. I loved that kid. But Cookie shook her head as she hung up her dress.

"Robert and I have already agreed. I'm going to help you with the case while he does what he can on his end. He's already gone into town to see if there have been any new developments."

"Cook, this is insane."

She walked to the sink to wash the glitter off her face. "Charley, we aren't going on our real honeymoon until after Beep's arrival anyway. It's okay." I sensed a ripple of apprehension go through Cookie when she mentioned her honeymoon. I'd sensed it almost every time we talked about it. If I didn't know better—and admittedly, I didn't—I would've sworn Cookie didn't want to go on a honeymoon at all.

Still, it was her wedding day, for heaven's sake. No bride should work on her wedding day. I was about 90 percent certain there was a law against it. Then again, who was I to argue?

"Okay, I need everything you can get. Friends. Social media activity. Phone calls lasting more than a couple of minutes."

"She's fifteen," Amber reminded me. "All her phone calls last more than a couple of minutes."

I smiled at her. "Excellent input, grasshopper." I'd make a PI out of Amber yet.

She flashed her pearly whites.

I took a few pages out of the file Kit had left with me. "I'll go check in with Rocket, inquire about Faris Waters's . . . status, and then comb through her texts. If I find anything suspicious, we can cross-reference them with her phone calls. If she was lured somewhere by a predator, I want to know."

Cookie's face brightened as though she'd been champing at the bit to work on a new case. It *had* been a while. We'd done some small side jobs that didn't require our presence, though nothing of this caliber for a long time. But I still couldn't shake the feeling that this had more to do with her honeymoon than with the case.

I reached over and brushed glitter off her cheek, regret consuming me nonetheless. No one's wedding day should be spent looking for a missing child.

"Do you think she's still alive?" Amber asked.

Cookie placed a hand on her shoulder as I glanced up toward the attic.

"One way to find out."

6

My death will probably be caused by being sarcastic at the wrong time.
—TRUE FACT

I left Cookie to get what she could on Faris's social life while Amber went to find Quentin. He was staying the night, since he didn't have to be back at the School for the Deaf in Santa Fe until the next day. While Amber wanted to help with the case, she decided spending quality time with the cutest boy on the planet—her words—would be more fun.

I walked to the end of the hall on the second floor, where another set of stairs led to the attic. Rocket had been staying up there since we moved here. We'd already had to replace the drywall twice. Rocket filled his days scratching the names of those who passed onto the walls. He knew the name of every person who'd died everywhere in the world. There was no way he really wrote them all. I'd read once that there were over 150,000 deaths worldwide every single day. So I wasn't sure why he chose to scratch certain names and not others, but for decades, recording the names of the departed had been what he considered his job. Who was I to argue? Surely there was a method to his madness. I'd have to pay closer attention someday, to see if the names he inscribed had any kind of connection to one another.

Just as I was about to ascend the stairs, I felt a rush of cold air at my neck. It whispered through my hair and caused goose bumps to erupt across my skin. I turned and saw her, the girl I'd been trying to talk to for months. Not the sobbing woman in my closet. She'd shown up just a few days ago. This other girl had already been living in the convent when we moved in. She was a young, almost childlike, nun, but her habit was of an older style than what they generally wore now.

I stopped and turned slowly toward her as one would do with a wild animal one was trying to capture. I didn't want to scare her off. She'd been trying to show me something; I was sure of it. Every time she appeared, she would hurry away from me, stopping to glance back every so often, as though making sure I was following her. But every time I did follow, I'd lose her in the forest.

"Not this time," I said as she turned away.

She walked quickly down the hall toward the main stairs and disappeared. I descended the stairs and went out the front door, knowing she'd be waiting for me. And she was, her expression full of fear, her lashes spiked with recent tears before, just like always, she ran away.

"I'm not losing you," I said to her back. She didn't acknowledge me.

We continued on the same path as always, the one that led in the opposite direction from where I'd been earlier, the way long since overgrown with vegetation, and as always, she disappeared from there. I stopped and whirled around in frustration. She couldn't have been more than eighteen years old. What was she trying to show me?

I continued deeper into the forest. "Where did you go?" I asked the empty air around me. Maybe I needed to have Angel tail her. Perhaps he could keep up. She was like Rocket, believing I could run through solid objects just as she could.

The last time we played hide-and-seek, I'd scoured the forest just to the left of the trail where it dead-ended. This time I went right. I stumbled over the uneven ground then got in some cardio when I passed through a spiderweb, flailing my arms and shuddering a lot. I heard growls in the distance. I stopped and the scent of lavender hit me. Very faint, but there nonetheless. Why would I smell lavender out here? After gaining my bearings, I realized I was getting closer to the border, but I still had a few yards yet. Or I did until I felt a sharp push from behind.

I toppled forward as the land slanted beneath me. Barely able to catch myself on a branch, I held on, but my feet had gone out from under me, the branch broke, and I was sliding down the side of the mountain. The trees around me blurred. They scraped and cut until I was able to grab hold of a root. The sudden stop jerked at my shoulder painfully. I had no idea the mountain was so steep on that side of the house. I fought to get my footing and was startled when someone reached out and grabbed me.

I looked up into the huge frightened eyes of the nun. She pulled and I struggled until I had crawled onto even ground. At first, I wondered if she'd pushed me. If so, then she wouldn't have helped me.

"Thank you," I said, dusting myself off. She didn't answer. "Did you see who pushed me?"

She just stared. I was getting that a lot lately. No matter. I had a very good idea I knew who had done the deed.

After scanning the area, I walked as close to the edge of the drop-off as I dared, keeping a death grip on a tree, because something had caught my attention moments before I went over.

There was one point I could see out over a clearing with a stream running through it. I'd never traveled down there, because it was beyond the border, but neither could Reyes travel that far. Yet there he was, standing pretty as you please by a group of bushes, talking to Angel. My Angel. My sidekick and lead—aka only—investigator.

First off, that was far past the border that Osh had staked out. Reyes should have been mincemeat. Second, what on earth would Reyes and Angel have to discuss?

I eased closer and squinted. The clearing was beautiful. It was one of those places perfect for a picnic. The sun hung low on the horizon, glistening across the field, elongating Reyes's shadow. He looked pensive, angry even, as he spoke to Angel. He no longer wore the tux jacket, and the top buttons of the starched white shirt had been undone, the sleeves rolled up.

He scrubbed his face with his fingers and turned sharply from Angel. He and Angel had never gotten along. Why would they be talking secretively now? Did he know about the Loehrs? Had Angel been spying on me earlier? Fear seized my lungs for a solid ten seconds before reality sank in. I looked awful with a blue face.

I filled my lungs and turned back to the young nun, but she was gone. And being left alone in the woods with someone who was clearly trying to kill me made me a tad uncomfortable, so I hurried back to the convent, doing my best to shake off the dread I felt. Was Duff trying to kill me? He'd said something earlier about pushing me, and I'd definitely been pushed. That couldn't have been a coincidence.

After sneaking back into the house, I rushed upstairs to change again since I was now covered in dirt and grass; then I headed back to the stairs that led to the attic. If the nun showed up again, I was not going to chase her. It was getting dark out, and there was a homicidal pusher roaming the countryside.

I took the steep stairs slowly. I'd been having a pain in my abdomen since my fall, and it was getting sharper with every step I took. I didn't think it was labor. It was too sharp and too concentrated in one area. I'd simply bruised myself on my trip down. Taking in a deep breath, I opened the door to the attic. Rocket was there, scratching a name into the Sheetrock.

He turned and brightened. "Miss Charlotte!" After lifting me into a hug that magnified the pain in my side, he set me down, turned back to his work, and started scratching again.

That was a short conversation. I leaned back against a column and said, "Rocket, I have a name for you."

"I have too many."

"Too many names?"

"Yes. Too too many."

"I'm sorry. Can you check on one for me?"

"I don't think so, Miss Charlotte."

"Why ever not?" I asked, massaging the pain.

"I have too many."

"That was a beautiful wedding." Strawberry stood beside me, holding her bald Barbie doll. "Cookie was so pretty. I wish I could have done her hair."

A sharp stab of horror washed over me at the thought. "Is Blue here, too?" I had yet to see Rocket's little sister. That girl was the best at hide-and-seek I'd ever seen.

"Yes, she's in the round room."

I frowned in thought. "What round room?"

"The tiny one."

"What tiny one?"

"The one downstairs nobody knows about."

This could go on for days. "Okay," I said, acquiescing. "Well, I just hope she's having fun."

"She likes it in there. It's quiet."

"Wonderful." I suddenly wondered if she was talking about the closet we couldn't get open. There was a door to a closet or a room or pantry in the laundry room off the kitchen. A door that was stuck. Or locked. Or both. Even Reyes couldn't open it. It became quite the challenge for a while; then we moved on to other, more interesting things.

What no one understood was that nothing, *nothing,* is more interesting than a locked door nobody could open. I had every intention of getting inside that room. I just didn't know how yet.

"Okay, seriously, Rocket. I need you to check on Faris Martina Waters."

He seemed to sadden. "Not on my list."

"Oh," I said, brightening. "That's good."

"Yet," he added.

That was bad. "So, soon?" I asked, knowing the answer.

"No breaking rules, Miss Charlotte." He continued to claw at the drywall.

And though I also knew the answer to my next question, I tried anyway. "Do you know where she is, Rocket?"

"Not where, only if. No breaking rules."

Damn it. "For your information, rules were made to be broken. Just whose rules are these, Rocket? Who gave them to you?"

He looked at me as though I were on the low end of the IQ totem pole. "Nurse Hobbs."

"Okay, and when Nurse Hobbs gave you these rules, what was she talking about?"

"Everything," he said, throwing his arms out wide. "But mostly pudding."

I had to ask. "Why pudding?"

"Because of that one time I tried to explain to her that the pudding disappeared yesterday and that Rubin took it, but she gave me the rules: Not when. Not who. Just if."

This conversation was not turning out as I'd imagined. "If?"

"If I took it."

I gaped at him. For, like, ten minutes. Was he kidding? After all this time, the rules weren't even about the departed or how he knew the names of everyone who'd ever passed, but about pudding? After absorbing that little nugget of gold, I said, "Rocket, I don't think those rules apply here."

A loud gasp echoed around me. "Miss Charlotte," he said, chastising me, "the rules apply everywhere. I told you. It wasn't just the pudding, but the corn bread, the honey, the turtle named Blossom—but that was only that one time—and the Thorazine."

I could not believe what I was hearing. All this time, I'd thought Rocket's rules came from some celestial manual or guideline or flowchart, something official—but all along, they were from a nurse at the mental asylum where he'd lived most of his life? Visions of the charge nurse in *One Flew Over the Cuckoo's Nest* came to mind. She was scary.

"Rocket, Nurse Hobbs was not talking about people who have passed away. You can tell me anything about them you want to."

"No breaking rules. You already broke all the rules."

He was scolding me for using my supernatural mojo to heal a little boy—and a few other people—in the hospital a few months back. He felt that using my gift to heal people was breaking the rules, but I saved people all the time. I found murderers and missing children and solved cases incessantly. How was that any different from healing a sick kid?

"Rocket, so I saved that little boy by touching him. So I saved a few sick people. How is that any different from what I do every day? I save people using my supernatural connections every other day. How is one breaking the rules and one not?"

"You probably shouldn't yell at him," Strawberry said, petting her doll's head.

I ignored her. "And I know darned good and well, Nurse Hobbs did not give you any rules regarding me, since I wouldn't be born for decades when you knew her."

"Nurse Hobbs was very smart," he countered as he scratched a *K* into the wall.

I decided to give it one more shot. "Okay, if. You can tell me if. So, if Faris Waters is going to pass away soon, where will it happen?"

"Not where. Only—"

"That's it!" I said, blowing up. "The next time you mention the rules to me, I'm going to take those rules, crumple them in my fists, and set them on fire with my laser vision." I didn't really have laser vision, but it would rock if I did.

Rocket gasped. "Miss Charlotte, you can't do that."

"Oh, I can. Just you wait and see." I rolled onto my tiptoes until we were nose to nose. "Just you wait and see."

He dissipated before me, his eyes saucers.

"You so don't have laser vision," Strawberry said.

"I might. I'm a god, in case you haven't heard."

She didn't buy it for a second. "Unless you're Superman, you don't have laser vision."

Before I could argue further, she followed Rocket's lead and left me standing alone in a dusty attic.

I looked up at the name he'd been carving into the wall and stilled. *Earl James Walker.* The man—the monster—who'd raised Reyes. He was currently living out the rest of his days drinking his meals through a straw in a nursing home. Reyes severed his spine when he'd tortured and tried to kill me a few months back, and now Walker was going to die.

I stood in shock a few seconds, wondering why the man was about to kick, before I realized it was rude to look a gift horse in the mouth.

The first thing I did when I got back to the bedroom was call Kit. She needed to know that her FedEx's niece was still alive. But I felt obligated to tell her that while we had some time, we didn't have much. We needed a break in the case soon.

They didn't have any more information, and all the leads they did have led to a dead end. They were going to question her classmates again, just to make sure they didn't miss anything.

"Charley," Kit said before we hung up, "you have to do your thing. We have to find her."

"I'm working on it. Promise."

I fetched my laptop, the file on Faris Waters, and a hot chocolate, and stretched out onto David Beckham to give my back a break. The pain in my abdomen was almost gone, but it was at that moment precisely that Beep decided to try out for the Olympics, showcasing her floor routine for the judges. I patted what I assumed was her bottom as I scanned the case file on Agent Waters's niece.

I had the distinct feeling I was being watched, but I'd had that feeling a lot lately, so I pretty much ignored it and kept reading the file. I read through all her texts and highlighted the ones that caught my attention. Cookie was working downstairs in my makeshift office. After a while, my hot chocolate got cold. I needed to check up on Cookie's progress anyway, so I went downstairs.

The place was almost good as new. Only a few of the wedding guests remained, and they were all in the kitchen or out back where the grill was. Thankfully, Cookie's cousin Lucille had gone. I headed toward the office but was cut off by Uncle Bob.

"Are you free?" he asked.

"No, but I'm on sale for a dollar ninety-nine."

He sighed, adding fuel to the fire.

"Do you have a minute?"

I patted my pockets. "Not on me, but I can go through the couch cushions."

"Charley." He pretended to be annoyed, but I felt the emotions tumbling inside him. He was happy. Completely content. It was not an emotion I felt from him often, and if Cookie had been there, I would've kissed her on the mouth.

I had to admit, however, I was a little surprised. I'd ruined his pre-honeymoon honeymoon.

"I'm sorry about tonight," I said.

"Don't worry about it. She's like you. Won't give up until she's got her man."

"That's true. She's a good egg. But you already knew that, I'm guessing."

"I did."

"You looked fantastic, by the way," I said. He'd changed out of the tux, but he'd looked amazing in it.

"Thank you." We were venturing onto uncomfortable ground. Compliments weren't part of our MO. Passive-aggressive insults were. Mild threats. A little nagging here and there. "You looked pretty amazing yourself."

My brows shot up. "I'm surprised you noticed, what with that goddess standing next to you."

He almost blushed. "You got that right."

"I hope the captain enjoyed himself."

"I think he did. He's quite . . . taken with you."

Though he didn't mean that in an attraction kind of way, I said, "Yeah, just don't tell the old ball and chain. So, what's up?"

"Well, we still haven't decided exactly where we're going on our honeymoon, and I thought you might know what she's thinking. She won't tell me. She wants me to choose where I want to go, but I want her to choose."

"So, you want me to flip a coin? See who chooses?"

"No, I want you to find out where she really wants to go."

I smiled and leaned into him. "See, that's the funny thing, Uncle Bob. She wants to go anywhere you are. You could book a vacation in Bosnia, and she'd be happy."

"You're no help whatsoever."

"Well, I do have one word of advice: Don't take her to hell. I've heard it's really dry there this time of year."

"You're worse than no help."

"I know. I really do. You haven't heard anything, have you?" He knew what I meant without my having to elaborate.

"No, hon. I'm sorry. We are working the forensics, waiting for lab results."

Unlike on television, real forensic work took weeks or even months. Knowing that didn't help. My impatience knew no bounds. Still, Ubie would have something new to chew on as soon as Mr. Alaniz sent in that anonymous tip about Vatican Boy. I would kill to be there during questioning. Not anybody important. I might knock off someone who groped women in the subway or talked in the theater.

I leaned in to give him a hug and whispered into his ear. "Puerto Rico."

He gave me a quick squeeze before letting me go with a wink and a grin.

Just as I was about to head toward the office again, I decided to take the opportunity to question my investigator about the recent, and rather disturbing, developments. What on earth could Angel have been talking about with Reyes? And why was Angel defending him? Last I heard, he hated the guy with a fiery passion. He'd never trusted him, so why the sudden camaraderie?

I summoned him, determined to find out. He appeared before me, his arms crossed at his chest as though I'd interrupted something important. The kid had been dead for decades. How important could his activities be?

"What are you and my other half up to?"

A hint of surprise flashed across his face, but he recovered quickly. "I don't know what you are talking about."

"Don't try to play the innocent with me. I saw you and Reyes talking in the field."

He lunged forward and pasted his hand over my mouth. "Shhhh," he said, scanning the area. "How did you see us?"

I peeled his hand away. "I looked. You were there. Reyes was upset. What's going on, and why all the secrecy?"

He cursed softly to himself. "I can't tell you."

"Angel," I said, stepping closer and giving him my infamous death stare, the one that frightened man and beast alike, "either you tell me what is going on, or I swear by all that is holy—"

"Please," he said, giving me a light shove of dismissal. "I'm more scared of him than of you, but only on days that end in Y."

"Wait, why are you scared of him? Did he threaten you?"

"No. He doesn't have to. Have you seen his angry side? Not something I want to mess with."

"Then clearly you haven't seen mine."

He scoffed. "Your angry side is like when Mrs. Cleaver burns the muffins."

"That is so offensive. I've never made muffins in my life."

"Whatever, *chiquita*. I ain't spilling, so take your threats and—ow!"

I'd taken hold of his arm and sank my nails into his flesh. "What?" I asked, forcing him closer. "What was that?"

"You can torture me. It won't help. I can't tell you, but just know everything he's doing is for you and your baby's safety."

I let go. "For Beep?"

"Yes," he said, rubbing his arm.

"Just give me a hint, then. Angel, if she's in danger—"

"If?" he asked, his voice incredulous. "Have you looked around? Of course, she's in danger. You both are. I'm not sure why that hasn't sunk in."

"It's sunk in. It's completely sunken, but—"

"I ain't talking. You'll have to ask Rey'aziel."

He disappeared before I had a chance to argue further. Damn it. I hated being left out of the loop. I loved loops. People didn't understand that about me.

I heard a loud crash coming from the dining room slash study. While we had assigned a small room past the dining hall to be our office, the dining hall itself had become our study. Reyes, Osh, and Garrett Swopes spent a lot of time in there, scouring over the texts Garrett uncovered, trying to find out how to kill the Twelve. Osh insisted they couldn't be killed. Only sent back to hell. So now they were trying to figure out how to do that as well. While it would be only a temporary fix, we would take what we could get.

I hurried there and came upon a very upset Garrett Swopes and a poor, innocent chair on which he'd taken out his frustration. He'd also knocked over a stack of notes, the same stack he'd been slaving over for weeks. He was funny when he was upset, so I almost didn't intervene. But he saw me anyway and gave me his back, embarrassed.

"What are you doing here?" I asked.

He was still in the nice button-down he'd worn under his jacket.

"I thought you had to leave early to work a skip for Javier."

"I did, but they picked him up this morning."

"Oh, well, that's good." I nodded toward the papers. "No luck?"

He shook his head. "None. There's nothing in here about how to kill the Twelve." He'd hired a doctor of linguistics to translate the texts, and although Dr. von Holstein didn't get through all of them, he'd gone through a good amount. It was all quite fascinating. Much of what this guy named Cleosaurius wrote was about me, aka the Daughter of Light, and Beep, whom he referred to as the Daughter. He did say on one or two notations that she would be a melding of light and darkness, me and Reyes respectively, and he prophesied that Beep, though he never called her that, would be the downfall of Lucifer. That she would destroy him. And while pretty much everything he wrote went against Revelations and the predictions written therein, some of it coincided with the ancient texts. The four horsemen, for example, although Cleo simply called them the bringers of great suffering.

He also prophesied about the Twelve and said what we'd been hearing over and over: Twelve would be sent and twelve would be summoned. So, then, who did the sending and the summoning? Surely Lucifer had sent the Twelve, the hellhounds patrolling our borders night and day. But who summoned the other Twelve? And how did they play into all of this? And how on earth did we kill them?

"I'm sorry, Charles," Garrett said just as Reyes and Osh were walking in. "There's nothing in the texts to indicate how to kill them. At least not in the texts Dr. V translated. There was a lot he had yet to get to. It would have taken him years to translate it all."

"It's okay. I'm going to give Sister Mary Elizabeth a call later. Maybe she found something." Sister Mary Elizabeth could hear the angels speak. Like literally. And though she couldn't interact with them, she did come up with some pretty good intel occasionally.

I sat on a chair and flipped through a few pages. Reyes sat beside me as Osh stood eating a BBQ sandwich. It smelled amazing and my mouth watered involuntarily.

"Food's ready," Reyes said as he studied me. His heat scalded my skin, and even though he was still wearing the white button-down and his hair had been neatly cut, he now wore a day's growth along his jaw. And he looked tired. His eyes had that sleepy look and, while incredibly sexy, Reyes just didn't get sleepy. He had infinite energy. Or that's how I'd always thought of him.

I still couldn't help but wonder what he had going with Angel. He recruited the departed to spy for him. Maybe he was doing something similar with Angel, but why spy on me? It wasn't like I could go anywhere. We were all stuck.

Perhaps that was why the air fairly crackled with tension. Why he was so blisteringly hot. Reyes was unused to feeling helpless, and now he was like a cornered wolf, ready to strike at anything that moved. While he was fantastic today, his energy seemed to be ratcheted tight, like he might explode given the smallest reason.

"Anything you want to tell me?" he asked, jump-starting my heart.

Did he know about the Loehrs? Or my interrogation of Angel? Or how I was pushed? I didn't think he'd seen me. On any of those occasions. And I wasn't about to give him a reason to explode. Not here. Not in front of everyone. I would explain about the Loehrs later, and he could decide what to do then. Besides, he was lying to me, too, in a way. He didn't let me in on what he and Angel were up to. He'd lied about the border, though that could have been Osh. But how was Reyes standing out in a field well beyond where Osh had marked the outskirts of the sacred ground? Was Osh in on it, too? And what was *it*?

"Not especially," I said, offering him my best smile. "Just wanted to make sure the helicopter is all set." We'd come up with a plan a few months ago. As soon as Beep was born, we were going to pile into a helicopter Reyes had chartered that was going to fly us to an island that had once been a leper colony. The entire island was consecrated, thus no hell hounds. We had no idea if it was going to work, but it was the best plan we'd come up with. And we'd come up with many.

"It's set. It's been set for weeks."

"Great." When he kept his gaze trained on me, I looked down at the documents. "What's this?" I asked, finding some notes in Garrett's handwriting.

"Nothing," Garrett said. "I've been trying my hand at translating the texts myself."

I was impressed, but Reyes seemed . . . blasé about it? It was as though he'd expected as much. Or he was still trying to figure out if I was lying.

"Is this about me or Beep?" I asked when I started to read.

"You, I think. Who the hell knows?" He strode back to the table and picked up the notepad. "From what I can tell, it's talking about the beginning and the end of something. I just don't know what."

"Hopefully not the world. Can you read this out loud?" I asked him, getting a new idea.

"A little. I don't know all the vowels, but—"

"Try it," I said, wanting to test a theory.

He picked up one of the documents. We'd had the original texts copied and preserved. They were thousands of years old and locked safely away in storage now, so Garrett was working off copies. After noisily filling his lungs to show his frustration, he stumbled through a couple of lines.

He stopped and glanced down at me as my mind mulled over his interpretation.

"One more time," I said. While I didn't know how to read every language ever spoken on earth, I knew how to speak them. All of them. Every single language, dead or alive, that had ever been spoken, or signed, on earth.

He picked up the sheet again and began.

"King!" I said, gazing up at him. "It's talking about a king."

"No," Reyes said, straightening in his chair. "A queen. If you take into account the first word of the sentence, it is describing a feminine subject. He's just saying the actual word wrong. It's queen." He looked up at Garrett. "Keep going."

Garrett picked up the chair he'd upended and sat down beside us to read the line yet again.

"That's not bad," I said. "I got it that time. The queen, though the first—"

"—will be the last," Reyes finished. Then he looked at me.

"You. It's talking about you, only using the word 'queen' instead of 'god.'"

"It makes sense," Osh said, joining us at the table. "He had to be careful what he wrote or be considered a heretic."

"Or in league with the devil," Reyes added.

Osh nodded. "Like a witch. He would have been condemned and most likely stoned to death."

"What a horrible thought."

"So, if you're the queen in this passage," Osh said. "How are you the first and the last?"

Reyes was staring at me, and I tried to ignore it at first because it wasn't a come-hither stare but more like a *you're a freak* kind of stare. Either that or I was projecting.

"What?" I asked him at last.

"It *is* talking about you," he said as though astonished. "You are the first pure ghost god."

I frowned. We'd had this conversation before. "I thought I was the thirteenth. What the heck?"

He shook his head. "You are the thirteenth god, but the first pure ghost god."

With as much dramatic flair as I could muster, I threw myself—mostly just my head—across the table. "You never give me the entire picture of anything. I'm so confused."

Reyes laughed softly. "Okay, here's what I know: There were seven gods, or what we would call gods, in your dimension. They were the original gods. They created everything there, like the God of this dimension created everything here."

I turned to him, trying to understand. "So, like another galaxy?"

"No," Osh said. "Like another universe. This one is taken."

"There are other universes?" Garrett asked.

"There are as many universes as there are stars in the heavens of this one."

Garrett sat back, as impressed as I was. "Okay, so in mine, there were seven gods. Not just one."

"Yes, for lack of a better term. They are actually very different entities, but we will go with 'god' for now."

"Gotcha. Going with god. And we have seven."

"You *had* seven. Eventually, through time, there were thirteen total entities, including you. But you are the only one left. The last of your kind."

I did the dramatic thing again and Reyes laughed again.

He pushed my hair out of my face. Tucked it behind an ear. "The original seven weren't like your god. They could procreate, but only once."

"Okay, I'll bite. Why only once?"

"Because once they created another god, what I'm calling a ghost god, they melded together and became one. They ceased to exist. Their union created another being—"

"Like Beep!"

"—like Beep, only they converged into one being, a single ghost god, with all the power of the two that merged to produce it. Therefore, the new entity is more powerful than the individual gods that created it. It's like two stars colliding to create a single supernova, one that can live forever and has an endless supply of energy. And now, in a process that took millions of years, or even billions, all of the original gods have converged, either with each other or with another ghost god, until there is only one left. And they were magnificent. They were great celestial beings floating in space with the power of a billion suns."

I sat back, impressed. "Okay, this is a really cool story."

"Thank you."

"But why am I the first as well as the last?"

"If you do that math—"

I gaped at him in horror. I had no idea there would be math involved. He ignored me. "—you'll realize that seven original gods, and the ghost gods they created, could only have produced a thirteenth if all of them had eventually merged. All seven of the original gods and three of the original ghost gods had merged until only two ghost gods were left. For the first time, two ghost gods, with the power of all those who came before them, merged and you were created from their union."

I squeezed my eyes and tried to envision the process. "I don't think you're very good at math."

"I'm very good at math." He took a pencil and paper and drew me a chart with X's representing the originals and O's representing their offspring, the ghost gods. He was right. Seven, when boiled down to one, was thirteen total. Seven original and six ghosts.

"So, it's like my mother and my father gave up their lives to create me?"

"Yes, and no," Osh said. "They still live inside you. If this is right, the power surging through every cell in your body could destroy this universe. Could destroy a million universes and everything in them. Thankfully, your species is very kind. I like to think the gods before you are sort of like—" He looked at Reyes for the word.

"Like counselors," Reyes offered.

"Exactly. They're like counselors. They're still there inside you, in the consciousness and memories that define your genetic make up. You're just a separate entity"

"So, to answer your question," Reyes said, "you are the first pure ghost god, the only one created from two ghost gods. And because there are no more, you are also the last."

"That's kind of sad," I said. "But they're all still here?" I placed a hand over my heart.

"Like advisors."

"Think about it, though," Osh said, gazing at me in awe. "All that power, all that energy, the potency of seven original gods, has been harvested and passed down to you."

Reyes looked at Osh and did something I'd never seen him do. He sought Osh's counsel. "This is where I get lost."

Osh nodded to encourage him.

"Why is she here on this plane? If she is the last god of her universe, of her people, the very last of her kind, why is she here?"

"That's something even I can't fathom."

"The first time we had sex," I said, making Reyes a little uncomfortable and Osh perk up, "I saw you see me." I looked at him. "I saw you pick me out of a thousand beings of light. They were all just like me. There has to be more of us."

"They were not all just like you. To give you a metaphor of what your dimension is like, imagine God, the god of this dimension, among his angels. He is not one of them. He created them. He has the power to reduce them all to ash with a single thought, but he still lives among them. And his angels, while more powerful than the mortal life in his realm, are not like him, though they are made of a similar substance. Of a similar light."

"So you saw me among my angels?"

"Metaphorically speaking. And, again, you have to understand, all of this took place over millions of years. Probably billions. The gods of your dimension are more ancient than any other beings I've ever come across."

I had an epiphany. "Then I'm older than you."

"What?" he asked.

"You may be centuries old, but I'm older. I'm millions of years old."

He grinned. "Yes."

"I robbed the cradle," I said, quite pleased with myself. "I wish I remembered all of this."

"From what I understand, you will once you know your celestial name. It's like a safety switch. But you aren't supposed to know your celestial name until your physical body dies."

"But I did die!" I argued. "When the Twelve attacked us. I stuck a blade in my chest and died, baby. I saw the heavens above us. Trust me."

"You died, but you came back," Osh said, struggling to understand himself. "That's the only way it makes sense. You didn't take up your position as the grim reaper like you're slated to do."

"So, the other grim reapers, the ones that reaped, for lack of a better phrase, before me, they were from my world as well?"

"Yes," Reyes said. "But they were like the angels. No god has ever taken on such a menial task."

"Then why leave the gene pool?" Garrett asked. "Why bring in a being—a god, no less—when you already have people for that?"

Reyes nodded, agreeing that the whole thing was utterly illogical. "Like I said before, it's like sending a queen to do the janitor's work."

"Or a god," Osh said, "to clean up someone else's mess."

Garrett sat in thought, then looked at me. "So, whose mess are you here to clean up?"

7

A friend will help you if someone knocks you down.
A best friend will pick up a bat and say, "Stay down. I got this."
—TRUE FACT

Cookie and I compared notes as we ate some of the wonderful fare Reyes
and Osh had grilled up. We came up with very little, unfortunately. She
was still waiting on information from Kit, and as long as I was stuck at
the convent, I just couldn't do much. I felt helpless, and the dread that
had taken up residence in the back of my neck concerning the Loehrs
weighed on me. I didn't know how to tell Reyes what I'd done.

I begged Cook to go, spend at least the night with her husband in a
nice place, but she was adamant about staying. Gemma and Denise were
still there, too. They'd been hanging out a lot. It was weird and a little
disturbing. Well, Denise was a lot disturbing, but she kept to herself
mostly. She picked up our plates and made herself useful. So there was
that.

Quentin and Amber went back to watching movies, which reminded
me, I needed to call Sister Mary Elizabeth before it got too late. If anyone had the lowdown on what was going on up top, it would be her.

Reyes got up from the table to clean the grill. Gemma found a plush corner in the living room in which to read. Uncle Bob had to get back to the city. Osh was nowhere to be found. That guy kept odd hours. Kit sent over the interviews they'd done with all of Faris's friends, and Cookie couldn't wait to dive in, so I took the opportunity to chat with Garrett, since we were the only ones left at the table. All our conversations were about prophecies and hellhounds. I wanted to know how he was doing. Kind of. Really I wanted to know how his son was doing and his baby mama, Marika.

I gestured him to move closer. He frowned suspiciously, then scooted his chair over. Like half an inch. Jerk.

"So?" I asked, drinking a cup of hot chocolate. Another one. Since I was officially off coffee until Beep was born, hot chocolate had become my friend. We weren't as close as me and mocha latte, but we were getting there. It took time to build a relationship. Trust had always been an issue for me.

"So?" he asked, drinking a beer, his beverage of choice.

"How's Zaire?"

One corner of his mouth went up. "He's good. I get to see him almost every week."

"And what about Marika?"

He lifted a shoulder and leaned back in his chair, straightened out his legs in front of him. "She's doing well. We've been talking."

I scooted closer. "And?"

"She wants to try dating again."

"Dude, that's great."

"I don't know. She used me to purposely get pregnant and didn't tell me."

"Of course she didn't tell you. What would you have done if she had?"

"Run in the other direction. But it's still not okay, Charles."

He was right, of course, but we all make mistakes. I decided to remind him of that. "Do you remember that time I was helping you out with a bust—?"

"You mean that time you butted into my stakeout because you wanted me to lick your coffee cup?"

"Exactly. And what happened?"

"The guy came home. I busted him. End of story."

"No, before that."

"You tried to poison me."

"No, after that." And I didn't try to poison him. I just wanted to know if my cup was poisoned. It tasted . . . poisony. Turned out, I just didn't rinse well. So much for my theory that my landlord at the time was trying to kill me.

He drew out his exhalation to make his point. A long, needless point. "Fine. I get it."

"No, what happened?"

"I went into that diner to get a cup of coffee."

"No. You went into that diner to try to get a date with one of the waitresses."

"I know the story."

"And why was I really in the same neighborhood as you?"

"Because you were staking out that diner."

"I was staking out that waitress. And why was I doing that?"

"Charles—"

I shoved an index finger over his mouth.

He glared.

"Why was I doing that?"

"Because you figured out she was spiking men's coffees with eye-drops."

"Yes. She had this weird vendetta thing going on and was purposely making men sick. I saved your ass. You could have died."

"I wouldn't have died."

"You could have gone into a coma like poor Mrs. Verdean's husband."

"So, where are you going with this?"

"You made a mistake hitting on that woman when your gut told you she was about as stable as a three-legged chair. We all make mistakes."

"What Marika did wasn't a mistake. It was quite intentional."

"I get it. I do. I just hope you give her a second chance is all. Especially now that she broke up with her boyfriend."

"She broke up with him?"

I nodded, knowing that would get his attention.

"I don't know, Charles. Chicks are crazy."

"Duh. That doesn't mean you can't keep trying."

"Maybe it could work. I mean, I've always wanted a family. And Zaire is great. Marika has her moments, too."

"That's the spirit," I said, punching his arm. "So, did you get it?"

"Is that the only reason you're talking to me?"

It wasn't, but I couldn't let him know that I genuinely cared about him. "Of course."

His mouth widened into a grin that made his silvery eyes sparkle. "It's behind that weird box." He nodded toward the potato bin.

"Sweet!" I scrambled up to check out my new toy. "I've always wanted a sledgehammer."

At about half my height, the handle wasn't bad. The head of the sledgehammer was about the size of a Big Gulp. All in all, it seemed pretty nonthreatening.

I took the handle and tried to pick it up, ignoring the skiptracer at the table. His snickers would not deter me from my task.

"Fine," I said, dragging it from behind the potato bin and across the floor.

"You aren't going to kill anyone with that, are you?"

"That's certainly not the plan," I said, huffing and puffing as it scraped along the tile with an awful, horror-movielike sound.

"You realize this floor is over a hundred years old."

I felt bad about the floor. I really did, but I couldn't pick the stupid thing up. "It's much heavier than it looks."

"Would you like some help?"

"Nope," I said, winded. I'd traveled about two feet. "I got this."

There was a tiny room off the kitchen with a wooden closet of some kind. Nobody knew what it was, even Sister Mary Elizabeth. It could have been a confessional, for all I knew. Either way, no matter what we did, we could not get the door open. Normally, that wasn't a big deal. But the more I thought about it, the more it ate at me. There could be anything in that closet. There could be a dead body. Or a mountain of gold. Or a staircase to a secret passageway.

After months of trying to pry it open, I couldn't take it anymore. This was my last hope. That door was coming open if I had to tear down the wall around it.

Garrett got up and followed me to the room that we had set up as the laundry room. Though I'd refused his help physically, he decided to help in other ways. He watched and chuckled and assured me I was batshit every so often. So, there was that.

After an eternity, we got to the door, a thick wooden thing set in the middle of a wall in the small room. The wall butted up against the room that Cookie and I had set up as our office, but we'd stepped the rooms off. There was a good five feet of space in between that wall and the office wall. So what was there?

I was about to find out.

As Garrett watched from the doorway, swigging his beer pretty as you please, I pulled with all my might to try to at least get the sledge-hammer off the ground. I wasn't weak. I could lift stuff. Heavy stuff. Well, heavy-ish. This thing was insane.

I set it back down just as Reyes walked up. He wore the same doubt-ridden grin as Garrett.

"Gonna get it open, are you?" Reyes asked, wiping his hands on a towel.

"Yes, I am." I set the hammer down to take a break. "We need to know what's in there. There could be anything. I mean, why is it locked?" I examined the door for the thousandth time. "No, *how* is it locked? There's no lock." I pointed to emphasize the absurdity of it all.

The door was massive. In a convent with regular doors and regular walls, why was this door—the same door that was impenetrable—so thick? So sturdy? Reyes had even tried to see into the closet incorporeally. He couldn't get in!

"I mean, aren't you even curious? What kind of room is impenetrable even to something that is incorporeal?"

I struggled to lift the sledgehammer again, but now I had an even bigger audience.

"She at it again?" Osh asked.

"Hardheaded as the day is long," Reyes said.

My frustration rose to new heights. "Okay, Mr. Smarty Pants, if you aren't going to help, what were you talking to Angel about?"

His gaze narrowed. "What do you mean?"

"In that field today. I saw you."

He straightened. "What were you doing out there?"

"I was following that sweet departed nun. She's been trying to show me something and then someone pushed me and I almost fell to my death and were you there? No."

A blast of heat hit me then, and I couldn't tell if he was angry with me or because someone had pushed me.

"What do you mean, someone pushed you?"

Oh, thank God.

"Who pushed you?"

"Why were you talking to Angel?"

"Is that what happened to you?" He took my arm and indicated a scrape down the back of it, his touch scalding.

"Probably." I shook off his hold and gripped the sledgehammer again. "And I have no idea who it was. I smelled something weird, though." I straightened and thought about it. "Like lavender or something." I bent to my task again.

He stepped to me, curled his fingers under my chin, and lifted my face to his. "Who was it?" The moment he stepped forward, I felt consumed by fire, like I'd been swallowed by a blazing inferno.

"What were you talking to Angel about?" When he didn't answer yet again, I stepped out of his grasp and pointed in the general direction of the living room. "Go stand in the corner with Mr. Wong."

Cookie had joined us then, doing her best to look over Osh's shoulder. "Is she trying it again?"

Reyes turned from me then as though frustrated. "Why is he here?"

"Mr. Wong? I have no idea." But I stopped to wonder as Osh and Reyes eyed each other. "Are you thinking what I'm thinking?"

"Why is such a powerful being in the house?" Osh asked.

"No. Well, yes—that, too—but I was thinking he needed to get out more. Maybe meet a girl. Try the singles scene. He seems awfully lonely."

I pulled on the hammer again, raising it about two inches off the floor, and swung with all my might. It tapped lightly on the door, the sound barely audible above the sound of the spin cycle.

Then someone else joined us. Gemma stood behind Garrett, but I didn't think the high-pitched screech that nigh drew blood from my ears was coming from her. Nope. It came from none other than my stepmother.

"What are you doing?" she yelled, pushing her way into the room.

Ignoring her, Reyes shook off his misgivings about Mr. Wong, the sweetest man alive, or, well, dead, and stepped to me again. "Are you okay?" he asked, taking my arm and caressing it.

His touch liquefied my insides. "I'm fine."

"A sledgehammer?" Denise howled. "What are you doing letting her lift a sledgehammer?"

"I'm calling Katherine," Reyes continued, unfazed by Denise's rant. "I think we need to be sure."

"Katherine the Midwife," I corrected. Since we couldn't take me to a medical team to give birth, we'd brought a medical team here. We even had one of the downstairs rooms outfitted with everything a modern midwife would need.

Denise ripped the handle away from me. "Do you know what that could do to the baby?"

Was she kidding? "The baby is the safest person in this room, Denise."

"Charley, you can't lift something this heavy."

"Yes, I can. Not very far, but—"

A slap echoed along the walls and I realized my face stung. The moment was so shocking, so surreal, everyone stood in complete silence. Even Denise. She seemed the most shocked of all.

Reyes reacted first. His heat exploded around me and I slowed time to watch a hand lift to Denise's throat. He would snap her neck in a heartbeat, before he even knew what he was doing, his anger was so great. I stepped in front of him, put my hands on his wide chest, and pushed with all my might. Then I allowed time to bounce back with my hands still on his chest, my body braced for impact.

It crashed around me, and Reyes, not expecting my influence, took an involuntary step back. I'd hardly fazed him. He started for Denise again, but I put my hands on his face and drew his attention to me.

"Mom!" Gemma yelled, tackling the big guys blocking the doorway to get inside. She didn't know what Reyes was, but she knew he was supernatural and she knew he was as deadly as they came. She got between Reyes and Denise and held up her hands to fend him off.

"I'm sorry," Denise said, trying to calm him.

"Reyes," I said, my voice soft, soothing. "It's okay."

His anger physically hurt, it was so hot.

"You have to calm down." I smiled, trying to lighten the mood. "You're boiling me alive."

He sobered instantly, his eyes shimmering with emotion. A telltale wetness gathered between his thick lashes as he glared at me. Then, ever so slowly, he came to his senses.

I wiped at a tear that slipped past its glistening cage, but he turned from me, embarrassed and furious and, I suspected, afraid of what he would do.

"Are you okay?" I asked Denise.

Both hands were covering her mouth. "Charley, I'm so—!"

"Get her the fuck out of my house." Reyes didn't turn around when he spoke.

"Come on," Gemma said, rushing Denise out of the room.

Garrett helped, ushering them out, and then he and Osh blocked the door in case Reyes changed his mind.

"I'm okay," he said to them, but they didn't move.

Cookie looked on the verge of tears herself.

"We're okay, hon," I promised her.

Even unconvinced, she took that as her cue to leave.

"Reyes," I said, placing a hand on the small of his back. It scorched my skin. "What is going on? You're so hot. Your temper is like a ticking time bomb. You leave and you're gone for hours. And then when you do come back, you stay away from me for the rest of the night. I don't understand." I couldn't even imagine how he'd react when I told him about the Loehrs. The very thought filled me with an all-encompassing dread.

"Tell her," Osh said, leaning against the doorjamb.

"Is it—?" I lowered my head, so afraid of his answer. "Is it me? Is it . . . how I look?"

His temper flared again as he faced me. "I can't believe you just asked me that."

"I'm pregnant, Reyes. I'm the size of a blimp."

The incredulous look on his face stopped me. He was astounded. "You're stunning. You've never been more beautiful. Don't you understand what you are? You're a god and I'm the son of your worst enemy."

I got over the beautiful remark, and asked, "What does that have to do with anything?"

"If you don't tell her, I will." Osh was pushing him. Now was not the time. Or was it?

"What is he talking about?" I asked Reyes as he glared at the Daeva.

"Okay, fine," Osh said. "I'll tell her."

The murderous expression he leveled on Osh made me wince.

He took a step closer to him, his movements dangerously smooth. "It will be the last thing to come out of your mouth."

Osh nodded. "'Bout time you grew some balls."

In the underworld, Osh had been a champion. Their best and fastest fighter. Even faster than Reyes, so my surly husband said. But he was not as big as Reyes. Not in human form. I wondered if that mattered, though.

Reyes took another step toward him. I stopped my husband with a hand on his chest, but only because he allowed me to.

Then I faced Osh. "Tell me."

The grin Osh wore was completely unnecessary. He enjoyed antagonizing Reyes far too much for my comfort. "He hasn't slept since the attack."

"What?" I whirled around. "What attack? When were you attacked?"

"The one eight months ago," Osh explained. "He would be useless in a fight now. If the Twelve somehow get across the border—"

"Eight months?" I asked, astonished beyond belief. "Is he kidding? You haven't slept in eight months?"

We were supernatural, sure, but we had human bodies and human needs. No wonder he looked so tired and disheveled all the time. I'd once gone three weeks without sleep. It about killed me. But eight months?

"Why?" I asked him.

"Oh, but we haven't gotten to the best part," Osh continued.

Reyes's jaw muscle leapt. "Don't do this. I stopped. It didn't work and I stopped."

"What?" I asked, squelching a shudder of fear.

"You stopped after how many attempts? A dozen? More?"

"I stopped, *Daeva*. That's all that matters."

I dug my nails into Reyes's biceps to remind him I was there. "Just tell me," I ordered Osh.

"He thought he might have found a way to kill the hounds." He glanced at me, his eyes twinkling with mirth. "He was wrong."

"To kill them?" I looked from Osh to my husband then back again. "And what way was that?"

This time Garrett spoke, but he did it minus the smirk. "He dragged them onto holy ground, thinking it would kill them."

The shock that jolted through my body was like sticking a fork into a light socket. I turned to Reyes, aghast and appalled and dumbstruck that he would even try such a thing. "You did what?" I whispered.

He didn't answer at first, and when he did, his demeanor was that of a schoolboy being chastised after having been ratted out. "I only tried it a few times. It didn't work, so I stopped."

"Fifteen," Garrett said. "He tried it fifteen times."

The thought of Reyes not only fighting a hellhound, but dragging one onto the consecrated ground—on purpose!—and then fighting it, sent the world spinning beneath me. Before I knew it, the floor disappeared.

"Maybe if he'd had a little sleep, he wouldn't have had his ass handed to him on a silver platter every time," Osh said into the darkness surrounding me. "Those fuckers can fight."

I sank to the ground as though in slow motion. The edges of my vision blurred, then three sets of hands landed on me until Reyes lifted me into his arms. Even though I weighed 1,014 pounds, he carried me with ease to the stairs and up to our room. Where Denise, Gemma, and Cookie were. This was not going to end well.

"She's still here?" I asked Gemma, trying to shake the fog from my head. "Are you kidding me?"

"I had to apologize," Denise said, both hands still covering her mouth. "Is she okay?"

The glare Reyes shot her would have shriveled a winter rose. But no one ever accused Denise of being a winter rose.

"I'm okay, hon," I said, gesturing for him to put me down.

He did so slowly, then steadied me until I had my footing. "I'm not leaving you alone with her, so don't even think about it."

"Reyes, it's okay. She didn't mean to slap the living shit out of me." I said the last bit while leveling my own glare on her.

She had the decency to look embarrassed.

"It's not her I'm worried about. Is that what you were doing in the field with Angel?"

He hesitated, then said, "Yes."

He was lying. I knew it, and he knew I knew it. I raised my chin and turned from him. After a moment, he left.

Then I turned on the woman who'd made my life hell growing up. "What are you still doing here?"

"I wanted to explain."

"Charley," Gemma said, "if you'll just hear her out, I think it would be good for both of you."

"Why? She has never listened to me. Why should I have to listen to her? I should mark her soul for Osh. Oh, wait, she doesn't have one."

"I don't have one?" she said from between gritted teeth.

There she was. I knew the helpful, nurturing routine wouldn't last long.

"You think I'm a big joke," she said, her face the picture of rage.

"Hon, you're not a joke. You're the punch line."

"You didn't even go to your own father's funeral."

Gemma gasped.

"You've been holed up in here for months like you're in witness protection or something."

"The only one I need protection from is you."

"That's it! Sit down! Both of you."

Denise sat on the bench at the end of the bed, while I crossed my arms over my chest again, showing just how defiant I could be.

Gemma reached over, grabbed my ear, and led me to the chair in the corner of our tiny room. "Ow, holy cow, Gem! Katherine the Midwife is not going to be happy with you."

"Her name is just Katherine. You have to stop calling her Katherine the Midwife."

She let go and I rubbed my abused cartilage. "How did you do that?"

"Sit down!"

"No, really. I'm having a kid. I need to know how to completely incapacitate someone by grabbing their ear."

"Sit down."

I sat down. "So, you'll tell me later?"

"You need to listen to what Mom has to say."

"No, I don't."

"She deserves that much, Charley."

"Wait, you were there. Right there through our entire childhood. You saw it. You saw what she put me through. And might I bring up the slap I just received."

It was the second time in my life Denise had slapped me in front of a crowd, and it was just as jolting and humiliating as the first time.

"I saw you both going at each other like children on a playground our whole lives."

"Yeah, but she always started it."

"That's not what I saw."

"What about the time she dragged me off my bike in front of all the neighbor kids because I didn't do the dishes? Or the time a boy threw dirt in my face, right in my face, and she turned away, refused to do anything about it? Or the time she tried to run me down with her car?"

Denise sucked in a sharp breath. "I never tried to run you over with my car."

"Oh, right, I just made that one up. But you admit to the other things."

"Charley, oh my God," Gemma said. "Can we stick with nonfiction here?"

"What? I needed backup just in case you didn't find the other events horrific enough. I know what I'm saying seems childish and ridiculous for me to be holding a grudge for so long, but she was like that every day of my life. In everything that I did. She never complimented me. She never took up for me. She never stopped nagging me about the stupidest things. It was like she made it her personal mission to make sure I knew I was less than she was. Mothers don't tear down, Gemma. They build up. Like she did with you."

"That's not true, Charley," Gemma said in her psychiatrist voice.

"She slapped me in front of all those people. I was five years old."

"Charley, look at that from her perspective. It was a horrible situation. You told a woman whose daughter had been missing for weeks that her daughter was in front of her."

"She was."

"We're mere mortals, Charley. We didn't know that. Mom was mortified. She was horrified and she panicked."

"Like a few minutes ago?" I rubbed my cheek. She had the decency to look ashamed. "Were you panicking then?"

"Yes," she said.

I looked at Gemma and scoffed. "Did you know that same woman sent me a bike after I led the cops to her daughter's body. Your mother wouldn't even let me have it."

Gemma looked stunned. "Of course. You helped bring her closure."

"Even a stranger believed in my abilities, and she—" I looked her up and down. "—made me feel like a freak every chance she got."

"I didn't think you should be rewarded for doing what you did to that poor woman. You had to learn that was wrong. You don't just blurt stuff out like that, even if it's true."

"Well, I learned, all right. Don't you worry about me. Is this over yet?"

"No," Gemma said. "Mom wants to explain."

"I was just trying to teach you."

"No." I stood and paced. "No, you were so indifferent to me. You hated me. That's not teaching. That's punishing."

"I never hated you."

"You were completely indifferent to me. If not hate, then what?"

"I wasn't indifferent."

"You were a monster!" I yelled. "Why are you even here? Why are you even talking to me?"

Her shoulders shook a moment before she cleared her throat and tried to gather herself. No way was she making me the bad guy in all this. Tears may have worked on my dad, but they would not sway me an inch.

"I wasn't indifferent, Charley."

A humorless laugh escaped me.

"I was scared of you."

I sighed, unable to believe she was pulling this shit.

"I was scared to death of you. You were something else, something . . . not human, and I was scared of you."

"Oh, so now you believe in all this?"

"Please listen to her, Charley. It's taken us a long time to get to this point."

"So, you've been counseling her? Five syllables: antipsychotic. They do wonders."

"You owe her at least a little of your time."

"She treated me like shit my whole life. The only thing I owe her is my middle finger and a cold shoulder."

"You're right," Denise said. "You're absolutely right."

"See?" I said to Gemma.

"If you will let me explain," she said, "I will leave tonight and I will never come back if that is still your wish."

"Can't beat that with a stick. Shoot."

Her cheeks were wet and her fingers shook as she stared down at her lap. "When I was little, my mother was in a car accident."

Not her life story. Damn it. I had to pee. This could take forever.

"They had her in ICU. They'd stabilized her, so they let me and my dad in to see her. It was so scary seeing her hooked up to all those machines."

I gazed longingly at the door, wondering if anyone would notice if I just slipped away for a few minutes. Beep was playing hopscotch on my bladder, and this was clearly going to take a while.

"My dad left to get coffee, and Mom woke up while he was gone. She looked at me sleepily and held out her hand right before the machines started going crazy. Her blood pressure dropped. The nurses and doctors came in and they tossed aside one of the blankets that was on her. A blue blanket."

Blue wasn't my favorite color.

"They were working on her, trying to bring her back. I guess she was bleeding internally. She woke up again while they were working on her, but the machines were still going crazy. She looked up at nothing and spoke. Just said things like, 'Oh, oh, okay, I didn't realize.' She had a loving look on her face. When I looked over, I saw what she was talking to. An angel."

I saw an angel once, too, but now probably wasn't the time to bring it up.

"He disappeared. Everyone had forgotten I was even there. They took her back into surgery, performing CPR on the way, but she was already gone. When my father came back, he dropped his coffee. I tried to tell them there was an angel, but all he saw was the blanket. He thought it was a blue towel."

I suddenly knew where this was going. When her father died, I was four. He came to me and asked me to give her a message. Something about blue towels. I was too young to understand. Later, I didn't care.

"They came back and told us she was gone. My dad broke down. I tried to tell him about the angel, but all he saw was a blue towel."

I was going to need a blue towel if I didn't get to the bathroom soon.

"He said sometimes a blue towel is just a blue towel. That became our mantra. Anytime anything unexplained happened, we repeated it. But we didn't talk about the actual event until about two years before I met Leland."

Wonderful. We were jumping ahead in time. I crossed one leg over the other and tried not to squirm. Gemma sat beside her on the bench and put a hand over hers. They were always so close. I'd tried to understand over the years, but some things were just impossible to explain. Like UFOs and bell-bottoms.

"My dad had a massive heart attack, but he survived. Then one day we were having dinner and he looked at me and said, 'Sometimes a blue towel isn't just a blue towel.' Sometimes it's more. But by that point, I'd grown up. I was a bona fide skeptic. And—" She ducked her head as though ashamed. "And I didn't believe him. After everything that had happened, I didn't believe him. I chalked it up to the medication they had him on. But then, right after I met your dad, I was in a car accident."

"So, the point of this story is to not get in the car with you or any of your relatives?"

"Charley," Gemma said, her voice monotone. Nonjudgmental. I loved psychology.

"Your dad rushed to the hospital. He had to bring you girls. They said I nearly died."

Nearly being the salient word.

"I guess because he was a cop, they let him bring you two in to see me." She laughed humorlessly. "I was pretty out of it."

Like now? I wanted to ask.

She looked at me at last. "That's when I saw it."

I had so many comebacks, it was hard to pick just one, so I remained silent.

"I saw your light, Charley. But only for an instant."

"I didn't know about your light," Gemma said. "Not until Denise told me."

"Join the club," I said. "I can't see it either."

Denise stared wide-eyed for a moment before continuing. "I just figured I was seeing things. Then about a year later, I was having dinner with my dad again and I told him what I saw. He tried to tell me how special you were. I scoffed and repeated our mantra. 'Sometimes a blue towel is just a blue towel.'"

"I'm not really sensing an apology here."

Gemma scowled at me. If only she knew about the bladder situation. It was making me cranky. I didn't want to go now, though. It would be my excuse to leave the room when they were getting ready to go home. I could hurry things along then.

"I slowly began to realize my dad had been right. You were special. Different. I didn't know your father was using you to help solve his cases, though. He hid it from me for a long time."

"I can't imagine why."

"It wasn't until the park incident with the missing girl's mother that I realized what he was doing. When I found out, I was livid."

"Because he was paying attention to me?"

"Because I was so against believing what I saw with my own eyes. Despite everything that happened, I had convinced myself that the angel was a figment of my imagination. That my mother did not go to a better place. That supernatural beings like angels and demons did not exist. It went against everything I was trying tooth and nail to hold on to. There was too much hurt and too much suffering in the world for me to believe that an omniscient being would allow it all to happen. I became an atheist. People are just good or bad. There's no devil making us do evil things."

"Well, I have to agree with you on the people front."

"But the devil front?" Gemma asked.

I let a slow smile spread across my face for Denise's benefit. "I'm married to his son."

"Charley, that's not funny."

This time I planted a serious gaze on my sister. "I wasn't trying to be funny, Gem."

She leaned forward and whispered to me. No idea why. "You mean—? Really? As in—?"

"Lucifer's son. Yes."

I was hoping that would send Denise running. Instead, she rambled on. For the love of—

"When you told me what my dad had told you that day in your apartment, the thing about the blue towels, my last desperate grip on atheism slipped through my fingers. I didn't know what to do. How to handle it. But then everything happened so fast with your father."

"After Dad died," Gemma said, "Mom started going to church."

"He's in a better place, right?" she asked, sobbing into a tissue.

"Actually, last I saw him, he was in my bathroom."

They both blinked up at me, their mouths forming perfect Os.

"What? I wasn't naked or anything."

"He's here?" Denise asked.

"No. Not right now." I glanced around just in case. "Not sure what's going on with him. But I really have to pee, so is this a wrap?"

"No," Denise said, her posture suggesting she was going to stand her ground. "I would like to ask for your forgiveness."

"My forgiveness?" I said with a huff.

"Charley," Gemma said, "you promised to listen."

"I did. I am. But that's all I promised."

"No," Denise said, patting Gemma's hand, "it's okay. Charley listened. That's all I can ask. I just want you to know that I am sorry for any suffering I may have caused you."

"There's something you're missing here," I said.

"Okay."

"You've known all along what I was. Or at least that I was special or had a gift or something along those lines. And you denied it and tried to make me feel like shit because of it. Is your knowing supposed to make me feel better? Because trust me when I say that makes you a bigger bitch than I thought you were."

Gemma lowered her head, then spoke softly. "Sometimes we just need to forgive. Not for that person, but for ourselves."

"You're right, Charley. I fought the truth. Fought you. Fought my father and your father and even our Maker. I have no one to blame but myself."

She stood, tucked the tissue in her handbag, then walked to the door. Without facing me, she said, "Thank you for listening. If you can find it in your heart, I want to be a part of your life. A part of Beep's life. I'll do anything you need me to do. I'll help you with the baby. I'll go to the store. I'll change diapers. Anything." Her voice cracked with her last plea. "Please think about it."

She walked out, but Gemma had one last thing to say. "It's taken her months to get through a whole day without crying about Dad. She's come a long way, Charley. She has no family but us. Please consider her offer."

"I'll think about it. After I pee."

8

When I got back from making number one, Katherine the Midwife was there waiting for me, gloves on, in her ready stance. Gawd, she liked sticking her fingers up Virginia.

"Hey, Katherine," I said. "Time for another torture session?"

Reyes was there, too, looking rather ashamed of himself. As he should. Picking fights with hellhounds was not something to be proud of. I would've kicked him out of the room, but I couldn't be too mad. I now had ammunition for when the time came to tell him about the Loehrs.

"Let's have a look at you," she said. "You fell?"

"Yes, in the woods."

"I see that." She lifted my shirt, and a burst of heat washed over me.

Confused, I looked in the full-length mirror and saw what Reyes saw. I hadn't even noticed it before. I had scrapes all along one side of my back and over my rib cage.

Reyes didn't say anything, but I could feel his desire to question me further.

"Okay, no broken ribs. You're breathing okay?" she asked.

I nodded.

She checked Beep's heartbeat, then said, "How about we do this right here? I'll just check to make sure everything is intact."

I knew the drill. She stepped outside the room while I removed my pants and my panties and draped the sheet over me. Then I lay down on the bed and called her back in. Reyes never took his eyes off me. His dark gaze was both reassuring and unsettling. He stared at me from underneath his lashes, his temper held in check by his own feelings of helplessness. I was right there with him.

Katherine the Midwife pushed my legs farther apart and did her thing. The lubricant was freezing and I jumped. "Sorry, hon. Let's see what's going on."

But a barrage of thoughts and images crashed into me as I lay there. The thought of Reyes dragging a hellhound, a fucking hellhound, across the border to try to kill it sank in. That and the fact that someone, or something was trying to kill me in addition to said hellhounds. I wanted to continue to hate Denise forever and ever, but her loneliness—I'd felt it. I'd been feeling it for months. I just lived in a constant state of denial. And the business with the Loehrs. What had I done? What would my actions do to my marriage? Would Reyes forgive me?

It all came bubbling to the surface at the worst possible time. Two fingers. All the way up.

I bit down, covered my eyes, held my breath, but the emotions swirling inside me, the stress of living with a dozen hellhounds just waiting to rip me to shreds—no, waiting to rip Beep to shreds—and being so utterly helpless to do anything about it were getting to me. That combined with everything else, mostly Reyes and his antics and me and my antics, wrenched a sob from my throat.

"It's okay, honey," Katherine the Midwife said. "I'm almost finished. You're dilated, but just barely. You're about a two right now."

She cleaned me up and pulled down the sheet, but it was too late. I covered my face with both hands and fought tooth and nail to hold back the emotions overwhelming me.

"This is a very emotional time, sweetheart," she said, patting my knee.

I felt the bed dip, felt the heat of Reyes near me, felt his fingers push a lock of hair from my face, and cried some more. It was like I'd turned on a faucet and broke the handle. I couldn't turn it back off again.

"I'll leave you two alone, but everything looks good. No damage that I can see."

I heard the door click closed as she left, and then Reyes pulled me into his arms.

"Freaking whore-mones," I said, and he held me tight as deep, cleansing sobs overtook me.

When I woke up, it was dark outside. I lay there listening to the sound of Reyes's breathing, deep and even, and I hoped beyond hope that he was asleep.

"I'm not," he said.

"What time is it?"

"It's only nine. You need to go back to sleep."

"I will if you will."

"Can't."

I rose onto an elbow and tried to make out his features in the dark. Moonlight streamed in from the open curtains and shimmered in his incredible eyes.

"Why can't you sleep?"

"I don't know, Dutch. I just can't. I can't make myself."

"You can't allow yourself. That's what this is about, but eight months? Really? How did I not know?"

"Because you sleep like you're comatose. And you snore."

"You can't watch me every second of the day. What good are you if something happens and you're too exhausted to fight?"

"I know. Trust me. I'm not doing it on purpose. I just can't sleep."

I frowned, worried about him. "Why were you talking with Angel? What's going on with you two?"

"He's doing a little reconnaissance for me."

"What kind of reconnaissance? You aren't putting him in any danger, are you?"

"No." He bent to nuzzle my ear. It sent warm shivers cascading over my shoulders.

"Okay, then tell me exactly what you're doing."

"No." He trailed tiny, hot kisses down my neck.

"Tell me or we are never having sex again."

He smiled behind a particularly sensual kiss where my pulse beat. "I'll put the tux back on."

My lids drifted shut with the thought as a ripple of desire shuddered through me. "Nope. You have to tell me first or that's it. We may as well call the lawyer now because it ain't happening."

"I'll do that thing with my tongue."

My gawd, I loved the thing with his tongue. I had to stay strong. "Nope," I said, my voice as weak as my resolve. "Not even then."

"Katherine the Midwife left the lube. We could try anal."

I stifled a giggle. "We are not trying anal." I rolled away from him and onto my feet. "I need a shower anyway. I just want you to know that whatever happens from here on out is your own fault."

"Really?" he asked, his expression full of interest.

"I tried to warn you. Don't blame me when this becomes a knock-down drag-out war."

"And just what do you plan on doing?"

"You'll see. And, mark my words, you will not be happy." I grabbed my robe from the closet with the sobbing tax attorney and left.

"Just remember," he said as I closed the door. "I was a general in hell. War is my middle name."

Oh yeah. This was going to be fun.

Hot water rushed over my skin, easing the aches from the afternoon's events. I'd already begun to heal.

I called Sister Mary Elizabeth on the way to the shower, hoping it wasn't too late. I'd promised to call earlier and give her an update on Quentin. He had been staying with them, but now split his time between the sisters and Reyes and me. We'd semi-adopted him.

"How's Quentin?" she asked before I could even say hello.

"He's good. He's still watching movies with Amber. Or doing crack. Not sure which. So, have you heard anything?"

"I couldn't find anything out about your nun, but we don't have access to those records. Much of that kind of stuff is archived in the Vatican."

"Wonderful."

"But I did find one very odd occurrence that happened at that convent."

"Hit me," I said, pulling back the shower curtain and turning on the water. It took forever to heat.

"A priest went missing there in the '40s."

"Really?"

"Yep. He was visiting and just vanished."

"Like, into thin air?"

"Not literally, but yeah, no one ever saw him again. There was a huge search. It was in all the papers."

"Okay, well, thanks for looking into it. Anything else on the other front?"

"Besides the fact that heaven is in an uproar? Did I mention that?"

"Yep."

"And did I mention how exhausting their chatter is?"

"Yep."

"And how I'm slowly losing my mind with all the chatter?"

"Hey, it's not my fault you can hear angels talking. Hellhounds."

"No, I haven't heard anything."

"Well, can you ask?"

"I don't ask and you know it. I just listen. It's not a two-way conversation. I can hear them. I can't communicate with them."

"Of course you can. You're a nun. You're pure and good and wholesome. Like Wheaties. They'll listen to you. All you have to do is ask."

"Do you ever listen to anything I say?"

"I'm sorry, were you speaking?"

"You're funny."

"Thank you!" I said, brightening. "So, I keep meaning to ask you something."

"Okay. Is it about abstinence again? I can't keep explaining—"

"No, it's about the night you found out I was pregnant with Beep. And now heaven is in an uproar. Why? I mean, are they mad at me?"

"Oh no. 'Mad' isn't the right word. More like . . . frantic."

"Why? Don't they know about the prophecies?"

"Absolutely, but prophecies are thwarted all the time. I think they were just surprised it was really happening. I mean, you're bringing something onto this plane that, well, maybe doesn't belong? No, that's not the right way to put it."

"So, Beep won't belong here?"

"I didn't mean that. It's more like . . . a birth like hers doesn't happen every day. I'm not sure how to say this without going to confession right after, but from what I can tell, they are saying the daughter of a god will be born here. But that's wrong. There is only one God, so I'm sure I'm misunderstanding them."

"Right. I'm sure."

"I did hear that she will change something that they hadn't expected to be changed. It's kind of freaking them out. It's like when you expect your car to run out of gas before you make it to the station, but you're still surprised when it does."

"Okay," I said, trying to grasp every nuance of her meaning. I gave up. "Bottom line, she isn't in any danger from them, right?"

"From heaven? Absolutely not."

"Oh, good. That's good. Hey, how do you have a cell phone, anyway? I thought cloistered nuns had to give up worldly crap."

"I'm not a cloistered nun, and I have a cell phone because, in my position, it's beneficial. It's all been approved."

"I'll need to see those documents."

"No."

"Have you ever considered the fact that the term 'cloistered nuns' sounds like an appetizer? Or a punk band?"

"Yes."

"Okay, well, let me know if you hear anything. I'd like to lead a normal life someday."

"Ten four."

Showers were God's reward for working hard enough to get dirty. I dried off, wrapped myself up in the plush robe Reyes had bought me, and stepped to a foggy mirror.

Before I could wipe it off, a letter appeared in the steam. I glanced around. No one was in there, but another letter appeared as though someone were tracing letters in the condensation with a finger. I stood back and waited for the full message to appear, then read it aloud.

"Spies."

What did that mean? There were spies here? Did we have a mole in the convent? And if so, who? No, the bigger questions would be, whom was the mole spying for? Whom would he report to?

I reached up and hurriedly wiped off the mirror. Two things came to mind immediately. First of all, that was my dad's handwriting. It was exactly the same, which was odd and a little disheartening that I'd have the same handwriting when I died. I had thought there was hope for me. I thought good handwriting skills were a perk of heaven. That maybe we'd magically know angelic script and have this fluid, flowing handwriting, but no. I was doomed. The second thing was that there were apparently spies among us.

But who? Who would be—?

It hit me like a nuclear blast. I strode down the hall back to my room. Reyes had left, but I knew one person who hadn't.

I opened the closet door to the agonizing sobs of the tax attorney. Reaching inside, I grabbed her arm and dragged her out. As long as I kept ahold of her wrist, she couldn't vanish.

She stumbled to her feet and raised a hand to her face, sobbing uncontrollably.

"Save it," I said, jerking her arm to snap her out of it. "Who are you spying for? Who sent you here?"

For a split second, I actually suspected my husband. It wouldn't be the first time he'd sent someone to watch me. But why would she be putting on a show like that?

No, I suspected it was someone who knew I'd try to help her, and they wanted her to get very close to both me and Reyes.

"Answer me, or I'll—" Crap, I had nothing. What would I do? I was a portal to heaven and threatening to send her there didn't seem like much of an incentive to talk.

But she stopped crying anyway and glowered at me.

"Who are you spying for?" I repeated.

Her glower twisted her pretty mouth into a defiant smirk.

Suddenly, I knew what to do with her. "I'll mark your soul. You will be devoured by a soul-eater and cease to exist."

A split second of fear flashed across her face, but she recovered quickly. "I'm not the only one," she said. "You have no idea what's coming."

"Enlighten me."

"Bite me."

"Hmm, no, I think I'll leave that up to Osh'ekiel."

Her jaw dropped open. "The Daeva? He's here?"

"You're not a very good spy." She tried to jerk out of my grasp, but I held her tight. "Once I mark your soul, there is nowhere you can hide that he won't find you." Then something else hit me. A scent. Lavender. It was coming from the closet and had seeped into her soul. "You pushed me!" I said, appalled, remembering the scent just before I went face-first down a mountainside.

She raised her chin and refused to talk.

Dang it. Where was a waterboard when I needed one? I wondered if an ironing board would work.

But then she had to open her big mouth and make me mad. Not a good idea. "She will never see the light of day on this plane," the tax attorney said, quite enjoying herself. "He'll eat her intestines for breakfast. You have no idea the plans he has for your daughter."

Anger surged through me lightning quick, and before I knew it, I'd marked her. I saw a symbol brand into her soul like a flash of light; then it was gone and all that remained was the burned imprint of the mark.

She gasped, looked at the mark on her chest, stumbled back, but I kept my hold.

Soon, Reyes and Osh burst through the door. Reyes was beside me at once while Osh fairly crooned when he realized what I'd done.

"What have we here?" he asked as the woman cowered away from him.

I turned from him to Reyes. "Your father has sent spies. We have spies! Did you know we have spies?"

Osh's gaze dropped with guilt. But Reyes's gaze never wavered from the woman's.

"Were you planning on telling me?" I asked my husband.

"Not today," he said.

I stood aghast. No idea why. The guy had more secrets than Victoria.

I thought Sheila was scared of Osh, and she was, but when her gaze landed on Reyes, she screamed and fought my hold. Just as she slipped through my fingers, Reyes took hold of her shoulders. "How many more?" he asked as he shook her.

"I don't—." She cried out when his fingers bit into her. "Two. Maybe three."

"What are his plans?"

"I don't know. I—I swear. He doesn't tell us."

He shoved her away from us, the revulsion he felt evident in every move he made. "She's all yours."

She caught herself, straightened, and raised her chin, resigned to her fate.

"Dinnertime," Osh said with a wolfish grin, and what happened next made me pee a little.

We looked on as Osh backed her against the closet door, not as though he were about to eat her alive, but as though he were about to make love to her.

"He's just waiting for the right moment," she said in one last act of defiance, one last attempt to scare us shitless. It was working. On me, at least.

"And what moment would that be, love?" Osh asked as he caressed her neck and lifted her face to his, his touch as gentle as a summer breeze.

She curled her hands into fists at her sides, waiting for the inevitable. "That moment when no one is looking."

He leaned into her, pressed his hips into her, ran his lips along her neck. "We're always looking, love."

The grin that spread across her pretty face was both sad and terrifying. Her gaze landed on me and her grin widened. "Not always."

Before I could ask what she meant, Osh bent over her and covered her mouth with his, the sensuality of the act surprising. And arousing. A shimmer of light escaped from between their mouths, and Osh pulled back from her, just enough for me to see her soul passing out of her and into him. His eyes were closed, his hands holding her head as she stared wide-eyed at the ceiling. She seemed to weaken almost instantly, her fists relaxing, her arms falling limp. Then her body grew more and more transparent. She began to dissipate. Pieces of her drifted into the air like ashes until she disappeared completely.

Osh braced an arm against the door and rested his head on it, his shoulders rising and falling with each heavy breath he took.

"How did you know?" Reyes asked me.

"My dad, I think. He told me there were spies and it just made sense. Mostly because she didn't make any."

"Any?" Osh asked, still panting.

"Sense. She didn't make any sense. She was way too put together, too smart to be so upset she couldn't even talk to me. And why in here? Where Reyes and I slept?"

"And talked," Reyes added.

I sat on the bench, Reyes still holding my hand as I said, "That was kind of amazing."

"Thanks for the meal," Osh said, crossing his arms over his still-heaving chest. His shoulder-length dark hair hid most of his face, but from what I could see, he was quite satisfied.

"I probably shouldn't have done that. Isn't that, you know, God's job?"

"You *are* a god."

"Not here. Not in this realm."

"Since she was sent from hell, I doubt he minded."

"From hell?" I asked, surprised.

Reyes looked down at me, his presence so powerful, I wanted to melt into him. "Who else would spy for my father?"

"You mean, she had been sent to hell and Lucifer sent her back? To spy on us? Is that even legal?"

"It would seem so," Osh said. He laid his head back against the door, still recovering.

"Can you take someone's soul who is still alive?" I asked him.

"Only pieces of it unless it's been marked. Otherwise, I have to wait until those who have lost their souls to me die." He bowed his head and looked at me from underneath his lashes, the wolfish grin back and darkening his features. "Then they're all mine."

"But, as per our agreement, you can eat only the souls of those undeserving of them." I knew that good people had lost their souls to him. I'd saved one from him a few months back and made him promise to be more selective.

He lifted a shoulder in agreement. A reluctant agreement, but an agreement nonetheless.

"Hey," I said, "I could mark my stepmother for you."

Reyes sat down. "You can't mark your stepmother."

"Just a little mark. Barely visible."

Osh laughed softly and stuck his hands in his pockets.

I grabbed a bottled water off my nightstand and nestled back beside the son of evil. "So, why do Daeva eat souls?"

Reyes spoke from beside me, his gaze hard on Osh's. "It's what they were created to do. Work. Fight. Entertain. Live off the suffering of others."

"And what were you created to do?" he asked.

"Send people like you to their deaths."

"Wait," I said, holding up a time-out sign. "When did this turn south? We were all friends a minute ago. Weren't we all friends?"

"It's all good," Osh said, sobering. "Rey'aziel tends to forget where he's from sometimes. And that we were created by the same being."

"But not in the same fires," Reyes said. "Not of the same substance."

Osh shrugged an eyebrow, unfazed.

"Maybe you're a spy as well," Reyes said.

"Maybe," Osh replied. "And maybe you know more than you are letting on."

"Maybe."

So, now we were playing the maybe game. What was going on? They'd been getting along famously, then this. I decided to change the subject.

"So, explain to me this whole marking thing," I said to Osh. "Are there others on earth who eat souls?"

"Yes," he said without elaborating.

"Are they all Daeva?"

"No. I'm the only Daeva ever to both escape and make it through the void."

He was right. Reyes's tattoo was a map to the gates of hell. It was how he could traverse the oblivion, the void between this plane and his. He was literally a portal to hell while I was a portal to heaven. And we hooked up. Stranger things had happened; I was certain of it. He told me once that most all of those who tried to get onto our plane from hell never made it through the void. They were stuck there, slowly going insane. I wondered what would happen to one of those creatures if it finally, after centuries of living in the void, actually made it onto this plane. What would it be like?

A shudder rushed through me with the thought.

"You know," I said, realizing something else, "all twelve hellhounds made it through the void and onto this plane. Someone had to have helped them."

Reyes nodded. "I would guess that whoever summoned them had a hand in that."

"But it took your father eons to create you, you who had the map imprinted on his body. He created a portal. Without the map that you and only you have, even he can't cross onto this plane easily. Is that right?"

He lowered his head in thought. "Yes, it is."

"Then how would he help them get here?"

"She's right," Osh said. "Whoever summoned them must have already been on this plane."

Reyes stood and started pacing as Osh bent his head in thought. They were trying so hard to figure out the puzzle. They had been for months. I still couldn't imagine why Osh was helping us. He hated Satan. I got that. But there seemed more to it than just hatred. He had an ulterior motive. I could feel it.

And why tell me what I could and could not do? I could destroy him with even the minute amount of information he'd already given me about my past, about my powers. I decided to learn more while I could.

"Why can I mark people?" I asked out of the blue. "I mean, why me?"

"Comes with the gig," Osh said, his head still bowed in thought. "Only the reaper can mark the souls of humans. Well, God can, of course, but why would he need to? And I think Michael can. And the Angel of Death, naturally."

"The Angel of Death? For real?"

"For real."

"Wow, so what else comes with the gig?" I asked, fishing. "I mean, what other marks could there possibly be?" He'd let it slip once that I had five marks, five avenues of judgment as the reaper. Since I can see into people's souls, I can see what they did with their lives and how they treated others, I had the ability to judge, jury, and execute. I wanted to know every avenue I had at my disposal.

"You have five marks, and what you say is law. Only God can supersede your decision on any soul." He looked up at me then, his brows knitting in suspicion. "Why?"

"I just want to know what I can do."

"You will know," Reyes said, "when you pass and you ascend to become the grim reaper. If you take the job."

"Why wouldn't I?"

"Because you are a god. You have an entire universe to run." He looked away from me. "Why would you stick around here?"

"Good point," I said, teasing him yet marveling at how matter-of-fact they made it all sound. How everyday.

"What other marks?" I asked Osh.

Osh eyed Reyes a moment before continuing. "You can brand a soul for heaven or for hell. You can brand a soul for termination, which is essentially what you do when you mark one for me. It's kind of like free game. You can mark one as a wanderer, a soul with no home who must wander the wilds of the supernatural realm, forever considering their mistakes. And you can give the mark of designation."

"Designation?"

"You can assign that soul a special purpose on earth, and no other supernatural being can argue with your decision."

"Like when the president appoints a chief of staff?"

"Pretty much. That soul can no longer be touched."

I was still confused on a couple of points. "So, if I marked a soul for termination and you weren't here to eat it, what would happen to it?"

"It would burn away over the course of a few days. It would be very painful. So, in a way, I'm performing a public service."

"Of course you are. And when I found you, what were you doing then?"

"Hey, everyone has to eat, and I can only bargain for souls. They must be given willingly."

"But you trick them into giving up their souls."

He spread his hands wide, acquiescing. "That was the old me. This is the new."

"You no longer trick them?"

"Oh, I trick them. Really, it's just too easy. But I only trick the bad ones, remember?" he added quickly when I scowled at him. "Child molesters and such. As per your request," he mocked.

"And people who talk at the theater. Don't forget people who talk at the theater."

One corner of his mouth tipped up. "I wouldn't dare."

Reyes walked to the window and looked out over the lawn. Even as dark as it was out, we could still see the departed.

"I once ate this woman—," Osh started.

"Dude, I don't think I should be hearing this."

"I ate her soul," he corrected.

"Next time, open with that."

"And she tasted horrible, like an ashtray with kerosene in it."

I fought my gag reflex. "No way."

"Crazy thing was, she didn't even smoke while she was alive."

"Then why? Surely she wasn't born bound for hell?"

"She was a very feared drug lord. Ruthless. Barbaric. She killed anyone who got in her way. A lot of people died in her crossfire. Even children. We are all tainted by the decisions we make."

"And the taste of our souls reflects that?"

"It does."

"Huh. I wonder what mine would taste like."

"Cherry pie." He grinned from ear to ear. "Very tart cherry pie."

"How would you know that?"

He ignored the threatening scowl Reyes had cast him and winked.

"You've tasted me? Oh my God, I feel violated."

"Please, it was just a nibble."

"I totally should have paid more attention in Bible school."

"I don't think they teach about the Daeva. We aren't important enough to merit a mention."

I narrowed my eyes on him. "Somehow, I don't think that's true. Are there more?" I asked Reyes.

"Exponentially more."

His shoulders took up the entire expanse of the window, so I nudged against him. He wrapped an arm around me and stepped to the side. He was right. Our shindig had grown exponentially.

"Do you think there are spies among them?"

"I do." He looked down at me. "But they could be anywhere. Anyone."

I nodded. "Is that what you and Angel were talking about in the clearing today?"

When he didn't answer yet again, I tsked. "Just remember, you brought on the wrath of the reaper all on your little lonesome. By the way," I added, looking at Osh. "I was just kidding about the people who talk at the theater."

"Damn it," he said, feigning disappointment.

Now if I could only figure out a way to convince my husband to get some rest. Too bad there wasn't a mark for that.

I stood and walked to the door to check on Cookie, but before closing it, I offered Reyes one last chance to come clean. "This is your one last chance to come clean," I told him, deciding not to mince words.

He sat on the bed, leaned back, and folded his arms behind his head.

"I mean it. If you don't tell me what you and Angel were talking about, why you were meeting, I can't take responsibility for my actions."

He grinned.

I tapped my toes in impatience.

He grinned wider.

"Okay, war it is. I have to warn you—"

Before I got much further into my intimidation process, a pillow slammed into my face. I stood there, eyes closed, mortified while the ball and chain laughed softly.

It was so on.

9

APPLICANTS MUST PASS AN ORAL EXAM BEFORE

ADVANCING TO THE NEXT COURSE.

—NOVELTY UNDERWEAR

I went down to check on Cookie. Uncle Bob was still in the city. Working. On his wedding day. I felt so guilty, though I didn't know why. I had nothing to do with his working. Just Cookie's.

"Hey, you," I said, watching Reyes in the kitchen from the corner of my eye. He was making us both a hot chocolate. God bless him. Chocolate had become my best friend in the absence of coffee, which I'd given up for Beep. Come to think of it, I'd given up a lot for her. I'd have to make sure she knew that. Remind her. Daily. "It's almost ten o'clock, Cook. You have to go to bed."

There was a small couch in the office, on which Amber and Quentin sat. Well, Amber sat. Quentin slept, his blond hair hiding his face, one arm hanging over the side, the other thrown over his head. He had a massive shoe on Amber's lap, but she didn't seem to mind. She sat reading, completely content.

"I've been going through everything," Cookie said, apparently ignoring my prime directive. That happened a lot.

Reyes brought my hot chocolate in. "Anyone else?" he asked, offering his own mug. A true gentleman.

"I'll take some, Uncle Reyes," Amber said, her smile flirtatious.

He chuckled and handed her his mug. "What about you?" he asked Cookie.

She was so engrossed in her work, it took her a moment to blink up at him. When she did, she stopped, blindsided by the picture before her. He stood in a pair of lounge pants, black and red plaid, with a dark gray, form-fitted T-shirt. I felt a flush of heat radiate out of her—a feat, considering Reyes's heat knew no bounds.

When she didn't answer, he flashed her his famous lopsided grin and said, "Hot chocolate, it is."

He winked at me before venturing back to the kitchen, and for a split second, I thought I saw odd lines across the back of his shirt, but I dismissed the thought when Cookie came back to earth.

"Did he say something?" she asked.

"He forgot the best part!" Amber said, scuttling out from under Quentin's enormous shoe and following after her uncle Reyes. "You forgot marshmallows!"

"He's getting you a cup of hot cocoa," I told Cook.

"Oh, right." She shook the fog out of her brain. "That man makes it impossible to concentrate."

"He does, at that. So, can I ask you something?"

"Of course." She turned in her chair to face me.

"It's about your pre-honeymoon honeymoon."

"Charley, really, it's no big deal."

"I think it is, but not in the way that you are letting on."

She shifted in her chair. "What do you mean?"

"It's like you were relieved that you didn't get to go."

"What? There is a missing girl. There was nothing for me to be relieved about."

"Which is exactly why I'm concerned."

"Well, don't be."

"Hey," I said, using reverse psychology, "at least when all this is over, you two will get the honeymoon of your dreams."

That ripple of concern shuddered through her again. "Absolutely."

"Cook," I said when she turned back to her computer, "what's going on?"

Her shoulders lifted as she filled her lungs before facing me again. After a quick glance down the hall, she said, "Robert is not my second marriage. He's my third."

A jolt of shock rocketed through me. "Oh my God, I can't believe you didn't tell me that!"

She slammed an index finger over her mouth to shush me.

"I tell you everything," I whispered loudly. "I even told you about that time Timothy Tidmore tried to use Virginia as a garage for his Hot Wheels."

"I know." She hung her head in shame. "I know. But my first marriage lasted all of two days."

"No way." I wiggled closer, suddenly very intrigued. "What happened?"

"Well, I was in Vegas with my aunt and uncle. It was my eighteenth birthday and they were there for a trade show. Anyway, my cousins and I had a lot of free time and, well, I met a guy by the pool and we had a really great day and we . . . um . . . got married."

I blinked, unable to reconcile the vision of a carefree wild child and Cookie.

"That night." When I didn't interrupt—I didn't dare—she continued. "So, we're in his parents' hotel room later that night, on what we were calling our honeymoon, and his . . . pants . . . kind of—" The longer she spoke, the softer her voice became.

"His what did what?"

"His pants caught on fire."

"Of course they did. He was eighteen."

"No, I mean, literally."

"Oh, like, *on fire* on fire?"

"Yeah. He'd spilled wine on his pants while we were having a candle-light dinner, at his parents' expense, naturally, and when I jumped up to help him, I knocked over the candle and . . . well, you get the idea."

"Oh, man. That had to hurt."

"I'm sure it did, but he was never the same after that. He was actually quite a jerk. Thankfully, his parents had the marriage annulled as soon as he told them what we'd done."

"Okay, so your first honeymoon didn't go so well. But surely you had better luck with Amber's father."

"My second honeymoon was worse."

"No," I said, intrigued again.

She nodded. "We lived together a whole year. Everything was wonderful until the day we got married. Everything changed."

"Cook, what happened?"

"Well, it started out okay. We had the wedding. It was a huge event. All the crazies from my side showed up, and his family numbered in the thousands. It was nice, but not really me, you know?"

"I do."

"I was so nervous that I drank a little wine before the wedding."

"Uh-oh."

"Oh, the ceremony went off without a hitch. I slurred my vows a bit, but other than that, perfection."

"Okay," I said, growing wary nonetheless.

"So, we had the reception and I drank some more."

That was never good.

"And we did the whole rice thing and left in a limousine for the hotel. We were going to stay the night, then fly out the next morning to Cancún."

"Awesome. Loving it so far."

"Well, I'd had a bit too much to drink, we both had, and Noah decided to moon the people on the freeway."

"Wait, who's Noah?"

"Amber's father," she said, suddenly annoyed.

"Oh, right, I knew that. Okay, so he's mooning everyone."

"Yes, but I started to get sick."

"Understandable."

"And I just reached for the closest door handle."

"No."

"Yes. I opened the door while he was mooning everyone. He fell out of the limo on I-25."

I sat stunned.

"South," she added.

I still sat stunned.

"Near the Gibson exit."

"Cookie," I said at last, "what happened?"

"He suffered multiple fractures, a ruptured spleen, and a mild concussion."

I slammed my hands over my mouth.

"I know. Things just changed after that. Even after ten years of marriage, we never found what we had again."

"I'm sorry, hon."

"I just don't have the best luck with honeymoons."

"No, that's not true. Those were total coincidences."

She smiled sadly. "You don't believe in coincidences."

I squeezed her hand. "I do now."

"This is so much better," Amber chimed as she skipped back to her seat.

"I can't believe you're that girl," I said softly as Amber tried to get back under Quentin's shoe and balance her hot chocolate at the same time.

"What girl?"

"The one who meets a guy and marries him twelve hours later."

"Nine."

I stifled a grin.

"And a half."

I leaned forward and gave her my best hug. "But now you have Uncle Bob. Nothing is going to change his mind about how unbelievably perfect you are."

She giggled. "You might be surprised."

"Never."

"What are you guys whispering about?" Amber asked, her hair in her face as she shimmied up the back of the couch under the weight of an anvil.

Cookie leaned back and wiped at her eyes. "We're talking about the boarding school we're going to send you to if you don't start earning your keep."

Amber blew her bangs out of her face. "You have to come up with some new material, Mom. That hasn't worked on me since I was three."

"She catches on quick," I said. "So, any luck with the information Kit sent over?"

The frustrated sigh that escaped her lungs told me everything I needed to know. "Nothing. Everything they have is right. Faris was supposed to go to the park after school, and then she and her friends were going to walk to a party."

"A party her mother didn't know about," I added.

"I don't get it, though," Amber said, scanning a handful of pages, and I realized she had been going over the case with Cookie. "Why are the cops so worried about that party or the park?"

"Because according to all her friends, that's where she was going."

"Which friends?" she asked as though we'd lost it. "Certainly not the one she was texting that day."

I straightened and walked over to her. "What are you talking about?"

She pointed to a copy of Faris's texts that were in the file. "Right here. Did Kit talk to this guy? Nate something or other? Because according to these texts, they were ditching the party and meeting at a skater hangout."

Cookie thanked Reyes as he handed her a piping hot cup, then stayed to listen in.

"Amber, where does it say that?" I asked.

She pointed again as I dialed Kit's number. I still didn't see it. She was pointing to a text that said,

COP at tunnel.

Feeling like an idiot, I said, "I don't get it, hon."

Before she could explain, Kit picked up. I put her on speakerphone.

"Okay," I said, forgoing the pleasantries, "you're on speaker. Who is this Nate kid that Faris was texting?"

"We don't know," she said, sounding exhausted but not sleepy. I hadn't woken her. "She has a friend named Nathan, but he says it wasn't him in the texts. Still, there were only a few texts from Nate, and they seemed pretty innocent."

"Nuh-uh," Amber said. "There were only a few from him *as* Nate. He also texted her as Caleb, Isaiah, and Sean. It's their favorite show."

"Yeah, we couldn't find any one of her friends with those names. What do you mean their favorite show?"

"*NCIS,*" she said as though we were daft. "It's right here." She thumbed through the pages and pages of texts. "Back when he was Nate the first time."

"The first time?" I asked, trying to see what she saw.

She rummaged through the pages until she got to a set of older messages. I'd remembered them talking about *NCIS,* but how on earth did Amber get the name thing out of it?

"Right here. He tells her if her parents catch on to let him know and he will switch to the next episode."

This was getting ridiculous. I was still young, for goodness' sake. I wasn't *that* out of touch. Was I? The text read,

If PAW, will start next episode.

Clearly I was. "You're going to have to explain."

"Don't worry," she said, sympathizing with me. "Okay, this says if your parents are watching, *P-A-W,* then I'll start the next episode. I'll go to the next letter. Thankfully, when the phone company sent a copy of her texts, they sent them in order instead of by user. That's how we figured it out, because right after that, like ten seconds after, Caleb wrote this."

She pointed at a text that read,

Starting next episode now.

"Caleb," I said, realizing at last what they were doing. I'd have to go back completely and find all the transitions and texts from this same guy. "But what about a skater hangout?"

"Right here," she said, pointing for the third time to the same text,

COP at tunnel.

"Isn't that just warning her away from a tunnel? That there's a cop there?"

"No, it says *C-O-P.* 'Change of plans.' And to meet him at the Tunnel. Aka, a skater hangout. Not that I've ever been there," Amber assured her mother.

My jaw dropped open. "How did we miss this?"

Cookie shook her head, flummoxed.

"We missed it, too," Kit said. "We just thought they were planning a little underage drinking and were trying to dodge the cops."

"Which is probably exactly what he was hoping we would think," I said. "This wasn't a crime of opportunity, Kit. If Amber's right, he planned this. Got to know her through texts. Spent weeks planning the abduction."

"And he sent her pictures," Amber said. "But that's not him." She held up one of the shots he'd sent. "I can't believe she fell for that."

"Why?" I asked. "Who is it?"

"It's the Target kid. The one who got famous when a girl snapped his picture and tweeted it to her friend? It went viral?" she said, trying to clue us in. "It was, like, everywhere? And this one," she said, holding up another, "is a kid who got famous on YouTube for doing 'Paparazzi.'" When we stared at her, she added, "Lady Gaga?"

"Oh, the song," I said, finally getting it.

"Seriously, though, they don't even look alike." She compared the pictures. "What was she thinking?"

I took the seat at my desk, the one opposite Cookie. "They'd been texting for weeks. She thought she knew him."

"She thought she could trust him," Cookie said; then she looked at Amber with a new determination. "That's it. Where's your phone? You're grounded from it for seven years."

"Mom," she said with a roll of her eyes.

Kit spoke up then, sounding more energized than before. "Charley, this is it. I think you guys are on to something."

"Not me," I said, waving a hand, then pointing at Amber. "Amber Kowalski."

"And Quentin Rutherford," she added, gazing at him adoringly. It took true love to overlook drool. "He was the one who caught the *NCIS* thing. He loves that show."

"We'll check out these numbers, see what we can get. I'm sure they're burner phones, but we might get a hit on one of them."

"He went to a lot of trouble to get to Faris," I said. "He had to have known her from somewhere. Became obsessed with her. Maybe a coffee shop she and her friends frequented or even their school."

"I'll call Agent Waters, now. We're on this."

I hung up and gave Amber a high five. "You may have just saved a life, Amber."

She smiled bashfully. "I hope so."

After scouring the texts one last time, making notes based on Amber's keen eye, we scanned them all and sent them back to Kit with our observations before wandering off to bed. I led Reyes to the communal bathroom and insisted he take a long, hot shower for two reasons. One, I wanted him to relax enough to fall asleep. Eight months without a wink? Unfathomable. How was I not married to a zombie? Two, I wanted to get a jump-start on this war.

Because the rooms were so tiny, we'd had to stash Reyes's clothes in the room next to our bedroom. I'd dubbed it his dressing room. He was a prince, after all. Sure, he was a prince of the underworld, but the title still counted. I hurried inside and carried out my dastardly plan, ransacking his dresser until I found every stitch of underwear he owned. I stuffed them into a plastic grocery bag—ever a champion of recycling—tiptoed back into our bedroom, and hid them in Beep's bassinet. Then, giggling like a mental patient, I grabbed the book I'd been reading and scrambled into bed.

My insides tingled when I heard him walk down the hall. Open the door to his dressing room. Pull out a drawer. Then another. I wiggled farther into the covers when I heard his footsteps get closer.

By the time he appeared at the door, a playful grin on his face, I lay reading in bed, completely innocent of anything he might accuse me of.

He folded his arms over his chest and leaned against the doorframe. "You wouldn't happen to know where my underwear ran off to, would you?"

I closed the book and thought. And thought. Then I crinkled my nose and thought some more. "Nope," I said at last. "Weird that you don't, though, since it *is* your underwear. This could get really awkward."

He dropped the towel and my gaze darted to his glorious nether regions.

"Not for me."

Damn him and his rock-hard body. I tore my gaze away and went back to reading as he pulled on a pair of loose pajama pants, the kind that tied in front, and a powder blue T-shirt, all the while watching me like a panther readying to pounce.

"Going commando?" I asked as he crawled onto the bed. The mattress sank under his weight.

Ignoring me, he read the title of the book I kept firmly between our gazes. "*Lover Awakened*." He nestled his head on my shoulder. "Weren't you reading this book last month?"

"No."

He raised a brow.

"Yes. I can't stop. I've read it twenty-seven times in a row."

He chuckled. "Do you need to be awakened?"

" 'Parently."

"You know, you don't need a manual for that. I can walk you through it step-by-step." He ran a finger down the curve of my neck, his heat licking across my skin, soaking into my nightgown.

"That's okay," I said, fighting a grin. "This author covers the basics. Her hero seems very well informed. I think I'm getting the general idea."

"But can he do this?" He slid a hand under the covers and over my knee. Separating my legs, he wrapped one of his around one of mine, locking mine apart as he pushed the other knee, distancing them farther. He kissed my shoulder and slid his fingertips over the delicate folds between my legs, parting them, easing inside. His touch was like liquid fire. It rippled over me, settled deep inside, melted me until the warmth pooling in my abdomen ignited. I curled one fist into the sheets and opened even wider, greedy for more.

"Well, I can't say," I said breathlessly. "I've never met him. But he seems very capable."

"What about this?" He peeled back my nightgown with his free hand and took Danger's hardened nipple into his mouth. Sucking softly, he did the tongue thing. The fucking tongue thing that set me on fire. He had me squirming in seconds, begging for release as he tasted and teased.

I reached down and took hold of his rock-hard erection through the pants. He sucked in a soft breath and even through the material I could feel the blood rushing beneath my fingers. I started to turn into him, but he pulled me up from the mattress. Locking me to him from behind, he walked me to the full-length mirror, pushed my gown over my shoulders, and let it drop to the floor.

When I tried to look down, he wrapped a hand around my throat from behind and forced me to look into the mirror, as though wanting me to see what he saw. But what I saw was a very large, very round woman.

He must have sensed my misgivings. He tsked softly and placed my hands on the wall on either side of the mirror. Then he pulled a chair over with one foot and lifted one of my legs over the back of it. My toes barely touched the seat and by that point, I was shaking visibly.

He wrapped a hand around my throat again and whispered into my ear. "Now I'm going to do things to you," he said, his voice deep and smooth and accented with a brogue, and I realized he was speaking in Manx Gaelic. "Very bad things," he added, his brogue almost as sexy as he. It set my soul ablaze. "And you're going to watch." He cupped Will. Kneaded her. "And you're going to learn." He grazed his teeth over my lobe, his warm breath fanning over my cheek. "And you're going to understand exactly what it is that you do to me."

What I did to him? Was he insane? I was just thankful for the wall; otherwise, I doubted I could have stood as his erection slid between my legs, so hard it pulsed there. I started to reach under and take hold of it, but he quickly set my hand back on the wall.

"Not yet," he warned, giving my wrist a firm squeeze.

Then he did the strangest thing. He pulled back my hair, sweeping it into one hand so he could caress my face with the other. He watched me in the mirror, and while I got the feeling he wanted me to see what he saw, all I could look at was him. His eyes shimmering beneath his long lashes. His mouth full and parted ever so slightly. His jaw strong.

He dropped my hair and moved to my shoulders. Ran his fingertips over them until he came from behind and cupped Danger and Will. Massaged as he nibbled on my neck. Skimmed his fingertips over their peaks, causing a spasm of pleasure to shoot to my core.

But everywhere he touched, he left a scalding heat, and I realized he was doing it on purpose. He could control his heat, at least to some degree.

I needed to see. I needed to watch him from the other side. From the supernatural side. And while I had yet to master the leap from one plane to the other, I released the breath from my lungs, relaxed my body, and concentrated until I saw the flames that forever engulfed him. I'd seen them a couple of times before, but never like this. While normally he had blue flames licking along his skin as though he himself were an accelerant, this time he glowed with a bright orange fire. And everywhere he touched, every part of me he stroked, he left a trail of flames in his wake.

I watched mesmerized as the prince of the underworld set me ablaze. Literally.

His hands brushed over my belly, infusing his warmth deep inside me, and my legs started to give beneath my weight. I lay my head back against his shoulder as he found the cusp between my thighs again. Holding me to him with one arm, he breached the folds, brushing softly, stroking until the tinder he'd ignited in my abdomen blazed to life. I clawed at his arm, wanting more, but once again he placed my hand back on the wall.

Then he was gone.

I opened my eyes and he was on his knees in front of me. My nails dug into the plaster when he opened me further and branded me with a fiery kiss. I gasped. Pleasure pulsed through me as his tongue caused stinging tendrils to swirl inside me like a dust devil struggling to become a tornado. I sought that peak, but I didn't have to look hard. He grazed his teeth along the sensitive apex, then feathered his tongue in sweet, short sweeps, stoking the embers, coaxing me closer and closer until a riptide of raw lust engulfed me. The orgasm rocketed through me, sending out pulsating swells of unimaginable pleasure to every nerve in my body. I plunged my fingers into his hair and held him to me as the tidal wave rose to exquisite peaks, then ebbed slowly, the sharp contractions tapering off.

With the release of all that energy, I almost fell against the mirror, but Reyes was behind me at once, his quest only just beginning when he pushed his pants over his hips and entered me from behind in one long thrust. A twinge of delight leapt inside me as the orgasm that had yet to ebb entirely reignited.

He captured my gaze in the mirror, daring me to watch, his eyes sparkling with unspent passion.

And how could I not? He was magnificent. His muscles strained against the T-shirt he wore as he buried himself again and again.

He pulled me back against him, locking me there as he whispered into my ear. "Come with me again," he said in the same Gaelic brogue, the fires around him fueled by the friction our bodies created. "See what you do to me, *my ghraih*." My love.

I focused on him as his powerful strokes fanned the flames around him. His brows furrowed, his expression one of almost agony as his own climax neared. He braced one hand on the wall, clenched his jaw. His breathing grew labored as a biting pleasure brushed over my skin, nipping and scratching in rapturous delight. He thrust harder, an exquisite hunger swelling inside me, as though he could siphon the pleasure from the very marrow of my bones.

I felt it the moment he erupted inside me. He groaned as his orgasm crested, as it surged from him and into me, and then I saw it. I saw him. He exploded into a sea of flames. They consumed him and engulfed me in a torrent so savage, so volatile, I wondered if I would survive.

The air left the room, and my lungs seized. My eyes rolled back as wave after wave of scalding fire crashed into me. The desire was overwhelming and earth shattering and wonderful.

I tumbled to earth slowly and blinked back to this plane. Disentangling myself, I turned to him and focused on his impossibly handsome face.

He still had a hand braced on the wall, struggling to catch his breath as one final spasm shuddered through him. Then he stepped closer until he had me pressed into the cool mirror. He placed his forehead on the hand braced against the wall and wrapped an arm around me.

"You saw?" he asked, and I felt the tiniest ripple of insecurity radiate out of him.

"I saw. It was amazing."

He wasn't so sure. Doubt settled deep in his core. I stroked his back to assure him that everything I saw, everything he showed me was incredible, but I realized his shirt was wet. Very wet. Too wet.

I lifted my hand and gasped. It was covered in blood.

Pushing him off me, I stepped away to see what had happened, but he quickly turned until he was facing me again.

"Reyes, you're bleeding," I said, trying to turn his body.

He steeled himself, his jaw working, his gaze hard as he stared down at me. He hadn't expected me to notice anything amiss.

"That's why you're wearing a shirt." It suddenly made sense. That little niggling in the back of my mind as he'd made love to me half dressed. That just didn't happen often. "Take it off."

"I'm fine," he said, jerking the pajama pants into place and tying them.

I did the same. I picked up my nightgown and slipped it over my head. "Wonderful. Then show me."

"Dutch," he said as though in warning, turning to face me when I tried to come around again.

But I saw the long streaks of blood in the mirror. Slashes that started at one shoulder, cut across his back, and ended under his rib cage. Claw slashes that only a bear or a hellhound could inflict.

I erupted in anger. "Take off your shirt or I'll take it off for you."

He knew I could. He knew I could completely incapacitate him with one word. But instead of the explosion I'd expected, he stilled. His lids narrowed, but not out of anger. An emotion more like pride spilled out of him. One corner of his sensual mouth tilted up, but he shook his head nonetheless. "No. You've seen enough over the past few months. I won't have you exposed to the depths of my stupidity."

The anger inside me dissipated immediately. "Mr. Farrow," I said, twirling my finger, instructing him to turn around, "the depths of your stupidity are the least of my concerns."

With a resigned sigh, he lifted the shirt over his head, his muscles bunching as he did so, and turned to face the mirror. And that was when I decided to take up gardening as I planted my face in the floor behind him.

"It's hormones," I said when Osh brought me a glass of water.

He had apparently been headed to the bathroom for a shower when he heard a thunderous crack and the ground shook beneath his feet—his words. Surely my fall wasn't that thunderous.

"I just got light-headed."

He winked at me, his signature top hat back in place, since the wedding festivities were over. Reyes held a cold rag to my temple, his expression severe. I'd scared him. I'd scared me too, but not for my own sake.

"I fell on Beep." I poked my belly, hoping she'd respond. "Do you think she's okay?"

"Better than you, *loca.*" Angel had dropped in, too, because I needed to be insulted as well as disoriented and humiliated.

"Angel Garza," I said, pointing at him threateningly. "I can do things now. Scary things."

He raised his hands, the boyish grin he wore perforating my heart.

"Duct tape?" I asked Osh.

He raised it, then tore off a strip to tape up Reyes's back. He'd been wearing duct tape under the dark gray T-shirt he had on earlier. I knew I'd seen odd lines across his back. But, thinking he'd healed for the most part, he peeled it off when he took a shower. He was wrong. His back bore two long slashes across it with four gashes each. One set extended from his shoulder to just under his rib cage. The other across the small of his back. The hellhounds' claws were like razor blades and the cuts were bone deep. Which would explain my sudden but blessedly short departure from reality.

"I think if I were you," Angel said to Reyes, "I'd stop trying to cuddle with hellhounds."

Reyes shot him a glare that didn't even faze him. Normally, Angel was scared to death of my husband. Clearly, they'd grown close enough in the last few months to give Angel's mouth free rein.

"If this happened yesterday," I said as Reyes bit down, steeling himself against the pain of Osh's administrations, "why are you not healing faster?"

Osh answered for him. "Because he's not sleeping. He hasn't been in stasis for months."

"Reyes," I said, drawing his gaze, "you have to sleep. Why aren't you sleeping? Eight months? How is that even possible?"

Osh applied one final piece of duct tape, then slapped it into place, causing a muted groan to escape his patient. "Good as new," he said. Then he grew serious. "But if this gets nasty, he'll be no use to us in this condition." He winked at me before grabbing his supplies and leaving.

"I'll be around," Angel said. "Just shout if you need me."

"Why?" I asked before he could disappear.

"Why?"

"Why are you here? What are you two up to?"

I didn't miss the warning glare that Reyes flashed him. He chewed on his lower lip, and said, "I'm just looking out for you."

Before I could push the subject, he vanished.

I crossed my arms over my chest and focused on my husband. "Why are you not sleeping?" I asked him, deciding to address his health instead of my curiosity about what Reyes had been up to with Angel.

He eased onto the bed, his large frame taking up most of its surface. "I can't let my guard down."

"Reyes," I said, straddling his hips, not an easy feat in my current state, "Osh was right. If you don't sleep, you won't be able to bring your A-game should things go south out here. It's like we're in a pot of hot water and someone is slowly turning up the heat. We can't stay out here forever. The hounds will figure out a way in. I can feel it."

His mouth widened into an appreciative grin when I crawled onto him, as though completely dismissing everything I'd just said. He rested his hands on my hips. "I'm learning about them," he said at last.

I leaned over him, tucked a lock of hair over his ear, ran my fingers along the outline of his lips. "About who?"

"The hounds. I'm learning how to fight them."

I bolted upright. "Is that why you continued to antagonize them even after you realized the holy ground wouldn't kill them?"

He lifted a playful brow. "Antagonize them?"

"You know what I mean."

"Something like that."

"But you're stopping, right? You said you're stopping."

"I'm stopping."

I lay down beside him. "What happened when you pulled them onto holy ground? I mean, did they writhe in agony?" I bounced up. "Did they smoke like the ground was burning the flesh off their bodies?"

He tucked an arm behind his head in thought. "That's just it," he said, his voice curious. "It didn't seem to faze them at all."

"I don't understand. The consecrated soil didn't hurt them?"

He shook his head. "Not even a little."

I lay awake, listening to Reyes's even breathing, but I now knew he was faking it. Had been faking it for eight months. My right foot was more asleep than he was. His revelation about the hellhounds kept my mind racing in overdrive. If the ground didn't hurt them, then why weren't they crossing it to rip out our throats? Maybe it did hurt them, just not visibly. They were freaking hard to see. Perhaps they were more focused on tearing my husband apart.

Or maybe they were simply waiting, patrolling the border to keep tabs on us. But why? What could they be waiting on?

My phone rang, but due to the limited number of electrical outlets in the room, Piper, my phone, was way across the other side. True, the room was tiny, but I'd still have to get out of bed to answer her summons.

I tried to roll out of Reyes's arms. He tightened his hold. I tried to lift an arm off me, but he clasped his fingers, essentially locking me in.

"Reyes," I said, stifling a giggle, "I know you're awake. You can give up the game."

"Never," he said into his pillow.

I laughed and leaned all my weight forward until he finally let go. By the time I got to Piper, my voice mail had picked up. It was Uncle Bob, so I put on my robe, tiptoed out of the room, and called him right back.

"Are you still at work?" I asked him, looking at the clock before I closed the door to a pretend sleeping Reyes. It was 1:32 A.M.

"We found him," he said, his voice hurried. "You won't believe this. He works for the Vatican."

"No," I said, adding a flare of astonishment to my voice.

"Freaking hell, Charley, did you already know that? Are you the one who called in with the tip?"

"No." Though I sounded super convincing, Ubie didn't buy it.

"Charley—"

"I suspected. It's a long story. So, what's going on?"

"We can't hold him, hon. He says he had nothing to do with the murder. Says your dad was following him, not the other way around. But we do have enough to charge him with stalking if you will press charges. Just say the word, pumpkin."

"Does he know anything about Dad's murder?"

Uncle Bob let out a long breath. "He says no. Says your dad threatened him if he didn't stop following you, then that's the last he saw of him."

"He's lying."

"How do you know?"

"Because, he wasn't just following me. Look at the pictures in his apartment."

"What pictures? There aren't any."

Damn it. He got rid of the evidence. Must have sent it all back to his boss at the Vatican. "He had pictures of Dad on his wall."

"You've been stuck at that convent for eight months. How do you know that?"

"I've been working with someone on it."

"Even after I asked you not to?"

"Kind of. He had pictures of Dad."

"Well, we got nothing now. And because he checks out, I can't hold him."

An idea hit me hard. As well as the corner of a hutch as I tried to traverse the house in the dark. I walked into the living room to hang with Mr. Wong.

"Put him on the phone," I said.

"Charley, I can't do that."

"Tell him who you're talking to and tell him Father Glenn sends his love." I'd suspected he knew Father Glenn, a man I'd helped with a nest of demons a few months ago, for a while now. He was the one who told me about the file the Vatican had on me. I wondered if they were connected somehow.

"Okay. Hold on."

After a few minutes, a timid male voice came on the phone. "Hello?"

"Hey, Blondie," I said, "been stalking anyone I know lately?"

"I don't know what you're talking about."

"Have you told the Vatican yet?"

"Told them what?"

"That your cover has been blown."

"Again, I don't know what—"

"How about we skip all this and get to the heart of the matter?" I didn't give him time to respond. I was hoping to disorient him so he'd slip up. "You tell my uncle, and you know damned well he's my uncle, who was following my dad. You had pictures of him and another man. Hand those over, and I won't tell anyone at the Vatican what a royal fuckup you are, *capisce*?"

He didn't say anything, which meant he was considering my offer.

"In turn, you can keep doing your Vatican crap, whatever the hell that's all about, and just do a few side jobs for me every once in a while, starting with a nun that died at this convent. I want her name and what happened to her. I also want to know what kind of trouble the priest that vanished was in."

"Which convent?"

"Dude, seriously, if you start playing games with me now, I will stop your heart in your chest. Funny thing is, you know I can do it. You've been stalking me for years. How do you think that makes me feel?"

Silence.

"Angry, Howard. It makes me feel angry."

"If they find out—"

"You'll lose your job?" I scoffed. "You're about to lose it anyway. You've been busted by your mark. A mark who is going to rain hellfire down on your boss's city. How do you think that will end?"

"I'm just an observer. I don't do research."

"Bullshit. Try again."

He sat thinking over his options, but the fact was, he didn't have any. Not if he didn't want to lose his cushy job.

"O—"

Before he could even finish the *okay* part, I said, "Get that picture you have of my dad and that other man to my uncle tonight and find out about the nun and the priest. You have two hours."

When I was met with only silence again, I said, "Howard, give the phone back to my uncle now. You're burning moonlight."

"What did he say?" Uncle Bob asked as he walked away from Howard. I could hear his footsteps in the background. "Is he going to cooperate?"

"He didn't have anything to do with Dad's death, but I think he might have a photo of someone who did. Dad seemed to be confronting a guy, and they both looked angry. He's going to give you that photo, but you have to let him go. Like immediately." I was so excited to be getting somewhere on my dad's case, I didn't want to waste another moment.

"You got it, pumpkin. What are you going to say if Reyes finds out you've been working on this case? He is afraid doing so will put you in danger."

"He won't find out. Don't worry about me."

"I like him. He's . . . a good man."

"Thanks, Ubie. I like him, too."

"Oh!" I almost forgot. "I'm sure he already knows it, but make sure Howard has my phone number. I'm expecting a call."

"Do I need to stay on him?" he asked.

"I don't think so. Once you get that photo and anything else he has on Dad, you need to come have sex with your wife."

"Charley," he said, and I could almost feel his cheeks heat up.

"I'm telling you, she's out here with three—no, four if you count Quentin, which why wouldn't you?—of the sexiest men on the planet. Just sayin'."

"I'll be there in an hour."

"It takes an hour to get here and you still have to get that photo."

"That's what sirens and flashing lights are for."

10

I decided to work on the door to the locked closet again while I waited for Vatican Boy's phone call. He'd better come through, or I was totally marking him. Not with anything bad. I'd give him a designation like head toilet bowl cleaner at the Pit, Albuquerque's sports complex. Man, that would suck. Though I was pretty sure the designation thing didn't exactly work that way, it was a thought.

I walked to the laundry room, this time with a flashlight, and studied the door from top to bottom. How was it even locked? There was no doorknob, no latch. And what would be the purpose of it locking from the inside? Then the occupant couldn't get out.

I gasped. That was it. Maybe someone was locked inside and they'd suffocated or starved to death. Maybe it was the priest. Maybe that was how he'd vanished.

This was getting exciting. I lowered myself onto all fours and shone the light under the door, hoping to catch a glimpse inside. Nothing. It was sealed tight.

Beep decided to practice the splits while I was down there. I crawled to the washing machine for leverage. Getting up was not so easy as it had once been. But since I was already in the vicinity, I decided to do a load of laundry.

Denise's voice scared the crap out of me. I startled when she said, "I was going to do that. I'm washing all the baby stuff and getting it ready."

"Wow, you don't give up, do you?"

"I have no intention of losing you."

Gemma was right. I felt Denise's loneliness cut through to my marrow. But whose freaking fault was that?

"Is Gemma with you?"

"No, I drove. Your friend Lando Calrissian gave me a room. It has a cot."

"Lando?"

"Long black hair, looks like he's still in high school?"

"Osh. His name is Osh. Lando is—"

"I know who Lando is."

"Oh. Well—"

"Are you taking your vitamins?"

"Yup."

She nodded. "Have you had cramping? Any spotting?"

"Nope." When she only nodded again, I said, "Okay, then. I'm going to go . . . do stuff. Other stuff. Somewhere else."

I couldn't miss the relief she felt when I didn't throw her out. I was not forgiving her. I refused. But she could do my laundry if she wanted. And, maybe, help with Beep when she arrived. All babies need a grandmother.

"You should get some rest," she said.

"I'm waiting on a phone call about a case. But the minute I get it—"

"A case? You're still working cases?"

" 'Parently."

She started to chastise me. I could see it on her face. She wore scorn like a trophy wife wore Louis Vuitton. Instead, she lifted a shirt out of a laundry basket that said DEAR DIARY, HAD TO CUT A BITCH TODAY and didn't say a word. No terms of aghastment. No scathing remark. It was weird, and I was more convinced than ever that she was possessed.

I decided to wait for the call in the theater room, which was really a few chairs and a television. I ended up curled into a recliner and watching an episode of *Andy Griffith* when my husband walked in. I eyed him. Yep, I could do him again.

He walked into the theater wearing the lounge pants and nothing else. Even his feet were sexy. But now I understood the scruffiness of his appearance. The sleep-deprived features.

"You're not coming back up?" he asked.

"I'm waiting for a call."

He nodded, picked up a magazine with Oprah on the cover, and sat in the chair beside me. "You know," he said right as Opie was going to knock some birds out of a tree. Such a bad boy. "You can tell me anything."

I snorted. "No, I can't."

He stopped and gave me his full attention. "Why would you say that?"

He was magnificent, and I didn't want to disappoint him. But now was as good a time as any. The thought of what I was about to do to him—to us—saddened me. I was about to turn his world upside down, but he needed to know what I'd done.

My nerves jumped to attention. My heart raced. He would hate me come morning. But where could he go? We'd be stuck in the same house for God knew how long, hating each other. Or, well, him hating me. I could never hate him. Not even if he ate the last Oreo, though that would be pushing it. "What if I told you—?"

My phone rang. I paused midsentence, swallowed back my fear, and picked up my phone. I had been given a momentary stay of execution, and I damned well was going to take it.

"It's Howard," the voice on the other end said.

"I figured as much. What did you find out?"

"There was a novice there, about to take her vows when she accused a priest of molesting her."

"Let me guess, the priest who went missing."

"Yes. But nothing ever came of her charges, and there's nothing about anyone dying there. Not a young nun anyway. The novice was excommunicated."

"Of course, she was." I stood and paced the room. "Coming forward to accuse a priest of misconduct back then usually meant excommunication." That would explain why her death had not been recorded. But how did she die? Did the priest kill her and then disappear? "What was her name?"

"Bea Heedles."

"Sister Bea?"

"I think she went by Sister Beatrice. So, is that all?" he asked.

"Did you get the picture to my uncle?"

The moment I asked, I heard a car pull up. That would be Ubie.

Reyes stood to open the door.

"Yes. I did as you asked." I could hear the resentment in his voice.

"Okay, then answer me this: Why?"

"Why what?"

"Why does the Vatican—I mean, seriously, *the Vatican*—have a file on me?"

"I'm just the observer," he said, trying to pull that innocent-as-the-driven crap again.

"Howard, if this relationship is going to work, we have to be honest with each other. So I, honestly, will let your heart keep beating if you stop bullshitting me."

He took a long moment to get back to me. When he did, his voice was a tad more reverent than before. I'd take it.

"All I know is that you are of interest to them. They— They have prophecies, and apparently when you were born, all the predictions started to come true."

"How did they find out about me in the first place?"

"We have people, too," he said. "People like you. People with gifts. They, they saw you, I guess."

I knew that they paid very close attention to what Sister Mary Elizabeth had to say. They'd wanted her in Italy when she was a novice, but she wanted to stay in New Mexico, near the girl causing all the uproar in heaven. Were there more like her?

"What about you? Do you have gifts?"

"No," he said.

Uncle Bob came in, gave me a peck on the cheek, then went upstairs to find his wife. Cookie was about to get a nice surprise. Reyes walked up behind me and draped his arms over the back of the recliner so he could rub my Beep bump. His hands felt wonderful. His heat soothing.

"What about other . . . people like me?" I asked. "Do you know about them?"

"There are no other people like you."

"No, I mean, what about other people they observe. How many are there?"

"Look, I was hired to observe you and report back. That's it."

"That doesn't answer my question."

"I know that your husband is special, too."

He had that right. He was busy nibbling on my earlobe, causing ripples of pleasure to race over my skin.

"Do you know what he is?"

"I know that he's from hell."

I stilled. That was more than I thought he'd know. "Is the Vatican aware?"

He'd grown more hesitant as the conversation wore on. I sensed a spark of fear in his voice, but he soldiered on. "Everything about you goes into my reports."

"Will they take any action?" What would they do, really? What could they do? But I needed to know if this was going to be an issue.

"I have no idea. I don't have that kind of clearance."

I believed him. I also believed that this guy was going to come in handy.

"Howard," I said, letting a smile spread across my face. "I think we're going to have a long and beautiful relationship."

"But I thought—"

"How many years have you been stalking me?"

After another long pause, he said, "Observing. Seven."

Holy cow, how did I not know these things? I was so oblivious sometimes. "Then the way I see it, you owe me seven years of indentured servitude."

"Crap," he said.

"You'll be like a double agent. It'll be fun!"

"I'm going to hell."

"Not anytime soon, you're not. I need you, buddy. It's you and me against the world. Oh, hey, so do you know how to kill a hellhound?"

Determined to stay up with Reyes—if he couldn't sleep, I couldn't sleep—I fell asleep in the theater room about five minutes after we snuggled together and he started rubbing my Beep bump again. I remember being lifted—and thankful that I was only dreaming that I was being airlifted—and carried to our room. I woke up a few hours later to an empty bed.

The sun was just breaching the horizon when I put on my robe and padded down the hall to find the community toilet. I peed and was in the process of brushing my teeth when I looked out the postage stamp window. I had a view from the back of the house. All the wedding goers had left and only an occasional flower or silken streamer remained as evidence of Cookie's special day.

I started back for the mirror, as my tongue was on fire—freaking cinnamon toothpaste—when I noticed a movement along the tree line. It was Reyes and he was sneaking out. To go fight another hellhound? Hadn't he proved that dragging them onto sacred ground wouldn't kill them? Maybe he was meeting that traitor Angel again.

I rinsed and spit, waving a hand in front of my face as I rushed into the darkened bedroom to throw on some clothes and hurried down the stairs. Denise was up, making breakfast. I ran, kind of, past her, then stopped and turned.

"You made bacon?" I asked, my mouth watering.

"It's veggie bacon."

"Isn't that an oxymoron?"

"Do you want to try it?"

I eyed it distrustfully. "I'm not sure."

"Sit down, I'll fix you a plate."

"No time. I have to catch my husband in the act." In the act of what, I had no idea, but I was damned well about to find out.

She pursed her lips as I grabbed a piece and ran, kind of, out the door. "Okay, I'll keep it warm," she said.

"Thanks!" I said, not too loud, though. I had to be like a grasshopper on the wind. No! I had to *be* the wind.

Initializing stealth mode: now.

I skirted the tree line to get to where I'd been the day before. I had a pretty good view from there. I really just wanted to make sure my psychotic, sleep-deprived husband wasn't wrestling hellhounds. That would have been such a great metaphor if it weren't real. I'd have to remember it. Use it metaphorically later.

I climbed through the trees, all the while keeping a sharp eye on the drop-off. It still boggled my mind that Reyes didn't notice me right off. If I was so bright, how could he miss me? But there he was, walking through the clearing that was supposedly beyond the border. Freaking Osh. He'd been in on whatever was going on from the first.

Reyes stopped in the middle of the clearing and Angel appeared. He'd summoned him! My investigator. I felt violated. Betrayed. Trampled on like a used napkin at the Frontier, my favorite restaurant.

The Frontier.

I started to drool again as I watched them. Easing over a fallen log and negotiating the uneven ground, I kept my head down and my breathing steady. No idea why. I totally felt like a sniper in the marines. Only I was pregnant. Other than that, and the fact that I couldn't snipe if they'd paid me to, I embodied all that a sniper should be. Stealth. Grace. The patience of a panther on the prowl. Gawd, I had to pee.

A face in my periphery caught my attention. It was the nun. She snuck up beside me and, following my lead, kept a close vigil on the men below. I finally got a good look at her, albeit from my periphery. I didn't want to scare her off.

She had a tiny, upturned nose, a soft face that still had the puffiness of youth, and a small, pretty mouth. The veil she wore covered her hair, but even through the grayness of her coloring, I could tell her eyebrows were light brown and her eyes hazel. We both kept our gazes locked on our targets as Reyes and Angel talked.

An idea hit me, and I finally turned to her. "Can you maybe pop down there and listen in?"

Without taking her eyes off me, she shook her head.

That was disappointing. "Can you read lips?"

No again, only this time she fought the twitching of a grin. Okay. Two could play that game.

"Then can you run up to them, jerk their pants down, then run away?"

She giggled softly. Then she was standing about ten feet from me. I decided to give up on my sniper career and see where Sister Beatrice took me today.

"Okay, but seriously, you have to wait for me this time. I mean it."

She kept disappearing and reappearing farther down the overgrown path. If it ever was a path. We went deeper and deeper into the woods, but I had yet to come across the string that marked the border. Even so, the growls in the distance grew louder with each step I took.

"Beatrice!" I said, calling out to her. I'd lost her again and I needed to catch my breath. But before that could happen, she appeared beside me. My heart tried to leap out of my chest. I pressed a hand to hold it in and took a few deep breaths. "All right, Sister. What are you trying to show me?"

She pointed down. I followed her line of sight to the ground beneath me and realized I was standing on slats. Wooden slats. I knelt down and brushed the dirt and leaves away. I couldn't be certain without a flashlight, but it could have been a well.

"What's down there, sweetheart?"

Her gaze dropped to her saddle shoes, her hands wringing nervously.

"Is it you?" I asked. Did the priest kill her and dump her body in a well?

Without looking at me, she shook her head.

It hit me then. I sat back on one leg. "Is it him?" I asked her. "Is it the priest?"

She closed her eyes as shame consumed her. I had to admit, I didn't expect that. Did she kill him? Or maybe he attacked her and she'd defended herself. It could have been any number of situations.

"Can you tell me what happened?"

She stepped forward and held out her hand. I took it, but wasn't sure what she wanted until she nodded and closed her eyes. She was allowing me access to her memories.

They catapulted me back to a moonless night slick with freezing rain.

I saw her journey through her eyes as she ran. Fear thundered through her. As she climbed as high and as fast as she could, her shoes slipped in the mud. But someone caught her wrist. Someone else was with her. Another young novice like herself. One whom she loved with all her heart and soul. It was hard to see her clearly through the rain, but the nun had features similar to Beatrice's. And she was just as scared.

Beatrice's fear paralyzed me. Her heart beat so hard, it hurt. He was going to kill her. He was going to kill them both. One of them, and he didn't know which, had written to the bishop, accused him of forcing himself upon her. He'd been drunk, he said. He didn't remember doing it, he said, let alone which girl it was. But he was not about to lose his entire career, his livelihood, over a whore. And since he didn't know which one he'd accosted, he was going to kill them both. They saw it in his eyes when he asked them for help with a pen outside. They'd gone with him, feeling safe since there were two of them. They'd been wrong.

He swung a hammer, hitting Beatrice's friend on the temple, and they ran into the night. Holding hands, they found a spot and hid from him. But he was not about to give up the search easily. He kept at it for what seemed like hours. Eventually, he found them.

The girl she was with motioned for her to run and then lunged at the priest. Beatrice couldn't, though. She couldn't run. She couldn't leave her friend. Instead, she attacked the man from behind. He was choking her friend. She beat his head with her fists and scratched at his eyes, but he elbowed her in the face. The force knocked her back against a tree and she lost consciousness for a precious few seconds. When she came to, her friend lay motionless, his fingers so tight around her throat, she'd turned blue.

He shook the girl, squeezing the last remnants of life out of her as hard as he could, then let her go and came after Beatrice. She no longer cared. She gaped at her friend, unable to process the fact that she was gone.

The priest walked toward her slowly, suddenly interested in her again. He would have his way with her before he killed her. Or after. Either way, he would win.

No, she thought. She brought out the knife she'd taken from the kitchen. The one she'd been carrying around since that night. To use on him. To protect herself. But she decided to use it on a part of him instead. The baby he'd left inside her body. He stopped and watched as she took the knife into both hands and plunged it into her abdomen.

He watched for a while, surprised, then shrugged. She'd done the work for him. When she fell to her knees, a searing pain paralyzing her, he walked back to the girl and dragged her higher up the mountain. Beatrice watched as he pulled back a wooden cover of some kind and dropped her friend into a well. He turned to come back for her, but the rain had softened the ground. He slid, caught himself, then slid again and toppled over the side and into the well.

She heard him groaning at first; then he came to and started yelling for her to get help. Instead, she crawled to the well, her hands and stomach covered in blood, and pushed the wooden cover with all her might until it canopied the entrance. His screams faded as the barrier slid into place, but they were still audible. So she worked for an hour, dragging dirt and grass and tree branches to cover the wood. To insulate the sound.

Finally, his screams were barely a whisper on the wind. With grief consuming her, she walked farther into the woods until the sun came up and drenched her in its light. Dreaming that it was God. Dreaming that he would forgive her, that he would touch her face as gently as the sun and welcome her home. She took her last breath thinking only of one person. Her twin sister. The girl lying at the bottom of a well with a murderer.

Her heart contracted for the last time, and then she was no longer cold.

I jerked away from her, fought to catch my breath, struggled to keep

at bay the wetness threatening to spill over my lashes. I lost. Fat, hot tears
streaked down my face as I looked at her.

"Beatrice, I'm so sorry."

She shook her head. Pointed to herself, and finger-spelled, "Mo."

"Mo? That's Beatrice in the well?"

She nodded.

"Are you Deaf?"

She shook her head, curled one small hand into a fist and held it over
her mouth.

"You're mute. And your sister?"

Her signing was archaic and not really American Sign Language. It
was a jumble of signs she'd probably done at home with her family,
gestures, and ASL. I did understand that her sister could talk, but that
night, she didn't want the priest to know which girl he'd raped. So she'd
refused to talk, refused to give away which sister was the threat. She'd
given up her life for her twin, who had been mute most of her life. The
priest knew that, and had believed that disability would keep her from
speaking up for herself. He'd been wrong.

"Mo, I'm so sorry."

She was crying, too. All the emotions I felt came straight from her.
Her heart had been ripped out that night. Her life and her happiness
stolen. But the worst part was the loss of her beloved sister.

She signed to me again, and it took three times for me to figure
out what she was asking. I felt stupid and inept for making her repeat
herself so much. But I finally figured out she was asking me if God
hated her because she let a man lie with her. Because she got her sister
killed and then killed herself. Because she took away the life he'd given
her.

"Can he forgive me?" she asked. "If I do something good?"

"Oh, sweetheart," I said, standing up, after some effort, and hugging
her. "He doesn't hate you. I promise with all my heart. You did do some-

thing good. You tried to save your sister." I set her at arm's length. "You can cross through me if—"

I heard something before I could finish. A crack. A sharp crack. Like wood. And I thought to myself, wouldn't it be crazy if—?

Yep. The cover broke beneath my weight. My eyes wide, I gazed at Mo. She gazed back. Then I dropped.

11

GOD GIVES US ONLY WHAT WE CAN HANDLE.
APPARENTLY, GOD THINKS I'M A BADASS.
—BUMPER STICKER

The wood didn't exactly break cleanly. It scraped across my back and arms as I fell, but I managed to grab hold of a slat on the way down. I hung there, my legs dangling. A jagged point had torn into my face by my ear and up across my forehead. I didn't realize it until my vision blurred due to the blood gushing from my head.

Mo tried to pull me up, but there was simply no way. I weighed too much. It was Beep's fault. Apparently, she weighed around eighty-seven pounds. My ribs burned and I had a difficult time breathing, but I took in a lungful of air and was just about to scream for my husband when the plank I held on to for dear life broke.

I dropped longer than I thought I would have, falling into a deep pit of darkness. In that instant, I prayed there would be water at the bottom. My prayers were not answered. I hit hard. My legs crumpled beneath me. My hips exploded with pain as my femurs drove into the sockets by the force of the sudden stop. The drop knocked the air from my lungs, and I raised my arms over my head, trying to catch my breath. Both those tasks caused jolts of excruciating pain in my side. I'd cracked a rib. Possibly more.

The ground was uneven beneath me, and in the back of my mind I knew I was sitting atop the bones of at least two people. I fell back against the side of the well. Most wells in the area weren't dug so wide. They were just wide enough for small children or animals to fall in. This was a bona fide well with lots of elbow room. I was lucky. I could have been stuck in a pipeline. Beep could have died.

Mo appeared beside me. My question was, why didn't Reyes? He loved to pop in when I was in mortal peril. What the heck?

There was just enough space for Mo to stand beside me. Had she been alive, it would have been terribly cramped. As it was, she could stand half inside the wall of the well.

I glanced around and could see two things. The round top of the well, which reminded me of a horror movie I'd seen, and Mo. I could've seen Mo no matter how much light I had. Or didn't have. But the light seemed to stop about halfway down the well.

Tree roots zigzagged across the opening above me. That would explain some of the burning I felt on my back and arms. And I honestly didn't know if I was sitting on more roots or bones. Either way, this was not a place I wanted to stay long.

"Reyes," I said weakly. Screaming for help was no longer an option.

"I'll go get help," Mo signed, but before she could go, Reyes appeared at last, his incorporeal form shrouded in a massive undulating robe. It filled any leftover space.

Mo fell back against the side of the well, her eyes wide.

"It's okay, hon," I said through gritted teeth. "He's with me."

His incorporeal form disappeared, and I heard someone running and then sliding to a halt above us. Dirt trickled down from overhead.

"What the hell, Dutch?" Reyes asked.

I was in too much pain to offer a smart-assed comeback. And though there was no water in the well, I was wet. Very wet. I closed my eyes, mortified. My water had broken. This could not be good.

I heard Reyes whisper above me, the sound echoing around me, the walls like an amphitheater. "Osh'ekiel," he said.

Osh would be there soon. He'd probably bring Garrett as well if he was still at the house.

I was safe. I knew I was safe. With that thought, I decided to drift off for a while. Regain my strength. Gather my thoughts.

Reyes yelled at me, but I couldn't stop my fall into oblivion. It certainly felt better there.

I heard arguing overhead. Every once in a while, a voice would drift down to me. Osh. Garrett. Uncle Bob. Poor Ubie. Reyes and Cookie argued with him. He wanted to risk it and have me medevaced to Albuquerque. He didn't understand the consequences of such an action. It might take the hellhounds a while to find me, but find me they would.

I didn't care at that moment, though. If it would save Beep, then we needed to risk it. I tried to tell Reyes that, but no one was listening to me.

"Charley!" Cookie called out to me. She was hysterical, racked with sobs. I felt bad that I was causing such uproar.

"I'm okay," I said, and looked over at Mo.

"What can I do?" she asked. Either that or she said I needed to dye my hair. Maybe it was time. I was getting older now. Had a family and a kid. Almost. I needed to be more adultlike. Dye my hair. Get my nails done. Go to water aerobics.

"What the fuck?" Osh asked me.

He grinned down at me from up high. It actually wasn't so deep as the fall that lasted forever would have me believe, but it was deep enough to make getting me out of there a problem.

There it was again. A pain across my stomach and abdomen that crept around to my back. Crap on a cracker. I was in labor.

"So, guys," I said, looking up at heads in a circle. It would have been comical if— Who was I kidding? It was comical. "My water broke. I'm in labor, so if we could just hurry this along. Also, I think I broke a rib. Or two. And possibly my hips. And my ankle hurts."

"The way I see it," Osh said, "you got yourself into this mess. You can get yourself out of it."

Cookie whacked the back of his head.

"Just kidding."

"Who's the girl?" Quentin asked, his signs difficult to read from my vantage.

I tried to sign back, to no avail. "Amber, can you tell Quentin this is Mo? She's mute but uses mostly home signs. I need a Deaf interpreter."

She relayed my message and I could hear Artemis whimpering in the background. I was surprised she wasn't down here with me. After a moment, Quentin nodded.

"Okay," I said, looking at Mo, "are there any neighbors close by with a rope of some kind?"

"Yes," she said, pointing repeatedly. I'd been at the convent all this time but had no way of visiting our neighbors. Even if I could have ventured out, we were trying to keep to ourselves, to allay any questions our new neighbors might have about why we were living there, so I had no idea what lay beyond our holy border. "Quentin, can you let her lead you to them? We need rope and boiling water."

"Why boiling water?" he asked.

"I don't know. They just always boil water when someone's having a baby."

"Not the boiling water," Reyes said to Quentin. "But we do need rope or ties or, better yet, mountain climbing gear, but that's aiming high."

He nodded and Mo disappeared to lead them to the closest neighbors. Hopefully they'd have at least one item on our list.

"Can you lift me out of here?" I asked Reyes, only half teasing.

He didn't smile. "How are you?"

"I'm okay. I need some ibuprofen. Or some morphine."

He nodded. "I've called Katherine."

"Katherine the Midwife. You have to say her full name."

"She's on the way," he continued without even cracking a smile. I was losing my touch. "But it'll take her almost an hour to get here."

"Okay. I'll wait," I said, just as another spasm ripped through me. It made breathing impossible with the rib situation. I grabbed hold of a tree root—hopefully—nearby and squeezed.

"Lower me down," I heard someone say. "I was a pediatrics nurse, and I even helped deliver a few babies in my day. I need to check her."

No way. They were going to put me in an enclosed area with Denise?

"This won't hold," Reyes said.

"It won't hold you, but it'll hold me. We're risking the baby's life."

"If it doesn't and you fall onto her—"

"I won't. I'm the smallest one here besides Amber, and I'm pretty sure she wouldn't know what to look for."

I drifted away again, wondering how far under the dirt the bones were. Someone needed to know that they were here.

I looked up to tell them, but found myself staring at a butt. A butt I'd recognize anywhere. It was Denise's, and she was being lowered with sheets that had been tied together. She was so going to fall on me. I closed my eyes as dirt tumbled down on me, and it felt good and I fell into oblivion again until an excruciating pain jerked me out of it.

"I hate labor!" I yelled, but it came out as a whisper.

"Here," I heard Denise say before feeling the rim of a water bottle at my mouth. She'd brought Katherine the Midwife's case with her. "I called Gemma. She's on the way, sweetheart. You just hang in there."

I pushed it away. "Were you possessed? Is that why you're being nice to me?"

She laughed softly. Like laughed. At something I said. Oh yeah. She was possessed. Bedeviled. Entangled in Satan's snare.

She lifted a bottle to my mouth again. "Just a tiny sip," she said. "Once you go into hard labor, you can't eat or drink anything. I need to see how far along you are, but it's too cramped."

"I was fine until you showed up."

"Can you get onto your knees?"

Now she was just expecting miracles. "My femurs have been shoved into my hip sockets."

"If that were true, you would be screaming in agony. You may have pulled some tendons, though, so be very, very careful."

She was standing over me and slowly slid to her knees. Moving one of my legs, she parted it at the knee, and while it hurt, it wasn't excruciating. She tried the other one, with the same results. "If I pull your arms, can you grab hold of my shoulders and get into a crouching position? It'll help with delivery if it comes to that."

"Delivery?" I asked, my voice an octave higher than normal. "No way."

"Hon, we may not have a choice. We need to be prepared."

"Like the Boy Scouts."

"Exactly."

"Okay, I can try."

"First we're going to have to get your pants off."

"Oh, hell no," I said, suddenly self-conscious. "We have an audience."

"And we," she said, smiling at me, "have a sheet. Several, in fact."

With Denise's help, I got onto my knees and we managed to get my pants off me.

"Can't the guys just lift me out of here with the sheets?"

"No, it's too big of a risk. If you fall again—"

"You could have fallen on me. Why was that not a risk?"

"Charley, every risk has to be weighed. It was riskier for you and for the baby for me not to come down here and check you. But it's riskier for you both if the sheets don't hold and you fall again. What is that?"

She pointed to my left. I'd been sitting on a skull. "So that's what that was. Killed my tailbone."

"Is that—?"

"A skull. Yes, we have to tell people. There are two bodies down here."

Even in the low light, Denise's face paled visibly. It was awesome.

"You okay?" I asked.

"Yes, We need to get a sheet under you, then I'm going to check you."

It took some creative thinking, but we managed to get the sheet mostly underneath me.

She'd brought gloves from Katherine the Midwife's stash and put them on. "Can you straighten up just a bit?"

I grabbed a protruding root and straightened as much as I could. A blistering hot pain shot through me. Every part of my body hurt, but she was able to get a hand between my parted legs. "Okay, you are at about a seven with ninety percent effacement."

"Should I push? I don't want to push too early. I've heard stories."

Reyes's heat felt good. I could feel it from where I sat.

"How long was she out?" she asked Cookie.

"About an hour."

"An hour?" I asked, surprised. "It felt like minutes." I fell onto my palms again, my head resting in her lap as a spasm of pain clawed at me and squeezed my midsection like I was a bottle of ketchup. I gritted my teeth and sucked air in and out through them. My hands curled around handfuls of the sheet until the pain began to subside.

"Charley," Cookie said from overhead. "I can't believe this is happening."

"Me neither."

"Do you remember that time we went to the movie and that woman went into labor but she wouldn't leave because she didn't want to miss the ending and then, bam, it was too late?"

"Oh yeah. That was crazy. That ending sucked."

"Right?"

"Do you want to tell me what you were doing out here?" Reyes asked.

"I was following you."

"Why?"

"You snuck out of the house and—" Anther spasm ripped through me and all I could wonder was why in the world had women been doing this for thousands of years? This was barbaric. This was torture. Never again. Never again as long as I lived would I have another baby, so Beep had better be pretty awesome.

"And what?" he asked me. I realized, of course, they were trying to take my mind off the pain. Off the situation.

"And you met with Angel again."

"Don't bring me into this," Angel said.

"Angel!" I said, happy to see him. Or hear him, since my face was planted in Denise's crotch. "Why were you meeting with Reyes?"

"I can't tell you. He's meaner than you are."

I lifted just to glare up at him. "Clearly you don't know me very well."

"I would go down there to be with you, but I draw the line at childbirth."

"Chickenshit."

"And proud of it."

"I would have told you," Reyes said. "You're holding my underwear hostage. I would've had no choice."

"Does that mean you aren't wearing any?"

"Your blood pressure is too high," Denise said. She'd checked me with one of those wrist models that fascinated me. She looked up. "We need that rope."

"Got it!" Amber called out. "He didn't want to lend it to us. He didn't believe we had a pregnant woman stuck in a hole. So he came to help."

"Hey, there," a man called down to me. A Native American, judging by his accent. "I'm thinking we might need to get some professionals out here."

"So, yeah, I'm not wearing pants," I said to him. "Sorry."

"I'm okay with it if your husband is."

Another spasm, this one harder than any of its predecessors, tried to tear me in half. I cried out between locked teeth and tried to breathe in a pattern. It didn't work.

"We need the rope," Denise called.

"I'm getting it ready," Reyes said.

"Got the board," Osh said as he ran up.

He put a wide board across the opening. "What's that for?" I asked. "It will just break like the ones before."

"Not this one," he said. "It's from your kitchen table."

"Oh, okay, that might work." I doubled over and clenched my fists so hard, my fingernails pierced the flesh on my palms. "There's so much pressure," I told Denise. "I feel like I have to push."

"Okay, sweetheart." She eased me back and reached between my legs to check again. "You're ready. If you have to push, push."

"But they can pull us out now."

She shook her head. "It's too late. We are going to have to do this here."

I glared at her. "I don't want my baby born in a well," I gritted out.

"I know," she said as I pushed with all my might. I couldn't not.

She instructed me on how to do it. Push to the count of ten, then rest. Push to the count of ten, then rest. It occurred to me that she hadn't done this in a very long time. They might have changed things since her day. Maybe babies were born differently now. Maybe ten was no longer the magic number. But I couldn't argue with her. I could barely speak through the labor.

She rubbed my back until it was over and I could take a breath; then she listened for Beep's heartbeat again.

"I need the rope!" she screamed; then she shoved me back against the wall, wedged her palms against my lower abdomen, and pushed up.

I cried out in pain and tried to get her off me.

She said something I didn't comprehend; then she did it. Again. For the third time in my life, she slapped me.

My temper flared and the ground shook beneath us, causing dirt to fall on our heads. It didn't faze her.

"Look at me," she said, her face inches from mine. "Beep is in trouble. If you push, she could suffocate."

Alarm sobered me instantly.

"I lost her heartbeat for a few seconds. The cord could be wrapped around her throat. You may have to have a C-section."

"We can't leave the grounds," I said, my agony ripping a sob from the deepest core of my being. "She'll be in danger."

"Charley, she already is. I don't understand."

"There are—" I stopped as another sob shook through me, my horror was so great. "There are beings who want her dead. Huge supernatural beings with large razor-sharp teeth and claws the size of Pittsburgh. They'll kill her the minute we step off this ground."

She gaped at me as though I were a child telling a tall tale. In her eyes, I could see the instinctive desire to chastise me for being ridiculous—then understanding dawned. "Charley, are you serious?"

"Trust me, I wish I weren't."

For a long while, she sat stunned, at an utter loss for what to do. My muscles seized again. She coached me through it again, pushed my abdomen to keep the umbilical cord from strangling my daughter. As painful as that felt, I could only be grateful. Then it hit her as I tried to catch my breath and get comfortable, both of which were impossible.

She nodded and straightened. "Lean back," she said, all business.

I sat on my heels, my knees spread as far as they could be in the cramped quarters.

She squatted down and perched elbows between my knees. "I'm going to reach in and loop the cord over her head. I'll have to push her back a little to do it. This is going to hurt, Charley."

"I've been hurt before," I said, determined to do anything it took.

Then Reyes was there, his incorporeal form scalding, the sensation welcome until he reached around me from behind and held me to the prickly wall of the well, forcing me back so Denise could do what was needed. She reached inside me and ripped me in two from the inside out.

I screamed, long and loud and guttural, as Reyes pinned my shoulders against the well wall. I clawed at his arms, but he was the only thing keeping me from doubling over as my stepmother pushed Beep back up and then searched for the cord. The sheet beneath us was covered in blood, as were my legs. And my shirt. And pretty much everything around me.

Another spasm hit just as she said, "I think I got it. I think she's in the clear." She listened for the heartbeat again with the stethoscope as Reyes kept his hold tight, this time monitoring the entire time I pushed. I grabbed a handful of his hair and gave it my all.

She sighed in relief. "I think she's okay. We can do this, Charley."

I heard the Native American man argue with Osh and Garrett. He was going to call an ambulance, but they insisted one was already on the way. They'd lied, but they had to hold him off.

"You're tearing, but I can't do anything about it down here."

"It's okay," I said, my entire body slick with sweat. "It's coming again."

"You can do this, sweetheart," she said.

I nodded and pushed when the spasm hit. I felt myself splitting as Beep's head passed through.

"Okay, stop pushing!" she said, taking one of the sheets and working on Beep. Then she took a sucky thing out of the bag. Though I couldn't see what she was doing, I heard a soft wail of annoyance waft up to me, and I let my head loll back against Reyes's shoulder. But Beep was still halfway in me, though, and I really needed to push. I fought the urge with all my strength.

"Okay, I'm going to pull her out one shoulder at a time. Don't push."

"What?" But with one final jolt of pain, Beep was out. And pissed as hell.

I covered my mouth with my hands. "Reyes," I said, unable to take my eyes off her.

"She's perfect," he said into my ear. Thank God he continued to hold me. I doubted I had the strength to hold myself upright anymore.

Denise worked to get our daughter cleaned up. I could relax and focus on the broken rib and the nigh-fractured hips and the blood still running out of my head.

I smiled at Reyes. "What a day, huh?"

He shook his head.

"So, do you still need the rope?" Osh asked.

"Yes, but not for a few minutes," Denise said. She cut the cord, clipped it with a clothespin from the looks of it, and wrapped our bundle in a clean-ish sheet. Then she handed her to me.

All I could see was a little round face still covered in spots of muck, but she was the most beautiful thing I'd ever seen in my life. Dark lashes. Full mouth. Stubborn chin. She was Reyes incarnate, and my heart swelled with pride. "She's so perfect," I said.

"Yes, she is, but we need to get you both out of here as soon as possible."

"Katherine the Midwife is here," Amber said. "Can I hold her?" she asked me.

"You'll have to ask Katherine, hon."

She laughed. "I meant Beep."

"You absolutely can, just as soon as we get out of here."

"One more thing," Denise said.

"What?"

"We have to get the rest out of you."

"What rest?"

I shouldn't have asked.

They lifted Denise out first while she carried Beep. Then the guys lowered Reyes to get me. He lifted me into his arms and they hoisted us both up at the same time using some kind of pulley system Garrett had jerry-rigged. I lost consciousness about halfway up, exhausted and broken, but as long as Beep was okay, I was okay. I knew she'd be well taken care of. She had a large family.

I awoke hours later in bed beside Reyes with a tiny bundle between us. One lamp fended off the darkness in the small room, and I could see Katherine the Midwife snoring in a chair close by. Though I didn't much care what time it was, I did wonder how long I'd been out. How many hours of Beep's existence I'd missed.

They'd dressed her in the first outfit Cookie had bought her. When I first saw it, I'd remarked that it looked too small. Babies couldn't possibly be that tiny. Now that she was wearing it, however, it looked too big. Beep didn't seem real. She was like a doll with thick lashes, a perfect nose, and a widow's peak. She was surreal and angelic and mesmerizing.

I rolled onto my side and loosened the blanket. Her tiny fingers splayed in reaction to my touch, and I marveled at her fingernails—exact replicas of Reyes's—as I counted them. An even ten. Just what the doctor ordered. I felt as though my eyes were glued to her. I couldn't stop gazing at this little person we'd been waiting so long to see. I fought back tears as I looked at her, ignoring the fact that I felt like I'd been run over by a train. I'd been run over by trains before. The tenderness between my legs, however, was novel. And nature wasn't calling. She was screaming, ranting and raving like a lunatic.

Unable to ignore my bladder any longer, I kissed Beep's head, then her cheek, then her hand, before rolling out of bed. I glanced at my husband, wondering if he was really asleep at last. He lay on his side with his head propped on one arm, the dips between his biceps forming deep, alluring shadows. His long lashes fanned across his cheeks, just like Beep's, and I stilled to watch them just a few seconds more, until I heard Denise.

"She's perfect," she said softly.

I turned to see her sitting in another chair they'd brought in. "She is, isn't she? She's so tiny. It's like she's not real. She's like a pink flower floating on a big blue sea."

"They're always smaller than you think they will be."

She and my dad had never had more children, and I always wondered why. Not enough to ask, but . . . "How long have I been out?"

"Since yesterday morning. About eighteen hours."

"Eighteen hours?" I asked, scanning the room for the clock. "She had to face the world without me for eighteen whole hours?"

"They said you were in stasis or something. That you had to rest to heal."

"Yeah, well, I don't think it worked this time." I tried to stretch. It was just too painful.

"Do you want to hold her?" she asked, stepping forward. "We finally wrangled her away from your husband long enough to let Katherine check her out. A pediatrician is coming tomorrow, though, just to make sure."

"Oh, good. Let me go pee, then she's all mine."

I grabbed my phone, then walked to the bathroom, my pace that of a snail in its late nineties. The soreness I felt was beyond anything I'd experienced before. My hips hurt the worst, then Virginia. Poor Virginia. She'd never be the same again. Then my ribs, et cetera. It hurt to brush my teeth and wash my face, too. I had a nasty bruise on the side of my head with a lovely gash in the middle and a black eye.

I checked messages while sitting on the toilet. Multitasking had always been a specialty of mine. And I peed forever, so I had a lot of time. I had a text from Mr. Alaniz, my PI, asking me if there was any progress on the home front. Meaning, had I told Reyes yet? I was going to have to tell him. The Loehrs had given me until tomorrow. Maybe now that we had Beep, he would understand what I did. Either way, I dreaded that conversation.

By the time I got back, Reyes was up with Beep. Shirtless, he held her in his arms as he turned to me, and my breath caught in my chest. Here was a man so powerful, he could make the earth quake beneath us, holding something as fragile as fine china. It was charming and endearing and sexy and exquisite.

I walked to stand beside him. He grinned down at me, pride evident in his every move.

"Did you get some sleep?" I asked, placing a hand on his arm.

"Sure," he said, lying through his teeth. His sleepy eyes and unshaven face awed me for a moment.

"I'll leave you two alone," Denise said, barely audible above Katherine the Midwife's snoring. Then she turned back to me. "You have some pretty great friends."

Reyes had just set Beep in my arms when I walked over to Denise. "You saved her life," I said, my gratitude limitless. "I don't know what would've happened if you hadn't been there today."

"Yesterday."

"Yesterday," I corrected.

She bowed her head. "I'm just glad I could help." She turned and left.

"And you," I said to the ball of perfection in my arms, "I have to show you something. Coming?" I asked Reyes as Beep and I left the room.

He followed us downstairs and outside, where we sat on two lawn chairs to gaze at the stars. I told her all about the constellations, pointing out each one and reciting its name, at which point, Reyes corrected me.

Naturally, I ignored him. "And see that star?" I asked her even though she had yet to wake up. "I'm claiming that one for you. It's all yours. Its name henceforth shall be known to all the lands as Beep."

"I'm pretty sure that one's already named."

I turned to Reyes as he lay beside us. Still shirtless despite the crisp night that didn't seem to faze him.

"And I'm pretty sure it's a planet, not a star," he continued, a playful grin lifting one corner of his mouth.

"Really?" I looked at Beep. "Did you hear that? Daddy is dissing your star. And he's wearing duct tape. Duct tape is so last June."

"Venus," he said.

"Beep," I volleyed with a stern brow.

He laughed softly. "Beep it is. I found something about her very interesting."

"Just one thing?"

His grin widened. "This is interesting in a different way."

"Really?" I asked, intrigued.

"Seven pounds, thirteen ounces."

I gasped and gazed at her wide-eyed, making everything I said and did into a Broadway production. Not sure why. "Did you weigh seven whole pounds and thirteen ounces? No wonder Virginia is under the weather." Then realization dawned, his point sinking in at last. I glanced at Reyes. "Seven original gods, thirteen altogether."

He lifted a shoulder. "Just found that interesting."

"I do too. Like, bizarrely interesting."

"You seriously need to hydrate and eat something. What do you want?"

"Dude, you can make eggs into a gourmet three-course dinner. Surprise me."

"Oh, I didn't say I was going to cook. I was just offering to hold our daughter while you cooked. I'm kind of hungry, too."

I laughed.

"Eggs it is. I have some red chile potatoes made up, too."

"My mouth is watering just thinking about it." Then I bolted upright. "Coffee," I whispered, the word like a delicate snowflake on my mouth. "I can have coffee now."

It was like the heavens had opened up and God smiled down on me.

"Aren't you going to breast-feed?"

And they closed again. "Yes."

He shook his head and went to scrounge us up some grub. I sat back in despair until I really examined the situation. Maybe it would be best for Beep if she built up a tolerance to caffeine now. Start her off young.

Reyes made breakfast, cooking eggs to go on the potatoes and chile, and brought me a huge plate. I handed Beep off to him.

Watching Reyes hold her, as though she were made of glass, afraid to wrap his arms too tight, was priceless. It amazed me to see how one tiny creature had the power to turn a man made of pure, natural prowess into a bumbling mess. Not that I was much better, but we'd get there. We had all the time in the world.

12

It was a sad and disappointing day when I discovered
my Universal Remote Control did not, in fact,
control the universe. (Not even remotely.)
—MEME

We went inside after we ate, not wanting Beep to get pneumonia. The house began to stir a couple of hours later. Kit and Agent Waters called soon after with news on the possible kidnapper.

"We tracked one of the burner phones from the text messages. It was still on and we traced it to a garbage can in the alley behind Dion's on Wyoming. From there, we traced where it was purchased and they had surveillance footage. We got him. His name is Colton Ellix. There's only one problem," she said, her voice tinged with panic.

"What?"

"He died two days ago in a car accident. He was trying to outrun a squad car that, at first, wasn't even after him. He thought they were, took off. The officers pursued, but he exited at Rio Grande during rush hour traffic doing at least a hundred. He killed a pedestrian as well as himself."

My heart sank. "She's still alive, Kit. You need to look into all his holdings, anywhere he frequented, his past. Where did he grow up? Does any of his family have land?"

"You're preaching to the choir, hon. We're looking into everything, but he didn't have any property. He was renting a small house in Algodones, but we searched it and the surrounding properties. The neighbors said they hadn't seen him in a few days."

"Where did he know her from?"

"He worked for my brother," Agent Waters said. "Did a few side jobs around the house for them and watched the dogs when they were out of town."

"He had access to everything."

"Exactly."

"Okay, then, what about your brother? Did he have any property that Ellix would have known about?"

"He had some land in Rio Rancho. They were going to build a new house, but there's nothing out there." When I didn't say anything, he added, "I'll get a patrol car out there immediately."

"In the meantime," I said, speaking mostly to Kit on this one, "I'll do what I do and see what I can come up with."

"And what is it you do?" Agent Waters asked.

"What I'm hired to do," I said, being as vague as humanly possible. "We need everything you have on him."

"Already en route," she said.

"Oh, and Beep's here."

A long silence ensued and I let it all sink in. Women had been having babies for years, though. It was all the rage. Not sure why it was such a difficult thing for her to digest.

"Well, say hi for us," Kit said.

"Okay."

"Oh!" she shouted. "Beep. *The* Beep. Oh my gosh, Charley, congratulations. Are you here in Albuquerque?"

"Nope, still out here at the convent."

"You had her there?" she asked, appalled.

"Yeah. In a well. It's a long story."

"Okay. Well, congratulations to you both."

"Thanks. Get us those files."

"They'll be there in an hour."

As soon as Cookie got up and got her hair under control, I set her to find out everything she could on our potential kidnapper. They found no evidence that he really took Faris, but I knew one way to find out for sure.

I had Denise take Beep to change her and lay her down for a nap. I was going fishing and she didn't need to be around when I caught anything.

I walked into the office while Cook was making coffee. I took a deep breath, closed my eyes, and summoned Colton Ellix.

Nothing. Either I was losing my touch, or he'd already crossed. And if he was kidnapping girls, then I was pretty certain I knew which direction he went. But that was the problem. He'd crossed and I needed to know where Faris was. According to Rocket, she was still alive. I checked. But again, the good news was given with a dire warning. She wouldn't be for long. That told me she was imprisoned where she was either going to suffocate or die of dehydration. Those were the most logical reasons for why she wouldn't have long to live. He could have hurt her, however, and she could be lying somewhere with an infected wound.

There was simply no telling, but I wasn't about to give up yet.

I took off in search of Osh. Only two beings on this earth knew my celestial name, and he was one of them.

I found him in the kitchen raiding the fridge. We still had a lot of food left over from the caterers and the cookout.

"No," he said before I could even get a word out.

"But you haven't heard—"

"No," he said again, standing up with his arms full of leftovers. "And that's final."

"How do you even know I want something?"

"It's how you walk. You have a determined walk, your footsteps harder, when you want something you know you can't have. So, no." He dumped his haul onto the countertop, since we no longer had a table, and went in search of a plate and utensils.

"It's a really simple request."

His shoulder-length black hair had been slicked back, still wet from a shower. It glistened almost as much as his dark bronze eyes. I'd never seen eyes quite that color before.

"Nothing is simple with you, love."

Glancing around, afraid Reyes might be near, I stepped closer and pleaded. "It's important."

He took a plate out of the simple cabinets and turned to me. "It always is."

"I need to know my name."

He stilled, looked me up and down, then asked, "Why?"

"The man who most likely kidnapped my client's niece," I said, trying to get him to connect with Faris, let him know she had family who was worried about her, "died two days ago, and she is being held somewhere. We need to find her. She's going to die soon if we don't."

Without breaking his mesmerizing gaze, he pulled a knife out of a drawer behind him. "No." He took out two pieces of bread, preparing to make a BBQ sandwich while I struggled to come up with some leverage or a trade or something, anything, to get him to comply.

"You said when I learn my name I will understand so much more. I will have all my powers. Everything I am capable of in a few, tiny syllables."

"And what would you do with that power?"

"I need to summon the guy from hell. I can't do that right now. I need more . . . mojo."

He shook his head as he took out some lettuce and tomatoes. On BBQ? Oh well, to each his own. At least he was eating a tad healthier than I did seven days out of the week.

"The kind of mojo you would get . . . it's not like you think. And besides. It's not my gift to give. It is something you will learn with your passing. Rey'aziel would never forgive me."

"Why would you need his forgiveness for anything?"

He paused, put both hands on the counter. "We all need forgiving at some point."

"Is that why you're doing this? Is that why you're helping? You need forgiveness?"

He turned to me then, as though I'd offended him. "What do you think?"

"I think you're not really afraid of Reyes."

"No, I'm not, but if we fought and I killed him, you'd never forgive me."

"I'm not worried about you killing my husband, Osh."

"Look, we don't know what will happen when you learn it. That's what he's really afraid of. He thinks that you might ascend. That you might quit your human body and become the grim reaper for real. That you might leave him. Or worse."

"What can be worse?"

"That you will go back to your dimension. That you'll leave him forever."

"But I wouldn't do that."

"There is no way you can know what you will and won't do once you have all your powers. Or what you can and can't do. Hell, love, *we* don't even know. Not really. You're not just the grim reaper. You're also a god. The first pure ghost god. Do you have any idea what that means? It makes Lucifer and all his power look like child's play."

"Then why not give me that power and end all this? Beep is in danger because of him. Because of the hellhounds. Why not just let me fix it so we can get on with our lives?"

"It doesn't work that way, love."

I was growing more frustrated by the minute. "Why? Why doesn't it work that way?"

"Because if you will notice, you have power over souls, right? You have the very rare ability to mark them."

"Yes, and?"

"That's it. We believe that when you agreed to come here to this dimension, you had to agree to abide by the rules of this universe."

"Man, you people love rules. And what rules are those?"

He slapped his bread together, turned to me, and took a huge bite of his sandwich. Mumbling, he said, "God gave humans the power over their own lives. They have the power to make their own decisions. To make their own mistakes. To follow the dark one or not. God kicked Lucifer out of heaven but not out of the game entirely. There's still a war raging, and you have no power to stop it. Only humans can really stop the war. Can really put an end to Lucifer. But, as you are well aware, there is a lot of evil in this world. Some people will always choose to follow him. And with every human he wins, his powers grow."

"So, you are telling me I have no dominion over Lucifer? Over his demons?"

"I'm saying you cannot destroy him. Only a human born of flesh and blood can."

"I'm human. Have been since the day I was born."

He grinned, took a huge gulp of water, then leaned into me. "You're no more human than I am."

"Wait. Are you telling me that is why all the prophecies say that Beep will destroy Lucifer?"

"She's human."

"With supernatural parents. Surely, if she is going to take on Satan, she has to have some of our powers."

"She does. She will. Just like you, her powers will grow as she gets older. But she was still created from the human sides of you and Rey'aziel. She was still born a human. She will ultimately have power over things you don't and never will. You can't break the agreement the God of this universe made. It's—" He stopped to think about his next words. "It's bad form."

"So that was it. That's why our Beep is going to face off against Lucifer?"

"That surprises you? After everything you've read? After everything we've uncovered?"

"I was just hoping—"

"To find a loophole."

I lowered my head. "Yes."

Osh bit down in frustration. "Yeah, me, too. Of course, there's something else you have to consider."

"There's more?" I asked, growing disheartened.

"You have to think about what you are, how powerful you are. If you learn your name before it's time, you might not be able to control that power. You could kill everyone around you in the blink of an eye."

"So, that's a definite no to my celestial name?"

His mouth formed a thin line. "Sorry, love. I don't want to have to kill Rey'aziel. Not yet, anyway."

This time I leaned in. "I think Rey'aziel can take you."

"Every other creature in hell thought they could take me, too. They were wrong."

I stole his sandwich and took a bite. "Then I guess it's a good thing you're on our side."

A sweet lopsided grin softened his face, and I had to remember once again that he only *looked* nineteen.

I walked upstairs to check on Beep. The trip was much easier now that I wasn't harboring the little fugitive. I wasn't about to give up on talking to Colton Ellix. I had a backup plan. It scared the hell out of me, and I didn't dare tell Reyes, but it was a plan nonetheless. Reyes wouldn't see it that way, though. He'd have me drugged and locked away so I couldn't carry out my plan until it was too late to do anything about it. But at that point, Faris would be dead. I was not going to let that happen if there was even the slightest chance I could stop it.

I tiptoed up to the door to our bedroom. Quentin and Amber were in there with Beep. Quentin held her much the same way Reyes had, like a crystal football in danger of cracking should he hold her too tight, while Amber taught him how to give her a bottle, an expert after only a day.

I longed to breast-feed Beep, but I was out for so long after the whole well incident that they'd had no choice but to bottle-feed her. I didn't know if she'd take me now, but I wanted to try. Not, like, right at that moment. Quentin might get embarrassed. But soon.

I watched Amber as she interacted with my beautiful daughter. She had a particular sheen about her. Her hair shimmered in the morning sun filtering in through the curtains. Her skin sparkled. Then I realized she still had some glitter on her face from the wedding. But she was so pretty. A wingless fairy, tall and strong with delicate features and an all-knowing sense of the world. Then again, she *was* a teen. They did know everything. The thing about Amber, however, was that she approached her worldly knowledge with respect.

Spiritualist, I thought as I looked at her. It seemed appropriate. Important, even. Her deep connection to all things around her, all things in nature, gave her a sense of the bigger picture.

She giggled when Quentin let the bottle drop too low. "Up," she said, pointing skyward. He obeyed immediately, his blue eyes sparkling as bright as the smile he flashed her.

"What?" Amber asked Beep as though the little rascal had spoken to her. She giggled again. "I think so, too," she told her. "His is bright and clear as a summer day."

Wondering what she was talking about, Quentin shrugged at her.

She signed to him. "She said your aura is nice."

He raised his brows and nodded, not believing her for a minute. I, on the other hand, was beginning to wonder. Maybe Amber really was a fairy.

She looked down at Beep again and nodded. "Okay. Okay, I promise. It would only upset her anyway."

"Upset?" Quentin said with his voice, deep and soft as it was. "Who?"

Amber pressed her lips together seeming to regret something that was about to happen. "Charley," she said.

Quentin knew I was standing there. He could see my light. He gave me a sideways glance, then went back to his duties. He also knew Mo was standing by them, waving to Beep, touching her face. Mo glanced up at me, her hands clasped at her chest in adoration.

I gave her a wink, then left them alone, my curiosity burning. Amber had a powerful connection with every living thing around her, but to have a conversation with a newborn? That was novel.

I felt a coolness waft over me and turned to see that Sister Maureen, or just Mo, as she insisted on being called, had followed me out.

"Thank you," she said, using a gesture of tipping a hat. She pointed to the bedroom. "She is beautiful."

"I agree," I whispered. "My contact at the Vatican sent a report to the higher-ups there. They will be looking into your and your sister's deaths as well as the priest's, naturally."

She thanked me again. "You told them? My sister tried to save me?"

"I told them everything, Mo." I walked to her, a deep sorrow for what she went through tightening my chest. "You can cross through me."

She lowered her head. "I— I don't think he wants me."

"Mo, of course he does. If he didn't, trust me, you'd be elsewhere."

"You don't understand. I sinned beyond redemption."

"Who hasn't? You should have been at my house Halloween night my senior year of college. You ain't got nothing on a French maid with a Jason Voorhees mask. That's what forgiveness is all about, and I have a feeling God will understand. We all get lost, sweetheart. He knows. I promise."

She gave in at last and took a hesitant step forward, then another, and another until her face brightened. I could tell she saw someone, most likely a family member. She looked at me one last time, her expression full of gratitude, then stepped through.

She'd seen her father gunned down in Chicago. The memory had the weight and force of a freight train behind it. It knocked the air from my lungs as I watched a gunman roar up the street in a classic Ford. He stuck his head out the window, his arms full of the automatic weapon he carried, a tommy gun, and showered bullets down on the pedestrians.

Sadly, he was after one man, a mob boss from a rival family. But Mo's father, a baker carrying a fifty-pound sack of flour, had been gunned down in the process. He didn't even know what hit him. He had the sack on a shoulder, holding it steady with one hand, and Mo's hand in the other. They were looking at the Christmas-themed pastries he'd made in the window. Santa. Christmas trees. Stars. All brightly colored and begging to be eaten. By her and her sister, of course, who was home with a fever.

One of her father's best customers was a man named Crichton, a crime boss, though she didn't know it at the time. The shooter wanted him, but the rival family had also wanted to make a statement, to kill anyone they could on the boss's turf.

Mo jumped when the gun went off, and she watched as the man, seeing her shocked expression, aimed the gun right at her. But the sack had fallen off her father's shoulder. He'd been shot in the head, and the sack took the two shots that were meant for her head.

The car sped off, leaving the agonizing screams of the survivors in its wake. Mo stood there in a cloud of flour with a death grip on her father's hand. But the angle of his grip was wrong. She turned and saw that he was lying facedown in a pool of his own blood.

The sounds died away. The cloud settled, looking like snow all around her. And her father lay motionless. Then everything went away for a very long time. She ended up spending several months in a psychiatric hospital. Her mother, thank goodness, refused to let them perform insulin therapy on her. She saw it no less barbaric than electroshock. When the doctors told her to just sign her daughter away to them, claiming she would never come out of her stupor, she took her daughter out that very day, brought her home, and made her chicken soup.

Mo felt to the day she died it was the chicken soup that had healed her, and though she never spoke again, she did find her way back to reality, slowly at first, and over time her mother and sister helped her recover.

She and her sister grew even closer. They made up signs, their own secret language, so Mo could talk to her, and while her mother insisted she learn real sign language, she never forgot the language she and her sister made up.

Her good memories hit me, too. Her cousin's birthday party where she ended up bringing a puppy home because her cousin was angry that it wasn't a pony. So her aunt gave it to her to teach her son a lesson. The boy had a pony a month later, thus her cousin learned nothing from the experience, but that was okay, because Mo and Bea had a puppy named BB, short for Big Boy, that they served tea to and taught to sneeze on demand. And I now had irrefutable proof that dogs did indeed go to heaven, because that was who Mo saw first when she stepped through me, followed by her sister and then her parents.

It took me a moment to recover after she passed. I was so happy for her, to be in the place she belonged, with her family again. I was also sad that it took over seventy years for her to be reunited with them, but from what I understood, time didn't matter much on the other side.

Cookie texted me asking me where I was at.

Right here. Where are you?

Right here. Why can't I see you? she asked, playing along.

I descended the stairs, still walking a little slower than I'd like, and strolled through the house toward our office.

Garrett was busy in the dining room, scouring a small portion of the text that he felt might be relevant to our situation, namely being held hostage by a group of angry hellhounds. I didn't dare disturb him, but Osh did. He was in there, too, and he tossed a Cheez-It at him. Garrett didn't acknowledge the Daeva or his antics.

Osh turned toward me as I walked past, his eyes narrowed. Had he figured out my plan? How could he have? It was a freaking awesome plan. No way would anyone figure it out. Not in a million years.

"So," Cookie said when I walked in, "I have a plan."

"Me, too." I sat in my chair and snatched the file papers out of her hand.

"This is everything I could find out about Colton Ellix. He has the usual. Poor social skills. Very arrogant despite it. He was accused of stalking a girl when he was in high school, but that was long before they took that sort of thing seriously. He told the principal they'd been secretly dating, and when people found out, she accused him of stalking. The principal laughed it off, chalking it up to teenage hormones."

"What happened with the girl?"

"That's just it. She disappeared about a month later. She was never found."

"So, he's been doing this awhile."

"I don't know," she said, pointing out another report. "He has never, not once, had another report filed on him. No complaints. Just always kept to himself."

"That doesn't mean he hasn't abducted more girls."

"True, but look at this." She lifted out a spreadsheet. I was allergic to spreadsheets, so I opted not to touch it. "I have a detailed account of everywhere he's lived. The high school incident happened in Kentucky. But his family moved around a lot, mostly in close range to other relatives. I get the feeling they were mooches. Once that relative got sick of them, they moved on to the next, claiming one hardship after another until someone new took them in."

"So, not a stable home life."

"Not at all, but I've searched and searched. There were absolutely no missing persons cases in any town they lived in. At least, not while he lived there. I even widened the search to a hundred miles. Nada. And that's taking into account when he left his family. He was only sixteen when he moved in with a friend."

"Still no missing persons?"

"Not one that wasn't solved. But here's the most interesting part," Cookie said, getting excited. "Look at the girl who went missing when he was in high school."

She showed me a picture of a girl who could have been Faris's twin. "Wow."

"Right? I mean, that can't be a coincidence."

I sat back and compared their pictures. Every feature was strikingly similar.

"You know what this means?"

"Yes," she said, nodding. Then she shook her head. "Well, no, not really."

"It means he was relatively new to it. He wasn't seasoned."

Her eyes crinkled at the corners as she tried to grasp what I was getting at.

"It means that he made mistakes. Probably a lot of them. Sure, he planned this. Thought it through. Went over every detail with a fine-toothed comb, but I promise you, he screwed up."

"Of course. He had to have. Repeat killers learn how to avoid mistakes as they go, how to cover their tracks better."

"They eventually screw up. They all do, but this guy had only done this once. And since he didn't do it again, I would say he probably didn't mean to kill the girl the first time. Maybe he genuinely thought that if he could just get her alone, he would win her over. When she either cried and scared him or tried to fight him, he killed her."

"Maybe she threatened him and he panicked."

"Could be. Either way, I think the first one was an accident."

"But when the guy he starts doing odd jobs for turns out to have a daughter that looks just like his former crush?"

"Those old feelings come bubbling up and he can't resist trying to win her again. I'm just wondering which feelings came to the surface."

"What do you mean?"

"Was it the old feelings of love or was it the feelings of betrayal? I think Faris's life depends on which emotion held more sway. So what's your plan?"

"I think you should go get him and drag his ass back here."

I sat speechless. "Cook," I said at last, my voice a harsh whisper, "how did you know what I was going to do?"

"No way," she said, just as shocked as I was. "I have to admit, I was mostly kidding. I mean, go where? He's already crossed, right? Then—"

This time she sat speechless. "You are not thinking what I'm thinking."

"Bet I am," I said with a wink.

"Charley, no." She stood, scanned the halls to make sure no one was looking, then closed the door with a soft click. She sat in front of me and whispered, "Charley, you can't be serious. I mean, he's . . . there. Look at what we are dealing with here. Hellhounds at our gates. Spies in the closet. Departed trying to push you down mountains. If that's what's up here, what do you think will be down there?"

I shifted in my chair. "I didn't think of that. I haven't really worked out the particulars, but, you know, it'll be a surprise. They won't expect me."

"That's for sure. I know you said Reyes went to hell to get that rock on your finger—"

I couldn't help a glance at the orange diamond on my ring finger, the cut stunning, the color surreal.

"—but he was born and raised there. He knew the layout. How on earth are you going to waltz in, find Mr. Ellix, interrogate him, then pop back out again without you-know-who finding out?"

"Reyes?

"Satan!" she screeched.

"Sorry," I said, testy thing. "Like I said, I haven't worked out the particulars."

"So, we're in agreement. That's a crazy idea and we will never have one like that again."

"Cook, all our ideas are crazy. That's setting the bar a little high, don't you think?"

She squared her shoulders. "Yes, but they aren't all *that* crazy. You know, batshit."

"Don't worry," I said, patting her knee. "I have insider information."

"From who?"

"Garrett."

"You're going to make him go to hell again, aren't you? That poor guy."

"What? No. I'm going to tell him . . . Well, I haven't gotten that far yet. It's a work in progress, but I'll figure it out. He can tell me what I need to know."

"This is the worst idea we've had yet."

"No way. Remember the time we tried to train that ferret to steal a file from that corporate guy's office and this guy died?"

"Oh, yeah. Okay, the second worst. Who would've guessed he was that allergic to ferrets?"

"I felt bad about that. And if he hadn't swindled the life savings from half the residents at Sunny Days Retirement Center, I would've felt *really* bad."

13

So, Mr. Ellix was pretty new to kidnapping. I could only hope he hadn't tried his hands at other parts of the gig. I prayed he hadn't violated her. If so, it would be even harder for Faris to recover. But it seemed like he'd wanted that girl's approval in high school. Her love. Maybe he was seeking the same from Faris. And raping her would not get her approval or her love.

That was a bridge I'd have to cross when I came to it. Right now, I needed a baby. And a beer.

I strolled into the dining room, carrying my beautiful daughter in my arms. I'd practically had to rip her out of Gemma's but I'd called dibs in the well, so she had to give in. I couldn't get enough of her. Of holding her. Of counting her fingers and toes, marveling at how long they were. She'd been swaddled in soft pink and gray and wore a crocheted beanie on her tiny head. Her fists were curled tight and resting on either side of her nose. It was the cutest thing ever. I'd been trying to figure out who she looked more like, but alas, I'd been in denial. Of course she looked like Reyes. Thick black hair. Impossibly long eyelashes. Straight, strong nose with a curve at the tip. Full, perfectly formed mouth. She was going to knock 'em dead. Like, literally. We'd have to teach her to use her powers for good.

Garrett looked up and didn't know which item to take from me first: Beep or the beer. He decided on Beep, then the beer. Probably a wise decision. As he bounced around with her, cooing about how she was going to save the world, I scanned the piles of copied documents. Many had Garrett's handwriting on them. Since going to hell, compliments of Mr. Reyes Farrow, he'd been obsessed with the prophecies. With the past, as well, and the future, and how Beep would one day destroy the underworld.

"So," I said to him, thankful that Osh had left the building. Or at least the room. "I have a question for you."

"No."

Damn it. Osh had gotten to him.

"Then give me back my kid."

He gasped at me melodramatically for Beep's benefit, though she slept through his whole performance. "Already using your child to get what you want out of people. That's shameful." He looked down at Beep. "Your mother is like everyone at the nuthouse rolled into one. She's a nut roll. Can you say 'nut roll'?"

Oh yeah. Garrett Swopes, the tough-as-nails bounty hunter who took bullets to the chest like others took splinters, had gone bye-bye.

I sat there for-like-ever while Garrett told Beep all kinds of stories about me that were mostly untrue. He tended to exaggerate. Honestly, like I would've gone out with Greg Nusser for backstage passes to Blue Öyster Cult. Not even. I went out with Brad Stark for the backstage passes to

Blue Öyster Cult. I went out with Greg Nusser for tickets to 3 Doors Down.

Denise came to get Beep then, saying it was time for her bath and I needed to learn how to bathe her. Like I didn't know already. Sadly, it was much more complicated than I'd thought, mostly because a wet Beep was a slippery Beep. And she did not enjoy that one iota. Denise said she would grow to love bath time. Until then, I was totally investing in those noise-reduction headphones.

Next Cookie came to hold her, because God forbid she feel the touch of a mattress on her back. Then she and Gemma took turns feeding then burping her all while I sat waiting for Reyes to go do something. He was spending all his time with Beep and me. What the hell? Did men do that?

It was a nice feeling, though. All of us together like a real family, as opposed to one being held together with duct tape and hellhounds. Reyes made the most adorable dad, especially when he let her sleep on his chest as we sat in the theater and exposed her to the world of hobbits. His heat, I was sure, kept her toasty warm on the chilly autumn day.

Then, when I least expected it, Uncle Bob came in for his turn at the little doughnut. That's what he called her. She looked more like a cherry éclair to me. Reyes checked his watch and made some lame excuse about going for a run. He didn't run unless being chased. And even then, running from danger had never been his strong suit.

"Okay," I said, a little too happy about it.

He was totally meeting Angel again. I could tell. I could see it in his eyes.

Oh well. His timing was perfect. I had a girl to save, and while I'd been hoping Kit would call with good news, we had yet to receive any news at all.

I called her just to make sure they hadn't found anything. They were still checking the area where Ellix had lived and worked.

With no other choice, I went into the laundry room. People went in there only if they had actual laundry to do. They rarely just showed up for no reason. This was the most likely place I could try this thing without being interrupted. With Reyes secretly meeting my traitorous investigator, now was the perfect opportunity for me to take my plan for a test run. But I needed a little assistance first.

I summoned Angel, just to make sure I wasn't missing something before risking life and limb to break into hell.

He popped in, his expression almost bored. At least he wasn't annoyed.

"Having a secret meeting with my husband?" I asked, my voice sharp with accusation and innuendo. Mostly accusation.

"Man, *pendeja,* you think that all I do is your husband's legwork?"

"So, you're not meeting with him right now?"

"No. What the hell?"

"Then who are you meeting with?"

"I was checking out the chicks at the mall."

"Coronado or Cottonwood?"

"Coronado, why?"

"I miss the mall," I said, suddenly nostalgic for the good old days when I could shop without being ripped apart. "Do they still have that store that sells those little ice cream dots? That is some crazy shit."

"I don't know. I don't eat."

"Right, so, can I visit someone in hell?"

"Dude, I'm not saying it again. You can do anything—"

I waved an impatient hand. "I know. I know. I can do anything. You keep telling me. But really, can I? And if you're not having a secret meeting with Reyes, who is?"

"Probably that old couple he keeps talking to."

I stilled. Like, for a really long time. Long enough for Angel to look worried.

"What old couple?" I asked at last.

"The one he keeps meeting with. I don't know their names. They're old."

I stilled again as my brain struggled for an explanation. Surely . . . No, he couldn't know about the Loehrs. It was impossible. I'd met them for the first time just two days ago. "And how long has he been meeting with them?"

"Couple of months. Why? Are you two getting a divorce?"

"What?" Alarm ran rampant over my nerve endings, much like five-year-olds on a sugar rush. "Why would you say that? Did he say that?"

"No," Angel said, stepping closer. "I was just hoping you'd ditch him for someone more your age."

"I'm millions of years old."

He stepped so close, I had to look up at him, though not terribly. He was only a couple inches taller than me. "Age isn't everything."

He had a gorgeous full mouth and clear brown eyes and if he didn't stop hitting on me, I was going to—

"Wait!" he said, sobering. "Did you say 'hell'?

"Yes," I said, biting my lower lip.

"You can't just go to hell. There's a void between here and there."

"But the map is imprinted on my husband's body," I explained.

"Yes, on his. Not yours."

It was now or never. I closed my eyes. "Lucky for me, I have an excellent memory. If I don't make it back, explain to Reyes I went to find Ellix." I opened my eyes again. "But I'll make it back. Give me two minutes."

I closed my eyes again, envisioned the map on Reyes's torso, the one that would lead me through the void, and I fell into darkness.

———

Admittedly, I didn't understand how the map worked. Not until I actually used it. There were paths, almost imperceptible paths, and I wound through them, meeting obstacle after obstacle, but knowing which way to turn, which opening to take. As long as I envisioned the map, as long as I let myself fall into it with complete and total faith that it would get me where I needed to go, I flew threw the void. It felt a lot like a head rush but it was all over my body. Tingling and cold. I hadn't expected the cold. I felt a frost form over my skin, and yet I didn't have skin here.

I looked down and it cracked when I moved my hand, only to reform, creating tiny crystals that spread over me, up my neck and over my face. But I kept envisioning the map, suddenly scared to death I'd get lost in the void. Reyes would find me, though. I knew he would find me if I did go astray. But another thing I didn't count on was the audience I'd gained.

I couldn't see them, but I felt their glassy eyes watching me, their hot breath on the nape of my neck, the prickling of their teeth. Were these beings the demons that had become lost in the void? Were they still trying to make it to the earthly plane, I wondered, and if so, how long had they been there?

In a heartbeat, I was standing on solid ground, a hot wind raked over my skin. It burned like acid, and my skin started to darken. As though I had a disease, I began to turn black, the top layers of my epidermis drying and floating off in thousands of tiny flakes. Wherever the skin peeled off and flew away, my flesh glowed a bright orange, as though I were made of molten lava on the inside. And I burned. Every breath I took scorched my throat, set fire to my lungs. My eyes calcified, leaving spiderweb cracks for me to see through. It was like looking at the desolate landscape through a shattered windowpane.

I stepped forward, the sound of a thousand screams swirling around me, carried on the blistering wind like whispers of agony. The ground broke beneath me, the top layer black with the same molten orange underneath. I tried to take another step, but I was melted to the spot. I couldn't move. Then I looked harder. In between the cracks of inklike crust were people. I could see faces screaming in pain, hands reaching out to me. I gasped and paid the price as the scalding air entered me again, turning my lungs to boiling acid, eating me away from the inside out.

I looked across the landscape again and realized what I thought were boulders on the horizon were people, melting into the maelstrom. They couldn't move either. All that was visible of them was their eyes. Wide. Terrified.

Sorry.

They were all sorry for whatever it was they had done. The screams started to make sense to me. They were a chorus of pleas, apologizing for what they'd done, begging for forgiveness.

I watched as my skin peeled away, just like what was happening to those around me who had yet to melt completely. The skin drifting off them was like fireflies at night. Horrific yet magical.

I had never imagined in my wildest dreams it would be like this. I knew it would be hot. Like my husband was. I realized I was on a surface that descended for thousands of floors beneath me. That was where Reyes was born. That was where Lucifer ruled.

I wouldn't be able to get back. I was stuck in hell, and by the time Reyes found me, I would be a melted glob just like all the others.

But I wasn't like all the others. I was a bit different. This place held no sway over me. At least, that's what I chose to tell myself. I lifted my foot and forced it out of the glassy quicksand. I lifted the other and then forced the fires off me with a thought. My skin began to heal. The darkness drifted off me one last time as I stood my ground. Finding anyone in this sea of condemned souls would seem an impossible feat, but I knew exactly how to get him to me. He was now a bound spirit in the underworld. I could summon it, just like any other soul.

I bowed my head and ordered him to appear in front of me.

The melting, fiery thing that materialized looked nothing like a man, though I could see its eyes, like saucers, afraid. Sorry. Begging for forgiveness.

I decided he'd need his mouth to talk to me. I reached out and touched what I'd hoped was a shoulder. He slowly re-formed and, now that he had a voice again, screamed in agony as a pain like none other consumed him. Continuing to heal him, I waited until he was able to stop screaming long enough to talk.

Once he was partially human again, his skin blackened but remained intact. I began my interrogation.

"Where is the girl?" I yelled at him. I had to yell to be heard above the wind and the screams.

He looked confused at first, then surprised. "You're here for her?"

"Where is Faris? Where did you take her?"

"You aren't here to get me out of this?"

"No," I said. I should have lied, but I didn't want him to feel any hope when Faris damned sure didn't. I didn't want him to have that luxury.

His shoulders collapsed the moment he realized he was going back.

"Where is she?" I asked, keeping my fingertips on him.

He glowered at me, his blistering features contorting under the heat. "Why should I tell you? What more can you do to me?"

I took my hand away and he cried out in agony as the lava took him again. What most people didn't know was that hell is only a temporary punishment. You simply ceased to exist after, but you burned for a limited amount of time, the amount depending on what you did to warrant a trip to the basement. After replacing my hand, giving him a small measure of relief, I leaned in. "Because I can make this last forever."

He knew he had no recourse. No bargaining chip. It was agony for a little while or agony forever. He decided to try to get in my good graces.

He lowered his head. "At my house. She's at my house."

"Liar," I said, my voice a husky version of the original, mostly because my throat had been burned to a crisp. "We've looked."

"There is a room. The fireplace pulls out. It's an old panic room. Solid concrete. She's in there." When he looked back at me, his face was full of remorse. "I didn't mean to kill her. Olivia Dern. It was an accident."

The girl from high school. "And what about Faris?"

"She was my second chance. A sign that I could make amends. I didn't hurt her. I swear. She's Olivia born again. Check her birthday. You'll understand."

I had no idea what he was talking about, nor did I care. I only wanted out of the literally godforsaken place.

When I let go, he lunged for me, but it was too late. He'd solidified to the spot and began melting back into the ground whence he came.

"Please take me with you!" he yelled, but his voice was distant and intermingled with the thousands of others.

I stepped back away from him and turned full circle. It was like an entire planet of just melting bodies. But underneath the melted faces at my feet, through the glowing glass, I saw the huge black eyes of demons. The razor-sharp teeth. The thick shiny scales.

They were coming for me. I had trespassed and they were swimming up through the bodies to get to me. I stumbled back and fell, the heat of the molten floor beneath me scorching the skin off my palms. Scrambling back onto my feet, I saw one of them. He walked straight for me, his skin blackening just like mine, his flesh molten just like mine. But this was no demon. He walked purposefully, his gait primal, as smooth as a panther's.

I stood transfixed, unable to believe my eyes until Reyes was upon me, his hand around my throat.

He didn't talk. He didn't say a word. He simply held me by my throat as fury surged through him. Even here I could feel it. His emotions. His palpable anger.

Then we were in the void. He'd never taken his eyes off me, and still didn't, even as creatures tried to follow us through the void. Reyes was too fast. His knowledge of the void now vast.

The blackened parts of his face faded and the frost was back. A thin layer of ice covered his mouth, spiked his dark lashes.

Then his heat blasted across my skin again and he thrust me against the nearest wall.

I didn't move. Instead, I allowed him to catch his breath. To remember who I was and what I meant to him. If he couldn't, if the beast he was in hell had come back in full force, I would have no choice but to disable him. But this was Reyes who held me. In all his glory. In all his rage. It was still Reyes.

He glared at me, his dark brown irises shimmering dangerously. He was trying to get his emotions under control. I let him. I gave him all the leeway he needed. His wide chest heaved and he moved at last, leaned into me, tightened his grip on my neck, but not enough to cause me discomfort. Quite the opposite. But he was too frustrated, too enraged to take advantage of the raw power rushing through his veins. He growled, a low and guttural sound, then hit the wall by my head with such force, he dented the drywall and broke a stud. It cracked loudly.

That was when I realized we had an audience. Osh stood near me as though to stop Reyes should he take it too far. Garrett wasn't far behind him. Angel stood off to the side by the washer, his face averted. Had he ratted me out? No matter. I'd gotten what I went in for.

Last but not least was Cookie. She stood, fear radiating out of her in waves. Fear for me and for Reyes. He could easily do something he would regret later. She didn't want that. Not for either of us.

The soft sounds of a baby breathing drifted to us and we both turned. Cookie was holding Beep, her sweet face like a salve on the stinging wounds we'd rubbed raw. Reyes's biting emotions shuddered through him. He turned from me, from us all, as wetness slipped past his lashes.

"We're okay," I said, placing a hand on Osh's arm to reassure him. "We're okay." I stepped to Reyes, and in a lightning-quick move, he grabbed hold of my arm. Not to hurt or scare me, but to slow time with me. In here, we could talk with no one the wiser.

"Why?" he asked, his voice hoarse.

"I needed information from that man."

"For a case?" he scoffed, and turned from me in disbelief. "You risked everything for a case?"

"I knew I wasn't in any danger."

He was in front of me at once. He dug a hand into my hair, his actions almost cruel. "You are a fool if you actually believe that."

I raised my chin. His opinion of me, of what I did, was a little more than I wanted to bear sometimes. "You keep telling me I'm a god. Why, if that's true, would I be in any danger?"

He let go and stepped back, and I understood.

"I wasn't in danger, but my body was. Is that it? If I accidentally brought one of those demons back with me and it killed my corporeal body, you think I will leave."

"I don't think, Dutch. I know. You'll have no choice. But it wasn't just that."

"Then what? I truly want to understand."

He bit down, welding his teeth together as he tried to explain. "I didn't want you to see . . . my world. I never wanted you to see where I came from. And I damned sure didn't want you to see me in that place. To see the monster."

How ridiculous and vulnerable he could be over the craziest things. I wanted to kick him. But mostly I wanted to rip off his clothes because that was the sexiest thing I'd ever seen. Reyes walking through smoke and ash, literally made of fire, his body startlingly powerful, his allure breathtaking.

His lids narrowed as he tried to read my emotions. Or maybe he'd already read them and thought he misunderstood. Stepping closer, braced both hands on the wall beside my head. Then he bent until his mouth was inches from mine. "You really are a god," he said, in awe of me when he had no idea the depths of my astonishment, of my awe of him.

"And you really were created in the fires of sin."

"You're repulsed?"

"Oh yes," I said, curling my fingers into the hem of his shirt and coaxing him closer. "Completely."

His reaction spoke volumes. He'd actually expected me to be disgusted. As if. Did he truly not understand the measure of his magnetism?

He warred with what to do next. He wanted to be furious. He wanted to rant and rave. But I could think of much better things to do.

Almost reluctantly, he looked to the side. "It's coming."

Time. He meant time was about to bounce back. Even a seasoned expert like Reyes could hold it for only so long.

My reaction to his world had thrown him. He glanced at each of the faces around us, then dropped his hands and strode out of the small room. I wanted to call him back. Mostly because I was in love with him beyond my wildest imaginings and I hated, *hated,* to see him in pain. But partly because in all the upheaval, I forgot to tell him something I'd learned while in his world: Lucifer was no longer in hell. He was here. He was on earth.

Cookie and I called Kit the moment I came to my senses. We sat in my office, then stood, then paced, each of us taking turns holding Beep. Agent Waters had argued with me at first. Furious Kit was wasting her time with me, he informed me every chance he got that they'd already gone through the house with a fine-toothed comb. I told him to quit being an ass and go save his niece.

The house was in Bernalillo and they were in Albuquerque, so Kit sent a squad car over there while they rushed that way. Cookie and I waited with bated breath. Gemma came in and waited with us. Then Denise took Beep to change her and brought her back. Still no call.

When the pediatrician arrived for the checkup, I was grateful for the distraction. We went upstairs and he asked over a thousand questions. Thankfully, Denise stuck around to help.

Reyes walked in, his expression sheepish yet stubborn after his brusque exodus earlier, and we watched as the doctor stripped her down—Beep, not Denise—for the checkup, and while she didn't like being naked one bit, it gave me a chance to look her over, too. I counted her toes and kissed the bottoms of her feet while Reyes tested the fine layer of hair that covered her body. We both marveled once again at how perfect she was.

"How strange," the doctor said in a thick Middle Eastern accent, and we both snapped to attention at his observation.

"What?" Reyes asked, his tone sharp.

"Oh, there's nothing to be concerned about yet, but this little sweetheart has dextrocardia."

I gasped. "Is it serious?"

"No," he said with a soft chuckle. "It simply means her heart is on the right side of her chest."

Right. I knew that; he just took me by surprise.

"I've never actually seen it." He poked around a little more aggressively, thoroughly perturbing his patient. "And it looks like all of her organs could be a mirror image. I'll have to order some tests to be sure."

"But she's okay?"

"Sure seems to be. We'll know for certain when you bring her in. How does tomorrow morning look?"

We both stood there, unsure of what to say.

"Tomorrow morning is great," Denise said for us.

"And she has a very unusual birthmark."

"Birthmark?" I asked, peering closer.

He used the light from his otoscope to examine a mark on Beep's left shoulder. "It's very light. I've never seen anything like it."

I had nothing. Both Reyes and I stood staring down at our daughter. So light, they were almost invisible to the naked eye were the tiny curves and lines that made up Reyes's tattoo. The map to the gates of hell. The key to Hades.

"Gosh, that is strange," I said, stunned.

"But everything checks out A-OK. You had a good midwife," he said. "I'll just need a sample of her blood, and I'll get out of your hair."

"You need my midwife's blood?"

"A sense of humor. That's good. You're getting around well, I see."

"Oh yeah, I'm a fast healer."

"Good. Good to know. My office will contact you with the results of the blood test, but I'm sure she's fine. Healthy, strong lungs, good heartbeat even if it is on the other side of her chest. I'll have my staff dig up some literature for you. It will be there when you arrive tomorrow." He took out a blood-collecting kit with a lancet and a small glass vial. "Just call my office around nine. Peggy will let you know when to bring her in."

"Thank you," I said, still taken aback by the markings.

The doctor took some blood from Beep's heel. And I thought she'd been pissed before. The minute he was finished, I wrapped her up and offered her a bottle. She'd had to be given one since I was out so long, and I didn't feel now was the time to try to switch her to a diet of Danger and Will Robinson. Maybe when she was a little less agitated.

After we bade the doctor adieu, I turned and gaped at Reyes. "How—? Why—?"

"I don't know," he said, indicating Denise with a nod.

"Right," I said under my breath. That would have to wait. For the moment, I satisfied myself with grilling Denise on dextrocardia.

"It only means there's a higher chance that she will have a congenital defect," she said. "Dextrocardia is, by definition, a congenital defect, but it doesn't mean there is anything wrong with her. Everything so far checks out perfectly normal. She just needs to be tested to be sure."

"Denise," I said as we headed back downstairs, "we can't. I told you." I looked at Reyes. Watched as concern hardened the lines of his face. "What do we do?"

"I don't know yet," he said.

"I'll take her in," Denise said.

I stopped on the stairs and looked up at her, as she was a couple of steps behind me. "Denise, Beep is in as much danger from the beasts I told you about as we are." After all, the prophecies that foretold of Lucifer's downfall were about Beep. She was his main threat. Not me. Not Reyes.

"Why—?" she began, then stopped herself. "Charley, she has to be tested. Dextrocardia raises her chances of other complications dramatically. We can't just—"

"We'll figure it out," Reyes said, ushering me down the stairs. But I could tell he was as worried as I.

When we got to the bottom, I took him aside as quickly as I could and said, "I meant to tell you, I found out something while I was . . . you know."

He bristled at the reminder of my trip to his hometown.

"Your dad isn't home."

After waiting for Denise to pass, he asked, "Then where is he?"

"From what I gathered, he's here."

It took a few seconds for him to respond. "If he's on this plane, we need to move quickly."

"We can't leave yet. Beep needs to be tested first. She could have a serious medical condition, and that's something we'll need to know no matter where we go."

He lowered his voice even further. "If they find her, it won't matter how healthy she is. She'll be dead before they can run a single test."

"Then they can't find her," I said, imploring him.

Before the hour was up, I was back to pacing. I couldn't sit still. Couldn't stop worrying about the tests Beep needed. Couldn't stop marveling at the map imprinted beneath her skin. Couldn't stop hoping they'd find Faris. Reyes paced, too, only he did it outside, his mind racing for a solution. Unless he planned on buying all the equipment the doctor would need, we would have to take Beep in for tests. We had no choice. Our escape-to-an-island-paradise plan would have to wait.

The phone rang at last and I lunged for it.

"She's alive!" Kit said before I even said hello.

I gave Cookie a thumbs-up and she rose out of her chair in elation— carefully, as she was holding Beep.

"Just barely, but we'll take it. Charley," she said, her voice cracking. "I just— I don't know where to begin. Jonny is very . . . appreciative of your help. We both are."

"Tell him it was my pleasure. And by the way, you realize he's still in love with you, right?"

The phone went silent for a moment before she spoke again. "He— He was never in love with me."

"You keep telling yourself that."

"Charley, I—"

"Celebrate. Take him to dinner tomorrow to celebrate finding his niece. If ever there was a reason . . . See where it goes from there."

"He'll be celebrating with his family, I'm sure."

"And you are a part of it."

"I have to know. How?"

Though I knew what she was talking about, I said, "That's a mighty broad question."

"How did you know where she would be?"

"I promise to tell you someday. But today, it's kind of a tender subject around these parts."

"I'm sorry, hold on. What?" she said, speaking to someone else. "Okay, I have to go, Charley. Thank you again."

"My pleasure. Give her a hug for me. And just so you know, he didn't— She wasn't violated. Not in that way."

A relieved sigh, then, "Thank you."

"Oh, one more thing. There's something about Faris's birthday and the girl he killed while he was in high school. Some kind of connection." After a moment of silence, I said, "Kit?"

"Charley, how did you know?" she asked.

"Know what?" I asked, suddenly intrigued.

"Faris was born the same day Olivia Dern went missing. The exact same day."

"That's what he meant. He took that as a sign that—"

"Who?" she asked.

Since Colton Ellix died two days ago, I couldn't exactly tell her the truth. Not yet, anyway. "My . . . gardener."

After another moment of silence, she said, "One of these days, you are going to tell me everything."

"Okeydokey. Go. Celebrate."

I hung up, then almost collapsed onto the couch we'd stuffed into the corner for just such occasions.

"Charley," Cookie said, "you realize you have to tell me everything. And I do mean everything."

"You sound like Kit."

"Charley Davidson—"

"I will. I promise. Once I absorb it all myself, I'll tell you. I don't know if you'll believe it or not, though."

"I've seen too much not to." She turned her attention to Beep. "Yes, I have," she said in an animated voice. "I've seen enough to make a grown man wet himself. And they don't wear diapers like you do."

I couldn't wait to tell her about the *birthmark*. That'd keep her up at night.

14

I HAVE COMPLETELY MASTERED THE RIGHT WAY
OF DOING EVERYTHING WRONG.
—T-SHIRT

Garrett, Osh, and I sat around the reassembled kitchen table and gazed down at little Miss Beep. She was trying to decide if she wanted to fuss or catch some Z's. It was a hard decision for most of us. She made baby sounds. Nothing on earth made sounds like that. They were a ruse. A ploy. A way to get adults to fall in love.

They worked really well.

But the reason our little moppet was lying on the table—on a blanket, of course—was so that we could see the birthmark. Or, more accurately, so that I could show them the birthmark. Barely visible, she had the lines, the map to the gates of hell, marked on her body just like her father.

"How?" I asked no one in particular. "I mean, those were put on Reyes when he was forged in hell. How did they transfer to Beep?"

Nobody answered. It was a fairly rhetorical question anyway.

And Reyes wasn't there to give his opinion. He'd been pacing outside, but I lost sight of him a while earlier. He was probably off dragging hellhounds around. I bet they hated that. And he was probably still mad at me. So, I went to hell. I'd needed information. That was the quickest way to get it. The *only* way to get it. And because of it, we saved a girl's life. Sure, it was dangerous, but that was my middle names. I'd assumed he was used to that by now. Figured he even liked that about me. Apparently not.

Of course, the thought of a family reunion right here on earth was the most likely culprit of his agitation. Coming face-to-face with one's evil father after centuries apart was enough to put anyone in a bad mood.

Speaking of bad moods, with all the unwanted attention Beep was getting, even she'd started leaning toward the fussy end of the spectrum, so I wrapped her up like a burrito, warmed up a bottle of breast milk I'd collected earlier, and walked around the house crooning and crowing about this and that. It was like dinner theater.

Uncle Bob had taken Quentin back to school in Santa Fe, and Cookie and Amber left, too. Amber had school in the morning, much to her chagrin, and Cookie wanted to get some shopping done. She'd been cooking quite a bit and bringing it out to us.

I thought about cooking once.

Beep and I walked around the house as she ate, partly to look out the windows in the hopes of seeing her daddy. And partly to work off some nervous tension. I'd hurt him by going to hell, and that was only the half of it. We wandered into the laundry room and I explained the washer and dryer as best I could. I turned on the dryer and put her on it. The vibrations lulled her to sleep again.

"Oh, no you don't," I said, picking her back up again. "You have to be burped. If I don't burp you, I'll get arrested by the burp police, and then—"

I stopped midsentence. The wall Reyes broke was adjacent to the locked closet door. He must've triggered a latching mechanism when he broke the stud, because it stood slightly ajar.

"At last," I said as we walked to it. "Are we ready for this?" I asked her.

She didn't reply.

I slid open the heavy door. It creaked along rusted tracks. It was a pocket door, which explained why it hadn't opened when we pushed on it, but as tall and narrow as it was, it had to be at least three inches thick. I peeked inside and, wow, was I not impressed.

"This is it?" I asked Beep. After fumbling in my pocket for my phone, I turned the flashlight on and took a closer look. It was a tiny round room, dusty and cobwebbed. Nothing special about it. The ceiling formed an arch overhead, so that was almost interesting. But there were no shelves. No nooks for storage. No dead bodies. Nada.

"What on earth is this for?" Finding no light switch, I stepped inside and, only a little fearful we wouldn't get the door open again as I'd seen how it latched, slid it closed. Then we stood there. Waited. Turned in a circle. Then I opened the door, utterly disappointed.

"Okay, then," I said, stepping out and giving it another once-over. "This is rather useless in the grand scheme of things."

I turned to leave and came face-to-face with everyone left in the house. They all stared at us with mouths slightly agape.

"What?" I asked, wiping at my face, then smoothing my hair down. "What?"

"Your light," Angel said at last. "It completely disappeared when you were in there."

"Really?" I turned back to give it another once-over. "That's odd, right?"

Osh stepped to the closet. "You have no idea. Your light is eternal. It's constant and boundless. Nothing can stop it from being seen from a thousand different planes."

"I can't see it," I said, my hand raised.

"Try it again, but be careful," he said, suddenly untrusting of the tiny compartment. It did seem a tad ominous. Maybe it was a portal to hell. Or a broom closet. I always felt broom closets were a little shady. Why would a broom need its own closet?

I stepped inside and closed the door again. Then I waited for the signal. Not that we'd decided on one, but surely they'd let me know when they were ready for us to come out. I was beginning to think we'd been punked when I heard a male voice from behind me.

"Hey, pumpkin."

Goose bumps erupted across my skin as I turned. "Dad!" I yelled, and threw my free arm around his neck.

He laughed and hugged me back, being careful not to squish my package. Then he looked down at said package, his eyes glistening. "My God," he said, his expression full of pride.

"Dad, how are you here?" I asked.

He sobered and smiled at me. "This is kind of like a safe room. No one from outside can see us in here. They would literally have to come inside this room to hear anything we say, even the departed, and you would see them."

"Really? This is the coolest room ever. But what happened?"

He smoothed my hair back. "No time for that, pumpkin. If you don't come out soon, that group out there is likely to rip the door off its hinges."

"Oh, you're right. Hold on."

I cracked open the door. Everyone was still standing in awe.

"I'll just be a minute."

Osh grew suspicious. It was like he didn't trust me.

"Why? What are you doing?"

"Reflecting."

I closed the door then turned back to my father. I touched his face and his cool skin reminded me exactly what state he was in.

"Now, what happened? Who killed you?"

"First, you have to know, there are spies."

"I know. I totally busted one. She was living in my closet."

"There are more."

I knew that. I'd known for a while. "Duff."

"Yes."

"More?"

"A couple on the lawn, I think. It's like the Cold War here."

"Wait, are you a spy for the good guys?"

He grinned. "I'm a spy for you, honey. I just had no idea." He glanced down at Beep again. "I had absolutely no idea."

"Okay, but really, who killed you?"

He shook his head. "I don't want you involved in any of that. You're too important. She's too important."

"Dad."

"Charley."

"Dad."

"Charley."

"Dad. And, yes, I can do this all day." I had taken hold of his arm. "And just so you know, you can't disappear as long as I'm holding on to you."

"Really?" he asked, surprised.

I raised my brows.

He turned away, as though unable to look me in the eye. "You know, you always amazed me. From the day you were born, you were different. I knew it, too."

"Dad," I repeated. We didn't have the time for a stroll down memory lane. I wanted to know who had killed my father, and said father was darned sure going to tell me.

"Just give me a sec, hon. You have to understand what happened before."

"Okay." I leaned back against the wall and bounced Beep, but didn't let go of his wrist. I didn't think I ever could again. I laced my fingers through his and waited for him to say what he had to.

It took him a moment. Tears swelled between his lashes. "Once you started helping me solve crimes, people noticed. They didn't know about you, of course, but somehow a few of the cops figured out I was getting . . . outside help. One was dirty. As dirty as they come. He told a businessman whose payroll he was on. As a result, that man became very interested in me."

"All this from my help solving crimes?"

"Yes. And no." He lowered his head, completely embarrassed. "You helped in other ways. Ways you were unaware of."

"Like what?"

"Charley, I wasn't always— I mean, I made mistakes. I— I got in over my head with a situation."

This time I lowered my head. "Did it involve the racetrack at Ruidoso Downs?"

"How did you know?"

I shrugged. "You changed after that. When you got home from your camping trip, you were devastated."

"Ah, yes, you can feel people's emotions, can't you?"

I nodded.

"Why didn't you tell me?"

"Like I wasn't enough of a freak."

"Charley, if there is one thing you are not, it's a freak. But that doesn't explain how you figured out what happened that weekend."

"It took me a few years to piece together, but I realized you'd gone to Ruidoso. There's only three things in Ruidoso: shopping, camping, and gambling. So, what happened?"

He lowered his head once more, embarrassed. "I had what we call in the gambling business a sure thing."

"But you weren't a gambler."

"Normally, no, but I got this tip. The guy said it was all set up."

"The sure thing."

"Yes. And I'd seen him win a fortune once based on a similar tip. So, I bet everything."

"And you lost it all."

"In the blink of an eye."

"Then how did you open the bar? I thought you did that with your savings?"

"That's where you come in. This businessman offered to pay me double what I lost for one name."

I gasped teasingly. "You used me."

"Charley, it's not funny."

"Right. Sorry. But, Dad, really, it's not that bad."

"It is, actually, and it gets worse."

"Oh," I said, understanding. "You gave him the name, and now you were indebted to him, only he knew you had a secret weapon."

"Yes. I led him to believe I had a confidential informant."

"What happened to the first guy? The first name you gave him?"

He bit down, embarrassed to say. "He was never found," he said at last.

"I'm sorry, Dad."

"As you can imagine, I retired soon after. I told him I no longer had access to my CI."

The gravity hit me. "Dad, he could have killed you."

A sad smile thinned his lips. "He did, actually."

That time, I gasped for real. "What happened?"

"He got himself in a bind, needed my informant."

"And you refused. So, your death was my fault, too. Just like mom's."

"Charley, you can't honestly say that about your mother. Not after what you've just been through."

He was right. Beep was worth the risk that went hand in hand with pregnancy.

"And my death was entirely my fault. I was never perfect."

"You were in my eyes." I leaned forward. "And you still are."

"Charley, I used you for years to advance my career. That doesn't exactly qualify me for Father of the Year."

"We work with what we got. Do you think I resent you in any way? I would do the same today. You never placed me in any danger. You caught bad guys that I led you to. We were doing a good thing."

"Yes, bad guys that I asked you to lead me to. That alone placed you in danger."

"Do you blame Uncle Bob for what he's doing? Special Agent Carson? Or her FedEx?"

"No, but you're older now, hon. It's different. You know what you're getting yourself in for most of the time. I just let you advance my career while leaving you completely in the dark as to what was at stake. And then there's the whole Denise issue."

"What about her?"

"I should have been harder on her. I shouldn't have let her treat you that way. But I could sense her fear. She believed, Charley. She always believed in you. For her, that *was* the problem."

"Denise and I are finding our way."

"And I want to thank you for that. You have a bigger heart than people give you credit for."

"Right?" I said in complete agreement. "Now, who actually pulled the trigger? And who is this businessman?"

"No. And I mean it. Your uncle is closing in, thanks to you and that anonymous tip. You've done enough." He smiled down at the little princess, and a soft squeak sounded.

"Uh-oh," I said to her, unlacing my hand to pat her mouth with the blanket. "Someone burped."

"Don't worry, Beep," Dad said. "What happens in the closet stays in the closet."

The door slid open then, and Spanky and the Gang stood in the exact same positions as when I'd closed it.

"We were getting worried," Angel said.

I turned, but Dad was gone. I could smell him on my clothes and on Beep's blanket.

Osh stepped inside and turned full circle. "Seriously, what the hell?"

"I don't know, but we need to have a powwow."

This time I hunted Denise down and gave her Beep for a while. She was more than happy to take her while Osh and I went hunting.

We went into the office, where it was quieter. No need to alarm Denise.

It didn't take us long to find him, since I could summon him right to me. I did so and immediately grabbed his wrist so he couldn't vanish.

"Wh-what's going on?" Duff asked, his eyes wide behind the glasses.

"How does this work?" I asked him.

"Wh-what?"

"And you can stop stuttering now," I added. "How does this work? Who do you report to?"

He looked down at his wrist, then back at me. "You don't know what it's like down there," he said, vying for the sympathy angle. "You are burned alive."

"I know. I visited recently."

He had the decency to look shocked.

"Don't pretend you didn't know that."

"I haven't been able to hang around much," he said, scowling at Angel. "Rey'aziel caught on. Sent the kid to babysit. Can't turn around without him watching me."

I turned to Angel. "Is that what all that was about?"

Angel shrugged. "We're also watching a few more."

"We?"

"Rey'aziel has a whole army of spies watching other spies."

"Why didn't he just tell me?" I asked, appalled. "I thought this was something horrible like you two were trying to figure out which asylum to have me locked in once Beep was born."

He snickered. "We decided that months ago."

Garrett walked in then. "Got him," he said, carrying a tablet. "Duff Newman, executed for killing a woman and her daughter in 1987."

Osh tsked. "Duff. That's not very nice."

Focusing on Duff again, I said, "Once more with feeling. Who do you report to?"

"If I tell you, he'll send me back."

"To hell?" I asked. "You're going back there anyway, sport. It's hot. You might want to plan for that. Take an ointment."

Osh spoke up again. "Why let him live at all? I could use dessert."

"You sure?"

"Positive." That wolfish grin was back, and Duff tried to jerk out of my grip, suddenly terrified.

"Wait," I said; then I turned to Angel. "No really, why not just tell me?"

He lowered his head. "You're too reckless."

"What?" I asked, completely offended.

"You're too careless," he said, unable to meet my gaze. "You risk too much for people you barely know. We couldn't—"

When he didn't continue, I finished for him. "Trust me. You couldn't trust me."

He didn't answer. He didn't have to.

"Well, that little decision almost cost me my life, thank you very much."

"Sorry."

Fury overrode every other emotion as I marked Duff. One thought was all it took, and the symbol appeared instantly. "He's all yours," I said to Osh.

The Daeva walked up to Duff, who decided right then to fight. He managed to slip from my grasp, but Osh had him around the throat in the blink of an eye. He pushed Duff against the wall, the exact same way he had with Sheila.

Osh squeezed Duff's jaw, doing some Vulcan mind meld thing to get him to be still. He froze as though he could no longer move.

"It's better than being burned alive," he told Duff.

Apparently, Duff didn't agree. He shook his head, fear consuming him. "Not this," he pleaded, and I couldn't help but wonder why. I'd been to hell. Why was this worse?

"I wonder if those people you killed said that."

Before Duff could answer, Osh braced a hand above the wall over Duff's head, pressed against him like a lover, then covered Duff's mouth with his own. And while the soul-sucking thing with Sheila had been hot, this was even more so. I felt a warm rush wash over me. It pooled in my abdomen as Osh kept a hand locked around Duff's throat, his mouth on his. Then he pulled back, just a little, just like before, and the light, a light blue glow, shone between them. Duff splayed his fingers and stared at the ceiling as Osh took everything he had to offer. Slowly, Duff dissipated, cracking and drifting away until there was nothing left.

Osh pressed his forehead against the wall, his chest heaving, his muscles weak, while I stood in a convent, in a house of God, with the most impure thoughts I'd had in a while. Boy-on-boy action.

"I need a shower," I said, suddenly warm.

Osh glanced over his shoulder at me. "You know what goes well with shish-kebabed Duff?"

"I don't want to know," I said as I started for the door.

"Cherry pie," he called out after me, laughing softly. "Tart cherry pie."

"Asshole." He knew how sexy that was. He was freaking doing it on purpose.

After about five seconds in the shower, I started groaning. Out loud.

I really did need one, if for no other reason than to work the kinks out of my muscles. I couldn't help but wonder where Reyes had gone off to. Maybe he was talking to that older couple again. Angel couldn't have meant the Loehrs. They weren't that old. Angel made the couple Reyes was talking to sound ancient. And he couldn't possibly know about the Loehrs. I'd only just found out about them myself, and he'd told me months ago he didn't want to contact them.

I turned off the water and wrapped a towel around me. Then I did the all-important phone check. No calls. No texts. Probably a good thing.

Hoping Reyes was okay and wondering if he would suck a guy's soul like Osh so I could watch—because, day-um—I wiped steam off the mirror and was just about to blow-dry my "in bad need of a trim" locks when my phone chimed.

The fact that it could have been Reyes made me a little too enthusiastic. I knocked the phone off the counter and watched as it headed right toward the toilet.

Without blinking, I slowed time, fetched it, then let time bounce back into place.

Being a god definitely had its perks.

Swiping a finger across the screen, I brought up the text and my world fell apart at the seams.

Do not move.

The first line of the text read like it'd been sent by some harmless creep playing a joke. That wasn't the part that slid the world out from under me.

Do not say anything.

The sender was unknown, a blocked number.

Do not alert your friends to this message.

Dread crept up my spine to settle at the nape of my neck.

Control your emotions or Ms. Kowalski and her daughter die.

Whoever was sending the texts knew enough about me and my friends to know that any spike in emotion could summon the cavalry. Not many people knew that.

But the next text contained an image, and the dread scratching at my neck exploded, awakening every nerve ending in my body as a sharp tingling sensation washed over me. My knees gave beneath me, and I sank onto the side of the bathtub.

They—whoever they were—had Cook and Amber. The picture showed them sitting beside each other in a dark room, a harsh light brightening only their features, their hands tied behind their backs, their mouths gagged, their faces dirty. There was a newspaper in their laps. I didn't bother trying to make out the date. No one would go to that much trouble without actually having the day's newspaper.

I couldn't take my eyes off them. They sat leaning in to each other. While Amber stared blankly into the camera, clearly in shock, Cookie looked up at her abductor, her brows scrunched in fear for her daughter's life. Her shoulder was in front of Amber as though she were trying to protect her. And then I saw why. The assailant, at least one of them, had a gun. I could barely see it in the upper right corner of the image. And it was pointed straight at Amber's head.

I covered my mouth with a hand to suppress an astonished sob as another text slipped underneath the picture.

I'm sure we have your attention. Calmly walk out the door, get in your car, and
go to the abandoned gas station at the bottom of the mountain, just before the turn

off in San Ysidro. If anyone follows you, if you alert anyone to the situation, they are
dead. You have ten minutes.

I dragged on my dirty clothes and burst through the door. Speed-
walking as normally as possible, I pressed my mouth together hard and
forced a smile when I saw Garrett come out of the kitchen.

He slowly made his way to the stairs, pausing to ask, "You okay?"

My keys to Misery, my cherry red Jeep Wrangler, were hanging on a
hook by the front door. I hadn't driven her in eight months, but Garrett
made a point to take her to work about twice a month to keep things
running smooth. Swallowing hard, I nodded and walked back to the
kitchen, waiting for him to ascend the stairs. The minute he was out of
sight, I rushed forward, grabbed the keys off the hook, and flew out the
front door.

The sun hung low on the horizon as I ran for Misery. I hopped in and
started her on one try. Backing out of the drive while trying to seem nonchalant was excruciating, but I didn't want to alarm anyone, so I took
my time. Hopefully, if anyone looked out, they'd think I was just moving my car to a different location. Dying inside. The fear coursing through
me was so powerful, I thought I would be sick. Clearly, I was not sup-
pressing my emotions, and yet Reyes was nowhere to be found. He must
have been angrier with me than I thought, but even at his angriest, he
would never leave me hanging. I couldn't imagine why he wasn't mate-
rializing beside me, but I was both relieved and concerned.

I raced down the mountain, taking the 25 mph curves at 75.

A motorcycle appeared out of nowhere, the driver waving me to
pull over. I ignored him and pressed the gas pedal until it would go no
farther.

He pulled ahead of me, missing an oncoming car by inches, and waved
again. I stared straight ahead. Was he one of the abductors? Two more
motorcycles appeared in my rearview, speeding up behind me. I consid-

ered slamming on my brakes to take them out, but I didn't want to lose the time. It took more than ten minutes to get down the mountain from where we were. I didn't have a second to spare.

Just as the last curve came into view, the gas station only minutes from there, the motorcycle swerved in front of me. My reflexes took over. I jerked Misery to the right and didn't have enough space to fix the overcorrection. I went headfirst into a shallow ravine, bouncing over the bumpy drop until crashing to a stop at the bottom. I flew forward, my seat belt biting into my shoulder as my head hit the steering wheel.

Then someone was knocking on the window, jerking on the door handle. I tried to restart Misery, to no avail.

"Charley, damn it!"

I finally turned and saw Donovan. Biker Donovan. *My* Donovan. It didn't make sense. Why would he be here? I looked back at the other two, and sure enough, his sidekicks, Eric and Michael, were also with him. They had lived beside the abandoned asylum Rocket grew up in. Artemis, my guardian Rottweiler, had originally been Donovan's. He'd led a rough life—most bikers did—but he had a heart of gold. If not for that whole bank-robbing gig, he would still have been in my life in one form or another.

"Move!" he shouted through my window a split second before he drove a leather-clad elbow through it. He reached in, unlocked the door, and dragged me out of Misery kicking and screaming. Eric, the one I'd always referred to as the Greek prince, was right there, helping him.

"What are you doing?" I yelled, pushing them off me once I'd gained my footing. "I have to go! They have Cookie and Amber!"

Donovan held his palms toward me, gesturing for me to calm down. "Who has them?"

My phone rang before I could come back with a biting reply. I pulled it out of my pocket, my hands shaking uncontrollably. It was from Cookie's number.

"Cookie!" I screamed, pressing a palm against Misery for support. "What happened? What do they want?"

"Charley, what are you talking about? What's wrong? Is Beep okay? Oh my God, did something happen to Beep?"

"No, what? Where are you? You've been abducted. You and Amber."

"What?" Cookie screeched. She dropped the phone, and I heard footsteps, a frantic voice, then more footsteps. "Charley, damn it," she said when she picked up the phone again, panting. "If this is a joke—"

"Cook, you haven't been abducted? You're— You're okay?"

"Of course we're okay."

"Amber's okay?"

"She's right here. We were just about to head out there. I was calling to see if you needed anything before we left Albuquerque."

I fell to my knees in relief. "Why did you pose for that picture?" I screamed at her. "What kind of sadist are you?"

"Charley, you're scaring me."

"Join the club. That was a horrible picture. And you had red eye in it."

"Honey, what picture are you talking about?"

Donovan was right beside me. He lowered himself onto one knee and kept a hand on my back.

"What's going on?" she asked, but I looked up at Donovan.

Donovan!

Donovan?

I blinked, knowing in the back of my mind that my mouth sat agape. Which couldn't be flattering. "What are you doing here?" I brought the trio surrounding me into focus.

Eric stood beside us, his lean frame at the ready.

Michael stood back as usual, coolness wafting off him as he rested against his Harley, arms crossed over his chest, an amused smirk on his face. "Still causing hell, I see."

I scrambled to my feet, then threw my arms around Donovan's neck. He lifted me off the ground and hugged me tight.

"What are all of you doing here?" I asked when he set me back down. "You're wanted men. You can't be here."

Eric nodded. "That's what we tried to tell that guy. Nobody listens to us."

I shook my head, trying to absorb a thousand layers of information at once. "What guy?"

Donovan grinned. "That man of yours, sugar. We've been holed up across the road from you, keeping watch."

"Reyes? Reyes asked you to come? Why? And keeping watch for what?"

"This," Michael said, smirk firmly in place. "Said you have a habit of running off when you shouldn't. Seems he was right."

I was so flabbergasted, I didn't even know how to respond. Why would Reyes bring these guys here? He knew I had a weak spot in my heart for them. A really weak spot. As in, Donovan-was-an-incredible-kisser weak spot.

Then something a tad more important hit me. Cookie and Amber hadn't been taken. Someone wanted me off the grounds, the sacred grounds. They wanted me dead. I whirled around, watching the road from where I'd just come, waiting for the sounds of paws tearing through the forest. For the sound of snarls and teeth gnashing as they drove closer and closer to the kill. Because I finally remembered why I was not to leave the convent. But the only sound I heard was the breeze whispering through the trees. A bird calling out overhead.

Slowly, realization dawned. There was a reason the Twelve didn't follow me. They were going after Beep. My hand flew over my mouth, and a paralyzing fear gripped me.

"Sweetheart," Donovan said, trying to coax me back to him.

"I have to go back. Now!" I started for Misery, but Donovan tucked an arm around my waist and hauled me toward his bike. "I'll take you. We'll come back for your Jeep later."

"Yes. Yes, good idea." I hopped on the back of Donovan's Harley and wrapped my arms around him. "Please, drive fast," I said before he brought Odin, his Harley, to life with a roar.

"My favorite way to drive!" he yelled back to me. Only after we started back did I realize I'd left Cookie hanging on the phone, probably frantic. And my phone lay somewhere between here and there.

15

The second we pulled to a stop, I tore off the bike and ran for the front door despite Donovan's insisting otherwise. When I got inside, I was met with exactly the scene I'd been expecting. The first things I noticed were the bloodied bodies of Osh, Garrett, and Reyes. Denise sat in a corner, her fear so great, she was probably crippled by it. And the hounds, the ones who couldn't come onto sacred ground, stood encircling Beep's bassinet.

My lungs seized when I saw their silvery black hides shimmer, then disappear, their massive heads more shadow than substance, and their razor-sharp teeth glinting off the low light. A terror of nightmarish proportions ripped through me so fast, I could hardly focus. With legs shaking, I lowered myself onto one knee.

I had so few options. With Osh, Reyes, and Garrett down, what could I do?

I could slow time, but they would only match it before I could reach Beep. I could let the energy inside me explode, the light like acid on their hides, but they'd recover too quickly for me to get to her. I could offer my life, but could hellhounds be bargained with? And Lucifer wanted Beep, all because of a few verses some guy wrote centuries ago. He wouldn't settle for me when he had the very being prophesied to destroy him at his fingertips. Or his hellhounds' claws.

Artemis took up position beside me, her hackles raised, a low growl reverberating from her chest.

Garrett was out cold, but Osh got slowly to his feet, a smile on his face as he dusted himself off. "I live for this shit," he said, but he wasn't looking at the hellhounds. In fact, the hellhounds seemed quite at ease. He was looking at Reyes as he followed suit and stood. He cracked his neck and rolled his shoulders before testing his jaw.

I blinked in confusion. Was Osh betraying us after all? Reyes hadn't wanted to trust him, but I thought we could. I really thought he was on our side.

I rose to my feet to try to reason with him. Osh, I could reason with. The Twelve, not so much.

"Charley, no!" Denise said. She started to get up, but I held up a hand to stop her.

Still, her cry was enough to get the attention of the others in the room.

" 'Bout time," Osh said, doubling over and panting as the bikers came in behind me.

Reyes watched Osh for a moment, turned his attention to the bikers, then focused on me. And I suddenly understood. The man before me, while in Reyes's body, was not my husband.

He stared at me a long moment, and what I saw was like something from a dream. Black fog drifted off his shoulders and down around him like a great cape. It pooled at his feet. His lips parted and he ran his tongue over his bottom lip. Or, Reyes's bottom lip.

Enough with the gawking. "Lucifer, I presume."

"You are more beautiful in your true form, but this isn't bad either. You'll taste good, I'm sure."

"What did you do with my husband?"

"You mean my son? The son I created to carry out a mission, and he couldn't even do that."

"And yet you don't seem disappointed."

Osh was easing closer to me. Lucifer offered him a disinterested glance, then asked me, "Why would I be disappointed when my son did exactly as I knew he would? He always defied my orders. Why should my order to kill you be any different?"

"So, you knew he would disobey you?"

"It's in his nature. He was never one to follow the rules. And I knew he would want to be with you, the Val-Eeth, the last of her kind, the most beautiful and the only pure ghost god ever to exist. He always was attracted to power."

"You know nothing about me."

"I know that you are the first god of pure light, the first pure ghost god born of two ghost gods ever to exist. I know you are the thirteenth. I know you have inherited all the power from all the gods ever to exist in your realm, and yet here you are, playing games with me. I am honored and appalled that you would think so much of these humans to risk your life for them. You must realize you have left your realm vulnerable. No telling what you'll go back to."

"What do you want?"

"So many things. Where to start?"

The conversation left me fighting for air. It was Reyes. It was his voice. It was his beautiful face. But absent his mannerisms and his convictions and his compassion. This being was nothing like my husband. And yet I couldn't help but wonder why anyone in this room, including my precious daughter, was still alive. Clearly, he could sic the hounds on us anytime he wanted. What was he waiting for?

"Actually, I have all I want right here. I've taken over my son's body, a feat that took some doing, as I first had to weaken him by making him worry about you and your creation so much he couldn't sleep. I had no idea it would take months to get him to the point where I could over-take him, but it was certainly worth the wait. I mean, look at this." He flexed and stretched, trying out his new body. "I do believe he is as beau-tiful as I was."

"More so, I'm sure."

"Well, there you have it. I made a good choice, because the other choice was to track down the champion, the escaped Daeva, and take him in-stead. I'm just not sure I would look good in teenager."

Lucifer's admission surprised Osh, who'd clearly had no idea that he had been an option.

"But don't worry, traitor. I have plans for you."

"Why do you need a body at all?"

"Have you seen the looks my kind gets in this world? Also, I didn't want to live like a vampire. We can live in the light only if we have a human host. But you know that. Do you also know that no human can contain me? So I created a son." He checked his nails and smiled in ap-proval. "You should understand before we go much further, I've been pre-paring for this very day for centuries. But one doesn't just escape from hell. One needs a map, so the mapmakers slaved for thousands of years to create a key to the gates that held me in. We lost millions to the void in the process. I couldn't risk it falling into the wrong hands, so I im-printed it on my son. In him, actually, thereby creating not just a map, but also a key, a portal. Then I destroyed the original and all those who helped create it, save one."

He focused on Osh again, accused him with a glare. "One was never found. Naughty boy. Did you eat my mapmaker?"

Osh said nothing.

"I wondered where he'd gone off to, but since you are the only Daeva ever to escape hell and make it to the other side, I'll assume you had something to do with his disappearance. And so," he said, refocusing on me, "I was stuck once again. I was hardly going to risk the void without the key, but then one day, I was minding my own business, melting the faces off a few thousand humans, when my son decides to risk a trip back home for that trinket on your finger."

The orange diamond. I pressed my mouth together to keep from gasping.

"Following him out of the void undetected proved far easier than I imagined. It's such a vast thing and he was traveling at the speed of light, him being a portal and all. And then I was free. Well, free-ish."

He hooked his hands behind his back as he explained, and I couldn't figure out what he was waiting for. Why was he telling me all this? Why he was stalling?

"I was quite tired of living in the shadows. The remedy for that was also easy. Weakening my son was not. But when one is plagued with nightmares of his wife and child being ripped apart by hellhounds every time he closes his eyes, he's bound to miss a few nights' sleep."

I leveled my best scowl on him. "You tortured him."

"Naturally."

Osh was about five feet from me, and I wondered what he was up to. Then I happened to look at Garrett and realized he wasn't out. He was faking. Great. They probably had a plan. I was so bad at plans, I wished they would have clued me in to theirs.

"You realize this is not going to end well for you," I said.

"And how can it not?"

"There's an ancient text that says our daughter will be your downfall."

"You humans," he said, the laugh that escaped him not even remotely similar to Reyes's, "stumbling upon words that mean nothing, trying to decipher the undecipherable. The man who wrote them was an imbecile."

"Yet here you are in all your glory to destroy her. Is that not a confirmation of the documents' legitimacy? You are going to fail here today." At least I hoped so. The more he stalled, the more I worried.

"My dear, I have contingency plan upon contingency plan. Even as we speak, there are twelve dormant parasites from twelve different dimensions waiting inside human hosts. They've been here for decades, in this realm, on this planet, and they are just now awakening. Trust me when I say they are very cranky when they first wake up."

"Twelve parasites? You sent the twelve? The *bad* twelve? Then who summoned the hellhounds?"

That was when I took a really good look at the hounds. They were not snarling at my daughter or snapping at her. They . . . they were protecting her. A new hope sprang to life inside me. The only person in the room they seemed focused on was Reyes. Their heads down. Their ears back. Their teeth glistening. But every single one of them was turned toward Reyes. No, not Reyes. Lucifer.

Then I noticed a man. Like the hounds, he was hard to see. His visibility shifted with the light. A shimmer of gold here. A glint of silver there. In fact, he seemed made of light. Pure and powerful.

One of the hounds nudged him, and he rested a hand on its head before disappearing into the shadows again. He was clad in armor like a prince from an ancient Asian dynasty.

"Mr. Wong," I said as I stood stunned by the mere thought of it.

Though not tall, he stood with the beasts, his shoulders wide, his stance sure and strong as his other hand rested on the hilt of a sword.

He bowed when I finally saw him, as though he'd been waiting. *"Tsu lah, Val-Eeth."*

He spoke in an ancient language that I recognized but didn't quite understand.

I thought back, tried to reconcile what I was seeing with what I knew to be true. The Twelve never actually attacked me. They attacked others, anyone whom they saw as a threat. Me, they simply tried to drag to safety. To keep me out of harm's way.

"Who sent you?" I asked Mr. Wong.

"You did. Before you became human, you sent me to be your protector, your sentry until you finished your duties here and went home."

"You are like an archangel, only from our realm?"

He nodded, accepting that analogy.

I wanted to run to him. To hug him. To beg his forgiveness for that time I tried repeatedly to put a lampshade on his head. But with the outcast up from the basement, salutations would have to wait.

Lucifer was actually quite interested in our conversation. I got the feeling he hadn't expected backup.

"What happens to the human hosts of these parasites?" I asked Lucifer. We were in a standoff, but he was taking it all in stride, letting us ramble and ask questions. I had a feeling he wouldn't normally do such a thing. He was biding his time, perhaps expecting backup of his own.

"They are all already dead."

I closed my eyes, horrified.

"Easier to control when they have no mind to fight back."

"I understand. But this is between you and me. Let my family go."

"We're bargaining now?"

"We have twelve hellhounds that I'm pretty sure would just as soon rip your face off as look at you. We have a testy Daeva with a score to settle. We have the equivalent of an archangel who loves to use that sword of his. And we have me, the Val-Eeth. Surely you'd be willing to make a trade."

"I'll give you the woman," he said, bargaining, again, to bide his time.

But so was I. I wanted Donovan and the guys out. And Garrett as well.

I glanced at Denise as she crouched in the corner. She gazed at me, seemingly grateful she was part of the deal.

With the barest wave of my hand, Artemis sank into the floor beside me then rose from the staircase right above Denise's head.

"Was the story real?" I asked her. "The one about the blue towels? About the angel you saw in the hospital? About your mother's car accident and your father telling you that sometimes a blue towel was more than just a towel?"

She frowned, confused, but couldn't help a quick glance at her boss. He didn't move. With a resigned sigh, she stood. "Yes, it was all real. But she was too much of a coward to tell you herself. Still, it was the perfect way to get inside." She looked at Lucifer. "May I have her now?" she asked.

"Manners," he said, scolding. "We have more guests coming."

My chest tightened the second realization sank in. He meant Cookie and Amber. And knowing Cookie, she'd called Uncle Bob. He was surely on his way back here, and possibly with Quentin. That's what he'd been waiting for. Because the more people I tried to save, the more chances he would have of getting to Beep. And if not him, then Denise. Or whatever was inside Denise.

Apparently the hellhounds had thought of that as well. Before I could say anything, one lunged forward, catching Denise by the throat. Artemis launched herself off the staircase and clamped on to Denise's arm.

I gasped and watched in horror as she changed. Her face stretched as a row of long, needlelike teeth grew out of her mouth. She shook Artemis off then latched on to the hound. It cried out, but another was on her back. It sank its teeth into her rib cage, until her fingernails grew into sharp, steely points. She fended him off her with one, clean swipe.

They turned on her, growling and snapping with Artemis right beside them as she did the same. The fact that Denise was a snarling, garish parasite wasn't that surprising. It was more the fact that she didn't kill Beep when she had the chance. She'd had ample opportunity, and I had no idea when she'd ceased to be Denise. Days ago, apparently. Possibly weeks. Then why wait? And how could a demon, a being of pure evil, pass so effortlessly as a human? It had delivered a human baby, for heaven's sake. It had quite possibly saved Beep's life. And yet we'd had no idea what she really was. Even Artemis didn't know.

The bikers had joined in the fight. Donovan, unaware of the hounds in the room, broke a chair over Denise's head, and Eric was using a fireplace poker as a sword. Michael just kind of stood back and soaked it all in. He was never one to rush into anything.

A third beast surrounded her, and I could tell she expected Lucifer to help her. How foolish to expect quarter from a man who would create his own son just so he could inhabit his body. Ethics were not his strong suit.

She hissed at the beasts, swiped as Eric got a little too close with the poker, and fell when the hounds converged, each ripping a piece of her apart.

I turned away. Even knowing the real Denise had probably been dead for days now, it wasn't easy to watch.

Once the beasts were finished with her, they slowly circled Lucifer. Only, that happened to be my husband's body they were about to rip apart.

I summoned Artemis back to me before glancing at Mr. Wong, now able to see the incredible power that encased him, and silently pleaded with him not to let the Twelve kill my husband.

"You sent me to protect you at all costs," Mr. Wong whispered to me, though I could hear him clearly. "He is a threat. There is no help for it."

Fine. I was back to fighting hellhounds.

"Hey!" I yelled at them, crouching down as though I would attack them.

"You would give up your life for his?" Lucifer asked.

"Of course, you idiot."

He smiled. "Rey'aziel is very, very unhappy about that."

"Yeah, well, he would be."

A hound snapped at him, and in that instant when his focus swept to the hound, Osh was at my side. He no longer had a choice. Reyes was about to die, and I was the only one who could send Satan back to hell and save my husband in the process. He wrapped his arms around me, leaned in, put his mouth at my ear, and whispered my celestial name.

What hit me next was like an epiphany times infinity. It all made sense.

In an instant, a power like I'd never felt before flowed through me like lightning in my veins. Just like Reyes told me, with the knowledge of my name came billions of memories. I remembered my realm, my people, the gods that came before me. The memories were like flashes of camera light, only a million at a time. Then another million. Then the next. I remembered the creation of my universe and every universe thereafter. I remembered the wars. So many wars. So many lives lost, both celestial and mortal, each species of intelligence a little different from the others, yet each capable of a love greater than life.

And I remembered my decision to shift onto this plane. Though Reyes had seen me centuries ago, I saw him first. Knew he was capable of greatness. Called dibs.

God promised to leave earth to humans, to leave them to their own devices. He could only intervene if asked, if prayed to. In His infinite wisdom, however, he found a loophole. Another god could keep Satan at bay. And that god's human child could destroy him.

I understood. I knew why my daughter—our daughter—was such a threat to Lucifer. She truly was born a human. She was conceived from both of our human sides. There was nothing supernatural about her conception. About her birth. She was human through and through. True, she would be a human with extraordinary gifts, but she was human nonetheless, and she would be his downfall. This was why I'd agreed to come. I knew my purpose, and I knew hers. I knew what she would be capable of.

But for now . . .

I smiled at Lucifer, at the monster inside my husband, and while he looked like the man I'd fallen in love with centuries ago, the man who would do anything for our daughter, for me, he was not. He didn't have a key to the void like Reyes did. Locking him back in the basement would give our daughter time to grow, to become stronger, to learn how to defeat her grandfather and destroy him forever.

Lucifer had raised his hand, blocking the light flowing out of me. Then he realized what had happened. He panicked.

"You have no jurisdiction over me!" he yelled, backing away. "Your ordination precludes authority over anything other than mortals. Only one born of humans can command me, can embrace or deny what I offer. Put simply, that was the deal."

"I *am* human."

"You are a god hiding behind the rotting layers of human flesh. You are no more human than I."

He had a point.

I walked over to him, grazed my fingertips along the hides of the hounds as I wound through them, and stood nose to nose with my husband's father. I placed a hand on his chest, moved it seductively to his heart. Interest leapt within him. Then I reached inside him, searching for the immortal being cowering there.

He grinned and wrapped one hand around the back of my neck and one on my jaw, preparing to snap my neck.

His voice grew hoarse. "Honey, in this universe, I'm the big, bad wolf," he said, enjoying the thought of my death. "That shit doesn't work on me."

I grinned back and every muscle in his body flexed as he twisted my head around. Or tried to. Even with all his strength, with all his incredible power, he was no match for the seven original gods residing within me.

I reached in farther and he grabbed my arm, fighting the agony I was putting him through, stunned.

He was even more stunned when I ripped him out of my husband's body. Reyes crumpled to the floor, unconscious as I held his father.

Lucifer was massive, his body taking up half the room, part demon, part grotesque, but a part of him was still an angel, too. The beautiful being he once was had become a shell filled to the brim with hatred, judgment, and indifference. Evil.

He was struggling to breathe under the pressure of my hold. "How?" he asked, his voice straining.

"Honey," I said, mocking him, "I'm a god. That shit works on everyone."

I looked to the side. The hounds had moved back, given me room to work. I leaned over Reyes, placed one hand on him, used his power, his key, to open the gates of hell.

Lucifer fought me, but it was like a gnat fighting an eighteen-wheeler. The gate opened, and with one last gesture—my sauciest wink—I tossed his ass off our plane.

The gate closed and I collapsed across Reyes, petting his hair, begging him to be okay. Just then, Beep started crying, and I rushed to her, relief flooding every nook and cranny of my body because she was okay. I took her to Reyes as he stirred. Osh had knelt beside him, too. Then Garrett and Artemis joined us.

Reyes opened his eyes and turned onto his back. I touched his face. Smiled. Told him we were okay. But the turbulence in my husband's eyes left little doubt that I was wrong.

16

"But I don't understand," I said as Osh and Garrett helped Reyes to his feet. He swayed a little, then repeated the words he'd ripped straight from my worst nightmare.

"We have to send her away. Now."

"You mean, we're going away with her like we'd planned. We're taking a helicopter to that island."

"The island doesn't matter anymore." He strode to the kitchen as we followed.

"I saw his plans," he said. "My father's. We— We have no choice."

He started throwing things in a bag, Beep's things, her bottles and formula.

"I saw his plans. He will not give up until she is dead."

"But I'm a god," I said, arguing with him. "I know my celestial name. Surely between the two of us, we can protect her."

"You don't understand. You *are* his plan. You are the beacon of light that is going to lead his soldiers right to her."

"Yes, demons. We've handled them before. We can do it again."

He stopped just long enough to tell me, "Not his demons. Not this time. Demons from other dimensions. Stronger. More powerful."

He made a call while ordering everyone around us to do this or that. They helped him pack Beep up. But I just wanted answers. I seemed to know everything I'd ever wanted to know, but suddenly it all meant nothing.

"So we fight them. Like always," I said when he got off the phone.

"He sent a group to lead them."

"Okay," I said, needing more.

"Gods from another dimension, three of them, and their dimension makes hell look like a water park. They are ruthless and powerful beyond belief, and they are more potent than even you."

"There is no such thing," I said, my temper flaring. The earth quaked beneath our feet.

He took hold of my arm to calm me. "More potent. Not more powerful. Not even close, but you have distinct disadvantages. You care about those around you. They care only about the destruction of anything and everything standing in their way."

"The gods of Uzan?" Osh asked, paling before my eyes.

Reyes offered a curt nod.

"Here? In this dimension? They'll destroy it."

"Exactly. They'll destroy everything on earth to get to her. My father is not going to give up until our daughter is dead. And your light, the same light that is a beacon of hope for the departed, is now a death sentence for our daughter. That is how they will find her." He forced another blanket into an already bulging backpack. "He planned for this, Dutch. All of it. He set this in motion centuries ago, from the time the prophecies were first written."

"If he wanted her dead so bad, why didn't Denise kill her when she had the chance? She could have done it at any time."

His mouth thinned. "He wanted to do it himself. At first. Now he doesn't care."

"This is insane," I said, scrubbing my face with my fingertips, unable to believe what was happening, but he kept working, ignoring my ideas, promising me we'd come up with our own plan once Beep was safely away. "Is this because you can't trust me? Because of my impulsive nature?"

"No, though it would serve you right."

I couldn't argue that, and I knew he wouldn't even consider such a move if there were any other option. "Surely, we don't have to send her away this minute."

"What do you think he was waiting for?" Reyes asked, facing me head on. "Lucifer, as he spoke to you, drawing out your conversation, stalling."

"The gods? They're already here?"

"They've been here, waiting for word from my father."

"But how? How can Lucifer command such beings?"

He went back to work. I wasn't even paying attention to what he was packing. "He doesn't command them, but you don't get to be the king of hell and not make a few nasty friends. We fought alongside them more than once."

"You fought with them?"

"Dutch, you saw what I am. That surprises you?"

"Everything about this surprises me."

A knock on the front door caught my attention. Uncle Bob answered it, his expression grave. The Loehrs walked in with Mr. Alaniz, the PI, trailing them. I sank into the nearest chair. Not this. Not now. Why were they here? What would this do to our already splintering relationship?

"Anything you want to tell me?" Reyes asked, his movements sharp and quick. "I asked you not to contact them."

"I know," I said, shame engulfing me.

"So I did it instead."

I blinked up at him. "What?"

"After a while, after the thought of Beep and having a family, I understood what you meant. They deserved to know what happened to me. So I contacted them months ago."

"But, how did you know I contacted them as well?"

He indicated Mr. Alaniz with a gesture.

I gaped at him. "You were in on it the whole time? From the beginning?"

Mr. Alaniz nodded, shame lining his face.

"Even the letter and the ultimatum that I tell Reyes the truth?" I said to the man I thought was *my* PI.

"I was trying to force your hand," Reyes answered for him. "You'd contacted them against my wishes. I wanted you to tell me. To be honest with me."

I wanted to apologize, but all I could think about was my daughter being sent away from me because I was the one thing in the universe that would lead to her death.

"I saw something else," he said, his voice thick with sorrow. "It was my father who had me kidnapped in the first place, taken from the Loehrs."

"Reyes," I said, aghast. "I'm so sorry."

"Don't be. They were my only contingency plan."

"What do you mean?" When he didn't answer, I put two and two together. "They're going to take Beep?"

"For now, until we can figure out our next step."

"But that would mean you knew this was going to happen. You prepared for us having to give up our child."

"I suspected. It was always a possibility."

"I didn't!"

He bowed his head. His sorrow was just as great as mine, his pain just as agonizing. "They're good people, Dutch. They'll take good care of her until all this is over."

"But they're going into this blind. They don't know who she is. What she's up against. They'll be taking her under false pretenses, and they'll be in danger."

"You're wrong," Mrs. Loehr said. I turned to her, studied her kind face, her olive skin, her hair, just as thick and black as it had been when she'd first lost Reyes. "We knew Reyes was a gift from God. We knew he was special. He told me his name the moment he was born. Rey'aziel."

" 'The beautiful one,' " I said, translating his name.

"Yes. That is one interpretation," Mr. Loehr said. "But it actually means 'God's secret.' "

I blinked in surprise. They were right. In the ancient angelic language, it meant "God's secret."

Reyes scoffed gently. "I appreciate the euphemism, but God did not send me."

"Actually, he did," Mrs. Loehr said. "And nothing you say will ever convince me otherwise." When her voice cracked, Mr. Loehr placed a gentle arm on her shoulder.

"You were an answer to our prayers." She focused on me then. "We will keep her safe until you come back for her. And then we pray we can be a part of her life."

My throat tightened at the thought. My heart ached, struggling to beat under the weight of my sorrow.

I looked at Mr. Wong as he walked up to me. He had allowed everyone to see him. A good thing since he'd taken a turn with Beep and, to everyone's chagrin, refused to give her up. Until now. He handed her to Mrs. Loehr, her eyes bright with emotion as she cradled my daughter in her arms. All I felt was the good in her. The love. The desire to help her son, her granddaughter, in any way she could.

It hurt too much to look at Beep, so I looked at Mr. Wong instead, suddenly very aware of who he was.

"You're like . . . like my second-in-command."

He bowed his head in acknowledgment.

"And your name is most decidedly not Mr. Wong."

"Just as your title is most decidedly not Your Majesty, Your Majesty. But, if I may be so bold, they will both do for now."

I smiled at him. "You knew Osh would tell me."

"I'd hoped, as I was forbidden to."

"By whom?"

"You."

"That's right," I said, remembering. "And the hellhounds?"

"They are yours to command," he said. "As am I."

I stood and walked to the hellhound I'd stabbed all those months ago, recognizing him. He'd hovered over me for quite some time after I'd stabbed him. I thought at the time it'd been preparing for an all-you-can-eat Charley buffet, but he'd actually been protecting me. All along, everything they had done was for my—and Beep's—protection. Even patrolling the border of the sacred ground was to keep me on it. Not the other way around.

I touched the wound I gave him. "I'm sorry for that."

His response was something akin to a purr but more like the low hum of an idling Bugatti engine. He nuzzled my hand, pushed his head into my side.

I heard a crash and turned to Reyes. He stood on unsteady legs, his expression blank, void of emotion. He'd knocked over a small table. The shattered glass of a vase shimmered on the floor. I doubted it registered.

"We're ready," he said to me, to the Loehrs.

We led them to the door, the room deathly quiet.

"They'll need protection," I said, glancing around at everyone who had gathered to say their good-byes.

I could now see imprints of light on people, like fingerprints. Their character, their pasts, their probable futures, all written in their auras. The lights shifted and danced on and around them and were as easy for me to read now as the morning paper.

Just like in the prophecies, there were twelve summoned and twelve sent. Mr. Wong summoned the hounds from hell for Beep's protection. Satan sent his twelve parasites, hid them among us. But he also sent the gods of Uzan. Reyes and I would have to become hunters. We'd have to find them before they found Beep. It would take time, but we had to succeed.

Still, the prophecies spoke of an army, Beep's army beyond the twelve. Her confidants who help her wage war on Reyes's father in the future. And they were there with us now. Every member of her army had somehow found us. Become a part of our lives.

I marked them all as we led the Loehrs to their car. The sentry, the scholar, the spiritualist, the healer. I even marked the three guardians, and it just goes to show that the bravest hearts often lie in the least likely candidates. No matter where Beep's path led, these people were destined to be in her life.

The departed who had gathered on the lawn watched. They'd just wanted to see her. They shuffled closer for a glimpse, their faces full of hope. Hope. It was an emotion I hadn't expected from them. Then one by one, they disappeared.

Sensing my distress, Mrs. Loehr granted me temporary custody. Holding her to me, fighting the sobs that threatened to wrench free, I looked at the Thirteenth Warrior, the one who, according to prophecy, would tip the scales either for or against her. The one who would be the doom of every being on earth if he failed: Osh'ekiel.

Beneath the powerful exterior lay the heart of a king. And he would love her. The question was, would she accept him? Would she see the good buried beneath the bad? Would she recognize that he was created that way? It wasn't a choice. It was an imposition. I marked him last as he ran a fingertip over the folds of her tiny ear.

The sob finally wrenched free as I handed my daughter back to Mrs. Loehr. I couldn't believe I was losing her after having just met her, but the thing that broke my heart even more was the fact that neither Reyes nor I would be there on that fateful day. The day she would challenge the devil to a duel. While I could see that as clear as the stars in the sky, what I couldn't see was why we weren't there for her at the appointed time. Would we die before it happened? Nothing other than death could keep us from her in her time of need, so then why would we not be a part of her army? Why would we not fight side by side with her?

Only time would tell—and fate could be altered. This could all be altered. I knew how the universe worked now. Time was anything but linear. Prophecies were anything but concrete. We could change it all.

They buckled Beep into her car seat and turned to say . . . what? What did one say in such a situation?

"Wait!" I ran into the house and grabbed Beep's registration form for her birth certificate and a pen. Then I stepped onto the porch and gestured for my husband to join me.

"What do we name her?"

He shook his head sadly.

"We need to name her after you."

"No," he said, a line appearing between his brows at the thought. "We can't name her anything that will lead my father's emissaries to her. Her name has to be completely untraceable."

"How about common? Or, at least, not completely uncommon."

I bent to write, and he nodded, giving me the go ahead.

"This is ink. No erasing."

"I trust you completely."

I tried to smile, failed, then wrote a name on the registry. My celestial father, for all intents and purposes, was named Ran-Eeth-Bijou. My mother, Ayn-Eethial. And my name, the name they gave me when I was created, was Elle-Ryn-Ahleethia.

My hands shook as I wrote Beep's real name: *Elwyn Alexandra*—a version of Reyes's middle name—*Loehr*. My vision blurred as I looked up at my husband for approval.

"It's perfect."

I folded the paper, put it in the envelope with a note I'd written Beep weeks ago, and took it to the Loehrs. As we stood below the starry sky, I couldn't watch them take Beep away. I closed my eyes, the act only encouraging more tears to fall. Then I just listened. I listened to the sound of the engine as the Loehrs backed out of the drive, tires crunching on pebbles and dried grass. I listened as they wound through the mountain pass, until their car was only an echo bouncing off the canyon walls. I listened until the only sounds I heard were the soft sobs coming from Cookie and Amber. The stalking-off of Osh. The beat of the hounds' paws as they followed the car. They would never leave her, and that was no small consolation. Then I heard the thud of Reyes's knees hitting the ground, his breath catching in his lungs.

I felt arms around me. Pats on my shoulder. Promises that it would get better. But my sorrow only grew. It built and spread and swelled until it swallowed me whole. I glanced up at the stars, at Beep's planet, and I could no longer suppress the force inside me. A primal scream surged out of me with the release, the energy bursting forth in a blinding flash, and I exploded into a million shards of light.

I pressed my fingers to my head, marveling at the agony therein, wondering why it felt like my brain had just exploded. I was on my back. I wondered about that, too. I didn't remember being on my back. I didn't remember being much of anything, my head hurt so bad. Pain rocketed through it in nauseating waves as I tried to figure out where I kept pain medication.

Then another sensation hit me. A biting cold like I'd never felt before, and I realized I couldn't remember where I was. Wondering if I'd sleep-walked, I tried to open my eyes. They wouldn't budge at first, but they were being pelted with ice-cold water, and I needed to find out why.

It took a minute, but I finally managed to pry them open enough to constitute two slits. Rain fell in huge, sleet-filled drops, stinging my face when they landed. I raised my arms to shield my eyes and saw a huge Rott-weiler standing over me. The moment my gaze landed on him, he whim-pered and licked my face. But his affection was just as cold as the rain.

A yellow light floated above me. A security light. Pebbles bored into my back and scraped my elbows as I struggled to a sitting position. I pet-ted the Rottweiler, assured him—her—I was okay. She finally let up and stepped back to give me some space. Still groggy, I looked to my left, then to my right. A dark alley stretched out in either direction. I focused on a faded sign that hung on a door directly in front of me. It read THE FIRE-LIGHT GRILL. To the left of that, a historical marker on the building itself read THE FIRE HOUSE, EST. 1755, SLEEPY HOLLOW, NY.

Okay. That answered that.

With legs made of lead, I took a crack at standing. Once I gained my footing, I stumbled toward the door. Even though it was a back door, I turned the knob and went inside, holding it open for the dog. That would garner a code violation and probably a swift kick out of there if they didn't call the cops on me first.

Thick brown hair hung in clumps over my shoulders and down my back. I had to push it out of my face repeatedly with blue, glacial hands. I could only imagine what the rest of me looked like. I glanced down at my waterlogged boots and shook my head. No need to worry about looks at the moment. There were more important things to consider.

I stepped inside a dark hallway and walked forward. A small room filled with supplies sat on the right, and a door with an OFFICE sign on my left. Ahead of me was a kitchen. I forced my frozen feet forward, taking it one step at a time. The café itself was dark, but one man was busy in the brightly lit kitchen, cleaning up for the night. A large man with a head of thick black hair slicked back, he wore a cook's apron as he emptied smaller garbage containers into one large one. He stilled when he spotted me. Reached for a weapon. Raised a spatula.

"What are you doing in here?" he barked, using a naturally baritone voice to his advantage.

I raised my hands. The blue ones that shook uncontrollably.

Another voice came from behind me. A female one. She must have come out of the office. "What's going on?" she asked, her tone sharp.

I turned to her. In her early forties, she was large, but she had bright red hair straight out of a box and a pretty round face that had probably seen a tad too much partying in its day. Her heavily lined brows slid together.

"I just need help," I said, showing my palms to her as well.

The dog whimpered, but they didn't seem to give a lick about her.

"You can't be back here."

"I know. I'm sorry, I was just— I mean, I was wondering—"

"Spit it out, girl, before you turn into a chunk of ice. I don't think I've ever seen that shade of blue on anyone before."

"Right," I said through chattering teeth. "I was just wondering . . . if . . . if you know who I am."

"Why?" she asked, jamming her hands on her hips. "You somebody special?"

"No. I mean, I was wondering if you know my name."

The man chuckled. "Don't you?"

I turned to him, hugging myself. "No," I said, my whole body quaking. "I— I don't have a clue."

Excerpt: Reye's POV

"I found her."

I turned to the kid, Angel, and tried to keep control of my emotions. I knew it wouldn't take him long to find her if she was still on earth. My fear was that she'd ascended. That she was no longer on earth and had taken her rightful place as grim reaper. Or even god of her realm. She'd come into her powers. There wasn't a damned thing I could do about it if that was her choice.

"Where is she?" the Daeva asked.

The Daeva's inquiry gained the attention of everyone else in the room, since they couldn't hear the mutt. Didn't know he'd gotten back.

Cookie, her eyes red and swollen, stood and glanced from the Daeva to me, then back again. Dutch's uncle Bob did the same while Amber and Quentin watched with wide eyes.

Gemma, who'd been sobbing almost uncontrollably, paced the kitchen floor, but she stopped and questioned me, her expression hopeful. "What? Did your guy come back?"

"Angel. Your sister's investigator. He's back and he says he's found her."

She covered her mouth with a hand, then rushed to Cookie and hugged her.

I turned to the kid. "And?"

"She's so bright now, it's hard to find her center. To find her in all that light. But she's in some town in New York."

"New York?" I asked.

"Like from the story. That town with the headless horseman. Sleepy Hollow."

"What the fuck is in New York?"

The kid shrugged as everyone once again turned toward me askance.

"I don't understand," Gemma said.

"Neither do I." Swopes was getting angry. The unknown did that to humans.

"She's only been gone an hour," Gemma said. "How could she possibly have gotten to New York in an hour?"

But the Daeva knew. He'd stilled the minute the kid said it.

I stepped to him, anger coursing through my veins like liquid fire. "Why are you surprised, slave? This is your fault."

He stood and stepped toe-to-toe with me. In all honesty, the fact that he looked like a kid meant nothing. He was centuries older than I and had been the deadliest Daeva in hell. On any other day, if he got really lucky, if the planets aligned and the tides shifted the gravity of the earth a centimeter to the left, he might have a snowball's chance of kicking my ass. Today was not that day.

He seemed to have something to say, so I fought the urge to break his neck outright.

He leaned in until I could see the minute details of his irises. "You'd been evicted, fuckhead. Daddy had taken over your digs and was about to kill your daughter. What would you have had me do?"

"Not that," I said, trying to suppress my natural inclination to rip apart first and ask questions later. He'd done the unthinkable. He'd told Dutch her name. Her celestial name. And now all that power coursing through her veins would be almost uncontrollable, as she'd proved with her trip northeast.

Swopes had moved closer to the Daeva and me, knowing what we were capable of.

A slow grin spread across the Daeva's face. "Afraid she'll figure out exactly what you are, what you've done, and leave your insignificant ass?"

The thought of a fight caused a spike of adrenaline. A welcome spike. "The only thing I'm afraid of is how much I'm going to enjoy burying your body tonight."

"You're nothing more than primordial ooze that slithered up from the basement, and she's a fucking god."

"A god?" Gemma asked, her voice thick with emotion. "Is that metaphorical?"

But the Daeva wasn't finished digging his own grave. I gave him all the time he needed. Handed him a shovel.

"Why would you ever believe yourself worthy of her?"

"There are innocent people in this room," Swopes said.

"Reyes," Cookie said. She'd stepped closer. Placed a hand on my arm. Looked up at me with those gorgeous blue eyes of hers. "Please, find her."

After a long and tense moment, I swallowed back my anger—and my sudden thirst for Daeva blood. She was right. We needed to find out what was happening with Dutch, not start a war.

"There's something else," the kid said.

I glared in impatience.

"I think she's lost her memory."

The Daeva, anger still surging through him, grabbed his dirty T-shirt. "What do you mean, you think?"

The kid pushed him. "Get off me, *pendejo*." He brushed his shirt, as though that would help, before continuing. "I mean she doesn't remember who she is. But, I don't know, maybe she remembers other things."

Quentin, who could see the kid as well as I could, was telling Amber what he could understand. Going by his signs, he'd pretty much nailed it.

Amber stood and walked to me. "Is that right?" she asked. "Charley has lost her memory?"

"What?" Now it was Gemma's turn to place a hand on my arm. "Reyes?"

I shook her off and grabbed my jacket from the back of a chair. "I'll find her."

"Wait," Gemma said. She sank into a seat at the table and spoke between sobs. "We need a plan. You can't just go up to her and force her to come home. If she doesn't know who you are, you could do more damage than good."

"I won't force her to do anything." I started for the door when the Daeva decided to press his luck again.

"Listen to her first," he said. He'd grabbed hold of my forearm, and the seething anger I'd felt before came back ten times stronger.

But Robert was beside me, too. "Please, Reyes," he said. "Gemma is very good at what she does."

After another long and tense moment, I'd calmed down long enough to sit at the table and listen to Dutch's sister go on and on about Dutch's psyche. About how fragile it had to be at that moment with everything she'd gone through. And now she vanished before our eyes only to end up somewhere in New York with no memory.

"She must have suffered a psychotic break, Reyes. We need to give her time to recover."

"I'm not leaving her up there alone," I said, making sure my tone spoke volumes on the subject.

"I'm not saying that." She blew her nose and then continued. "I'm just saying, we need to reveal her past to her slowly, to let her try to find her way back on her own."

"So, what's your plan?" Robert asked her.

She thought a moment, then glanced at him. "How much vacation time do you have saved up?"

"As much as I need."

She smiled. "Okay, here's what we do."

We got as much information from the kid as we could about where Dutch was and who she was with; then Gemma laid out a viable plan for us. One that involved most of us going to New York. Amber and Quentin had school, so they would stay back, but the rest of us were headed to the Northeast. I chartered a plane. We would leave in seven hours. Not soon enough, in my opinion, but the others had to make arrangements.

The longer we waited, however, the more danger Dutch would be in. With no memory of who she was—of what she was—she was more vulnerable than ever before, and my father had emissaries out there just itching to separate her head from her body. Not to mention the three gods of Uzan. Throwing them into the mix was like bringing nuclear weapons to a knife fight.

Everyone left to clear their schedules, leaving me alone in the house with the Daeva. He stood without saying a word and started for the stairs.

"You're wrong," I said.

He stopped but didn't turn around.

"I've never believed myself worthy of her."

"At least we have that in common." He took the stairs three at a time, and I couldn't suppress my doubts about him. Why was he here? What did he have to gain? I'd been suspicious of him from day one, and my suspicions grew stronger by the minute.

Finally, after a long wait, I said, "You can come out now."

Dutch's father appeared in front of me. He was almost as tall as I was. Thinner, though. Lighter. "I'll keep an eye on her until you get there," he said.

"I have the kid for that."

He hesitated. "I'll help."

"How did you know about the spies?" I asked him. I'd been very curious since he told Dutch about them. How had he known about them in the first place?

He shrugged a bony shoulder. "You understand how it is. You hear things on this side."

Before he knew what I was up to, I grabbed him by the throat, making it impossible for him to disappear, and shoved him back against the fireplace. I couldn't actually choke him, since he was already six feet under. I just felt better with my hand around his throat. "I won't ask again."

He scoffed. Fought my hold. Failed. "What can you do to me that hasn't already been done?"

With a smile as sincere as a used car salesman's, I leaned in to him. "I can send you to hell."

He stilled, but only for a minute. "Bullshit. You can't send someone to hell."

"I'm the portal. I can send anyone anytime."

"Look," he said, giving up the struggle. "It's not what you think."

"Enlighten me."

"I had no idea what Charley was. I swear. Not until I died. Only then did I discover that my wildest imaginings didn't even come close. I mean, seriously? A god? But you know what your father is planning for her. And for my granddaughter."

"Better than anyone."

"Well, I did what I do best. In my early years on the force, I went undercover, sometimes for months at a time. I collared more dealers than anyone in APD history."

"Ah, so you're undercover. Doing what, exactly?"

"I'm a spy. What else?"

His treachery stunned me. "You're spying for the very people who want your daughter dead?"

His mouth formed a crooked smile, mostly because I still had him by the throat. "I am. I told you, I'm undercover. And I know who Duff was reporting to. The man in the black Rolls. I've seen him. He's one of your father's emissaries."

"You're not impressing me, Mr. Davidson." I prepared to send him back to hell. He was better off in hell than spying on his daughter for my father.

"Think about it," he said. "You knew me before I died. Do you really think I went to hell?"

He had me there. He was a good man for the most part.

"It took me months to get in with them. To convince them I'd been sent by the big man downstairs. And the more we talk about it, the more likely you'll blow my cover. So if you wouldn't mind getting the fuck off me."

He shoved my arm and I lost my grip, but he didn't disappear. Least he had balls.

"Still don't believe me?"

"Your word is not evidence," I said, giving him a long leash. If he disappeared now, I'd know he was lying, and next time there'd be no exchange. I'd throw him into hell before he knew what hit him.

"In your room, underneath the slats on the bed."

Fine. I'd bite. I strode to our room, the one Dutch and I had shared for over eight months, and lifted the bed off its frame. A picture floated to the ground. I stepped into the square bed frame and picked it up, though I didn't need to look. It was the picture Dutch had of me when I was around fourteen, the one she'd managed to get from a crazy old lady who lived in a building I'd once inhabited growing up. The man who raised me, Earl Walker, used to take pictures of his handiwork. This one was of me tied up, bruised and bloodied. But I'd endured worse. Still, I felt the emotion that charged through my wife when she looked at it. I wondered why she kept it. She'd even brought it here. Why?

"To remind her," Leland said. He'd appeared beside me. "She thinks she is going to prevent anything like that from happening to you ever again. She thinks she is your savior, and it's going to get her killed. Just look at what she tried to do tonight. She tried to trade her life for yours."

As gratingly right as he was, he hadn't convinced me of a damn thing. I put the picture in my back pocket and started to pack. "This isn't evidence."

"I was just making a point."

"And that point is?"

"That the man who did that to you—the man you made a quadriplegic and who you think is in a care facility drinking his meals through a straw—is the man in the Rolls."

He'd caught me off guard. I shot around to face him.

He nodded. "The emissary has been inside him for weeks. Who better, after all? He knows more about you than anyone. Knows how you think. Your weaknesses. Your habits."

"No one knows how I think."

"But Earl Walker knows better than most. The beast inside him, the emissary, finally killed him yesterday and now has complete control of his body."

"Thank God for small favors."

"Those things are bloody hard to kill once they've burrowed inside a human host. These aren't your average demons."

"I know that. I was there, remember? I saw what one did to your bitch wife."

"Then why didn't you know about Earl Walker?" he asked me.

I stopped.

He nodded. "I think your father let you see exactly as much as he wanted you to see. There's still a lot you don't know and a lot I can help with. I'm in, Reyes. Let me do what I do best, but first let me help with Charley. She's my daughter. I have a right."

There was no denying that Leland had been a good man when he was alive, but death did things to people. Their good nature didn't always survive the trip into the supernatural world. I was beginning to think, however, that Leland's did.

"I want reports every two hours," I said, stuffing a handful of shirts into a duffel bag.

"You got it. But, Reyes, there's a reason I told you all this."

I gave him my full attention. "More good news, I assume?"

"Not really. I just find it odd that Charley ended up in Sleepy Hollow, New York, of all places."

I shook off the dread clawing its way up my spine, and asked, "Why?"

"Because that's where Earl Walker is now."